$\mathcal{A}$
BURNABLE
BOOK

Bruce Holsinger is a professor of English language and literature whose books on medieval culture have won major prizes
from the Modern Language Association and Medieval Academy
of America.

He is also a Guggenheim Fellow and recipient of research
fellowships from the National Endowment for the Arts and the
American Council of Learned Societies.

He lives in Virginia with his wife and two sons. *A Burnable
Book* is his first novel.

For more information visit BurnableBooks.com

A
BURNABLE
BOOK

BRUCE
HOLSINGER

HarperCollins*Publishers*

HarperCollins*Publishers*
77–85 Fulham Palace Road,
Hammersmith, London W6 8JB

www.harpercollins.co.uk

Published by HarperCollins*Publishers* 2014
1

Map of London and Southwark © Nicolette Caven 2013

A catalogue record for this book
is available from the British Library

ISBN: 978 0 00 749329 6

Set in Sabon by Palimpsest Book Production Limited, Falkirk, Stirlingshire

Printed and bound in Great Britain by
Clays Ltd, St Ives plc

MIX
Paper from
responsible sources
FSC FSC C007454
www.fsc.org

For my mother,
Sheila,
who taught me to write

CAST OF CHARACTERS

ENGLISH ROYALS, MAGNATES, AND RELATIONS

Richard II, *King, son of Prince Edward (the Black Prince)*
John of Gaunt, *Duke of Lancaster, brother of Prince Edward*
Henry of Bolingbroke, *son and heir to John of Gaunt*
Joan, *Countess of Kent, mother of King Richard II*
Robert de Vere, *Earl of Oxford*
Stephen Weldon, *knight of Oxford's faction*
Katherine Swynford, *governess and consort to John of Gaunt,
    sister-in-law of Geoffrey Chaucer*
Robert Braybrooke, *Bishop of London*
William Wykeham, *Bishop of Winchester*
Michael de la Pole, *Baron de la Pole and Lord Chancellor of
    England*
Isabel Syward, *Prioress of St Leonard's Bromley*

OFFICERS OF THE CITY OF LONDON AND SERVANTS OF THE CROWN

Thomas Pinchbeak, *serjeant-at-law*
Ralph Strode, *common serjeant of London*

James Tewburn, *his clerk*

Thomas Tyle, *King's Coroner of London*

Nicholas Symkok, *clerk to the King's Coroner*

Richard Bickle, *goldsmith of London, beadle of Cheap Ward*

Thomas Tugg, *keeper of Newgate Prison*

Geoffrey Chaucer, *controller of the wool custom*

Philippa Chaucer, *his wife, sister of Katherine Swynford*

COMMON WOMEN OF LONDON AND SOUTHWARK

Eleanor/Edgar Rykener, *maudlyn of Gropecunt Lane*

Mary Potts, *maudlyn of Gropecunt Lane*

Agnes Fonteyn, *maudlyn of Gropecunt Lane*

Joan Rugg, *their bawd*

Bess Waller, *bawd of the Pricking Bishop; mother of Agnes and Millicent Fonteyn*

St Cath, *maudlyn of the Pricking Bishop*

TRADESMEN, FREEMEN OF LONDON AND SOUTHWARK, AND COMMONERS

John Gower *of Southwark, esquire and poet*

Will Cooper, *his servant*

Simon Gower, *his son, clerk to Sir John Hawkwood*

Mark Blythe, *mason of Southwark*

George Lawler, *spicerer of Cornhull*

Jane Lawler, *his wife*

Denise Haveryng, *widow of Cornhull*

Nathan Grimes, *master butcher of Cutter Lane, Southwark*

Tom Nayler, *his first apprentice*

Gerald Rykener, *his second apprentice and ward; brother of Eleanor/Edgar*

Millicent Fonteyn, *singlewoman of Cornhull; sister of Agnes Fonteyn*

Sam Varney, *gravedigger*

IN OXFORD

Peter de Quincey, *keeper of the books of Durham*
John Clanvowe, *knight of the King's Chamber*
John Purvey, *curate of Lutterworth, disciple of John Wycliffe*

IN FLORENCE

John Hawkwood, *mercenary knight, chief of the White Company*
Adam Scarlett, *his chief lieutenant*
Jacopo da Pietrasanta, *his chancellor*
Giovanni Desilio, *doctor of the Studium Generale, Siena*

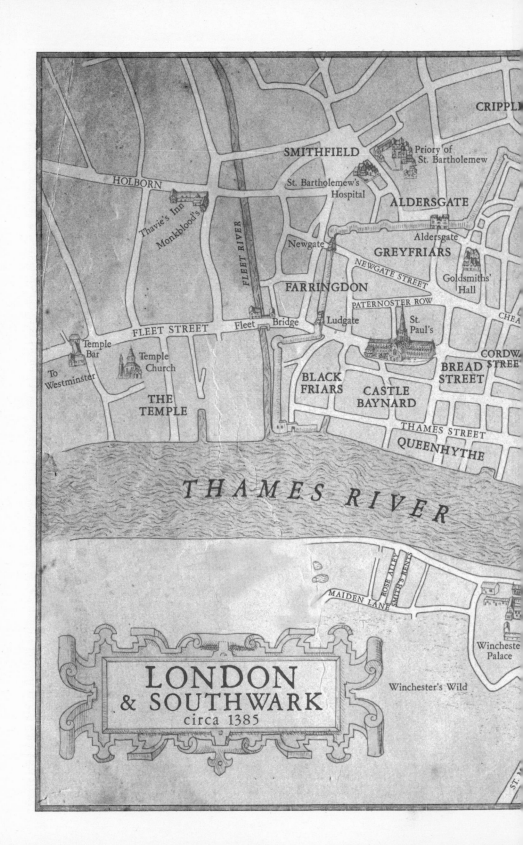

LONDON
& SOUTHWARK
circa 1385

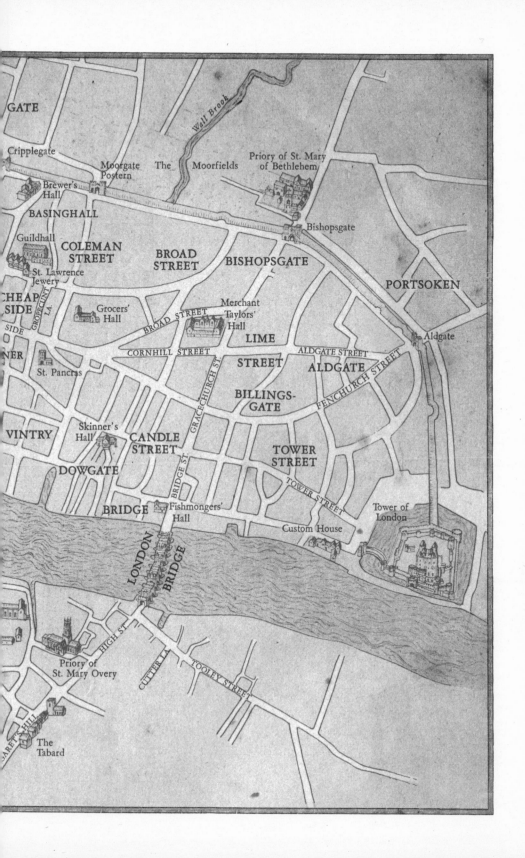

GATE

Cripplegate

Well Brook

The Moorfields

Priory of St. Mary
of Bethlehem

Moorgate
Postern

Brewer's
Hall

BASINGHALL

Guildhall

COLEMAN
STREET

BROAD
STREET

BISHOPSGATE

Bishopsgate

PORTSOKEN

St. Lawrence
Jewry

CHEAP
SIDE

SIDE

CROPGATE LA.

Grocers'
Hall

BROAD STREET

Merchant
Taylors'
Hall

CORNHILL STREET

LIME
STREET

ALDGATE STREET

Aldgate

NER

St. Pancras

GRACECHURCH ST.

ALDGATE

FENCHURCH STREET

BILLINGS-
GATE

VINTRY

Skinner's
Hall

CANDLE
STREET

BRIDGE ST.

TOWER
STREET

DOWGATE

TOWER STREET

Tower of
London

BRIDGE

Fishmongers'
Hall

Custom House

LONDON BRIDGE

HIGH ST.

CUTTER LA.

Priory of
St. Mary Overy

TOOLEY STREET

ARET'S HILL

The
Tabard

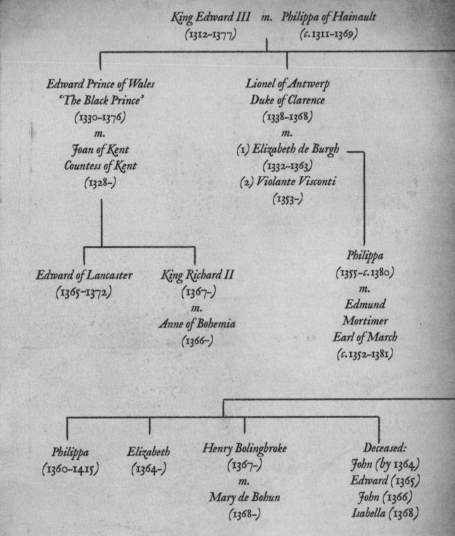

King Edward III m. Philippa of Hainault
(1312–1377)   (c.1311–1369)

Edward Prince of Wales
'The Black Prince'
(1330–1376)
m.
Joan of Kent
Countess of Kent
(1328–)

Lionel of Antwerp
Duke of Clarence
(1338–1368)
m.
(1) Elizabeth de Burgh
(1332–1363)
(2) Violante Visconti
(1353–)

Philippa
(1355–c.1380)
m.
Edmund
Mortimer
Earl of March
(c.1352–1381)

Edward of Lancaster
(1365–1372)

King Richard II
(1367–)
m.
Anne of Bohemia
(1366–)

Philippa
(1360–1415)

Elizabeth
(1364–)

Henry Bolingbroke
(1367–)
m.
Mary de Bohun
(1368–)

Deceased:
John (by 1364)
Edward (1365)
John (1366)
Isabella (1368)

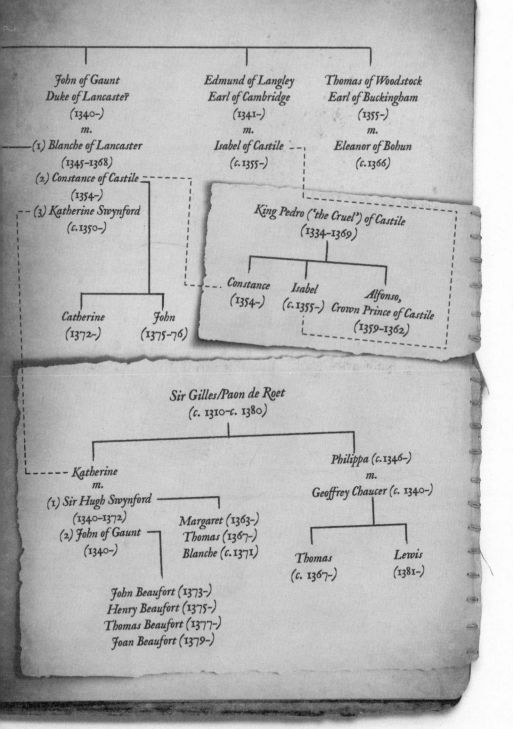

John of Gaunt
Duke of Lancaster
(1340–)
m.
(1) Blanche of Lancaster
(1345–1368)
(2) Constance of Castile
(1354–)
(3) Katherine Swynford
(c. 1350–)

Edmund of Langley
Earl of Cambridge
(1341–)
m.
Isabel of Castile
(c. 1355–)

Thomas of Woodstock
Earl of Buckingham
(1355–)
m.
Eleanor of Bohun
(c. 1366)

King Pedro ('the Cruel') of Castile
(1334–1369)

Constance
(1354–)

Isabel
(c. 1355–)

Alfonso,
Crown Prince of Castile
(1359–1362)

Catherine
(1372–)

John
(1375–76)

Sir Gilles/Paon de Roet
(c. 1310–c. 1380)

Katherine
m.
(1) Sir Hugh Swynford
(1340–1372)
(2) John of Gaunt
(1340–)

Margaret (1363–)
Thomas (1367–)
Blanche (c. 1371)

Philippa (c. 1346–)
m.
Geoffrey Chaucer (c. 1340–)

Thomas
(c. 1367–)

Lewis
(1381–)

John Beaufort (1373–)
Henry Beaufort (1375–)
Thomas Beaufort (1377–)
Joan Beaufort (1379–)

At Prince of Plums shall prelate oppose
A faun of three feathers with flaunting of fur,
Long castle will collar and cast out the core,
His reign to fall ruin, mors regis to roar.
    By bank of a bishop shall butchers abide,
To nest, by God's name, with knives in hand,
Then springen in service at spiritus sung.
    In palace of prelate with pearls all appointed,
By kingmaker's cunning a king to unking,
A magnate whose majesty mingles with mort.
    By Half-ten of Hawks might shender be shown.
On day of Saint Dunstan shall Death have his doom.

The thirteenth prophecy, from
Liber de Mortibus Regum Anglorum
('Book of the Deaths of English Kings')

Prologue

Moorfields, north of the walls

Under a clouded moon Agnes huddles in a sliver of utter
darkness and watches him, this dark-cloaked man, as he questions the girl by the dying fire. At first he is kind seeming,
almost gentle with her. They speak something like French: not
the flavour of Stratford-at-Bowe nor of Paris, but a deep and
throated tongue, tinged with the south. Olives and figs in his
voice, the embrace of a warmer sea.

He repeats his last question.

The girl is silent.

He hits her.

She falls to the ground. He squats, fingers coiled through
her lush hair.

'*Doovay leebro?*' he gently chants. '*Ileebro, mee ragazza.
Ileebro.*' It could be a love song.

The girl shakes her head. This time he brings a fist, loosing
a spray of blood and spittle from her lips. A sizzle on a
smouldering log. Now he pulls her up, dangling her head
before him, her body a broken doll in his hands. Another
blow, and the girl's nose cracks.

'*Ileebro.*' Screaming at her now, shaking her small frame.

1

'*Nonloso!*' she cries. '*Nonloso, seenoray.*' She spits in his face.

He releases her and stands. Hands on his knees, he lets fly a string of words. Agnes can make nothing of them, but the girl shakes her head violently, her hands clasped in prayer.

'*No no no, seenoray, no no no.*' She screams, sobs, now whimpers as her softening cries fade into the silence of the moor.

When she is still he speaks again. '*Doovay leebro?*'

This time the girl hesitates. Moonlight catches the whites of her eyes, her gaze darting toward the dense foliage.

In the thick brush Agnes stiffens, ready to spring. The moment lengthens. Finally, in the clearing, the girl lowers her head. '*Nonloso.*' Her voice rings confident this time, unafraid.

The man raises a hand. In it he clutches a stick of some kind. No, a hammer. 'This is your last chance, my dear.'

Agnes's limbs go cold. *Perfect gentleman's English.* More than that, she knows this man's voice, has heard it close to her ear, though she can't summon the face. One of a thousand.

Now the girl throws back her head, lips parted to the dark sky, the dread ascending in a last flux of words: '*Though faun escape the falcon's claws and crochet cut its snare, when father, son, and ghost we sing, of city's blade beware!*'

English again, brushed with an accent, confusing the night with these strange portents hurled at the stars. She's taunting him, Agnes thinks. He hesitates, the hammer still in the air.

Finally it descends. There is a glint of iron, and a sound Agnes will never forget.

⁙

For hours Agnes waits, as the moon leaves the sky, as the din of night creatures falls slowly into a bottomless silence. Now dawn, birdsong mingling with the distant shouts of

2

workingmen within the city walls. The priory rings Lauds, and light rises across the moor.

Time to move. She arms aside a span of branches, scoring her wrists on dense clusters of twigs and nubs. A tentative foot out among the primrose, a pale blanket of scent.

Her gaze glides over the clearing: the lean-to, the remnants of the fire, the body. Her killer has stripped the girl to the flesh. Not with unthinkable intent, but with a deliberation that makes clear his aim. He was searching her, picking at her, like a wolf at a fresh kill. No rings on the delicate fingers, no brooch at the slender neck, though a silver bracelet circles her wrist. With her right hand Agnes clumsily unclasps it, admiring the small pearl pendant, the delicate chain. She pockets it. The only other item of value is a damask dress, tossed over a rotten log. Too big and bulky to carry into the city, and too fine for Agnes to wear.

Her left arm, still pinned at her side, aches. The small bundle has been clutched too tightly to her breast, almost moulded to her body. A thousand thorns wake her limb as she examines what the doomed girl thrust wordlessly at her hours ago. A bright piece of cloth, tied in leather cord, wrapped around a rectangular object of some kind. She collapses on a high stone and rests the bundle on her knees. With one tug the cord comes free.

A book. She opens it, looking for pictures. None. She tosses the thin manuscript to the ground.

What she notices next is the cloth. A square of silk, the embroidery dense and loud, the whole of it still stiff with the volume's shape. She spreads the cloth to its full span. Here is a language she reads: of splits and underside couching, of pulled thread and chain stitch, an occulted story told in thread of azure, gold, and green. At the centre of the cloth appear symbols that speak of ranks far above hers. Here a boy, there a castle, there a king; here lions rampant, there lilies of France; here a sword, there a shield.

Agnes knows something of livery, suspects the import of what she holds. A woman has just died for it, a man has just killed. For what? She remembers the girl's last, haunting words.

> *Though faun escape the falcon's claws and crochet*
> *cut its snare,*
> *When father, son, and ghost we sing, of city's blade*
> *beware!*

The rhythm of a minstrel's verse, one she has never heard. Yet the rhyme will not leave her mind, and she mouths it as she thinks her way back through the walls. Which road is less likely to be watched, which gate's keepers less likely to bother with a tired whore, some random maudlyn dragging it into London at this hour?

Cripplegate. Agnes takes a final kneel next to the dead girl and whispers a prayer. She retrieves the book and wraps it once more in the cloth, hiding them both in her skirts.

Soon she has left the Moorfields and traced a route below the causeway, circling north of a city suddenly foreign to her, though she has spent nearly all her life between its many gates. She enters London dimly aware that she holds things of great value on her person and in her mind, though unsure what to do with any of them, nor what they mean, nor whom to trust.

A cloth, a book, a snatch of verse.

Which is worth dying for?

PART ONE

The Prince of Plums

*Day xv before the Kalends of April
to the Ides of April, 8 Richard II
(18 March–13 April 1385)*

ONE

Newgate, Ward of Farringdon

If you build your own life around the secret lives of others, if you erect your house on the corrupt foundations of theirs, you soon come to regard all useful knowledge as your due. Information becomes your entitlement. You pay handsomely for it; you use it selectively and well. If you are not exactly trusted in certain circles, you are respected, and your name carries a certain weight. You are rarely surprised, and never deceived.

Yet there may come a time when your knowledge will betray you. A time when you will find even the brightest certainties – of friendship, of family, even of faith – dimming into shadows of bewilderment. When the light fails and belief fades into nothingness, and the season of your darkest ignorance begins.

Mine fell in the eighth year of Richard's reign, over that span of weeks separating the sobriety of Lent from the revelry of St Dunstan's Day. London often treats the passing of winter into spring with cold indifference. That year was no different. February had been an unforgiving month, March worse, and as the city scraped along toward April the air seemed to grow

7

only more bitter, the sky more grey, the rain more penetrating as it lifted every hint of warmth from surfaces of timber and stone.

So too with the jail at Newgate: a stink in the air, a coating on the tongue. I had come over the bridge that leaden morning to speak with Mark Blythe, jailed on the death of his apprentice. I had come, too, as a small favour to the prior of St Mary Overey, the Southwark parish that Blythe once served as head mason. For years I had let a house along the priory's south wall, and knew Blythe's family well.

We had been chewing for a while on the subject of the coming trial, and whether I might help him avoid it. No fire in the musty side-chamber. I was losing my patience, and more of my vision than usual. 'You have no choice, unless you want to hang, or worse,' I told him. 'And there is worse, Mark. I've seen it. I've smelled it.'

'It was an accident, Master Gower.'

'So you've said, Mark. How could you have known the axle would break?' Despite the prison chill a bead of moisture, thick as wheel oil, cleared a path down his cheek. Blythe had lost three fingers, two from his left hand as well as his right thumb, his body marked with the perils of his craft, and Newgate's heavy irons had scored his forearms. I softened my voice. 'But the axle did break. The stones, half a ton of them, did spill out and crush that boy's legs. Your apprentice did die, Mark. And the soundness of that cart was your responsibility.'

'Not's how I saw it, and as for the axle . . .' His voice trailed off.

I heard a sigh, realized it was my own. 'The problem, Mark, is that the law sees different kinds of accidents. You can't claim accidental injury when your own negligence – when your carelessness has been taken as the cause of death.'

Blythe's hands dropped to the table.

'Please don't make me tell your wife you've just put your life in the hands of a petty jury.'

His eyes widened. 'But you'd stand for me, wouldn't you then, Master Gower?'

'I'm not an advocate, Mark. What I have are connections. And money. I can put those at your service. But not before a jury.' Poor timing, I didn't say. Before the crackdown last year I could have bribed any jury in the realm.

His shoulders slumped. 'No trial, then. How quick to get me out?'

I hesitated. 'You'll be here until next delivery. June, I would think.'

'More time, sir? In *here*?' He shook his head. 'They'll send me down, sir, down to the Bocardo. They press them down there, it's said. Sticks them with nails like Jesu himself, do abominations each to the other. Don't want the Bocardo, Master Gower, not by the blood.'

My hands settled on Blythe's mangled fingers, stilling them against the wood. Mutilated, cracked, darkened with years of stonework, these fingers had shaped their share of useful beauty over the years: a lintel, a buttress, the pearled spans of a bishop's palace, the mortaring so precise you would never know from beyond a few feet that what you saw was not a single stone. 'Mark, I will do what I can to—'

'Have an end!'

I flinched at the yawn of old hinges and half-turned to the door. Tom Tugg, keeper of Newgate, a cock in the yard. He swung a ring of keys, each a gnarled foot of iron. 'Fees to be tallied and collected presently,' he crooned, and two turnkeys did their work. Blythe moaned, the irons biting his swollen wrists.

It took a moment, but finally Tugg saw my face. Even in the scant light of three candles I caught his gape.

'Whatsit – who let this *fiend* speak to my prisoner?' He spun on his men. 'Who put them in here?'

Your deputy. A small threat for a small thing. The turnkeys just shrugged.

9

'Take him back,' Tugg ordered, a spit of disgust. He looked at me, and got my heartiest smile. He licked his lips. 'Come along, then.'

I gave Blythe's broad back a pat before he was pulled in the opposite direction. Tugg led me along the passage to the outer gatehouse. A fight had broken out in the women's chamber, a crowd cheering the crunch of bone on the stone floor. At the gatehouse door Tugg turned on me. 'Well?' His chin was pocked, unshaved.

'I would like Blythe transferred to Ludgate until delivery.'

Tugg wrinkled his heavy brow. 'Ludgate, you say?' The new prison, recently completed at the western gate and now under the custody of the city chamber, housed those accused only of civil offences. So pleasant were its conditions that stories were circulating of inmates striking deals to remain jailed. 'You've got to understand my *situation* here, Gower,' he said with a slight twinge of his jaw. 'Newgate's abrim with spies.'

'So I've heard,' I said, prepared for this. 'Secret alliances with the Scots, French agents lurking behind every door.'

'Twenty of them at last count, held without surety.'

'All the more reason to move Mark Blythe, then, for he's no spy,' I said. 'Relieve the overcrowding, put a petty criminal out of your mind.' Almost there. 'You can say it was your idea, sound leader that you are.'

He blew out a breath. 'A pound, Gower. It'll take a pound to move him, what with that touchy keeper they got, dealings with the Guildhall—'

'Wonderful,' I said. 'We'll deduct it from your balance.' Tugg was still down to me many pounds; another handful of shillings would make little difference.

'See here, Gower—'

'Nothing to see, Tugg. I have your debt, I have your note. And I have the most horrendous bit of—'

'Ludgate, then,' he said, with another thick sigh. 'He'll be there till delivery.'

I gave him a hard look. '*Live* delivery.' He nodded.

Outside Newgate I retrieved my pattens, then trudged through the walls and up the muddy way to Holbourne, breathing shallowly on the bridge as I neared the outer reaches of the ward. Before the churchyard at St Andrew a wild-haired man preached to the drizzle, his only parishioners a crescent of nosing goats. I caught a snatch of verse as I ducked into the narrow alley just east of Thavie's Inn.

> 'Full long shall he lead us, full rich shall he rule,
> Through pain of pestilence, through wounds of
>   long war.
> Yet *morire* is matter all sovereigns must suffer.'

All kings must die. True enough, and the lines were well wrought, though the preacher soon lapsed into the usual fare. Corruption, gluttony, lust, the coming holocaust of the unfaithful. I wondered how long the poor man would last before joining Blythe in his cell.

At street level Monksblood's stood open to the weather, a brick wedged beneath the alley door. I leaned in and gave a nod to the keeper. He tossed me a jar. At the foot of the stairs sat his daughter, a slight thing of about eight. With her foot resting on the next cask, she angled my jar beneath the tap and carefully turned the bronze spigot. I dropped a few pennies in her little palm. A wan smile, tired eyes bright for a moment beneath her shining brow, then she looked past me and up the stairs, waiting for her father's next fish.

With the sour ale on my tongue I surveyed the undercroft tavern, lit weakly by a row of lanterns dangling from heavy beams. The tables were nearly empty, just two groups of men clustered along the hearth. Masons, fresh from work on the bridge. I got a few sullen looks. Steam rising from damp clothes, the muffled clatter of boots overhead.

In the far corner my friend sat alone, frowning into his jar

11

as his finger traced a slow arc around its mouth. He seemed coiled on the bench, his brow knit, his eyes narrowed in concentration, the whole of him tensed against some unspoken thought.

'Geoffrey,' I said, and moved forward.

Half-turning with a start, he rose, his face blossoming into a smile. '*Mon ami.*' He spread his hands.

As my arms wrapped his frame I felt the familiar surge of anticipation: for court gossip, for poetic banter, for news of mutual acquaintances. Yet beneath the thin coat I also felt ribs, hard against tightened skin. Chaucer had lost a couple of stone that winter; there was less to him since his latest return from abroad, and his unfashionable surcoat, of undyed wool cut simply with straight sleeves, lent an almost rural aspect to his bearing. Normally he would dress like a bit of a fop. I wondered what explained the change.

For a while we just drank, saying nothing, two hounds sniffing around after a long separation. Eventually he leaned over the board. 'How has it been, John? You know . . .'

I looked away. 'Let's not bleed that wound, Geoffrey.'

He let that hang, then touched my elbow. 'I hope it has started to heal, at least.'

'I had her things removed and sold at Candlemas – most of them.' Candlemas: purification, purging, the scouring of the soul and the larder. I thought, as I hadn't in weeks, of Sarah's prayerbook, its margins and flyleaves full of her jottings. It was one of the few of her possessions I had kept.

Chaucer moved his hand away. I asked about Philippa. He picked a splinter from the table. 'Keeps to court, hovering around her sister and the Infanta. It doesn't help that I'm travelling all the time. Calais, the cinque ports.'

'And this recent trip, to Tuscany and Milan? The custom was able to spare you?' Back in November Chaucer had arranged for a deputy to step in for him at the customhouse. His trip south had been planned hastily, and for reasons he had kept to himself.

'Some negotiations for the chancellor: a bribe here, a false promise there.' He pushed a lump of talgar across the table. The Welsh cheese was an epiphany on my tongue: tart, rich, deliciously illegal. 'Though this trip was a bit less official than the last. *Inglese italianizzato, diavolo incarnato.*' He feigned a sinister smile.

An Englishman italianized is the devil incarnate. 'A judgment you inspired, I suppose?'

'You've been practising!'

I hadn't, though the odd lesson from Chaucer in recent years had taught me a few useless phrases. '*Donde il formaggio?*' I said awkwardly, pretending to look around for the cheese.

He smiled. 'It's *dov'è il formaggio*, John, not *donde*. Where *is* the cheese, not where is the cheese *from*.' He pushed the talgar my way.

'*Dov'è*. Right.' I knifed another wedge.

He went on about his trip. 'And the books! In the Visconti libraries you can't reach out a hand without—Speaking of books, I've brought you a little something.' From his bag he removed a volume and set it between us. '*Il Filostrato*. A work that has reminded me of you since I first read it years ago, though I can't quite say why. It's a tragedy of the Trojan War, and a story of love. Not to your usual tastes, though I have a feeling you'll enjoy it. And it will give me an excuse to teach you more Italian.'

I thanked him and stroked the embossed spine and cover. Calf, dyed a deep purple, cool and smooth. 'The writer?'

'Giovanni Boccaccio,' he said. 'I tried to meet him once, but he wouldn't see me. A recluse, practically a hermit.'

'Boccaccio.' A name, like the talgar, worth savouring. I mouthed the rubrics as I leafed, admiring the ghostly thinness of the abortive vellum. No full-page illuminations, but the larger initials were ornate, with gold flourishes, a full palette of inks, descenders reaching out to curl around the peculiar

13

beasts in the margins. There was a poem on the second leaf, a single stanza in a hand I knew well.

> *Go, little book, to our unfathomed friend,*
> *Above his silvered head to build a shrine,*
> *Retreat of Wisdom, Ignorance to mend.*
> *Full oft there shall you comfort and entwine*
> *His long limbs in bookish fetters benign.*
>   *Thou shalt preserve those aquamarine gems,*
>   *Or Gower's friend shall cast you in the Thames.*

As always Chaucer's verse captured its subject with the precision of a mirror. My thinning hair, shot through with spreading grey. My long frame, which had two lean inches on Chaucer's, and he was not a short man by any measure. Finally the eyes. 'Gower green,' a limner I once knew named their shade, claiming no success in duplicating it. Sarah had always likened them to her native Malvern Hills at noon, though she had died without fathoming the truth about these eyes, and their diminishing powers. Only Chaucer possessed that knowledge, expressed in a touching bit of protectiveness in the couplet.

I looked up to see him staring vacantly at the far wall. I closed the book.

'Why did you want to meet here of all places?'

'I'm less known in Holbourne,' he whispered, in French, teasing, 'where there's smaller chance of recognition than within the walls.'

'Ah, I see,' I replied, also in French. 'I am the object of a secret mission, then. Like your visits to Hawkwood and the Florentine *commune.*'

His smile dimmed. 'Hawkwood. Yes. You know, I spent some time with Simon while I was in Florence.'

'God's *blood*, Geoffrey!'

He looked uncomfortable. 'You didn't write to him after Sarah died.'

14

'No.'

'He's your son, John. Your sole heir.'

The child who survived, when three others did not. I drained my jar, signalled the girl for another.

'Have you heard from him?' he asked, reading my thoughts.

A fresh dipper, and I drank deeply. 'Tell me about your sons instead,' I said, in a feeble change of subject. 'How is Thomas faring at the almonry?'

'Well enough, I suppose,' he said.

'And little Lewis?'

'With his mother, the little devil.' He gave a half shrug. 'Some call *him* the devil, our Hawkwood. But I suppose our king knows what he's doing when it comes to alliances.'

'What few of them he has left,' I said.

He looked at me, smiling. 'No King Edward, is he?'

I held up my jar. 'Full long shall he lead us, full rich shall he rule.'

His smile faded. 'Wherever did you pick that up, John?'

'A preacher, versing it up out on Holbourne just now.'

'Our sermonizers are quite poetical these days, aren't they?' he scoffed. There was a certain strain in his voice, though I thought nothing of it at the time.

'Fools, if you ask me, to versify on that sort of matter,' I said.

'Better to stick to Gawain and Lancelot, I suppose.'

'Or fairies.'

'Or friars.'

We laughed quietly. There was a long silence, then Chaucer sighed, tapped his fingers. 'John, I need a small favour.'

Of course you do. 'Go on.'

'I'm looking for a book.'

'A book.'

'I've heard it was in the hands of one of Lancaster's hermits.'

I watched his eyes. 'Why can't you get it for yourself?'

'Because I don't know who has it, or where it is at the moment.'

'And who does know?'

He raised his chin, his jaw tight. I knew that look. 'Katherine Swynford, perhaps. If a flea dies in Lancaster's household she'll have heard about it. Ask her.'

'She's your sister-in-law, Geoffrey.' I felt a twinge of misgiving. However innocent on its face, no request from Chaucer was ever straightforward. 'Why not ask her yourself?'

'She and Philippa are inseparable. Katherine won't see me.'

'So you're asking me to approach her?'

He took a small sip.

'Why me?' I said.

'How to put it?' He pretended to search for words, his hands flitting about on the table. 'This job needs a *subterranean* man, John. A man who knows this city like the lines in his knuckles, its secrets and surprises. All those shadowed corners and blind alleyways where you do your nasty work.'

I gazed fondly at him, thinking of Simon, and so much else. It was one of the peculiarities of our intimacy that Chaucer seemed to appreciate talents no one else would value in a friend. Here comes John Gower, it was murmured at Westminster and the Guildhall; hide your ledgers. Hide your thoughts. For knowledge is currency. It can be traded and it can be banked, and more secretly than money. The French have a word for informers: *chanteurs*, 'singers', and information is a song of sorts. A melody poured in the ears of its eager recipients, every note a hidden vice, a high crime, a deadly sin. Or some kind of illicit antiphon, its verses whispered among opposed choirs of the living and the dead.

We live in a hypocritical age. An age that sees bishops preaching abstinence while running whores. Pardoners peddling indulgences while seducing wives. Earls pledging fealty while

16

plotting treason. Hypocrites, all of them, and my trade is the bane of hypocrisy, its worth far outweighing its perversion. I practise the purest form of truthtelling.

Quite profitably, too. The second son of a moderately wealthy knight has some choices: the law, the royal bureaucracy, Oxford or Cambridge, the life of a monk or a priest. Yet I would rather have trapped grayling in the Severn for a living than taken holy orders, and it was clear that my poetry would never see the lavishments from patrons that Chaucer's increasingly enjoyed. Yet I shall never forget the thrill I felt when that first coin of another man's vice fell into my lap, and I realized what I had – and how to use it. Since then I have become a trader in information, a seller of suspicion, a purveyor of foibles and the hidden things of private life. I work alone and always have, without the trappings of craft or creed.

John Gower. A guild of one.

'You can't be direct with her about it,' Chaucer was saying. 'This is a woman who takes the biggest cock in the realm between her legs. She's given Lancaster three bastards at last count – or is it four?' He waited, gauging my reaction.

'What is this book, Geoffrey? What does it look like? What's in it?'

His gaze was unfocused and vague. 'To be honest with you, John, I don't know. What I do know is that this book could hurt me.' He blinked and looked at some spot on the wattle behind me. Then, in a last whisper of French, 'It could cost me my life.'

Our eyes locked, and I wondered in that instant, as I would so often in the weeks to come, what price such a book might extract from my oldest friend. He broke the tension with one of his elvish smiles. 'If you can do this for me, John, get me this book, I'll be greatly in your debt.'

As you are so deeply in mine, he did not say; nor did he need to, and in his position neither would I have. I left

17

Monksblood's that morning bound to perform this 'small favour', as Chaucer had called it, for the one man in all the world I could never refuse. The man who knew my own darkest song.

TWO

Gropecunt Lane, Ward of Cheap

Eleanor Rykener grunted, spat, wiped her lips. The friar covered his shrivelled knob. Wouldn't meet her eyes, of course. Franciscans, they never liked to look. He dropped his groats on the straw. 'Why thank you, Brother Michael,' she said, her voice a sullen nip. The friar stared coldly at some spot on her neck, then shrugged on his cowl, edged around the old mare, and left the stall.

When she had dressed, Eleanor stepped out into the light rain, looking down toward the stone cross before St Pancras. The friar wouldn't give that a glance either as he slunk around the corner of the churchyard toward Soper Lane. She raised her face to the sky, cleansing his piety from her tongue.

'Regular as these little oinkers here.' Mary Potts leaned against a post, gesturing to a dozen pigs nosing street muck.

Eleanor tossed her gossip a tired smile. 'And never has the good grace to render me confession after I grant him service.'

They stood in silence for a while, watching the flow of late-afternoon traffic up along Cheapside, the creak of old wheels, the low calls of sheep, the urgings of hucksters, though the din seemed always distant from the ladies of Gropecunt

Lane, a quiet byway of leased horsestalls and abandoned shopfronts that absorbed sound the way a dry rag absorbs ale, and as central as St Paul's to the human business of London. Every now and then this business would be theirs, as some desiring man, face to the ground, mind on slit, would make the turn and find a maudlyn to take his groats and squirt. Despite the lane's reputation, the girls kept things tidy, raking the dirt and pavers themselves, cleaning up after animal and man alike. It was their own small piece of the city, where jakes plucked coin from their purses and maudlyns tucked it into theirs, the ordinances be damned. A simple thing.

'Afternoon, m'pretties!'

Eleanor turned. Joan Rugg lifted her skirts as she hopped from stone to stone in a vain attempt to avoid the mud.

'What now what now what now,' Mary Potts murmured.

With a final grunt, Joan heaved herself on to the pavers fronting the stalls and straightened her dress, a shapeless thing of stained wool. The Dun Bell, Joan's girls called their bawd, with three chins stacked against her neck, lips full and always moist, beady eyes that moved more quickly than any other part of her, and a mass of matted hair entwined through the band of a wide hat she never removed. This, a splendid circle of leather and wool adorned with flowers of faded silk, had been given to her by a lover in her youth, she liked to recall. On that misty day its perch lent her large form an air of botanical mystery, as if the viewer were approaching a mountaintop garden above the clouds, or some strange, Edenic island in the sea. 'You ladies seen our Agnes?' she asked.

'Not today,' said Mary Potts.

'Thought you sent her up Westminster on Tuesday,' said Eleanor, suddenly concerned. As far as she knew Agnes Fonteyn had been consorting with one of the king's substewards, a long-time jake who would request Agnes's company for a few days at a time during royal absences.

'Didn't come through.' Joan raised her sleeve to scratch at

20

her forearm. 'But I had a particular request for her this morning, from a fine gentleman of the Mercery. And a procuratrix'd like to make arrangements, right?'

'You talked to her mother down Southwark?' Mary asked.

'Sign of the Pricking Bishop,' Eleanor added quickly, naming a common house in the stews where Agnes's mother had long peddled flesh.

Joan scoffed. 'Would've had to wait in line a half day to get a word in. That whore's swyving makes her daughter look like St Margaret.'

'Did you try her sister?' Eleanor said. 'Lives up Cornhull.'

Joan wagged her head. 'Took a peek in her fancy house, asked about a bit in Broad Street, but no sight of her ladyship.'

A dungcart turned up from St Pancras on the way to the walls, banded wheels groaning under the weight, the waste of man and beast souring the air. When the clatter receded, Joan turned back to them. 'Can't have my maudlyns vanishing on me, not with Lents about to pass, appetites built up as they are. Forty days of nothing, then a week of everything, in my experience.'

Mary groaned, her arms wrapping a post. 'Shoulda been a nun, shouldn't I, maybe took vows with them Benedictines?'

'Ah, but then you'd *really* be getting it in every hole, my dear,' said Joan wisely.

The two of them shared the laughter for a bit, attracting a few looks from other girls up the lane as Eleanor clasped her hands in worry. Joan put a hand to her chin. With a sidelong glance at Eleanor, she said, 'Agnes got a little spot, though, don't she? Out in the Moorfields.'

'A small walk short of Bethlem,' said Eleanor with a natural shudder. 'I've been there with her.' This was Agnes's 'lair', as she called it: an old hunter's blind outside the city walls where some of her wealthier jakes liked to take her, along with any other maudlyns they could cajole. They were, for the most part, young, reckless men with too much time and coin on their hands. Or fellows whose names might start with *Sir*.

'Go have a look then, will you?' said Joan. Her sweetest wheedle.

Eleanor hesitated. 'Rather not go alone.'

Joan heaved a shoulder at Mary. 'Take the child with you. Be back bell of six, or shortly after. Sky looks to be clearing, so we'll likely be busy tonight, the blood of London rising strong.'

Mary, playing the genteel, crooked her elbow. Eleanor took her arm, and they left Joan Rugg standing beside the stalls. 'Bell of six now,' the bawd called after them. Eleanor waved an acknowledgment, only too glad to escape her sticky work for a few hours, though quite worried for Agnes.

A muddy trudge in the drizzle took them along Cheapside past the Standard at le Vout, where two vagrants hunching in the stocks chewed at tack as a one-armed boy softened the biscuits in ale. A straight course up Wood Street and they were at Cripplegate. Eleanor looked up as they passed beneath the gatehouse, the prisoners idling behind the high grates, the keepers giving the two mauds barely a glance. Agnes likewise would have strolled from the inner half of the ward to the outer without a second thought from these men. Strange, that she would have let off her work for longer than a few hours, let alone a full day; she seemed always wanting more shillings, the busiest girl on Gropecunt Lane and happy about it.

Strange, too, that she'd said nothing to Eleanor about her plans, for the two maudlyns had long been intimate, swapping jakes, lending a coin here and there, looking out for one another in their carnal trade, and always mindful of the situations that had led them to it: Eleanor, an orphan, her younger brother apprenticed to a Southwark butcher who beat him mercilessly; Agnes Fonteyn, who had fled her mother's bawdy house in the stews for a higher cut of her skincoin. *Tightest yoke a' mauds you'll ever see*, Joan Rugg liked to say, and it was true.

Once past Cripplegate they skirted the northern wall past the bricked-up postern at the foot of the causeway and soon came to the edge of an overgrown orchard. Here the lane opened out into the broad expanse of the Moorfields, a linked series of marshy heaths that formed London's nearest hunting grounds, mostly deer and fowl. A few drier, higher bits could handle cows at pasture, though for the most part the whole area was a fen. That late afternoon Eleanor and Mary saw no one moving among the high tufts of moorgrass.

The first path off the causeway led to a spot beneath a large, lone oak. From there a smaller path branched off to the east. Ahead loomed the mass of Bethlem Priory, its walls heightened and buttressed since the order started taking in lunatics the year before. Eleanor recalled her last visit to Agnes's lair, the mix of routine coupling and utter terror. The desperate gropings of an ageing squire, the loose spread of his gut on her back like a jelly blanket – then a sound that shrivelled the squire's cock, and her own as well: a lunatic's scream, echoing from the Bethlem walls. Since that night Eleanor had heard similar accounts of the priory's madmen, fighting their chains as the canons extended their charity to the wrong of mind.

Eleanor saw the white rock that marked the final turn. They pushed through the heavy foliage until they reached a high wall of hawthorn. A strong scent of primrose masked a sweeter, sicker smell beneath. Mary touched her arm. Eleanor held her breath and stepped into the dense brush. A flash of bare skin on the ground, glistening, moist. Eleanor pushed aside the last branches. They saw the body.

She was face down in the wetness, naked, her skin marbled with mud and rain. Her hair, caked in soil, had spread into three slicked highways from the crown of her crushed head, opened to the vermin. Beside her left hand lay a shoeing hammer, its handle resting carelessly over a root. Eleanor, in a daze, picked it up, felt its killing weight. As she stood feeble guard, Mary, with a heavy sigh, squatted in the mud beside the body. 'Oh, you poor thing,' she said. 'Oh, Agnes you were so lovely, oh my beautiful.'

'Turn her over then, get her face out of the peat,' said Eleanor, hammer still at the ready. Something didn't make sense. Agnes's hair—

Mary pulled at the girl's shoulders. With a suck of mud she came free. Once she was flipped Mary used her hem to wipe the dark patches from the girl's ruined face.

They stared down at her, at first disbelieving what they saw. Eleanor glanced into the hunter's blind. A pile of women's finery thrown over a stump: an ivory busk, a taffeta cape trimmed with fur, more silk than she and her fellow maudlyns could ever hope to afford, all in a style that Eleanor – who had a poor girl's eye for new jet, could tell you who in town sold the latest dresses from Ghent and Bruges – had rarely seen in London. She looked back at the face.

This dead girl was indeed lovely. She was not Agnes Fonteyn.

THREE

La Neyte, Westminster

Wat Tyler. Jack Straw. The city as powerless as a widow, Troy without its Hector, the commons running like barnyard animals through her streets, taking her bridges, torching her greatest houses, storming the Tower and murdering the lord chancellor and the lord treasurer. Though it had been four years since the Rising swept through London, the memories still haunted our great but tired city, pooling beneath the eaves, drifting along narrow alleys with the continuing threat of revolt.

No one had been more affected by the events of those grim weeks than John of Gaunt, Duke of Lancaster. After stealing everything worth taking, Tyler and his gang burned Gaunt's Thames-side palace to the ground, and the ruins of the Savoy would sit along the Strand for years: a charred reminder of the brute power of the commons, and the constant threat embodied by the city's aggrieved poor.

Now the duke avoided London as much as possible, centring his life and his business around the castle of Kenilworth far to the north. When his presence was required in the city Gaunt would appear for a few days or a week at a time, the grudged

25

guest of those magnates willing to tolerate his household, and betting on his survival. Often he would lodge at Tottenham, though that Lent he was residing at La Neyte, the Abbot of Westminster's moated grange a mile up-river from the abbey, and it was there I would be granted an audience with his sometime mistress, arranged the day before.

The duke himself was just leaving the abbot's house as I arrived in the upper gateyard, his retainers gosling along behind him. He half-turned to me, his brow knit in fury as he acknowledged my bent knee with a curt nod. Those around him knew better than to speak, as did I.

In the summer hall I moved slowly along the wall, mingling with the line of bored servants as thick hangings brushed my cheek. The chamber teemed with lords of various ranks who had been seeking a word with the duke before his abrupt departure, and I tried to go unremarked by those remaining. My eyes, uncooperative, failed to spy a drip bucket, full of rainwater from the porous ceiling. It surrendered its contents to my left foot, then clattered across the floor. There was a hush. It was Michael de la Pole who broke it in his graceful way. 'Not to worry. The abbot has ordered some silken buckets,' said the lord chancellor into the silence, giving me a slight nod. Laughter, though not at my expense, filled that portion of the hall, and the baron resumed his conversation.

Standing behind the baron, shifting a little as the hubbub returned, Robert de Vere, the Earl of Oxford, gave me an ugly look. I glanced away, though not before noting his discomfort. De Vere had likely been the target of Gaunt's ire, and now here's John Gower, come to brew more trouble, as if the particular group of magnates clustered in the hall at La Neyte that day did not promise enough. A duke, an earl, and a baron, a tensile triangle of mutual suspicion and dependence. Gaunt was still furious at de Vere for turning the king against him at the February tournament at Westminster, where a plot against the duke's life was only narrowly averted – and this after all the business the year before at the Salisbury Parliament, where Gaunt's supposed plot against his royal nephew nearly led to the duke's hanging on the spot. The plot was spun of gossamer, of course, the invention of a Carmelite friar who was afterwards seized on the way to his cell and tortured to death. One year, two imaginary plots, and great trouble for the realm. De Vere, the young king's current favourite and a notorious flatterer, was taking every advantage he could of the widening rift between the king and the duke, gathering nobles to his side in an open attempt to wrest power from the much older Lancaster. Caught in the middle of it all was the Baron de la Pole, chief financier to old King Edward and now lord chancellor, determined to keep the peace at all costs – and, it appeared to me, losing ground by the day.

Oxford had now turned his back on de la Pole, suggesting that he had taken the chancellor's kind gesture toward me as an insult to him. Sir Stephen Weldon, chief knight of the earl's household, noticed his lord's vexation and excused himself. I set my face for the encounter. This took some effort, for Weldon's most distinguishing characteristic was a crescent scar on his chin, a jagged curve of whitened skin. Whenever I saw it I imagined a line of Oxford's wretched tenants hooked by their necks, swinging in the wind.

'Gower.'

'Sir Stephen.'

'Our fine town should consider itself gilded indeed whenever John Gower deigns to abandon Southwark to tread Westminster's humbler lanes.'

'Even as these avenues acclaim your own passings through with their every voice.' How I hate this man.

Weldon assessed me, a peculiar glint in his eyes. 'You look awful, Gower. I'd thought it was your wife who was sick.'

I stared at his scar. 'Sarah died last year. The week of Michaelmas.'

He raised a hand to his mouth. 'I'd not heard.'

I said nothing.

'You must forgive me, John,' he insisted. 'It is inexcusable.'

'Though unsurprising, Sir Stephen.'

His eyes narrowed. He was about to say something more, then thought better of it. They usually do, even the higher knights. He inclined his head, spun on a toe, and rejoined the cluster around Oxford, leaving me wondering why the man had approached me in the first place.

Someone coughed, stifled it. Katherine Swynford was descending from the abbot's chambers, given over to Gaunt for the duration of his stay. Her skin glowed with the duke's recent departure, the cut of her gown too low by a coin's span, her hood trimmed in a silk brocade that matched her emerald eyes. Stretching her compact frame, she looked about until her gaze settled on me. With a subtle toss of her head she directed me to the wide oratorium off the summer hall, where a group of five other ladies sat at their embroidery.

'Why did you want to see me, John?' she said when I joined her. She glanced over her shoulder, already impatient.

I recalled Chaucer's anxious state at Monksblood's. *You can't be direct with her about it.* I opted against obedience. 'Apparently Geoffrey thinks you might know about a book he's seeking.'

She let me stand in silence, leaning over to correct a companion. 'Unravel that. Less of an arc, more of a triangle. Lovely. Then pin out the *roet*.' Dame Katherine never failed to amaze me in those days, commanding the duchess's ladies-in-waiting as if they were already her own.

At length she gave me her attention. 'Always on the lookout for the next little book, isn't he?'

'Too true.'

'What's special about this one?' She took up a narrow strip of cloth of gold, which she proceeded to pick apart from the edges.

28

'It's – delicate,' I said, hiding my ignorance behind a veil of discretion.

'Well of course it is, John, or it wouldn't be you standing before me but my own brother-in-law!' She continued to pick. 'What a worm.'

I silently conceded the larger point. Gaunt's subtle favouritism toward Chaucer was well known and had been ever since Geoffrey composed an elegy upon the death of Duchess Blanche some years ago. Katherine viewed him as an unworthy rival for the duke's attention. The current duchess certainly wasn't getting much of it, despite Gaunt's vow after the Rising to forsake his mistress in favour of his marriage. The duke had seen the rebellion as a warning from God to put away his long-standing consort, and indeed for several years the two had succeeded in avoiding one another's presence, even as the duke plied her from afar with luxurious gifts, properties, and pounds. Now, by all indications, things were boiling up again, their liaisons increasingly out in the open, as they had formerly been for so many years.

Yet I remained one of Dame Katherine's greatest admirers, both for her restraint and for her admirable fortitude in the face of so much calumny from her detractors. Despite what must have been nearly irresistible pressure from Lancaster, she had never broken her vows while her husband lived, even when Sir Hugh Swynford was abroad. That Lancaster was now breaking his own was the duke's problem, not hers. She seemed determined in those years to see him through another duchess, whatever the cost to her reputation and prospects.

'So . . . what makes him think the book is here?' she said, giving me a look.

'He heard it indirectly from one of the duke's hermits, so he says.'

'Oh? And did he bother to say which one?' She swept an arm toward the terrace doors. 'Lancaster has hermits to spare. Richard of Chatterburn, John of Singleton, Gregory of Bishop's

Lynn – David of the Ditch, Tom of the Tavern, Peter of the Privy, as common as friars. Dozens of them, popping their heads out of their holes like rabbits, sniffing for nobles whenever Gaunt opens his purse.'

'He didn't say.'

Her gaze lingered for a moment. 'Will you play cards, John?' From a side table she removed a stack of parchment ovals.

'Cards?'

'You haven't played such games?' She spread the cards across the table at her knees, and I marvelled at the colourful shapes: blue swords, golden hawks, red plums, and purple thistleflowers, all arranged in differing numbers and patterns. 'They are quite popular in Paris, though this pack comes from Florence. A gift from Chaucer, and now it's my second.' She pointed to another deck, stacked neatly on the table, and to all appearances identical to the one she held.

I asked how the game was played.

'There are many games of cards; it seems I learn a new one every week.' There were four suits, she explained, each numbering thirteen. Pips from one to nine, then the four faces in each suit: the Prince of Hawks, the Duke of Plums, the Queen of Swords, the King of Thistles, and so on.

'Fifty-two cards in all, then,' I calculated.

'Plus the trumps, a dozen of them.' She laid out another row. 'The Wheel of Fortune, the Magician, the Bleeding Tower, and this is the Sun.' An exquisite rendering of Apollo in full splendour.

'What part do the trumps play?'

'They wrestle with the pips and one another in various ways, depending on the rules of the particular game.'

Like the queen in chess, I observed.

'Though the queen has worthy rivals.' She laid out more trump cards. 'Fate, the Devil, the Fool – and, most powerful of all, Death.' A skull, leering at the viewer, the skeleton mounted on an emaciated horse. She explained the rules to a simple game involving points doled out for each pip and face card, with the trumps acting as foils. For some time we played in silence, and I noticed her agility with the parchment shapes, a sleight of hand that involved a deft use of her palms and knuckles to deal and reposition the cards in play. Eventually, as I learned the rhythm, I relaxed back into the conversation.

'Perhaps the Earl of Cambridge might know something about this book?'

Swynford raised a shoulder. She caught me looking at her bare skin, didn't seem to mind. 'Our dear Edmund Langley?' She played the Four of Hawks, a shrewd move, evidently.

'The Infanta and her sister are at court this month, I've heard.' The wives of Gaunt and Langley, the eldest of Edward's surviving sons. I went to take her four but flubbed my draw. She smiled as she swept the table clean in one movement and laid out a new play.

'Ah yes, the *hermanas español*. Those dark bitches are my little hell.' Swynford looked up with a worried smile. 'What a tangled web you spin for me, John Gower. Are you here to torture me or amuse me?'

'Your choice.'

She narrowed her eyes. 'Let's have a different game, a simpler one.' She picked up the cards again and laid ten of them face-up on the table. 'Choose one. Any card at all.'

'What determines my choice?'

'Merely the condition of your soul.'

Feeling mischievous, I leaned forward and tapped the Devil.

She puckered her lips. 'But that is Chaucer's card.'

We shared a laugh as she gathered the cards into a loose pile, though just as quickly her face clouded. 'I know something about this book.' She looked across the hall to the humming circles of gentry. 'There have been whispers of a theft. A strange manuscript, stolen from La Neyte last week.'

'Silver I could understand, or plate. But who would steal a book?'

'It was a young woman, passing as a lady-in-waiting to the Countess of Bethune. Now she's dead.'

I stared at her.

'Someone skulled her, out on the Moorfields.'

'The Moorfields? I can't imagine—'

'And, John,' she breathed, leaning forward, her eyes attractively wide, 'I think I may have seen her. Coming out of the abbot's private chapel, right before she lifted it.'

'What sort of a book?' I asked, trying to keep up.

'I know nothing of its content, I swear to you. Only rumours.' To my surprise I believed her. 'And now Braybrooke is involved, asking my duke all sorts of ugly questions. You know how suspicious everyone is since the council, and that crazed friar's rantings last year. As if my duke and the king are mad dogs in a ring, circling one another, waiting for the next chance to lunge for a neck.'

This gave me pause. 'Why would the Bishop of London be after the same book as Chaucer?'

'Suppose it's less innocent than you suspect. Not one of those romances everyone is reading. Not a saint's life. But a book of prophecies.' She narrowed her eyes. 'Heretical prophecies.'

'Prophecies.' I recalled the preacher spewing his verse out on Holbourne, and Chaucer's agitation when I recited the man's words. 'Wycliffe's work?' John Wycliffe: a heretic, thoroughly condemned and recently dead, but all the more dangerous for that.

'Lancaster doubts it, though—'

Swynford's chin lifted. She stood. I twisted my neck as I rose to see the figure of Joan, Countess of Kent and the king's mother, standing at the arched doorway. Greying hair pulled back from slivered eyes, widow's weeds on a figure to make any man pause despite her considerable age. High cheekbones,

32

set beneath a wide brow, and cobalt eyes that flashed as they settled on Swynford.

'Where is my brother?' she demanded as she approached, four of her attendants stepping aside. 'He summons me up from Wickhambreaux, yet I am kept waiting at Westminster half a day.' I winced inwardly at Gaunt's treatment of his sister-in-law. In the nine years since the death of Prince Edward, Gaunt's elder brother and former heir to the throne, the countess had seen her status slowly decline. Had her husband survived the ancient King Edward, she would have ascended to queen consort, and helped the younger Edward rule with the same flawless grace and deliberation she had shown so many times on public occasions. Though still the most beloved woman in the realm, Joan was becoming more and more of an afterthought.

Katherine put a hand to her breast. 'He just left us, Countess. An appointment at Fulham.' She straightened her skirts and retook her seat, the other ladies doing the same; a subtle insult.

Joan's lips tightened. 'Tell the duke my patience wears thin. I shall return to Wickhambreaux tomorrow.'

'I will tell him, Countess,' said Swynford.

Turning to leave, the countess looked at me. She sucked in her cheeks. 'John Gower.'

I bowed deeply. 'Your servant, Countess.'

She regarded me closely. 'I've gazed into your mirror, Gower.'

'My lady?'

'I have read your great work, the *Mirour de l'Omme*.'

My cheeks flushed. 'You surprise me, Countess.'

'Why is that?'

'I would not expect such a humble work to make its way to so noble a reader as yourself.' Nor its writer's name to be remembered.

She waved a hand. 'Rot, Gower. The breeding of Death and

Sin, the bastard births of Hypocrisy and her sisters – why, you could be describing the household of Lancaster!'

Swynford gasped, staring in hatred at her lover's sister-in-law.

The countess gestured with her chin and turned away. Chaucer's book forgotten, my head swimming with the rare flattery, I followed her through the gauze curtains and out on to the small terrace.

'I am too hard on Lancaster, you know,' she said as we circled. 'It was a unique humiliation for a man like Gaunt, to bounce his king on his knee.' She walked along the parapet, pausing to pick dead leaves out of a pot. 'Though it has to be said that there are not many so powerful yet so willing to sacrifice their ambition. You would agree?'

'The Duke of Lancaster's modesty is universally admired, my lady.'

She spun on me, eyes darkened. 'Watch yourself, Gower. The ears of Westminster are as plentiful as scales on a herring.'

'Yes, Countess,' I said, chastened.

She stared at the lines of barges plying the Thames in the distance. 'My son has many enemies. Enemies who openly question his legitimacy.'

She paused with the ruffle of curtains. In the open doorway to the upper gallery stood Swynford, the gauze draped across a bare shoulder. One of her sons had wandered to the terraces, it seemed, his gaze now following a bird. Gaunt's youngest child, a girl they had perversely named Joan, she held by the hand. Seven and counting, some Gaunt's, others her late husband's – the entangled promises of a future none could yet foresee.

Swynford, after an amused glance between the countess and me, whisked her children away. The countess watched the curtains flutter in their wake.

'Be inventive with your next work, John Gower,' she murmured as the curtains stilled. 'To see my son stand before

34

Parliament, with his slutting uncle at his side? A spectacle worthy of the mysteries.' With that she left me.

In the distance the river was a plane of drifting pieces. Barges, wherries, a raft of sawed logs soon to be swallowed by the city below. To my weakening eyes they appeared as so many living forces, moving against each other in ways I could then only dimly understand: an enigma in motion, like Swynford's foreign deck of cards. I stared at the water with a growing unease, thinking of a dead girl and a missing book, wondering what strange burden Chaucer had laid on my shoulders.

FOUR

Cornhull, Ward of Broad Street

'Please put it on my tally, Master Talbot.' Millicent Fonteyn nodded at the spicerer, willing him to wrap her purchases before his wife came to the shopfront. Between them sat four equal measures of prunes, almonds, currants, and dates. 'Oh, and a measure of the apricots,' she said, unable to stop herself.

George Lawler reached for the jar, shook his head as he tonged them out. He twined the lot together. 'Last time, Mistress Fonteyn.'

'You're kind, Master Lawler. We'll settle after Easter, if that suits. Now—'

'Oh, that suits us fine, m'lady, just fine.' Jane Lawler pushed through the alley door. She was a spindly woman, with dark brows set close and a small nose she fingered at will. 'Fine to settle after Michaelmas, fine to settle after All Saints, and, by Loy's bones, it'll be fine to settle after Easter. Why, it's only coin, isn't that right, Georgie? And if we lose it all, why, we'll get the Worshipful Company of Grocers to provide out of the common money, aye?'

Lawler sheepishly handed Millicent the bundle.

'Why, that's it, George!' his wife went on. 'Let's pack up

some raisins for her ladyship. Saffron, too, cypress root, nutmeg – why, let's crate it all for the virtuous madam and have done with our livelihood.'

Millicent, shamefaced, turned to leave, Mistress Lawler tagging her heels. 'After Easter, she says. After Easter!'

Millicent was on the street.

'As if the Resurrection of our Lord'll be enough to put a single farthing in her graspy little palm.' Millicent took a sharp right out of the shop, her shoulders stooped with humiliation. 'You walk 'neath this eave to pay your debt, Millicent Fonteyn, nor never walk 'neath it again, nor any grocer's eave of Cornhull!'

Londoners turned their heads, cruel questions in their glances. Millicent kicked through a cluster of hens by the well before St Benet Fink, fluff and feathers scattering with her haste. She stopped on Broad Street, calming herself with her back on the rough wood of a horsepost. The damp air settled around her, drawing the moisture from her skin. By the time she pushed herself off the post her dress was soaked through, with dark stains at her middle and beneath her arms.

Millicent's house fronted the longest row of tailors' shops in London. For two years now the Cornhull house had been hers, the annual lease financed by Sir Humphrey's lust and largesse, and the dwelling had matched her aspirations in every detail: a keyed door, two floors, a glazed window at the front. She loved the walk along West Cheap and through the Poultry, her back to St Paul's as she strolled along the widest street in London, with its double gutters and raked pavers. A singlewoman without profession, kept by a wealthy man for his weekly dalliances. There were far worse fates for the elder daughter of a Southwark maudlyn.

Or so she had once thought. Two pounds five was the happy sum she had possessed on the day of Sir Humphrey ap-Roger's death. Now it was nearly gone, with no provision made in the knight's will for her keep. His homely widow had got every penny of his fortune and every hand's width of his lands, leaving nothing to keep the woman he had truly loved free of penury. Millicent picked a spiced apricot out of the grocer's package, chewing but not tasting it as she approached her home. She removed the chained key from her neck.

'Why *there* you are.'

Millicent tilted her forehead against the door, sighed, then put on her best smile as she turned. Denise Haveryng, proprietress of her own late husband's thriving shop and a boastful freewoman of the city, wandered over with a tray of flans. 'Dame Haveryng.'

'You've been to Lawler's, I see.' She inspected the opened package in Millicent's hands, clearly disapproving of the indulgence. The weeds on this widow were dark only in colour: gauze sleeves flounced at her wrists, a belted sash with a leather buckle that almost glistened at her waist, and the damask lappet on her brow beneath a short-coned hat would not have looked out of place on an earl's wife.

Millicent, though not hungry, reached for a flancake.

'You've had visitors,' Dame Haveryng began. 'Three of them.'

'Ah?' Millicent opened her door. Denise herded her inside.

'Been like the Whitsunday procession. First there was Master Pratt, third time this month.'

The house's owner, clerk to the merchant taylors' guild, after her for weeks over the lease.

'Very well.' Millicent removed her hood, once a subtle latticed affair trimmed in silk, now fading and patched.

'And Jacob. To see about back wages, the poor dear.'

Millicent winced at the reminder. Even her former servants were her creditors now. 'And the third?'

'Your sister.'

Millicent froze.

38

'Takes after you, though dresses a bit downward from your station.' Denise paused in her glee. 'Wasn't aware you *had* a sister, dear.'

'We – we are not close.' Their last meeting, nearly two years before, had been a chance encounter on the wharfage, Agnes waiting to board a common wherry, Millicent and Sir Humphrey passing by to hire a private barge. They had exchanged quick smiles; Millicent remembered Agnes's hand jumping from her side, though she had settled for a furtive nod before turning away.

Ignoring the flan tray, Millicent pushed Denise from her house and shut the door. Out back she took the stairs two at a time. The door to the rear bedchamber was ajar. She entered to see her sister huddled against the wall, clutching a bolster, wrapped in a coverlet.

'What are you doing in my house, Agnes?'

Her sister looked dreadful, her skin ashen, her hair a tangled mess. Her eyes would not meet Millicent's until she had walked over to the bed and sat, the old straw pallet giving beneath her weight. Agnes looked up at her sister, her eyes darkened with sleeplessness and, Millicent thought, fear. 'I'd nowhere else to go, Mil.'

'Not to our mother's?'

'Said I'd made my choice, now I'm on my own, like I wanted it.'

'Why do you need anyone's help?'

'"Though faun escape the falcon's claws and crochet cut its snare, when father, son, and ghost we sing, of city's blade beware."'

'Are you sick, Ag? You're talking no sense.'

'She gave it me before she died. That's what she yelled.'

'Our mother has died?'

'"*Doovay leebro*", he said to her. "*Doovay leebro*", like he was singing.'

'Who was singing? Is our mother dead, Agnes?'

She shook her head. 'Not Bess Waller. That poor girl by the fire. Man with the hammer killed her.'

'Man? What man?'

Over the next while, as Millicent sat with her sister and calmed her down, Agnes haltingly told her all that had happened: her assignation in the Moorfields with the abbot of Bethlem, the holy man's departure after a short swyve, the silence as she dressed, then the crash of shrubbery before the beautiful girl burst into the small circle of firelight. 'She tried to talk, to tell me something, I could see it, but the poor thing was out a' breath, and the man was just behind her. So she shoved me her bundle and pushed me into the hawthorn and put a finger over her lips. Then he was there.' Finally the girl's death: the exchange of words in two tongues, the fall of the hammer, the killer's silent departure from the clearing.

Millicent listened with a growing disbelief, torn between sympathy for Agnes's plight and fury at her sister for bringing this darkness into her home. When Agnes had finished she stood and staggered over to a large chest, one of the last household items Millicent had to sell. She reached down behind it and withdrew a rectangular object wrapped in a heavily embroidered cloth. She looked down at the bundle for a long moment, then handed it to Millicent.

'I suspect he'll be wanting it back.'

FIVE

St Laurence Lane, Ward of Cheap

Joan Rugg slapped the constable's wrist. 'Not so pinchy there!' she cackled. The constable gave the bawd a hard shake as he led her toward the beadle's shop, where two men bearing heavy sticks stood to the sides of the door. Joan goosed them in the ribs. 'Valued jakes of the ward, these ones,' she teased. 'My best regulars.' The men traded denials.

Eleanor Rykener entered the shop behind them, a heady mix of ash and smelt in the air. An image of St Dunstan hung over the door out to the smithy in back, while wooden shelves at various heights displayed the goldsmith's newest wares. Gleaming plate, necklaces with inlaid gemstones, silver spoons laid out on silk. On the facing side were objects brought in for repair: a bishop's crozier, a set of clasps, embossed cabinet panels, a rich man's wine jug. That jug alone would buy my cock and arse for a year, Eleanor mused. Joan, she could see, was having similar thoughts about the rings.

Two apprentices tooled a brace of gold plates. For a while, as the constables shuffled their feet, the maudlyns sat and listened to the *tap tap tap*, the rough joining of common tools and precious metal, until the guildsman came in from the back. Eleanor looked up and into the nose of Richard Bickle, beadle of Cheap Ward and richest goldsmith north of Cheapside. The eyes and ears of the ward, a man who knew everything about anyone worth knowing anything about. Past master of the city's guild, Bickle was wrapped in a gown of red wool trimmed in sable, his lean face atop a neck chafed by a recent shave. 'Ladies.'

'Master Bickle,' said Joan.

'Let's cut through the elegances.' Bickle's voice was clipped, severe. He rubbed his palms. 'Two of your unspotted virgins been seen, Joan, heading into the Moorfields, coming out all spooked. Now we got a dead lady found not a hundred yards from where they come out the moor.'

Eleanor toed at a gap in the rushes.

'Hope you'll see it as we do, Joan. Girl's killed in one ward, possible witnesses whoring it up in another. City politics be a tricky business.' He spread a paternal smile. 'But no need to take this to the Guildhall, yeah? Avoid complications. Wouldn't want to shut down Gropecunt Lane again, send you and the Blessed Sisters of St Pox down Southwark way for trimming your hoods in budge.'

'Course not,' said Joan, wagging her head. 'Who's the dead girl?'

Bickle shrugged. 'Not for the likes of us to know. Some intimate connection to mustard, is all I'm told.'

'French girl then?'

'Looks like to the coroner,' said Bickle. 'Some fancy lady taken to the Moorfields, brained in the prime of life, left for the crows. Sad story, but not ours.'

'Right right.' Joan fingered her chin. 'And why they pulling your poor knob into this mess, Master Bickle?'

'Pressure from above and beside: the alderman, getting it from the mayor, getting it from the bishop, getting it from the – ah, St Tom only knows. I do as I'm told.'

42

Joan turned to Eleanor. 'What about it, El? Tell the little man what he needs to know.'

Bickle bristled at *little man*, but held his peace. He turned to Eleanor. 'Good then. Firstwise, what were you doing out on the Moorfields that time of day? Bell of five, was it?'

'Thereabouts,' said Eleanor, in no hurry to help.

'What brought you to the moor? Strange place for a pair of mauds to go a-wandering.'

She shrugged. 'Sometimes the men like it, that little shed out there near Bethlem. They can be – free with themselves.'

'Lets them scream for the teat, like the hungry babes they be,' Joan put in helpfully.

Bickle's scowl softened. 'Haven't changed a bit, Joan Rugg.' She gave him a girlish grin. He turned back to Eleanor. 'So you were heading out that way with some jakes, you and—'

'Mary Potts,' said Joan.

'You and this Mary Potts, right, taking some fellows out there, was it?'

Eleanor shook her head. 'We were looking for somebody.'

'Looking for somebody. And who were you looking for?'

Eleanor said nothing.

'And who were you looking for then?'

'Tell him, Eleanor,' said Joan, her voice hardening. 'You tell him or I will myself, girl.'

Eleanor hesitated, feeling protective of Agnes.

He edged closer. 'This isn't only about a murder, now. This young lady went and stole something from the very Duke of Lancaster before she got herself killed. A book, is what it was. A *valuable* book. And from what I seem to be hearing from your pretty little mouth, could be your *somebody* went and stole it from *her*, yeah? Went and stole it from that girl, then killed her, yeah?' Bickle grasped her chin and turned her face to his. There was a plug of mint in his lip, his breath strangely pleasant, though his hands smelled of metal.

43

Eleanor tried to shake her head. 'I know less than nothing about the Duke of Lancaster, nor about some old book.'

'Could be, could be,' said Bickle. 'But I suspect your *somebody* might.'

'I – I couldn't say naught about that, Master Bickle.'

'You couldn't say naught.' He leaned in. 'A dead lady's one thing, *Edgar*.' He spat her man name in a tone that terrified her, then gripped her forearm. 'French lady of means dead on the Moorfields, you got the whole city asking questions: constables, subconstables, beadles and aldermen, the coroner and his deputy, all the way up to the king's household wants to know.' His grip tightened. 'But a dead maudlyn? Who'll give half a mind to that, hmm?' His gaze swept her face. She saw the flicker of revulsion. 'Dead swerver like you, floating in the Walbrook with the cats?'

Swerver. And that's what I am, like it or not. A man in body, a woman in soul. One day a *he*, the next a *she*, a stiff cock for some, a tight arse for others. Provided they could pay, Eleanor would do all and be all for her loyal jakes, and she had plenty who liked taking it and giving it every which way. Sometimes as a man, sometimes as a woman, sometimes as both at once, though that could get complicated. Why, just last week there was this gongfarmer, big-muscled and hairy as you could like, but get him in the stall and he starts to whinny like a gelding. Or a mare, more like, wants to take—

'Speak to the man, El,' said Joan Rugg. 'You speak, or I will.'

As Eleanor sat on the goldsmith's bench, her own life threatened over the death of a stranger, she felt her fear turn slowly to resentment, then to anger. She knew it wasn't Agnes who killed that girl on the Moorfields. Yet who's Agnes Fonteyn to leave such a mess for Joan's mauds to clean up behind her? A book, the beadle says. A *valuable* book, stolen from Lancaster. And now Agnes has it. What's that whore doing with a book? Worse, she's keeping it to herself, after all I've done for her these years, the coin and bed we've shared, now here *I* am on a beadle's bench, getting *this*?

Eleanor's lips were inches from Bickle's ear. 'Agnes,' she said. 'Her name is Agnes Fonteyn.' And Eleanor Rykener, she did not add, will find her first.

SIX

Florence, near Orsanmichele

'You leave tomorrow. You will join the delegation at Bologna.'
Adam Scarlett found a more comfortable position on the stool,
one of four in the low single room that served as the friar's
occasional dwelling. His left foot rested on the floor, his right
on the hearth, scattered with ash and meal. As he spoke to
Paolo Taricani he rocked himself slowly back until his head
touched the stone wall, the cool on his neck a pleasant contrast
to the chamber's stuffy heat.

'I will not do it.'

'Of course you will.'

'No.'

'Brother Paolo—'

'Send Teti. Or Efisio. Efisio makes sense. He is quick, young.
Gets it up and in and twisted before the florin hits the floor.'

Scarlett ignored the hurried pleading. 'But you are the best,
Paolo. And Ser Giovanni knows it. That is why he has chosen
you for this extraordinary task.'

'I am *Il Prescelto*, then.' Taricani's sarcasm was thick, and
Scarlett worried this could get difficult.

He sighed, recalling what Hawkwood had told him. *Take*

him as far as you can, Adam. If he's still balking bring him to me.

He tacked right, appealing to Taricani's ego; left, to his civic pride. Nothing worked. Finally Scarlett stood. 'Let's go, Brother Paolo.'

The man frowned suspiciously. 'Go where?'

'San Donato a Torre.' Hawkwood's villa that season, a short ride to the north.

Taricani shook his head, still showing no fear. That could change, and quickly, but for the moment Scarlett let him prattle on. 'I will not go. I will not do this – this "extraordinary task", and I will not go with you.' He spat on the floor. His own floor. He looked tense, about to spring. His hand moved to his belt.

Scarlett spread his arms, slowly, and raised his hands to his sides. He gave the man a conciliatory nod. '*Bene,*' he said, and left the tenement, hating what he had to do next.

Taricani's house sat at the ass end of a narrow alley leading south from Orsanmichele. At the other end waited three of Hawkwood's roughest men, unmounted at the moment, their horses posted out in the piazza. Scarlett gave them the signal, then went to wait in front of the church, selecting the sharp corner at Via dei Pittori as his spot. The crumbling house of the Bigallo loomed overhead, knots of thirsty pilgrims draped around the plinths, waiting, like Paolo Taricani, for a miracle that would never come. On a high scaffold an old painter and his apprentice were at work retouching a David, hurling his stone at the giant. Scarlett wondered whether the outmatched Paolo, too, would fight, and if so, for how long. The man had too much to lose, though, and it was not long until he stumbled into the piazza, his hands bound at his waist, one eye blackened, the other cut and swollen.

Hawkwood's men had fared no better. One of them had earned a long gash across his cheek, which he wiped with a quiet fury as the others threw the friar over a horse and set off across the piazza. Scarlett took his time, arriving back at San Donato a full hour after the others. Hawkwood had waited for him, though, and as Scarlett walked through the yard toward the house the *condottiero* was just coming out the villa's entrance. The men had bound Taricani to a chair, an ornate, high-backed seat brought out from the hall, and the man's thin face now showed a few more bruises, a second black eye.

Hawkwood stood before the chair, fixing Taricani with a friendly smile. 'You were Bernabò Visconti's swiftest knife for years, Brother Paolo. Why he let you retire I'll never know.'

Taricani shrugged. 'The *signore* has his methods, Ser Giovanni.'

'Indeed,' said Hawkwood. 'Might be interesting to plumb them with you someday.'

Taricani bunched his lips, exuding confidence. 'At your pleasure, Ser Giovanni.'

Stay humble, Scarlett silently warned the man.

Hawkwood knelt in the dirt. He placed a palm on each of Taricani's knees, looked up at his face. 'You have a beautiful woman, Brother Paolo.' He let that sit, then, 'And a daughter who ripens by the day. My men have seen her at the markets, Paolo. She can't be more than, what, ten, eleven?'

Taricani nodded, his eyes darkening.

'And her name, Paolo. It is memorable, isn't it, but I seem to have forgotten it. Help an old man, Paolo. What is your daughter's name?'

'Pic-Picco-Piccola-Piccolamela, sire.'

Hawkwood chuckled at Taricani's difficulty. 'Piccolamela. Now I remember! "Little apple" in my native tongue. An exquisite name for an exquisite girl, this virgin bastardess of an uncelibate friar. Did you choose this name yourself, Paolo?'

'My – her mother chose it, sire.'

'Well good for her. Piccolamela. How about that?' Hawkwood clapped his palms on Taricani's thighs, reading

48

the new terror on his face. 'Though it's a strange coincidence. For do you know what my favourite fruit is, Paolo?'

Taricani shook his head.

'Can you guess?'

He shook his head again. Less confidence this time.

'Apples, Brother Paolo. I like apples best.'

Taricani's tongue flickered across his lips.

'And you know how I like my apples, Paolo?'

The assassin was still.

'Green, Paolo. I like my apples green.'

Taricani pressed against the ropes, then the pleas started. *No, Ser Giovanni, you wouldn't, Ser Giovanni, she is only a girl, Ser Giovanni, oh mercy, Ser Giovanni, mercy mercy mercy!* Scarlett listened for a while, then looked off into the hills until the begging faded into the familiar moans of a newly broken man.

Hawkwood stood, all business. 'The fate of your daughter's virtue is entirely up to you. If you refuse us we'll have her in hand this evening, and your whore as well. I'll make you watch, Paolo Taricani. I'll taste your little apple first, then hand her to my man Scarlett here, then we'll bring the garrison up from the river. I'll cut off your eyelids if I have to, but you'll watch every man take her, one by one, and in every way imaginable. You know I'll do it, too. You've seen me do worse. By God, you've *helped* me do worse, Paolo. And if you fail in your mission, if I get word you've bungled the thing, or fled, why – why then I will take your Piccolamela to Venice and sell her to the Turks. Little apples fetch a handsome price in the doge's slave markets.'

He bent over the puddled friar. 'On the other hand, Paolo, if you do this, know that I will take care of your daughter, and your woman too. They won't be short of florins, and no one will lay a hand on them. And if you don't come back I will still protect them. Your daughter, though the illegitimate spawn of a half-lapsed friar, will marry well.'

49

Scarlett could see the resignation on Taricani's face, the defeated angle to his shoulders. But only for a moment. Taricani was a professional, after all, and this was a job like any other. Just a job. Scarlett watched him take a deep breath, nod at the ground, and look up at Hawkwood, his eyes lit with the cold flame of a born killer. 'At your service, Ser Giovanni.'

Hawkwood clapped the man on the shoulder. 'Very well, then.' He started to untie the knots, freeing Taricani from his chair. 'The rendezvous is set for Bologna. You'll have four spears of ours, in addition to any accompanying the delegation. From Bologna up to the Aosta pass and over to Geneva, then on the Rhine from Basel to Cologne. Next a hard ride to Hamburg, where you'll sail to Dover. The French are likely massing in Flanders, so there's no getting through by land to Calais.' Even as Hawkwood rattled off the sites along the itinerary Scarlett could hear the mix of wistfulness and anticipation in his lord's voice, thick with longing to make this journey his own.

'You will arrive in London the third week of May or thereabouts, and the thing is set for – well, Scarlett here will fill you in on the details. Should be a beautiful spring day.'

Hawkwood walked inside. Scarlett spoke to Taricani for a while longer, then hailed several of the men who had brought the man up from Florence. 'See him back to Orsanmichele. And, Paolo, this is for your woman, and for Piccolamela.' He tossed a purse on the dirt. Taricani rubbed his wrists, reached for it, and peered inside. He looked up at Scarlett. A grim nod. The job would be done, and done well, despite the cost. With that Paolo Taricani was taken back to Florence, for a final farewell to his family.

Inside the villa Hawkwood was staring up at the arms of his father, Gilbert Hawkwood, now his brother's: a lion rampant above a bend, the tendrils curling up the sides and the centre. The Inheritor, Hawkwood liked to call his brother.

The *condottiero*'s own arms, much more prominently displayed on the east wall, consisted of a lone falcon poised above a tangled forest of vines.

'My father was a strange man, Adam,' Hawkwood said into the gloom. 'Imagine having three sons, and naming them all John. The eldest son, heir to the name, and all that comes with it. The youngest, also John Hawkwood, has the luck to die young. And the middle son? That's right: John Hawkwood.'

He sniffed. 'Middle John, my mother called me. "Does Middle John want his cider now?" "Time for Master Middle John to get him to his lessons!" And it all stacks on, doesn't it? Thornbury and the others, fled back to suck on Lancaster's teat with scarcely a word of thanks. My son-in-law takes my daughter away and now sits in Parliament, one of the highest men in Essex. Then all this business with Chaucer . . .'

'You've bought up half of Essex, John,' Scarlett said. 'Sible Hedingham, the lands around Gosfield.' He put a hand on Hawkwood's shoulder, a gesture to frame the familiar use of the *condottiero*'s first name. Hawkwood permitted it when they were alone, though Scarlett rarely took advantage. 'You own more of England than your brother ever could, let alone Coggeshale.' The son-in-law. 'Are you absolutely sure this is the wisest course? This is what you want for yourself, to reclaim your legacy under such circumstances?' He had been trying for weeks to turn the *condottiero* from his dark purpose; one last try, however weak, could not hurt.

Hawkwood reached up and patted Scarlett's hand, clasping it tightly as he nodded at his family's arms. 'It is not about me any more, Adam. It is about my son.'

'Your – your son, sire?'

'He's in Donnina's belly. I can *smell* him in there, baking away.'

This was news to Scarlett – and, he suspected, a bit of wishful thinking.

'The next Sir John Hawkwood will be a baron, Adam.

Perhaps even an earl, belted by the king himself. And I won't curse the poor fellow with a brother, either. Perhaps I'll name him George.' He smiled, looked at his friend. 'Or Adam.'

Scarlett felt it, more deeply this time. The warm glow of inevitability and fate. Sir John Hawkwood was a hard man, the hardest he had ever known, but this plan of his, despite its ruthlessness, was melting the great mercenary into a soup of sentiment. 'His given name hardly matters, John. It's his surname that will bear his nobility.'

'Well spoken, Scarlett.' Hawkwood turned back to his family's arms, his eyes verdant with the ambition of a much younger man. 'England, Adam,' the *condottiero* said. 'It is time to go home.'

SEVEN

Temple Hall

Dozens of struggling lamps cast a hellish glow on the huddled apprentices, all stomping their feet against the raw air, their eager faces greyed by the smoke lowering down from those few chimneys rebuilt in this precinct since the Rising. I slowed in the middle of the courtyard and just watched them: their pent-up energy, their fear of rejection, their tentative pride at this rite of passage, all readable in the nervous poses struck as they waited. Forty young men, no more than half to be utter barristers by the evening's end.

Fifteen years had passed since my own, less formal initiation at the Temple, yet the occasion could still raise the hairs. As I stepped beneath the row of arches along the cloister a familiar voice stopped me. 'Is that you, John Gower?' I turned to see Thomas Pinchbeak hobbling along from Temple Church, with Chaucer holding an arm. 'Wait there.' He wiped his high forehead, exposed by the tight-fitting coif worn by his order. A capped stick bore part of his fragile weight.

'Good evening, Thomas. Geoffrey.' I took his stick and his other arm, my hand brushing the silk rope belted around his banded robes. Pinchbeak was a man who had grown into his name, with a long, sharp nose that jutted forward above lips pursed against some unnamed offence. Behind the serjeant-at-law's back Chaucer gave me a meaningful look, which I returned with a subtle shake of my head. We hadn't spoken since Monksblood's, I had no real news yet about the book, and I didn't want him to think I was avoiding him.

'Lurking at the fringes, I see,' Pinchbeak said to me, and I smiled at the ribbing. My ambivalent ties to the legal world were a matter of occasional amusement to Pinchbeak, newly a member of the Order of the Coif, one of the most powerful lawmen in the realm and now a royal nod away from appointment to justice of the King's Bench.

'You are one to talk.' I gestured across the lane at the last of the crowd straggling into the hall. 'Late, as always.'

'Ah, but I have the excuse of a wound,' he said, though something in his eyes belied his easy manner. A compact and wiry man, Pinchbeak had taken an arrow in his left thigh at Poitiers yet stood and fought for hours after, an incident that had rendered him both lame and legendary. When he gave the gold and ascended to serjeant not a soul in the realm begrudged him the honour. Yet his face that evening was troubled, and he seemed about to say something more when a small group of other serjeants-at-law surrounded him, hustling him gaily into the throng.

Chaucer watched him go in, then turned to me, his face lined with concern. 'Nothing?'

'Not really.'

'What did Swynford say?'

'Very little,' I said, deciding to mention nothing about the book's theft, nor about Swynford's peculiar suggestion regarding its prophetic nature. I needed to learn more first, and I was not in the business of giving away information, even to an intimate friend. 'She doesn't have it, if that's what you want to know. She'll do some discreet asking around.'

'I see,' said Chaucer, looking at me dubiously.

'I've only started searching, Geoffrey,' I said, wanting to give him something. 'London is a big place. A book could be anywhere.'

He gave me a tense nod.

'Just one question.' I pulled him out of the human flow. His eyes darted to the hall door, then back to the lane as I leaned into him, my mouth inches from his ear. 'What do you think this book is, my friend? What do you know about it that you haven't told me?'

I felt his breath on my cheek. 'Less every day, it seems.'

'And you're aware you're not the only one looking for it?'

'I suspect not,' he said. 'But I need you to find it first, John.'

I backed away, found his eyes. 'You know me, know my skills. If it's there to be found I'll find it.'

His shoulders rose slightly, and he grasped my arm before turning for the feast. We parted at the arched doorway into the great hall, where hundreds of lawmen were already at table, ladling soup, picking flesh from lavish trays of sauced cod and porpoise. At the front of the space stood the pageant wagon, covered in a cloth that obscured everything but the wheels. As I found a seat the men around a far table lifted their glasses in song. The crowd joined in, the din rising to the rafters and the darkened spaces high above.

> *Twice two full quarts we lawyers need,*
> *To fill a legal jug.*
> *With one, we're gay, with two, we teach,*
> *With three, we prophesy.*
> *And four good quarts it takes to bind*
> *Legal senses, legal tongues,*
> *A lawyer's hands and mind.*

Cups and flagons clashed on the last word, drink sloshed, the sobriety of Lent set aside for an evening. The clamour stirred a familiar longing. Though I had spent two formative years at the Temple, my father had not allowed me to remain in the profession. For an esquire's son the practical application of law was regarded in those days as a rather low trade. Had I been born ten years later I might well have been sitting that night with Pinchbeak and the serjeants instead of on that crowded bench, shrouded in ignorance.

The line of nervous apprentices formed for the tap. As the first hopeful presented himself, the presiding master leaned forward and plucked at his gown, the mark of unsuitability. The young man turned away, his eyes already moist at the prospect of another year before his next chance at admittance. Other unlucky souls followed him out over the next little while until the successful class stood at the front of the hall to great applause. A few pompous speeches, then, with cake and ale served out, the main event began.

Up stood Stephen FitzWilliams, master of the utter barristers. Delighting in his role, he pushed himself on to the pageant wagon, his legs swinging freely between the wheels, his gown hanging loosely on a gaunt frame. He spread his hands above his head, gathering silence.

'Gentlemen of the law,' he intoned. 'I bid you fair evening, and good fare made of our moot!'

'*Huzzah! Huzzah! Huzzah!*' the crowd replied.

'As your new-appointed liege, your sovereign, your emperor and king—'

Someone threw a fish spine.

'Leave that off!' He loudly cleared his throat. 'It has fallen to me to determine our evening's weighty matter, to be mooted before you.'

'*Huzzah!*'

'Last year on a similar occasion we mooted some obscure clauses of the Statute of Merton, did we not?'

'*We did!*'

'Our disputations involved the writ of redisseisin. In the Latin of our beloved Parliament, *Et inde convicti fuerint* et cetera et cetera. Which is glossed, in our Frenchy cant, *Ceo serra entendu en le breve de redisseisin vous vous cadew hahoo haloo* and thus and so. Shall we revisit this well-trodden ground, as dry as pestled bone?'

'*Nay!*'

'Perhaps we should dabble in the assize of novel disseisin.'

'*Nay!*'

'In default of a tenant *en le taile*?'

'*Nay!*'

'In the wrongful appropriation by a tortious patron?'

'*Nay!*'

'In theft?'

'*Nay!*'

'In misprision?'

'*Nay!*'

'In the law of bankruptcy?'

'*Nay!*'

'Well then, you leave me no choice!' A master of delivery, FitzWilliams had brought me and everyone else in the great hall to the edges of our seats.

'Our subject for this year's moots shall be a matter of universal and urgent concern.' He leaned forward, an air of suspense in his thrown whisper. 'Methinks the matter of our March moot, my matriculating men, must be . . .' The pause lengthened until finally FitzWilliams, his head bent back, his nose pointing to the ceiling far above, screamed, '*MUST BE MURDERRRRR!*'

A collective whoop went up from young and old alike, followed by a round of sustained applause. As the claps and stomps faded and the men retook their seats, I glanced over at the upper benches, where the serjeants-at-law sat in high station. Thomas Pinchbeak, I saw, was leaning forward and speaking with some urgency to two of his colleagues. I could understand their consternation, as even the more festive moots generally treated the finer points of property and torts. A murder trial would not be unprecedented, but it would require the substitution of mere spectacle for legal rigor. I was somewhat surprised that the young men had opted for such a subject.

FitzWilliams hopped down and grasped a corner of the drapery. 'Servants of the law,' he shouted, his eyes wild, 'I give you the evening's bench!' In one flourish he pulled off the canvas. The applause was thunderous as the crowd took in the mock court on the wagon: the stern judges in a ponderous line, the pompous bailiff, a hunch-backed recorder, and finally the accused, bound standing to a rail by his legs and wrists, his teeth gnashing, his face twisted in mock agony at the imagined hanging in his near future.

The most remarkable part of the spectacle was the scene laid out on a narrow platform jutting forward from the left front of the wagon. A scraggly hawthorn bush, potted in an oaken tub, suggested the outdoors, as did several inches of loose dirt spread around it. On the soil, face down, lay a young man, his torso bare, his waist and legs clad in a flesh-coloured costume, the buttocks exaggerated with padding.

'Our victim, if you please!' FitzWilliams called out over the roars of approval. The actor rose to his knees, cutting a ghoulish figure. His chest had been shaved clean and painted with wide crescents traced to suggest breasts. Between the legs of the suit had been sewn a triangle of animal pelt. And from his head, adorned with a wig of long, dark hair, a dried shower of red paint descended in a glistening path, its source a crusted wound mocked up in gruesome detail.

I looked again at the cluster of serjeants. At least five of the powerful men were now visibly agitated, their gestures conveying strong displeasure at the subject of the performance. There was clearly some disagreement, though: I guessed that several of them wished to halt the murder moot, while others felt reluctant to take action, with all the objections this would raise. Yet why, I wondered, was this spectacle provoking their concern at all, given the usual tenor of plays at the Temple? Such pageants were notorious for their bawdy and even violent content, some of them ending in blows; this one appeared no different.

FitzWilliams had pressed a cluster of utter barristers into service as the jury. He held up his hands.

'Let us review the facts of the case,' he said. 'First: before us lies a young woman. A virgin, I'm told – though I have not, personally, performed the requisite inspection.' He put a finger in the air, drawing earthy calls.

The victim sat up, pursed his rouged lips in a kiss, then, with a wan wave, collapsed. 'Her head crushed,' FitzWilliams continued, 'her fair body stripped of its dress, her raiment laid carelessly over a rock. So far a straightforward matter, no? A fair maiden wandering in a place where a woman should never venture alone. Attacked. Perhaps ravished. Surely killed.'

An exaggerated frown. 'But consider the complexities of the case before us. First, where did this act most foul occur? Not in London, but outside the walls – indeed in the Moorfields, hard by Bethlem Priory, where the wood are wont to wander.'

A crowd along a side wall sent up a wolfish howl, and my skin went suddenly cold. Katherine Swynford, at La Neyte. *It was a young woman . . . Someone skulled her, out on the Moorfields.*

My vision blurred as FitzWilliams continued. 'The location of the crime introducing, then, the matter of jurisdiction, which some will place under the abbot of Bethlem. Others will contend that the Moorfields as a whole lie within an outer ward of the city. In what court, then, and by whose authority shall this matter be adjudicated?'

A movement to my left. Pinchbeak had summoned two pursuivants.

'More central to our purposes this evening, though,' FitzWilliams continued, 'shall be the nature of the crime: how are we to determine whether we are facing a killing *ex malicia praecogitata*, or an accidental death? Was she killed with a club to the skull? Or' – he held up a knife, then placed the blade against his chest – 'with a steely thrust to her heart?' At this last word FitzWilliams plunged the knife into his chest and doubled over.

A few shouts of alarm from the more gullible and drunk, but mostly laughter as he withdrew the wooden blade. For me the moot had lost all its humour.

'Ah, but wait!' The murmurs died down. 'We must now reveal the identity of the accused.' He dug a hand into a pocket. 'Why, what's this?' He pulled out a parchment, waved it before the room. 'The indictment, honourable gentlemen! Inscribed by His Honour himself, Justice Beelzebub Barnes of Brixton!' He stood at the top of the aisle between the rows of tables. 'In this document,' he shouted, 'is written the very name of the accused!'

'*Huzzah! Huzzah!*'

'As well as his profession, our next matter for rumination. And what is the profession of our accused, you may ask? A moment . . .' He held the document up to the lamplight. 'Our alleged killer is – a highwayman?'

'*No!*'

'A street vagrant, then?'

'*Nay!*'

'How about – how about a friar?'

'*The friar! The friar!*'

FitzWilliams shook his head, shining an exaggerated sadness around the great hall. 'Incorrect, gentlemen of the bar, the killer is not a friar!'

General laughter, and as it crested, then ebbed, I noticed a small stir from afar, rendered peculiar only by its timing. In the hall's north corner Chaucer rose from his seat, nodded an apology to his benchmates, and ducked through the low doorway leading to the buttery. As the door closed to on his back FitzWilliams adopted a more serious look. 'Our alleged murderer is not a priest, nor a bishop, nor a cardinal. He is neither a cooper nor a cordwainer, neither a mercer nor a shipwright, neither a pinner nor a—'

'Let's just have it, then, Fitzy!' someone shouted from the back.

FitzWilliams looked up, affecting offence. More titters. I sat forward, confused by Chaucer's departure at the height of the apprentice's spectacle. With a flourish, FitzWilliams gazed across the crowd. 'Have it we shall. Our murderer is, rather, a p—'

'*Huzzah! Huzzah! Huzzah!*'

Loud shouts, drowning out FitzWilliams's revelation with the force of a gale. The serjeants-at-law, twenty strong and with Thomas Pinchbeak hobbling in the lead, rushed the pageant wagon as a single dark-robed mass, their gowns spread above their heads like bat wings as they mobbed the players. Three of the younger serjeants climbed on the wheels and proceeded to demolish the set, kicking apart the flimsy rails, ripping the robes from the judges, releasing the accused from his bonds. Two others grappled the 'victim' off the side platform and stripped the costume from his flesh, leaving him only in his braies, then sent him into the crowd with a jar of wine over his head.

Utter pandemonium: screams of delight and alarm; cups, jars, and flagons flying overhead, to shatter against the walls; serjeants and apprentices alike screaming to the rafters, some enjoying the skirmish, others frightened nearly for their lives; the wagon overturned on the floor, its spoked wheels and siderails broken on impact; the melee thrown in long shadows by hooped candelabra casting pantomimes of disorder against every surface.

Even the wildest revels must end, however, and eventually,

as the tumult subsided and the barristers and apprentices surveyed the results, there was a general quieting through the hall, an almost embarrassed assessment of the state of things. I watched and listened to the reactions. Many held that the disruption had been coordinated between the utter barristers and the serjeants, perhaps as a staged commentary on the poor quality of the recent moots. Others avowed that the serjeants saw murder as inappropriate for mooting, and broke the spectacle up accordingly. There were still others who had observed what I had during the lead-up to the interruption: the anger of the serjeants-at-law, the whispered conferrals among England's most powerful lawmen, the decision taken to rush the players before their moot had even begun.

Yet there was something more that had disturbed me about the spectacle, something I would scarcely admit to myself as I lingered in the great hall. I sat at my bench for a long while, watching the overturned wagon as the space emptied of barristers, of serjeants, of apprentices and guests, until only the servers were left. Around me they swept up broken bits of glass and clay, gathered the leavings of the students' extravagance into buckets that would now feed pigs, dogs, their children in the tenements. As the hall emptied my certainty deepened, and a tingling of unease began at the bottom of my spine, moved up my back, and settled into my heart as a coiled suspicion.

My memory replayed the course of the abbreviated moot: the introduction of the case, the gaudy spectacle of the victim, Chaucer's unexplained departure through the kitchen door – and finally, the naming of the accused. In that moment before the serjeants shouted him down, I could swear with a near certainty that one final word had escaped FitzWilliams's mouth. *Our murderer is, rather, a p—*

It seemed unlikely in the extreme that the man had suggested such a thing. Yet I had heard it from his lips, was sure of it: the one word that could most have affected me as I took in the lewd spectacle of a young woman's violent death. *Our murderer is, rather, a p—*

One word: *poet.*

⁜ ⁜ ⁜

Worshipful Sir, and Our Most Intimate Friend,

Your muse finds herself in peril. Upon your return from Rome you will fondle not her supple skin but this rough parchment. Here on the banks of the Arno it will await you, just as my flesh awaits reunion with your own.

Those pleasures must be delayed, for in the morning I leave our Tuscan Eden for the coast. From there I shall arrange passage to that faraway island our histories call Albion, and you call home.

You are a lover of stories. Stories of love, lust, and loss. Of wars, rivalry, and revenge. Of the commonplace and the unlikely. The story I must now tell you is woven of all these threads, and more besides.

You know its characters, some better than others, though you cannot know, as I do, the depths of their perfidy and the heights of their nobility. Even to commit this tale to writing is to subject you, its reader, to the same peril that stalks me now. For Hawkwood's talons are sharp, his vision is keen, and his enemies tend to die young.

I can delay no longer. Time is short, and there is much to relate.

Here, my only heart, is the story.

⁜

Once, along the Castilian marches, beyond the Crown of Aragon, there lived a knight. Not a great knight; no one would have mistaken him for a Lancelot, a Gawain, a Roland, though where he fell short of these famed knights in ferocity, he matched every one of them in honour. To his lord he was a model of duty. To his own men he was the very mirror of chivalry: swift of sword, moderate in judgment. Toward his people he acted fairly and wisely in all things.

Our knight kept a castle. Not a great castle; no one would have mistaken it for the alcázar of Pedro the Cruel, nor for Avignon's papal palace, nor England's palace of Westminster. Yet its walls of broad stone and heavy mortar kept our marcher lord well defended from the occasional marauder.

Our knight had a wife. A beautiful wife indeed, so beautiful one might well have mistaken her for Helen, or Guinevere, or for the Laura of Petrarco. She was the daughter of a minor count of questionable lineage. A family of Moorish blood, not a few whispered, keeping the faith of Mahound while miming love of the Cross. Yet as the knight was trusted by his people, such whisperings were soon quieted, his small, dark wonder of a wife accepted into the circles of Castilian ladies gathered on occasion at court.

Soon a daughter arrived. She was, like her mother, dark and small. She captivated her parents. The knight, of course, wanted a son. The wife was still young, and though the years went by with no further issue, there was little doubt that God would someday reward them.

It came to pass, when the daughter was approaching her seventh year, that the knight was summoned by his lord to battle. Not a minor border skirmish, but a major campaign in a larger war that threatened to conscript every able-bodied man from the Pyrenees to the port of Cádiz. You will know of this war: of Pedro the Cruel and Enrique de Trastámara, of brothers divided against themselves. When Pedro called, our knight gathered the might of his men, leaving only a small garrison behind.

Word soon came of a bloody battle in Nájera, a battle in which King Pedro won back the crown of Castile from his bastard brother. Though this victory was to be short-lived, the tidings brought considerable joy to the castle and town, despite the additional news that the lord's return would be delayed many months as King Pedro led his army to further battles against the lingering enemies of the crown. In her knight's long absence the lady saw to the needs of his property and people, with an added touch of feminine grace that delighted those around her.

On the Day of St Dominic, as the lady and her daughter strolled in the castle's herb garden, the scents of rosemary and lavender mingling in the hot calm of an August afternoon, a blotch on the northern hills caught the little girl's eye. She squinted against the sun.

Dust, yet not from a storm. The road from Burgos was dry, and any single horse would kick up a mass of saffron powder that might linger for hours.

The cloud she saw now filled the horizon. Forty horses, perhaps fifty. She tugged at her mother's dress. They gazed together at the approaching force, their hearts lifting against a darkening sky.

The Day of St Dominic. The day the strangers came.

EIGHT

Rose Alley, Southwark

The Pricking Bishop. Edgar Rykener shook his head at the painted sign, amazed that the Bishop of Winchester allowed such pictures in his liberties. Lord Protector of Whores, they called him up on Gropecunt Lane, defending his right to run as many houses as he pleased across the river in Southwark while the hard-working maudlyns of London got constantly harassed by the law. Joan Rugg would go on about it for half a day. Unlike Gropecunt Lane, the stews of Southwark embraced their natural filth, the half-pipe gutters stopped up with brackish water of a murky green, the conduits to the river long forgotten by the bishop's underworked ditchers. Wobbly shacks had been built out into the streets to claim space for shops, while the oblong fishponds at the western end walled off the great houses on the riverbanks beyond. No sweepers or rakers to maintain the streets, nor regular dung carts to haul away the most offensive waste.

On the Bishop's front steps sat a withered old maudlyn, barely there beneath her shift and smock. St Cath was her name, Edgar recalled, still alive after half a century on her back. A dozen cats wandered in and out of the half-opened door, pressing against St Cath's side or darting past while she ignored them.

'Is Bess about?' Edgar asked her. The old woman said nothing. 'Bess Waller, be she about?'

St Cath shifted against the step. 'Bess Waller,' she said, as if speaking the name of a stranger. Her face, crossed by a thousand lines, registered no emotion.

Edgar tapped his foot.

St Cath spat. 'The matter of it?'

'Not your concern.'

'Nor be Bess Waller none of yours.'

Edgar stood on his toes and peered into the doorway.

'Not a peek more,' said the woman, pushing away one of the cats and struggling to stand, 'but you proffer your pennies like the fine gentlemen of the parish.'

He snorted. 'For the love of St Thomas, woman, all I'm about here is looking out for Bess's daughter.'

'Millicent?' she said quickly. 'Hunting Millicent Fonteyn in the stews?' St Cath shook her bent frame and wheezed, wagged her small head. 'Won't find that knight's trull in Southwark. Best look up Cornhull for Millicent. *Duchess* Millicent by now, for all we knows over here.'

Edgar thought over the woman's response. Something about it didn't sit right. 'It's not Millicent I'm about. It's Agnes.'

'Agnes?'

Not this again. 'Yes, Agnes, you withered hag, sometime maud of the Bishop. Is Agnes Fonteyn about, or'd your witch-craft turn her into one of these cats?'

St Cath glared at her. 'Agnes hasn't been about since Epiphany time.'

'That's right.' Bess Waller, bawd of the Pricking Bishop, leaned against the doorsill looking Edgar over. Despite two daughters and years of swyving, Bess had angles to her face that could only be boasted by the mother of Agnes Fonteyn;

68

also the same lithe form, the same golden hair still radiant as she neared fifty. 'You're El—Edgar Rykener, are you not?'

'I am,' said Edgar. They'd met last year, soon after Agnes had left the Southwark stews and joined Joan Rugg's crew in Cheap Ward. Bess Waller had come after her younger daughter with a club while the bawd was away, trying to beat Agnes back to the Bishop, pleading the strength of family and roots. But Agnes had stuck to Gropecunt Lane, and now she was pure London.

'As I was telling your lovely serjeant-of-the-gate here, I need to have a word with Agnes. She about?'

'She's not,' said Bess. 'We miss her round the stews though, that right, St Cath?'

The old woman nodded. 'Miss her all right.'

'Agnes had the cock lining up at the door,' said Bess. 'Something in the sweet air off her, that way she got with her head. That toss, you know?' She mimicked it perfectly. 'And always had since she's a girl. Sweet piece of sweetmeats, that one. Still sucking it off up Cheapside?'

Edgar rested a foot on the step, stretched his tired thighs. 'Our bawd's Joan Rugg.'

'Joan Rugg!' Bess cackled. 'Taught that fat hen everything she knows about the cock. How to fondle it like one of St Cath's kittens here, how to clamp it atween her thighs for the while of a paternoster. The gentle cock's your false idol, Joan, I tell her, and treating it right will bring you all the riches you can want. A fast learner, by St Bride. Just like Agnes.'

And what a homily to motherhood Agnes had in you, Edgar thought. 'So,' he said. 'Not a sight of her, then?'

Bess wiped her nose. 'Why you seeking out my Agnes?'

'Had some little business to pestle with her.'

'Business.'

'Thought she might've stepped over the river. If not, then . . .'

'Then . . .?' Bess raised her eyebrows.

Edgar took a step back, his gaze moving up the façade to the second-storey windows, one of them wedged open. A giggle, a slap, a moan.

Bess clucked. 'Best you be off, pretty boy. Got some gentlemen coming by next bell. Don't want my jakes inconvenienced.'

'I'm thinking the same,' said Edgar, also thinking there was more going on here than Bess Waller would reveal. He gave the bawd a meaningful look. 'You tell Agnes her Edgar come by, though.'

'Sure sure,' said Bess. 'Though could be Easter, could be All Souls all I know. But I'll tell her you were by. You give Joanie a Jesu palm on the arse from her Bess, hear?'

Edgar turned and walked down Rose Alley to the bankside. There he paused and looked back at the Pricking Bishop. Bess Waller's arms were in the air, her face beet-red as she let St Cath have it, for what he didn't know.

On the bridge he purchased a farthingloaf and pinched off pieces of coarse bread, washing them down with some warmed beer. As he crossed the Thames he thought of the peculiar twinge of suspicion he'd felt on first telling St Cath why he was there. What was it about the old woman's words that had unsettled him?

Millicent.

Bess Waller's older daughter, Millicent Fonteyn, lived in a decent house along Cornhull, had some money and wanted more. She'd had nothing to do with her mother nor her sister for a long time. While Agnes had only recently left her mother's stewhouse for the streets of London, Millicent Fonteyn was no more than a distant memory on Rose Alley. Yet the moment Edgar had asked St Cath whether Bess Waller's daughter was about, the old woman had responded swift as you please.

Millicent? Hunting Millicent Fonteyn in the stews?

Which meant what? Which meant St Cath, flustered at

Edgar's prodding, was covering for Agnes. He nodded, sure of it now. Agnes has been at the Pricking Bishop, he thought; may be there still, the little tart. And who, he wondered for the hundredth time, was that poor dead girl on the moor?

NINE

Westminster

Two appointments set for that morning, the first with the wife of a disgruntled notary to the king's secretary with a copy of a royal writ to sell. We met in an alley above the stone wharf. She had brought a maidservant along for appearance's sake, and perhaps to impress me. As the servant dawdled at the end of the alley she sidled up close, wanting to flirt. She was an attractive woman, with soft curls peeking from beneath a loosened bonnet, full lips, cheeks pinched a bright pink, and I felt an unfamiliar stir that I promptly pushed aside.

'The writ?' I finally said, taking a small step back.

'Here, sir,' she said, offering it to me. The original, or so her husband claimed, had been sent under the king's own signet, a sign of Richard's increasing tendency to bypass set procedures in the administration of the realm. I read the hurried copy carefully, scanning for that useful detail. *The king to Sir Richard de Brompton, greeting. I command you to do full right without delay . . .* A knight of Shropshire, a mercer of Shrewsbury, and a debt of nearly two hundred pounds. Yet I knew Brompton, a notorious debtor I'd had occasion to pluck a few years before. This was nothing new.

I shook my head. 'Sorry.'

She looked at me, a promise in her moist eyes. 'Not even a shilling, Master Gower?'

I suppressed a shudder. 'Nor a farthing, I'm afraid. But do tell your husband to be on the lookout for this sort of thing. You never can tell what might rise to the top. He knows how to reach me.'

She mumbled something, tightened her bonnet, then slunk off toward the palace with her maidservant. I followed them at a discreet distance and watched as they merged into the crowd around the south doors.

In the great hall I looked about for Ralph Strode, my second appointment in Westminster that morning, but when I reached our meeting place before Common Pleas at the north end a sudden silence swept the chamber. King Richard, in from Eltham Palace for the day, showing himself off. I went to my knee like every other man in the massive space, watching as the king came to the centre of the hall, paused with a practised deliberation, then gestured for all to rise and go about their business, though as always in his presence the talk was subdued. He wore long robes cut in the French fashion, a wide collar squeezing his thin neck. His fair hair, shoulder length and uncovered, swept from side to side as he spoke to his minions and those seeking a word. The king's impromptu entries into Westminster Hall were of a piece with his increasing love of ceremony, these portentous shows of authority that brought him in ritual touch with his subjects as often as he liked. If he caught your eye on one of these occasions you took a knee, no questions asked.

Yet there was a strange gentleness in the young king's bearing, a warmth of gesture and look I had never felt from his father, whose princely arrogance had surpassed even Gaunt's among old King Edward's sons. Though barely into his nineteenth year, this man had real reverence for the crown and its regal history, in ample evidence around the space. King

Richard had recently commissioned statues of England's past kings to be installed around the hall, with his own likeness culminating the series. The Confessor already stood in splendour against the south wall, his robes and crown gilded luxuriously, and a limner at work on his feet.

I leaned unobtrusively against one of the hall's great pillars, watching the king, when his head turned in my direction. His eyes found mine, and sparkled with what looked like affection. It took me aback: since his coronation I'd had perhaps three brief interactions with the king, none of them remarkable in any way. Surprised by this sliver of royal attention, I went to my knee and held the pose until King Richard released me with a slight, boyish smile and a swivel of his chin. It was a moment of genuine connection I would hold in my mind in the weeks ahead, as I learned of our intertwined fates.

'Quite a mess up there.' Ralph Strode had come up behind me. He grasped my arm. We gazed together into the vaults, the moist flakes of sawdust descending in thin streams, stirred up by work on a platform high above. For years there had been talk of an entire new roof, though for now all was timber and shingle, the ceiling playing a constant game of catch-up against rain and birds, bats and wind.

King Richard left the hall, the accustomed din rising again in his wake. As I turned to walk with Strode I was struck by his appearance. The common serjeant's skin was deeply veined, his eyes rheumy, his skin puffy and pink. He barked a wheezing cough into his sleeve.

'You're the busiest man in London, Ralph. I appreciate the time.'

He shook his head. 'For you I'd renegotiate the date of Easter with the Greeks!'

We strolled along the booths as I told him why I was there. For months I had been tangled up over my lands east of Southwark. A wealthy merchant, building a house on a neighbouring lot, had sued for ownership, claiming that certain

74

acreage fell within the boundaries of his property. Though the case hardly threatened my livelihood, it was requiring more of my time than it deserved, and I could find nothing to use against the man. Strode had just the sort of urban pull to finesse a transfer of jurisdiction from the bishop's court across the river. He was one of the few men in London's upper bureaucracy I could honestly call a friend, and he owed me a stack of favours as high as the north tower. 'The short of it, Ralph, is that I want to get this moved to Westminster, into Common Pleas.'

'You'll need a writ of *pone*, then,' Strode said.

'There may be some complications.'

He asked about the deeds, security, documentation, clarifying several matters. At the end he shook his head dismissively. 'None of this should present a problem for writ of *pone*. I'll put James Tewburn on it when I get back to the Guildhall.'

I inclined my head. 'You're a big gem, Ralph.'

'Believe me, it will be my most pleasant task of the week, and if I can use it to avoid other entanglements . . .' His stride stiffened a bit, a hint of trouble in his eyes. 'Especially this Bethlem mess.'

'Oh?' He was turned away and didn't see my reaction.

'The killing up there,' he went on. 'Quite a foul business.'

'So I understand.'

'Didn't help to have the whole thing played by those student hoodlums the other night. For days I've heard clusters of barristers bragging on the affair: the first moot ever busted up by the serjeants! The mayor's courts at the Guildhall are buzzing with it, then I come out here and the murder and its mooting are the talk of Westminster.'

There did seem to be a certain thickness in the air, several animated conversations nearby clearly occupied with more than the usual legal matter. Michael de la Pole, whom I had last seen at La Neyte, stood in the middle of one of them.

The chancellor gave me a slight nod when I caught his eye. 'Has the killer been apprehended?' I asked Strode.

'No, nor the victim's identity discovered. No name, no associates, no claimant to her body.' His voice lowered to a near-whisper. 'She was last seen alive at La Neyte. Now it's rumoured she was an agent of Valois.'

'A spy? Here in England?' I thought back to that moment with Tugg at Newgate, which was supposedly filled with French spies.

'So it seems.'

'Why do they think she's French?'

He shrugged. 'Her clothing, for one. And those who heard her speak claimed her accent smacked of Provence. Avignon, perhaps.' A word with grim associations: the schism of the church, a holy empire divided against itself, and France's ally against the true pope in Rome.

Our circles had brought us through each arcade twice, and we now approached the opened doors to the north porch, looking out on the yard. Strode gazed across the line of tents pitched along the hedges. 'War's coming, John. You can see it in the king's face. All this business with the Scots, the truce nearly at an end.' The royal delegation had recently left for negotiations to extend the peace, though no one expected anything to come of them. 'Imagine a French fleet, an invasion force, pulling its way up the Thames.' He looked over the shapeless mound of his nose and across the space. 'Ten thousand Frenchmen set on revenging their countrymen starved at Calais, or slaughtered at Crécy. What would such a host do to Westminster, to our children?' He leaned over a balustrade, elbows on the stone. 'To have their spies infiltrate London itself? Unthinkable.'

I needed more. 'And the girl?'

Strode shrugged his heavy shoulders. 'At La Neyte she was flitting from room to room, admired but unremarked. She was there a whole day, pretending to be a lady-in-waiting to the Countess of Bethune, one of Gaunt's guests. Bethune and the countess had already left for Kenilworth, you see, so no one was there to discredit her. And her story was unassailable. She stayed behind, she told everyone who asked, in order to procure a particular variety of Flemish cloth desired by the countess. At last, by asking the right questions of the right people, the girl found what she was looking for. She stole it and fled, presumably to hand it over to another spy. No one knows whether she succeeded.' He licked his lips. 'Then she was killed.'

'In the Moorfields.'

'Yes.'

'Who found her body?'

'I don't know.'

'Who examined it, attempted an identification?'

His nostrils flared. 'Tyle.' The coroner of London, Thomas Tyle, a man Strode had long despised. Lazy, incompetent, sloppy in his record-keeping, Tyle was an intimate of the king's chamberlain, and let everyone within hearing know it at every opportunity.

'Strange,' I said into the clamour of starlings angling toward the riverbank. 'A murder in the Moorfields? That's outside the walls. Not Tyle's jurisdiction.' Ralph knew this as well as I did, and as I studied his face I could tell the irregularity had been gnawing at him.

He looked at me. 'Nor Tyle's usual practice, to show up and do his actual job.'

'True.' In cases of unnatural deaths, it was the subcoroner who nearly always performed the inquest. Why, then, had Tyle himself taken over the scene? I posed a final question, trying to keep my tone light. 'And what did our French beauty steal out from under Lancaster's nose?' Katherine Swynford had already told me, but I wanted to test Strode's knowledge.

He gazed through the cloud of starlings, black slashes against the sky. 'A book.'

TEN

Broad Street, Ward of Broad Street

'A nun and a maud, and here we are together again.'

Millicent looked at her sister, huddled in the darkness.
Agnes had stayed in the Cornhull house that morning while
Millicent went out to sell the bracelet her sister had found
on the body in the Moorfields. The tiny piece had fetched a
few shillings on Silver Street, enough to keep them fed for
a week or two, though what they would do after that was a
mystery. She sighed. 'I was hardly a nun, Agnes.'

'Well, you lived among them out at St Leonard's Bromley.
Got their speech, learned to read like a master.'

'Not quite,' said Millicent. 'But I darned their robes,
smoothed their wimples.' She stared at the book, wondering
at the peculiar motivations of its maker. 'Then Sir Humphrey
ap-Roger came along, and they put me out as a concubine.'

'Girl who lives as a nun *is* a nun, leastwise in my book.
Not that this is my book now, by the cross.'

Millicent had just struggled through a second reading of
this dark work: a difficult book, filled with words and turns
of phrase the Bromley sisters had never taught her. *An educated
laity is our order's highest aspiration, Millicent*, Prioress Isabel

had reminded her many times. *To know that God's teachings are well water to the thirstful – this is one of the central works of our contemplative life.* Millicent had cut her teeth on the devotional texts made available to her by the Bromley sisters, though she had never read anything like this. The verse was bumpy, like her heartbeat, with repeated letters throughout and four hammering thumps to each line. Like a minstrel's romance, sung in the halls of lords.

> *The bone that he breaketh be baleful of harm,*
> *Nor treachery's toll with treason within . . .*

> *A woman with womb that woes him to wander*
> *For love of his lemman, his life worth a leaf . . .*

Such lines, as she murmured them to her sister, carried dire threats, each one of them tuned to the fate of an English king. Yet much of the work remained obscure, its lines heavy with symbols she couldn't decipher. Hawks, swords, thistles, and much else.

'So what's it all mean, Mil?'

Millicent thought for a while. 'Twelve prophecies, and I think I've undressed most of them. From the songs the minstrels sing, the plays they put on at Bromley Manor, St Paul's, everywhere.' The sisters knew these stories well, as did all Londoners: lays of olden kings, ballads of Harold and William the Conqueror, the story of the Lionheart, dying in his mother's arms. 'Twelve kings of England, Ag, all dead in the very way the minstrels say they went. Age, battle, disease, a poker in the arse.'

'Kings can die a lot of ways, eh?' Agnes shook her head.

'The great question, though, is, what will be the *next* way?' Millicent found the passage on the final pages that most concerned her: twelve lines of verse, speaking with a terrifying force of her own moment.

Agnes looked confused, so Millicent read through several of the prophecies and glossed along the way. 'I hardly know all our kings, Ag, but as for the ones I do know, the book seems to have it about right. And now we have here, in these last lines, the thirteenth prophecy.'

'The thirteenth prophecy?'

'The death of King Richard himself.' Millicent recited the most baleful passage in the work.

> '*At Prince of Plums shall prelate oppose*
> *A faun of three feathers with flaunting of fur,*
> *Long castle will collar and cast out the core,*
> *His reign to fall ruin, mors regis to roar.*
> *By bank of a bishop shall butchers abide,*
> *To nest, by God's name, with knives in hand,*
> *Then springen in service at spiritus sung.*
> *In palace of prelate with pearls all appointed,*
> *By kingmaker's cunning a king to unking,*
> *A magnate whose majesty mingles with mort.*
> *By Half-ten of Hawks might shender be shown.*
> *On day of Saint Dunstan shall Death have his doom.*'

'There it is then,' said Agnes, her face brightening.

'There what is?'

'It lays out the place of the killing, doesn't it? "In palace of prelate" and "by bank of a bishop". A palace by a river. A bishop's palace.'

'Braybrooke?' Millicent remembered a float with Sir Humphrey to the Bishop of London's riverside residence.

'Or our own Wykeham,' said Agnes. William Wykeham, the Bishop of Winchester, whose palace in Southwark stretched along a fair span of the Thames. 'Then it gives the killer's method, aye? Nesting with knives in hand, then springing forth—'

'"At spiritus sung",' Millicent finished for her. 'What's that mean, then?'

Agnes shrugged. 'Prayer, could be, ending in *spiritus*. Like a signal.'

'A signal.'

''Cause they'll have help, won't they?'

'From a "kingmaker",' said Millicent. 'A magnate whose majesty is mingled with *mort*.'

'Who's this Mort?'

'Not who but what, dearheart,' Millicent said gently, stifling a laugh. '*Mort* is France's word for death.'

'Ah.' Agnes frowned. 'But the book tells who wants the king dead, or at least how to know them for what they be. The shenders'll show themselves by "Half-ten of Hawks", whatever that might betoken.'

'Five hawks, then,' Millicent said.

Agnes frowned. 'Why not say five?'

'*Half-ten. Hawks.*' Millicent emphasized the common first letter of each word. 'It's the verse.'

'So the killer of our king will be carrying five hawks on his arm?'

'That's a lot of hawks for one arm,' Millicent mused.

Agnes crawled forward on the rushes, took the cloth that had covered the book in hand, and spread it over the floor. 'Five hawks, the book says, and there they are, clustered around the shield. Now I see it, Mil!' She turned round to her sister. 'It's like wool and a spinning wheel.'

Millicent squatted by the cloth.

'Without the wheel, the wool is just wool.' Agnes cradled an imagined basket. 'What good be a basket of wool if you haven't made it into thread yet? But once you've wound it on the spindle, started turning your wheel' – her hands spun the air – 'why, the wool starts to twist itself together, and soon you got so long a length of thread as you like.'

'I don't see it.'

'It's all on the cloth, isn't it?'

Millicent had thought little of the piece of embroidery apart from the shilling or so it would fetch on Cornhull. Yes, it was an extraordinary sample. But what did it have to do with the book?

She surveyed it now, looking more closely at the marks of livery embroidered across its span. She had noted them earlier, when Agnes first unwrapped the book for her, yet now their significance hit her with real force. Around one of the shields had been embroidered a careful pattern – a circle of five hawks – while the other sat in the midst of a triangle formed by three delicate white feathers. The cloth, she realized, told a story, a story whose main characters were embodied by the livery set between its edges. And what a story it was!

If she had learned her reading from Isabel of Barking, Millicent had learned her heraldry on the lap of Sir Humphrey ap-Roger, who had loved to point out the subtle variations signifying relations of rank, status, and depth of lineage: fields and divisions, charges and crests, beasts rampant and supine. In the difference between a blue lion on an argent field and an argent lion on a blue field lay whole histories of conquest and submission, Sir Humphrey taught her; *learn these histories and the livery that tells them, Millie darling, and you'll go far.* Yet the heraldry on this cloth required no great knowledge, for she recognized most of it instantly. The colours of the king and his uncle were depicted in a battle of some kind, with swords, knives, and arrows surrounding their emblems and supporters.

Millicent clasped her sister's hands. 'Without the wheel, then, the wool is just wool.'

Agnes nodded. 'And without the cloth,' she said, continuing the thought, 'the book is just . . .'

They said it together: 'A book.'

There was one final piece. Millicent read the last line of the prophecy to her sister. '"*On day of Saint Dunstan shall Death have his doom.*"'

'Dunstan's Day,' said Agnes. 'Nineteen May, or I'm a fool.'

Millicent calculated on her fingers. 'Six weeks, Ag,' she said into the darkness, the meaning of the prophecy chilling her limbs. 'Our king has but six weeks to live.'

They had sat in silence for a while, absorbing the prophecy's dire meaning, when Millicent saw a flicker of something cross her sister's face. 'What is it, Ag?'

'The faun,' she said, a faraway look in her eyes.

'What about it?'

'Right before that man killed her. She looked up at the sky, and she cried it out. A rhyme. 'Though faun escape the falcon's claws and crochet cut its snare, when father, son, and ghost we sing, of city's blade beware!' I remember it like my Ave Maria, her voice was so clear. It felt like she was screaming it to me, *to me*, while she's kneeling there, waiting to die. It's been stuck in my head since, just like that man's *doovay leebro, doovay leebro*. So what's it mean?'

'Say it again.'

As Agnes repeated the rhyme, Millicent scratched it on to the last page of the manuscript with a nub of coal in her unpractised, spidery script. The words did nothing to clarify the rest of the prophecy, but writing them down seemed to calm Agnes somewhat.

'Whatever it means it's only words, Ag. And we can't eat words.' Millicent stood, the manuscript falling from her lap. 'Nor a cloth, nor a damned book.' She slammed the chamber door behind her, clomping down the outer stairs, her hopelessness rising with each descending step. Her sister in her bed, the two of them together for the first time in years, yet Millicent felt more alone than ever. City's blade indeed.

ELEVEN

Basinghaw Street, Ward of Basinghaw

In London, if you die of unnatural causes, your corpse will be inspected not by the coroner himself but by his deputy, who gathers witnesses, orders the beadle to summon the jury from around the ward, and performs the inquest at the site of demise. The procedures are well established, and in theory should function smoothly.

Things are somewhat messier in practice. Though he works on behalf of the city, the coroner reports to the king's chamberlain, not to the mayor – a bureaucratic peculiarity I have found immensely useful over the years. Officials of city and crown can always be stirred against one another, and divided loyalties are to my vocation what a hammer is to a smith's. Since the last year of Edward's reign, the commons had been complaining regularly in Parliament about the coroner's office and the mischief this arcane arrangement could cause. To have a city official unbeholden to the mayor of London? A scandal, and an opportunity.

As usual Thomas Tyle, king's coroner, was absent when I arrived at his chambers on Wednesday of Easter week. The location spoke of the office's tenuous relation to the city government: just outside Guildhall Yard but within shouting distance of the mayor's chambers, and the common serjeant's, though I had sent a boy ahead to confirm the common serjeant's absence from the precincts. Seeing me here would raise uncomfortable questions in Ralph Strode's mind, and I needed him on my side.

Two clerks, facing one another over a double-sided desk. Neither looked up.

'Is Symkok about?'

The one to the left raised his jaw slightly, eyes still on his work. 'He's in there.' The back room, which I'd visited more than once. It was a dark space despite the bright day, the shutters closed nearly to. I found Nicholas Symkok, chief clerk to the subcoroner, hunched over the end of a table, a ledger opened before him. A crooked finger followed a column downward. The curve of his back seemed part of the furniture, a bony arc some carpenter hadn't thought to trim.

Nick Symkok was my first. It still startles me to think of how natural it all seemed when it began. Just a few years after the great dying, half of London beneath the soil, the city abuzz with news of the Oxford riots. That summer I found myself performing occasional clerical work in the Exchequer under the chancellor's remembrancer. Though I hardly needed the money, my father had promised my temporary services to the treasurer, to whom he owed a favour.

It was during the Michaelmas audit when one of our counters came to me with a messy sheaf of returns from Warwick's manors near Coventry. It seemed a sheriff had been drastically undercounting the number of tenants in his hundred, with the resulting decline in revenues from that part of the earl's demesne. I received permission from the remembrancer to take a discreet trip out to the Midlands to investigate. A careful comparison with the original returns soon showed that nothing was amiss in the earl's record-keeping. The guilty party, I realized, had to be one of our own.

85

A few days of digging back in Westminster turned up Nicholas Symkok, an auditor responsible for the embezzlement of nearly twenty pounds from the king's treasury over the last several years. Not only that, but Symkok had been using these enormous sums to purchase the flesh of the boy choristers singing for a prominent chantry attached to St Paul's.

When I confronted Symkok he melted in front of me, begging me to say nothing to the chancellor or the remembrancers – asking me to save his life. I agreed, on one condition. Symkok, I told him, would hereafter provide me any and all unusual information that came across his desk: the shady business of earls, the questionable holdings of barons, the conniving of knights. He was to digest all of it, slipping me anything of possible interest. I paid him, though just enough to keep him dangling on my hook. For several years after I left the Exchequer, Symkok was my main conduit, giving me my first clear look at the private lives of the lords of the realm.

Those years taught me much about the peculiar arts of *chantage*, and it was from the steady flow of copied documents in Symkok's hand that my small reserve of knowledge gradually expanded to encompass the vast store of information it would become. The arrangement seemed to crush Symkok, though, and he was never the same man. His ambitions stifled, he had spent the last twenty years floating through a series of clerical positions in the London and Westminster bureaucracies, all of them happily useful to my own purposes, if not to his career. At present he worked for the coroner of London, counting corpses.

I watched him until he felt my presence. He turned slowly on his bench. His eyes widened. 'Gower.'

'Hello, Nick.'

'What brings you here?'

'Death, of course.'

'Whose?'

86

'A girl's.'

'Lots of dead girls in London.'

'Not like this one.'

'What's her name?'

'Medusa? Persephone?' I said wryly.

'Name unknown, then?'

'To me it is.'

'And when did she die?'

'A week ago, perhaps more.'

'How?'

'Clubbed, or stabbed,' I said. 'I'm not sure.'

'Murder, then.'

'Yes.'

'Where did she die?'

'The Moorfields.'

It was as if a flame blew out in his eyes. His face went flat, expressionless.

'She was killed in the Moorfields, two weeks ago or more,' I repeated. 'I take it you know the circumstances?'

Symkok looked down at the ledger, his jaw rigid. 'Can't help you, Gower. Not on this one.'

A dog barked from Guildhall gate, a muffled sound that carried through the outer room. I let the silence linger. 'But I think you can, Nick.'

He shifted on his bench. A vacant stare toward the shutters, and finally that reliable nod. From a cupboard at his feet he removed a wooden box and placed it on the table, then reached inside and withdrew a heavy roll. He spread it across the surface, the worn wooden handles gleaming with the polish of many hands, until he found the entry in question.

'Be quick about it.' He left the room, with the coroner's roll opened on the table. In this document would be transcribed the original report, which was written out at the scene of the inquest. The roll, then, was the official copy of all the coroner's investigations of unnatural deaths in London during the term of his appointment. A rich and morbid archive, I had found over the years. I read the inquest report.

Friday the eve of Lady Day, ao 8 Richard II, it happened that a certain woman, name unknown, lay dead of a death other than her rightful death beside a certain low wood building in the Moorfields, in the rent of the holy priory of St Bethlem. On hearing this, the coroner and the sheriffs proceeded thither, and having summoned good men of various wards – viz. James Barkelay, Will Wenters, Ralph Turk, Thomas de Redeford, mercer, Simon de Saint Johan of Cornhull, draper, Laurence Sely, Simon Pulham, skinner, John Lemman &c. – they diligently inquired how it happened. The jurors say that on some unknown day before said Friday, said woman was beaten in the face and struck on the head and bloodied, feloniously murdered by an unknown assailant. When asked who found the dead body, they say a certain Adam de Hoyne, carter, did raise the hue and cry upon discovering the lady in her natural state. Upon inquiring further they did learn that no witnesses were found to be present at the said woman's death, nor did they find that anyone about knew her name, nor her station, nor her land of origin.

The corpse viewed &c.

Clothing appraised at 2s.

The surrounding inquests contained nothing out of the ordinary. I read the report again, memorizing certain details. The body had been discovered some days after the murder, it appeared. The woman had been beaten, her death apparently caused by a blow to the skull. She had been found 'in her natural state', or unclothed. No witnesses, no identifying

88

belongings. The appraisal of her clothing was high, though not unusually so.

In the outer chamber Symkok was conferring with his fellow clerks. When I emerged he gestured me outside. We reached the middle of Cat Street before he opened his mouth. 'So?'

'Seems simple enough,' I said.

'Murder usually is, in my experience.'

'Tyle himself held the inquest?'

He nodded.

'Bit unusual.'

Symkok shrugged. 'Though not unprecedented. When an earl dies on us, or a knight—'

'A nameless girl, stripped to the smooth? Hardly an earl, Nick.'

He wouldn't meet my gaze.

'Tell me, Nick.'

He straightened his back, his chin high. 'Nothing more to tell, Gower.'

We stood for a time, Symkok squirming in his discomfort.

'Do some digging, then,' I quietly said. A cart passed behind him, a low groan from its wheels. 'I need to know why Tyle took this one. Who told him to do the inquest himself rather than fob it off, like he usually does? And what did he find?'

He swallowed, his lined neck rippling with the effort.

'Be discreet about it, Nick.'

He swallowed again. 'Always am, Gower, at least where you're concerned.'

I left him there, gnawing at his past.

⁕

Back at St Mary Overey a letter awaited me in the hall. I took it up from the tray where Will Cooper would leave all my correspondence, expecting a bill from a local merchant, or a report from the bailiff of one of my estates. I was surprised at the letter's weight until I turned it over and saw the heavy seal. The wax bore the impress of Robert Braybrooke, Bishop of London.

Rather unusual, to send a sealed missive across the river when the bishop's messenger could have said a simple word to my servant. After a moment's hesitation I broke the wax. The note was short and to the point, and in his chief secretary's hand. The Lord Bishop of London requested my presence at Fulham Palace this Monday, at the hour of Tierce, upon his return from a visitation up north. The letter left the subject of the appointment unmentioned. London and I had had our moments, though all of that was far in the past, and I wondered what the bishop could possibly want with me. I thought about it for a while, ticking off a mental list of current complexities but coming up with nothing aside from Katherine Swynford's brief mention of Braybrooke at La Neyte, and his distress over the book sought by Chaucer.

Whatever its subject, the bishop's was an invitation I was in no position to decline. In my study I scribbled a reply at the foot of the letter, melted some wax, and left the missive in the tray for Will, who would arrange its delivery for that afternoon. Five days, then I would know more.

TWELVE

Cutter Lane, Southwark

The knife landed in muscle with a wet spit. A second blade quickly followed, nearly touching the first. The carcass swayed, and Gerald Rykener clapped his hands roughly on his tunic. 'Have that, Tom.'

The other apprentice stepped up to the line, a blade pressed between his fingers. His wrist bent, his arm rose, and with a flash of metal the knife was buried in the flank just inches from Gerald's. The second landed a half foot higher on the beef, missing its target. '*Damn* it to queynting hell,' he said, then with a scowl handed Gerald a coin.

Eleanor watched her brother pocket it, and for a moment the simple joy of victory on his face turned him back into the sweet boy she remembered. Then Gerald saw her.

'Ah, by St George. Swerving again,' he muttered to his companion, his contempt for her undisguised.

The other apprentice looked over to where she stood by the fence. 'What do you think, Gerald? Your brother a mare or a gelding?'

'A mare with a cock?' Gerald taunted. 'A gelding with a queynt?'

'Either way she-he's got enough riders to keep him-her filled with oats 'n' mash till the trumpet sounds, from what I hear.'

'Aye that,' said Gerald, ignoring her as his fellow turned for the barn. Gerald wiped a long crimson smear across his cheek, then from beneath the carcass removed a bucket of blood. He took it to a heated cauldron at the far end of the yard. Gerald was fourteen, yet already moved with a trades-man's confidence that would have been endearing if he hadn't turned so foul. His apron was cut small in the style of the craft. *We butchers pride ourselves on leaving our aprons white*, he'd explained in those days when he cared. Now it was stained a brownish red, his loose breeches slimed with gore.

When he returned to the fence she saw the latest bruises had faded. His lip, too, had mostly healed. He was close so she went for his neck, the line of faded scar tissue running from his jaw to his nape. He knocked her hand back but she reached for his head and felt a new knot. Size of a peach pit. 'What's that about?'

He ducked away. 'He swings the mallet around, you know, got those teeth on it. It's wood, though, so. But Grimes'd never hit me with the metal one. Not ever.'

'Not yet,' she said. 'And when he does you'll be dead as that beef side hanging behind you.' Why Gerald took his master's part so often she couldn't reckon, though Nathan Grimes had been his effective father for going on three years, and children could develop peculiar loyalties.

He looked at her purse. She handed him the coins she'd come to deliver. 'It's hardly much. A shilling and five. Keep it somewhere, use it only in your most needful moments. Not for candied gingers on the bridge, now.' She half-turned to go, but something in his eyes held her back. 'What is it?' Trying to sound impatient: she needed to be tough with him, tough as he was with her, or he'd never make it to his majority. 'What is it, Gerald?'

He snarled and spat in the filthy straw. 'No matter. Go away, Edgar.'

As her brother returned to his work Eleanor watched him sadly, marvelling at how much the boy had changed. They had been separated since their mother's death, when Gerald was seven, Eleanor thirteen and starting to discover her second life. A man in body, but in soul a man and a woman both, a predicament that made her wardship a domestic hell: a wife who tormented her with the hardest household labour, a husband who wouldn't leave her alone once he found out what she was. She had taken to the streets at sixteen. Gerald, though, had seemed to be getting by, floating from guardian to guardian, some good, some bad, yet all carefully regulated by the city, with appearances before the mayor himself once a year. Eleanor managed to see him nearly every month as they grew up. Finally, at his eleventh birthday, the office of the common serjeant arranged for his apprenticeship to a freeman of London and master butcher, and all appeared set.

Then, not six months after his apprenticeship began, the city passed the butchery laws, and Gerald's master moved his shop across the river to Southwark to avoid the fines and fees. There not only butchers but guardians operated on their own authority, with little legal oversight from the town, and no common serjeant to take the orphans' part. 'Never heard no law against a butcher moving shop to Southwark,' Grimes had said when Eleanor confronted him. He turned instantly cruel upon the move across the Thames: Gerald was on his own there, surrounded by meat yet starved for bread, beaten regularly and with no recourse. Eleanor had tried to intervene, but the laws of London, it was said, have no house in Southwark.

Soon enough Gerald was turning into one of them, these Southwark meaters, a nasty bunch of Cutter Lane thugs without guild or code, sneaking rotten flesh into the markets and shops across the river. The Worshipful Company of

Butchers, London's legitimate craft, had been trying for years to quash the flow of bad flesh into the city to no avail, and now that Gerald had been caught up in their illegal trade he, too, was slipping down the path to a hanging. It often seemed to Eleanor that Gerald's entire self had changed, as if the Holy Ghost had sucked out his soul and the devil had blown in another.

'Best be off,' she said. He shrugged indifferently. From behind her, a whisper of straw. A pig, she thought. Gerald's back was to her as he scraped at a pile of hardened dung. 'May be a stretch before I can get out here again.' She recalled the beadle's questions, the threats, and thought of Agnes. Two sparrows perched on the side of the stall flitted off. Gerald started to turn. 'There's been some trouble on the lane, and I might have to be—' He faced her now. His eyes widened.

Eleanor's neck snapped back, her hood wrenched violently downward by an unseen hand. She was spun around into the face of Nathan Grimes, taking in his ale-breath. 'Trouble on Gropecunt Lane? For a lovely boy-princess like yourself?'

'You let my brother go, now!' Gerald screamed, backing away. 'You just let him go, Master Grimes!'

Grimes was a stout, boar-like man, with well-muscled arms that flexed as he held her. 'I'll let it go all right.' With a hard push against her head, he shoved Eleanor to the stall floor. She backed up against the boards, then came to her feet, her breath shallow.

Grimes gestured toward Gerald. 'Get inside, boy.' Gerald stayed where he was. Grimes raised a hand. '*Inside*, boy.' Gerald looked at Eleanor. She gave him a reassuring nod. He backed away, pushed open the pen gate, and walked reluctantly toward the house. The butcher leaned over Eleanor, toying with Gerald's knives.

'I know what you be, Edgar Rykener,' said Grimes, with a small lift of his chin. 'No place for swervers in a respectable butcher's shop, now. Let your brother learn his craft in peace.'

'Peace?' said Eleanor under her breath; then, more loudly, 'He getting any peace by *your* hand?'

'Getting fed, isn't he?' Grimes retorted. 'Getting schooled in hogs and calves, learning the way of the blade, got some thatch over his head. More'n you can say for lots of boys his age, in London or not.'

'And getting a mallet to the skull in the bargain.'

Grimes spat in the dirt. 'Boy needs to learn respect he wants to be a freeman like me.'

'You took an oath, Master Grimes,' she seethed. 'In the mayor's presence himself you swore to God you'd protect my brother, keep him from harm. Now you'd as lief kill him.'

Grimes lifted a cleaver, fingered its edge. 'Never cut up a maudlyn in all my day.' He looked over at the beef carcass. 'Can't imagine there's much trouble to it, though.' He smiled. 'Now get back to London, sweetmeats.'

She edged out of the stall with a final glance at Gerald. He stood in the doorway to the apprentices' shack, his face so much older than it should have looked. Once she was gone Grimes would paint it good. The burden of it all settled on her: a murder, a missing friend, a brother liable to be brained at any moment and clearly troubled by something he wouldn't reveal.

Yet there was one man who might be capable of putting things right for Gerald, Eleanor speculated as she walked up toward the bridge, get him out of all of this. A kind man, from all she'd heard. A man with the authority to remove her brother from his Southwark dungeon and put him with a kinder master in London. As she passed back over the bridge she thought about this man, knowing, at least, where to find him; trusting, for she had to, in his kindness.

THIRTEEN

St Mary Overey, Southwark

On the morning after Low Sunday I rose early, awakened by the buzz of the priory bell, cracked and unreplaced since the belfry fire two years before. My appointment with Braybrooke would not be for hours, but I left the house anyway, absorbing the quiet din of these Southwark streets at dawn, already alive with the work that sustained the greater city over the river. Here the trades commingled with none of London's attempt at logic, the shops of haberdashers and carpenters, tanners and tawyers, fishmongers and smiths, coopers and brewers all side by side, spewing smells and sounds and petty rivalries even as small creeks of rubbish spilled out of alleys between them. I stepped into a baker's shop and purchased two sweetbuns for the trip. At the river landing I paid my pennies and hopped on a common wherry, joining a few others westward bound.

I found a seat for the float to Fulham, and as the wherry passed St Bride's on the north bank I squinted across the wide span at a group of young men in skiffs. They were tilting, I realized, their target a square of beaten tin suspended from the lampstick of an anchored barge. Four oarsmen per skiff made wide circles around the craft, the lanceman at the bow, loose on his knees; then, a speedy approach, the lance held at the shoulder, the skiff keeping steady over the rises; and finally impact, as the dulled point of the lance struck the tin, the noise carrying over the water. An awkward game, yet several of the young men were quite skilful with their lances, taking the applause of their mates with exaggerated pride.

These, I thought with a shudder, would be the first Englishmen killed were a French invasion force to sail up the Thames from Gravesend and destroy the bridge. How would these boys spend their final moments? Would they turn tail, ditching their skiffs on the bank, fleeing through the streets? Or would they stand and fight, tilting at warships in a futile attempt to save London?

At the quay of Patrisey I changed wherries and thought ahead to my appointment with the bishop. Knowing Braybrooke as I did, I could expect a meeting full of venom and insinuation, of parries and feints. Tread softly, I warned myself.

With a slow turn toward the north bank, we passed lines of oak and elm towering over the terraced lawns leading up to the bishop's great house, which commanded an enviable position over the river. Above the dock was a pavilion trimmed in banners of silk, cloth of gold, and sable, displaying Braybrooke's mascles over his personal barge.

As the bank came into view I saw not only Braybrooke's colours, but the Earl of Oxford's as well. The wherry bumped in just up-river from Braybrooke's barge, and as I stepped up the bank I saw Robert de Vere striding across the lower terrace. Normally Oxford moved about with a larger retinue, yet his only companion that day was Sir Stephen Weldon. I bowed as the earl approached. He looked me over, his discomfort apparent as he waved me to my full height.

'Gower,' he finally said.

'Your lordship.' I nodded to Weldon. 'Sir Stephen.'

Weldon returned the nod.

'How is his lordship the bishop?' I asked them.

'Supervising plantings on the upper terrace,' said the earl, forcing a smile. 'Seems there are some questions about the rigor of the vines he's got in from Bordeaux. But he's still determined to pull a decent *clairet* from our English clay.'

I winced. *'Prêtres anglais ont toujours aimé le vin.'*

'As long as I'm not forced to sample the result,' said Oxford.

Weldon feigned choking, a comic gesture that broke the awkwardness. 'I do miss the wines of Italy,' the knight said, his eyes crinkling with the memories. For years Weldon had served with Sir John Hawkwood before his permanent return to England in the fifth year of Richard's reign. Weldon was taller than Oxford, and thinner, with a studied casualness to his stance. He wore little in the way of livery, a small badge on his right breast the only mark of his station. 'Perhaps England's next war might be fought over France's vine rather than its cities.'

'A welcome suggestion,' I said, choosing to take Weldon's courteous demeanour as sincere. 'For that I'd happily lift a sword.'

With these elevated nothings we parted, and I was left wondering what business the earl could possibly have at Fulham. To my knowledge, all Oxford and London shared was a mutual hatred of John of Gaunt.

I was directed to an upper side terrace, reached after a circuitous route through a network of gravel walks. I found the Bishop of London on his knees, thinning roses. At a discreet distance stood two servants bearing bowls, flagons, and gardening tools for the bishop's use, and, closer, four additional men holding his robes, mitre, and cap: two friars, a canon of some kind, and Fulham's head gardener, the last with his hands crossed tightly in front of him as Braybrooke assaulted his art with the unpractised hand of a knight shearing sheep. The canon, noticing me, cleared his throat. Braybrooke turned.

'Gower.' The bishop was a man of awkward, treeish height;

98

to see him on his knees, his meaty hands scooping dirt from the ground, was something new.

'Your lordship.'

Braybrooke loosened a stone. 'How's Gaunt?'

'I would not know, your lordship,' I said. 'I caught a passing glimpse of him the other week at La Neyte, but that is all.'

Another stone, a spray of soil. 'Can't be comfortable for the duke, can it, being a constant object of suspicion?' I listened as the bishop muttered over the royal troubles of the last year, still the talk of the realm. He had been at the council tournament in February, and I learned a new detail about the aftermath of Oxford's plot against Lancaster. If not for the peacemaking interventions of Countess Joan, the bishop claimed, either Gaunt or King Richard would surely have been dead by now. And with the king still young, always gullible, and increasingly unpredictable in his alliances, things could only worsen.

'What about you, Gower?' the bishop said. 'You're content with your own alliances?'

'I'm for the king, your lordship,' I said cautiously. 'From whatever faction he comes, I'm for the king.'

'An easy vow.' He packed dirt into the new hole. 'For a man who takes such stark moral stands in his verse, you're remarkably reluctant to choose sides.'

My jaw tightened.

'The lines are being drawn, Gower. Two popes, two churches – some would say two kings.' The bishop looked up, his eyes cold. 'Your friend Geoffrey Chaucer, too, would do well to clarify his allegiances. Not a lover of friars, that one.'

I glanced at the two Dominicans. 'Chaucer is a lover of the good,' I said. 'He loves good friars, as he loves good bishops such as your lordship. Good wine, too, and good lawyers.'

Braybrooke barked a laugh. He clipped and dug for a while, then looked up at me again. 'This book you're looking for has a name.'

I blinked.

'You think I'm a fool, Gower? You make a wide-eyed request of Katherine Swynford, the yawningest mouth in the realm, and you expect her not to gossip?'

'A fair point,' I conceded.

'*Liber de Mortibus Regum Anglorum.*'

'My lord?'

'*Liber de Mortibus Regum Anglorum.* That's what this work is called.'

'"The Book of the Deaths of English Kings",' I translated.

'A book of prophecy, written by a certain Lollius during the reign of the Conqueror.'

'That long ago? What relevance could a book three centuries old have in our day?'

'The *De Mortibus* prophesies the death of every English king since William. The houses of Normandy, Plantagenet, with the circumstances of each royal death rendered in detail. The time, the place, the means.'

'I've never heard of this Lollius. Are people taking this seriously?'

'The book is being read by Wycliffe's minions, Gower. They gather in conventicles and recite the prophecies one by one. Thirteen kings, thirteen prophecies, thirteen deaths, all foretold and retold as a goad to revolt.'

'I loathe Wycliffe's teachings as much as the next fellow, your lordship. But he never questioned Richard's legitimacy.'

'I suggest you learn a bit about this book before you dismiss it, Gower. One of my friars here has mingled with the Wycliffites during their readings. He's got a bit of the work in his head.' He looked over his other shoulder. 'Brother Thomas, a taste. The death of King William, if you please.'

One of the friars stepped forward with a bow. At a nod from Braybrooke, he spoke the requested lines.

'A bastard by birth, of Brittany bane,
A duke rendered king by Deus decree,

100

With fury so fierce all England will fight,
Shall matins and masses restore to all men,
Then in Mantes to muster his might shall appear.
Unhorsed by his hand this sovereign full hale
On pommel full pounded from saddle shall pitch,
And goeth to ground to giveth the ghost.
At sovereign of swords in death swoon he will,
No more to flee mors, his reign an end make.'

The friar stepped back, assuming his position, still by the tree. Something about the lines sounded familiar.

Braybrooke sat on his heels, prompting the gardener to step forward hopefully. The bishop waved him off. 'Thus shall die the first of thirteen English kings.' Braybrooke wiped his brow. 'Let me correct myself: thus *did* die the first of thirteen English kings, this one at the great battle at Mantes, of which we read in our chronicles.'

'Of which this Lollius read in our chronicles, unless I'm an utter fool,' I muttered, unswayed by the bishop's lofty tone.

He glared at me. 'If you're sceptical, Gower, keep listening.' He nodded to the friar, who began a second series of lines.

'With seven of swords to swing at their will,
To chasten with chattel, and chase their king down.
In Gloucester will he goeth, to be gutted by goodmen
With rod straight of iron, in arsebone to run.
With pallet of pullet, his breath out to press,
And sovereign unsound for Sodom be sundered.'

My hand went to my gut. 'The second King Edward.'
'And his disgusting execution,' Braybrooke said. 'Lying on a feather pallet, a poker shoved up his arse. A fitting death for a Ganymede king. And finally the more peaceful death of good King Edward.'

101

The friar spoke a third time. I could not hide my surprise at his opening words.

'Full long shall he lead us, full rich shall he rule,
Through pain of pestilence, through wounds of long war.
Yet morire is matter all sovereigns must suffer.
This long-lived leader, beloved of all,
At three of thistles shall suffer his fall;
Gold bile shall him bite, with bitter wound wide,
At Sheen will be shent, last shrift there to render.'

Braybrooke scrutinized my face as I remembered where I had heard these lines before. At Holbourne cross, shouted into the drizzle by that deranged-looked preacher. The man had spoken this very verse.

'Some say the gomoria took him,' the bishop said, turning away with a smile, 'though I believe the old fellow had a simple stroke.' With the rocks removed and the ground cleared, he knelt to address the large rose bush before him. The gardener was trying not to weep.

'The prophecies, if that's what they are, are full of enigmas, Lord Bishop,' I said, wondering how Braybrooke could be swayed so easily. 'What are the "three of thistles", the "seven of swords" in the account of Edward, or the "sovereign of swords" in William's case? These sorts of symbols don't appear in the chronicles, not in the ones I've read.'

The bishop pricked a finger, brought it to his mouth. 'The thistle is important to the Scots, I'm told,' he said with a smack of his lips. 'Perhaps some new Robert de Bruce is on the rise.' His voice sounded almost jocular now, as if he were putting me on.

I looked at his rounded back. 'With respect, your lordship, the work your friar just recited is written in a modern fashion – its style, its rhythm. It sounds like the story of King Horne, or that vision of Piers the Ploughman that was so much in

102

favour around the Rising. I have to say, I'm surprised so much is being made of an obvious forgery.'

He turned to look at me. 'The thing could have been written by anyone schooled in our nation's chronicles. Is that what you are thinking, Gower?'

Finally some sense. 'The church is familiar with false prophets, my lord.'

With an audible crack of his long spine, Braybrooke stood, flicking dirt off his hands. 'Your scepticism is admirable, Gower, and matches my own.' An attendant stepped forward with a bowl. Braybrooke dipped his hands and wiped them on a cloth. He turned to the friars and canon, who robed and capped him. He waved off his mitre like a cat refusing tack.

'We are men of the law, Gower,' he continued as we walked to the river. 'I serve the church now, but I still have faith in our earthly institutions. The crown, Parliament, even the courts. You know all too well how my trust was once challenged in this regard, John, and I'm still grateful for the compassion you showed.'

It was a rare moment of candour from Braybrooke, whose ambition often outstripped his memory. I murmured my thanks.

He puffed his cheeks, blew air. 'My contempt for Lancaster is no secret.'

'I've witnessed it.'

'Heresy and war arrange us in peculiar alliances.' He said nothing of Oxford, though I assumed he was thinking of the earl. 'If the reports I have received are accurate, the thirteenth prophecy is known only to a few.'

'The thirteenth prophecy?'

'England has had thirteen kings since the conquest.' He waited a moment, then said, 'Thirteen, *including* William.'

'Yet if William—' I stopped walking, finally understanding, and feeling like a fool.

He stepped down on to the Fulham quay. 'Now you know

why a man in my position would be anxious to root out this book before the thirteenth prophecy becomes known, let alone realized. My friar, Brother Thomas back there, has heard only whisperings of its content, but apparently it implicates someone quite close to the king. Who that might be we don't yet know, though one can guess. So you see it hardly matters whether the *De Mortibus* is a genuine work of prophecy or a clever forgery. If word of the last prophecy were to get out . . .' He looked at me.

'Yes, my lord.' A missing book, a girl murdered in the Moorfields, and now this. 'The thirteenth prophecy, then, concerns—'

'The death of King Richard. Still a boy, really, but with all the world on his shoulders.' He gazed across to the far bank. 'Whatever Chaucer is paying you to find this book, I will give you double if you bring it to me instead, Gower. Triple.' With that the Bishop of London turned from me, walked up the embankment, and was gone.

FOURTEEN

Cutter Lane, Southwark

Hook out the belly, knot up the guts, snip out the anus – all that was fine, but Gerald still had trouble with the hiding. How to keep it one piece when it wants to split apart at the shoulders, that was the thing. As Grimes liked to remind him, a split hide wasn't worth half a whole, *and you'll get the hole, boy, get it right through your pate 'f you split another vellum on me.*

This time it worked. Gerald grunted happily as he felt the spine, pared to the haunch, begin to loosen against the gored skin. Spines had their own smell, too, that chalky air of fresh bone. He pulled it free. Hard part of this calf was done. He felt his arms loosen, the knife working its magic as he sliced and split with the ease of a stronger, bigger man.

Gerald loved butchery, felt he was born to cut up these beasts. Only bad part was Grimes. His master was inside now, prattling with that priest. He'd first shown up two weeks ago. This was his third visit. Gerald could hear them all the way from the cutting floor, their voices raised in an argument of some kind. Same as last time.

The priest's comings and goings were putting Grimes in a

bad state, even worse than usual. More blows to the cheek, more boxes to the ear, more threats of worse to come. Part of him knew his brother was right – well, his sister – his broster, his sither, whichever way in God's name Edgar–Eleanor was swerving these days, it was true that Grimes's shop wasn't a safe place for a boy Gerald's age. Better to be back in London, with its laws. But what could *he* do about it? What could Edgar do, for that matter – let alone Eleanor? He shook his head, trying to put it all out of his mind and concentrate on the carcass swinging in his face.

Tom Nayler came in, wiping his hands. 'I'm off, then,' he said, tossing his chin in the direction of the high street. 'Got a coney to slit up the market. This'll wait, yeah?'

'Suit yourself,' Gerald said, wondering who the lucky girl was this time. Tom had a way with the daughters of oyster-mongers and maudlyns. 'I'll finish this one up. Not a lot left.'

Tom ambled off. Gerald sliced and cut contentedly for a while longer. Flanks, legs, heart, with the offal for the dogs. The master's shop had grown quiet, though he hadn't seen the priest leave. He stepped off the floor and glanced up the alley. Tom Nayler was long gone. After a look in the other direction he wiped his blade, set it down on a board, and stared at the shop, his thoughts churning.

What was it with Grimes and this priest? Wasn't a parson of the parish, that was sure. Gerald knew the local parson, just like he'd known the parson at St Nicholas Shambles in his younger days. No, this one wasn't a Southwark man. Not even a Londoner. A northerner, maybe. Or a Welshman. Talked with a gummy twang, like his words were tangled up in brambles and couldn't get out.

The only window on this side of the shop was shuttered, as usual when important visitors came to talk to Grimes. The butcher liked to keep his inquisitive apprentices at bay. Taking his time, Gerald walked over to the shop, found the right spot, and pressed his ear to the gap between the boards. More than once he'd saved his hide this way, catching snatches of the master's complaints about his apprentices and correcting himself accordingly.

He heard the priest, speaking low. At first none of it made sense. A lot of talk about how Grimes had to listen, had to do this and that, think about his future. Then, a stream of verse. 'Listen to it, Nathan Grimes. It's you this prophecy is talking about, you and your cutters over here.

> *By bank of a bishop shall butchers abide,*
> *To nest, by God's name, with knives in hand,*
> *Then springen in service at spiritus sung.*

Butchers, Nathan. Butchers bearing knives. They're to be the blood of it, and you the heart.'

Grand words. But what did they mean? Gerald heard Grimes clear his throat. 'Lots of butchers in London, Father, over in the Shambles and such. There's nothing in the verse to say it's to be a Southwark meater, is there?'

'Not exactly, no,' said the priest slowly. 'But "bank of a bishop"? And later it reads "In palace of prelate with pearls all appointed." That's Winchester's palace, my son, you know it as well as I. And who's the closest master butcher to Winchester's palace? Nathan Grimes, that's who.'

'Nathan Grimes,' said the butcher, tasting his name.

'That's right. "By kingmaker's cunning a king to unking." Do you see?'

'Well—'

'It's plain as the shining sun, Nathan Grimes. Look in the glass. You're to be the kingmaker, sure as I'm standing here.'

'The kingmaker,' Grimes repeated.

'Wouldn't be the first time you've been at the centre of such great events,' said the priest, lowering his voice. 'You were on the bridge with Wat Tyler, Nathan. You walked right behind him. And I saw you myself on Blackheath, standing at Ball's feet. You could have taken out King Richard at Mile End, with a cleaver or a long knife.'

Gerald felt a chill, finally understanding the priest's cryptic talk. It had been four years since the Rising, when the commons of Essex and Kent, infuriated by the poll taxes and the harshness of their levy, had flooded London by the thousands, burning buildings, beheading bishops and treasurers and chancellors, imprisoning the young King Richard himself in the Tower and nearly executing him at Smithfield.

The butchers of London and Southwark had marched along with the rest, and Gerald could still remember the exuberance on the streets as word spread of John Ball's sermon on Blackheath. *When Adam delved and Eve span, who was then the gentleman?* Words of hope, and a promise of a better life for England's poor. Though things were now much the way they had been before the Rising, its wounds were still fresh, the city and the realm braced with suspicion of the commons. You could still see it on the faces of the beadles and aldermen, in the tense stance of lords and ladies as they rode through the streets, trading hostile glances with clusters of workers breaking stone, or lame beggars idling by the gates.

Now, it seemed, the talk of treason was back. That priest in with Grimes, he was trying to convince the master butcher to raise arms again, and this time have a real go at the king. He thought of the priest's verses. *By bank of a bishop shall butchers abide.* Not *one* butcher, not Nathan Grimes alone, but *butchers.* So what did that mean for him, Gerald Rykener?

The scrape of a bench. Gerald turned his head so his eye was against the gap. The priest rose and clapped Grimes on the back. 'This is fate, my son. It's prophecy, as sure as the Apocalypse itself. God sees our futures and our glories in ways we mortals cannot, Nathan. This is yours. Embrace it, my son!'

Grimes sat there, staring at the far wall of his shop, kneading his swarthy chin. Gerald watched him, almost seeing the muddled thoughts in his master's brain, like a rocker churning cream. Then the butcher looked up at the priest, a gleam in his eye. He stood, inhaled deeply, and nodded.

'I'm in, Father.' His nod strengthened as his certainty swelled. The priest stepped in and embraced him.

Gerald felt his stomach heave. He turned away, his eyes cast at the ground as he trudged back to the kill shed. He leaned against the rough board wall, pondering what he'd heard.

The butchers of Southwark. A new Rising. Knives and cleavers and axes and a crowd of meaters, massing over the bridge, intent on killing the very King of England. To what end? He shook his head, the answer as clear as his memory. A rain of arrows, the swish of a garrison's swords, and it would all be over. A slaughter in the streets, the blood of the poor running between the pavers. Just like last time.

And who would the hangman come for first, once the king's men discovered who sparked this certain treason? Gerald looked up, the fear clenching at his middle so he could hardly stand straight. Nathan Grimes, that's who – and his two apprentices, all of them about as safe as the butchered veal calf hanging there before him.

FIFTEEN

Broad Street, Ward of Broad Street

A rock, hitting the streetside shutters. Millicent did her best to ignore it but then another struck the wood, throwing a hollow *crack* into the back room where she lay with Agnes. She glanced at her sister, who was still asleep, then threw off the covers and walked to the front room, pushed open a shutter, and leaned out. On the lane stood a young woman in a faded wool dress, hands planted on her narrow hips.

'What is it?' Millicent called down.

She looked up, her hand angled against the sun, tendrils of dark hair circling a moonish face beneath her hood. 'Millicent Fonteyn?'

'Who wants to know?'

'Eleanor Rykener. Searching out your sister. She about?'

Millicent willed herself not to look over her shoulder. 'Agnes hasn't been up Cornhull in five seasons.'

'That right?'

'What do you want with her?'

Eleanor lowered her voice. 'Beadle of Cripplegate's been asking questions, and she's been gone for a while now.' Millicent said nothing. 'Tell her I been by. I'm worried for the poor thing.'

Millicent was about to reply when Denise Haveryng came out of her shop, making clear she'd been listening to the exchange.

'Saw her last at the wharfs, if I remember,' said Millicent quickly, trying to end the conversation before Denise opened her mouth.

'That right?' said Eleanor.

Denise loudly cleared her throat. 'Though you might check up Gropecunt Lane, or Rose Alley over the bridge,' she called out. 'Those be more her haunts. Millicent's as well, I imagine, before too long.' She looked up at the window with a sweet smile, as if expecting Millicent to thank her for saying nothing about Agnes's presence in her house.

Millicent slammed the shutter, jammed her palms against her eyes, and leaned back against the sill, cursing her sister and her own penury for the tenth time in as many days. Ever since Agnes showed up in her bed with that damned book Millicent had felt frozen, unable to make a decision about anything, even what food to purchase with her few remaining pennies. Nor was Agnes any use, huddled up as she was, afraid to set foot on Cornhull, let alone return to Gropecunt Lane and earn her skincoin.

They'll be after me, she had sworn up and down. *Constables, sheriffs, the man who killed that girl. Don't make me leave, Mil. Let's stay here. I feel safe here, Mil.*

She wasn't, of course. For someone wanted this book enough to kill for it – and if one man wanted it so badly, surely others did, too. Yet here they were, sitting like harts in a field as the hunters closed around them. Even that Eleanor Rykener had known where to look, and if what she'd just said was true, the authorities in Cheap Ward were now asking after Agnes.

They were in danger. Something had to change. She took a deep breath, and the decision stole demon-like into her mind. She woke Agnes.

'We sell it, Ag.'

'Whah?' Agnes yawned, rubbing her eyes.

'The book. We sell it to the highest payer.'

Agnes shook her head, coming awake. 'Having it here in your house's already a dangerous thing, Mil. Like holding a flaming log. And now you want to sell it, spread the fire when the source be us? Better to toss it in the Thames.'

'Wrong.' She pressed her sister's hand. 'We have to sell it, and sell it soon. It's the only way out of this hell, Ag. My debt, your life – why, sell it to the right man and we'll have riches to spare.'

'But who would purchase such a thing, Mil?'

Who indeed? Through the morning hours Millicent thought through every interaction she could recall with members of noble retinues from her years as Sir Humphrey's consort. Since his death these connections had been entirely broken, for a singlewoman without blood, wealth, or station could hardly seek the company of counts, knights, and ladies and expect to meet anything but disdain. It was not the nobles themselves they would approach, she decided. Rather it was the working members of their households: the armourer to the Baron of Yorkshire, the steward to the Duke of Lancaster, the clerk of wardrobe to the Earl of Oxford. The men with the most intimate access to their lords, and the means to persuade them that this book of prophecies would be a most worthy purchase.

Agnes still looked doubtful. 'Suppose they turn us over to the constables, or the beadle?'

'They won't,' Millicent said confidently. 'Who'd believe them, claiming some maudlyns are going around London peddling a book of prophecies?'

'I suppose you're right,' said Agnes. 'Though we don't have to do this, Mil. Our mother, she still might take us in. Even you, even after all these years.'

'A generous soul, that Bess Waller,' Millicent scoffed.

'You're her daughter too, Mil. Could be she'd give us our old rooms to ply the swyve, let us keep more of what we earn. The Bishop wasn't so bad, and we'd be together. Our mother's got, what, another ten years, then the place can be our own.'

Millicent shook her head furiously. 'I'm never going back. Never. And you can't live the life of a maud into your old age. You want to turn out like St Cath, that withered sheath? This book, this is all we've got.'

'Not true, Mil,' Agnes pleaded. 'We got these' – she grabbed her breasts – 'and this' – palmed her crotch – 'and as long as they work we'll get skincoin. You know that well as I!'

Millicent looked at her sister, her small body still unruined. Agnes had always carried her beauty well. When their mother started selling Millicent's flesh at fifteen, all those quick, rough lessons in womanhood, Agnes had slipped about the Bishop with a beguiling sense of her own virginal charms that provoked Bess Waller's eager jakes. 'I'll wait for *her*' was a common refrain, their eyes following Agnes even as their legs followed Millicent.

Only one man had ever openly preferred her to Agnes: Oswald, the prior of St Mary Overey. Millicent had come as close to loving him as she had any man, even Sir Humphrey. An old Austin canon of forty-eight when she met him, what he wanted most was to run his nose and fingers up her bare sides and along that warm space between her breasts, never get inside her and grunt away his groats like all the others. She remembered the gentle ambitions of his lips and fingers, the firm pleasures of his clerical tongue. He talked to her of his life, his sin, his ambitions for a bishopric that would never come – provoking jests from her about bishops' pricks and why he'd ever want one in the first place, given how soft they all were.

One morning Prior Oswald asked her what *she* wanted most. She told him: a way out. So he purchased it for her, and gave her the news the last day she saw him. *You shall be a laysister of St Leonard's Bromley, my dear Millie. You'll learn to garden, to embroider, perhaps to read – and you'll never have to spread your legs for another man (though if the prioress herself demands a ride, you probably shouldn't refuse).* He had made the arrangements that very week. She never saw him again.

In the years since Oswald's death, Millicent had come to understand the fragility of it all, and her dependence on the wealth of flawed men for the needful things that had given her life whatever coherence it held. Prior Oswald had lifted her from the life of a maudlyn, buying her a position in a revered religious house. Then Sir Humphrey ap-Roger came along, giving her access to the greatest halls, to say nothing of this house and its furnishings. Yet his wealth, too, had been a passing force in her life.

First her prior, then her knight, and now – who next? Who would step into this frightening void and fill it with apricots, and almonds, and good meats, and a strong tongue, and wine and houses and—? Yet even as she asked herself such hard questions she was filled with guilt at the stir of gluttony and lust and covetousness in her soul. She heard the voice of Prioress Isabel ringing through her mind. *God frowns on extravagance, Millicent. You must temper your desires for worldly things, stamp them underfoot along with the demons who provoke them.*

Millicent closed her eyes, vowing to heed Isabel's warning, the moral charge of the nun's sobering words. She would live a measured and moderate life, yes she would, just as soon as she could afford it.

She turned on Agnes. 'We sell it, or I'll burn it myself.'

SIXTEEN

Gropecunt Lane, Ward of Cheap

Eleanor had slumped herself over the low fence, trying to ignore the soreness in her feet. It was early afternoon, not a jake in sight, though the tedium only sharpened her worry. For hours she had been hanging next to Mary Potts, going over the same ground as her foot traced lines in the dust. Agnes still missing, her brother's life threatened by a cruel master, that girl's body never leaving her inner sight.

At the moment her thoughts were all on Gerald, though she couldn't help commingling her concerns. '"Only a wooden mallet," he says. "Never hits me with the metal one!" You hear that? He's got to get out of that cutter's shop, Mary. Grimes'll brain him sure, or he'll lose an arm for bad meat. But now I'm afraid to leave Gropecunt Lane in case Agnes comes back, not that there's much chance of that, plus then the beadle'll start asking more questions. But if I don't seek out the common serjeant soon, get Gerald moved back to London – why, he's dead sure as we stand here, like that girl on the moor!'

'Just *go*, El,' said Mary. 'You been twisting your teats about the thing for days now. What's the worst can happen? Mayor'll throw you out on Cat Street and you'll be right back here, doing what you love. I'll be here the whole time, waiting on Ag.'

Eleanor felt a nudge of hope. 'You'll cover for me with the Dun Bell?'

'If Joan asks I'll say you went off with King Richard and Bolingbroke to teach those boys how to keep their young wives happy.'

Eleanor kissed her, grateful for Mary's practicality. She snuck off through an alley; replaced her dress and bonnet with the breeches, hose, coat and cap she kept hidden behind a horse stall; manned her hair and face in a trough; and was soon in the crowded precincts surrounding the Guildhall. It was market day, though despite the morning fires the western-most hulk of the college threw the loud press of Basinghall in a cold shadow that pimpled his arms. Passing the eastern gatehouse Edgar came out between the chapel and the library into the more open expanse of Guildhall yard, where he paused to survey the inner precinct.

The common serjeant might have been anywhere, so Edgar chose a position outside the west doors to the side of the porch, edging near a clutch of women selling hand food. He was used to leaning against posts watching men's faces for long stretches of time. No different than swyving. He settled in for a wait, studying the trawl of tradesmen and bureaucrats and hucksters moving in and out of the doors and gates.

Edgar had encountered the common serjeant of London once before, at the procedure terminating his wardship upon his majority. An ample man. Reddened cheeks. A massive nose. The man had treated him with a genuine if cursory kindness on that earlier occasion, and Edgar's hope was that he would be similarly disposed toward Gerald.

Now here he was, coming right toward him. There were three men, deep in conversation, and as they stepped up to the porch Edgar took a few idle steps in their direction, picking up a fragment of their exchange.

116

'. . . could not have been clearer,' one of them said, 'though the mayor's lost his patience.'

'All of us have.'

'Don't have much of a choice, though, do we?'

The shortest one walked through the Guildhall door with a grim nod to the others. Ralph Strode and the first man huddled together, their voices too quiet to make out, then the other man followed his colleague into the great structure. Strode turned about and made his way along the south side of the building, waving off the hucksters thrusting buns and pies at his face. Edgar followed him as he angled for a cluster of lower timber buildings at the far side of the Guildhall.

He quickened his pace. 'Master Strode.'

Strode looked down at him but did not slow. 'Busy just now.' They passed along the western edge, the scent of roasting chicken in the air from the spits in the side yard.

'Pardon, Master Strode, but there be a matter of some urgency that requires your attention,' said Edgar, trying to sound proper.

'Some urgency,' Strode said, his voice strained. 'How many times have I heard those words this week?'

'It concerns my brother, Gerald. He's but fourteen, sir, and I worry for him.' He stayed at Strode's heels through a narrow passage between two of the outbuildings. 'He was one of your charges, Master Strode, an orphan of the city. Now he's a butcher's apprentice and his master beats him, beats him somewhat awful. With a *mallet*, sir. I fear for his life.'

Strode stopped in mid-step, his frame swaying like an over-filled cart. Slowly he turned. 'Tell me your name,' he said, his robed bulk looming over Edgar in the shadows.

'Rykener. Edgar Rykener, and my brother's Gerald Rykener, butcher's apprentice of Southwark.'

'Rykener.' A voice resonant and deep. 'Edgar Rykener. And your brother is Gerard, you say?'

'Gerald, sir. Gerald Rykener.'

He waved him along with a heavy sigh. 'You've found the right functionary to your purpose. Step in here. We'll have the matter out.'

Edgar followed him into a two-room stone-and-timber building with parchment windows on the outer walls. In the front chamber were three desks, a small hearth currently cold, and a generous amount of crammed shelving. Two of the three desks, the largest one against the far wall, were occupied by four young clerks, one huddled over each side and all busy scribbling on to the parchments, papers and ledgers spread before them. Iron-looped oil lamps dangled from chains of varying lengths, like a strange tree bearing fruits of smoky light.

The clerks sat up at the common serjeant's entrance. Strode summoned one of them with a raised hand and a snap. 'Tewburn.'

Edgar started and blushed, recognizing the clerk immediately. James Tewburn was one of her more frequent mares. Liked to take it as a woman, mouth and arse alike. But he was always tender, always paid well. He didn't recognize Edgar in mannish garb. Not yet.

'Mark what this young fellow says, James,' Strode ordered the clerk, without noticing Edgar's discomfort. 'Take his name, the location of his brother's shop in Southwark, the name of his master – all the pertinent details. Write them up as an appeal to Wykeham and keep at it until the matter is resolved.'

'Yes, Master Strode,' said Tewburn, looking right at Edgar, though still without a trace of recognition.

Strode flashed an easy smile. 'Pardon the lawyerly cant, Edgar. I've explained to Tewburn that we must make an appeal to the Bishop of Winchester, William Wykeham, in order to transfer wardship of your brother into the City of London. Southwark is out of my jurisdiction. But I know Wykeham well. I can't imagine he'll have a problem with our request.'

Edgar nodded, overwhelmed by the man's generosity. 'I – I

don't properly know what to say, Master Strode, nor how to thank you.' He could think of some improper ways, though the common serjeant didn't seem the sort.

He waved a hand. 'Keeping our city's wards free from harm is my greatest duty. I do it happily. Just confer with Tewburn here, and he'll have it settled.' He disappeared into the inner chamber.

Tewburn led him over to his desk, where Edgar stood as the clerk shuffled through a mess. The man was younger than he looked, with shoulders already sloped and a discernible hump midway up his back. His eyes, small and round like little black beads over his thin whiskers, took Edgar in with a bureaucrat's scrutiny.

'Your brother is apprenticed to whom?' he asked, his swollen knuckles poised above a ledger.

'Nathan Grimes, master butcher.'

'Of?'

'Cutter Lane in Southwark.'

'Your brother is to be a butcher, then?'

'Yes, sir.'

'And he's in what year of his apprenticeship?'

'His third, sir.'

'Age?'

'Fourteen, sir.'

'I'll take up your brother's wardship as quickly as I can,' said Tewburn, a ready warmth in his voice as he discerned the depth of Edgar's concern. 'Come round in a week or so.' Still no flash of recognition, and Edgar left Guildhall yard with a tentative hope that Tewburn would truly help his brother.

Later Eleanor crossed the bridge to risk another visit to Grimes's yard, where she found Gerald alone, shovelling dung. His arms, bare and glistening with sweat, showed a patchwork of fresh bruises, and a gash on his brow had recently scabbed over. His eyes when he looked at her were empty, his shoulders slumped.

119

After she greeted him he wiped a forearm across his brow. 'Might be time after all.'

'Time for what?'

His shifted on his feet. 'To find me another station. Butcher's shop back in London.'

She slapped him, hard. 'So *now* it's time, is it, when I been saying the like for two years?'

Gerald shrugged, not defensively but with a sort of sullen fear, the coldness gone from his eyes. 'Grimes got himself in some deep stick, Edgar. *Real* deep.' He looked over his shoulder at the butcher's streetfront office, separated from the slaughterhouse by a series of narrow pens, each containing a few animals just shy of the knife. 'You got to get me out of this, and right soon.'

'What kind of stick, Gerald?' she said, not wanting to hear the answer.

'This priest, he shows up time to time. Been four, five times now, to meet with Grimes. They pray and get to talking about another Rising. Grimes was on the bridge, you know, with Wat Tyler. He's still got plate he took from the Savoy before they torched the place.'

'But that's wood talk, Gerald,' she said, wanting to believe it.

'They say Wat Tyler should've quartered King Richard when he had the chance. Now it's like to be *their* job. They're butchers, after all, quick with a knife. Grimes keeps mumbling about his fate, how he's been chosen for it by God. That's what the priest told him, so he says when he's in his ales. Butchers, biding by a bishop's bank, then springing out to kill the king.'

Eleanor took this in with a mix of contempt and fear. On the one hand, the notion of these Southwark butchers plotting rebellion was ludicrous on its face. Yet when it came to treason the king's men wouldn't deal in niceties. If a butcher was conspiring on the death of the king they'd take his apprentices along with him, and happily hang them all. 'Grimes is a lunatic,

Gerald,' she said, trying to sound convincing. 'Man doesn't have the brains to start a revolt of the mutton against the cows.'

'Still,' he said, 'I want out of Cutter Lane, Eleanor. Get me back to London, yeah?'

She looked at his face, set with genuine fear. Gerald only called her by her she-name when he really wanted something. 'It may be a stretch of time before I can get it done, Gerald.'

'But soon, Eleanor,' Gerald said. He hefted his shovel. 'Soon, yeah?'

Eleanor swallowed, the fear for Gerald eating at her as it never had. 'Soon as I can, Gerald. Then you'll be free.'

SEVENTEEN

Colbrokes Quay on the Thames, Tower Ward

The Ides of April, and the river's surface churned beneath a pale sun as I walked the last length of the wharf toward the customhouse, a hard knot in my chest. The book was out of Swynford's hands, God knew where it was, and Chaucer had no business with it. Seditious, Braybrooke had called it. A traitor's book. The sensible part of me wanted to warn Chaucer off before the whole thing got us both strung up at Tyburn.

Yet my motives were hardly pure. From everything I had learned the *De Mortibus Regum Anglorum* could become the single greatest piece of information I would ever acquire. To possess this book of prophecies and learn the identity of the king's supposed assassin? The manuscript would open doors I had been working to unlatch for years: to the Privy Council, to the lord chancellor, to the court's uppermost magnates. It was clear that Chaucer had been less than honest with me about this book – and I had little enthusiasm left to put it in his fumbling hands.

The door to the customhouse stood open, though no one was inside. Around the near quay a crowd had gathered beneath the highest crane on London's waterfront. The Goose, the machine was called, its charge to raise with pulley, crank, and the sweat of ten men the most massive arrivals at the city's port: great slabs of Kentish stone, casks of iron shot, the occasional mast. Chaucer stood there waving his arms up at the crane. From its hook, over the wide deck of a merchant barge, was suspended a large bale of cloth, the subject of a dispute. I went inside to wait.

Surveying the office, I marvelled that the crown collected any customs money at all. I'd long been amazed at the administrative burden Chaucer had taken on with this post. Virtually no surface was free of the slips that marked every collection of fee in the port going back years. There were thousands of them, spilling out of drawers and crates, papering the seats of stools, leaving a single narrow path across the floor. *The countless cockets crowding my craw*, Chaucer once put it. The line hadn't made it into his verse.

As I looked across the littered office of the wool custom, it occurred to me how closely this documentary rat's nest resembled the disordered sprawl of Chaucer's poetry. Stories of mundane dealings between men, accounts of every imaginable human exchange, recorded on these slips of skin just as they filled his poems with the endless flow of his imagination.

On the far end of the desk sat the quire I had sent over a few days before. It was our private game, the difficult glue of our friendship. Months could go by between our poetical swaps, yet then we'd sit right down, berating one another for a tenuous metaphor, an ill-chosen trope, a lazy rhyme. That morning Chaucer was to critique some of my elegiacs, fragments of a long Latin work I had been composing since before the Rising and still had not completed. I expected to leave the customhouse with some new writing of his.

Nothing, I felt confident, would divert us from this ritual we had both come to cherish. Not even murder. Not even treason.

'John, you're here!' Chaucer stepped into the customhouse,

his eyes going to the bag at my side. He gave a few instructions to a waiting clerk, signed a bill of some kind, and sent the man back to the wharf. 'Let me dig out my little book.'

The air thickened immediately. He wanted to know. But our practice was always to begin with the poetry. He dug through the mess on his desk and emerged with his 'little book', as he called it: the familiar pigskin bifold in which he would keep only those quires of parchment currently in use. It was Chaucer's custom, once he had filled an existing quire with his writing, to remove it and slip a fresh one within the covers. So familiar was his old, faded bifold that it took my poor eyes a moment to see he had replaced it with a new one.

'Lovely, isn't it?' he said, showing off the elaborate tooling and the shiny leathern cover, dyed a striking red. 'It's goat. From Africa, swears a leatherworker I know in Florence. He does great work for the Bardis.' He opened it and took out two loose quires wedged between the fixed pages. 'These verses are a small taste of a larger compilation I've been tossing around. The idea is a pilgrimage, a – well, the frame is unimportant. Two tales here, each to be preceded by a prologue. One is earnest, the other's all game, and next time I'll expect a devastating *sed contra* to both.'

I tucked the parchment quires into my bag while Chaucer started humming distractedly and knuckling his desk. I waited.

'Have you read them, Geoffrey?'

He frowned.

'My elegiacs, on the virtues and vices?' I felt almost child-like, waiting for his attention.

A reassuring smile. 'Of course, John. Pardon my distraction.' He sorted through the loose sheets on his desk, found my own booklet of verse. 'Here we are. Let's just see . . .' He scanned his notes in the margins, his lower lip tightening in displeasure. 'Rather stark, wouldn't you say?'

'The lines weren't written to be light, Geoffrey. Not like these fabliaux.'

'As you'll soon learn.' He gestured at my bag, and the work he had given me. 'Honestly, though, they could use some leavening.' He took on a preacher's voice, gazing at me over the folios as he spoke my Latin lines. '"The schism of our church has cursed us with two popes, one a schismatic and the other legitimate." And the next couplet: "France worships the schismatic and holds him in awe, but England is a defender of the true faith."' He set the booklet down, a wry challenge in his gaze.

'Should I be amused or offended by your tone?' I asked him. 'The church *is* divided: we're allied with Rome, France with Avignon.'

He shook his head. 'Take these next lines, on bishops. Listen to yourself, John.' He went on in my Latin.

> *'As I seek for followers of Christ among the*
> > *prelates*
> *I find that none of the rule survives that was once*
> > *in force.*
> *Christ was poor, but they are overloaded with*
> > *gold.*
> *He was a peacemaker, but they are war-mongers.'*

His voice had taken on a sing-song cadence, rising before the caesura, then falling toward the end of each line, as if my elegiacs were some child's rhyme.

> *'Christ was generous, but they are tight as a closed*
> > *purse.*
> *He was occupied by labour, they have an excess of*
> > *leisure.*
> *Christ was virginal; they are like maudlyns.'*

He stopped. 'I won't go on – nor, I think, should you.'

I felt my fists clench, and my vision starred. 'You're parroting my lines, as if their faults chirp for themselves. I thought you approved of taking the clergy to task.'

Chaucer squinted down at the quire, wetting a quill. 'Perhaps if you lightened up a bit, added a dash of humour to your biting satire?' He dipped, blotted, scratched. 'We've talked about this before. In your poetry, everyone is either good or bad. There's no room for moral ambivalence, no accounting for the complexity of character that renders us the fallen humans we are. It's as if you are firing arrows blindly at the entire world.'

'Are you saying the lines aren't true to their subject?'

He sighed, then turned to me. 'Much worse, John. They are not true to *you*.' I blinked. He leaned forward, his hand clutching his crowded desk. 'You're a dazzling Latinist, John, and your elegiacs could be taught as paradigms of the form. But why can't you take some *risks* in your work? Your verses always preach the upright line while you spend your own life scurrying through the shadows, ratting up useful bits of information you turn to your own advantage. Do you write this way because you see yourself as some white-clad incorruptible, standing on a high place upheld by excellent moral foundations? I hardly think so. Do you pen lines like these to obfuscate, to keep us all looking away from what you do? Because no one who writes like this could be as devious as John Gower, *mon ami*. Whatever your reason, your making doesn't come from your heart, from that place that makes you *you*. It doesn't ring true. It never has.'

I could say nothing. He looked at me for a long moment, a mix of puzzlement and affection in his eyes – and, as I think back on it now, a shadow of pity. 'You are a stubborn man, John, and the stubbornest poet I know.' He nudged me back my booklet and turned to his desk, straightening a small corner of the untidy surface. 'Keep writing like this and you're bound for oblivion.'

Though his responses to my poetic making could often be

harsh, Chaucer had never spoken to me like this. I sat there, goaded into silence by this cold assessment of my work, feeling something between long regret and immediate fury. Then one of Chaucer's clerks put his head in the door, asking several questions about the transaction down at the quay.

When he was gone I plunged straight in, my voice tight with anger. 'The book you're looking for is a work of prophecy. You didn't think to tell me this?'

'Prophecy,' said Chaucer, his bright eyes unreadable. 'What sort of prophecy?'

'Braybrooke claims the book is treasonous.'

He bent his neck and looked at the rafters. '"Treason" is a word tossed around like pigshit these days. Though considering the source I suppose I shouldn't be surprised. For the Bishop of London, thought itself is treason. Pose a few curious questions about the sacrament, get a hanging for your trouble.'

'Don't cling to Wycliffe, Geoffrey,' I warned him. 'Gaunt adored the man for some reason, but he was a heretic, and a dissident. His teachings have been roundly condemned.'

'God help us. And now Braybrooke is convinced this book is heretical? From everything I have heard it's just a light satire. A well-crafted look into England's royal past, with a peculiar twist here and there.'

I shook my head. 'Believe me, Geoffrey, this is not a book you want to be associated with. There's already been loads of trouble about it: at court, at the inns, with the bishops – foul circumstances that surround it on every side. Even a young woman's death.'

'*What?*'

'Murder, Geoffrey.' I told him what Swynford and Strode had told me, and reminded him of the disrupted pageant at the Temple Hall. I said nothing about the business with Symkok, keeping that bit of information to myself.

His hand went to his mouth. It trembled there, then went back to his side. 'Who was the young woman?'

'An agent of the French crown, by all appearances.' He was still. 'So you see, it's not Katherine Swynford who is responsible for the disappearance of the book. This is much bigger than her.'

He stared at me. Were those tears welling in the corners of his eyes? 'But *why*, John? Why would anyone kill a young woman over a book?'

'The work concerns the deaths of kings,' I said, pushing on. 'Of *English* kings.'

He blinked. Yes, tears. One of them escaped, tracking down his left cheek.

'By statute of Parliament it's treasonous to compass or even *imagine* the death of the king,' I went on. 'Yet this work – and I've heard parts of it, with my own ears, from Braybrooke's friars – this work prophesies the deaths of England's last twelve sovereigns, as well as—'

'Ha!' He gave a short, frantic bark of a laugh. 'How is it that a work can prophesy deaths that have already occurred?'

'I asked Braybrooke the same question. According to the bishop, it was written many years ago.'

'Yet again, how—'

'Its prophecies reflect the chronicles accurately. Consider the prophecy on the death of the second Edward.' I repeated the memorable lines I had heard from Braybrooke's friar.

'In Gloucester will he goeth, to be gutted by goodmen
With rod straight of iron, in arsebone to run.
With pallet of pullet, his breath out to press,
And sovereign unsound for Sodom be sundered.'

As I spoke the lines Chaucer stood and walked to the opened door, where he leaned on the sill, his shoulders rising and falling to the shouts on the embankment, the clap of boards from an unloading barge.

I gazed at his back. 'I haven't told you the worst. The thirteenth prophecy foretells the death of King Richard.'

A dismissive cluck. 'No no no, that's wrong, Richard does not—' He froze, his eyes widening as he turned to me. His face paled, going the colour of sunbleached bone. I approached him and took his hand, the earlier cruelty forgotten for the moment. 'Geoffrey, what is it?'

'It cannot be,' he said, his voice just above a whisper, the tears giving way to something I took then as fear. 'This explains – but it simply cannot be.'

'You are making no sense, Geoffrey.'

'But of course. Of *course*!' Tears streamed down his face, his entire frame shaking with the strangest abandon.

Baffling. 'Why are you laughing? These are grave matters.' And what are you not telling me?

Chaucer calmed himself, placing a hand on my shoulder as he wiped the other across his eyes. 'The book, John,' he said. 'Get me the book, and all shall be well.'

'This is blind idiocy, Geoffrey. The Bishop of London himself says it: this is a burnable book, a work of high treason certain to destroy any man who holds it.'

'Get me the book. At any cost.'

'You're acting like a little boy now. Do you want to see your reputation ruined over all this?'

'*Reputation*,' he said, as if the word were a rotten river oyster. 'My *reputation*, you say?' Suddenly back from wherever he had been, Chaucer leaned into me, his face a red mask of cruel intention, his neck a foreign bulge of tendons and veins. 'You *will* find this book for me, O Moral Gower. I know it, and you know it. In a city where everyone owes John Gower, Esquire, a favour, Geoffrey Chaucer may be the only soul to whom he owes one himself. Quite a large one, too. And in a city in which John Gower, Esquire, has information on nearly every man of importance, it may be useful to call to mind the small matter of your son's count—'

'*Enough.*' I stepped away. 'How *dare* you threaten me like this?'

He grabbed a pile of cockets from his desk and threw them in the air. The parchments snowed around our heads. His lips curled into a puerile sneer. 'Call it a threat if you like. Whatever the case, your position is exceedingly weak. Do not test me, Gower.'

I stared at him, waiting for him to retract the malicious threat behind his words, but his lips seemed frozen in place. 'You've finally stripped the veil, my friend,' I said, a trembling whisper. 'Now you are no better than I am. At last you know what it's like, to have a man's soul in your hands.'

The look Chaucer gave me then was the coldest I had ever seen. 'Poets don't traffic in souls. That is the work of priests. The sooner you learn the difference the better a poet you shall be.' On that cruellest of notes he turned away. 'Find the book. Find it, bring it to me, and just maybe you will see your son in England again.'

As I left the customhouse and paced back along the wharfage, I carried Chaucer's words as a profound weight on my spirit. Yet from our abrasive encounter one deeper question lingered, a question that concerned neither the viability of this deep friendship nor its tenuous basis in our poetry. The question concerned, rather, the young woman on the Moorfields, this alleged French agent murdered over the very book my difficult friend sought with such singular focus – and to whose death he had reacted with such exaggerated surprise that it seemed feigned. It was a question about Geoffrey Chaucer himself, and it had been haunting me for a week and more. A question no longer avoidable.

Could Chaucer kill?

The dust cloud grew as the company approached, massing into a great orb that filled the northern sky, as if God had obliterated a portion of the earth from His sight. Even from that distance the lady could recognize the arms borne by the herald: the livery of the king. The gate, she ordered, was to remain open, the defences unprepared. Castile is arrived, she told her husband's men and her servants. Make the castle ready! Open our larders and cellars to his needs! Her orders carried out, the company arrived, to be greeted with the lady's open arms.

Yet once they had reached the castle gates and their leader stood before her, she realized she had been deceived. This was not King Pedro, nor was her husband among the company. These men wore livery she had never seen, spoke in a language she could not comprehend. The banners of Castile they flung carelessly to the ground.

Their lord, a prince from a northern land, was a hard man, with a pale face that might have been cut from stone. A forked beard fell from his chin like two waterfalls of molten lead, and in him the lady sensed a certain cruelty, a flow of dark intention beneath the rituals of courtesy the situation demanded. He groused loudly of King Pedro's unpaid war debts, and the poor condition of his troops.

The prince had arrived in the company of his younger brother, a duke. Taller by half a head, this lord was a man of few words. He was of nobler bearing than the prince, and seemed almost ashamed by his older brother's disposition.

For weeks the lords remained in the castle, their troops garrisoned along the walls. The lady learned that a much greater force, thousands strong, was encamped near Burgos, growing hungry and ill as the foreign prince awaited payment of Pedro's debts. As the unwelcome visit lengthened, the prince let the lady know her place at every opportunity.

Your husband is in my debt, he said. And your husband's lord, and his lord, and his lord in turn – all are in my debt. All that your husband claims to own shall properly be mine. Mine the harvest gleaned from the earth beneath your feet. Mine the flocks rutting and grazing in these fields. Mine the small treasure guarded in this castle's hold. And mine—

The prince did not say it, but from the moment of his arrival she had felt it. His eyes upon her constantly, his conversation crudely suggestive, his hand lingering too long upon her own at their moments of formal greeting.

She made sure she was never alone, trailing her daughter with her wherever she went, ordering a maidservant to remain in her bed through the night. She bent her back to please the visitors. There were slaughters to order, hunts to organize, horses to water and feed. Her husband's senescalo went nearly mad as the soldiers' demands increased.

The lady called on her villagers to help, appropriating their animals, their grain, their bodily labour to ensure adequate food and drink for the visiting lord and his men. All shall be returned to you in droves, she promised them. They gave willingly, that their lady's honour might remain intact.

Yet those hardened folk of the Castilian marches, their wisdom deep as the soil, understood what she did not. The darkest law of chivalry.

When a great lord arrives at the home of a lesser, whether his vassal or not, the lesser shall consider all he owns to be the just property of the greater. All should be surrendered to him freely and without objection.

And what the lord does not receive willingly, he is entitled to take by force.

✜　✜　✜

PART TWO

Faun of Three Feathers

*Day xiv before Kalends of May to Nones of May, 8
Richard II
(18 April–7 May 1385)*

EIGHTEEN

St Mary Overey, Southwark

Two stories: one of lust, one of murder. One of revelry, of adulterous love, of untroubled joy in the flesh. The other of a young boy's faith, of treachery, death and resurrection.

In the first story, a randy student seduces a carpenter's wife, deceives him with a false prophecy of a second flood, and causes a household disaster. There is also a parish clerk, a fop who seeks the wife's favours for himself yet wins only a fart as his reward. The tale is told by a miller, who delights in the flaws of every character he portrays.

In the second story, a young chorister hears a sacred song being performed by older boys and vows to learn this gorgeous antiphon on his own. As he moves back and forth through a Jewry, the song fills his throat. The offended Jews conspire against him, causing his murder and throwing his corpse in a privy. As his mother searches for him, the boy is miraculously resurrected. The narrator of this tale is a prioress, a holy woman leading a community of Christian nuns.

Two stories, both scrawled in Chaucer's loose hand in the quire he had given me at the customhouse. On a first reading no two stories could have been more unlike. The thought of compiling them within a larger work made no sense, yet such was Chaucer's plan, inspired by the same Giovanni Boccaccio who wrote the tragic romance Chaucer had brought back from Florence.

The more I thought about these stories, though, the more I came to see what, in Chaucer's bent imagination, they might have in common. Both dealt with the consequences of sin and fallen flesh. Though the prioress's story more directly concerned death, martyrdom, and persecution, this miller's tale cast its own shadows: another Noah's Flood, the degradation of the marital sacrament, hints of sodomy. As art, then, the stories seemed congruent, eerily so. Once again Chaucer had proven himself a superior teller of tales.

Or a compelling liar. I sat back, my spine finding its worn place on the study wall. We had spoken often over the years about the proximity of poetry and deception. To write a great poem, Chaucer insisted, you have to be a greater liar. You must convince your readers that your characters are flesh and blood rather than words on dead skin, that their loves and hatreds and passions are as deep and present as the readers' own. Your task is to delight, to pleasure, to lift your reader to another sphere of being and then strand him there, floating above the earth and panting for more lines.

This long struggle with my own poetry? Perhaps it's just that, I thought: I don't deal in colourful lies, but in plain truths, however coarse and hidden. What need is there for deception when the truth is so much more compelling, so much darker in its attachments?

The truths before me now, though, were hidden beneath an impenetrable veil, despite all the damning facts and obscure information I had accumulated over the years. A prophetic book I hadn't read and couldn't find. A murdered woman I didn't know and couldn't name. A friend I couldn't fathom and shouldn't trust. And all the while a city I thought I'd mastered suddenly strange and alien to me, coiled like a serpent across the river, its tongue whispering a threat I could not comprehend.

Caught up as I was in these clouds of enigma, it took me a few moments to notice the hard knock from the front of the house, followed by faint voices and the stomp of boots. A visitor, admitted by Will Cooper at the hour I defended most fiercely for my writing. I sighed, looked down at my quill, and stood. Thick clouds had been toying with the sun that morning, casting the interior of the house into peculiar shades that created illusions of presence in empty corners. It was for this reason that I thought at first I had imagined the man in the lower hall, as if a phantom of his form had flared up from Hell to burn through my very door.

He turned, looked everywhere but into my eyes, his smile tinged with everything that had passed between us.

'Father,' he said.

✤

Nearly three years had passed since that dreadful Trinity Sunday, a feast Sarah particularly loved. She would order up everything in threes for the supper. Three soups, three wines, three meats, three sweets, enlisting every taste in the celebration of Father, Son, and Holy Ghost. The messenger arrived mid-morning, as we were returning from early Mass. Our house stood back from the priory walls on Overey Street by a good twenty feet, with two broad yew trees towering over a gated yard paved with riverstone. A young man waited within the courtyard. I recognized him as one of Chaucer's clerks from the wool custom.

He bowed slightly. 'I must speak with you, Master Gower,' he said, his eyes wandering toward Sarah. 'I come direct from Master Chaucer, and at his orders.'

There was an awkward moment which Sarah smoothed over by going inside. No one else was about, save a few churchgoers gathered farther down. The shops were closed, the street appropriately silent for the morning of a feast day.

'Is Chaucer in some kind of trouble?' It would not have been the first time.

'Not – not Master Chaucer, sir. I'm here about your son, Master Simon.'

'Simon? What has Simon got to do with your business at the wool custom?'

'It might be best to leave such questions for Master Chaucer.'

I pressed the man as we walked to the Southwark wharf and boarded the waiting skiff.

'There's been a killing, sir.'

My heart thrummed in my ears. 'Simon?'

He shook his head. 'Your son is safe.' He would say nothing more, and my worry turned to dread as we floated toward the Tower. I sat back on the board seat, willing the small boat across the river.

Chaucer was waiting at the quay. Above the water, as the skiff angled toward him, he stood still as a carved apostle, his face pale, his eyes swollen with exhaustion. When I stepped up he broke his stance and grasped my arm. We walked in silence to one of the warehouses down the wharf. At the door Chaucer stopped me. 'Go easy on him, John.'

The air inside stank of sheep. Bales of wool were piled high to the rafters. A thin shaft of sunlight outlined a peculiar shape on the floor, reflecting upwards to create a luminous sphere around Simon's bowed head. He sat at the end of a long counting bench, nearly doubled at the waist. Low moans came from his chest, his body shaking with pain and fear. Against the near wall, just inside the door, rested the corpse: a form wrapped in sailcloth, a thatch of dark hair visible at one end, a trace of blood on the board floor.

Chaucer signalled to the watchman to leave us, then shut the door from within. I approached my son.

'What have you done?'

Simon was filthy, his clothes torn, his flesh reeking of ale.

138

He looked up. His face was an utter mess. 'I killed him, Father. And . . . there's more.'

The moment stretched, my rising anger mingled with a helpless confusion. I turned to Chaucer. Back to Simon. Finally I approached the corpse and uncovered the face. I recognized it as belonging to a constable of Tower Street Ward, a man I had encountered once or twice, though I didn't know his name.

Simon, in his stuttering way, and with Chaucer filling in the last several hours, revealed everything.

For some months, Simon told me, he had been involved in a counterfeiting ring, forging half-nobles with the help of a goldsmith and an under-master at the King's Mint. The smith would concoct a weak alloy, the under-master having snuck one of King Edward's obsolete stamps out of the Tower, and Simon would rough up the fake coins with bricks, trading them up for genuine nobles or down for groats and pennies. Too many of the three-shilling-fourpence coins appearing in London all at once would arouse suspicion, so Simon had arranged for quantities of them to be put into circulation at the markets in York, Hull, and Calais, as well as on deposit with two of the Italian banking houses on Lombard Street.

As he explained his logic and actions, I stared at his mouth, spewing these numbers and calculations as if he had been born a criminal. I had always hoped Simon's prodigious talent with numbers and words would open doors to a respectable career, perhaps on the logic faculty at Oxford, or in the law. Never would I have imagined my son conspiring with such men to forge a royal likeness on gold coins. Yet the scheme had been turning a handsome profit for some months, due in large part to Simon's astute sense of the money supply.

Their luck turned when a constable of Tower Street Ward stumbled on to their operation while chasing down a petty thief, who had taken refuge in the back of the goldsmith's shop. Rather than turning the three counterfeiters over to his superiors, the constable had attempted to extort part of their profits, threatening them with exposure should they refuse him. So, with the approval of his partners, Simon had arranged a large payoff, setting the exchange for just after curfew at a rough alehouse on the wharf. The negotiation had grown heated and was taken out to the bankside, where the men came to blows. Simon described the fight, his fists flying at the man's face, taking his own hits, then delivering the final blow that sent the constable reeling backwards on the wharf, his head meeting an iron shipping-hook as he fell. Hearing the commotion, two watchmen at the wool wharf had come running, one of them tackling Simon to the ground, the other attempting to revive the fallen man.

Too late. Rather than summoning the authorities, they had sent for Chaucer, controller of the wool custom and something of a tyrant in his management of the wharf. At his direction the watchmen had hauled Simon inside, along with the constable's body, and there they had waited for Simon to recover from his drunkenness before questioning him about the incident.

'I made him tell me all of it before I sent for you,' Chaucer explained. 'I thought it best to limit the surprises, make sure Simon had all of this straight so we could get to the truth without a lot of hemming and hawing.'

I nodded vacantly, the enormity of it all dawning on me. My only surviving child, a counterfeiter, and a murderer.

Simon broke again, burying his face in his hands. 'I'm sorry, Father, you – you have to appreciate my—'

'You'll get no appreciation from me, Simon. Nor forgiveness. *Counterfeiting*? Did you think for one moment of your honour, and my reputation?'

He looked up at me, his eyes lit with a righteous clarity that seemed drastically out of place. 'You're right, Father. Perhaps I should have pursued a more honourable trade. Are you taking apprentices?'

I hit him. Not a smack but a hard punch that sent him flying backwards to land on the filthy surface.

'*John!*' Chaucer rushed forward and reached for Simon, who was sprawled across the floor. Chaucer helped him to his feet, then stepped back, grasped my arm, and led me out to the wharf. He pushed me roughly against the side of the warehouse. 'If Simon is taken – if there's even an inquest – he'll be hanged. Perhaps not for murder, my men will attest it was an accident, but for the coining. It's treason to counterfeit the King's Mint.'

'Treason,' I said, the word bitter on my tongue.

'We can fix this,' Chaucer said in an angry whisper. He looked up the wharf. 'The constable never told anyone else what he found out – otherwise he couldn't have used the information against Simon. Do you see?'

I nodded tightly.

'As for my men, they'll stay silent. They're well paid, and God knows they keep enough secrets as it is. So really this all comes down to destroying evidence, and staying mum.'

Chaucer's focus on the practical had a calming effect. I looked at him. 'So what do you suggest we do?'

There was no real choice in the end. The corpse was disposed of by the watchmen. A sack, four large stones, a skiff up to Stepney Marsh, the weighted body over the side and into the reeds. Simon, too, needed removal from London lest tongues start to wag. Chaucer would make all the necessary arrangements: passage to Tuscany; a letter of introduction to his old friend Sir John Hawkwood; a promise to check on Simon within a twelvemonth, as his business for the king would surely take him back to Italy before long.

With dire threats, I forbade Simon from speaking any word about the matter to Sarah. I would tell her of an unexpected opportunity for him in the south, an offer of employment in the king's service, working on behalf of Hawkwood, the great mercenary and Richard's newly appointed ambassador to Rome.

He left for Italy without bidding farewell to his mother. I thought it best that she remain ignorant. Within five days of the killing on the wool wharf, and with barely a whisper of notice in London, Simon's presence in Southwark, and in our lives, was only a memory.

✢

Now, with all this coming back to me in an unwanted rush, I watched Simon unbuckle his belt, remove his surcoat, line up his boots on the doorside block in the same way I had seen him do hundreds of times. The elegant movements of his hands, the distinctive lines of his face, the almond curves of his eyes, curls as neat as if an iron had pressed his hair: all still spoke of that insolent boy who could never please his father. Yet Simon's gaze was not, as it had been the last time I saw him, floating toward Gravesend for a new life in Italy, defiant or proud. Instead it was tired, or defeated. He wouldn't meet my eyes.

'Why have you come back, Simon?'

Simon bowed his head. He was wearing a short gown, the sleeves long and wide in the Italian style. 'I should have written ahead, Father, but with the roads, the French – I decided to come ahead on my own. I have taken a leave from Hawkwood's service, with his consent, though I am not at all sure whether I shall go back to Italy. When Chaucer told me my mother had died I couldn't help thinking of you, and of our home.' He looked around at the hall, though still would not show me his gaze. 'I don't imagine I shall be much comfort to you, but it seemed the right time to come back to England, after so long abroad. I should like to find a position in London, or if you don't want me that close I have contacts in Calais. I think my skills could be useful there.'

He continued on in this vein, and more than anything else it was his pathetic curiosity about Sarah's death that began to stem my anger. When did she first show signs of sickness? Did she speak lucidly to you, Father, in her final hours? Did she have any last words for me? Because Chaucer never said.

Was her suffering great? It was as if Simon, within his first hours back in Southwark, became the voice of my own, unspoken sorrow, now so mingled with his.

It was at some point in those hours that I found myself thinking of the Duke of Lancaster, and wondering where in his tangled relations he found the most comfort in the face of so much loss. John, Edward, the second John, Isabel, four of his children with Duchess Blanche, all of them buried in Leicester years ago; another John with Duchess Constance, felled by fever before his second year. Such childhood deaths harden a man, whip his heart with chill and heat even as he bites his lips to keep the pain from speaking for itself. Now this one boy who had somehow clung to life was here, with me, and despite all that he had done the feeling that almost overwhelmed me in that moment I can only describe as a grateful, joyous calm. The calm of kin, I suppose.

We sat in the garden, eating a midday meal I barely tasted. As Simon devoured his food I turned the conversation to his life in and around Florence, at the service of the English *condottiero*. His position, as he described it, seemed to consist in a variety of clerical tasks for Hawkwood's company: contracts for service, purchases of supply, provisions for garrisoned troops around the peninsula. At one point in our conversation his face darkened.

'What is it, Simon?'

He hesitated. 'I should tell you as well, Father, that I was betrothed.'

'Was?'

His lips tightened. 'She died. Fever. We never made it to our vows.'

'How long has it been?'

He slightly shrugged. 'Months. But every day I wake up imagining she's still alive.'

'What was her name?' I asked, thinking she might have died right around the time Sarah passed.

He closed his eyes. 'Her name . . . her name was Seguina.' He could barely utter it, and when he had he started weeping, not the cry of a man with an eye to his status, nor a boyish mewl, but a ripping keen, the phlegm pouring from his nose to glisten his lips and chin, his chest and shoulders heaving in a haphazard rhythm, animal-like chokes barking from his throat. In a strange way I found myself feeling almost jealous of his pain, its comfortless depth. I had never wept with such abandon for Sarah.

'Seguina,' I finally said.

'Seguina d'-d'-d'Orange,' he hiccupped, still a boy in that moment.

'A beautiful name,' I said, and just like that it was settled. I still marvel at the ease with which Simon slipped back into my daily life, like a hand-warmed coin into a silk purse. Often I wonder how everything would have turned out had I gone with my first impulse, sending him away from Southwark with an oath and a boot. Or if I had demanded to search his meagre luggage.

But Simon was my sole heir, as Chaucer would not stop pointing out, and with all the stir around the book and the Moorfields killing, the lingering emptiness left by Sarah's death the year before, I suppose I was looking for some source of comfort in those turbulent weeks. No one can be blameless in such circumstances, and I now understand why I remained ignorant – was kept ignorant – even as the clouds thickened above. Yet as I look back on our reunion that day I can still be sickened by my self-deception, my blithe acceptance of its terms.

That, I am afraid, was my own doing. For never once did I think to question the timing of my son's return from Italy. Nor its meaning.

NINETEEN

San Donato a Torre, near Florence

Adam Scarlett, hungry, muddy from the road, in no hurry to deliver his news, leaned against the stable wall and watched the battle unfold. Three lancemen, shields held high, began their charge at the small artillery company, who waited until the last moment to launch the payload. Clods and stones peppered the attackers, then the trebuchet broke, sending a cracked feed bucket rolling between the ranks. The five boys traded screams and blows, coming together in a loud melee before collapsing in a heap of giggles and sweat. The farrier, mumbling about the yearlings, came out and chased them off.

Scarlett turned away and started his ascent to the villa, the scene replaying in his mind as the scent of freshly turned dirt rose from beneath his riding boots. War never ended in the communes, it seemed, every season grinding its hundreds of young men into the clay. Soon enough these boys, most of them sons of bought soldiers, would be riding out themselves, bound for a seasonal cattle raid, or another pillage in the Romagna.

In the gallery Hawkwood was dressing down one of his chief men, a *tenente* from the garrison near Perugia. Scarlett had arranged the man's summons and transfer to Florence several weeks before, after Taricani's departure, and now he was here to face due punishment. Private deals with a Jewish banker, sums moved off the books. Scarlett found his usual place along the south wall, within easy sight of the *condottiero*. With the mess he had in hand he was happy to wait.

'Please, sire, if you would only—'

'Silence, pig.' Hawkwood was enjoying himself, and the kneeling man seemed to know it. Scarlett watched as the soldier's cheek paled, his fright like a layer of wash swept over a fresco.

'You think I haven't had enough of this from my countrymen already? First Cocco, pulling his little *truffa*. And now you, Antonio?'

'But, sire, the Raspanti—'

'Ah, the Raspanti. Blame it on the poor, shall we? That's the best you can do?'

'Yes, sire – I mean no, sire—'

'Enough,' said Hawkwood, quietly this time, and in English. 'Enough.' He turned and his gaze found Scarlett, who gave his master the slightest of shrugs. A *what-did-you-expect?* sort of shrug. The *condottiero* widened his eyes in agreement, his irises white flecks on brown, hues of frosted mud, of winter campaigns and Yule sieges.

Hawkwood reached down to his side for the stick. *La Asta*, the Rod, a notorious forearm's length of hard elm, its core drilled out and filled with a pour of lead. He palmed it gently, looking from his hands to the *tenente*, now a whimpering dog waiting for a boot. With one movement Hawkwood brought the stick up, across, and the man's head whipped to the side with a hard crack of bone. Wretched moans, lots of blood, and when he brought his head back to centre Scarlett could see the ruined jaw hanging by a slab of torn skin and ripped muscle. Hawkwood leaned forward and cupped the broken bones, shoving them back into place with an excruciating thrust. Scarlett winced for the *tenente*.

'Keep this shut for a while, Antonio,' he said, back in Italian. 'Take the silence I've imposed on you as an opportunity, hmm? To think about virtue, about service, about loyalty and the consequence of what you've done. We'll talk again next year, when your mouth works again.' He jerked the loose bone to the side, and the *tenente* fell to the floor, writhing in pain.

Later, after Hawkwood had sorted through the day's correspondence with Pietrasanta, his chancellor, they walked through the gardens, looking at the week ahead. Scarlett was procrastinating, and badly. He listened to his master going on about the Perugia situation.

'I've grown sick of these southern men, Adam. The heat makes them lazy, and now all this conjuring with the Jews. Really, I've taken all I can take. Give me an Englishman over these rude peninsulars any day. Or even a Scot.' He paused to look across the ravine to the north. 'It will be good to see London, won't it? And after so many years.'

Scarlett took a breath, another, then said it. 'The book has disappeared.'

Hawkwood froze. 'When?'

'Five weeks ago Monday, my lord. Our messengers have just brought the news from Westminster.'

Scarlett told him the rest of it: the incident at La Neyte, the pursuit in the Moorfields, the fear spreading like fire among the English gentry. The messenger had been sent on his way within a few days of the theft, with instructions to spare no expense in bringing the news to the great *condottiero* in Florence with all due speed.

'I shudder for the poor horses,' Hawkwood said absently. He turned and looked at Scarlett. 'You're telling me, Adam, that a French spy has stolen the book from under our beak, and Lancaster's?'

'All we know is that it was pilfered by an unidentified woman,' said Scarlett, letting the implication sink in. 'Now she's dead.'

'A woman.' Hawkwood's eyes widened. 'Could it be—'

'That is my assumption, sire.'

Hawkwood considered this for a while. 'Resourceful little thing, isn't she?'

'Wasn't she.'

Hawkwood smiled thinly. 'And the others?'

'That's not known,' said Scarlett. 'Yet.'

Hawkwood continued walking. 'The last dispatch spoke of the work's popularity among these Lollers.'

Scarlett paced behind, watching his master's face. 'The late Wycliffe's disciples, and friends of Lancaster. Some of them have it by rote, and by the time of its disappearance it had become the most notorious writing in England. A book of ghostly prophecies, with dark portent for the fate of the realm! But now no one can find the original manuscript, nor the cloth. And I worry – well . . .'

'Tell me, Adam.'

'I worry that this may be Il Critto's doing.'

'Oh?'

'I do not like coincidences. First Il Critto takes a leave, suddenly, and without warning. Then this young woman, who was nearly betrothed to him, disappears without a trace from her father's house. Next your slinky poetical friend comes back from Rome. You know the gossip, sire. He was seducing her. Then *he* leaves us – quite distraught, from the servants' reports. And all of this just a few weeks after the book leaves our hands. A book now missing.' They took a few more steps. Scarlett was the one who stopped this time. 'I don't like it, John. I don't like it at all.'

Hawkwood's face was hard to read at that moment, though it soon broke into a serene smile. 'Well, there's little we can do about it now, eh? And in some ways the theft may be the best thing that could have happened.'

'Oh?'

'This will only draw more attention to the book. Soon

enough every man and woman in London will be singing these prophecies from the towers. Then what will our long castle have to say for himself? This changes nothing, Adam.'

Scarlett could see Hawkwood's point about the theft, though he did not share the *condottiero*'s confidence that all would be well. With the book on the loose and the prophecies bandied abroad, there was no telling where all of this might end up.

He thought again of Il Critto, as they had dubbed him soon after his arrival in Hawkwood's circles. Young, ambitious, sizzlingly brilliant. A charmer, but Scarlett had distrusted him from the first instant. Il Critto had distrusted Scarlett as well, especially after that unfortunate misunderstanding over the faked dispatch from London. It was merely a loyalty test, and the young man had passed it admirably, though he had taken the whole thing as a personal affront, an assault on his honour. Scarlett had tried to make peace, but Il Critto would hear none of it, and the young man had spent the next two years in Florence despising the sight of him.

It had been weeks since Scarlett had given Il Critto more than a passing thought. Now he was concerned. *Non tenet anguillam, per caudam qui tenet illam.* A bit of wisdom ground in by long experience among these venomous communes. 'He who holds a snake by the tail doesn't have it under control.' And at the moment, Scarlett worried, we don't hold even the tail.

Hawkwood, feeling none of this, gave his most faithful man a fond smile. 'And now, Adam, you will join your kingmaker in a game of cards.'

TWENTY

St Paul's churchyard, Ward of Farringdon

'Will he recognize you?' Agnes Fonteyn asked her sister.

Millicent ignored the question as she gazed across the expanse of the great churchyard, where swift clouds bowled shadows among the hucksters, pilgrims, guildsmen, and idlers. With her gut tightened in fear, every sight and sound reached her with an acuity that cast the peril of their situation in sharp relief. The line of swearers spilling out the south door, clutching contracts as they awaited their turn at the altar to sign or make their mark. Construction at the south end on a line of dwellings for canons: the pounding of hammers, the loud claps of boards, carpenters' swears. The banter from the steps, bakers' daughters and fishwives hawking from their leased stations around the broken cross, and every word bounced off the stone.

River mallard, roast bittern, five roast larks for two, here here, sir.

Cristina Walwayn's pigeons're putrid, sir, hardly fit for pasties.

Don't y'purchase from that station, good sir. That's Evota there, Our Lady of the Stale Buns.

Fish, sir, roast fish? Henry Holdernesse be my master,

150

trustiest monger in town, sure. Not like Tilda Cooke over there, she'll sell you a flat a' pigshit and call it a herring-cake. Mine goes down easy, sir, and sells easy as well.

Though selling a book, Millicent had discovered, was more difficult. Over the last week she and Agnes had become industrious fishers of men, posing as middling singlewomen of Cornhull, their hook baited with the only worm they possessed. This book, Millicent firmly believed, would bring a high price from the right man – a man ambitious enough to use it for the unique sort of personal gain its contents promised. A few whispered conversations at service gates, furtive proffers at tavern doors, a handsome profit.

Yet none of these men had taken the bait. Not a one of them had even understood the significance of what she was offering them, nor the grave threat the book represented to the realm. That morning Millicent had made a decision. Their next prospect would be a greater man. Not a lord, but something like a lord: a man belonging to the Order of the Coif, a serjeant-at-law with deep connections in the king's affinity.

Thomas Pinchbeak had once been close with Sir Humphrey ap-Roger, who had relied on him for a number of legal matters. She had met the lawman at a mummers play along the embankment, Sir Humphrey showing her off on a Midsummer Eve, the shore fires painting the river with a devilish sheen. That was nearly three years ago. Pinchbeak might recall her face, though surely not her name, as she hadn't encountered him again since well before Sir Humphrey's death. What would he think of her, she wondered, approaching him with such a peculiar offer – or, depending how he received it, such an unsettling threat?

With the book concealed in her coat lining, Agnes turned to wait at the top of the south stairs while Millicent approached the gate. Pinchbeak stood with two of his fellow serjeants-at-law within the parvis, a low-walled area before the portico enclosed as a small courtyard. The lawmen were engaged in a light-hearted dispute of some kind, with Pinchbeak the wry observer and mediator, two of the younger serjeants more animated. On the stone benches that lined the sides of the parvis sat several other lawmen conferring with visitors – two wealthy burgesses and a knight. To the side of the gate stood a young man of perhaps seventeen, gangly, tall, puffed with his minor station.

'A word with Master Pinchbeak, please,' Millicent said, giving him her most winning smile.

He spat in a gutter. 'The serjeants have little time for hucksters or women, nor women hucksters. Be off with you.'

Millicent looked down at her dress, now shabbier than any garment she had worn since St Leonard's. 'But it's known that the serjeants-at-law gather in the parvis to serve *all* the citizens of London. You'd deny a freewoman of the city such privilege?' Her raised voice attracted the attention of the lawmen. Pinchbeak approached the low gate, then leaned out to address the young man.

'Let her in, Dawson.'

The young man bowed his head. 'As you wish, Master Pinchbeak.'

Pinchbeak gestured to Millicent to follow him, and she matched his slow progress toward the far wall of the parvis. He walked with a stick, topped by a carved skull of ivory that looked small beneath a massive hand, which belied his compact frame. He didn't look at her until they had taken a seat, and he said nothing once they were settled, merely raising an untamed eyebrow.

Millicent reached into her bodice and removed her medal, the silver replica of St Leonard that still identified her with Bromley. She displayed it for Pinchbeak. His expression softened. 'As you see, Master Pinchbeak,' she began, 'I was once a poor laysister of St Leonard, no more than a peeler of roots to that great house. Yet I come to beg the indulgence of a lawman famed across England for the wisdom of his counsel.'

Pinchbeak, ignoring her flattery, studied her face, his gaze wandering freely over her features and down to her breast. 'We've met before.'

'I don't believe so, Master Pinchbeak,' she quickly said. She stole a glance at his collar, a band of chained silver about his neck with a pendant badge below, bejewelled with the livery of his affinity: a single white star, opposed fields of gold and red, the whole surrounded by ornate tangles of vines, leaves, and flowers, the subtlest metalwork to be had in London. The gifting of this collar had been a sign of singular distinction, marking Pinchbeak as a prestigious member of that extended network of knights, squires, freemen, and servants orbiting Robert de Vere, Earl of Oxford.

Pinchbeak tilted his head. 'I'm rarely wrong about such things. But no matter. State your business. Always happy to help out a sister of Bromley, whether lay or avowed.'

She spoke of the book. His face remained impassive as she described the volume and its poetry, the dark histories inscribed in its strange verses; the cloth and its heraldry, the incriminating livery woven in its strands. She recited the four bits of prophecy she had gotten by rote, including the one that mattered most, on the death of King Richard. She said nothing about the manner in which the book had come to her, nor about the murdered girl. This piece of the story, she suspected, might prove more useful at a later point.

All the while Pinchbeak observed her with a practised calm, his fingers steepled before his sharp nose. She could not read the lawman's eyes even as well as she had read the book, though in their depths she sensed genuine concern. The hollow of his neck created a dark well of stubbled skin that pulsed as he listened. She was watching a vein throb beneath his chin when he finally spoke.

'To whom else have you uttered these lines?' He leaned forward slightly.

'You are the first,' Millicent lied. 'The very first, Master Pinchbeak.'

She waited. With a shuddering groan, the bell struck in the St Paul's belfry far above, wrapping Millicent in its deep throb and shaking her guts like jelly in a bowl.

Pinchbeak remained still through the last of the clamour, his gaze on Millicent far from kind. 'You deal rather freely with these prophecies,' he said into the final, dying tone.

'Though freely is not how I hope to part with them, Master Pinchbeak,' she countered.

His frown was severe. 'You haven't the devil's idea what unholy hell you've dug yourself into, Mistress—'

'Rykener,' she said on an impulse, thinking of the Gropecunt maudlyn showing up at her door. Through the parvis gate she saw Agnes, lingering by the stairs. 'Eleanor Rykener is my name.' Her sister would flay her if she knew she had betrayed her friend in this way, yet giving her own name would lead the authorities right to her door.

'Mistress Rykener,' Pinchbeak said, attempting patience, though she could now see the cords in his neck standing out against his skin, which had coloured to a deep purple, 'I've heard noises from others about this book. A hideous thing, and if what you say is true, if you really have it, why, you've dug yourself a pretty little hole. The very words you've uttered in my presence – the words alone are treason.'

Millicent subtly smiled. She had Pinchbeak just where she wanted him. 'Though they are not my words, good sir. Nor my treason described in the prophecy.'

'Not your words,' Pinchbeak said, sitting back. There was a challenge in his gaze, perhaps even a small degree of admiration. 'Yet whose words are they? That's the question, hmm?'

She shrugged. 'Though to my purposes a useful one only insofar as it aids me in their sale.'

'Your purposes will best be served by bringing this book to me. You'll receive a handsome fee, I assure you.'

At last. 'And the size of this fee, Master Pinchbeak?'

He thought about it. 'Four marks.'

Millicent sniffed. 'Four marks? Four marks, when a prince's ransom would hardly suit? Think of your own reward, Master Pinchbeak, should you deliver this book of prophecies to your lord. And the penalty should he learn that you were presented with the opportunity to recover it – but failed.'

He sputtered for a moment, but he knew she was right. 'Let us be clear on this, Mistress Rykener. The line you quoted concerning the day of the regicide, the feast of St Dunstan. The thirteenth prophecy is clear on this matter?'

Millicent nodded and repeated the two lines:

'By Half-ten of Hawks might shender be shown,
On day of Saint Dunstan shall Death have his doom.'

Pinchbeak rose with some difficulty, his right arm shaking on his stick. 'What's to prevent me from having you seized this very moment?' he asked. 'Here you are, *femme sole* in the presence of a serjeant-at-law, with no husband to shield you. Newgate is full of traitors this season, man and woman alike.'

Millicent had anticipated this. 'I have made certain arrangements for the disposition of the book in case I'm taken, Master Pinchbeak. It's safely hidden.'

'I see,' he said, looking sceptical. 'And you intend to approach every prominent man in London with this book until you find one ready to snap it up?'

'Only those known for the keenness of their discernment. Their wisdom in making difficult choices.'

He gave her a thin smile, then leaned forward awkwardly, his breath warming her cheek as he wedged his stick between his chest and the parvis pavers. 'Come see me next Friday, Mistress Rykener, in my rooms at Scroope's, the serjeants' inn at Ely Place. By then I will have inquired about these prophecies. If I learn there is anything to them we'll discuss a suitable price.'

Millicent, delighted, rose from her bench while Pinchbeak

turned away for the company of his fellow serjeants. She rejoined Agnes at the south porch and they headed back to Cornhull, talking excitedly about the fortune that awaited them. Though she felt a nagging worry that Pinchbeak's inquiries might lead him to spurn her offer, Millicent had been stirred by the encounter, and had no intention of waiting until the next week to inquire with Pinchbeak about his price. Why, the serjeant-at-law could make an offer for the book along with other gentlemen interested in its purchase. They had settled on the next wealthy man to approach when Agnes tugged her sleeve.

'What do you suppose he wants, Mil?'

'Who?' The turn for her house was just ahead.

'Man over there. Spicerer, looks like.'

Millicent looked to see George Lawler, standing before his shop and urging them over. He was agitated, his gaze shifting left and right. Arm in arm, the sisters crossed over and cleared the gutter. 'Yes, Master Lawler?' Millicent said when they reached him.

'Men've come.' He peered back into his shop. 'To your house, and also here.'

'Pratt, sure, and his son,' Millicent said. 'He'll have what I owe him, as soon as I've settled with you.'

'Not Pratt.'

'Who, then?'

'Loy if I know. Constables? But not of our ward, that's certain. Had the long knives at their sides, no badges. Asked after the sisters Fonteyn, do I know them, know their whereabouts.'

Millicent gasped. 'The *sisters* Fonteyn?'

'Knew that one of them, the rich one, frequented Lawler's. With a fondness for sugared things. And that the younger one's a mau—' He stopped himself. 'Didn't know you had a sister.'

Millicent turned to Agnes, her fury rising. 'And how could

they have known, Agnes? Spreading rumour of your famed chastity about the city, hoping it would burnish my name?'

Agnes stepped back as if struck. 'I been gone from Gropecunt Lane weeks now, Mil. So they're looking for me, looking for the b—'

'Stop!' Millicent cried.

They all turned at a harsh laugh from Lawler's shop door. Mistress Lawler, arms folded, taking it all in. 'Look at the shiny side of the coin, your ladyship,' she said as Millicent felt herself redden. 'Least now you'll have an honest way of working off your debts.'

Millicent turned and strode off, Agnes hurrying behind her.

'Never had a doubt about that one, Lawler,' she called to their backs. 'A maud's a maud, wherever she gets her pennies. Let that be a lesson to you, George. The wisdom of wives, deep as the sea is green.'

'Aye,' she heard Lawler mutter. 'And just as cold.'

They reached the corner. Millicent had to force herself to place one foot in front of the other.

'Mil,' said Agnes, working to keep up. 'Mil, what if the men are still about? Shouldn't we get away from here?'

The visitors had been thorough in their inquiries. It seemed London's entire cloth industry was staring at them as they slunk past the colourful displays and hangings lining the lane: dresses, smocks, hoods, coverlets, and a host of other goods that now made Millicent feel trapped by the opulence rather than a part of it. Finally they reached her house.

The door stood ajar. Heedless of Agnes's warnings, Millicent entered, surveying the destruction. In the front room, chair cushions had been torn apart, feathers and straw scattered across the floor, wooden shelves torn from the walls, leaving gaping holes in the plaster; in the kitchen larder, already-empty barrels were broken on the floor, her recent purchases from Lawler's studding the rushes. She raced up the back stairs and into the rear bedchamber. Her trunk lay in pieces, hacked apart with an axe or sword. It seemed that nearly every garment she still owned had been sliced in two and tossed about the room.

She turned to Agnes, who had followed her up the stairs. 'Dearheart,' Agnes said, holding out her arms.

Millicent pushed her away. 'This is on *you*.' Her fall from wealthy consort of a peer to penniless sister of a Gropecunt Lane whore had been short but steep; now it was complete.

'But, Mil—'

'*Shut* it, Ag.' Millicent's hands shook as she gathered up those few items that were whole and stuffed them in a handled basket she kept for laundering.

Agnes was peering down at the street through a gap in the front shutters. 'They'll be after us, sure. Folks are already staring up here, lot of talk in the street.'

Millicent nodded tightly. 'We'll go then,' she said. They left her house for the last time, stealing along the alley to Spinners Lane. There they paused as Millicent adjusted the load and hefted the light basket that contained all her earthly possessions: an extra bonnet, two faded dresses, the few shillings left from selling the dead woman's bracelet, and the book, still wrapped in its cloth.

There was only one place to go, a destination neither of them had to name. They walked silently to the river and over the bridge, then made the turn past St Mary Overey. Millicent felt her shoulders sag with defeat, and as they entered Rose Alley it seemed that every raw moment of her former life as a maudlyn assaulted her with a thickening of memory and shame.

The neighbourhood hadn't changed a bit. Same drab store-fronts and sagging overhangs, looming over the lane like sullen birds of prey. Same sluggish gutters, carrying filth from house to pond and pond to river, filling the air with the stink of dead fish and tired whores. Same forlorn women and girls affecting cheer as they peddled their flesh to tradesmen, friars,

158

and worse. No better than slaves, Millicent thought, and though I swore I would never return, now I'm all but one of them again.

She glanced over at Agnes. Her sister walked tall, no shame on her face, appearing almost excited to be coming back to their childhood home. The strength of the girl, Millicent thought. Where does she get it?

Finally they were in front of the Pricking Bishop. Millicent nearly gagged at her first sight of St Cath, the spirals and slashes of withered skin. The old woman looked at Agnes, then at Millicent, letting her wizened gaze wander slowly over her breasts and down to her thighs and feet.

St Cath snickered, bobbing her chin. 'It'll be an honour, Lady Queynt, an honour to put your fair cheeks and teats to work again for the Bishop. Bess'll be thrilled.'

'Thrilled and gashed and swyved,' said Bess Waller, appearing at the door. Millicent looked at her mother's face for the first time in five years. More lines in her skin, more grey dusting her hair, but the Southwark bawd was as fetching as ever.

Agnes seemed about to say something but Bess held up a hand. 'Middle back room up top. Yours for a fortnight, but after that it's suck or scram. Hear?'

'Yes, *mère*,' said Agnes, nodding dutifully.

Millicent could not make a sound. Her mother stared at her with something between pity and contempt, then let out a thin whistle. 'My, my, my. How the wheel of Lady Fortune turns.'

Millicent gritted her teeth and pushed past her mother, entering the Pricking Bishop and hating herself for having to.

TWENTY-ONE

St Mary Overey, Southwark

We quickly settled into a pattern. Always an early riser, I nibbled at bread in the kitchen, where I would sit by the hearth until Simon came in from the hall. We would exchange a few words, he would eat a little something, then he tended to go to the solar to read or scratch on a tablet for the rest of the morning. The first few days he never left the house. I would catch him staring vacantly out of a window, or sitting in a dark study by the hall fire. Invariably his smile would return when he noticed me, and soon enough he would start peppering me with questions about my affairs. He wanted me to take him to St Paul's and Westminster, where I could introduce him around. Despite my reluctance I gave in the third time he asked.

Simon had a new and easy way about him, open yet respectful as we spoke with these familiar clutches of lawmen and bureaucrats. He never seemed too free, his bearing modest and unpresumptuous, and I began to think these changes in him were genuine. Within days of his return to Southwark Simon was simply *there*, my natural son and only heir, more a part of my daily life than he had ever been before that night on the wharf. If his crimes were not forgotten they had diminished with time, miniaturized, I suppose, by the simple fact of his presence, and the brittle persistence of his mother's last words.

✤

There is a particular image of Sarah that can slip from my memory for days or weeks at a time, only to reappear at the most unguarded moments, taking away my breath, nibbling at my conscience.

It was Epiphany time, over fifteen years ago now. We had lost Elizabeth to fever the week before, this after the death of John, our eldest, that autumn. Now our two younger children, Alison, eight, and Simon, just shy of six, had fallen ill. Simon's birth had been difficult. There would be no others. Unable to sleep over the rattles of his troubled breaths, I had crept from the lesser bedchamber down to the parlour, using the outer staircase so as not to disturb Sarah.

My feet were carelessly bare. I remember the rough edges of cold stairs, the indifference of a January moon. In the parlour I slouched on a long bench against the western wall, thinking blankly of our dead, our barely living. At some point I drifted off.

When I awoke Sarah was at the east window, framed against the night. We would often leave that window unshuttered, as it gave on to the far corner of the churchyard, and was thus in that part of the Overey house that lay within the priory's walls. There was a high stool there, nestled in an angled nook that allowed its occupant to lean against a broad wooden post. It had been Bet's favourite place to sit. Birds watering at the polygonal fountain, new buds on the gillyflower stems, Austin canons sneaking past to slip her a plug of mint: over this private world our elder daughter had sweetly reigned for most of her eleven years.

Standing there in her nightclothes, washed by a half moon,

161

her mother looked like a glassed saint in a church window, pious and steady, every strand of her thick hair tucked properly beneath her night bonnet. Since our elder son died I had grown increasingly resentful of Sarah's composure, which seemed only to have strengthened with Bet's passing. She would reveal nothing of her grief, greeting friends and family with a sympathetic smile and a warm embrace, as if *they* were the ones needing comfort. My own state over those months could hardly have been worse. I would find myself weeping at a moment's notice, bawling in a corner like a whipped schoolboy.

Not Sarah. *Great in a crisis, our Sarah*, it was said among the women of the parish. A new Job. She had always been so, a tower of womanly strength as she bathed the foreheads of the dying, comforted the living with rote phrases from the prior. That night, as I watched her stand before the window, I felt a flash of fury and wanted to shake her, to scream some feeling into that placid skull. Instead I simply sat, mute and still, as if nailed to the bench, diminished by my wife's stout quietude.

Then the contortions came. Her entire frame gave a single heave. A choking sound rose from her throat, stifled as soon as it began. This convulsed her further, her arms spasming like the bound limbs of a criminal on a noose.

Thinking she was ill, I was about to rise when she went to her knees and reached for the window. Her fingers stretched along the sill. She put her face to the bottom of the opening. Her cheek moved slowly along the rough board. I watched her, the strange sweeping movements of her hands as they whisked from the wood to her face, as she sniffed like some chained lunatic at her fingers and palms.

It came to me then, the meaning of Sarah's actions. She was gleaning the dust of our daughter. Discovering those places where Bet's hands had played, gathering the last particles of her skin, the final remnants of her scent as they lingered on the windowsill. As if to take them in, and store them somewhere until the two of them could meet again.

My breath stopped, yet I was too stunned by the change in my wife to go to her, despite the rush of sympathy swelling my lungs when I could breathe again. Sarah next turned away from the window and clutched the wooden stool. Flattening her cheek against the surface, she embraced the legs so tightly I thought she must be hurting herself. All the while she continued to draw indistinct moans from somewhere in her chest, which hummed with the pain of a dying animal.

Now she was prone, writhing on her stomach, clutching at the rushes. Now on her back, groaning at the ceiling beams. This went on for an indeterminate time until I thought she was done. She had curled herself against the wall, still heaving, puddled in grief. I took a deep breath, preparing to rise.

Then her voice, stealing from some shattered place, broke the room's silence. 'Not Simon . . . please not Simon . . . not Simon too . . . oh God not my Simon not Simon not Simon not Simon . . .'

I frowned. What about Alison? Why wasn't Sarah praying for our daughter, just as close to death as her brother? My thoughts darkened. Simon had always been Sarah's favourite; it was obvious from the moment of his birth. She had been a model mother to all the children, in her way. Yet our youngest she treated differently. Lifted him more often, shouldered his governess aside at night, gentled him in ways she never had the others.

It showed in him, too. Simon was a defiant, stubborn boy. Spoiled, coddled, contrary. Though astonishingly quick at his lessons, he could be an incorrigible brat, the object of numerous complaints from his schoolmasters and tutors, never willing to sit still and learn, whether sums from his teachers or bits of wisdom from his father. The very opposite of Alison, my child of light, seemingly born to please with her delicate embrace, her shy nods, her willing smile. She had been my only source of comfort over those awful months, as her older siblings died and her mother grew increasingly remote from everyone but her son. It was as if our family had been separated by some fathomless chasm, Sarah and Simon teetering on one side, Alison and I on the other, the voices of our departed sounding from the void, willing us to jump.

Yet here we are, still among the living, and we must manage somehow. The thought guided me back to the present. Despite the favour Sarah had always showered on Simon, I could not believe she would ask God for his life over Alison's. I waited for a prayer for our daughter. None came. Sarah continued her moaning for Simon, a thousand desperate pleas thrown into the night. Still nothing for Alison, not a motherly word.

I ground my teeth, close to screaming at her, cursing her for preferring Simon even at a time like this. Instead I remained silent, and channelled my fury into my own, darker prayer. No, Lord God, I prayed inwardly, take him. Spare *her*, God. Spare my daughter, I beg of Thee, and take my son. In the name of Your own Son, my God, grant me my daughter's life. Take Simon if You need another, so long as Alison lives.

At the time these words seemed only natural, a bid for Alison's life against her mother's wishes. I imagined our warring prayers mounting to heaven, curling into God's ears, and I felt a rush of righteousness as I asked Him for the life of my beloved daughter, at whatever cost.

Sarah never saw me sitting there that night, feebly watching the spectacle of her sorrow.

Alison died the next morning. My reaction was a tearless silence, as I shuffled about the Overey house, heavy with failure. Two days later Simon's fever broke and he was out of bed, jumping about as if he had never been ill. Instead of joy in his recovery all I felt was the bitter unfairness of it, that Alison should die so Simon could live. For it seemed to me then that Sarah had traded something for Simon's life that night, that some vital portion of her spirit had passed into him with all those spasms and wracks and grotesque snifflings, none of which she had spared for Alison.

So I turned against her, against the good and against life, embracing the nothing that belongs to this world. She had God on her side, after all. She certainly didn't need me. That chain of early deaths pulled me from my moorings, dragged me downward into that amoral place where I have dwelled for so many years. Once a loving husband who doted on his wife, I became a reserve of cold severity, indifferent to the comforts of intimacy and the pleasures of the marriage bed. Once a fair and judicious father even to Simon, I became distant, demanding obedience from a son whose very life I secretly resented. Once a poet of youthful love, I became a scribbler of cranky moralism, my writing nothing more than a means of access to high men and hidden information, much as I had once wished to craft such things of beauty as Chaucer gave the world.

As for Sarah, Alison's death and Simon's survival seemed to have no effect on her, and as the years passed and our sole child grew from a boy to a man, she remained unflinchingly loyal to him, even as he proved himself again and again unworthy of her indulgence, drinking in the street, consorting with maudlyns, boxing with labourers, trying his thumb on the blade of the law. It would come as no real surprise when his juvenile indulgences culminated in the killing of another man. A fitting turn in a life of such frivolous waste.

Then, within eighteen months of his departure for Italy and

Hawkwood's service, another death. A shallow cough one day, a fever the next, and Sarah was gone. There was a moment near the end, as I sat beside her, when she reached for my hand, her own a patch of warm parchment, loose against my palm. I blinked at her fading eyes, leaned down to catch a ragged whisper. 'Try to love him, John. Just try.' My head bent in a feeble nod. She never spoke again.

Regret paints the memory in infinite hues, all blurring to a leaden grey with the passing of time. What future would have become possible had I gone to my Sarah that night in our parlour, had I pulled this wracked woman into my arms, cleared her nose with my thumb and finger, helped her gather up our daughter's invisible dust? What could our remaining life have been, had I shown a half-ounce of compassion for this shattered mother, praying for one small life out of four?

For only now do I see how much greater Sarah's burden was than my own, and what Simon's survival must have cost her. Only now do I see that her turn to God that night was done out of desperation, not spite or unthinking preference for one child over another. That her prayer for Simon's life was in part a prayer for me, for our family, for the survival of the male heir by which every man judges his worth and ensures his legacy. That in that darkest of places she remained the most loyal of wives, even to the extent of praying to God, in the only way she knew how, for the survival of her husband's name. That Sarah Gower, unlike her husband, never asked for a child's death.

Now, with her son back in our home and so many past roads converging, I found myself burning to speak to that shimmering woman in the window one last time, and ask for her forgiveness. Not for the way I treated her all those years. Sarah, in her stolid goodness, would not need to be asked for that measure of grace. I had seen it in her eyes as she passed, and knew it was mine to take with me to the grave.

The forgiveness I sought was on behalf not of Sarah, but

of Simon. For half a lifetime I had blamed my son for the extinguishing of his sister's life, and for the slow moral decay of my own. All his life Simon Gower had carried that heavy load I had laid on his narrow shoulders so many years ago: the impossible burden of the unchosen child.

Try to love him, John. Just try. I felt the womanly pressure of Sarah's last words, the charge they gave me to live up to some modest ideal. *Just try.* That, at least, I could do.

✥

Word from James Tewburn arrived from the Guildhall. There was now definitive news on my property matter, and he hoped to deliver it in person. I called for Simon, thinking to bring him along, but he had already left the house. By noon I was on Basinghall Street, then in Guildhall Yard, which was busier than usual that day.

There was a long board bench along the pavers outside Strode's chambers. On it sat a typical collection of Londoners seeking attention: three starved-looking children, their clearly drunk guardian giving them the occasional head slap; a short row of bored apprentices over on legal business from Westminster or the inns, their robes hiked up to their knees to gather air; a young man tapping his foot, likely a ward nearing his majority; and a hollow-eyed man in faded hose clutching a sheaf of documents. All had business with the common serjeant's office, and all had arrived before me.

Ignoring the glares, I leaned in. Four of the common clerk's scribes filled the cramped space, busily filling ledgers and rolls with the city's affairs. Though employed by the Guildhall, these were also scribblers for hire, young fellows with good eyes, men you could rely on to copy out a quire or a book when you needed a quick and steady hand. I had commissioned their services more than once in recent years, so my face was well known around these inky precincts. 'Is Tewburn about?'

The nearest clerk shook his head. 'Been summoned to Westminster.' He turned. 'Chancery, Pinkhurst?' he called to one of his counterparts.

'Chancery, right,' the man called back. 'Expect him back at two or thereabouts. But you'll catch him before then at the Pin-and-Wheel.' Sometimes it seemed that London's clerks and lawmen spent half their lives in taverns.

At Cat Street the way narrowed and bent to such an extent that even an experienced Londoner might find himself lost, though I never minded this part of the city. Nowhere else were so many trades practised, so many goods sold and resold with such spirited rivalry. Silks of Lyon, hanging from poles of polished elm jutting out over the close lane; olives of al-Andalus, displayed in shortened barrels and scooped out with great pomp by a shopkeeper's girl; cinnamon and cloves from who knew where, filling the air with exotic scents – and all available at a stone's throw from the knit hose and rough leather work-gloves crafted across the river in Southwark.

Outside a leatherworker's shop, as I stooped to examine a row of tooled belts, I saw Ralph Strode coming up Cat Street from the church of St Lawrence. With him was Sir Michael de la Pole. James Tewburn walked behind them, and as I watched the trio approaching I wondered what would bring the chancellor to these precincts. The baron's finger was aimed at Strode's wide chest as they walked, thrusting sidewards to reinforce his points. All three appeared agitated, Tewburn's face in particular clouded, the corners of his mouth pulled back in what looked almost like physical pain. Not wanting to get caught eavesdropping, and with nowhere to conceal myself, I stepped from behind the display.

'Gower!' Strode called, suddenly all cheer. The chancellor's manner had also transformed, and after my bow arms were grasped all around. Tewburn, said Strode, had good news.

The clerk turned to me with a forced smile. 'Only this morning, Master Gower, I secured the writ of *pone* necessary to move your property matter into Common Pleas.'

'I'm pleased to hear it,' I said. 'Thank you, James, for taking care of it so quickly.'

'I'd wager your adversary will drop the matter soon.'

'Let's hope so,' I said.

The clerk bowed. Strode dismissed him. Tewburn's face fell again as he turned for the Guildhall, giving the impression of an unresolved conflict. Strode watched Tewburn's back until the man disappeared. 'A peculiar one, our Tewburn,' he said distantly. '*Deficit ambobus qui vult servire duobus.*'

'Surely he regards you as his primary master, Ralph,' said the baron.

'Perhaps,' said Strode, his face clouded. 'In any case . . .'

'Yes,' said the chancellor with a brisk tone. 'Thanks as always for your counsel, Ralph.'

'At your pleasure, your lordship.'

The baron turned to me, his brow arched. 'I understand your son is back from Italy, Gower. He sounds like a promising young man.'

'Thank you, my lord,' I said, wondering how such information could have reached the chancellor so quickly. The Baron de la Pole was by reputation and action a fiercely independent man, one who had earned the friendship of old King Edward and now spoke for the House of Lords with persuasion and quiet force. It was he who had arranged King Richard's marriage to Anne of Bohemia several years before, and though he came from a lesser family than most of those in his circle, there was no one in the realm who commanded more respect. I decided to be direct. 'You know, my lord, he is eager to find a position in the government – perhaps too eager, given that he's just returned.'

'Do send him my way, will you?' said the baron. 'With all the ruckus over levies it would be good to have some steadier hands among the ledgers. The court of Chancery has never been busier.'

I bowed. 'Simon would be delighted to serve in any capacity, my lord. He'll call at your chambers tomorrow.'

The chancellor said his farewells. We watched as two of the baron's guards, who had been shadowing their master as he walked along Cat Street, converged on the chancellor in the middle of the lane and proceeded with him toward the river.

'Simon is back in England?' Strode asked when the baron had left us. 'When did he return?'

'Not a week ago,' I said, still wanting to know the purpose of his colloquy with de la Pole.

Strode glanced down the street. 'The Bent Plough, if you aren't pressed for time, John?'

'If *I'm* not pressed?'

'Be good to have a sip,' he said. 'Hear your news, your latest connivings.'

Ralph Strode was hardly one to spend the middle of a workday in idle chat. Yet he seemed eager to speak, though I would have to tread lightly. I gestured back toward St Lawrence. 'The chapel would be fine, if you wouldn't mind.' Strode used the chapel of St Eustachius within the church as a secondary chambers of sorts, conducting all kinds of business from the dim space. If we went to the tavern, as he had suggested, I would get nothing else done that afternoon.

'So be it.' His heavy arm wrapped my shoulders and we made our way into the church. The nave was mostly empty, though the clink of silver from up ahead suggested some lingering business. In the Eustachius chapel I half-sat on one of the misericords, a row of narrow seats that had been moved to the side after their replacement some months ago. Eight of the displaced wooden chairs, grouped in two rows of four, rested vertically along the chapel's north wall, their underseats carved with scenes of rural life: a wife wielding the distaff against her cowering husband, a rotund fellow at the hurdy-gurdy, a ploughman sodomizing a goat.

'You look troubled, John,' he said with no preface.

'Simon's return has me a bit thrown off, I suppose.'

'Not a pure source of joy?'

Strode knew nothing about the accidental death on the wharf. 'For the last two years he's been working in the White Company. The clerk of a mercenary, blood for hire. Not the career I would have chosen for him.'

'I had understood that his position with Hawkwood was more in the clerical line.'

I leaned against the cool wooden back of the misericord. 'Sir John hires out his troops to anyone. His last client before Florence was Clement of Avignon, when he bought himself a papacy. The man led the slaughter of an entire village in the Romagna. To imagine Simon notarizing and sealing bills for such an alliance of convenience – not a settling thought.'

'I speak from experience when I say that the servants of great bureaucracies rarely have an effect on their policies. Don't be too hard on him, John.'

'I've already been too soft. When I saw him standing in my hall I wanted to strangle him.' I shook my head. 'To return from Tuscany with no message ahead, no warning?'

'"For youth," as our good friend writes, "shall have neither guide nor straight line".'

'"Nor old age dewed grapes to pluck from the vine",' I replied, completing Chaucer's couplet.

Strode chuckled and sat back. It was time to broach the other subject. 'You know, Ralph, may I draw on your knowledge for a moment? I need the ear of an Oxford master.' Before moving to London and taking up his current office, Strode had enjoyed a long career as a theology fellow at Merton, where his connections were still quite deep.

'You flatter me, John,' he said, looking amused.

'There's a certain author I need to know more about, an

171

ancient writer,' I said. 'You know I'm not boasting when I tell you I'm pretty well read in the authorities. But this man is an utter mystery. I've never heard of him.'

Strode shifted on the misericord. 'What author?'

I watched Strode's eyes. 'His name is Lollius.'

He blinked.

'The name means something to you?'

Strode toyed with a loose button, his jowls working a tooth. 'You're testing me, I can see it in your eyes. Yet I know you well enough to take no offence. So I'll take your test, then you'll tell me whether I've passed it.'

Pleased at the frank reaction, I grasped his near arm. 'You just did, Ralph.'

'Good, then.' He cleared his throat. 'When we met at Westminster, I mentioned a murder. A girl, slain in the Moorfields.'

'I remember.'

'What she took from La Neyte, it's said, was a book. This book contains a number of prophecies written by this Lollius. Twelve of them foretell the deaths of our past kings.'

'And the thirteenth,' I added, 'the death of King Richard.'

Strode studied me. 'You are well informed.'

'Braybrooke.' This prompted a brisk nod. 'The bishop is confounded, has no more idea about Lollius than I do. Without having seen the work I can't speak to its accuracy, of course – but I have my suspicions.' I lowered my voice. 'From all I have heard, this *Liber de Mortibus Regum Anglorum* must be a forgery.'

He frowned. 'A forgery?'

'To write a prophecy about times already past is hardly a challenge,' I said. 'What would prevent a living man from tracing back through our chronicles the means of these royal deaths, and "prophesying" accordingly?'

Strode nodded slowly. 'Then simply writing a new prophecy about King Richard.'

'What better way to trouble the realm than to predict the manner and means and even time of its sovereign's death?'

Strode's eyes caught flecks of candlelight from the chapel's altar. 'I have thought about the name "Lollius" a good deal myself. Is there a taste for Lollius's work in Wycliffe's circles, among these Lollers?'

'Braybrooke thinks so.'

'I'm not surprised, though I've heard nothing of it from my former colleagues in Oxford.'

'I can't help but think I might have better luck than Braybrooke's men in identifying this Lollius. But I need an excellent library, Ralph. A library with the – ah, the muscle to bear up under the inquiries of a dogged man.' I thought of Chaucer's account of the Visconti library, the immense holdings that had furnished him with the Italian writings that inspired so much of his current making. 'The problem is, there's little time, and I can't go abroad.'

Strode, always up for an intellectual challenge, adjusted his bulk and sat forward. 'There are libraries aplenty in Oxford, Gower, of more variety than even the great monkish collections at Bury or St Albans. In fact, now that I think on it, there may be a collection of books in Oxford uniquely suited to your purpose.'

'At Merton?'

'No indeed,' Strode said. 'The library I'm thinking about is in an outbuilding behind the Durham grange. A roomful of trunks and crates. I know little about the collection beyond the fact of its existence. Yet I do know its keeper. A cantankerous old man, but we are on friendly terms, and I'd be happy to write you a letter of introduction. The man in Oxford you'll want to see is Peter de Quincey.'

'And he'll admit me, even though I'm not a monk?' Durham was a small Benedictine college, and the order was jealous of its privileges.

Strode shook his jowls. 'Quincey is a lay brother to the order. His late master was Richard Angervyle de Bury.'

'Bishop of Durham?'

'And a great lover of books. You'll have read his *Philobiblon,* of course.'

I gave a chagrined frown, feeling ignorant as I often did in Strode's presence. 'I haven't, though the title intrigues me. Do you own it?'

'I do,' said Strode. 'I'll have my copy sent round to St Mary's in short order. As for the collection, well.' He looked up at the vaults, as if searching the ceiling for the appropriately lofty words. 'The most mysterious collection of books in England, some say, though I've never plumbed it. Few in Oxford have, though it's the subject of endless speculation.'

'And Angervyle himself?' I asked.

'He was quite the figure: Clerk of the Privy Seal, a noted emissary at Avignon before this disastrous break with Rome. Peter de Quincey was his most trusted clerk. He's an old man now, though with a letter from me he should give you a friendly hearing, despite the whiff of suspicion in the Oxford air these days.'

This took us to the subject of rising heresy, and the disturbing news out of Oxford. Strode had mixed feelings on the matter of Wycliffe's emergent sect. 'The condemnation of Wycliffe before his death has divided my colleagues on the faculties of logic and theology,' he said, getting to his feet. 'Every syllogism is now parsed for heretical content. The old freedoms are being threatened.'

He led me out of St Lawrence and on to the street. 'The effect is chilling, Gower. You have to wonder how long it will be before the same scrutiny comes to the inns, and infects how we teach the very laws of England.'

'It surely won't come to that,' I said, considering this dire possibility. I struggled to match his pace. 'Would you

174

recommend against this visit to Oxford, then? This Lollius could be anyone.'

'One has to start somewhere,' said Strode. 'Take our students, who must entertain absurdities of the most outrageous sort when they're first learning to theologize. "Suppose God revealed Christ not to be His Son. What then would be the authority of the sacrament?" "Suppose it were discovered that the faculty of intellection resides in the stomach. Could a hungry man think well?" Such inquiries aren't threatening. They merely *pretend* to question our beliefs precisely in order to strengthen them. Consider the nature of the irrelevant proposition. Such a proposition must be greeted with scepticism, and yet we cannot discard it entirely, can we?'

I hesitated, not sure where Strode was taking me. 'I suppose not.'

'Suppositions are exactly the point in the case of an irrelevant proposition. If the proposition proves useless, we simply ignore it. If, on the other hand, it proves itself worthy to think with, why, we should do everything we can to exploit its use. There's hardly heresy in that.' We had reached the porch at the Guildhall, where Strode indicated that he would leave me for an appointment with the mayor. 'It's a lesson,' he said, 'we would all do well to remember. In dialectic, even what seem the most irrelevant propositions can lead us to the truth.'

'Or truths,' I muttered, feeling glum.

Strode paused on the first step, towering over me. 'Tell that to Braybrooke, Gower. The Bishop of London should cultivate a taste for tolerance to match his enthusiasm for gardening.' He took the shallow steps in one move, his long robes fluttering in his wake.

Back through Guildhall Yard. A flash of colour before the eastern gate, and a few scattered laughs. On approaching I saw the cause: a bit of street theatre of the sort often seen in the city's larger gathering places. With Strode's concerns still preoccupying me, I paused, distractedly, to watch.

The mimes were performing a play about the first King Edward. Longshanks, the Hammer of the Scots. The company had reached the deathbed scene, performed with the king prostrate on a mat, his lords gathered round. The speaker stepped to the front to interpret the scene for the crowd.

> 'As he lingers his last, with lords all about,
> By six-less-two swords he shall say as he dies,
> "My heart you must heft toward heaven on earth,
> To Jerusalem journey, joy to enjoin,
> And my bones against Bruce to be borne into war,
> My gravestone to graveth: Leave Gaveston gone."'

The mime playing Longshanks put a hand to his forehead, chortled out a last breath, and expired, to the warm applause of the circle of Londoners gathered around the actors. He leapt to his feet, the mimes collected small coins in their caps, and the scene broke up as quickly as it had gathered, the company heading for St Paul's or the bridge with the heat of the day.

My own skin had gone cold. *By six-less-two swords he shall say as he dies.* Seven of swords, sovereign of swords, prince of plums, three of thistles – and now six-less-two swords, another numbered symbol echoing with the voice of the *De Mortibus* prophecies. Even this rough street spectacle of Longshanks's death had drawn its language from the book, which now seemed to be everywhere I turned. A street preacher, the bishop and his friars, the common serjeant, and now the mimes of London, all speaking the morbid idiom of Lollius, the whisper of kingly deaths on their lips.

It was at that moment that I started imagining the prophecies as a kind of pestilence, raising boils on the vulnerable body of the realm. Despite the laughter of these Londoners, the image stayed with me the rest of that day, as the book spread its ill portents through the city and the realm.

Men of our time have a peculiar fascination with a form of story. It is the story of raptus, of ravir, of ravissement. It has various names, in the Moorish tongue the muwashshah, in Spanish the serranilla, most commonly in French the pastourelle.

A simple story, always the same. A young shepherdess strolls in a field or on a road. A knight on horseback swoops in and seeks to seduce her, beguiling her with poems, or clever words, or promises of fame. She resists his advances, resists yet more, until eventually his desire goads him to force himself upon her, destroying her virtue. There are variations here and there: the shepherdess is carried off by an evil knight or a murderous giant, so her gallant rescuer saves her life even as he sullies her flesh. Often there is a rival involved, and one knight must defeat another to win the lady.

Yet however the matter falls out, the young lady remains silent about her rape, her tongue as useless as Philomel's after it was severed by Tereus. So acceptable a part of lovemaking is this vile act that even Father Andreas, in his Art of Courtly Love, enjoins noble men to delight in it without thought: 'Remember to praise them lavishly,' he writes, 'and should you find a suitable spot you should not delay in taking what you seek, gaining it by rough embraces.'

Yet where is the woman's sovereignty, her choice in the matter? The woman never writes her own story. She is rather like the lion in Aesop's little fable, who sees a painting of another lion being strangled by a man. But who paints the lion? Tell me, who?

He who paints the lion claims to know the lion, and with his brush he may colour whatever lies he wishes. The power of the teller, you see, is inestimable.

And so it is with women in these pastourelles, these tales of rural virgins who know not their own desire well enough to keep from resisting the rapes they must suffer with all the inevitability of death. I have heard them in the langue d'oïl, I have heard them in the langue d'oc, in the tongue of Juan Ruiz, in the tongue of Dante, and translated from the tongue of the Jews. In every human language, it seems, men have depicted the joys of ravishment, and never with consequence for the ravisher. Just one time I would like to hear a version with a righteous end, one in which the perpetrator—

—I flee my matter.

One morning, as the girl sat with her mother in their bedchamber, learning to pin out a broad stitch on her frame, there came a pounding at the outer door. They heard voices, then one of the servingwomen entered.

'The prince requests an audience, my lady.'

'Very well.' The lady gathered her embroidery and placed it in a basket. 'I shall receive him in the salon.'

As she left the bedchamber she turned, stooped down, and held her daughter by the chin. 'Stay here, my sweet. Just here. Do not come out until I call you. Do you understand?'

The girl nodded. Her mother kissed her nose and walked out of her private rooms, closing the door behind her.

Through a knot the daughter watched as the foreign prince entered the salon. Her mother called for her maidservant, moving in frantic circles as she sought to elude his grasp. It happened so quickly: a brief struggle, a hand clamped over her mother's mouth, her dress torn from her shoulders, the horrific sight of the lord in his nakedness.

Through it all the girl obeyed her mother's last command. 'Do not come out until I call you.' And she did not. What could she have done?

The prince, dressing himself, left his victim on a cushioned chair, weeping with pain and humiliation. At the sight of her mother's bruised thighs, her reddened breasts, the little girl let out a whimper of sympathy.

The prince's head whipped round. Before she could move he had flung open the door to the bedchamber, grabbed her small arm, and pulled her violently to the middle of the salon. He drew a knife, madness in his eyes, and made ready to cut the girl's throat.

A crash of splintered wood, and the door to the upper hall burst open. In the opening stood the foreign duke, a short sword in his hand. He took two long strides and held the blade at his brother's throat. No words were exchanged, though the thunderous tension between the brothers filled the salon. Finally the prince shrugged, smirked at his younger brother, and left the room.

That evening, as she walked with her mother through the lower hall, the girl sensed a movement behind them. She turned.

There, in a doorway, with his grey, fish-like eyes, stood the prince. His arms were crossed over his doublet, pointed with the same lions and flowers depicted on his shield. His eyes took in her mother's form, surveyed the bruised and battered flesh he had ravaged. Then he looked at the girl. She gave him her cruellest glare, surprising herself with her childish defiance, and on his face she saw it: a flinch, a smear of utter shame at what he had done.

She felt a dark and secret thrill. For all his brutality, she recognized in that moment, for all his shows of strength, what defines this man above all is his weakness.

A weakness I shall never show.

TWENTY-TWO

The Guildhall, Ward of Cheap

The gentleman the clerks called Gower had departed the Guildhall a while before. Edgar Rykener wondered whether he, too, should put his head in the doorway and ask them for assistance. But he'd overheard that James Tewburn wasn't about, so he gave his name to one of the other clerks and returned to the bench. The wall's dark stone cooled his blood, easing him into an upright slumber untroubled for once by thoughts of all that pressed him: that mess with Bickle the beadle, the dead girl on the Moorfields, his worry about Gerald, the missing Agnes.

He was deep in a dream when a hand on his shoulder shook him gently. 'Edgar? Edgar Rykener? You are here to see me?'

'Ye—yes,' he stammered, waking to the sight of James Tewburn. The clerk's threadbare coat was cinched too tightly, giving his thin fingers no quarter as he kneaded the chapped skin at his neck. His eyes shifted about, darting from Edgar's face to the chamber door. 'As I was in the precincts of the Guildhall, I thought—'

'Right, yes yes, of course,' said Tewburn.

Edgar glanced up and down the passage between the buildings. The bench had emptied during his slumber, though voices floated from the structures on either side.

'Master Strode's chambers are in heavy use today,' the clerk continued. 'Let's find a more suitable spot.' He led them in a circuitous path around several more buildings to a remote corner of Guildhall Yard, obscured from view by a high privet hedge. Had Tewburn recognized him this time? Edgar wondered.

'Here,' Tewburn said. There was a short stone bench slightly apart from the wall. The clerk sat forward with his elbows on his knees. 'There have been some, ah, difficulties in the matter of your brother's wardship,' he rasped.

'Difficulties?' Edgar said with alarm. 'Is Gerald well? Is he safe?'

'I believe so,' he said, though Edgar could hear the doubt in his voice. 'His master knows nothing about the transfer, and he won't know until the day it's to take effect. Our common serjeant is scrupulous.'

'I see,' Edgar said weakly. 'And what's caused these difficulties?'

Tewburn shrugged. 'London and Southwark are discrete cities, with distinct laws, distinct manors, distinct courts. Master Strode has no jurisdiction on the far bank, and though his arm is long, there are limits to the speed and force with which even he can negotiate with his counterparts there. In Southwark he's nothing.'

'But what—'

'We must find an accommodating judge in the Southwark manor court wielding jurisdiction over Grimes's shop. And even to determine in whose authority Cutter Lane lies presents a considerable difficulty. The lane runs along the boundary between two Southwark boroughs, dividing them as prettily as Pythagoras himself could bisect a circle.'

The flood of details overwhelmed Edgar, for what did he

know of borough courts and jurisdictions, of bisected circles and Pythagoras? What he did know was that Gerald needed to be moved out of Nathan Grimes's shop, and moved soon.

He also suspected there was something Tewburn wasn't telling him. The clerk's voice was stiff, too proper even for a Guildhall man. For Edgar knew Tewburn, in that way he knew his most frequent jakes: knew his voice and his manner, the way he responded to certain gestures and inflections. 'When will you know more, Master Tewburn?'

'We should receive official word by Monday, I'm told, Tuesday at the latest, and we fully expect a resolution—'

'James,' Edgar said, his voice soft but severe.

Tewburn stopped, then turned slowly, his eyes widening with recognition and desire. Tewburn knew that tone, asked for it every time.

'I – how—'

'James,' he said again. 'If you have something to tell me, tell it now, or there won't be much of this in your future.' He took Tewburn's hand and put it on his breeches.

The clerk's face reddened, his tongue flicked his upper lip, then he sprang to his feet.

'What is it, James?'

He put a hand to his eyes. 'Ah, hell with it all.' He gazed through the privet, making sure they were not being observed, then blew out a long breath. 'The truth is your brother's mixed up with some foul men. The butchers seem to control that whole manor over there. They've paid off the judges, the bailiff, the prior for all I can tell. They're a hard bunch, waylaying cattle and sheep before they're driven to market, scaring off the inspectors. No one knows who's in charge, and whenever I push for an answer on who has the authority to approve the transfer I get a spin on somebody's finger.'

Edgar considered telling the clerk what he knew but decided against it. Too risky. No reason to muddy the waters with all

Gerald's talk of treason, which could interfere with the transfer of wardship. 'Anything else?' he asked.

Tewburn shrugged. 'I'll know more in a few days, after I've met with one of the Guildable justices. It looks to me like Gerald's kept himself clean, but Grimes is thick in it. I'll have it sorted by Monday. We can talk then.'

'Here?'

'Better that I come find you. Our usual place?' Tewburn took the sacrament most often in the north churchyard at St Pancras, a disused and overgrown spot of land lying between Gropecunt Lane and Popkirtle Lane and running nearly up to Cheapside. The newer yard to the west of the church was now the parish's burial plot, so the maudlyns tended to use the older one with certain jakes who were uncomfortable coupling in the horsestalls.

Edgar nodded and stood. 'Monday, then, just after the Angelus bell.'

Tewburn peered through the privet, then back at Edgar, going to his knees with a questioning glance. Edgar allowed him to reach up and unlace his breeches. The clerk was eager, and within the short whiles of three paternosters, said in his mind while he was sucked by Strode's clerk, his seed was in Tewburn's mouth, Tewburn on his feet, and they were winding back through the mayor's outbuildings. Edgar refused his offer of a groat. This one, he told the clerk with a grateful smile, is on my tally.

As he left Guildhall Yard Edgar pondered the troubling encounter. Whatever Tewburn had learned across the river about Grimes and his gang of butchers couldn't be good for Gerald. He shuffled along Cheapside back to Gropecunt Lane, his gloom returning. Perhaps Master Strode, for all his might and goodness, wouldn't be able to help after all.

No surprise there. Tewburn, after all, worked for the City of London, and Strode worked for the City of London, and

Bickle the beadle worked for the City of London – yet the City of London, Edgar Rykener thought with a grim sense of his own place in this hateful town, most surely did not work for him.

TWENTY-THREE

St Mary Overey, Southwark

Distraction, deception, subterfuge, mendacity, all those unspoken tools of the subtler crafts: government and trade, diplomacy and finance. For someone in my line of work these are tools ready to hand, and I wield them with an implicit confidence in my own mastery of any given transaction. Only rarely are they used against me, and when they are I generally recognize them before any harm is done.

But not always.

'You could write an algorism for it,' said my son.

'What is an algorism?'

Simon looked at me almost pityingly. 'A procedure for calculating something. Put an equation together with a few rules and you have an algorism. Named for al-Khwarizmi, one of the great mathematicians of Araby.'

'Oh.'

'The metre of a poem is a measurable quantity,' he went on.

'Right,' I said.

'Whenever you choose a word or a combination of words in putting together a line, you're also choosing numbers. Any given elegiac couplet contains six feet, then five feet, with a finite variation in syllable count across the couplet.'

'Finite. Like my patience.'

Simon laughed, though I could tell he would not give it up. It was the day before the St George's morrow feast out at Windsor, and we were eating a sparse midday meal together in the hall. Onion soup, drawn beans, a loaf of wastel, and a tart with an orange conserve that Simon had purchased at a spicerer's on Bridge Street. An extravagance, I thought, but he intended it as a small gesture of gratitude; I decided to take it in that spirit. We had discussed his new employment with the chancellor, and he had just been asking me about my latest writing. I had complained about the drudgery of elegiacs. He was responding with this arcane defence of poetic metre.

'An algorism would allow you to calculate rate of change in the metre, whatever sort you're employing.'

'But what would this information give you?'

'A glimpse of the poet's mind as he writes. How often does Cato craft an irregular line? With what frequency does a poet writing in elegiac couplets choose a spondee as opposed to a dactyl as the first foot of the hexameter?'

'Again, though—'

'You could do it with chronicles, too, starting with very simple calculations. What's the most frequently used dactylic word in Vergil? *Numine*? *Volvere*? *Omnibus*?'

'So one could tell a lot about a poet's taste in images, say.'

'Exactly. Or whether there's less metrical or syntactical variety toward the end of a work.'

'Suggesting what?'

'That the poet grew lazy the closer he got to the end?'

I looked at him, sensing a subtle shift in tone. 'I take it you had lots of time for this sort of thing in Italy.'

He shrugged. 'It's how my mind operates, I suppose. At the

moment I'm working through a similar sort of puzzle for the chancellor's secretary.'

'Oh?' Simon's appointment with de la Pole's office had gone well, and the chancellor had given him some materials with which to assay his skills.

'He asked me to prove my accounting skills on an old audit book.' He rubbed a palm over the worn leathern cover of a small booklet. 'Reconcile this sum, justify that expense, and all of it's written in the most crabbed hand you can imagine, with these unique abbreviations I have never seen before. It's like a code. Quite a mess, though I've almost got it cracked.'

He went on for a while in this vein, and as I watched him eat his tart I wondered at this strange combination of genius and whimsy that defined so much of his person. Simon had killed a man, and his history of counterfeiting spoke to a capacity for deception that could still give me chills. Yet as Chaucer had once pressed me to recognize, the death was unintentional, an accident, and Simon had clearly been changed for the better by his two years in Hawkwood's service. Gone was the arrogant self-confidence, the defiant puerility. In this new role as the dutiful son, he was capable of helping me to forget, even for a few hours, the subject of Chaucer's murderous book.

The respite ended abruptly when Will Cooper came in with a small bundle under his arm. 'A delivery from the Guildhall, Master Gower. Compliments of the common serjeant, the Honourable Ralph Strode.'

'Ah, the Angervyle.' Remembering Strode's promise, I eagerly untied the rope thongs binding the cloth around the volume and started to browse.

'What is it?' Simon asked, craning his neck.

I hesitated, unsure how much to say. 'It's a book about loving books, I suppose. The *Philobiblon*, by Richard Angervyle of Bury, who was once the king's envoy to the papal curia in Avignon.'

We spent the next several hours in the solar, Simon sprawled in the south oriel overlooking the priory garden, I seated on a broad-backed chair along the northwest corner absorbing Angervyle's bracing account. Written in Latin prose of an easy gait, the *Philobiblon* began with several straightforward chapters on the affection due to books, the wisdom they contain, their considerable cost. 'No dearness of price ought to hinder a man from the buying of books,' Angervyle wrote, 'if he has the money that is demanded for them.'

Angervyle possessed a strong sense of history, citing examples of renowned book-buyers from the past, including Plato and Aristotle, as well as some negative *exempla* of those who spurned their volumes. There was also a long discussion of the treatment and storage of the bishop's own books. Dripping noses, filthy fingernails, pressed flowers, cups of wine brought too near the precious folios: all of these represented destructive forces to the volumes in his collection, which he sought to preserve and protect against the ravages of their many potential abusers. To this end, he wrote, his plan was to endow a hall of books at Oxford, a chamber that would lend out his collection, rendering it a great public good to the entire Oxford community. 'The treasures of our books,' he wrote, 'should be available to all.'

Eventually I came to a chapter containing stories about certain notorious haters of books. I read it, then read it again, associating Angervyle's story with the events of the last several weeks: prophecies, threats, the burning of books.

An old woman came to Tarquin the Proud, the seventh king of Rome, offering to sell nine books of prophecy. But she asked an immense sum for them, so much that the king said she was mad. In anger she flung three books into the fire, and still asked the same sum for the rest. When the king refused, again she flung three others into the fire and still asked the same price for the three that were left. At

*last, astonished beyond measure, Tarquin paid for three
books the same price for which he might have bought nine.
The old woman disappeared, and was never seen again.*

My thoughts raced. The story of Tarquin spoke directly to
Angervyle's interest in books of prophecy, and his acute
awareness of the value of such volumes even to kings. Could
one of his own books have contained the prophetic work of
Lollius, this manuscript it seemed everyone in England was
seeking – this work that had already led to a young woman's
violent death? Despite my conviction that the *De Mortibus*
must be a forgery, the cryptic mode of Angervyle's treatise
was giving me a taste for the hunt.

'Prophecies, Father?'

I looked up, realizing I had been murmuring. I tend to
translate aloud as I read, an old schoolroom habit, and Simon
had caught a word that tickled his curiosity.

'Just an old Roman tale,' I said.

'Though I'd be happy to hear it, if you wouldn't mind.'

'Well – fine then.' I translated Angervyle's account.

'Fascinating,' said Simon.

'How so?'

'I was just doing a little calculation here, for the chancellor's secretary, on the price of barley during a drought year.'
He tapped the book on his table and set aside the tablet he
had been using for his sums. 'The smaller the supply, the
greater the cost – or so you would think. In fact, though, like
the old sibyl's books in your story there, the price will often
stay constant even when the supply diminishes suddenly. What
do barley and books have in common? Well, if we look at
your typical bill of sale . . .'

And we were on to another exchange about the predictive
virtues of numbers and algorisms, the weak proofs of mere
words. Soon enough I was caught up in it myself, amused by

his serious tone though aware of how much he knew about a subject utterly foreign to his father.

What struck me most about that afternoon, though, was the distracting ease of our conversation, despite following so closely on Simon's unexpected return. I realize now how pathetically grateful I was for his renewed presence in Southwark. I even felt reluctant to depart for Oxford in a few days' time, so warmed was I by his company after those bleak months. My guard was down, the air thick with questions I never thought to ask: what Simon was scratching on his tablet, the nature of the book he held throughout our long hours together, the purpose of all this talk about algorisms and the price of barley.

Surely, I see now, this was Simon's intent. For by the time I returned to reading, the one moment of curiosity he had shown about Angervyle's book was entirely forgotten.

TWENTY-FOUR

Watelyng Street, Cordwainer Ward

Eleanor spent the afternoon preceding her rendezvous with Tewburn away from Gropecunt Lane, taking it from a wealthy merchant down from Coventry. Joan Rugg had sent her to the man's inn at half-Sext, and by Vespertime her tongue, her lips, her arse, even her cock ached from a day of hard use. She needed cider, and she needed it cursed soon or she might's well nail herself to the side of the stable and let every freeman of London have his turn with her corpse. She shed her dress and pulled on her breeches. It was that sort of a day.

The Painted Lion off Watelyng Street was fairly packed at that hour; seemed half the workingmen of London lined its benches, calling for ale. Edgar was able to nudge himself a space on the broad hearth, where he sipped contentedly and watched the crowd.

The talk was all of labour statutes and poll taxes. He heard names and titles he recognized, all spoken in contempt. The Duke of Lancaster, the Earl of Oxford, the Duke of Dung and let him rot in his privy.

My brother Joseph, farms out Suffolk way for Sir Rillardain. What he tells me, the pollers are counting his very children.

192

Twelve groats per to the royal coffers, if you please, and not a penny left for bread.

Where's the injustice in that, hey? Suppose if you be the mighty Duke of Lancaster you need gold to pave the steps of your new palace, the Savoy being torched and all.

Can't have our dukes goin' penniless now, can we?

Nor our good king.

Where'd our England be without the king has enough gilded hawks to hunt Waltham Forest?

And enough of our blood to spill for the sodden fields of France?

But thank St Lazarus we got the Parliament to sort it for us.

Got me there. A blessed shining lot of common profit for the nonce.

A handsome statute it was, too, the poll tax. Makes a fleet of good common sense.

Your married pardoner paying twelve shill, your Mayor of Chester paying forty and six, your widowed second cousin of the third son of the alderman's clerk-in-chief of Bridge Ward paying three shill four – why, what could be simpler than them sums to figure up in the Ex-cheker?

Edgar laughed along with them, raising his jar to the Prickling Pickled Pricks of the Poll Tax, though the men's words went right around and over his muddled head. The workings of Westminster and the Exchequer were a fathomless mystery to Edgar; no reason to start plumbing them now. For a while longer he sat with the labourers, listening to the discontented talk of tax and toll, of collections and conscriptions, until he reckoned it was time.

The Angelus bell had already sounded from St Martin le Grand by the time he turned up Soper Lane toward St Pancras. The ward watch generally left the maudlyns and their jakes alone after curfew, though he didn't want to risk further delay. He angled on to Popkirtle Lane, avoiding Joan's crew and the prying eyes of the bawd, then went through a narrow gap between storefronts and over the low wall.

Beneath a waxing moon the St Pancras churchyard could assume an unearthly cast, as if the bodies below its soil were reaching up for the ankles of those who passed above them. Long grasses whisked at his hose. Under his shoes he could feel forgotten graves, and there was a faint musky smell carried on the churchyard air. When he reached the meeting place he stopped and leaned on a tilted slab, a stone rectangle that served well for coupling. No sign of Tewburn yet. It was a peaceful night in the parish. The gentle breeze was cool on his face and a blanket of quiet settled among these stones.

Too quiet. Normally at night, until hours after the curfew bell, the churchyard would hum with the giggles and groans of maudlyns at their labour, with catcalls from the two whoring lanes to east and west as jakes wandered their length. Even on slow nights the ladies would fill the air with a low chatter that could easily be heard in this grassy space behind St Pancras. That night Edgar heard nothing.

A rustle in the grass, low and to the right. He turned and backed away, heart pounding. Only a bird, picking at something – a carrion bird, at its foul work. It gave him an ugly look as he stepped toward it. He stamped the ground. The scavenger flew sluggishly away.

Edgar moved forward several feet, then retched in the high grass. He turned back and looked. Before him lay the ruined body of James Tewburn. His head had been half-severed from his neck, now a gaping valley of torn skin and blackened flesh. The skin above, pale under the quarter moon, was a ghoulish lantern, glowing brightly among the looming stones. One of clerk's eyes was already gone, the bird's easiest meal.

Squatting in the grass Edgar closed his eyes again and said a prayer. After a careful look around he stood and crept between the stones to a gap in the western wall, thinking only of reaching the safe company of his fellow maudlyns. A few more steps brought him out to Gropecunt Lane.

He shrank back with a gasp, now understanding the silence. The narrow street was abandoned, as if Joan Rugg's sturdy gaggle of maudlyns had simply fled. Doors sat askew, their hinges broken apart. A pendant-lamp lay on the pavers, its glass shattered, the frame bent. No candlelight from the stalls or beneath the eaves.

Edgar huddled against the corner of a horse barn. Sure, the mauds got their share of grief from the authorities. Once a season or so the alderman might send his men down to make a few arrests, usually at the behest of an abbot or prior. Curfew violations were a way of life, though every once in a great while there would be some trouble about it.

Yet this was more than the typical hassle from the constables. The maudlyns were simply gone. Vanished, like Agnes Fonteyn, and now James Tewburn was dead in the churchyard.

From the darkest shadows to Edgar's left a figure stole out on to the narrow lane. From his belt he pulled a short sword, the blade glistening in the moonlight. Edgar quickly calculated the distance between them. He looked over his shoulder at the churchyard. Back at the man. The stranger paced slowly forward, peering beneath the eaves.

Then, from the top of the lane, a flash from a torch. Night watchers, patrolling the ward. 'You there!' one of them shouted, seeing the man in the lane.

For a moment it looked as if the intruder would turn and run, but he decided against it, clearly not wanting the entire parish after him. If he was Tewburn's killer, Edgar thought, flight would cast immediate suspicion on him once the body was found. He discreetly sheathed his blade and approached the watchers, his hands raised. 'Just out for a bit of queynt, good fellows. Where are all the mauds?' A gentleman's voice.

The first walker clucked his tongue. 'Not here, that's sure. Popkirtle Lane and Gropecunt Lane both. Busted up earlier today, sluts hauled away, and who knows when they'll be back.'

'How unfortunate,' said the man.

'Aye,' agreed the first walker with a rough laugh.

There was a pause. 'Sir Stephen, if I'm not mistaken?' said the second.

'The very same,' said the man, his voice taut with the recognition. Edgar heard the jangle of coins as the man prepared to pay off the walkers for their poor memories.

As the chatter continued Edgar edged backwards, away from the arc of lamplight, until he was at the end of the alley leading back to the churchyard. He took a final glance at the trio on Gropecunt Lane. At one point the stranger shook his head with a laugh, and it was then Edgar saw it.

A hook on his chin, a whitened scar. And a face he would remember. *Sir Stephen*. Edgar turned and made for the wall.

TWENTY-FIVE

The palace of Windsor

On the evening following the Feast of St George the palace
was lit like a box of polished jewels, the guests just as gaudy.
Simon and I had arrived from Southwark late that afternoon
and were staying at the mill inn by Windsor Bridge, and had
joined the crowd streaming through the west gate. The secretive St George's festivities on the eve and the feast day itself
had been restricted to the twenty-four knights and twenty-odd
ladies of the Order of the Garter, as custom dictated. Over
the last four years, though, and at King Richard's initiative,
an additional, much larger feast had been thrown on the
morrow, largely to show off the extensive renovations at
Windsor. Each of the Order's lords and ladies was permitted
ten guests for the closing feast, though the size of the crowd
indicated that the figure had been interpreted rather loosely.

That year and the last I had been the guest of Sir Lewis
Clifford, a Knight of the Garter who had happily approved
the addition of Simon to his list. Next to Gaunt himself,
Clifford was perhaps Chaucer's greatest supporter in these
high circles, a friend to poets of diverse quality and fortune,
and it was Geoffrey who had introduced us years before

during my time at the Temple. Clifford and I had an interesting history: a missing shipment of Lyonnaise silk, a discovered bribe, a quiet conversation about one of his crooked associates. In gratitude he became my entrée to these circles, a trusted source when I needed him, and a fount of unending courtesy when I did not. When we entered the great cloister I saw him near the grange, speaking to Nicholas Brembre, Mayor of London and one of numerous royal and civic officials present at the annual gathering.

'A stew of bureaucrats and secretaries,' I mused to Simon.

'Generously spiced with aristocrats,' he said quietly.

The Windsor steward had opened up the tower at the top of the Spicery Gatehouse to the guests, who moved up and down the stairs as sconced torches lit the darkening sky. The tower commanded a vast panorama of the surrounding countryside, which was settling into dusk. Outside the walls and far below, the commons were already ankle-deep in mud, enjoying the order's bounty: casks of ale, spiced cider, roasted mutton by the score. The lower tables stretched into the night, the nearby hamlets and villages emptied of their residents as the king purchased their goodwill toward himself and the Garter. We descended to the hall for Richard's entrance. Despite the deepening factionalism in the realm, for these few days the cream of English chivalry was to set aside its squabbles and resentments and unite for a festival of prayer, unity, and reconciliation. A charade, of course, though always a useful one.

'Why are you smiling, John Gower?' Katherine Swynford, sidling up as Simon wandered off. She wore an uncharacteristically modest dress, a taffeta of deep purple cut just below her neck, an arched and almost coif-like hood covering all but the frontmost span of her hair. With her stood Philippa Chaucer, also dressed down, though where Swynford wore modesty as a peasant wears ermine, on Philippa this understated attire looked natural. Chaucer's wife had a prominent chin below a pleasant, honest face, and eyes that sparkled with a wit whose quickness she shared with her sister. 'Plotting some nasty satire, I suppose?'

I bowed to the sisters. 'Simply admiring the royal view, my lady, and appreciating the feel of the royal stone beneath my humble feet.'

Swynford tightened her lips and dismissed me, looking around for someone more important. Not difficult at Windsor. Everyone knew that Gaunt's mistress aspired to the Order, and these occasions gave her the opportunity to win favour with the knights in hopes of getting her name put before the king once Lancaster was in a position again to ask for royal favours. Swynford's attention was on the terrace doors and the duke's coming entrance. She stood several feet in front of us, showing no interest in our talk.

'You are looking well, John,' said Philippa, her soft voice patterning a warm familiarity.

I inclined my head. 'Nice to see you down from Lincolnshire, Philippa.'

'Have you heard from Simon? How is he faring?'

I was used to hearing this question from Chaucer's wife, who had no knowledge of my son's dark past. 'Why don't you ask him yourself?'

She looked surprised. 'Simon is back in England?'

'Right there, talking with Ralph Strode.' I nodded at him, standing nearby with the common serjeant. 'Geoffrey hasn't mentioned it to you? Perhaps he hasn't heard either.'

'The things Geoffrey Chaucer fails to mention to his wife would fill an ocean.' She did not say it bitterly, though her eyes hinted at her sadness. Over the last two years Philippa had been spending more and more of her time at Kettlethorpe Hall with her sister rather than in London with her husband. 'But I'm glad to hear you are reunited with your son, especially now.'

'Thank you, Philippa.'

'Has he brought a wife back from the south?'

I hesitated. 'Actually he had been betrothed. The young woman died. Fever.'

Philippa put a hand to her neck. 'And Simon so young!'

'Though I must say, she seems to have changed him for the better.'

'What was her name, the poor dear?'

'Seguina. Seguina d'Orange.'

As if a keg of powder had exploded behind her, Katherine Swynford's nose traced a swift arc through the air until she faced me, her torso twisted in the effort. She glanced at Philippa, then our eyes locked, and for an instant hers scorched me, a loss of composure so uncharacteristic of the Swynford I knew it left me breathless. Her gaze lingered another instant, then, recovered, she spun from me and walked toward the gate.

I turned to Philippa, who also looked unaccountably troubled. 'Seguina d'Orange. What does that name signify to you and your sis—'

The trumpets sounded, and my question faded into the loud stir from the gates. Heralds stepped forth first, announcing the royal entry into the king's cloister, eight trumpets blaring as the king and his queen, the duke and his duchess moved out among the kneeling crowd. The company fell into two double-deep ranks. I joined the second, all eyes on the young man whose life seemed so delicate as his subjects pressed around him. The king's fair skin set off the feeble beard. His robes were pounced with heraldry, white harts in chase around his shoulders and waist. The queen, a tiny scrap of a woman who rarely spoke, wore a gown trimmed in a sable-silk brocade that she fingered absently as she paced.

King Richard walked slowly across the room, pausing before every third or fourth visitor to speak a few words. Lancaster and the duchess followed, the duke's mouth fixed in a tight frown.

Behind them walked a large company of magnates, the

200

most important among them the earls, including Thomas of Woodstock, Earl of Buckingham and Gaunt's younger brother, and the Earl of Oxford with his burgeoning entourage, including Sir Stephen Weldon. Other knights of the king's affinity followed – Philip la Vache, Nicholas Dagworth, John Clanvowe, Richard Abberbury, and Simon de Burley, all jostling for position in the press of bodies, cloth, livery, and banners as the throng slowly moved through the fawning crowd of lower gentry.

The last man out, appearing as the lines were already disintegrating, was Chaucer. He walked alone, his gaze on the spectacle before him bemused and authorial. Spying me with his wife, he raised his chin and approached.

'Philippa,' he said.

'Geoffrey,' she said, and walked away. Chaucer looked after her, resigned rather than offended.

'The height of courtesy, as always,' I said, his cruelty at the customhouse still on my mind. 'What gives you licence to treat her like that?'

The skin around Chaucer's eyes creased. 'There's a fine line between licence and licentiousness, John. I've crossed it more than most: to the stews of Rose Alley, to Gropecunt Lane and back again, mistresses taken with her full knowledge.' He looked away, a hint of regret in his stooped shoulders. 'Philippa thinks our marriage is a pageant, nothing more. Since that Cecily Chaumpaigne mess she won't let me touch her.'

Chaucer's notorious troubles with women had sparked more than one unfortunate episode over the years, including a disturbing accusation of abduction and rape some time ago. The young woman, a baker's daughter, had officially released him from the initial charge before things got too serious. I was away from London that season and had never learned the truth of the matter, though I had seen what he was capable of in other contexts and had long wondered whether the accusation were true.

'Candour suits you, Geoffrey,' I said. 'Though you could have shown more of it earlier in your marriage.'

'Perhaps,' he conceded. 'But then, candour goes only so far, don't you think? There must also be love.' A shadow passed over his face, a hint of longing or regret in that sad smile. 'Ah,' he said, tripping past the admission, 'and here is Weldon. What about *your* many loves, Sir Stephen?'

'Too numerous to count, and always more in line.' Weldon's scar was at full jut. Ignoring me, he gave Chaucer a pointed look. 'I need a word.'

'You may have a dozen or so,' said Chaucer. He turned to me. 'If you will excuse us, John, a customs officer's duty is to his dutifulness. Oh –' he stopped, his voice measured as Weldon strolled ahead – 'and that surely wasn't Simon I saw just now, having a chat with Ralph Strode?'

'It was,' I said, with a hint of defensiveness.

'I thought so.' He looked at me strangely, then turned away and strolled with Weldon toward the palace. I watched them recede into the crowd, then went to look for Simon. It took a while to find him, and by the time I did the bell had sounded for the feast.

As the ladies separated for the lesser hall, we retired into the St George's range, a space of opulent magnificence that seemed to be trying too hard to awe those who entered. There were a few courteous words from the king, a prayer from the arch-bishop, then the chatter resumed. Simon sat to my left, and to his left was Thomas Pinchbeak, who peppered both of us with news from Westminster and the Inns as we made our way through a roast piglet, the crackled skin slipping easily from the tender flesh. Chaucer was seated at the next table. I felt for the queen and the duchess, the only women remaining in the great chamber. They ate in gloomy silence next to their husbands on the dais. They never spoke to one another as far as I could see.

The extravagance of food and plate was distracting, and it was not until much later, with the serving of cakes, sweet wafers, and a spring pudding as minstrels and players filled the front of the hall, that I thought again of the book. It was Pinchbeak who did it, leaning before Simon to ask me the most peculiar question.

'And the blood, Gower?'

'Pardon?' I said, assuming I had misheard him. Simon was sitting back, trying not to interfere with our exchange.

'The blood, on the robes.'

I stared into Pinchbeak's eyes as the words of the coroner's inquest came back to me: *said woman was beaten in the face and struck on the head and bloodied, feloniously murdered by an unknown assailant.* 'What about it?'

'Your son and I were debating the point. Are they using wine for the blood, do you suppose?' He nodded toward the front of the hall. I turned my head and realized Pinchbeak was referring to the pageant playing out before the dais. A play of St George and the Dragon, with one boy taking the part of the sacrificial virgin and four others bearing the painted beast on their shoulders. Two robed youths, bloodied, dead, trying not to wriggle, lay sprawled on the floor before the dragon.

My pulse slowed. 'Beet juice, I'd guess.' Pinchbeak gave me a vague smile, then turned to the man on his other side with a comment about the cakes.

'Too dark to be sheep's blood,' Simon mused.

It all came back then – the book, the murder, the play at Temple Hall, broken up by Pinchbeak and his fellow serjeants. As I looked around at the babbling guests I wondered how many of them knew of the *De Mortibus*, of the alleged French spy murdered in the Moorfields, of the king's prophesied death. The exchange reminded me to visit the coroner's chambers to have another word with Nicholas Symkok, who had acted so dodgy with me. I wouldn't have time before my Oxford trip, though it would be at the top of my list upon my return.

After Richard's departure the crowd started to thin. Lancaster remained on the dais, enjoying the attention, though the duchess excused herself, as did several of her attendants. Swynford entered with a small clutch of other ladies. The doors to the lower stairs were propped open; guests began to drink more seriously, many filtering out to the yards; and a pleasant evening cool descended on the hundreds still remaining.

I wandered among them, speaking to acquaintances, until I came upon Sir John Clanvowe, a knight of Richard's chamber and a poet of modest accomplishment. He stood with Sir Lewis Clifford, our host for the evening, before the entrance to the Spicery stairs.

'I understand you'll be travelling to Oxford?' Clanvowe asked me. The knight's loose cotte, dyed a simple grey, bunched around the belt girding his waist. Of my height and age but a wiry stick of a knight, Clanvowe was like an eager bird, his head moving in small, distracting jerks at each phrase. His voice was high and sing-songish, falling at the end of every sentence like a crow's fading caw.

'I am, John,' I said without the honorific, as Clanvowe preferred. 'I leave at dawn, and Simon will be going back to Southwark.'

'You know, I will be in Oxford by Wednesday or Thursday,' Clanvowe said. 'Travelling with Clifford here, who's taking up the constableship at Cardigan. I'm on my way back to Hereford for the summer. Perhaps you'll let me feed you one evening while you're in town?'

'I'd be delighted,' I said, meaning it, for I had always felt a companionable warmth toward Clanvowe, a man of real wisdom who was never his best at court. We parted with a promise of supper the following week in Clanvowe's rooms at the Queen's College, and I thanked Sir Lewis again for his hospitality in inviting us to the great occasion.

Growing tired, I started to search out Simon, wandering past a canopy festooned with gay flags and branches of flowered crepe. Beneath it, in the glassy light of four hanging lamps, Katherine Swynford sat at a low marble table, laying out her

204

cards. Her opponent in the game was Sir Stephen Weldon. A crowd had gathered around their table to watch, and there was much murmuring about the beauty of the cards. I recalled the rules of the game Swynford had taught me, though this one was different.

Swynford laid down four cards. I leaned in to see which they were: the Two of Thistles, the Eight of Swords, and the Four and Duke of Hawks. Weldon countered her move with a trump card, the Wheel of Fortune, which Swynford took with the King of Thistles. Weldon's next play was the Prince of Plums.

I stared at the card, my vision starring.

The Prince of Plums.

I went cold, nearly breathless with the realization. As the game continued lines of verse burned through my mind, the letters searing my memory like a hot coal on skin.

> *With seven of swords to swing at their will . . .*
> *At sovereign of swords in death swoon he must . . .*

Seven of Swords. Sovereign of Swords. Three of Thistles. The strange phrases from the prophecies referred not to arcane symbols or figures of allegory, but to the suits of the playing cards of the sort dealt by Katherine Swynford.

The faces of the guests gathered around the card table took on a sinister cast. In the front rank stood Robert de Vere, the earl's mouth set in a bemused grin at the sight of his knight losing badly to Lancaster's concubine. Behind him loomed the imposing bulk of Ralph Strode, taking in the game with a slight frown as Thomas Pinchbeak watched over his shoulder, bent forward like a raven at a fresh corpse. Beside him Sir Michael de la Pole, the chancellor, cold in the April evening, arms wrapping his frame. A dozen others surrounded the pair, all transfixed by this unfamiliar game: the cards from Tuscany, the strategies from Lombardy, yet the players wholly English in their allegiances.

I imagined myself watching them from above, these lords,

205

magnates, diverse bearers of the nation's fortune. Had anyone else with knowledge of the *De Mortibus* made the association with the cards? Or was this my knowledge alone, shared only with those plotting against the king? And, I now wondered, was Katherine Swynford one of them?

'Not if I can help it, *damn* it all to hell, and now with all the rest . . .' A familiar voice, raised and angry, had barked from the cluster of shrubs at the range-end before fading into a loud whisper. Heads turned.

Chaucer, his features twisted in anger, strode past me without a look. At the sight of the lofty crowd beneath the canopy he recovered himself and affected a tired smile. He bowed to the assembled company, then without a word shot through the gateyard postern. I turned back to see Simon slinking away from the foot of the range. The light was such that no one else in the vicinity seemed to note my son as the target of Chaucer's wrath.

Later, as we left the palace grounds and rode to the mill inn with a small company of other guests, I struggled for words. I suspected I knew the source of the dispute but wanted to make sure.

'Simon,' I eventually said, my voice low. At my initiative we were riding last in the group and wouldn't be overheard.

'Yes, Father?'

'You had words with Chaucer.'

'I did.'

An owl hooted somewhere behind us.

'We talked about Hawkwood, and my homecoming,' said Simon. 'Chaucer had – Chaucer *has* warm feelings regarding my decision to return to England.'

'What feelings?'

'Hawkwood—' He let out a breath, his head angled skyward. 'Chaucer feels I haven't acted in good faith toward the White Company. That I've made him look terrible in Hawkwood's eyes.'

'Ah,' I said, my suspicions confirmed.

'Chaucer said it wasn't easy to set me up in Hawkwood's service after – after what happened,' he said, stumbling. 'Said he had to call in quite a large favour with Sir John in order to obtain a position for me. And that my unexpected return to England suggests that I haven't shown the trustworthiness he would expect. That it smacks of youthful indecision, as he put it.'

'He has a point,' I said wryly. 'Rather a strong one.'

'I suppose he does,' said Simon. 'But I was truthful with Hawkwood about the reason for my departure. He told me he would be happy to accept me into his service again if I return.' He turned to me. 'Have I acted in bad faith?'

I thought for a moment, pleased by this unexpected request for fatherly wisdom. 'Not toward Hawkwood, at least. You have given him two years of good service, and he's invited you to return. But you *have* acted in bad faith toward Chaucer. The courteous thing would have been to write him in advance, informing him of your decision to return. Seeing you at Windsor while thinking you were still in Italy? That must have been quite a shock.'

He nodded. 'I see that. But what can I do to make it up to him?'

We had reached the courtyard door and now stood in the road. The other palace guests were handing off their horses to the stabler and his boy. 'If I know Chaucer, it should be a simple matter. A letter. Doesn't need to be long. Short and sincere. Once he reads it he'll forget the whole thing.'

'Let's hope so,' said Simon, holding the heavy door.

Simon slept deeply the first part of that night, snoring on his bolster as I thought back through the Garter feast, wondering what I had missed. It had been an evening of tense encounters and interrupted revelations: Swynford's peculiar reaction to the name of Simon's lover, my epiphany about the cards and the prophecies, that ugly spat between Chaucer and Simon. Though I knew more about the prophecies than I had that morning, I felt my ignorance like a bad meal in the stomach. For the first time in my life, it seemed that knowledge, which had always been my privileged coinage, was failing me. There were things I was not being told, knots my mind seemed incapable of unravelling. And always before me the murder on the Moorfields, and the deaths of kings.

It was at some point during the smallest hours when I awoke to the bark of the keeper's talbot in the courtyard. The dog was quickly silenced, and I realized that Simon was no longer in our bed. I sat up, listening intently, and heard a series of low murmurs from below. One of the voices belonged to Simon. The other was too soft to recognize. I could make out nothing of the conversation. I went to the door and opened it a crack.

The hinges threw an angry squeal across the courtyard. The talk ceased abruptly. I crept back to bed and waited until Simon climbed the stairs, then listened as he pissed, loudly, from the upper landing down into the courtyard. He cleared his throat, spat. He entered our chamber quietly and slipped beneath the covers.

'Everything all right?' I whispered.

'Just a trip to the privy. That onion soup . . .'

'Right,' I said, feeling uneasy.

Hours later I awoke with a start, the sound of Simon's piss, and his obvious lie, ringing in my ears.

TWENTY-SIX

Rose Alley, Southwark

Eleanor wedged herself between the barrels, her attention back on the Pricking Bishop's alley door. No sign of Agnes yet, but she'd seen Millicent, airing a blanket out the second-storey window. It was only a matter of time before the sisters would make their move. And when they do, she vowed, I'll make my own.

Out of a larger house along the bankside stepped a rail-thin woman, a basket of laundry in her arms. She set it down on the street side of the gutter. A boy followed her out. They walked together toward the high street, leaving the basket of clothing for a servant to wash. Eleanor glanced up and down the lane. She stepped across and pulled a few garments from the basket. In the far alley, bouncing on her toes to avoid the filth, she shoved first her left foot, then her right down the stolen breeches. The grey doublet fit snugly.

It was not an hour later when Edgar finally got what he'd been waiting for. The Fonteyn sisters, their hoods cinched tight, left the Pricking Bishop and strode with purpose toward the bridge. Despite the welter of affection and relief he felt at seeing Agnes alive and well, Edgar was also newly furious at her, and he was tempted to jump out and confront her right there, though he remained in place. When they had turned he took a deep breath and walked across Rose Alley.

St Cath sat at her usual place. A loud snore shot from the old woman's mouth. He waited for another, then stepped around her and slipped inside.

He stood in a small antechamber, dim with no windows. As his eyes adjusted he heard the choir: soft moans from the room to the left, rhythmic thumps from above. He crept through the lower level to the makeshift bakery. A squat oven, where Bess Waller's crew baked wastel and other breads for illegal sale across the river in London. A cutting block with an upside-down mashing bowl. Two high tables with four stools. The heavy door to the rear yard was bolted shut, though the trapdoor to the undercroft stairs was open. From the space below rose a pale cone of candlelight and two voices.

'Pickled twenty pots and here it be George's week with only two on the shelf?'

'Girls like the leeks and garlic, Bess. Gets the blood up, stiffens the cock.'

'Tell them to ease off a bit.'

'Sure.'

'And you'll see about the cod? Half a barrel gone to rot, and the Bishop out good coin. As to the cider . . .'

Edgar stopped listening as he surveyed the room. He made his way carefully along the walls, peering into the shelves past the crockery, the warmth of the oven on his skin. On a shelf above the hearth rested a small array of pious items: a copper candlestick, a small pewter cross, both of which he pocketed; a wood painting of the Magdalene, which he left. He had nearly circled the room when his foot struck a pan, sending it to clatter across the floor.

'St Cath! That you?' Bess Waller hollered up the cellar stairs.

Edgar held his breath.

'Agnes? Mil, that you, girl?' Bess's bonnet came into view. 'Can't let a damned bawd sort her cellar without a rotting racket, by St Bride.' She looked up. '*You!*' she screeched, legs already pumping.

Edgar bent down to lift the edge of the cellar door. Bess ran up the stairs to beat him to it. He took more than a few splinters in his fingers as the trapdoor rose from the floor. When it passed the midway mark he let go of the heavy board.

Whump. The board slammed down on Bess's hand. A rough scream from the bawd, who slipped her fingers from beneath the weight. Edgar stomped on the board to the pounding of Bess's shoulders and fists from below. He reached for the cutting block and dragged it until it rested halfway over the trapdoor.

The women's cries were muffled now. Given the kitchen's separation from the main house there was little chance those within had heard the commotion. Nor was there a direct street entrance to the cellar, as far as Edgar knew. He had some time. He resumed his look through the shelves, peering into pots and pans, knocking plate and crockery to the floor with an abandon that gave him more angry satisfaction than he'd felt in weeks, since finding that corpse on the Moorfields.

Four grain barrels occupied the final bit of floor space beneath the shelves. He knocked the first barrel to the floor and reached for the next as the brown dust of wheat flour filled the air. Two more barrels, and now millet and barley dust rose in great clouds. The final barrel, quarter full with rough-cut and mouldy oats. He knocked it down, then stood, panting in the bready air. No dust from the oats, but a lot of mess on the floor, take a full day to—

He saw it. A lump beneath the rancid grain. Pushing his dusted hair aside, he bent to the pile and pushed through a few inches of oats. He felt cloth. He grasped a leather thong and pulled, recovering a thin rectangular bundle, wrapped in

211

embroidery. He felt its width and length, pressed his palms on the flat surfaces.

A book.

He stared down at it, scarcely believing his fortune. The girl in the moor, stripped of her clothing, creatures at her flesh; the beadle of Cripplegate, Richard Bickle, his gold-smelling fingers grasping Eleanor's cheek; poor James Tewburn, slain in the churchyard with no one about. And this book, a book Edgar couldn't read to save his soul, yet a treasure worth a lot of killing and coin.

Edgar wiped flour from his eyes. After a last glance around the kitchen, he crept back to the Bishop's front, squeezed on to Rose Alley, and headed for the bridge, the oldest maudlyn in Southwark still snoring in his wake.

TWENTY-SEVEN

Holbourne

Coming up from the Fleet River the sisters slowed, looking across at the imposing façade of Scroope's Inn and the armorial bearings on the windows, the tracery spidering from the central medallions. The inn of the serjeants-at-law was a solid block of stone, framed by two gardens and two small houses but with no front courtyard welcoming visitors. It would have to be entered directly from the street, in open view. Two wagons came from the left, a cart and a few riders from the right, though the wide street was relatively deserted on this sunny day. Millicent took Agnes's arm, crossed to the high door and, no one stopping them or asking a question, pushed against the heavy oaken barrier.

With a deep yawn of old iron, the door yielded, giving way to the cold gloom of a long rectangular chamber. Little light penetrated through from the high windows. Before them on the east wall was painted the figure of a massive robed woman, a cloth binding her eyes, a set of balanced scales hanging from her left hand. IUSTITIA, the Latin inscription above her read. In Scroope's Inn, Millicent mused, justice isn't a pretty painting, for here the law sees everything, and the scales are always tipped.

It could be no mistake that Pinchbeak had directed them to his own domain, the chambers of the serjeants-at-law, the most powerful legal officials in the land. There were fewer than thirty of them, king's appointees all, with their own set of privileges, their own style of robe and coif, their own grand inn up on Holbourne. Sir Humphrey ap-Roger had known several of them, dined with them in this very inn as a guest on occasion, though even he, a knight of ancient lineage, had felt intimidated in the serjeants' company.

Doors off the front hall led out to a central courtyard, where a series of covered staircases on the outer walls rose to two levels of apartments. They reached another chamber, smaller though equally high. In an alcove off the far corner stood three writing desks arranged around an aged clerk, his bent form crammed between them. A mounted arc of candles hung chained from a lower rafter, rendering the man's head, uncapped and bald, as a glowing orb.

He did not look up at their approach. At his desk Millicent said, 'We seek Master Thomas Pinchbeak, sir, serjeant-at-law. Where may we find him, if you please?'

Still without moving his head, the old man replied, 'First back stairs, top level, eastern corner rooms on the south side.' Then he looked up, taking them in with something like terror. He sputtered a bit, shook his head, and gave them a stern frown. Millicent could almost hear his bones creak as he rose. 'Women are not permitted in Scroope's, nor in any of the inns of our art. You must leave at once.'

'But Master Pinchbeak himself summoned us,' said Millicent. 'And here we are.'

'Summoned you, did he?' the man thundered. 'Summoned the pair of you, and not tell old Wilkes? Couldn't be bothered to – not that I – well . . . ahhhh.' His voice weakened and his eyes shot upward, catching the flames. 'Though do I recall something about . . .' He grimaced down at his desk, his hands sorting through the loose sheaves around him. 'Your name?'

214

'Rykener,' said Millicent. 'My name is Eleanor Rykener.'

Agnes gasped. Millicent silenced her with a look.

'Eleanor Rykener, Eleanor Rykener,' the old man intoned, patting around his desk. Millicent heard the clink of coins. He help up a felt purse. 'This is for your troubles, an advance left for you by Master Pinchbeak. The serjeant had an urgent matter at the bench.'

Millicent, torn between frustration and greed, took the purse, opened it, then showed it to Agnes, who reached inside and pulled out a small handful of coins.

'Two marks of silver, that be,' the old man said, 'and not a farthing less. With the balance to be paid upon delivery, says Master Pinchbeak.'

Millicent started to protest. They hadn't brought the book with them, fearing some form of deception on the serjeant-at-law's part. Their plan had been to gauge Pinchbeak's seriousness and see the money before returning to the Pricking Bishop to retrieve the manuscript.

'And this balance, good sir?' Agnes asked in her pleasantest tone. 'Its size?'

He pursed his lips. 'Master Pinchbeak said nothing to me about its size, my pretty. He requests your return tomorrow with the item in question.'

Outside they considered the exchange as they walked back through the walls and toward the bridge. 'Merely an advance, that man said,' said Agnes. 'And tomorrow we'll collect the balance, eh, Mil?'

'So it appears,' said Millicent, though without her sister's optimism. If Pinchbeak truly wanted the book, why would he have left a mere two marks, and why would he have put them off like this? Something about these dealings with the serjeant-at-law didn't sit right, though Millicent couldn't sort it before Agnes started pressing her about the Eleanor Rykener business. Millicent explained, telling her sister about Eleanor's visit to her Cornhull house, then her use of Eleanor's name in her meeting with Pinchbeak at the parvis.

'It just happened, Ag,' she said. 'I couldn't very well use my own, could I? Hers was in my head, and it spilled out when Pinchbeak asked me my name.'

Agnes, visibly furious, said nothing all the way to the bridge, then across to Southwark, with Millicent tagging her heels. On Rose Alley their steps slowed at the sight before them.

A small crowd of maudlyns, spilling on to the lane. The girls, some of them wearing only unlaced shifts, had gathered unexpectedly in the street, while others had dressed themselves in their shabby finery; few heads were covered.

St Cath, arrayed in a faded purple gown and a hood four sizes too great for her shrunken head, sat with a cat on her lap, glowering up the alley. As her daughters approached Bess Waller turned to face them, her arms crossed tightly, her jaw set in anger.

'What is it?' Millicent asked, fearing the worst.

'Thing's gone.'

'What's gone?' Agnes asked. 'What thing?' Millicent asked at the same moment.

'The book,' Bess said. 'Nor will you credit who's robbed us of it.' She told them the details: Eleanor Rykener, all manned up, sneaking by St Cath and appearing in the Bishop's kitchen. The slammed cellar trap. The spilled oats. Finally Bess's release by one of the girls.

Millicent spun on Agnes. 'And it had to be that Eleanor Rykener, didn't it?' she spat, no longer regretting her use of the maudlyn's name with Pinchbeak. 'I hope that swerver hangs for treason.'

Agnes gasped. 'What – how could you—'

'She stole it from us, Ag. Out from under our chins. And with it our only chance at a future.'

The sisters turned away from one another, silent in their mutual fury.

'So there it is, then,' said Bess eventually. 'What's a biddy maud like Eleanor Rykener hope to do with a cursed stack of parchments?'

It was at that moment that St Cath looked up from her trance. Her face shone with the confidence of a prophetess. 'Only one place in London an unlettered maud could hope to sell a book,' she croaked. 'Leastwise in my experience.'

They all looked at her, wondering what strange memory had provoked the old whore's intervention.

'And where's that, St Cath?' Bess Waller asked her with the patience the woman's years deserved.

'Ave Maria Lane,' St Cath went on with a sage nod. 'Hard by St Paul's. Had it off there with a limner and his apprentice upon a time.' Her eyes sparkled with the recollection. 'Or Paternoster Row. That's where I'd look for the tarred slut.'

TWENTY-EIGHT

Broad Street, Oxford

'How much for the copying?'

'Three and two.'

'And the subwarden let you have it for the week?'

'"One of only two copies of Master Albertus in Balliol," he tells me. "Mind it well, young Pelham, mind it well."'

'And you will?'

'I'll keep it chained to my wrist.'

'And basted with your annotations.'

'Basted, roasted, ruminated—'

'And shat on Shitbarn Lane.'

'Into the privy of theology—'

'We call Balliol College.'

The three students erupted in laughter as they walked by, sparing no glance for a robeless Londoner seated on a stone wall. One of them looked a bit like Simon, the same sparkle of wit and ardour in his eyes, brains and charm to burn. They passed beneath the arched gate into Balliol yard.

With a heavy sigh I rose, feeling, as always in Oxford, like the slow third wheel of a swifter cart. Though I had travelled here several times in recent years, I was neither a former

218

student nor, like Ralph Strode, a master, my education having led me to the Temple rather than to Oxford or Cambridge. I knew men who had studied in both towns, Strode among them, and Chaucer always swore I could have been a fine philosopher or logician. But I had admitted to myself years before that certain dimensions of these disciplines were beyond me.

Though what, I wondered as I looked up Broad Street at yet another ruined façade, can come of theology when its greatest home lies in rubble? The town of Oxford seemed to have declined since my last visit into a haven of thieves and whores, stealing and swyving in the empty plots and fallow fields along the London road, keeping company with the hanged. Yet as the keeper of the inn at St Frideswide's had remarked, for every structure being pulled down outside the walls another two were going up on Cornmarket Street. Even the Durham monks had ambitions to expand their manse into a full-fledged college, with its own degreed faculty. As Will Cooper had observed to me on our way along the high street, Oxford was a confused town, it was plain to see: uncertain about its future yet eager to scrape away its pestilential past, caught in that strange land between decay and renewal.

I walked through the outer doors of the Durham *hospitium* as the monks were concluding Tierce. The voice of the abbot dismissed the monks to their work, and outside they broke up into smaller clusters.

One of the last to leave the oratorium was an old man in lay garb. His hose were cut tight around his ankles, tucked into rough boots that wouldn't have looked out of place on a ploughman. He wore a loose jacket of thin brown wool, unbuttoned over a simple shirt dyed a dark red, and from its collar jutted a neck of remarkable length made all the more striking in contrast with its owner's head, which seemed to block the sun as he approached me from across the quadrangle. Though deep crags lined his brow, his skin lay

219

drum-tight against his cheeks, as if pulled by an unseen force somewhere behind his ears.

'Master John Gower?'

'The same.' I half-bowed to the man. 'You are Peter de Quincey?'

'All my life,' was his reply. 'Come to sniff through the bishop's books, have you?' He asked a few other pointed questions, referring to the letter from Strode I had sent around the day before. Apparently satisfied, he led me to a far corner of the outer manse, where a narrow doorway opened to the dormitory passage.

'Bishop Angervyle, Strode tells me, was a great man,' I said to his back.

'The greatest,' said Quincey as he stepped along the narrow passage. 'His lordship served as the king's cofferer, as dean of rolls, as bishop of Durham, even as envoy to Avignon, to say nothing of his station as lord chancellor. A lustrous life.'

'Though I've heard, too,' I said, sensing his eagerness to expand, 'that Angervyle was instrumental in the deposition of the second King Edward. That he was forced to hide out in Paris for a time.'

A secretive smile over his shoulder. 'I will not deny it. He was a man of powerful associations. An adviser and emissary to kings, emperors, and popes. But above all Richard Angervyle was a devoted collector of books. An *amasser* of books, one of unparalleled devotion. You undoubtedly know about the more immense holdings in our realm. Bury St Edmunds, St Albans, the libraries at Winchester and Worcester . . .' We left the grange through a rear door facing on the walls. Fields and orchards beyond, workers toiling in the distance. 'And the great libraries of Christendom: the holdings of King Charles of France, the curial libraries at Rome and Avignon.'

'Yes, of course,' I said, thinking of Chaucer's account of the Visconti collection. Our apparent destination was a small, detached building positioned against the north wall and surrounded by a thick cluster of trees and shrubs. The building's walls formed a hexagon of timber and stone.

'Yet these libraries, while great in number, have no *soul*.' Quincey pulled a long key from its dangle by his waist; it reminded me of Tom Tugg's grotesque key to the Newgate cells, though more finely wrought. There was a click, then, with a reluctant breath, the door swung open on well-oiled hinges.

'Such collections,' Quincey continued as he stepped inside, 'are rich men's baubles, serving the purposes of vanity. Even the most sober monks regard their books as a reflection of their order. These men, Master Gower, collect books as the Duke of Lancaster collects palaces. And bastards.' He gestured for me to enter.

The first thing I noticed about the dark space was the smell: rich, deep, gorgeous. Cardamon, I thought, and cloves and cinnamon – and old parchment, and leather, and boards, and dust. It was overwhelming; I had to step back out for a moment to sneeze. Quincey, meanwhile, had taken a pair of wicksnips from a shelf and busied himself lighting several new candles. Despite the opened door the room was not well lit, the shutters having been nailed fast. Old, rickety-looking shelves lined five of the chamber's six walls. All were empty. Angervyle's books, I assumed, were stored in the many trunks arranged around the room, of varying sizes and laid out like a labyrinth of low walls.

'You'll pardon the spice,' said Quincey. 'An excellent preservative of books.'

Though perhaps not in such quantity, I thought.

'Bishop Angervyle's library was different. Distinctive in every respect. Richard de Bury, you see, collected only those books that matter most to our modern minds.' He rubbed his hands and approached one of the closer chests.

'I've been told that the bishop was quite particular about his selections,' I said. 'No law texts, for example.'

Quincey nodded. 'The bishop had no patience for law, nor even for much theology, and those subjects he did favour did not exactly endear him to his superiors. The abbot here in Oxford – and this was before Angervyle's elevation to the bishopric – was unwilling to give over a room to his manuscripts. He regarded the books, and also Angervyle himself, as vulgar.'

'Vulgar?'

'Supposedly it demeaned the order to be seeking out wisdom in the works of pagans. In lewd poems, in the spectacles of Seneca, even in the obscenities of Juvenal, one of his particular favourites. So here they are, left to rot in chests, with no dedicated library to house them, despite the talk of all the new building to come. I worry that these, these *monks*' – he shuddered, as if swallowing a spider – 'will ruin his legacy. That on my death the collection will be destroyed.'

I surveyed the chamber, wondering if Quincey would let me buy the whole lot.

'Or divided, with some books going to one college, others to another. The bishop's fondest wish was to have all his books housed in a single room, made available for lending.'

'So he writes in the *Philobiblon*.' I looked around at the many chests, feeling greedy. 'Did he make a catalogue?'

'After a fashion. But the bishop's own lists were organized into rather eccentric categories: books lending themselves to happiness, books sorting virtue from vice, books concerning animals. So I took it upon myself in the years after his death to systematize the collection. Even so, the handlist I've assembled leaves much to be desired, I'm afraid.'

He led me to a standing desk. On it was a volume of moderate thickness, its clasps locked, its binding chained to the wall. Quincey inserted a small key into the clasp lock, and the tight straps sprang apart at the buckle. 'Here, then.'

222

I peered down at the neat lists, alphabetized by the author's name if known, by the work's opening words if not. 'This will be enormously helpful,' I said as I scanned incipits.

'I hope so, Master Gower.' He modestly bent his stick-like neck. 'Though perhaps you might save yourself some time if you tell me what you are after. A particular work?'

'Well, I suppose you might know of the author I'm looking for.' I watched the man carefully. 'What significance does the name "Lollius" have to you, or did it have to Angervyle?'

'Lollius, you say.' He rubbed his nose, looking everywhere but into my eyes. '*Lolliuslolliuslolliuslolliuslollius*,' he intoned, his voice running an unmelodious gamut from high to low and back again. 'Do I recall a moment in Petronius, perhaps, or was it Sallust?' He squinted. 'Horace,' he said at last, with a snap of his long fingers.

'Horace?'

'Wrote a famous *epistola ad Lollium*.'

'A letter to Lollius?' I said. My hand twitched.

'And an ode. Do you know Horace?'

'A bit.'

Quincey walked to a trunk against the far wall and came back with a moderate volume opened to a middle folio. With a growing excitement, I moved to a position near the door and sat on a trunk to read the Horace as Quincey puttered around the chamber, dusting the empty shelves, straightening the trunks, fooling with the latches. Lollius, I discerned from the ode's first lines, was evidently a judge, consul, and well-regarded public figure in Rome. Horace had written the ode as a kind of promise to save the man's memory from oblivion. The lines were also a paean to good and virtuous service for the state: Horace praised Lollius for his keen sense of ethics in his work, bending decisions to the right, turning away from bribes, facing down death while spurning the rewards of wealth.

I turned the page and frowned. Where I had expected more

lines to Lollius, a new poem began, this one the epistle to the same man, which the scribe had inserted between the two Horatian odes. I read it quickly. It largely duplicated the content of the first ode; the second was addressed to another man altogether.

Neither the epistle nor the ode said anything about Britain, nor kings, nor cards; not a word about prophecies, nor assassinations, nor conspirators. Horace's Lollius, as I should have realized when Quincey first mentioned him, could not possibly be the same man who allegedly authored the *Liber de Mortibus Regum Anglorum*. The Roman poet was writing during the lifetime of Christ Himself, fully a thousand years prior to the demise of the Conqueror, the first kingly death prophesied in the *De Mortibus*.

No cause for despair, though. I had been in Angervyle's library all of a quarter hour and had already acquired a significant bit of information. I looked over at Quincey, who was inspecting a binding. 'Do you know of this Lollius's poems?'

He shook his head. 'Only his memory, and only in that Horatian ode and letter.'

'No other Lollius, then? An English one, perhaps?'

'Doesn't clap a bell, I'm afraid.'

'Though perhaps his works are mentioned elsewhere in Angervyle's library.'

'Anything is possible, Master Gower.' With this enigmatic reply Quincey set the volume back in its trunk and rose, brisk and businesslike. 'In any case, you're free to inspect the collection at your will.' He pointed to two trunks near my knee. 'These crates contain all the bishop's holdings in *historia*. Chronicles of England, of times past, and the writings of the ancient historians of Rome, Lucan and such. And here we have books of science.' Four trunks, arrayed against the western wall. 'Aristotle's *Physics*, treatises of Galen and Hippocrates, even the works of al-Kindi on astronomy and cryptography, translated from the Arabic.'

'Cryptography?'

Quincey gave me a queer look, his left brow edging up his broad forehead. 'The art of secret writing, Master Gower. Transpositions, ciphers. Such techniques are employed mainly by alchemists, dabblers in magic, that sort. And spies, of course.'

I felt a quiet thrill. Tom Tugg at Newgate, Ralph Strode at the Guildhall, and now Peter de Quincey here in Oxford, all quick to invoke the shadow of spies, unnumbered and anonymous, spectres of treachery and deceit in a time of war. I thought of the dead girl in the Moorfields – a French spy, according to Strode – and again I had the sense of a connection unmade, of knowledge hidden beneath veils I could not part.

Quincey soon left me alone in the chamber – as alone as I could be with hundreds of books around me. I decided to begin with the histories, selecting four volumes from the first trunk and taking them to the reading desk. Settling on the stool and adjusting the candles, I arrayed the four manuscripts before me, admiring the unique embossments tooled on covers of various shades.

No time for pleasure, I reminded myself. My king prophesied to die, and here I sit, plucking at chronicles. Secret writing indeed. First the Bede – no, Geoffrey of Monmouth. With a sigh and a squint at the crabbed script, I read, my vision, for once, unclouded.

✢ ✢ ✢

The strangers had arrived on the day of St Dominic. They departed on the Saturday following the Feast of the Assumption of the Blessed Virgin.

At first the lady would not admit the truth to herself, and in the early weeks it was easy enough to ignore her condition. The first time she missed her menses she put it off to the trauma of her rape, the evil humours the foreign prince had left within her. After the second time she examined her frame in a glass. Her belly was undeniably growing.

The daughter watched as her mother cursed her fortune, tore her hair, beat at her breasts. She swallowed anise, birthwort, chamomile by the mouthful, hoping with these herbs to abort the child. At one moment she reached for a knife, planning to tear out this foul life. At another she vowed to throw herself off a chalk cliff. Yet each time she would relent, unable to abandon her daughter.

Soon enough it became impossible to hide her condition. The lady sensed her people turning on her. Oh, they would still serve her, carry out her commands in their dutiful way. Yet she had lost their goodwill.

A lady in these times, bearing the child of a lord not her own? Unthinkable, and yet there she was.

With her sixth month came new tidings of the war. A miserable defeat for her lord's king, and as this bleakness descended the lady gave in fully to her despair. On the morning chosen for her death, she sat for a while in the outer courtyard, dandling her daughter one last time. The girl knew something was awry. Yet even as they kissed their farewells, they saw in the distance a cloud of dust, smaller than the last, moving slowly across the marches. The lady squinted against the scorching sun. Bevelled or and sable, six hawks argent ascending the middle rank.

The livery of her lord and husband.

The lady locked herself in her apartments and for two days would

226

not see him, despite his pleas. Nor would his men nor his servants tell him what they knew, though in their averted eyes he read a calamity.

Had she been ill, with pestilence or some other malady? Was she sick even now, afraid to pass on a mortal blight to her lord? Was she disfigured?

Yes, the lady thought. Disfigured. She stripped to her thin shift and threw open the door, awaiting the sword.

Call to mind, my heart, the story of Joseph's trouble about Mary. It is not a story to be found in the Gospels, where Joseph thinks for a mere verse about divorce but then accepts the truth of the incarnation. I speak of the Father Joseph we see in the minstrels' pageants. This is the Joseph our knight knew best: the foolish Joseph, the husband convinced his pregnant wife has sinned with another man.

An angel came to you? Is that your claim? Ha! A man in the likeness of an angel, say I, come to cuckold me in sight of my relations – and you, my fresh wife, claim to be carrying the Messiah, though still a virgin?

Yet even in this Joseph finally relents, his anger calmed by the angel into a cool acceptance of his fate as the earthly husband of the mother of our Lord.

The mores of the time dictated that the knight should have cast her out of his home, exiled her as a harlot and a whore. Instead he listened to his lady's account of her attack by this foreign prince. Though her swollen body was there for all to see, the knight would not put his wife away, as even Joseph was tempted at first to do. Wondrously, he wept with her instead, promising her his enduring love and protection.

It was not to be. On the Tuesday after Pentecost, in the last year of Pedro the Cruel's reign, God poured spirit into the body of an infant boy, and extracted it from the flesh of his mother. The little girl would hear her mother's death-screams for years to come.

The new child looked so much like his mother – and, the girl could plainly see, his malevolent father. Yet from the moment of the boy's birth the knight took him as his own. One of the most self-sacrificing, self-denying loves in all history was this lord's for a son not his own. They made a strange family, these three, yet there was a certain nobility to their devotion that inspired awe from more charitable souls.

Love can be sustaining even in the worst of circumstances. Bare life, though, can be passing hard to endure. As the infant grew into a boy, the people started to look upon their lord with ill will. Betrayed by a strumpet of Mahound! And this bastard will be our lord's heir, and thus our own future lord?

No longer did they treat the knight with such solicitous fealty. There were whispers of insubordination, and gossip in the town.

The situation could not stand. So the knight gathered his most loyal men, no more than thirty in number, and with his children left their home. This best of lords gave up his castle to become a wanderer, a knight errant served only by the few dozen men who would join him on the road.

Though weakened in spirit, our knight was still strong in body, more than capable of leading a company of men in battle. He could sell these skills. He became a knight for hire, peddling the might of his men in the wars of that era, from the Straits of Gibraltar to the ports of Marseille and Toulon, adding other wayfaring men to his company as they went.

The knight taught his daughter well in the course of their wanderings: how to butcher a hart, how to fight with her fists and teeth, how to ward off brigands with a knife. By the age of twelve she was a fierce, rodent-like thing, unrecognizable as the daughter of a wealthy lord.

La Comadrejita: the Little Weasel, as she was known among the camp women. Small, lithe, quick on her feet, always sneaking up on the warriors and their women, dodging grasps and slaps, lifting coins and shiny objects from pouches and shelves. These she would give to her brother as tokens of their love, extracting solemn promises from the little boy that he would do her bidding in all things.

From her father's men his growing daughter learned the many

tongues spoken around the great inland sea – not only French and Italian but the languages of the Jews and the Moors, and the mixed tongue of sailors. She took a new name, too, after an old Roman town in the Dauphiné where her father's company wintered one year, and after the orange scarf she wore in her hair.

For eight long years she roamed with her father's company among the hills and rivers of many lands. If not the happiest of girls, she was content, though the memory of her mother's ravishment stayed with her always, like an aching tooth too frequently tongued.

Sorrow comes in waves, it is said. In her sixteenth year the girl fell ill along with her father, her brother, and many of their company. The fever slew the weakest among them: a half-dozen ageing soldiers, two camp women heavy with child – and her brother. He was buried on a high cliff above the sea, with no priest to say Mass. So she said it herself for this sweetest of boys, murmuring through narrowed lips those rote snatches of unknown Latin heard so often in her life.

In his bleakness at the loss of his son, and seeing his daughter's devastation, her father made a decision. His child needed a home, a chance at a life worth living.

He had heard tidings of a large company of mercenaries serving the signore of Milan, a much larger assemblage than his own, well managed and organized. So the knight travelled with his diminished company to Lombardy. There he sold himself and his men to this company, a wealthy band of mercenaries hiring their might to the most powerful magnates in the land: kings, dukes, popes.

The leader of this company was a fearsome lord, tall, haughty, quick of wit and quicker of cruelty. Yet he was revered by his subordinates, and feared by those who hired his engines and his men.

His name was Ser Giovanni Acuto. In your tongue, my sweet, Sir John Hawkwood.

✜ ✜ ✜

229

TWENTY-NINE

San Donato a Torre, near Florence

'It's remarkable, Sir John,' said Adam Scarlett. 'And alarming.'

Hawkwood, fresh from his weekly bath, had thrown on a loose robe. He peered into the mottled glass, shaving his neck. 'Perhaps it's nothing,' he said.

That morning a servingwoman and her husband had been cleaning one of the smaller *villette* to make room for an envoy from Rome. Four of the chancellor's clerks had vacated the week before, having made a mess of the outbuilding, and it needed a top-to-bottom scrubbing. Her husband had been shovelling old coals from the main hearth when he came across a half-burned quire behind the grate. The edges were badly charred, several pages rendered unreadable. Yet there were at least a dozen nearly full sheets with legible letters and mysterious signs scribbled across both sides. The man had promptly brought the quire to the *condottiero*.

'The hand matches Il Critto's, I'll be bound,' said Scarlett, paging through the quire and eager to examine it further. 'This could only have been his work.'

Hawkwood towelled off. 'So what did our friend leave behind?'

Scarlett shook his head. 'Hard to tell, sire. Only one of these pages makes any sense to me. It's in Italian, if it even deserves the name.' Scarlett read it aloud. A short set of awkward sentences conjugating the verb *nascondere*. *I nascondere, si nascondono, si nasconde* . . .

> *I hide my knowledge beneath my words.*
> *You hide your ignorance beneath your power.*
> *He hides his treason beneath his loyalty.*

The fumblings of a man still practising a tongue not his own.

When Scarlett had finished reading through the grammatical exercise Hawkwood shrugged, reached for his hose. 'So he was honing his Italian. What does this prove, Adam? We've never had reason to doubt his loyalty.'

'Nothing, Sir John. Merely that he used this quire for casual writing in addition to his ciphers. As for the rest . . .'

'Well?'

'It's like reading pebbles on sand. None of it means anything to me, and I don't have the quality of mind capable of sorting it out. Il Critto kept his ciphers to himself.'

'As I warned him he should, on peril of his life, and damn me for a fool!' He laughed gruffly, then considered the matter. 'I suppose we need some help, then.'

Scarlett agreed. That afternoon he left for Siena, where he asked around at the *studium*. He was back two mornings later with the sharpest mind on the faculty. A purse, a polite request, a few vague threats: there had been little resistance. With Hawkwood there rarely was.

In the gallery the *condottiero* invited the dazed man to sit with him on the padded bench he used at his desk. The wide surface was taken up in large part with a marked-up map of Tuscany, Lombardy, Romagna, and the Veneto: troop movements and garrisons, debts owed to the company, the intricate web of Hawkwood's empire. He liked to hold his strategic conversations here, where his power could be spread out before him for the benefit of his visitors.

'In what discipline is your training, Maestro Desilio?'

'Law, Ser Giovanni, at Bologna. Though logic is my greater strength.'

Hawkwood glanced at Scarlett. 'Well good, then. We need a logician's mind to crack these rocky nuts. Did my man Scarletto explain all this to you?'

'He did not, Ser Giovanni.'

So Hawkwood did. 'What you see before you, sir, this mess of scorched parchments and half-burned papers? This is all that was left behind by one of my associates.'

'Associates, Ser Giovanni?'

'He left our service earlier this year. His mother dies, he's the sole heir, he thinks of home – the details don't particularly matter. Though his profession mattered a great deal to me, as it soon shall to you. You see, this man was my cryptographer, Master Desilio.'

'Your – your cryptographer?'

'Il Critto, we called him,' said Hawkwood. 'The man responsible for taking my dispatches and letters and casting them into cipher for delivery abroad. To my garrisons, to my contacts in Rome, Paris, London. You are familiar with cryptography?'

Despite the peculiar situation the logician looked intrigued, provoked by the intellectual challenge. 'I am, Ser Giovanni. At the *studium* we have several books on this craft. By Master Roger Bacon, by al-Kindi the Moor, the latter translated into Latin. I've not studied them carefully, but I know the rudiments, and I can certainly loan you these books.'

'Excellent,' Hawkwood said, nodding eagerly. 'Though I have a different sort of loan in mind.'

Scarlett watched them for a while, the way Hawkwood had of warming up his visitors, making them feel comfortable in his presence, even when he was delivering unwelcome news. Yes, you will be my guest here at San Donato, at least for a time. No, you won't be going back to Siena today, nor tomorrow. Better to write a letter, requesting that the books in question be sent back with my man. You will certainly be paid well, and the *studium* compensated for your absence, however extended it should prove.

'Do you have any further questions or concerns about this arrangement?' Hawkwood asked him.

The man paged through the quire, his mouth at a rueful slant. 'Only that this task, Ser Giovanni . . .'

'Yes?'

'These sorts of ciphers do not lend themselves to expediency. Breaking them could take – it could take months.'

Hawkwood's smile stiffened. 'Months I don't have. Weeks? Perhaps. Days? Even better.'

The logician, knowing better than to shake his head, took a heavy breath. 'I will do my best, Ser Giovanni.'

Scarlett watched Hawkwood incline his head. 'I know you will, Maestro Desilio.'

THIRTY

Paternoster Row

From the northwest corner of St Paul's churchyard Edgar peered across the busy lane, his head filled with the muddle and din, his stomach rumbling with hunger. He'd hardly eaten in days, relying on the sparse alms of the parishes as he skulked around the city, trying to elude the constables, and that hook-scarred man on Gropecunt Lane. Swyving was a hard business, yet it was nothing compared to the week he'd experienced as one of the city's thousand beggars: sleeping in abandoned horsestalls, mouldy bread plucked from gutters, the cold anonymity of London's poorest souls, trying to stay invisible or feign lameness so they wouldn't be put out at the gates. Yet now it was time.

He pushed himself off the booth and walked toward Paternoster Row, past several parchmenters' shops. Halfway down the street a shop matron, hair tied back in a simple scarf, bargained with a neat-looking man over a bundle at her feet. A reeve or steward, Edgar guessed, commissioned to purchase parchment for his employer.

'That's too high, Mistress Pinkley,' the man wheedled. 'The brothers of the Charterhouse toil for the Lord, not for themselves.'

'The sum wasn't too high for my late husband, nor too high for me. You should get a smell of what I charge the friary.' A harsh cackle. 'But for this stack of lambskin? Four shillings a dozen is passing fair for the holy disciples of the Grand Chartreuse, and I'll have not a penny less. The finest lambs of Sunbury-on-Thames in these skins, nor will you find a thinner lot on Paternoster Row.'

Edgar waited while the man paid and trudged off with the parchments. The parchmentress turned to him with a ready smile which faded somewhat when she saw this vagrant at her shop door.

'What is it?'

He looked down at his hands. 'A book, mistress. A book to sell.'

'A book to sell, eh?' She took in the shoddy hose, the frayed cap. 'Most come to Paternoster Row looking to purchase books, not sell them. And what's a bairn like you doing with a book?'

'Came into my possession, willed me by my mother, bless her,' he lied. 'I have no reading to speak of and don't know the matter of it but I believe it's a valuable thing.'

The parchmentress grinned. 'A primer is it, a painted book of hours that's been in your family? A Bible perhaps, or the blessed Psalter?'

Edgar held it out. The parchmentress looked down at the book and took it briskly. Untying the thong with an adept tug, she gave the embroidery an admiring glance, handed the cloth back to Edgar, then smoothed her hands over the volume's covers.

'Thin little thing.' She flipped through the pages without, it seemed, reading a word, inspecting the thickness of the parchment, fingering several of the leaves with an expert feel for quality. 'Heavy, the skins are. Could be scraped, I suppose, yield a clean book to write anew.' She closed the manuscript and slapped it against an open palm. 'Six pence.'

235

Edgar felt his jaw slacken. Six pennies, for a book sought by half of London? He shook his head. 'Not for this book, madam. Five – nay, six nobles, and I'll have not a penny less.'

The parchmentress just stared, listening to her own words used against her, then burst into great peals of laughter, slapping her leg. 'Six nobles, he says! Not a penny less! Why, aren't you a gamey little fella! Tom! Get out here, friend!'

The neighbouring shopkeeper appeared in his doorway. Edgar reached for the book. The parchmentress released it with a little shove, accompanied by a delighted recounting of Edgar's demand for six nobles and he'll have not a penny less, Tom, not a penny less. Edgar turned away and made for the corner.

So parchmenters, he'd learned, would find no interest in the book. Their interest in books was like men's in maudlyns: of value for the outer aspect, the fineness of the skin. Not so much the words – and it was the words, Edgar suspected, that gave this book whatever value it had.

He was now on a smaller byway cutting down from Paternoster Row. Three-storey houses with shops at the street level, a glaze of sulphur on the air. The tradesmen here seemed to specialize in painting pages with all the florid colours in God's creation. Illuminators' shops displayed fine samples of their work pegged on to smoothed boards hooked beside their doors. Several painters had pulled their stools and desks out on the lane that dry day, and the sun had reached a point in its arc that allowed their work to show to its best advantage. He paused behind a painter crafting an enormous page filled with black marks in square and oblong shapes. At the top left side of the page a cluster of singing monks stood inside a letter *P* – yes, a *P*, Edgar knew that much, and the *P* was coloured in a shade of blue-green he imagined as the hue of the southern seas.

His shoulders sagged as he walked to the end of the lane.

For these painters, books were things of beauty. This one had no beauty to it, that was for certain: no pictures aside from the hurried sketches at the edges of the pages, no great letters filled with holy men or dragons, no blue-green hues to ravish you with longing for the oceans of the earth.

He stepped on to a slightly wider lane. Here at least a dozen men sat at desks, in shops and out on the street, pointing ink on to surfaces of varying size. Like Master Strode's clerks at the Guildhall, Edgar thought, putting letters to skin. A street of words.

Halfway up it he stopped to look over the shoulder of a younger man practising his script on a large, rough sheet: a smooth line, a delicate curve, then he scratched it all out and started again, then again, until he noticed Edgar's presence. He half-turned with a friendly smile. 'Help you?'

'You're – you're a scriv—a scrivener, yes?' he stammered.

'This be the shop of Roger Ybott, master stationer of Creed Lane,' he said. 'Tom Fish is my own name, sole apprentice to Master Ybott. Pleased to help you, whatever your wish.'

He considered his reply. 'Is your craft in the words of books then?'

He frowned. 'The words of books?'

Edgar squinted at the writing desk. 'These parts of London by St Paul's be filled with the bookish crafts, all different bits of it. Those that scrape the skin, ready it for writing—'

'Parchmenters on Paternoster Row, sure, sure,' said Tom Fish, head bobbing. 'Though they don't do their scraping in the city, just come here to sell out of their shops.'

'Then there be the painters, colouring the pages with every shade you ever—'

'The limners along Creed Lane.'

'And in this street there's writing,' said Edgar. 'Those who lime and scrape, those who paint, and here be those who write.'

'We do our share of the writing, sure,' said Fish, finally

237

getting his meaning. 'A commission from an abbot or an earl, we'll put pen to vellum quicker than you can say your Ave Marie here on Ave Maria Lane.' He laughed at his own joke. 'Stationer's work's important work, important as you'll find in all London.'

Edgar pulled out the book. 'Would you be so kind as to value this, Master Fish?'

Fish looked surprised, though also pleased to lend his expertise. 'Let us see here,' he said, taking the book and handling it with a careful adeptness. 'Mm . . . hmm . . . ahh, yes . . .' he murmured, showing off. Like the parchmentress, Tom Fish seemed to be examining the book at first only for its physical make-up, tugging at the pages, holding the spine against the sky. Then he started reading from the beginning, at first with a neutral curiosity, then with a slight frown, then, as he read on, with a widening of the eyes that made Edgar want to turn and flee. At one point he gasped softly. He flipped ahead to the final pages and scanned. He took a large step backwards, holding the book out in front of him as if it were a serpent about to bite.

He looked at Edgar, eyes wide with fright. An older man walked out of the shop. 'What's this then?' he demanded. The shop's master stood only slightly taller than his apprentice, though his hewn face matched his craft, his eyes narrowed in a permanent squint, deep lines reaching for his ears. On his thinning hair he wore a round hat of blue silk, embroidered letters in black and white filling every inch.

Tom Fish turned to his master. 'This young fellow here, Master Ybott, he – he wished to have this book examined, and so I've been about it for the last little while.'

'To sell, Master Ybott,' Edgar clarified. 'I have no reading, so books be of no use to me excepting what price they might fetch.'

Ybott took the book from Tom, taking no notice of his apprentice's state. He read selectively through the thin volume until he, too, went pale. He looked at Edgar, then at Fish. 'Well now,' he said, his voice husky. 'Not a book to bandy about, is it? And you've been carrying this on your person? Just walking along with it, not a care for your head?'

'Yes, sir – I mean no, sir,' said Edgar. 'I know not the words nor the meaning of it. But it it *must* be worth more than sixpence, yeah?'

'More than sixpence,' said Ybott, staring at him. Recovering himself, he cleared his throat, leaned toward Edgar, and rested a firm hand on his shoulder. 'How came you by this book, young – what is your name, young man?'

'I am called Edgar, sir.'

'How came you by this book, Edgar?'

Edgar crossed his arms. 'That be no man's affair but my own, sir. The book be rightfully mine now, and I mean to sell it for what I'm able.'

Ybott gave him one of his deep squints. 'You don't know what pile you've stepped into, Edgar. You best come inside.' He held out his other hand, gesturing toward his shop.

Edgar stood his ground, recalling the encounter with Bickle, the beadle of Cheap Ward. He had no desire to enter yet another man's shop, nor to be assayed further about this damned book. 'I'd rather not, sir, if it be all the same to you.' He stuck out his jaw. 'Now give me back my book.'

Ybott tilted his head, holding a tense smile. 'As you wish. Be warned, though, this book is a dangerous thing to its owner, whether an illiterate vagrant, a Cambridge master' – he paused – 'or a young woman taking on a man's role.'

Edgar shrank away from him. Ybott had got it wrong, but not by much.

'We're in the business of books,' the stationer said, pressing him. 'We know what's best when it comes to the worst, yes?' Sensing his hesitation, Ybott went on: 'You appear hungry, or lost. There's a desperate look about you. Come inside, please, and let me lend you whatever bookish wisdom I possess.'

Could Edgar trust him? Even as he supposed the man's warmth to be motivated by something other than Edgar's well-being, he felt his suspicions dissolving – foolishly, perhaps. Yet Ybott was not a constable, nor a beadle, nor, he trusted, a murderer. So he allowed himself to be guided into the stationer's shop, the apprentice close behind. Once the three of them were inside, Tom Fish shut the door. At the sound of the latch Edgar shuddered, wondering what lay before him.

THIRTY-ONE

Ave Maria Lane

From the top of Paternoster Row, Millicent Fonteyn watched the stationer guide Edgar Rykener into his shop. The apprentice followed them inside, his worried glance in both directions telling Millicent all she needed to know.

She surveyed the narrow lane. The trio had attracted little attention from the neighbouring craftsmen, all busy at their work. Yet there was one of them, a man standing in front of a shop just across the lane, who had witnessed the interaction. He was staring at the door with a hard intensity that gave Millicent a prickle of concern. She and Agnes weren't the only ones searching London for a book. There were others on the watch, others working on behalf of whatever forces or factions sought to use its perilous contents to their advantage. Others looking to take, and to kill.

She stepped out and signalled for Agnes to join her. Two other girls waved in relief as Millicent dismissed them with a grim nod. For days now, and at Bess Waller's orders, a clutch of Southwark mauds had taken turns lying in wait for Eleanor Rykener in these precincts, some watching Paternoster Row itself, others surveying Ave Maria Lane, still others keeping an eye on Amen Lane above Pembroke's Inn. All setting a net for the wretched little fish, the swerver who'd stolen the book out from under Bess Waller's nose and now sought to sell it for whatever it would bring.

Now they'd found her. Him.

Yet it appeared they were too late. How could Edgar be so foolish? Did he have no idea what it was he possessed, how much of his own future might turn on the fate of the book he'd stolen, and now sought to sell to half the book-makers of London? For soon the master stationer would realize he had little choice but to inform the authorities that a book prophesying the death of King Richard had come into his possession. Nor could Millicent steal it from the stationer as Eleanor had stolen it from the Pricking Bishop, for all the master's attention would be on the volume for the duration of its stay in his shop.

Could she and Agnes take the thing by force, grab a few logs on the way in and have at it? Hardly. A master and his young apprentice, hale men both, would be more than a match for them, even if the sisters took them by surprise. Besides, she reasoned, the streets in this neighbourhood were so narrow escape would be impossible. The guildsman would raise the hue and cry, summon a constable. It would all be over within minutes, the sisters taken before they got as far as the Boar's Head.

'So,' said Agnes. 'Let's walk in.'

'What's that?'

Agnes looked at her. 'Let's walk right in there, talk to Eleanor. She'll give it back, come with us.'

'Have you gone wood, Ag? She's the one stole the book from us!'

'She'll listen to reason, if I know Eleanor Rykener. She'll listen to me.'

Millicent scoffed. 'Listen to that man's coin, I'll be bound. That's what he – what she's here for.'

'Eleanor's not like you, Mil.' Agnes's tone was suddenly hard. 'Sure, she wants good shills like any maud of London. But that's not what's most important to her.' She looked away. 'Not like you.'

Millicent, stung, stared at her sister's profile. 'Well,' she said, then looked back up Ave Maria Lane. 'Maybe you're right.'

'No maybe about it, Mil. We go in there, get her, get the book, she'll come right along.'

Millicent smoothed her dress, held out a hand. 'Come, then.'

They walked up Ave Maria Lane with locked arms and furtive looks at the work of the scriveners on either side. When they reached the shop door, Millicent turned to face the oaken surface, which was free of tracery and grillwork; nor was there a lock. Blowing out a breath, she pushed it open.

A one-room shop. Clean, well lit, books displayed on single shelves. Two writing desks faced one another in the middle of the shop. The scrivener, seated at one of them with his apprentice and Edgar standing before him, looked up in surprise. On the desk the book lay open.

'What's this?' he demanded.

'We came for that,' said Millicent, pointing. 'Our book, just there.'

'*Your* book?' Ybott looked from the sisters to Edgar. 'The young man here tells me it's his.'

Edgar raised his chin. 'That it is, sir.'

'Then you two best be on your way,' said Ybott.

'The book is ours,' Millicent insisted. 'It was given to my sister by – it was given to her, weeks ago. You hand it over or I'll summon a ward constable.'

'Will you now?'

'Get out, Ag,' Edgar snarled. 'Both of you, now, *get out!*'

'You know better than that, Eleanor,' said Agnes, conciliation in her voice. 'You know I be your good gossip.'

'That right, Agnes Fonteyn?' said Edgar. 'Leaving me high

and dry on Gropecunt Lane, finding that killed girl, that bloody hammer with her brains still on it? That how you treat your "good gossip"?'

Millicent winced at Edgar's use of her sister's full name, and the incautious crowing of their profession. The scriveners, she saw, were taking it all in. Gropecunt Lane, a bloody hammer, a dead girl.

'We are taking the book,' she said quickly. 'This one stole it, and now we're taking it back.' Ybott started to protest. Millicent raised her hand and stepped right up to him, threatening. 'Think about it. Think about a constable, or the ward beadle stepping in here once you summon him. What do you suppose he'll do? Comes in a stationer's shop to find this book of prophecies in your possession, what do you suppose he'll think?'

'Now, look here, by what right—'

'That it belongs to a few maudlyns wandering by, trying to scare up cock on Ave Maria Lane?'

Ybott was speechless. Tom Fish shot a fearful glance at Edgar, then at Agnes.

'Would *you* believe such a thing, sir, if this one here' – Millicent pointed at Edgar – 'hadn't slunk up from St Paul's to sell it to you himself?'

A feeble shrug.

'What you *would* believe is what's before you: a London stationer closeted in his shop with a treasonous book, trying to pin the blame on some poor maud he brought within to swyve of a spring afternoon.'

Ybott turned away. Millicent approached the writing desk, lifted the book, and dropped it in her coat's broad inner pocket. She turned on her heel and walked to the door.

'Wait, Mil.'

Millicent turned back to her sister. Agnes approached Edgar, whose face registered a mix of confusion and fear. Agnes reached forward and put a hand on his cheek. Edgar's response was considerably less gentle: a hard slap to Agnes's face that rang through the small shop.

'Where you been, Agnes?' he demanded, his voice hoarse with rage. 'Not on Gropecunt Lane, nor on Cornhull, nor in Southwark, nor lying dead on the Moorfields.' He stomped a foot on the rushes. 'Like that girl I thought was *you.*'

Agnes shook her head against the tears. 'Oh, Ellie, I don't know what to say to you, dearheart.'

Millicent opened the door a crack. The tradesman who had been watching from across the street was gone. She stepped forward and grasped Edgar's wrist. 'Come along. You be a part of this now as much as I am myself, and Agnes here.'

He tried to pull away. Millicent tightened her grip. 'Don't be a child.'

Millicent felt Edgar's acquiescence in the loosening of his muscles. She tugged, and he finally allowed himself to be led from the shop. By the next bell they were halfway across the bridge.

They passed the following days at the Pricking Bishop, stowed in a third-storey room overlooking Rose Alley. It was sour in there, the linens strewn across the pallet crusted with the spent passions of the men who dried their parts on them every day. The book rested in an alcove beneath a low shelf, just within the door. Thomas Pinchbeak, Millicent felt certain, was determined to purchase it, despite the delay caused by Eleanor Rykener's theft, and she was equally determined to sell it for the greatest sum she could extract.

✢

On the fourth night, in the stillest hours, they awoke to hoarse shouts on the street below. Cracking a shutter, Millicent looked out to see five men on horseback, dark hoods and cloaks obscuring any features. They were clustered up by Smith's Rents, their animals circling in the darkness. One of them dismounted and approached the Pricking Bishop, his short sword glistening at his side.

The shouts had come not from him, though, but from his unexpected antagonist.

'Y'aren't Southwark men, that be sure.'

Millicent leaned out. Down below stood St Cath, yawping in the lantern-light, a withered arm in the air, her shift billowing obscenely in the night breezes. The old woman pointed up the alley in the direction of the palace. 'By what right do you trounce in the bishop's liberties? By whose warrant?'

St Cath's crazed bravery soon brought company. Three maudlyns joined her on the street to confront the armed man. They were joined in turn by a dozen girls from the other houses, all shouting at the company to leave the stews the way they had come. Soon nearly twenty maudlyns of Southwark had encircled the men, cackling a righteous din to fill the stews. More lanterns were brought out, the lane filling with a shimmering glow.

Millicent moved for a better view, and her elbow pushed the shutter slightly to her right. The movement drew the man's attention. He looked up. His face was covered, all but his eyes and forehead wrapped in a black scarf tucked between his doublet and cape. For a long moment, in the glare of the lamps, she stood frozen by his stare. His eyes, deep and cruel, smouldered as he memorized her face. Then he looked away.

Now more distant cries, the echo of metal on metal, the clatter of hooves, and everyone's attention was drawn up Rose Alley. Joined by Agnes and Eleanor at the window, Millicent heard before she saw the opposing company bearing down hard past the Vine. The man on foot turned and sprinted back to his horse, joining his fellows in a mad dash in the opposite direction.

For these were the Bishop of Winchester's liberties, the unannounced intrusion by the strange company a violation of ecclesiastical jurisdiction. The bishop did not take such incursions lightly, nor did his men, a company of which had been dispatched from the palace's main guardhouse into the stews. It was an unfair fight, for though the strangers had the advantage of surprise, Winchester's men were greater in number. Within minutes the violators had been chased through Bishopspark and into Winchester's Wild, where they would scatter themselves to the winds.

Once the street had calmed there were sounds of shutters slamming along the way. Bess Waller appeared at the door, her cheeks ruddy in the candlelight. 'You need to leave, all you, at first bell. They were here for that book, plain as the sun.' She did a circuit of the room, shoving their few things into a basket and sack.

'But where are we to go, *mère?*' Agnes asked her as she pulled on her shoes. 'We have no place, nor coin.' Eleanor huddled at her side, watching the exchange.

'Not her concern, Ag.' Millicent was pulling on her own shoes, the once-elegant skins by now full of holes, not all of them patched. 'Our good mother doesn't bother herself with inconveniences like the welfare of her daughters.'

Bess came to stand by the bed. Stooping, she pressed something into Millicent's hand. Cold, metallic. Millicent looked down, hoping for coins. She saw a key.

'Ditch Street by the Split Shill, just within Aldgate,' said Bess, her night breath foul on Millicent's cheek. 'Small place there I've leased four years now. It's empty, has been a good while. They won't look for you there, that's sure.'

This, for Bess Waller, counted as generosity: the loan of an unused hole across the river. Millicent looked at her mother, wondering what moral world those unwavering eyes saw when they peered into a glass. Though I suppose I'm not one to judge, she thought. She closed her eyes, then her hand over the key.

THIRTY-TWO

Logic Lane, Oxford

Sir John Clanvowe, standing at a trestle table, poured wine from a silvered flagon. 'We will have an additional guest this evening.'

I masked my displeasure with a small sip. A seventh unproductive day among Angervyle's book chests had put me in a sour mood. 'Delightful. The wine, I mean, though I'm sure your guest will be as well. Who is he?'

'I shall let it be a surprise.' Clanvowe spread the frayed ends of his coat across his uncushioned chair. 'Let me hear about your week in Oxford. Have you enjoyed yourself?'

'Not particularly,' I said, opting for honesty. Over the first several days I had felt like a starved man at a king's feast. So many new books to plumb with the raw excitement of a child, losing myself for hours at a time in these authors formerly known only by name and reputation. Yet the search had soon grown monotonous, as each new book failed to reveal anything about the elusive Lollius. After all that time among Bury's books I had started to experience the dark building behind the Durham grange as a hermit's cell.

In airing all of this for Clanvowe, though, I stayed vague,

248

telling him I was in Oxford to track down some texts related to my next major work. We sat in his parlour, sparsely furnished with several chairs, a writing desk, and a short shelf of dusty books against one of the whitewashed walls beneath exposed timbers. Paid well for his service as a knight of the chamber, Clanvowe had been a stalwart in Gaunt's campaigns in Aquitaine, Castile, and France, and he was known to be quite rich. Despite his wealth, though, he lived like an Oxford student – if a well-armed one.

His finger traced the lip of our glass. 'There must be more to it than that, John, to pry you out of Southwark. There are plenty of books in London. What is it you hope to find among Bury's manuscripts? What brought you here, to Oxford?'

'I would ask you the same question.' I took the wine. 'I'd have thought you would spend every hour out of court at Radnorshire, honing your Welsh.'

His face loosened into a smile. 'And it's well honed indeed by this point, what with all the diplomacy I'm performing up and down the border for the king. The marcher lords are a restive bunch. Master connivers. As to my own purpose in Oxford? *Byddwch yn dysgu cyn bo hir*, my friend. And I asked first.'

'Impressive,' I said. Clanvowe's yellow whiskers were tensed, gathered in a thick bunch. 'You won't translate for me?'

'You'll learn soon enough,' he said.

'Learn what?'

'That's the answer to your question.'

'Which question?'

'Both of them, I suppose. Now,' he said, leaning forward to refresh the glass, 'to the purpose of your visit.'

I looked away, thoroughly muddled, already exhausted with all the effort. I took a long drink of wine and watched the flickering shadows play on the knight's eyes. Sir John had come to Oxford fresh from the political turmoil of London, where all the talk was of war, spies, and factions. He was also a knight of the king's chamber, and though he was a friend, there was no question where his loyalties would go should he learn of a threat to Richard. This was precisely why I wanted to speak with him: however Clanvowe might react to the existence of the prophecy, he would do so with the king's best interests in mind. Yet by divulging the existence of the *De Mortibus*, I would be bringing its dark prophecies into King Richard's affinity for the first time, an irrevocable and potentially perilous step.

Making a decision, I turned back to my host. 'Do you know Horace?'

Clanvowe's brow dropped. 'Slightly. Peasants, slaves, philosophizing merchants. Not to my taste.'

'The odes are great achievements, though.'

'Is that so?'

'But very hard to find. Angervyle's must be one of a handful of copies in England.'

'Do you have a favourite?'

'The ninth ode of the fourth book.'

'What is its subject?'

I waited a moment. 'A poet named Lollius.'

Clanvowe flinched. I have you, I thought, pleased with myself. 'You know it, then?'

'I don't,' he said, recovering quickly. 'Though perhaps there's more you want to say about it.'

I was saved from accepting the challenge by the arrival of Clanvowe's other guest, signalled by a soft knock at the outer door, then a quiet exchange with Sir John's sole servant. We stood as the third man entered the parlour.

A priest, capped and robed in russet, a simple belt at his waist. No other adornment, though the uncompromising blue of his eyes forced attention, as if roundels of lapis lazuli had been painted around his pupils. A beard, bushy and long, caped his neck. I recognized the man, had seen him on at least one occasion but couldn't place him. Clanvowe made his hostly bow and spread his hands. 'Master John Gower, Esquire, let me present the curate of Lutterworth, Father John Purvey.'

I maintained enough presence of mind to reach forward and clasp hands. Purvey was a young man, his grip on my arm strong with the righteous confidence of the fanatic. Secretary to John Wycliffe himself until the master's death the prior December, Purvey was known as a preacher and scholar of radical leanings, and if what I'd heard was true, he had had the main hand in Wycliffe's recent translation of the Bible, a notorious work that was even now being circulated among the conventicles.

The conversation remained superficial until a weak sop was served, at which point Purvey turned to me with a mischievous smile.

'We have much in common, Master Gower.'

'In what way, Father?' The broth, light and unsalted, tasted vaguely of almonds.

'We are both writers, for one.'

'Though our respective subjects speak to our differences.'

'And our commonalities. Your *Mirour de l'Omme* has struck a chord among the men of our persuasion.'

Our persuasion? I swallowed. 'How is that?'

'Well, for one, you're not shy about criticizing the church, even its most powerful sects.' Then, to my horror, Purvey quoted my own French: '"The friars preach poverty to all, but they're always stretching forth their hands for coin. They love their worldly comforts, but never do they seek employment. Instead they wander about in the habit of vagrants."' He sipped, smacked his lips. 'Truer words have never been written about the friars. Not even by Master Wycliffe himself, bless his soul.'

Clanvowe laughed gruffly. Purvey tittered, and I met their amusement with an uncomfortable smile. 'You came prepared this evening, Father. I'm impressed.'

251

The conversation moved on, the remainder of the meal consisting of overdone rabbit in a mealy pie, with old mustard on the side. I picked at my portion, imagining that every bite had to be taken carefully, as if my very teeth might grind with heresy, though Clanvowe and Purvey were now chatting amiably about the priest's new living. 'Now that I'm at Lutterworth, it's difficult to get back to Oxford as often as I would like. But that may be for the good.' He looked down at his rabbit. 'It's time I remain in one place for a while, tend to the souls in my care.'

'A fine suggestion,' I said. 'After all, priests are as numerous as stars in the sky. But unlike stars, only two of a thousand know how to shine.'

Purvey gave me a nasty look. 'You question my sincerity, Master Gower.'

'Only your memory, Father Purvey.'

He wiped his lips. 'Take Wykeham, your Bishop of Winchester. The man has twelve livings to his name, all going to fund his castle and his liberties in Southwark, his fishing ponds and his whores. Yet how often do you think he visits those parishes? Once a year, if it suits his schedule?'

'He's a busy man,' I pointed out.

'If the priest of the parish can't live a virtuous life, how is he supposed to teach his parishioners to avoid sin? If gold rusts, what about iron? It's like a shepherd smeared with shit herding a flock of sheep, trying to keep them clean.' He pounded the table. 'This is the problem with the higher clergy, Gower. They've become barons, building obscene castles for themselves, taking on concubines and mistresses and God knows what else. This is why I support their disendowment so strongly. Why should our spiritual leaders also be our wealthiest possessioners?'

I looked at the nearest candle, amazed the man would say such a thing in my presence. 'That position has been condemned by the pope, Father. As you well know.'

'Which pope would that be?' he responded.

I looked at him, now truly shocked. To speak of disendowing the clergy was one thing; to question the English alliance with Rome against Avignon and France was quite another.

'These are high matters, gentlemen,' said Clanvowe, waving a hand as if to dismiss them all. 'Matters between our king and his uncle, between parliaments and popes. If Father Purvey errs too far on the side of the crown against the church, others – Sudbury, say – err in the other direction. Yet that's not why we're here this evening.'

'Then why are we here?' I asked, suddenly wary.

He hesitated. 'I am going to be honest with you, John, and I hope you'll forgive me for luring you to my house under false pretences.' He took a deep breath, exhaled. 'I've known all along why you were coming to Oxford.'

I reared back.

'You're after the *De Mortibus*. You and half of England.'

'How—'

'Chaucer told me. At Windsor.'

'But how did Chaucer—'

'That's unimportant,' said Clanvowe. 'The point is, I've invited our guest here this evening to refute to your face the vile rumours connecting Master Wycliffe and his teachings to these prophecies. Your word carries weight in London, John. It's crucial that you understand the difference between honest theological disputation and open rebellion. Wycliffe had strong opinions, true. But he was hardly a traitor, and neither are his followers.'

'I know what Braybrooke must have told you,' said Purvey, leaning in. 'That we commissioned the work's copying, encouraged its circulation. Perhaps even wrote it ourselves, maybe to inspire rebellion against King Richard, install our ally the Duke of Lancaster on the throne. But these are lies, Gower, intended to destroy Father Wycliffe's legacy. However strongly Ralph Strode and his ilk dispute us on matters of endowment, possession, and so on, I'd step into my own grave before promoting or even imagining the death of our king. This *Liber de Mortibus* has nothing to do with our teachings. Why, I believe that the king, not the pope, is the vicar of God! It's from the king alone that the bishops derive their authority and jurisdiction.'

Plain blasphemy. I remained silent, wishing I had a clerk's transcription of the whole evening.

'These so-called prophecies are worth less than the sheep-skins they're scribbled on,' Purvey said, pressing on. 'They offend me. They offend me as a Christian, as a citizen of this realm, and as a priest. Most of all, though, they offend me as an intellectual. They are utter trash, the work of a *jongleur*, not a prophet.'

Clanvowe's brow shone as he moved in the candlelight. 'As a poetic maker like you, John, I also have a pretty low opinion of this work. Like our friend here, I regard it as tripe.'

'At least there we can all agree,' I said, sitting back. Despite my better judgment I found myself believing Purvey's account. It was true that this outspoken priest and his ilk had the potential to do great harm in the realm, and I had long wondered what merit Lancaster saw in Wycliffe. Yet the late theologian had never shown himself disloyal to the crown. Then, just as my mind was settled on this version of things, I realized its obvious implication.

'You two seem to know the *Liber de Mortibus* quite well,' I said. 'Well enough to judge the quality of its poetry, the value of its prophecies. How have you gotten so familiar with such an execrable work?'

A church bell struck for Vespers, struck again, then another sounded in the distance, both carried on the evening air and filling Clanvowe's hall with a low thrum. It's always unsettling to be away from home, where you can't name the bells. Purvey was fingering a last bit of flesh, teasing it round a circle only he could see. He looked up at Clanvowe with the faintest of nods.

Clanvowe grunted. His tight smile broadened when he met my gaze. He said, 'I made a copy.'

THIRTY-THREE

Ditch Street, near Aldgate

'The stews of Southwark be watched.' Eleanor turned from
the slitted window, looking down on what had to be the nar-
rowest, filthiest alley in all London. In the bare room behind
her Millicent and Agnes sat huddled beneath a blanket on an
old furze pallet, the rough gorse spines crackling with their
every move. It had been a chill afternoon, and for a fourth
day the three women had remained inside, waiting for a constable's pounding at the door. One of Bess Waller's girls had
been bringing food and drink to the room, which had seen its
last consistent use two years before as a comfort station of
sorts for travellers from Colchester on the Mile End Road.
No proper beds, just a stack of old linens for warmth. Though
the new ordinances had forced closure of this small venture
in the flesh, Bess Waller still leased the filthy tenement on and
off as a way of maintaining a foothold in this part of the city.

'Gropecunt Lane's being watched,' Eleanor continued. 'The
parvis is being watched. Same with Paternoster Row and St
Paul's. The eyes of all London are looking about for three
maudlyns and a poisonous book.'

'So it is,' said Millicent. 'And we've nearly lost our chance with the one man who has interest in its purchase – thanks to you, Eleanor Rykener.'

They glared at each other. Eleanor didn't trust Millicent Fonteyn the width of a hen's beak, yet here she was, imprisoned in this cursed hole with the uppy trull, and seeing no way out. Unlike Eleanor and Agnes, who'd been living on so little for years, Millicent had plummeted from a condition of genuine wealth and comfort to this dire state. There was a wild, threatened desperation in the woman, like some caged bear on the bankside, baited with a dog, and yet she acted sullen and secretive, casting furtive glances at the book and the stair. Nor did she seem to have any concern for Agnes, who had brought her the book in the first place, put it right in her hands. She treated her sister like a servingwoman, as Eleanor saw it, giving her little commands as if she were some lady at court.

'Selling this book isn't like peddling meat-pies on the bridge,' Eleanor said. 'Why, I seen a man whipped in the street for selling bad herring. Constables catch us at *this*? We'll be lucky if they throw us in the Tun for a month.'

'We can't hold it against Pinchbeak that he was away on king's business when we went to Scroope's Inn,' Millicent disagreed, rubbing her hands together. 'Pinchbeak has wealth beyond our reckoning, ladies, and I for one wish to give him opportunity to lavish it on us.' The two marks were still nearly intact, and Millicent's hope, Eleanor knew, was to multiply the sum twentyfold or more.

Eleanor shook her head, determined to resist Millicent's lust for riches. 'If Pinchbeak had as much interest in this book as yourself, wouldn't he have had something more waiting for you when you went to Scroope's? Besides, you think it's chance that Gropecunt Lane got broken up so soon after you met him at the parvis?'

'Oh, so you think it's my doing now, is that it? Listen to the little thief, Ag, just listen to her!' Millicent taunted.

257

'Oh, *I'm* the thief, is that it, then?' Eleanor's hands balled hotly into fists. 'You two been striding about London these weeks, peddling some other man's book, and Eleanor Rykener's the thief is it?'

Eleanor was now inches from Millicent's nose. Millicent pushed her roughly, then stepped in, ready to strike. Agnes sprang up. She wedged herself between them, a hand on each chest.

'Shut it, you trulls,' said Agnes. 'You want the ward-watch on us?' She gestured to the window. London parishes were small, everyone knew everyone's business, and it would not do to have theirs known by their temporary neighbours. 'If we're not together on this all shall be lost.'

Eleanor turned away, her eyes screwed shut. Millicent's loud breaths slowed.

'Now,' said Agnes, 'let's talk it out. Mill, clamp it for a half-bell and let Eleanor speak her thing. It's the least the girl deserves after what we put her through.'

Millicent shrugged.

'Eleanor, say what you want to say,' said Agnes.

Eleanor calmed herself and spoke. 'There are men we can trust in the city, at the Guildhall. The common serjeant, say. He's helping Gerald, and I don't doubt he'd help us with this matter of the book.' She thought of Ralph Strode, wondering if he had learned of Tewburn's death. 'We can take it to him. Lay out the whole matter as it's pulled us in.'

'Turn ourselves in, then?' said Millicent incredulously. 'Hand the book over, and our bodies with it?'

Millicent's rebuttal began another round of argument that stilled with a sudden noise from the alley.

'Jonah's *cock* it be a hellish walk, and me joints faring poorly.'

A familiar voice, the suck of shoes in mud. The three of them froze, then scrambled about for weapons.

'Bear up, Joannie, bear up,' another voice replied. Equally familiar; more reassuring.

Eleanor walked to the door and opened it a crack. Bess Waller, and behind her trudged Joan Rugg, panting heavily, her great dress half-soaked with her exertion. She stopped when she saw Millicent.

'Ah Lord, Bess, you didn't' – she paused to catch her breath, pushing her hands against her lower back – 'didn't tell me to expect her ladyship'd be about.' Once inside she looked around in the candlelight, then chose a stool against the inner wall. 'What finds a grand lady like Millicent Fonteyn dallying with two common women, albeit one her sister?'

'No whore be commoner than yourself, Joan Rugg,' said Millicent.

'Won't give you a *sed contra* to that, my dear.' Here she looked at Bess. 'I'd suppose between the two of us we've sold half the queynt of London over the years, hey, Bessie?' She shifted her bulk on the stool, allowing a slow fart to escape her mounded form.

Eleanor wrinkled her nose.

'There's no body fouler than your own, Joan Rugg,' said Bess.

'Nor no mouth shaped so like a privy,' Eleanor murmured.

Joan showed her suburban rival a charming smile and farted again. 'A verse for you, my dear:

> We *swyve with pride in Londontown,*
>   *Those Sou'ark men be thine;*
> For *city pricks be long and thick*
>   *Yet Sou'ark's thin as twine.*

My invention, I'll have you know,' she said with considerable pride. 'There be other lines too, if you fancy a hearing on 'em. Now,' she said, turning to her basket, 'how about some supper?'

As Joan Rugg dug out a quantity of bread, cheese, and dried meats, she told the others of the dark events on

Gropecunt Lane over the last week. Eleanor listened carefully, as Joan's story explained a lot. A raid, Joan said, the street broken up, every one of her girls hauled in for questioning – though not by the constables or the beadle's men.

'It weren't king's or mayor's men, I'll be bound,' Joan said, lipping a stale crust. 'Maybe Lancaster's, maybe Oxford's, or Warwick's for all I know. Four men I never seen before. They hauled us up to Cripplegate jail, cleared out a room for themselves to assay us one by one. Wore no badges, nor said a word about their affinity or allegiance. Kept us for three days they did, all packed in a cell like a barrel of Bristol herring.'

Eleanor recalled the broken lanterns on Gropecunt Lane, the unraked piles of dung.

'Then, the very day we're back at swyving,' Joan continued, 'the constables find a body down Pancras. A clerk of the Guildhall, murdered like that poor thing in the Moorfields.' She looked at Eleanor, her voice lowering. 'That's when I knew, girls. When I seen the coroner down in the churchyard, a crowd of the beadle's men around him – and then the alderman himself shows up.'

'Maryns?' Eleanor asked in surprise.

'Grocer and alderman, the very one,' Joan said with a sage nod. 'Now what, I asks myself, has the alderman of Cheap Ward got to do with it all? Where did my Agnes get herself to, and what about that Eleanor Rykener? And who killed that girl, and that Guildhall clerk? A chain of strange happenings, Joan Rugg. Must be more to the matter than it appears.' She raised her chin, proud of her deductive skills. 'That's when I decided it might be well on time to pay a visit to Dame Bess Waller here. Figure we queen bees need to consort when numbers of us start disappearing and folks start getting themselves killed. Parliament of whores is what we need. So I step across the river, find me in Rose Alley for the first time in, oh, must be ten year. And there she is, the cheeky little virgin: Bess Waller, in the incarnate flesh of her, and St Cath as well, fresh as the dew on the fleece!' It was at the Pricking Bishop that Joan learned the same company of dark-cloaked men had also paid a midnight visit to the Southwark stews.

'But the Guildhall usually keeps its hands off your lot,' Bess observed. 'So the question is, what's that clerk's killing got to do with all this trouble for us? What's the damned connection?'

Eleanor took a deep breath. 'I am.'

They all turned to her. She told them about her first visit to the Guildhall, how Strode had put her with Tewburn, who promised to get Gerald moved back to London. Then, during his subsequent visits, the intransigence of the Southwark authorities, and Tewburn's troubles with the butchers. 'Tewburn was set to meet with the Guildable justices the very day he was killed. And Gerald thinks Grimes and his boys are up to something. They want the Rising to start again, and this time to kill the king. You should hear the way Gerald went on about it. Butchers, biding by a bishop's bank, then springing out with their knives.'

Millicent's head whipped around, her eyes wide. She looked about to speak when Joan intervened.

'That explains the little lurker on Gropecunt Lane, then,' she said.

'What lurker?' asked Maud.

'This one's brother,' said Joan, nodding at Eleanor. 'Didn't recognize him at first. He shows up that first day back, mean as you could like. Asks about for Edgar the swerver. 'The swerver' he calls our Eleanor, and his own brother! I told him she hasn't been about, he'll have to come back he wants some of that weird queynt. Guess that wasn't what he was after, though by the—'

'Hold it!' said Millicent, springing up and coming to Eleanor's side. 'What did Gerald say?'

'Said that Grimes and his boys—'

261

'Not that. The part about the bishop's bank.'

'Just what I said,' said Eleanor, taken aback by Millicent's intensity. 'Buncha butchers, biding by a bishop's bank, springing forth with knives.'

Millicent looked sharply at Agnes. 'That's it, then.'

'Sounds like,' Agnes agreed.

'What are you on about now?' Bess demanded.

Millicent went to the low shelf by the door where she had placed the manuscript. Tearing off the cloth, she paged quickly to the final folio and read.

> *'By bank of a bishop shall butchers abide,*
> *To nest, by God's name, with knives in hand,*
> *Then springen in service at spiritus sung.'*

She looked at Eleanor, whose eyes widened with the realization.

Agnes said, 'Seems what your brother's on about is bigger than a lot of talk, Ellie. What do you want to do?'

Eleanor looked at Joan Rugg. 'Did Gerald say where to find him?'

She gave a broad shrug. 'In the Shambles, he tells me. Didn't think much of it at the time. Why would one of my mauds go looking for a little jake like that in the Shambles, of all places? But he says you'll know where to find him if you want him. He'll be there on Saturday morning. Says he can get off of Cutter Lane and over the bridge for a while. Says you'll know the spot.'

She did, and Saturday was the day after tomorrow – though would it be safe? She moved again to the doorway, the fear biting at her. She peered out at the gathering night. 'There's no safe place now, not for any of us been privy to the matter. And I keep seeing Tewburn's eyes pecked out, and that man on Gropecunt Lane.'

'What man's that?' Joan asked.

'The man she saw near St Pancras, the night she found Tewburn,' said Millicent.

'A hook-shaped scar on his chin,' said Eleanor, repeating the description she'd given the others. 'Name is Sir Stephen.' Millicent had sworn she'd seen such a chin before, though she couldn't place the man, or so she had claimed.

'Best to lay low,' said Bess Waller, 'give it another week or two, and this whole thing's like to pass by. Forget about the book. Look to yourselves.'

It was Agnes who saw the great moral flaw in their talk. 'Wait, now,' she said. Eleanor watched the beautiful girl as she stepped to the middle of the room, her face aglow with her sincerity. 'We're all thinking about profit, about coin, about Lady Meed and what she'll do for us if we sell the book to the right man,' said Agnes. 'Thinking on our own lives, as if our bodies be the only bodies worth keeping from the grave. Yet here we sit with a book and a cloth speaking the murder of our very king two weeks hence, and what are we *not* thinking about?'

Eleanor nodded slowly, ashamed of herself but with a surge of love and admiration for her friend. 'About King Richard.'

'And our having the means in hand to save him!' said Agnes.

Millicent snorted. 'It's not our lot to save his neck. This whole matter is far above our heads, and has been from the beginning. With the book we can buy our lives back, and wealth for ourselves. *That* should be our aim, and no other. Let someone else look to the king's sorry life.'

'That's not right, Mil,' said Agnes, shaking her beautiful head. 'Just not right.'

'You'd throw away our one chance at new fortune?' Millicent demanded. 'To what purpose, Agnes?'

Agnes tossed her head, her loose hair a noble bonnet of gold. 'To save our king.'

263

Joan Rugg threw back her head, cackling incautiously. 'Who'd have thought it?' The bawd smoothed her dress over her generous thighs, her chins aglow in the lamplight: a bull-frog's throat on a moonlit pond. 'The very King of England, by the cross, and his life in the hands of five whores!'

THIRTY-FOUR

Ditch Street, near Aldgate

Lifting the blanket as gently as she could, Millicent moved
to the edge of the bed and set her feet on the floor. Agnes
stirred beside her; Eleanor lay motionless against the wall.
Millicent reached for her shoes. The book rested in its nook,
hidden by a dirty cloth. She'd oiled the garnets the night
before, telling the others she was doing it for their protection:
if the watch were about and they needed to flee, better to
have the advantage of silence. Before cock-crow, she stole
out of the small tenement.

She moved through the city in the pre-dawn darkness, her
destination the landmark described on the note she'd sent
to Thomas Pinchbeak yesterday. With a stub of coal, Millicent
had scribbled the note on to one of the book's blank flyleaves,
sliced from the manuscript with a dull knife and folded into
a small square, a stableboy on Leadenhall and a farthing
enough to get the note to Pinchbeak, who, she felt sure,
would show himself at the appointed time and place – or,
more likely, send one of his minions.

Reaching the cross above the Puddle-wharf, she peered
down upper Thames Street into the rising dawn. A narrow

slice of river glistened in a thin, red line. A heavy breeze from the waterfront pushed her skirts hard against her legs. The bells of St Andrew-by-Wardrobe rang Prime. Few Londoners moved along the broad, unpaved expanse wending down to the water.

She heard a shuffled foot on the pavers, then the roll of a kicked pebble, ticking against the base of the cross. At last, she thought. She took a last turn around the cross and lifted her head with a ready smile.

Eleanor Rykener, her arms folded on her narrow chest, wide eyes flashing in the dawn. 'What's this, then?'

'I'll have none of your suspicion, Eleanor Rykener,' Millicent shot back. 'Look at yourself, why don't you? Taken to following me, tracing my every step.'

'Only when your steps lead the rest of us under the wagon,' Eleanor retorted. She looked her up and down. 'Where is it?'

'Where is what?' Millicent said, not meeting her eyes.

'The book, you cold slut.' Eleanor took a step toward her. 'Where is it? Brought it here to sell, did you?'

'And if I did?' said Millicent defiantly.

'Then we'll have it back, sure,' said Eleanor. Another step. 'And now.'

From around the corner of St Andrew's came a loud flock of sheep, bound for the Friday markets at Smithfield. A river of wool flowed around them as a boy slapped at flanks, his dog skirting the flow in a wide semicircle, nipping with the confidence of an earl. '*Cumbiday, cumbiday,*' the boy called to a few lingerers. In the wake of the sheep walked a man Millicent recognized immediately.

'Watch, now,' she warned Eleanor. The man followed the sheep to the top of St Andrew's Hill, making directly for the cross.

He was no less than a barn's width from the cross when Millicent remembered who he was. Not Pinchbeak but the rude young man from the porch of St Paul's: that gutter spitter who'd tried to bar her entry from the parvis. He stopped ten feet in front of them, hands at his sides, and gave a mocking bow as the last of the flock passed by. 'Fair ladies,' he said, his contempt undisguised.

'Your name,' said Millicent. 'Say it.' He had come alone, it appeared.

'Robert Dawson,' the man said with a pompous air. 'Steward to Master Thomas Pinchbeak, serjeant-at-law in the service of King Richard. You have the book?'

'You have the coin?' Millicent shot back.

Dawson reached into a pocket and withdrew a small sack. He jangled it before her, the coins within mixing dully. He tossed it on the pavers between them. 'Direct from Master Pinchbeak himself. Forty marks, all in gold nobles and halfs.'

Forty marks. Not a fortune, but easily enough to lease a house in Cornhull or anywhere else for a long while, keep them all in food and clothing, purchase their way into a craft of some kind – as seamstresses, embroideresses, or what have you – and take on their own apprentices. Enough to buy a new life.

Millicent felt her shoulders relax for the first time in months. Such a sum was unimaginable for a book, no matter its content. There must be great and wide belief in these prophecies, she reasoned, or a man like Thomas Pinchbeak would never offer such an exorbitant price. 'What do you think?' she said, turning to her still-hostile companion. 'Forty marks – a suitable sum for our effort, and our prize?'

Eleanor glared at her. 'Though if forty, why not a hundred?'

'A good question,' said Millicent, turning on Dawson, feeling giddy. 'Why not a hundred marks, Robert Dawson?'

'Forty marks, says the serjeant, nor a penny more, my lovely ladies.' He leered at them in a manner that stretched his face to look like one of those stone monsters on St Paul's.

'Very well.' Millicent reached into a side pocket and pulled out the book. The embroidered covering was smooth in her hand, and as she palmed it she realized neither she nor Dawson had mentioned it as part of the exchange. As casually as she could she untied the thong and stuffed the cloth back into her pocket. She took a step toward the man and held out the manuscript.

Dawson flipped through the book, then slipped it into a pouch at his side. He said nothing about the cloth. Dawson looked at Millicent for a moment, his eyes narrowing in amusement. With a nod, he turned from them and made his way past the cross and up Thames Street, soon disappearing along the ward's dim byway.

'Well, pillory me,' said Eleanor, shaking her head as she looked after him. She turned to Millicent with a look of bewilderment. 'Forty marks.'

'Forty marks,' Millicent repeated, squatting for the parse. With the coin in hand, she allowed herself to feel some affection for her sister's wily companion, and of regret for endangering her life. For Eleanor had come through her own hell: forced out of her livelihood, pursued through the streets of London half-starving, she'd stolen a book from a brothel and found a corpse in a churchyard – and yet here she was, still standing, about to receive a small fortune. Feeling generous, Millicent shook the purse. 'And a third yours, Eleanor Rykener. Thirteen marks and change? That's a lot of cock, if memory serves.'

Eleanor smiled grudgingly, and together they walked back toward the precincts of Aldgate. 'You were right all along, I suppose,' said Eleanor. 'What do we do with all that coin, now we got it?'

'We'll buy us some finery, purchase our way out of this pottage,' said Millicent. 'I'll teach you and Agnes to speak like ladies instead of mauds, find you a squire to share between you. Agnes will have him on even days, you on odds, and you'll hump him together at the Nativity, Easter, and All Saints. How's that?'

They stepped up Fenchurch toward the walls, neither of

them giving mind to the moral charge Agnes had placed on them. *To save our king.* Yet in the presence of all that gold, now clutched in Millicent's hands and filling their minds with heady visions of new lives, it was all too easy to forget the dark prophecies whose writing and sale had put the heavy purse in their possession. Millicent listened with a new contentment as Eleanor spoke of a future that now seemed miraculously possible. 'Maybe I'll become a chandler, and Gerald'll cut me out the fat – sheep fat, cow fat, pig fat, goose fat, goat fat – and our candles'll be purchased up and down Cheap and Cornhull, maybe even Calais, why not, and by priors and canons and merchant taylors and all of them.'

As Eleanor spoke of her dreams Millicent untied the heavy purse. As soon as her fingers grazed the first coins she knew – and should have known earlier, during the handoff, when these coins had echoed not with the bright ting of gold, but with the deadened clank of lead. She pulled one out and bit it, leaving toothmarks across its centre.

As she clutched the worthless plug her hands began to shake, yet she said nothing to Eleanor, who walked before her with the bounce of imagined wealth in her step. But when? When should she tell her, and tell Agnes, that she had traded their only hope for a bag of lead, fit for the lining of a conduit, or the smelting of a cheap cross for a country church?

They had reached Ditch Street. Millicent looked up through her tears and into an unearthly scene. A large crowd had assembled in the small patch of dirt before Bess Waller's tenement. From the conversation around them they gathered what had happened. A woman's scream in the dark – the neighbourhood roused, lanterns put alight in the rising dawn, the hue raised around the ward against a fleeing man, though no word yet on the outcome of the pursuit.

As they watched dumbly from the edge of the crowd, the victim was borne out to the street, a spill of golden hair, a river of crusting blood along a whitened arm and a reddened hand that seemed to beckon them forward.

Agnes.

Millicent pushed through the crowd and grasped her sister's arm. Eleanor cradled her head, and the crowd pressed in around them.

'*Doovay leebro. Doovay leebro,*' Agnes moaned.

'Oh, Ag—'

'The – the crochet, Mil,' said Agnes. '*Doovay leebro.* It was him.' She raised her hand to her chin, then looked into Millicent's eyes, her own now delirious with pain, and darkened with memory. 'The maid on the moor, her yelling at the moon like that. It's the crochet. His face. 'When father, son, and ghost we sing, of city's – city's blade . . .' Her eyes froze. A final breath.

Millicent heard a splintering keen as she sank to the ground, the sack of lead plugs making a dull thud beside her. A red dawn cast the tenements in a hellish blush, and the sobbing was her own.

THIRTY-FIVE

The Oxford Road

Bone-weary and still five miles out from Newgate, I heeled the mare's flanks and caught up to Will Cooper. He handed me his skin, the warmed ale doing little to lift my spirits. I had left Southwark determined to ferret out the truth behind the prophecies of Lollius. Now, with nearly two weeks passed and the work in hand, I was filled with doubt. Clanvowe had stunned me with the revelation that he had made a copy of the *De Mortibus* after it fell into his hands in London. Yet the knight had offered little advice on what to do with the volume.

Surrender the book to the agents of the king? Hardly: even its possession put me in a perilous situation given the current factionalism in the realm. In my saddlebag was a book that imagined the violent demise of England's king, a work enumerating royal deaths just as Swynford's cards enumerated fates. Despite reading the work a dozen times, I still had not puzzled out the link between the poem and the cards, and there was much in the thirteenth prophecy that made no sense – though some of its words danced before my eyes with a taunting clarity. *Long castle will collar and cast out the core.* It was with this line, and all it implied, that I would begin my return to the city.

As the towers of Westminster loomed before us, I ordered Will ahead with our packhorse. 'I'll be at Overey for a late supper. Ask Simon to join me after the Angelus bell.'

'As you wish, Master Gower,' said Will.

By dusk I was in Guildhall yard. Ralph Strode, as I'd expected, was in. I gave him Quincey's greetings from Oxford. He bent to remove a bottle from a chest at his feet, then poured us a jar of dark wine before easing his bulk on to a chair that groaned with the accommodation.

I looked at him. 'I have the book, Ralph.'

Strode tilted his head, frowned. 'The book.' His eyes widening. 'You mean the book of—'

'*Liber de Mortibus Regum Anglorum.* I have it, Ralph, and I don't know what to do with it. Nor with myself.' I set Clanvowe's manuscript on the desk, where it sat for a long while. Strode stared at the leathern cover as if the book were a dead pig in his bed. At last he sighed, arranged his candles, and opened it.

Ralph Strode was generally a sonorous reader, known to grunt and murmur while shuffling through the many depositions, writs, and other documents that constituted the material regime of his office. Yet he read the *De Mortibus* in silence, the only sound in his chambers the rough whisper of parchment on his thumb. Finally he closed the manuscript and handed it across his desk.

'Your persistence is admirable, Gower.' Robed arms folded at his chest, a still width in the candlelight. 'You found it in Angervyle's library?'

I drank slowly, considering how much to tell him. 'The only whiff of a Lollius to be found among Bury's manuscripts came from the works of Horace.'

'"Oblivion, dark and long, has locked them in a tearless grave",' Strode quoted Horace in Latin, his eyes dark and inscrutable slits. 'Of course.'

272

'That's right.' Though impressed as always by the common serjeant's prodigious memory, I felt, too, that Strode's reaction was skewed, as if I had offended propriety by bringing this book back to London.

'How did you get it, John?'

'It's a copy,' I admitted. 'Made by a friend of ours.'

He narrowed his eyes. 'Clanvowe?' At my nod he looked away. 'I thought I recognized the hand, should have suspected his role in all this. Sir John's connections among Wycliffe's minions are as deep as Lancaster's.'

'We have to take this to the mayor, Ralph, or the chancellor,' I said. 'St. Dunstan's Day is less than two weeks away.'

Strode pushed the volume across his desk and angled his frame toward the wall. 'Are you mad, John?' Closing me off.

'What?'

'I can't have anything to do with this. Nor with you, if you insist on taking this up the ladder.'

'But, Ralph, don't you see it? "*Long castle will collar*"? You and I both know what this means. You have to see reason here—'

'*Reason?*' Strode thundered, coming to his feet. 'You speak of *reason*, and yet you bring this poison into the Guildhall? This work has been circulating among agents of the French, John, I told you that *weeks* ago. And meanwhile you've been picking at justices, bishops, clerks, coroners, Lancaster's own whore, threatening them with God knows what so *you* can find it. To say nothing of the maudlyns.'

'The maudlyns?'

'The corpses are stacking up, John.'

'What corpses? What the hell are you tal—'

'You've heard about Symkok?'

This stopped me. 'Nick Symkok?'

'Took a header off the bridge. An accident, Tyle's saying.'

The clerk for the subcoroner, the man who'd been feeding me some of my best information for nearly twenty years. 'He

273

knew something,' I said. I'd seen it in his eyes that day at the coroner's chambers. Why hadn't I pressed him sooner? Then it got worse.

'And my man Tewburn. Asks a few questions around Southwark and gets a slit throat for his troubles.'

'James Tewburn is dead?'

'Murdered, Gower, and left for the birds in the St Pancras churchyard.'

'Ralph, I don't know what to say. Are you sure—'

'Now I learn you've been conjuring with Clanvowe, a known affiliate of Wycliffe and his strongest voice in Richard's affinity! Why do you think the man was sent off to Wales last week?'

'*Conjuring*?' I protested, rising and jabbing a finger at his massive face. 'You listen to me, Ralph. *I'm* the one who's been trying to keep this whole mess from exploding in our faces. This isn't even the original stolen from La Neyte. It's a copy.'

'And all the more seditious for that,' he said, giving me a breath of the half-eaten pie on his desk. 'The talk of a plot against the king is growing more feverish by the day. Now you return from Oxford, from an evening with Sir John Clanvowe, of all people, with the work that sparked it all. I don't suppose Purvey broke bread with you? I hear he's in Oxford. But not even you could be that stupid, John.'

I hesitated.

'No,' he said, backing away.

'Wait – Ralph—'

'Oh for Bart's skin!' he howled at the rafters. 'Where the hell is your mind, Gower? Our nation is on the verge of war again, and you're dallying with budding heretics?' His breath slowed, his voice laden with quiet warning. 'Let's hope those buds don't bloom, Gower, at least not until Dunstan's Day is safely passed.'

With that he dismissed me, his stony silence and averted gaze like twin weights on my shoulders as I left Guildhall yard. The hour was late, and I was badly shaken, in no state for another appointment that evening, though it couldn't be avoided. My suspicion had sharpened since leaving Oxford with Clanvowe's manuscript, and there was one line from the prophecies rattling my skull with the racket of rocks in a jar – the line I had just recited to Strode, provoking his fury. *Long castle will collar and cast out the core*. The 'core', I was convinced, was *cor*, Latin for 'heart', and signified King Richard's personal emblem, the white hart. 'Long castle' was equally obvious: longcastle, longcaster, Lancaster – a young boy could make the connection, and 'Longcastel' was a spelling I had seen on more than one document in Lancaster's own hand.

Worst of all, I had seen this bit of wordplay before. In another poem, an elegy, written some years ago after the death of Gaunt's first wife, Duchess Blanche. And in the great liturgy of information and deceit, coincidence is an unknown song.

I pushed on to Leadenhall, which I took to the city's easternmost gate, still open to the few stragglers making their way into the city from Bethnal Green or Whitechapel, their features alight with the torches along the inner gate. Aldgate loomed over me like a midnight eagle from its eyrie, its single eye a lone candle high above, shining through a glazed window that might have been Chaucer's parlour. The stairways and apartments climbing Aldgate created a labyrinthine ascent to the top, where I went down a quarter-stair and passed through an arched walkway giving on to the high landing before Chaucer's apartments.

I took the heavy knocker in hand, intending to tap lightly, but the bronze lozenge escaped my grasp. A booming concussion echoed through the precincts of Aldgate. The heavy door opened to reveal the frown of a servant. The man looked me up and down, his face twisted with displeasure. I inquired after Chaucer and got a curt reply. 'Master Chaucer's away from London till Monday, sir, his affairs takin' him to port a' Dover.' Three days. I left strict instructions for Chaucer to contact me on his return.

Now over the bridge, the narrow way between shops and stalls. As I passed the open parts of the span, the water rushing darkly below, my hand moved more than once to my bag; I felt a mounting temptation to cast Clanvowe's manuscript into the Thames and be done with the entire affair.

I knew something was wrong before I reached the gate to Overey close. Will Cooper stood just outside, a sputtering lantern suspended from his fingers. When he saw me he moved in big strides up the lane. One of his eyes was blackened. A line of blood had crusted on his upper lip.

'Master Gower!'

'What is it, Will?'

'They've taken Simon, sir.'

'Who?'

'King's men, looked like.'

'Whatever for?'

'Treason's what they said.'

'*Treason*?' My hand went to my mouth. The counterfeiting. Someone must have slipped news of Simon's transgression to an agent of the crown, and after all this time. As I stood there I vowed revenge – even on Chaucer, if he proved my betrayer. 'Did they have a warrant?'

'Not's I saw.'

But of course they didn't. The thought chilled my bones. If they'd taken Simon for treason, a warrant would be unnecessary. He might already be dead.

'We had a bit of a struggle, we did,' Will went on, 'with two of 'em having to hold me back. I got a beating, 's you can see.'

'Where did they take him?' I asked. 'Marshalsea?'

He shook his head. 'Newgate, was what they said.'

Fresh shoes, a quick supper on my feet. It was well past curfew. I bought my way across the bridge.

Newgate. Tom Tugg, roused from sleep, had wrapped himself in a surcoat when informed of my arrival, and now stood yawning at the gatehouse door.

'What is this, Tugg?' I demanded. 'Treason?'

He looked at me strangely. 'You know the rub, Gower. Imagining and purposing falsely and traitorously t'destroy the Royal Person of the king, and therewith t'destroy his Realm.'

'I can quote the Statute of Treasons as well as you. But what are the charges? Is there a writ you can show me, something more specific?'

Tugg gave a slow shrug. 'I am a jailer, not a judge.'

'Yes, but—' I stopped pressing him, realizing I would get nowhere with pleas alone. I reached for my purse. 'How much will it take, Tugg?'

'Take?'

'To see my son.'

The keeper stepped back, his head shaking. 'None a' your shillings now, Gower, not a king's ransom for a mote a' time with a traitor.'

'It's counterfeiting, Tugg, not exactly an attack on His Highness's person. I'll credit you a full pound.'

Tugg frowned at me, intrigued – but ignoring the offer. 'Heard nothing about counterfeiting, Gower.'

I instantly realized my mistake – an inexcusable one, for I'd just revealed to the keeper of Newgate prison the secret crime that could still hang Simon at Tyburn, and exposed my own role in covering up the evidence. Trying to recover from my error, I made a more exorbitant offer. 'Ten nobles, Tugg.'

He stared at me, now looking worried for my sanity, then plucked the heavy purse out of my palm. 'That'll do.'

'Good. Now take me to my son.' I tried to push past him.

Tugg wedged himself into the opening. A guard stepped up behind him. 'Can't.'

'What are you talking about?'

'He's not here.'

'*What*? You told me—'

'I told you nothing. You're the one bellowing about treason, counterfeiting, your son. Newgate hasn't swallowed a new morsel since last week.'

I stared, and it struck me almost violently how far my poise and skill had plummeted over the last weeks. And how pathetic it must have appeared that John Gower, who fashioned himself the great trafficker in men's secrets, had freely handed three of his own to the keeper of Newgate. Then Tugg slammed the door in my face, leaving me to imagine the worst. Flaying, whipping, a cruel surgeon with a dull knife. With these and other tortures pressing my thoughts, I walked home through a city dark with night, knowing my son was somewhere in its foul grip.

THIRTY-SIX

Spitalfields, outside Bishopsgate

The three of them stood in the May drizzle as Agnes's grave
was carved in the earth. The strikes of shovel in soil were
comforting in their way, though the digger's glossing didn't
help. 'Pull a skull out the pit every day, it seems,' he said
during one of his breaks. 'Reckon half of hell be filled with
Spitalfields souls.'

Eleanor, shivering, could sense them there, waiting for the
resurrection, when God would call them up, so the preachers
said, when all the decayed flesh and old bones would rejoin
their souls like some meat puppet in heaven.

They owed their presence at Agnes's burial to Joan Rugg.
In the commotion following the murder, Eleanor and Millicent
had slipped out of the Aldgate neighbourhood and back to
the Bishop before the questions started, avoiding the gathering
of the jury and the coroner's inquest. A beadle recognized
Agnes as one of Joan's crew and, after summoning the bawd
to the inquest, released the body for a pauper's burial at the
Spitalfields, where Joan's cuz, Sam Varney, worked as under-
digger. Joan sent word to Bess about the timing, and the three
of them came across that morning. They bound Agnes in a

rough shroud and loaded her on to the digger's cart for the haul out to the burial yard.

As the hole deepened they gathered bluebells from the far corners of the churchyard and carried them to the edge of the pit, with stems of thyme to give Agnes safe passage to the world beyond, and some separation from the other bodies in the partially exposed pit. The gravedigger made quick work of lining the floor, the bluebell stems in the direction of her feet, the thyme a cushion for her head. Finally he coaxed his nag around to the top of the grave and pulled Agnes out by her feet, sending her shrouded form through the air. It landed on the bluebells with a muted finality. He shovelled dirt on top of her. Soon she was gone.

Bess Waller fell to the ground, smudging her dress in the morbid soil. 'Oh, the beautiful little dear! Oh, the most precious body what ever lived!'

Eleanor, silent in her own desolation, watched Millicent. Her face was blank, though Eleanor could feel her fury at her mother as a living thing.

'Stop it, Bess,' Millicent finally said. 'Just stop it.'

Bess's voice hitched. 'Stop it, you say?'

'Your sorrow is *feigned*,' Millicent said, the last word shot at her mother as an arrow of contempt. 'Where was your concern for this "most precious body" when Ag was a girl? Your "beautiful little dear", her arse split open by half the friars of London.' Millicent's voice shook with hatred. 'Agnes was nothing to you but pennies for her queynt.'

Bess pushed herself off the ground. The digger paused in his shovelling.

'Was you who killed her.' Bess shook a finger. 'You who took the book away to sell to Pinchbeak's man, leaving her in those rooms with nothing to bargain for her life. And for what? Bag of lead plugs, and a cold grave in the Spitalfields. So don't you talk to *me* about concern for my

Agnes. By St Agnes herself, don't you say a word. You're the one put her in the ground.'

Millicent raised a hand, then turned away, clutched her stomach, and vomited on the soil. All her reserve left her then, her face losing its frozen pride in a bare moment. Eleanor stepped forward, but Millicent waved her off, shaking her head wildly, retching between words.

'She be – she be right, an't she? Bess Waller be as – be as right as the cursed – cursed rain, don't she? I killed me Agnes, right as if I bladed her meself.'

Eleanor stared at her in wonder. From the refined diction of a knight's courtesan Millicent's speech had lowered itself to the rough patter of the stews. She sounds like me now, Eleanor thought; no, like Agnes.

'That's not true, Mil,' she said, but Millicent backed away, arms held before her face. She fled from the churchyard and disappeared beyond a distant garden.

Bess Waller turned back to the grave, ignoring her. After a final look at the soil covering Agnes, Eleanor made her way out of the Spitalfields yard. All her thoughts were on Gerald, now her one intimate in all the world.

She went through the city walls at Bishopsgate, then westward, to the Shambles. To her left were slaughterstalls once the largest in London, now diminished by Parliament and the city, though still redolent with mingled breaths of shit and death, halved cows hooked four to a beam, gutters spattered with new blood aglisten in the full sun. A few sheep, cows, and goats occupied the far stalls, while the walls of the abattoir were lined with the knives and cleavers for killing time.

Finally she reached the church. St Nicholas Shambles, the stenchiest in all London, and the only one that was ever hers. Her parents had been steadfast parishioners all their lives, and their parents, and probably theirs for all she knew. Eleanor knew its crumbling stairs, its skewed porch, its plain rood screen like she knew her own teeth. After their mother's death she and Gerald had come every day for alms, along with the rest of the parish's poor, until the parson realized they were orphans and turned them over to the city.

Inside the church was silent, the air familiar despite her long absence from its damp and smell. Her brother stepped from a dark recess near one of the side chapels. He'd lost a bit of his sneer, and let Eleanor grasp his arm and lead him to a bench near the west door.

'That fellow from the Guildhall you sent around,' Gerald began. 'Grimes didn't like it much, when he got wind of the transfer, and all the questions.'

'Grimes killed him, then?'

'Not Grimes.' He looked off. She grabbed his chin, turned him toward her.

'Who then?'

He shrugged. 'Don't know their names. They're the ones that bring the priest around and spread coin. The priest that has them all convinced it's God's will that the butchers of Southwark lead the new Rising, reading to them all from a prophecy, he calls it. Their destiny it is, to save all England with their flaying knives! Then I hear them in Grimes's house, talking about Tewburn. He learned something, Tewburn did, something about the plot. Heard them saying he has to go or he'll bring them all down. So they killed him. And now they're all set to kill the king, kill King Richard! And they have a day set, too. They're to do it on—'

'Dunstan's Day,' she finished for him.

He looked at her, his eyes wide. 'How'd you know that, Eleanor?'

She whispered it. '*On day of Saint Dunstan shall Death have his doom.*'

He swallowed, and she told him about the book, from the murder on the Moorfields to the deaths of James Tewburn and Agnes Fonteyn.

'Same as the parson says, and Grimes believes it,' said Gerald. 'It's all true, then. There *is* a prophecy.'

She gazed into the far end of the nave, through the gloom beyond the screen. 'A prophecy, a plot, a pickle. Who knows? What I do know is, a maudlyn and a butcher's boy don't have any business meddling with a king's death. This be far above us, Gerald.' She took his hand. 'When you go back to Grimes you can't let on that you know anything, you hear? Play it humble, like you're his ass or dog got smacked into obeying. Do anything he says. Meanwhile I'll figure it out from this end. If we want to come out of all this with our heads, and the king with his, we best find someone with sway. Some real weight.'

'Father Edmund?' Gerald asked, referring to the old parson of St Nicholas.

'Not him,' said Eleanor, who had already discarded the thought. Though kind, Father Edmund was elderly and frail, and the parson of the poorest parish in London could hardly command the needed attention in royal circles. She looked at her brother. 'But I know just the man.'

THIRTY-SEVEN

Bankside, west of Southwark

The days following my return from Oxford were some of the darkest of my life – as dark, in many ways, as that bleak time around the deaths of my children. Simon, seized in the night, facing torture and who knew what else, if he even remained alive. My greatest friendship, threatened with a treasonous book and a dead girl. Three murders, none of them comprehensible, yet all related in a way I could not yet see. I had lost, too, the trust and goodwill of Ralph Strode, and of other powerful men of the city and the court. I could only imagine the whispers in the Guildhall, at Westminster, in the parvis at St Paul's, at the inns and the Temple, the sneers of derision from the likes of Sir Stephen Weldon and Thomas Pinchbeak. *Gower's finally got his due*, they would say; *serves him right, too, after the way he's built his fortune and his name.* Though terrified for Simon, for the realm, and for myself, I felt frozen with indecision, and moved through each hour in an almost gluttonous torpor, feeding only on my desire for self-preservation.

On the first Sunday I roused myself early, intending to listen to the dawn office. Instead, without thinking, I made my way past the docks and on to the broad river path running west from Southwark. Soon I had left London far behind, passing Westminster on the far shore, skirting the great houses along the banks, walking as I hadn't in years, from village to village, sometimes on the high road with the horses and hackneys, then along the narrower way by the river, among sheep and cows taking water. For hours I ignored my hunger, the pains in my legs and feet, and it was well past midday when I looked ahead and realized I had come as far as Staines Bridge, a river crossing easily twenty miles from London. The stone marker was there on the bank, leaving me stunned at how far I had walked, and walked alone, despite the dangers. The keeper at the inn gave me a heavy lamb sop with bread and a cheese. The food did nothing to revive my spirits. I thought of borrowing a horse for the return, thought twice, then set off on foot as the parish bell tolled for None.

Several hours later, as I neared the ferry at Putney under the last afternoon glare, the storm clouds gathering behind me made their first distant rumblings. I had expected to find the quay nearly empty, as it had been that morning. Instead a large company of infantry filled the road above the embarkation point, visibly anxious to secure passage to Fulham and the highway to London before the coming storm. The ferry stood thirty feet out, but the ferrymen and his helpers would not bring it to shore. The unexplained delay was causing a growing resentment among the soldiers, several clearly drunk. Conscripts, I guessed, commoners without a knight or squire among them. Not the sort of armed crowd a lightly guarded ferryman would normally put off.

'Haul it in, Linton!' one of them called out, crashing his worn shield against a companion's.

'Bring her to, you wastrel!'

'Want a boot to the neck, ferryman?'

The situation was growing uglier by the minute, and I kept

my distance. Many of these conscripted garrisons were no better than loose gangs of highwaymen. I could smell the days of travel on these men, the crusted stink of a forced march. One of the rougher men approached a boy sitting on a post.

'See here, Linton!' the man called across the water, unsheathing a knife. 'Tasty-looking son you have here. Shall we cook him up for our supper, have victualling from his flesh?' The boy leaned away, terror in his eyes.

'Let him go, now!' Linton called from the water. His servants started arguing among themselves. Within moments the quay and the vessel had erupted in a loud melee. Swords were drawn, knives unsheathed.

Then, out of nowhere, a trumpet, and a call ahead: 'The king's guard! Make way for the king's guard!'

King Richard's chief herald, a clarion voice I would have recognized anywhere. There was a general shuffle as the rough crowd parted to allow the chargers through. Three knights looked down from their slowing mounts on to the double ranks of soldiers, all wearing neutral expressions as they obediently made way for better men.

Cavalry and infantry, the eternal hierarchy of war, and now it had likely saved a life. The advance guard approached the quay and called out to the ferryman, whose boy was already helping his father ready the ropes for the vessel's arrival on the shore, explaining the delay. The ferryman had been waiting for these members of King Richard's household, and had been unwilling to bear the infantrymen across the river for fear of incurring their wrath.

The situation was still tense, however, and I was about to call out for their protection of the boy – and myself – when the clatter of more hooves sounded from the high road. Eight more knights, riding two abreast, and between them King Richard and Bolingbroke, his cousin and Lancaster's son. Every man went to his knees, doffed his hat or helmet.

'All hail the king!' one of them called out.

'All hail the king!' came the echo.

As he passed through, King Richard slowed his mount long enough to speak small words of encouragement, of the sort I had heard him deliver on other occasions to high and low alike. Bolingbroke wore a bored look, bemused, as if sharing his father's disdain for any relations of noble and commoner beyond the barely necessary.

I knelt in an outer rank, my dress separating me from the crowd of infantry, though I wasn't expecting to be noticed. I caught the king's eye, assuming he would pass without a second look, though I also recalled his probing gaze at Westminster a few weeks before.

He pulled his charger to a stop. 'Why, is that John Gower?'

'It is, Your Highness,' I said, hiding my reluctance. The crowd parted to allow the king full view of his hailed subject.

'Come forward,' Richard commanded me. I went to the horse's side, my nose at the level of the king's waist. Richard dismounted, signalling to Bolingbroke to do the same. He handed off his reins. 'Walk along with us,' the king said. I obeyed, though not without fear for my head. Richard's behaviour had grown increasingly erratic by all accounts, and I worried that he would draw on me in his barge just as he had on Braybrooke not three months before. Did he know anything about my involvement in the search for the book, or about the seizure of Simon? The horses were led on and lashed at the ferry's bow. 'You'll cross with us, Gower?'

'I would be delighted, Your Highness, if it's not too much of an imposition.'

'Hardly! I tire of my cousin's dismal company.'

Bolingbroke forced a smile. 'We could use some sharper wit to get us over the river. These knights are a grim lot.'

Richard stepped on to the ferry, looking back at the infantry. 'Unfortunate to make these men wait.'

I followed him on to the shallow vessel. 'They are eager to cross before the storm, Your Highness.'

Richard looked at the low clouds now settling to the west. 'You are far from home, Gower, and on foot. You live in London?'

'In Southwark, Your Highness.'

'Southwark – well! So we'll be taking you *out* of your way, then,' he chuckled. The ferry cast off; the knights standing forward gathered into a loose cluster, listening to Bolingbroke as he regaled them in his vivacious way. For a while, as the shouts and work of the crew got us moving, I watched the king observe his cousin, his emotions unreadable. For the Duke of Lancaster the lack of a crown had seemed always a burden, as if he were weighed down by the continual failure of ambition. For his son this lack seemed a relief, an easing of expectation, perhaps, that gave him confidence in his high status without the desire or need to move beyond it. As a result, young Henry was more natural in front of a crowd than Gaunt, able to speak with older knights and gentlemen with an ease and grace that eluded his father. Richard, who shared Lancaster's reserve, seemed to perceive this freer quality in Bolingbroke. I had often wondered whether the king wished he were more like his cousin.

There was a moment then, as the ferry reached the middle of the wide waterway, when I nearly told the king everything. Years afterwards I would look back on that river crossing with some regret, for speaking up might have forestalled all that would follow. Perhaps the king already knew everything there was to know about the prophecies, I reasoned then; on the other hand, he might be ignorant of the whole affair, and saying something to him would elevate the matter far above where it now stood. Richard and Gaunt were already at one another's throats; who was I to insert myself into this running quarrel? So I said nothing, whether out of fear or self-doubt or lack of confidence in the young king's wisdom I don't know. How to present a king with the prophecy of his own death?

King Richard looked across the water. 'And what are you composing these days, Gower, in your mind or on parchment?'

I stumbled a bit, mentioning my notion of a romance of sorts, though a moralized one, then sought to deflect the question on to him. 'What sort of work would please you, Your Highness?'

King Richard shrugged. 'I find biblical stories tedious. I do like Ovid, at least the chunks of him I've read. And modern stories that make us question ourselves, our motivations and character.'

'Question ourselves, Your Highness?'

'Think of the tale of Sir Lancelot *en la charrette*,' the king said, warming to the popular story. 'Smitten with Guinevere, on a quest to rescue her from her abductor, Lancelot finds himself on foot. He's on the road, fully armed, hardly able to walk – and horseless. Suddenly a cart comes by, a humble cart, driven along by a dwarf. Lancelot begs a ride. Now he's a knight in a cart, entering a city as if a traitor, or a murderer. But Lancelot loves Guinevere so severely that he'd do anything to keep on task, including enduring the humiliation of himself in front of an entire city. The story is about the extreme condition of love, teaching us the consequences of following its commands too blindly, and without regard for our reputation.'

'Quite right, Your Highness,' I said, impressed with the young king's skills as an interpreter. 'Lancelot embodies the danger of excessive love.'

'Perhaps,' the king said, tilting his head. 'But do you know the detail of that story I like most, Gower?'

'What is that, Your Highness?'

'Do you recall the moment when the dwarf, driving the cart, invites Gawain to join Lancelot?'

I confessed that I did not.

'The dwarf invites him into the cart,' Richard continued. 'And when he does, he says to him, 'If you are as much your own enemy as is this humiliated knight, sitting here in my cart, why, climb on in, and I shall take you along.' Gawain refuses, of course, for as he knows very well, it would be the height of dishonour for a knight to exchange his charger for a mere cart.

'Yet Lancelot has already done it. He has climbed into the humble cart, put himself in a base position while Gawain stays proudly out of it, disdaining the thought. But what if Gawain *had* joined Lancelot, as the dwarf asked him to? What if he had made a different choice, gone in a different direction than what his pride told him was right? And what if we, in turn, followed his example? "Are you Sir Lancelot, or are you Sir Gawain?" the poet seems to ask. Will you abase yourself for the sake of something vitally important to you? Or will you stand aside like Gawain, loftily removed from the squalor, even as a greater man climbs within, risking it all?'

I nodded. 'I see, Your Highness. The choices of the characters mirror our own choices.'

'Exactly,' he said, his young face brightening. 'The best stories, it seems to me, are those that force us to ask the most difficult questions of ourselves. They want to be mined for these questions, even as they want our soul to be mined for its will, in the way a priest mines it at confession. The poet is asking us to become our own confessors.'

'Well said, Your Highness.'

The king looked off the stern, then back again, regarding me closely. 'Though in the end, I think, the best story is always the simplest one. For your next work, Gower, I hope you will craft such a tale. Write it for me, your sovereign. Make it a confession, whether of a lover or a saint I don't much care. We need more confession in the realm, don't you think? More disclosure. More truth.' His eyes shone with a righteous lustre, and a shudder moved over my limbs. I braced myself, once again almost spilling it all and appealing for Simon's release, then the moment passed, and the king moved forward to speak with his cousin.

The river lapped at the ferry like the tongues of a thousand eager dogs. We were nearing Fulham Palace, the great house of Bishop Robert Braybrooke in the gardens of which I had learned of the existence of the *De Mortibus*. What a distance I have travelled in these weeks, I thought. Since that first meeting with Chaucer I had been mired in complexity: conniving gossips at court, arcane prophecies of kings' deaths, an unused library at Oxford. Yet what if this story, as the king had put it, were a simpler one? If Chaucer himself were to write this story, I mused, where would it go, and what would be its ending?

Before the Fulham wharf I had begun my bow to the king when he grasped my arm. 'Will I see you at Wykeham's feast?'

'How is that, sire?'

He hailed a page. 'Be sure Master John Gower here is on the bishop's list for the feast on St Dunstan's Day. On my name.'

'Yes, sire,' the page said with a bow.

It caught me from the flank, as if a predator stalking me all day along the river had finally pounced. I almost shouted in the king's face, so violent was my reaction. 'Thank you, Your Highness,' I managed to say.

'At my cousin's urging, I am trying to calm the wrath between my uncle and the prelates who despise him,' he said, appearing not to notice my discomfiture. 'All those bishops and archbishops Lancaster has mortally offended over the years. I am doing my best to gentle the roiled waters separating our factions, but the Bishop of Winchester is a difficult man.

A poet's presence is a calming one on such occasions, Gower. Minstrels of the page, as I think of you and your scribbling ilk. And since you are a Southwark man you may easily step right over to Winchester Palace and join our company. Your friend Geoffrey Chaucer will also be there, at my request.'

'Again, sire, I thank you for your courtesy,' I said. 'I shall be happy to attend.'

'I'm delighted to hear it,' said the king. A gentle impact, ropes pulled to, the clank of metal on tack and stomps of hooves as knights led their mounts to the quay and up to the high road in the direction of Westminster and London. I waved off the offer of a horse. The storm had blown over, and though dusk approached I would easily make it on foot to the gates by sunset, then home on a wherry.

Bolingbroke gave his horse a final turn back toward the river, waiting for his cousin with the rear guard behind him. Four knights, still against the sky. The king spurred the charger ahead, the guard falling in behind. 'Until St Dunstan's Day, then,' King Richard called back to me.

As the company receded into the distance, I puzzled over the whole exchange, my pulse calming as I began the walk toward Westminster. Since reading the book in Oxford I had known when King Richard was to meet his fate by the terms of the prophecy. *On day of Saint Dunstan shall Death have his doom.* Now, thanks to the king, I knew where the assassination was to take place.

By bank of a bishop shall butchers abide . . .
In palace of prelate with pearls all appointed.

The 'bank of a bishop': the precincts of Winchester Palace, the Southwark home of William Wykeham, Bishop of Winchester, one of the great prelates in the realm. On the Thames adjacent to St Mary Overey, the palace was as familiar to me as St Paul's or Westminster, even more so: the priory and the palace shared the same span of wharfage, and Wykeham's episcopal offices at the palace had long served as the administrative hub of Southwark.

I thought it through. *Pearls all appointed.* The phrase had to refer to the oyster-and-pearl reliefs that Wykeham had commissioned during a past expansion of the great hall. The Blessed Virgin is like unto an oyster, he would say in his pretentious homilies: the Christ child is the precious pearl of her womb, created miraculously within, as a pearl within its shell. Matching his treasure to his theology, the bishop had commissioned a team of masons – led by Mark Blythe, still imprisoned at Ludgate – to craft stone chains of oyster and pearl along the inner walls of the hall. The carvings had been duplicated by Blythe and others on the palace's main outer wall facing New Rents, lined with subtle reliefs in the same pattern, mortared to the wall's uppermost span on either side of the gate. The *De Mortibus* even predicted the very moment of the attempt on the king's life: the killers would spring forth 'at *spiritus* sung' – a phrase that had to be a reference to 'Ave Dunstane, prae-sulum', a popular carol proper to St Dunstan's feast day.

King Richard's death, then, was to take place at Wykeham's palace, during the episcopal feast on Dunstan's Day, at the procession preceding Mass. The prophecy put the plot squarely on Gaunt's shoulders, identifying 'long castle' as the traitor casting out the *cor*: deposing the king. Yet who was the 'kingmaker', and who precisely would attempt the murder of Richard? How would it happen? Who were these 'butchers', and what role would the cards – the Prince of Plums, the Half-ten of Hawks – play in the unfolding of the plot?

In the wherry the story of Lancelot came to me, in the form of King Richard's memories of Arthurian tales. My mind resounded with the questions he had posed on the ferry. Are you loyal to those you love, loyal to the point of humiliation?

293

Or are you feckless in your love, unwilling to risk the shame that lies in blatant self-sacrifice? Are you Lancelot, or are you Gawain?

Neither, I told myself with a creeping sense of my own blindness – yet knowing the answer was almost within my grasp. You are, in fact, the dwarf.

In the service of Sir John Hawkwood, the knight settled with his daughter into a life as stable as any she had known since childhood. In those years, as now, Hawkwood shifted his alliances like a ram changes mates — by summer he might be found fighting for Florence, by fall for Milan, in winter for the pope, in spring for the anti-pope. Despite all the political turbulence around them, though, the girl was provided for by her father in every way.

The knight chose a new wife, a kind woman from Hawkwood's homeland who took her in hand and reshaped her from the wild rodent she had become into a lady fit for an earl's table. Where this girl's father had taught her mannish things, her stepmother instructed her in the domestic graces of femininity: the correct way to do her devotions, the virtues of the wardrobe, the proper running of a household. She hired a tutor, as the wealthier families do, to instruct her stepdaughter in the reading and writing of Latin and the vulgar tongues, especially her own.

Her stepmother took particular pride in the girl's skills with the needle. You are a natural embroideress, she told the younger woman. Your handiwork will yield things of great beauty, perhaps help win you a husband.

One of the most artful items crafted by the girl — a budding young lady of sixteen now — was a needlework depiction of her most vivid and horrendous memory. She started it the very morning her father told her the news: Prince Edward of England, her mother's ravisher and the father of her brother, had met his end. A sickness, it was said, of mind and body both.

The tidings of the prince's death brought back images of her mother, brutalized by an honoured guest. Of the prince, in all his naked cruelty. Of his brother the Duke of Lancaster, saving her life and her mother's with a blade held to the prince's throat.

With this last scene newly alive in her mind, she resolved to embroider it. Two lords, clad in simple tunics and hose, their arms pointed out on shields poised above their heads, details of livery and falconry added as she pleased: three ostrich feathers around the prince's shield, five hawks around the duke's. She used the false hood of an old priest's silk cope as her base. Already bordered with ornate vines, leaves, and flowers embroidered by a more skilful hand, the cope made the perfect ground for the play of her memory. When she had finished her work, she snipped away the embroidered square and loosely pinned it to a large tapestry of a merchant's festival at the Tribunale, hanging in her father's gallery. There it remained for years, a constant reminder of the cruel lusts of men, and the nature of true nobility.

Such reminders were useful in Ser Giovanni's circles. Hawkwood had a reputation as a singularly brutal man. There were numerous stories of his cruelty. Some shrivel the ears.

Two of his men, having sacked an abbey, stood arguing over the flesh of a young nun found cowering in the dormitory. The matter was about to come to blows when Hawkwood strode up and demanded an explanation.

'She is mine,' said one, 'and I shall have her.'

'Nay, I shall have her,' said the other.

Hawkwood drew his sword. 'You will each have half.' He cut the nun in two, leaving her body divided on the tiles.

Such stories put the lie to chivalry, a myth she had seen violated so many times she could scarcely credit anyone still believed in it. Even her father, so noble in her sight, turned a blind eye to Hawkwood's ways. 'War is war,' he would say after hearing of some new atrocity. Hers was a world defined by men and their means, vicious spirals of brutality in which the flesh of a woman was utterly expendable, as cheap as pigshit on a paver.

She had suitors, of course. Though none of them interested her, her father pushed her toward a match. A gentleman of London, as her stepmother described the smooth young man. Suitable in every way.

He was a minor clerk in Hawkwood's chancery. Il Critto, they called him, a sobriquet reflecting his facility with numbers and ciphers. He served the great condottiero as a cryptographer, he boastingly confided to her when they met, dedicated to unravelling secret codes of all kinds, whether the signals of an approaching army or the rhythms of a lady's batting eyes.

Il Critto was young, handsome, quite obviously brilliant. She liked him enough at first, and the more time he spent in her father's house, seeking her company in the gallery, the closer she came to accepting the inevitability of a married life. He was tormented with love for her, or so he claimed.

Smitten. Tortured. Goaded. Martyred. Oppressed. Not a wordsmith like you, I am afraid, though the poor man tried.

Yet there was about him a certain blankness, some quality of sincerity or directness that seemed to be lacking, no matter how earnestly he spoke, and that caused her to question inwardly the wisdom of the desired union.

Nevertheless, he spoke well, and flattered her father with gifts and kind words. It is likely she would have been betrothed to him within a month's time – had not her world changed in an instant.

PART THREE

Half-ten of Hawks

*Day viii before Ides of May to Nones
of June, 8 Richard II
(8 May–5 June 1385)*

THIRTY-EIGHT

Priory of St Leonard's Bromley

To save our king.

The words of Agnes rang in Millicent's ears as she stood before the gate, the abbey's door to the secular world. A bored-looking porter leaned on the walls. These were now gap-toothed in places, collapsed into piles of rubble. Millicent had heard about floods doing some damage to St Leonard's properties, though she had had no real comprehension of the extent of the devastation. Several dykes along the Lea were collapsed, as were a few of the lesser structures on the outer grounds. The malting shack still stood, and the woodhouse, though the big barn's thatched roof was sinking in places. A pair of carpenters were at work up by the old manor house, their labours desultory, as if done in their sleep – an attitude shared by two men in the near field leading skinanchors of fuel, brought from woods that had receded a shocking distance from the walls. It seemed half the forest of Essex had been denuded, still another sign of how much had changed since Millicent's departure in the arms of Sir Humphrey ap-Roger.

She slipped a coin to the surprised porter and passed through the priory's main gate, each structure and passage laden with memories. The porch of the Lady Chapel, where the nuns performed the mystery play on Innocents' Day solely to themselves. The narrow cloister, through which the Mass priest, chaplain, and acolytes would pass on their way to the common room, bearing small ale past the mincing sisters. The scriptorium, where Millicent had acquired the gift of reading over long months with Isabel, now prioress – the nun whose withering attention she would soon endure.

'Millicent?'

She turned. Sister Heda stared in bewilderment. Millicent embraced the nun. Beneath its wimple the narrow disc of Heda's face possessed the same sweet clarity she remembered, if lined with passing years, and the abbey's recent troubles. Millicent pulled her around the corner of the dormitory. 'Where is the prioress today, Heda?'

'The prioress?' Heda's eyes widened still further. 'You wish to see the Reverend Mother?'

'Right away, my dear.'

'She is in her chambers today,' said Heda. 'The bishop has a visitation scheduled for next week. I've been appointed cellaress, you know, and there being so few of us now and it being so close there seems little we can do, so . . .' She looked around in near despair. St Leonard's was in no state for one of the occasional rounds of official visits from its presiding bishop, Robert Braybrooke of London. Heda and her fellow officers of the house would be hard-pressed to make the place presentable in the coming days.

'Will you lead me there, Heda?' Millicent pleaded. 'I won't be stopped if you guide me.'

Heda hesitated, eyes shifting toward the gate. Then the nun silently turned and led her straight past the refectory, where the day's loaves lay stacked on the tables between meals. Left through the kitchen passage, redolent with river eel. Another left across the herbal, its springtime offerings of sage, thyme, and dill. Down a gentle stair into a low, cold

302

building of riverstone. The chapterhouse, the heart of St Leonard's, with voussoirs of banded fleurs-de-lis tracing high arcs along the vaulted entryway. The chamber was empty at that hour, though it would soon fill with the rustle of habits and the singing of Tierce.

Outside the prioress's private apartments stood a young novice. Millicent didn't know the girl, though her face was vaguely familiar. The girl started at the sight of an unknown laywoman in St Leonard's inner sanctum. Heda gave the novice Millicent's name and requested an audience.

'Your business with the prioress?' The novice's voice, like her face, betrayed nothing.

'She must see me,' Millicent said. 'It's a matter of grave importance for Bromley, and for the realm.'

The girl's smile was – bemused? Cruel? Just throw me to the she-wolf, was Millicent's impatient thought.

The novice held up a finger, then pushed open the door to the prioress's parlour. Heda backed away, her brow showing a single worried line beneath her habit, then disappeared around the corner. Millicent heard a few mumbles. A piercing *Who?* The outraged ejaculations of a voice she knew all too well. The novice returned, pale-faced, saying nothing as she held the door.

The prioress's parlour was a lushly furnished space with three glazed windows, a writing desk, and a rug of black-dyed wool thrown over paving tiles bearing the Syward arms. Dame Isabel Syward, the Prioress of St Leonard's Bromley, gazed down from her raised chair with an air of taut disdain. Millicent lowered herself, remaining still until the leader saw fit to speak.

'You have—' Isabel's voice was gravelly with bile. 'You have come home at last, my dearest daughter.'

Millicent looked up in surprise, but the prioress's expression belied her welcoming words.

'And what a glorious homecoming it is,' Isabel continued.

'Perhaps you've reconsidered the wicked ways that led to your expulsion. Perhaps you've decided to be grateful for the gifts this house gave you. Food, shelter, rescue from a life of raw swyving, how to rap your Ave Maria on your knuckles. And reading. Oh! I taught you myself, didn't I? Every letter, holding your hand as your fingertips traced patterns in the letterbook. For hours, for weeks, for *three years*, Millicent, I taught you how to read, how to think, how to pray, how to *live*.'

The prioress put a hand to her mouth and sat back, seeming shocked at her own outburst. There was a glistening in the corners of the great woman's eyes. She wiped them and went on.

'Yet you threw it all away. And for what? A fat old January! At least you could have fallen for a squire, strong of arm and stiff of cock. Now *that* would have been understandable, given our sisters something worthy to aspire to, an actual challenge. Instead, what do you do? Why, you settle for the first easy target that comes along, making *yourself* easy in the process, then *off* you go, abandoning the community that opened itself to you. Now you expect the same openness from Bromley? You think you can simply show up, demand an audience with the prioress, get a handout? *Bah!*'

The prioress spat. Millicent lay crumpled on the floor, stilled with the truth of all the woman had said to her, and with wrenching sorrow at the loss of this place from her life.

She squeezed her eyes shut. What could she say that might rein in Isabel's contempt, at least long enough for her to appeal for the help she sought? 'Reverend Mother,' she began, 'if you please—'

'But I know you, Millicent Fonteyn.' Isabel's voice was flat now, devoid of passion. 'I know you to be the most calculating, self-interested woman in all England, a woman who would spare no thought to betraying friend and family alike. It is simply who you are, my dear.'

Millicent thought of Agnes. The prioress could not know the horrible accuracy of her judgment.

'So I suppose you would not have the spine to show yourself here if you didn't have good reason, and I suppose I am bound to hear it. "A matter of grave importance for Bromley, and for the realm." How grand. Tell us. Then get out.'

Millicent left nothing out, and when she was done the prioress studied her with an intensity she remembered. 'I'm very sorry about your sister, Millicent,' she said with lowered voice. 'Such a loss is difficult, even in these times when we lose so many to war and pestilence. To know that your own greed murdered her – that doubles the guilt, and triples the pain. May Agnes be at rest in God's hands, her sins washed away in the waters of purgation.'

'Thank you, Reverend Mother. Your words are kind.'

Isabel stood with a sigh. She walked to the window looking up to the manor house. 'I have heard of this book from other sources in recent weeks. It is the talk of our order. The bishop has made inquiries about it to the houses in his diocese. A burnable book, Braybrooke calls it. The timing could not be worse, with Pope Urban's delegation set to arrive from Rome before Trinity Sunday.' She turned, her look incredulous. 'Yet you, Millicent Fonteyn, of all people, have read this book?'

'I have, Prioress. Several times.' *Trinity Sunday. Pope Urban.* Millicent thought, with a fleeting confusion, of her sister's death, and the words she had scribbled in coal inside the book. *The crochet . . . father, son, and holy ghost . . . city's blade . . . doovay leebro.* Why were these phrases coming to her now? She had assumed that Agnes, in her own throes, was echoing the last words of the girl in the Moorfields, the couplet thrown into the night sky while Agnes watched from the shrubbery. For weeks she had dismissed Agnes's recounting of the doomed girl's dying utterance. The book and the cloth: these could be sold, after all, while words were just words, and there seemed little reason to credit the girl's final call as

305

anything more than a cry of dread as the hammer fell. Yet now she caught herself wondering if there was something to these words after all, even if Agnes herself had never discovered their meaning. The Holy Trinity, a city's blade – but what was it?

'This house is in enough peril already,' the prioress was saying. 'Our fortunes the property of the manor, our income shrunk to two hundred marks in the year. We've been forced to enclose the park, and lost a thousand acres in Dagenham. And here you are, slinking back like one of King Edward's dogs, with this news. I'd be within my rights to have you cast in the brew cellar, and the key thrown in the Lea. If our cellaress hadn't lost the damned key,' she muttered.

'I would have thought,' Millicent began, 'that the Reverend Mother's close relation to the crown—'

'Oh, yes, of course. We've had the corpse of Elizabeth of Hainault, old King Edward's sister-in-law, mouldering in our chapel for ten years. Why, we could sell it for relics! Why hadn't I thought of that? St Leonard's piss is liquid gold!' Her hands dropped to her sides. 'I'm afraid we're no more protected from the threat of ruination than the shrinking forest around us.'

'Prioress—'

'Show me the cloth.'

Millicent reached within her skirts and pulled out the folded embroidery. Isabel spread it in her lap. She ran her fingers along the sides, where the thistleflowers, hawks, plums, and swords were arrayed in numbered sets. She stroked the heraldry arrayed against the king's arms.

'You say Pinchbeak has the book?'

'I handed it to Robert Dawson, his man. Pinchbeak wasn't there.'

The prioress put a slender finger to her lips. 'So we have this book of prophecies, one of them auguring the death of our king and pointing a finger at his uncle. We have the cloth,

306

identifying the chief conspirator beyond doubt as Lancaster. And we have mere days until the feast of St Dunstan.'

'Yes, Reverend Mother.' Millicent watched the prioress's eyes, felt the shrewd calculations taking place behind them.

'I'm told you've been living up Cornhull.'

'Yes, Prioress.'

'I assume you've kept up your embroidery, then, given the neighbourhood.'

'Well, I can't say that I—'

'An orphrey of fine needlework is what we need, and the most ingenious we have ever made.' She stretched the cloth to its full width. 'It must be identical in every respect to this vivid sample, with one difference – well, two.' She pointed to the coat of arms emblazoned on the figure attacking the boy king. 'Do you see these colours, just here?'

The Duke of Lancaster's. They were nearly identical to the king's, the only difference being the ermine label above. 'Yes, Prioress.'

Isabel squinted at it. 'Hand me that glass.' The prioress pointed to a low table in the corner. Millicent walked over and lifted a triangular magnifying glass, set in a bone frame with a wooden handle below. Isabel took it from her and scrutinized the cloth further.

'The brick stitch around the border is remarkable, as is the infilled foliage. And the waffling is superior, must have taken weeks. *Look* at that work. The ground is Italian, or I'm a pregnant goat. But in the middle, the figures of the duke and the king are – well, they're nicely done, but their quality doesn't come close to what I am seeing in the base. And these smaller emblems – the thistleflowers and hawks and so on – wouldn't pass a seamstress's eye in Cornhull, let alone at court.'

Millicent came to the prioress's side, catching a faint waft of rosy perfume from the older woman's neck. Not all luxuries had been abandoned in Bromley, it seemed. She leaned over

307

the prioress's shoulder and peered through the glass at the cloth. She saw immediately what Isabel's expert eye had discerned. At the edges of the cloth the stitching was tight and uniform, the product of a practised embroideress working slowly and patiently to embellish the borders with an elaborate pattern of vines and flowers. The figures of Lancaster and King Richard, as well as their arms, had been pointed into the cloth in an entirely different style. Looser stitches, higher loops. Skilful and not incompetent, not by a long stretch, but – *youthful* was the word that came to her mind. Finally, the figures of thistleflowers, hawks, swords, and plums surrounding the central figures had been done hastily, with inferior threads and with no regard for the surrounding ground. Three hands, then, working at different times, with different materials, and with varying degrees of competence.

The prioress leaned back. 'This cloth is clearly a fake,' she said, 'cooked up to point a finger at the duke. Besides, Lancaster wouldn't come near a book of the sort you describe. The man eats self-preservation for supper. So who would create such a thing to wrap around a manuscript of prophecies, implicating him as a conspirator against the king?'

Isabel stared at the wall for a moment, then shook her head. 'Well of course. Who else?' She took up the cloth, picked at some threads. 'This work is too tight to unravel without damaging the ground. You, Millicent, will create a new shield for this fellow here, with new arms altogether. In the first quarter, we must have a silver mullet borne upon a field gules.'

Millicent's eyes widened. 'Do you mean—'

'I do.' The prioress's eyes sparkled, and she allowed Millicent the slightest of smiles before returning her attention to the cloth. 'The other must be similarly altered, though with different arms. Here, parti per fesse gule, and on the chief of the second there must be – ah, what is it?'

'A demi-lion, rampant of the field,' Millicent said, remembering the shield. A tournament two years before, she on Sir

Humphrey's arm in the stands, the Earl of Oxford mounted below.

'Exactly. Now.' Isabel clapped her hands three times, summoning the young nun from the other side of the door. 'Bring us thread of silver, gold, azure – all of it. We haven't a moment to spare.'

Soon Millicent found herself in her old place at Isabel's feet, frame and needle in her hands. Following the prioress's instructions, she pinned out a portion of the pattern within the smooth frame: the demi-lion, a complex figure to execute, though Millicent felt confident she could complete it in good time, at least as well as the earlier embroideress had pointed in the arms of Gaunt. The pull of the needle, the occasional click of the thimble against the frame: though her fingers soon ached with the unfamiliar labour, it was a good ache.

'Reverend Mother?' she said at one point, tentatively.

'You may speak, Millicent.'

Her given name from the prioress's lips: a balm over a forgotten wound. 'How can we know this will work?'

Isabel gave her a bland stare. 'There is a great conspiracy in the land to slay our king, my child. We can be sure of nothing. But we must do what we can to foil the plot. To bring this cloth before the king on St Dunstan's Day, and from a credible source, we must put it in the hands of someone in the inmost circles at court. Someone of unassailable standing.'

'Your relations?'

The prioress snorted. 'The concubine of the king's second substeward has stronger connections in the court than my relations these days. No, I have in mind one of our dear sisters. Just there.' She nodded toward the door. 'Margaret is her name. She's properly a nun of Barking, but we've taken her in for a few months given the unpleasantness between the king and his uncle. Abbess Matilde wants her to disappear for a while, at least until after the bishop's round of visitations.' Barking, the much greater house several miles to the east, would often impose on St Leonard's for 'gifts' of space and provision, taking undue advantage of Bromley's diminished numbers and extra dormitory space.

The girl, no more than fourteen, stood out of earshot in the half-opened doorway, her head pointed demurely to the floor.

'I don't understand, Reverend Mother,' said Millicent.

'Her mother has an intimate connection to John of Gaunt,' said Isabel.

Her mother. 'The Infanta?' It was a guess. Millicent knew the young woman had looked familiar, though the face of Gaunt's Castilian duchess didn't seem a match.

The prioress glanced up. Blinked. 'Hardly. She's Margaret Swynford, daughter of the late Hugh Swynford. And her mother is Katherine, Lancaster's whore.'

THIRTY-NINE

Church of St Lawrence Jewry

Edgar Rykener joined the small knot of beggars gathered at the foot of the St Lawrence steps. Some gave him unfriendly glances, taking him for an interloper who would diminish their proper share of charity. He ignored them; the wait wouldn't be long. Master Strode was to appear at the first stroke of the Sext bells, he'd been assured at the Guildhall. The common serjeant likes to take a walk around the ward, one of his clerks had said, before returning for his midday meal with the mayor.

The St Lawrence bell struck, Mary Magdalene soon followed, then Bassishaw, the three parishes competing for the proper ringing of the hour. Still no Strode. Edgar thought nothing of the delay at first, yet as the minutes wore on his concern mounted, until finally he pushed himself off the wall and stepped up on to the porch.

The interior was nearly silent, a heavy wheeze the only discernible sound. It came from one of the side chapels, a half-lit space with shuttered windows and several rows of old seats wedged askew against the walls. Ralph Strode sat on one of them, a silent mound of concern. Even in the dim light

311

Edgar could see his face was ashen. His wide chin sat propped on his knuckles, robed elbows on his knees. The man could have been one of the painted statues, but for the whistley breaths from his guts.

'Master Strode,' said Edgar, his voice a small thunderclap.

Strode's opening eyes caught the glare of the lone candle on the chapel altar. No other movement. Finally he half-turned, his brow bent in a distant frown. A slow nod. 'Edgar, is it?'

'Yes, Master Strode.'

'Came about your brother a few weeks back.' He seemed mildly pleased that he had remembered.

'Yes, sir. James – Master Tewburn was a great help.'

'Tewburn.' Strode shook his head. 'Senseless. A senseless loss of a good young man.'

'Yes, Master Strode. I'm sorry he had to go and die, sir.'

Strode's gaze found him in the gloom. 'You heard, then?'

Edgar nodded, casting about for what to say.

'For my life I can't figure out what is happening in London,' he said. 'Factions moving in stealth through the streets, with their feints and counter-feints. Young men being plucked off the lanes, tossed off the bridge, throats slit in churchyards, dragged from their homes and thrown in nameless pits, all for baseless suspicions from above. London is being torn apart at the seams, and despite my office I am feeling powerless to stop it.'

Edgar took a deep breath, then said, 'It was I found his body.'

His eyes widened. 'Tewburn's?'

'Aye, sir.'

'It was you who alerted the constables, then?'

'Not – no, sir.' Strode was staring at him. 'I found him the day before the coroner's men took him from St Pancras.'

He sat forward. 'Yet you let his body lie there for another day?'

'We had us a time, you see, to meet in the churchyard, and—'

312

'Tewburn was at St Pancras to meet *you*?' Strode clapped his knees, fixing him with the fiercest stare. 'Whatever for?'

'Master Tewburn said he'd have some news for me about getting Gerald a wardship in London. Said he'd tell me that night when we met. But the justices over there, in the manors—'

'Guildable Manor.'

'Master Tewburn says they were giving him all kinds of grief just to find out how to transfer Gerald's wardship from Grimes's shop. And Gerald says the butchers are stirring up bigger trouble in Southwark. Got a priest riling them up, with Grimes taking the part of Wat Tyler, and the other butchers—'

'*The butchers*. My God.' It was as if the common serjeant had been struck with a seizure of the heart. The large man came to his feet with a surprising agility. He turned to the side, and with his body facing the chapel altar whispered a portion of verse.

> '*By bank of a bishop shall butchers abide,*
> *To nest, by God's name, with knives in hand,*
> *Then springen in service at spiritus sung.*'

Edgar gasped. The last time he'd heard these lines they'd come from the mouth of Millicent Fonteyn, who'd read them from the very book Agnes took from the doomed girl in the Moorfields. Now here was Ralph Strode, common serjeant of London, speaking the same verse.

He had to press him. Strode was staring off toward the upper nave, a haunted slackness to his face. 'That verse, sir. You think it's Grimes and his men set to kill King Richard?'

He barked a laugh. 'It's not what *we* think that matters. It's what others can be *made* to think. The perfection of art is to conceal art, so Quintilian tells us.'

'Sir?'

'We have two sets of butchers before our eyes.' He stooped, hands on his broad thighs. 'Butchers in this prophetic verse,

313

and the butchers of Southwark – and one dead clerk. I am not a believer in coincidence, Edgar, not by a far sight. You say you talked with Tewburn about your brother, yes?'

'A few times, sir, he was very helpful, always—'

'Wait.' Strode grasped Edgar's shoulders, his eyes wide. 'What did you say?'

'That Master Tewburn was ever so helpf—'

'Before that. About the snatch of verse I recited.'

'Oh . . . yes. If you thought Grimes and his men were to be the butchers to kill the king.'

Strode's stare was deep and cruel, as if a hand were reaching out from his eyes, down into Edgar's bowels. 'And how did you know?'

'Sir?'

Strode's grip tightened on his shoulders. 'How could you possibly have known those three lines referred to the slaying of King Richard?'

His jaw loosened. 'Well, I – I suppose with the bishop, and the knives, and all that, it just seemed—'

'Don't lie to me, boy.' Strode shook him. 'You've heard someone else speak those lines, haven't you?'

'Please, Mast—'

'What do you know about these prophecies, about the book?'

His hands squeezed harder. Edgar flinched with the pain. Could he trust him, after all, this great man of London, so many spheres above his own?

Edgar left nothing out. The Moorfields, the murder, Millicent, the man with the hooked scar on Gropecunt Lane, the death of Agnes. He even told him about the couplings with Tewburn, and his life of swerving – all of it. Strode breathed deeply when he was done, his lips sucking and blowing the stale air of St Lawrence. The common serjeant's face was calm now, his eyes agleam with a certainty Edgar wished he could share.

'Will the king die, Master Strode?' he asked, and looked into that confident gaze.

'It's not the king we need to worry about,' said Strode. 'No, Edgar – or is it Eleanor?'

He shrugged. 'As you wish, sir.'

A smile, tentative but serene, played on Ralph Strode's generous lips. 'No, Eleanor, I'm afraid we have a smaller life to save.'

FORTY

San Donato a Torre, near Florence

Jacopo da Pietrasanta stood at the door, clutching the letter.
Scarlett watched with some amusement as Hawkwood's chancellor worked up the nerve to speak. 'Sire,' he finally said.

'What is it?' said Hawkwood, focused on the game.

'An urgent message, Ser Giovanni. From your brother-in-law.'

'Lodo?'

'Carlo, sire,' said Pietrasanta.

Hawkwood took Scarlett's four. 'Read it.'

Scarlett looked at his lord. With the coming departure for
England Hawkwood had grown increasingly impatient with
his Italian functionaries, even Pietrasanta, and it was all he
could do at times to control his sharpness when addressing
them.

The chancellor cleared his throat. '*We send this to inform
you that in Milan the hateful count Giangaleazzo Visconti
has unrightfully seized our beloved and magnificent lord
Bernabò Visconti, as well as our beloved brother Lodovico.
We are holding here at the fortress in Crema, and we have
the castle at Porta Romana under our protection. We urge
you to gather your garrisons and march to our comfort and*

defence in Milan. You will be amply rewarded for your effort. The time has come, Giovanni Acuto, to prove your mettle.'

Hawkwood made him read it again, and when he had finished his lips curled up into a sneer. 'He's taunting me, the hammy little shit.'

Pietrasanta flinched at the epithet. Scarlett knew what the man was thinking. The Visconti are the most powerful and ruthless clan in Italy, more than a match for this northern roughneck. Who is he to hurl such insults at *la famiglia lombarda principali*? 'How would you like to respond, Ser Giovanni?'

Hawkwood shrugged. 'We're in no position to respond, Jacopo.'

'Ser Giovanni?'

'I am in Florence. Our brigades are massed in Bologna. Bologna still owes us, what, twenty thousand, thirty? What does Carlo expect, that I'll pull up stakes and hoof it up to Milan at his bidding? It could take weeks, months, even, to prepare for such a relief effort.'

'What should we tell Ser Carlo in the meantime, Ser Giovanni?' Pietrasanta was working hard to keep his voice measured, Scarlett could tell.

'Write nothing for now.'

'Ser—' Pietrasanta began.

'There is no hurry, Jacopo.' Hawkwood turned on his chancellor, his eyes grown cold. 'This is a family squabble, nothing more. We'll bide our time.'

There was a heavy pause as Pietrasanta absorbed the *condottiero*'s decision. Hawkwood's chancellor had no idea what his master was planning, nor the bearing of these plans on his own future. Within a few weeks the dirty wars of the Visconti would be only a memory to the man they had both served for so many years. And Pietrasanta would be out of a job.

'Very well, sire.' Pietrasanta turned to exit, pushing past a young man entering from behind him. Desilio's boy, sent up from the *villetta*.

'What is it?' Scarlett asked him.

'Master Desilio requests your presences, good sirs,' said the breathless youth.

'Oh?' Hawkwood's eyebrows arched up, and he turned to Scarlett with an intrigued grin. They walked together to one of the *villette*, the line of small cottages in a line down the hill from the main house. The grapevines reached from the path up the sweeping rise to the south, and the late afternoon had settled into a mellow glow. My last season in Italy, Scarlett thought, whispering a quiet prayer.

In the *villetta* they found Desilio wedged among several piles of books on a trestle table, which was covered with scribbled papers arrayed in an unpatterned mess around the quire. The scholar's eyes gleamed with excitement as he stood, though he maintained a respectful silence until Hawkwood asked him to speak.

'I have broken the first cipher, Ser Giovanni, and will soon break the second.'

'Is that so?' said Hawkwood, his gaze shifting between Desilio and the table. 'Sit, please, and explain what you've found.'

Desilio took his chair, Scarlett and Hawkwood each to one side.

'The key was the first cipher. Without it everything else in the quire means nothing. It took a bit of thought and effort, but I was able to decipher these first pages without difficulty once I realized what was before me.'

Scarlett peered over his shoulder. 'And what is it?'

Desilio waited a moment, letting the curiosity build. 'Sardinian,' he finally whispered.

'*Sardinian?*'

'Yes. Nothing complicated or encoded, just Sardinian. He used it as the first of his ciphers.'

'So you read the language yourself, Maestro Desilio?' Hawkwood asked.

'Hardly,' the logician scoffed. 'I asked around among your men, and one of them knew another who was from that island. I read him the first few sentences, as well as I was able—'

'You *what*?' Hawkwood exploded, his hand poised to strike.

Scarlett put a hand on his arm. Desilio was wagging his beard. 'Nothing to worry about, I assure you, Ser Giovanni. The ciphers mean nothing in isolation. The man had no idea why I was even pulling him in here.'

Scarlett felt Hawkwood relax, and took it upon himself to move the conversation along, reaching over Desilio's shoulder to turn the page. 'What about here, and here?' He pointed to the script on the facing folio. The alphabet was Roman, the hand legible, but the words themselves were clearly nonsense, full of letters bunched seemingly at random, and what looked like extra vowels and consonants, such as an X within a circle.

'It's an extraordinary thing,' Desilio said, a touch of pride in his voice as he looked up at them. 'He was inventing a *lingua ignota*, as I've heard such things called.'

'A new language,' Hawkwood murmured.

'It's rudimentary, of course, without declined nouns or conjugated verbs, and the tenses are rather primitive. But a few hundred words is all one needs to put together fairly sophisticated messages.'

'But how would the recipient know the meaning?'

Desilio smiled. 'A glossary, owned by both parties, translating each word back into Italian. Or any other language. The only way to decipher the code without such a glossary would be through an analysis of letters and their frequency, but for that to work you'd have to have a much larger sample of the language than the mere four pages here.'

'So then,' Scarlett said, confused, 'how were you able to decipher the unknown language?'

Desilio rubbed his palms. 'It all begins with the Sardinian, the simplest of the ciphers. It's merely another language, and anyone who knows it can crack the code, which I've now done with the help of your man. And as I've discovered in the process, the Sardinian is in effect the glossary to the *lingua ignota*. The Sardinian, that is, provides the key to the next cipher.'

'Explain yourself,' said Hawkwood.

'Certainly, Ser Giovanni. Look here, at the beginning of the first column. It reads, "Word seventy-nine is *míntza*" – and *míntza* is Sardinian for "spring". The next sentence reads "The twelfth word is *bidduri*" – Sardinian for "hemlock". Once I had all of this translated I was stymied. The seventy-ninth word of what? What twelfth word is he talking about? Then I realized what your cryptographer was doing here. What he's telling us is that word seventy-nine of the secret language – *the next cipher in the quire* – is "spring". And word twelve is "hemlock". And so on and so forth. And now, by translating the *lingua ignota* as the key, I believe I am opening the lock to the *next* code, which follows in the quire. The Sardinian unlocks the secret language. The secret language unlocks the numbers. Do you see?'

Hawkwood nodded, all admiration. 'Indeed I do, Master Desilio. You are Theseus in a labyrinth of sorts, with each cipher a length of rope guiding you to the next corner, and the next solution.'

'A perceptive analogy, Ser Giovanni. I should have the solution to the subsequent code worked out as soon as I have transcribed and recombined the *lingua ignota*.'

'And what is this next cipher?' Scarlett asked him.

Desilio turned back to the manuscript, showing us the next three pages, filled with scribbled numbers stacked in equations and scattered along lines, shapes, and angles. Once again they meant nothing to Scarlett.

'The next one is numerical, drawing on the mathematics of

Master Gersonides,' said Desilio. 'A Jew, and an astronomer of moderate renown. I believe your cryptographer was constructing a cipher based on some of Gersonides' more arcane calculations. Extraction of square roots, binomial coefficients, that sort of thing.'

Hawkwood laughed lightly, slapped him on the back. 'Ah yes. Binomial coefficients. I eat them with my rabbit.'

'It sounds more complicated than it is,' Desilio said modestly. 'This mathematics is several generations old, nothing I cannot untangle. A few more days, Ser Giovanni, and I should be ready to tackle the final cipher.'

'And this final cipher? Do you have an inkling as to its solution?'

'Not yet, sire, though I am confident I'll get there.' He thumbed through the booklet's last few pages and set his finger in the middle of one of them. 'Your cryptographer organized the last cipher around four discrete images, arranged in different combinations across these pages. Here is what looks like a falcon, perhaps. This one is clearly a sword, the next a flower – a spindly one, like a thistle. And here we have a grape, if I'm not mistaken.'

'A plum,' said Hawkwood, his voice suddenly taut. 'It's a plum.'

'And the bird is a hawk,' said Scarlett, seeing it at the same instant. Hawks, thistleflowers, plums, and swords. The four suits of Hawkwood's cards, written in neat rows and columns across the last four pages of the quire in small groups of two – each group, Scarlett suspected, a letter or a word. The phrases came back to him, like pinpricks along his arms. *At Prince of Plums shall prelate oppose . . . By Half-ten of Hawks might shender be shown . . .*

He should have seen it during his own scrutiny of the manuscript, yet these symbols had blended in with all the other mysterious writing in the quire, and he hadn't taken the time to examine them in their own right before extracting Desilio from the *studium*. How differently all this might have turned out, Scarlett would think later, if he had.

Hawkwood, who always carried a deck of cards slung in a purse, removed them and spread the painted ovals out on the table as they explained to the scholar what the two of them had noticed. Desilio nodded eagerly, getting it right away, and promising to let them know as soon as he had untangled the mathematical cipher and turned to the cards.

'I am entrusting you with my favourite deck, Maestro Desilio,' Hawkwood said as they prepared to leave him there. 'Treat it well.'

'I shall, Ser Giovanni.'

As they turned into the lower gardens Scarlett repressed a shiver. Hawkwood knew him too well to let it pass.

'What is it, Adam?'

'Think about it, John,' he began. 'A book that just happens to survive a deliberate burning in the *villetta*, yet with enough of its pages intact to allow the ciphers to be broken. The first cipher is simply a translation into Sardinian – a tongue Il Critto could have heard spoken in the streets of Florence more than once. It would have been a simple matter to hire a Sardinian man and have him translate the words he needed. The next cipher, Desilio tells us, relies on mathematics that's years, maybe decades old, presumably solvable by anyone with university training. And the final cipher? The only way to break the encryption is with your own cards, John. Doesn't all of this feel too convenient somehow – too easy?'

'Well, I suppose one could—'

'It almost seems as if . . .' Scarlett paused on the garden path, a hand to his mouth.

'Say it, Adam.'

'As if he *wanted* us to find the damned book. Find his book, and break his ciphers.'

'To what purpose?' said Hawkwood, intrigued, though not as troubled as Scarlett wanted him to be.

'Betrayal?' The first word that came to him.

'Or information,' Hawkwood rejoined, his gaze on a distant hill. 'Something he wanted to tell us before he left, and this was his only way.'

'If that's the case, why not simply speak to us in person?' Scarlett said. 'He had an audience in the hall the day before his departure. Why the need for secrecy, when he could have spoken privately while seeking your permission for his trip?'

'Well,' said Hawkwood, taking Scarlett's arm and moving on toward the main house, 'if Il Critto wanted us to break his ciphers, he wanted it for a reason. And I, for one, am determined to nose it out, wherever it takes us.' The *condottiero* gave Scarlett's arm a squeeze. 'Let Desilio continue his work, Adam. All we are after is the truth.'

The truth. Scarlett pondered this weak notion as he resumed his day's tasks. England seemed as far away as ever, and the more he thought over the content of the half-scorched quire, the more he convinced himself that the breaking of the final code would be the last thing in Sir John Hawkwood's interests, or his own. The truth, he sensed with a warming fear, would prove a devastating lie.

FORTY-ONE

Aldgate

On the fourth morning after Simon was taken, I crossed London Bridge at first light and walked once more to Aldgate. From the landing before Chaucer's door I looked far down into the still silence of a London dawn, experiencing the everyday smells and sights – a baker's wife airing a tray of cakes, a smith assaying his coals – with the kind of acuity that comes only with true clarity of purpose. It was time to confront my darkest suspicions.

Chaucer's face was always hard to read. That morning it might have been written in the script of the Moors. He greeted me in the front room. Sparse furnishings, dust-filled cloths on the wall, short shelves of tarnished plate and silver placed at irregular intervals around the interior. The room spoke of Philippa's long absence from the Newgate house. Chaucer had chosen a troubled frown to frame his opening words. 'Simon is missing, I understand.'

'Who told you?'

'That hardly matters.' Chaucer pulled a chair around for me. 'What matters is his safety, and his return.' His ready knowledge of Simon's peril only made me more furious, though I was determined to show nothing.

'Did you know this would happen, that Simon would be taken?'

He pushed a second chair beneath him and sat, gesturing for me to do the same. 'I worried it might come to this,' he admitted.

'The counterfeiting?'

He shifted on his chair. 'Not that. It's the other matter, I fear.'

'The other matter.' I looked at him blankly.

'Our matter, John.'

I frowned. 'Surely you can't mean—'

'The book.'

'Why? Is there a connection between Simon's abduction and the prophecies?'

'I suspect so, though I have no proof.'

I took the twin chair, maintaining my composure as this sank in. 'I need to know more about the book, Geoffrey. I need to know it now.'

He looked away. In the silence that followed I took Clanvowe's manuscript from my bag and set it on the octagonal table between us. Chaucer stared at it for a moment, then picked it up and leafed through. He grimaced, set it down. 'Clanvowe?'

I nodded.

'I recognized the hand.'

'So did Strode.'

'Though a different hand wrote the book you've been seeking.'

'Whose?'

'It's – complicated, John.'

'So you've known all along.'

'Not entirely.'

'You knew the content of the *De Mortibus* down to the last prophecy.'

'Well—'

'I'll wager you have the thing by rote.'

'Not quite.'

'Yet you sent me chasing after it without bothering to tell me anything.'

'John—'

'And now my son has been taken, probably murdered like Tewburn, or poor Symkok. Will they come for me next, Chaucer?'

'Please, John—'

'And all for a small favour, as you called it. A little thing, John. You'll help me, won't you, John? Help me avoid all that unpleasantness with Swynford, will you, John? And there sat John, didn't he, like a schoolboy waiting for the whip. So deeply in your debt that he couldn't refuse you, not if his life – his *son's* life – depended on it.'

'Simon was—'

'You think because you saved it once his life is now yours to throw away?'

'I couldn't tell you because—'

'Because my ignorance was amusing to you?'

'Because—'

'Because I'm your mouse, a little creature you can tease and claw till it dies?'

'Because—'

'Because you assume that John Gower—'

'*Because I wrote the damn thing, John!*'

At last. I let his words linger. 'Say it again.'

He looked at me, eyes watering. '*Liber de Mortibus Regum Anglorum*. The book is as much my invention as the book of Duchess Blanche, or the *Parliament of Fowls*.'

I sat back, a cold rage running through my veins. Then my joints relaxed, my vision starring as I stood and moved away from him. I honestly did not think he would admit it. Now that he had, I realized how keenly I had wanted it not to be true.

'John—'

'Go to hell, Chaucer.'

'John, as your friend—'

'You are no friend. You are a curse.'

'—as your friend, John, I beg you to see all this from my angle.' From behind me I heard him rise, his shoes crackling the rushes. 'There are constraints on my position. My wife is Swynford's sister. To have revealed my hand in the composition of this work . . . it's difficult to imagine the disaster that might have befallen the duke and his family.'

'And *my* family, Geoffrey?' I said faintly, still turned away. 'Why didn't you trust me with this information in the first place? Did you think I'd betray you to Westminster? You know me better than that.'

'As well as you know me, John.' I turned. Chaucer almost cringed; there were still things he wasn't saying.

'What about this Lollius, then? What was his role in writing the prophecies?'

Chaucer lifted a vase from a nearby shelf, wiping at the dusty brass. 'Lollius is also my invention. A Latinist of real distinction, and his stories are only now being translated into English. He's the *auctor* of what will be my own great work someday, a romance of Troilus.'

'Simon is missing, Chaucer,' I spat. 'Perhaps you might worry about your precious poetry some other time.'

He set down the vase, looking perplexed by his own narcissism.

'And the Lollius of Horace, the poet I chased through Oxford?'

'No relation,' he said. 'Though certainly an inspiration. To blame it all on Horace's Lollius, an unknown poet from ancient Rome? I couldn't pass it up.'

'But to write a poem prophesying the death of our king? You can't be ignorant of the treason statutes, Geoffrey. How many times have you heard them read aloud on the street? To compass or even *imagine* the death of our king: treason pure and plain. You *know* this. I cannot imagine what might have motivated you to write this sort of thing. And "long castle"? You used the same wording in your book for Duchess Blanche. You might as well have signed the damned thing!'

Chaucer was tapping his foot. 'But I didn't – ah, what can I tell you, John, that you won't discover for yourself soon enough?'

'There's *more*?'

'I wrote the *De Mortibus* in Tuscany, John. In Hawkwood's company, during that visit last year. It was a jest, an amusement that took me a few mornings. I never intended it to circulate. But then it went missing.'

'Tuscany.' My skin prickled into gooseflesh. 'Simon knew you'd written it, then.'

He nodded.

'Did he read it?'

'Oh, he read it quite carefully, I should think.'

So Simon knew the *De Mortibus*, had known of it all this time. There was something in Chaucer's tone, though, that bothered me. 'Are you suggesting Simon stole it from you, brought the manuscript with him from Italy?'

He looked at his shoes, a gesture I took then as a sign of shame. Despite his newfound forthrightness, he was still deceiving me, protecting me from knowledge he feared would destroy me. 'The timing doesn't work. It's true that those who took Simon must have made a connection between the book, his service with Hawkwood, and his return to England. But the *De Mortibus* came to London weeks before Simon's arrival.'

'Suggesting what?'

Chaucer's eyes clouded. 'Suggesting there are other forces at work here, John. Larger forces, with motives far from poetical.'

'Isn't there a simple solution?' I said. 'You wrote the prophecies, after all. You can prove it, for the original manuscript is in your hand. And you have the good will of the duke. Why can't we go to him and lay bare what you've done?'

'Impossible.'

'Why?'

'It's gone too far.'

'How so?'

'Well, for one thing, there are already multiple copies circulating. This one you've brought me is in Clanvowe's hand. I assume there are others. Who would believe I wrote it, even if I *were* to confess?'

'So you'll let another man be quartered for your own vanity?'

'It's not so simple.' Chaucer stepped close to me. 'The knowledge of this book reaches deep into Richard's faction. Some of the most powerful men in the realm are arrayed against Lancaster. Warwick, Arundel, Oxford, Buckingham, who knows how many others, all of them convinced that the thirteenth prophecy will shatter the duke's faction, pull the king away from his uncle. If it's known that the *De Mortibus* was written by Geoffrey Chaucer, betraying the king's affinity on the duke's behalf, why – that would be just the wedge the earls need to drive apart Lancaster and the king, breaking an already fragile truce between Richard and Gaunt. Imagine it: Chaucer and Clanvowe, scribbling seditious prophecies at the behest of the recently deceased John Wycliffe and his chief supporter, the Duke of Lancaster. A scandal of the highest order.'

'So it all comes down to politics? Factions and alliances, title and power, government and gossip.'

Chaucer waved a hand. 'Easy for you to say, John. You're a man without a faction – the one fact about you everyone knows. The reason you were chosen for this task was precisely your neutrality. Your ability to do all your dirty work regardless of faction.'

'I "was chosen"? As if the passive voice somehow excuses *your* choice of me as your tool?'

'Oh, you weren't my choice.'

I froze. 'Then whose?'

Chaucer's eyes closed.

'I am sick of your petty secrets. Who suggested to you that I be sent on this fool's errand?'

Chaucer puffed his cheeks, looked at the ceiling. 'Strode.'

Of course. 'And how long has Ralph known that you wrote the prophecies?'

'Since my return from Italy, the week before our meeting at Monksblood's. It was Ralph who convinced me I needed to recover the book. He believed it was already too late to confess I wrote it, which I was prepared to do. We needed your help, your skills. But then, when Simon returned, it was felt that you were too compromised. That you were both in danger.'

I thought again of my trip to Oxford, that earnest conversation with Strode about the allure of false propositions. Strode had been tantalizing me, then, with his *own* false proposition, encouraging my trip to Oxford, even going so far as to write a letter to Angervyle's keeper to help me find a book he knew I would never discover in the bishop's collection. The only factors he had not controlled were my meeting with Clanvowe and the knight's copy of the prophecies.

'Strode was protecting you,' said Chaucer. 'Getting you out of town when things were at their hottest. He continues to protect you, and me as well.'

'*Protect* me? From what? I don't need protection, Geoffrey. My *son* needs protection. He's the one suffering for my sake, as we stand here jawing about your ridiculous prophecies.' I felt short of breath.

'We all need protection,' Chaucer gently said, risking a hand on my back. Despite myself I did not knock it away. 'Don't you see? The book is an axe at our necks. I wrote it in Italy. Simon read it there, and he's missing. You are Simon's father, and you have a copy of the *De Mortibus* yourself. You received it from Clanvowe while dining with Purvey, Wycliffe's closest disciple. Barely four hundreds lines of my doggerel, and they threaten us all.'

'And King Richard.'

'And King Richard,' he agreed.

'Who is behind all this, Chaucer?'

'Hawkwood.' A blood-soaked name. 'I believe he's plotting a return to England. He wants to ensure his legacy, win a greater title for his descendants. Rather than retiring happily to Essex, though, he plans to destabilize the realm by implicating Lancaster in this plot against the king. Hawkwood has Oxford in his pocket, you see. His ties to the de Veres go back two generations, and that's a family that would do anything to heighten its status. Weldon is the go-between. He's now Oxford's man, but for years he served Hawkwood in the White Company. He led the massacre at Cesena, the slaughter of an entire town.'

I thought of the scar on Weldon's chin, the butchery of which the man had long seemed capable. 'And now Weldon is doing everything he can to see the plot to its completion.'

'It's why Simon was seized, I believe, because he's associated with Hawkwood, and knows his plans.'

'As do you, Geoffrey.'

'Even Strode isn't safe,' he continued. 'The only thing to do now is to recover my copy, hunt down any others, and hope for the best. Unless—'

I looked at him. 'Unless?'

'Unless we can find the cloth.'

'What cloth?'

'An ornate piece of work, embroidered with the livery of Gaunt, the alleged conspirator, raising a sword against King Richard. It travelled with the book from Italy.'

'Who made it?'

He looked away and breathed deeply. 'It fits the *De Mortibus* as a glove fits a hand,' he said, ignoring my question. 'From Strode's inquiries we know that the book has been separated from the cloth. Whoever puts the book with the cloth, then—'

'Will destroy the realm.'

'Or save it,' he said. Then he actually smiled. 'There's one final wrinkle.'

'Why am I not surprised?'

'I have it from Strode that the book was brought into the city by maudlyns.'

'*Maudlyns?*' A stir of the absurd.

'Apparently some whore got ahold of it just as I was asking you to find it for me. You'll remember the girl's murder, outside the city walls—'

'In the Moorfields,' I said.

'They sold the book, or tried to. Strode doesn't know who paid them for it. He's trying even now to find out, asking all kinds of questions. The cloth, on the other hand, has not been seen.'

'So they still have it.'

'Presumably.'

I thought about this. 'And I suppose there's no one more suited, in Strode's opinion and yours, to extracting this cloth from the maudlyns of our city than one John Gower.'

'Well, if it's any comfort, you may be the only one looking for it.'

'Where should I begin?'

'Gropecunt Lane, I imagine. Or Southwark. Perhaps Rose Alley, in your own neighbourhood.'

'And how does one go about prying cloth from maudlyns, in your expert opinion?'

Chaucer turned to me, his brow a world-weary arch. 'Drag a sack of silver through the stews and there's no telling what you might find.'

He said it lightly, provoking me with a familiar humour that obscured those deeper truths he still had not revealed.

You will remember, my soul, that Dante Alighieri, the great poet of Florence, first saw Beatrice at a feast. He was only nine at the time, as was she, yet even then the arrows of Amor penetrated him deeply, inspiring wild thrums and tremblings and pulsations in his heart despite its tender age.

Our young lady was fully a woman when she first saw her love, though the effects on her soul were no less childish, no less urgent for her greater maturity.

It was an autumn evening on the feast of St Luke, just after the procession of the physicians along the square before San Simpliciano. The last company had passed by, the raucous shouts of the children following in their wake, the oily whiff of torches in the air. As the final cluster of drunk doctors walked past she looked across the open space to the opposite rank of spectators – and there he was, in the smoky light: a fair-haired man, twenty years her elder, she guessed, broad of chest, long of leg, a face that brightened the air as if some new Apollo had deigned to troll the streets of Florence.

The man spared her no glance, turning from the procession and walking along the edge of the crowd.

She saw him again the next week, at the Broletto, pausing at a tinker's table while she examined silks. That day he wore a loose shirt of thin wool, a rough thing hardly fit for a clerk. As she passed behind him she glanced at his hands, those long fingers stained with gall. A man given to writing, despite his unslouched back and clear-eyed gaze at everything around him. He smelled of balsam, of honey mixed with ale.

How she pined for him! How she ached to feel his touch, to guide his blotchy fingers in making of her very skin his vellum and his books.

Then, as she watched him stroll across the market street, he was stopped and embraced warmly by a man she knew quite well.

Il Critto! They were countrymen, of course, though there were so

334

many Englishmen in Florence that she had not thought to ask her suitor about the one she most desired.

'Who was that old fellow I saw you with at the Broletto?' she casually asked him the next morning. They were in the upper gallery, finally usable after a months-long repair to the flooring, seated on the long bench beneath the Tribunale tapestry. Her stepmother sat with several visitors at a proper distance. Embroidery and gossip.

'An envoy from Westminster, and an intimate friend of my father's,' he said, suspecting nothing. 'He arranged my current position with Hawkwood, in fact. I owe him a great deal.' He was proud of his knowledge of Hawkwood's relations with the English envoy, whom he seemed to admire tremendously. He told her a bit about the man's employment (royal customs official), purpose on the peninsula (some discreet diplomacy), obsession (poetry), and wife (estranged).

With a frown and a strange tilt of his head, he pointed over her shoulder. 'Why, look there! Those are the arms of his greatest supporter.'

She turned, her gaze falling on the old cloth embroidered with the opposed livery of the foreign duke and prince. She felt it: the breath of Fate on her neck. To learn that the man she desired was in favour with the duke who had saved her life so long ago – this was a destined match. Everything else would naturally follow.

So she dropped a hint, a mild suggestion, and the next day Il Critto (poor fool, she thought) dutifully brought the older man with him to her father's house.

It was a simple matter to put her ambitions in play. A half-hidden smile here, a dropped kerchief there. The Little Weasel no more, she had developed into a captivating beauty, one of the true gems among the ladies of the Commune. Soon enough his visits became the most longed-for part of her day.

They discovered in one another a mutual love of stories and poems. His verses were artful and urbane, pleasuring some hidden part of her with their depth of knowledge and craft. He whispered, too, from some of his more lecherous lays, comparing his desire to a written map of the

335

world, himself to a cold fish marinated in the spicy sauce of her favour. She became an avid listener to this Narcissus of the North, his impenetrable self-regard only warming her further.

The ambassador wrote his poems not on wax but in little books, parchment quires folded within a worn cover of faded leather. Each time he filled one of these booklets with his notes and drafts he would remove it from its cover and place a new quire within. He wrote constantly, rejecting nine out of ten of his own crafted lines. She marvelled at how one man could waste so many words.

Her own stories she spun from the tales of the Moors remembered from her mother. She was his Sherazade, filling her accounts with flying horses and evil viziers, moaning ghouls and poisoned fountains. The only tale she never told him was the story of her life.

One of their favourite entertainments was trading in riddles. Enigmas, he called them, word puzzles in which simple truths are disguised and things are never what they seem. He would slip them to her on torn lengths of waste paper, and she would have to guess their solution before his next appearance.

Some were trivial, riddles about roofless houses and eggs, or chairs and silent goats.

Others were obscene, written to raise a blush on her fair skin.

I am a long rod swinging by a man's leg. He likes to shove me into familiar holes. Who am I? No, not that. A key.

Between two curved legs I quiver, a twist of eager flesh, singing sweetly when fingered. Who am I? No, not that. A harpstring.

The one that most provoked her was an enigma of the moon. He slipped it to her on the second Sunday in Advent, during a procession outside San Lorenzo.

> Whisper the middle of a moon,
> Think the wheel of a wagon,
> Trace the beginning of a king,
>   And mine own shall be yours.

For a full week she puzzled over its meaning, parsing each syllable, looking for that hidden kernel. And on the eighth night, as she slept, a wagon wheel spinning in her dreams—

—she awoke, and she had it. A wheel? The letter O. The 'beginning of a king'? 'King' is 'rex' in Latin. The letter R. And the 'middle of a moon'? A half-moon, of course. The letter C.

'Cor.' Latin for 'heart'. And mine yours, she silently promised him as she drifted back to sleep, and my flesh as well.

Stories, riddles, sin: her father and stepmother were hardly pleased. Florence was starting to whisper, and consorting with this Englishman would only sully her reputation. Il Critto is the son of a landed gentryman, her stepmother scolded her, an upper esquire. This man you favour is merely an esquire en service, with no lands or rents to his name – and married!

Il Critto, too, took notice of her growing attachment to the older man, coming around less frequently and casting dark looks on the two of them from afar. She ignored them all.

Though she recognized the older man's poetical genius (as, indeed, what living man or woman could not? you are surely thinking), some of his making struck her as facile and unserious. She coyly told him so, infuriating and delighting him at once. He told her of his plan for a greater work, a collection of tales in the manner of Boccaccio.

'Though this work, unlike the Decameron, shall be framed not with pestilence but with pilgrimage,' he said. 'The pilgrims shall all tell their own tales as they travel from city to town. Two stories each on the journey out, two on the way home. The narrator will be a pilgrim as well, his feeble talents serving to convince us that the whole compilation bears the ring of truth.'

She taunted him: 'Your readers must be gullible indeed, to fall for such poetical tricks.'

He waved a hand. 'In this land poets are considered akin to prophets. Look at Florence's own Dante, writing of a journey to Hell and back, telling us plainly it is all a lie even as he inks his tercets at his desk.

337

And yet the people credit him as a true visitor to the underworld! Readers will believe anything they are told to believe.'

She looked at him, a provocation in her gaze. 'And you would be the new Dante? Spouting visions and prophecies with the ease of a sibyl?'

'Prophecy is a game like any other, no more complex than our exchanges of riddles and enigmas,' he said. 'Show me a lunatic with a quill and I will show you a prophet.'

'Prove it,' she said.

'I shall rise to your impertinent challenge,' he vowed, and began a work that promised to redeem his talents in her eyes, and win her to his bed. 'It shall be a book of kings,' he told her. 'A book of kings, and their deaths. Once I have completed it, you must quite me with a work of your own. For then it will be your turn to write for the gullible.'

Less than a week had passed when, on a bright winter morning, the ambassador appeared at her door.

'The work is done,' he told her, pleased with himself. He pulled out his current booklet, which he had filled to the last folio with a rough copy of his creation. 'Take me within, muse, and I shall read it to you.'

Just then his young rival appeared at the end of the street. Il Critto's eyes darkened as he strode forward, his jaw a hard knot of envy. But her love put a kindly arm around the younger man's shoulders and drew him into her father's house, as if nothing was amiss. The three of them went up to the gallery, and it was there that she heard the prophecies.

As her lover recited his tuneful lines, she listened with a thrilled amusement to these beguiling prognostications of royal deaths. How he laughed over his own audacity! The work was an amusement to him, its mortal prophecies cast in the gentle light of his wit.

He had even thought to include an actual game in his prophecies: the thistleflowers, hawks, swords, and plums painted on the oval playing cards he often brought with him to her father's house. Yet to

338

anyone else hearing the work, these prophecies would appear genuine, the true products of some latter-day Jeremiah foretelling the deaths of twelve kings, from poor King William to the late King Edward.

Il Critto laughed with them, his boyish grin easing their concerns that—

Ah, but I must drop the pretence of story, my heart. As I think back on that fateful morning, all I see now are Il Critto's owl eyes gazing over my shoulder at the cloth, those mole's ears resounding with your baleful verse. The eyes and ears of Simon Gower, a serpent coiled in envy and plotting his revenge.

FORTY-TWO

Gropecunt Lane

Years ago, soon after the deaths of my elder children, I once followed the Bishop of Ely up Soper Lane, watched him hand a few coins to a maudlyn, and waited as he disappeared into a stall. I confronted him that same afternoon with the evidence of his sin: a copy of the whore's confession, purchased from a clerk at Guildhall after her arranged arrest. For a pound it can all be forgotten, I said. The archbishop won't have to know.

I'll never forget the look he gave me, half scornful, half amused as he leaned against a column in the west end of St Paul's. Know what, Gower? That I just swyved his favourite whore?

What I learned that day was that episcopal visitations with whores were not only not off-limits but commonplace. Unusable. I never again bothered with maudlyns.

So despite my easy familiarity with the underside of London, I felt a bit awkward as I stood at the foot of Gropecunt Lane that afternoon, wondering how it all worked. I did not have to speculate for long. Fewer than five steps into the lane I was confronted by an aggressive young woman who stepped

340

from the shadows of a horsestall. 'Fancy a bit, good sir?' Her hair, unhooded and wild, swept from her brow in a tempestuous wave. Her eye sockets had been blackened with coal or pitch: a Gorgon, her cheeks painted in a red shade rubbed into pink circles. I shook my head tightly and walked on.

Several more maudlyns accosted me on my way up the lane, chirping of their smooth skin, their fair breasts, their shapely buttocks, ripe for you, sir, ripe for you. Near the end of the lane one final woman stepped forward. Her hair had a reddish sheen and she was small, delicate. She put her arms around me, pushing her lithe form against mine. 'I've a young body for your use, good sir,' she said. 'Youngest you'll find on this stretch, sure.'

I gently removed myself. 'Fourpence to talk.'

'Talk?' She pulled away. 'Want to talk to me that way, do you? Price be the same, though.'

'Not that kind of talk. I need to ask some questions.'

'Like them constables?'

'I'm not an arm of the law. Not even a finger.'

She squinted up at me, scrutinizing my intentions. 'You'll want me bawd,' she said softly, putting a hand on my chest, and I felt in the lingering pressure a gentle warning as she hurried down toward St Pancras. She returned with a large, triple-chinned woman wearing a dun dress of shapeless wool and a hat covered in embroidered flowers, all faded with the years.

'This be Joan Rugg, sir.'

I nodded my thanks, then half-bowed to the bawd. 'Mistress Rugg.'

She beamed. 'Your first time on Gropecunt Lane?'

'It is,' I admitted, strangely abashed, as if I should have been expected to possess more experience of whoring.

'Well,' she huffed. 'We're a mite careful up this way with strangers.'

'I understand.'

'Your purpose?'

'I seek a young woman.'

'Queynt?'

'Questions. It will be worth her while to meet with me.' I jangled my purse.

Joan Rugg eyed it. 'What sort of questions?'

I took a risk; time was short. 'Questions about a book. And a cloth.'

Her eyes narrowed into doughy crescents. 'We're not much for books up this way.'

'I don't imagine you are,' I said, watching her. 'Though this book is a special case.'

She considered this. 'You're not the only one asking questions about such matters.'

'Oh?' I said, acting surprised.

'We've had constables, beadles, brigands of a sort.' She was boasting about it. 'Busted us up something good, shut us down for a bit – though the well be full again already, appetites of cock being what they are.'

'Your maudlyns are in danger, Mistress Rugg.'

She put a hand to her chins. 'You puts me in mind of Master Gartner, good sir, the great lover of me youth. Been departed this earth these many year, though not a bell tolls without his face comes to my imagining. Knew the ways of queynt, Master Gartner did. Played me jolly body like a sautrie, and the pole on him would do Gawain's charger proud.'

She took my stunned silence as an invitation to continue.

'It was Master Gartner purchased me this hat by Haberdasher's Hall.' Fingering it. 'Bands of silk, leather for the brim, the most curious flowers here, and here' – her wide arms rose together as she pointed at the faded buds – 'and all for his ladylove. This hat, for all its beauty, Master Gartner says, be the unworthy gloss of your own beauty, Joan Rugg. Let it ever rest upon your fair head as testament of our cherishing. Let it have humble place there, Joan Rugg, its role ever

342

to shade thy fair skin from the ravages of sun and rain. And ever there it has sat, good sir, nigh on twenty year, and there it will sit even to me grave.'

She stared off in a silent reverie that I ended with a gentle cough. The bawd snapped her head around and saw the quarter noble between my fingers. She snatched it. 'Didn't tell them any of it, nor did my girls breathe a word.'

'Tell them what?'

'But I suppose I'll tell you who might tell you who has it. Or tell you who might tell you who might tell you who has it, as the case might be.'

Patiently I said, 'And who would that be?'

'Bess Waller,' she whispered. 'Queen whore of Southwark. Sign of the Pricking Bishop, Rose Alley.'

Rose Alley. The Bishop of Winchester's liberties, up the bankside from St Mary Overey. Joan Rugg had named a bawdy house not a hundred steps from my own front door.

I arrived within the hour to find the narrow lane nearly deserted. Grateful for the lack of idle eyes, I approached the Pricking Bishop and gave a nod to the old woman seated in the low stone entryway. Her skin, pitted with pox and age, twisted into a quizzical frown when I announced myself.

'Gower, flower, hour, power – your name makes no difference to me,' she wheezed. 'Now, coin? That'll open St Cath's ear, sure as a morning stiffie opens her legs.'

I tossed her a groat then stepped into an empty front room, the only furnishings a low table swirled with old candle wax, a rough bench against the far wall. A narrow door gave on to the next room, where a young woman wearing only a shift lay on a pallet, snoring loudly. Despite the open window the space reeked of couplings. The maudlyn's eyes fluttered open, then narrowed as she put on an alluring smile and, keeping her gaze locked on to mine, rolled on to her back and raised her shift.

I looked away. 'Cover yourself.'

343

'As you please,' she said, coming to her knees. 'Most like to start right off, but I don't mind the wait.'

'Is your proprietress about?' I asked.

'Eh?'

'Bess Waller?'

She fixed me with a cold stare, then got to her feet and put her head out the window. '*Besswaller!*' One animal-like burst of sound, then another: '*Gen'manforyou!*' With that she stalked out of the room, leaving me alone. I paced the width of the chamber, trying to ignore my surroundings.

'Sir.'

I turned. In the doorway stood a woman of uncommon beauty despite her age. Her hair fell loosely about her shoulders in ringlets that clung to a long neck rising from a yellow dress. This was faded, austere, but shaped closely to her slim form.

'Mistress Waller?'

'The same.' A sharp, inquisitive voice; no need for niceties here.

'I've come to make a purchase from you.' I held out a purse.

She looked at it with some irritation, then back at me. 'Want a girl to carry along, take home to bed? That's not my trade, sir, not been these five year. The law of the bishop's stews makes plain: swyving permitted in his houses only, not yours.'

'It's not flesh I'm after. It's a cloth.'

She started, tried to hide it. Turning away, she went to the window and laid her hand on the sill. 'Yet you come here unarmed.' She gave me a wistful smile. 'Joan Rugg sent you, I'll be bound.' Her voice had dulled, tinged with sorrow.

'She did.'

'All my slits been chased from this house on account of that damned book. Constables, king's men – St Loy knows what they were.'

'A cloth?' I prompted. She said nothing, and still looked

344

suspicious. 'We're fellow parishioners, Mistress Waller. I let a house from St Mary Overey, and have for some ten years.' Though I had never seen the bawd at the priory, parish identity is nearly as strong as blood. We are neighbours, I was telling her; you can trust me.

She sighed. 'You'll be wanting my daughter.'

'Your daughter.'

'Millicent,' she said. 'Millicent Fonteyn. Got herself in a muck of trouble, she did, and my Ag as well. My younger. Buried her in Spitalfields, poor little maudlyn as she was.' Her eyes teared.

I waited a suitable interval. 'Was your daughter the woman slain in the Moorfields this March?'

She shook her head. 'But Ag's the one saw that girl die, sure as light from lamps.'

I recalled the barristers' play at Temple Hall: the wig, the paint, the furore of the serjeants. 'Where is Millicent now?'

'Not up Cornhull, that's sure.'

I shook the purse. 'Where is she?'

She looked down at the purse, then into my eyes. She exhaled. 'St Leonard's Bromley.' Bess Waller turned and departed the chamber, leaving the purse in my hand.

FORTY-THREE

St Leonard's Bromley

In the parlour Millicent sat at the prioress's feet, watching John Gower. A tall man, quiet but confident, handsome if somewhat gaunt, with a neatly trimmed beard and a peculiar cast to his aquamarine eyes. These were piercing yet somehow clouded and he blinked frequently at times, as if warding off a troublesome gnat. Millicent had heard the name before, a whisper of disapproval from Sir Humphrey ap-Roger in one of his frequent fits of pique at the vagaries of courtly politics. She could tell Gower was troubled, or else hadn't slept in weeks. Dark crescents smeared beneath those curious eyes, his spine a tired arc. Yet he seemed to have the trust of the prioress.

With her work obscured by Isabel's robes, Millicent listened as the two of them discussed it all. The book, the prophecies, a futile search at Oxford, the fate of his missing son. It was amazing, what he said. For during the same span of weeks in which she had sought to sell the book, this man had been searching urgently for it, and would have been happy to part with a great sum to procure it – yet Millicent had never crossed paths with him, nor even heard of his existence. Now here they were at St Leonard's Bromley, neither in possession of the manuscript, yet both intent on forestalling the threat to King Richard this evil work embodied.

'You haven't seen the book yourself?' Isabel asked him.

'Not the original,' he replied. 'Though I have read the *De Mortibus* in a copy.'

'And you believe we have this book here at Bromley?'

'No, Reverend Mother. Not the book.'

'You've come about the cloth, then.'

'I was told by a certain – well, a certain procuress of my acquaintance—'

'A *procuress*, Gower?'

'—a bawd of Rose Alley—'

'A *bawd*?'

'—by a bawd of Rose Alley—'

'Not of your *warm* acquaintance, I should hope.'

'I only met her yesterday.'

'And she told you what?'

'That I should ask after her daughter, Millicent. That I would find her here, at St Leonard's.'

'And what is the significance of this cloth, Master Gower?'

'I have been told that it is embroidered with the livery of the supposed conspirators against King Richard. That it reveals their identity without question.'

'So this cloth must be revealed, to preserve the life of the king against his would-be assassins?'

Gower hesitated. 'Or be destroyed. This entire affair, I believe, is a fabrication, an attempt to make an innocent lord appear guilty of the worst crime imaginable.'

'Oxford's doing, of course.'

Gower stared at her. 'How—'

'Oh, you're not the only one with good sources, Gower.' She cast a sidelong look at Millicent.

'Yes, Reverend Mother.' He cleared his throat, blinked those eyes. 'In any case, the feast of St Dunstan is in a week. The

347

king will appear at a great feast at the Bishop of Winchester's palace. The details of the prophecy suggest the attempt on Richard will happen there.'

'When, precisely?'

'The prophecy maintains that the assassin will spring forth "at spiritus sung". I believe this refers to a processional proper to that day. Evidently the attempt on Richard's life will take place during its performance. At "Prince of Plums", so the prophecy reads.'

'A curious phrase, Prince of Plums.'

'I believe it refers to a game of cards.'

'Cards.'

'Playing cards, Prioress. They're all the rage at court. Swynford herself owns a deck, and is known for inventing new games. The plums, thistleflowers, hawks, and swords are suits – with cards ranging from one to nine in each suit, and face cards ordered as princes, dukes, queens, and kings.'

Seven of Swords, Millicent thought with a thrill, finally understanding the strange symbols positioned around the centre of the cloth.

'So then.' She tightened her habit, spreading the material tautly across her knees. 'It all comes down to the cloth.'

'The cloth is the key to the book. If we can—'

'We have it.'

A pause. 'I suspected as much, Prioress.'

'Allow me to present Millicent Fonteyn, one of our laysisters. She brought the cloth here several days ago. Millicent, explain how it came to you.'

Millicent stood and Gower raised his chin, watching as she haltingly began her account. She watched his face in turn, noting the flickers in his eyes, the changes in his colour as he heard her story. He interrupted her to ask questions, probe the details, and it was in those moments of heightened attention that his eyes remained open and unblinking. He was taken with her intricate memory of the prophecies, which seemed to match his own knowledge. When she had finished she bowed her head and waited.

Isabel said, 'Show him the cloth.'

Millicent reached for her work.

'The other one.'

She turned to Isabel's great chair and lifted the original cloth from the back. She held it out for Gower's inspection, seeing through his eyes the violent scene of treason limned in thread of so many hues: the boyish face of a crowned prince or king, his brows knit together, his mouth opened in a cry of surprise; the long knife pointed at his heart; the bearded face of the attacker, scowling as he aimed the weapon at the royal breast; the heraldry of England's greatest magnate, poised against the royal livery of his victim.

Gower slowly shook his head. 'Lancaster, of course. The obvious suspect.'

'Quite,' said Isabel. 'The cloth is clearly an attempt to incriminate Gaunt, to make him seem the prophesied slayer of his nephew.'

'Though—'

'I don't believe it for a minute, of course, and neither do you. Yet what we believe is hardly at issue. What our flighty young king can be made to believe? That is another matter.'

'The cloth must remain hidden, Reverend Mother. If anyone puts this with the book there will be no mercy for Lancaster.'

Isabel turned. 'Millicent, show Master Gower your work.'

'Yes, Prioress.' Millicent stooped and gathered up her embroidery: a shield and badge, crafted in the style of the cloth, and nearly ready for careful boring into the original.

Gower stared, his high brow lined in thought. As Millicent watched, the creases grew shallower, his skin smoother, until his lean face took on an almost beatific smile. Finally he looked up, his hand on his stomach, and laughed the laugh of a man unused to merriment. A crazed and joyous sound.

When he recovered, Gower looked at the prioress, his

sobriety returned. 'How will you get the altered cloth into the right hands?'

'Millicent will pass it to Lady Katherine Swynford just before the feast,' said Isabel. She explained the abbey's connection to Gaunt's mistress. 'Lady Katherine will be expecting the cloth, and we'll depend on her to reveal it at the right moment.'

Gower shook his head. 'With respect, Reverend Mother, I don't believe relying on Swynford is wise.'

Isabel was unused to being contradicted, especially in her own parlour. 'You have a better idea?'

A slender finger to his chin. 'I have in mind an unusual alliance, Reverend Mother. An alliance that only the direst threat to the realm could create.'

The prioress tilted her head. 'Tell me, Gower.'

FORTY-FOUR

St Mary Overey

Southwark suffered the vigil of St Dunstan beneath a soaking spring rain, the clouds low and close, the house damp with cold as I spent a day alone at my writing desk. Scribbles, pen trials, some scattered rhymes in French and English were the extent of my accomplishment, distracted as I was. I drank far too much wine at supper, also taken alone, and retired early with an ache in my head and a tightness in my gut, fearful of what the feast day would bring.

Though the fear, I discovered, was not as acute as the ignorance. Having gone through most of adulthood in firm control of nearly every aspect of my life, it was jarring to anticipate an event of such magnitude that was entirely out of my hands. No one to threaten or bribe; no whispered scandal to use; no idea whether my son lived or suffered; no certainty about whether the entire course of events over the last weeks had been anything more than a phantom.

That night, sunk in a deep slumber, I saw a tower on a hill, and below it a field stretching to the horizon. On the field were hundreds of ploughmen, toiling silently in unison, digging in the soil, though for what wasn't clear. All they turned up was rock, heavy stones they would shove to the side before going back to their holes for more. The ploughmen worked for what felt like hours, days, weeks. Then, like a scythe cutting through a lawn, sleep overcame them all simultaneously, and they fell to the ground.

It was only then that I realized I was one of them. My hands were filthy with the muck of the field, my back an aching quarter moon, my joints exhausted and worn after a fruitless search for the unknown.

At one point in my dream I had the distinct sense of an obscure figure hovering over me. I could not make out any features, as a luminous arc shone from behind. An angel? Its touch was warm, its breath moist on my skin. It spoke. *I am sorry, Father. Sorrier than you will ever know.* An urgent whisper, a gentle hand on my cheek.

I woke with a start, drenched in fear, my heart fluttering beneath my ribs. No one there. Or was that—? A presence I knew. The smell of my son.

Simon. There, in the doorway, backing out. 'I – I am sorry, Father,' he murmured, seemingly to himself. 'Forgive me, Father. You must forgive me. So – so sorry—'

I came fully awake only to see him turn and stumble forward into the gallery. I called after him but his footsteps were already on the back stairs, clomping down to the rear garden. The slam of a door. I threw open the shutters. He was in the priory sideyard, awash with silver beneath a newly cloudless sky, making diagonally for the high street. I called out again but he ignored me. He ran with a limp, a new injury, his hand clutching a dark bundle against his side.

I lit a candle and walked through the house, sensing his traces in every room. An overturned chair, a table set at an unfamiliar angle against the hall wall.

I immediately saw why. High on the western face of the hall hung the Gower arms, the colours and crest of my father and his father, embossed on an oaken shield that had once hung in our family seat. The shield had been torn from the wall and now hung by one corner, exposing a small recess gouged from wattle and daub between the timbers. I stood on the table and reached into the hole, feeling only the rough boards on the house's street side. The hole was just the right size to hide a large purse, a box of gems, perhaps a silver cross.

Or a book.

FORTY-FIVE

New Rents, before Winchester Palace

The poor of Southwark could smell out a feast from a league's distance, and here they were, all shapes, sizes, and ages, crowding Eleanor's way, though also masking her from anyone who might be watching for her. Closest to the palace's great outer gate stood the usual clutch of old gossips, making a din that competed with the hoarse shouts of the men ranked behind.

'First and third argent? That's Buckingham, sure.'

'And there's Warwick's dragons, I'll be bound.'

'Ah, Lady Anne!'

Earls and bishops, knights and squires, even the untitled were recognized and named as they rode through the gates and into the palace grounds. Most slowed to hand out coins or purses, some more liberally than others.

Midway through this procession of gentry there arrived an armed man on horseback whose appearance raised a less welcoming note from the crowd. A knight, Eleanor saw: lean, tall on his horse. She couldn't see his face from that angle.

He turned his head. Eleanor gasped. From his lip to the lower part of his chin a wide scar traced a crescent, the only flaw on his ruddy skin. With a thrum of fear, Eleanor recognized him: the man from Gropecunt Lane, the man she felt certain had killed poor James Tewburn. Sir Stephen, the night watchers had called him.

With her own face hidden, chin at her chest, Eleanor leaned over to the bonneted woman to her left. 'Who's that, the knight just there?'

'Sir Stephen Weldon,' she replied with a look of disgust. 'Most generous man in England, gifted my purse with an entire farthing last of Wykeham's feasts. He'd pinch a dead babe's face for the coin in its eyes.' Eleanor watched Weldon carefully as he made his way through the guarded gate.

She looked down the high street, along the market rows, waiting for Gerald and thinking about the meaning of Weldon's presence at the feast. Eventually, through a gap in the crowd, she spotted the butchers making their way up New Rents. As Gerald had told her, the bishop didn't like too many fires going at once on the grounds, least when the king was to be present. So twenty lambs and six piglets would be spitted by Wykeham's cooks in a shallow firepit along Cutter Lane, to be carted to the palace for carving, and now here they were. Ten butchers and apprentices processed with the cooked flesh, guarded by bishop's men on either side to keep the hands of the poor off the tender meat, which wafted a delicious scent throughout the market. Grimes himself was in the lead, a pompous air about him, full of his own status as the unofficial leader of the guildless Southwark meaters. Eleanor saw the wild look in his eyes as he fingered the two large knives strapped to his side. Gerald walked at the rear of the bunch, loping after the last cart as it drew toward the smaller postern a ways up from the gate.

Eleanor dashed to the far side of the street past the fishwives' tables, the custard-mongers and bakers along the drainage. After a careful look in both directions, she stepped forward and grasped Gerald's arm as Grimes disappeared through the postern.

Gerald looked at her, surprised. 'Not a place for you to be, Ed—Eleanor,' he murmured beneath the market din. 'Not today, at all rates.'

'Nor you, Gerald,' she whispered, pressing his arm. 'It's all known to the bishop's men.'

The third butcher and his apprentice wheeled the second handcart through the postern.

'What's known?'

The third cart was stuck, a wheel wedged between two stones. Three of the men worked to free it. 'Give a hand, Rykener,' grumbled one of them, seeing Gerald idling with a woman.

'All of it,' she said. 'Who, how, when.'

He looked at her as he backed toward the postern, a shade of doubt in his eyes. She stepped toward him, chin out as she breathed a last warning into his ear. 'And they're *ready* for it, Gerald. You have to get out of this somehow, prophecy and Grimes be damned. Disappear, while you can.'

'What's the hold-up, boys?' Grimes, his greasy face re-appearing at the postern. His eyes darkened when he saw Eleanor. 'Get that swervin' ganymede outta my boy's way,' he said to one of the guards. He pulled Gerald inside the walls.

A guard pushed her roughly from the cart, now freed and rolling forward. The bell of St Mary Overey shuddered above them. The guard started closing the door from within. As she backed away from the postern Eleanor caught a last glimpse of her brother's face, a wan circle of fear.

FORTY-SIX

Winchester Palace

Luke Hodge had served William Wykeham as chief steward
for nearly twenty years, rising to a position of quiet promin-
ence in the official life of Southwark. Our early acquaintance
had involved a sensitive matter regarding Hodge's daughter
that had left him breathless with gratitude. Despite the pre-
feast frenzy, the bishop's steward was glad to invite me within
the palace's service gate to observe the final preparations.

As the first arrivals streamed through the gates the inner
gardens and hall were abustle, the large staff garlanding
shrubs and trees, setting tables with servingware and glass,
arranging chairs. On the lawn a large tent was being raised,
and in the hall, where the wide doors sat open to the inner
court, I noted tables set up in the northeast corner for games
and amusements. On the dais the bishop's high table beneath
the baldachin was arrayed with serving dishes and a ship of
salt-pot and cutlery. A dozen ewers stood in a line along the
south wall.

I found an inconspicuous spot by the outer passage to the
bishop's kitchens, massive chambers filled with smoke, yells,
the clatter of roasting pans and utensils. A company of

butchers arrived with spitted lambs, which they flung on boards and proceeded to carve with a determined energy, flashing knives glistening with grease, competing with the bishop's own cooks as they loaded the results on to large platters held by the servers. As I watched them at their work I started to notice several of the men trading peculiar looks, as if sharing an unspoken secret among themselves. Others were pale in the face as they carved, and I wondered for a moment if they might be ill. Then one of the butchers, a large, beefy man who seemed to be the leader, started to move among the others, patting their backs, speaking softly into their ears, getting grim nods in return, though one young man, perhaps his apprentice, received a hard smack to the ear, and an order to get to it.

By bank of a bishop shall butchers abide.

The line came to me with the force of a hard sneeze. *Butchers.* A metaphor, I had thought, signifying a clutch of armed men primed to attack the king during the feast. Yet what more efficient, more sinister plan could one hatch than to enlist a company of butchers, already armed to the teeth, in the slaying of a royal? The lower trades of Southwark had acted notoriously during the rising, none more so than the butchers. What if the butchers named in the prophecy as Richard's killers were not soldiers or knights after all but . . . just butchers?

I moved quickly out to the kitchen yard, where Hodge stood on a tree stump and addressed a crowd of servants. 'The hour before the king's arrival there will be games and amusements in the hall,' he called out. 'Beers, wines, bird tarts. Aim here is to refresh the ladies' cups as often as possible.'

A few gruff laughs.

'Upon the arrival of His Highness the company will proceed to the gardens. Then Mass for St Dunstan, with the bishop presiding. Craddock, the mass pavilion?'

A man to the steward's left visibly winced. 'Cracked post,

sir.' He held up his axe. 'But we felled us that small elm before the gates at sunrise—'

'Yes, I heard you at it – as did the lord bishop.'

'Ah!' the man said to scattered chuckles. 'So his worship'll know we got it down, then. Tent'll be upright sooner than a cock at a maud's mouth.'

'Glad to hear it. The bishop's pulpit?'

'Already in place, carted out last night.'

This went on until the steward had ticked most of the way through his list, then he clapped his hands. 'A word more.' Hodge straightened himself, spreading a wise smile to all corners. 'We are to have an additional guest or twenty at our feast this day. With the bishop's consent, His Most Indisputably Charming, His Most Esteemed, Generous, and His Most Faultless and Unimpeachable, His Most Excessively Irreproachable Excellency the Duke of Lancaster will be present for the festivities.'

A low murmur from the servants, some calls of scorn. Wykeham and Lancaster despised each other, a sentiment shared throughout the factions of the two magnates, from the lowliest stableboy to the uppermost baron. The domestic servants gathered here would be especially keen in their bitterness toward Gaunt, whose notorious contempt for the commons flavoured every mention of the duke among the city's servingmen.

'I'm told that His Highness King Richard wishes to put an end to the enduring hostilities between our households,' Hodge continued. 'His esteemed uncle, his most trusted bishop – these men should be allies, not enemies. And for today, at least, they shall.'

'Bah!' came a call from the crowd's edges. Hodge shrugged.

'Look to your work. It's not your pounds paying for the puddings.'

'Just our backs,' someone muttered.

Hodge dismissed them all after a few words with the head cook. I followed him into the hall, where he wiped out a silver soup basin as I approached him. 'Gower!' he said, looking up. 'Settling in for a long day?'

I hesitated. 'Keep a hard eye on those butchers, Hodge.'

He looked at me strangely. 'Why's that?'

Challenging me, as if he knew already what to expect. Taken aback, I stumbled a bit, then said, 'Keep an eye on them, will you?'

A thin smile. 'Already am, Gower. Already am.' He left me there, feeling rather foolish, and only slightly reassured.

In the lower lawn the accoutrements of the bishop's Mass had been arranged at the east end of the pavilion. Most notable was Winchester's moveable pulpit, an ornately crafted thing of polished wood with ivory inlays that had been carted out to elevate the bishop above the congregation for his St Dunstan's sermon. I stopped in front of it. In addition to Wykeham's arms, two chevrons sable between three roses gules, the front panel had been carved with the same pearl-and-oyster pattern visible on the stonework above the hall. *In palace of prelate with pearls all appointed.* I stared at the woodwork. Even here, at the site of the bishop's holy Mass for St Dunstan, the signs of King Richard's death.

FORTY-SEVEN

Pepper Alley, Southwark

Millicent waited in the noontime shadows not far from the southern end of the bridge. Southwark was too small a town by far, and though she hadn't swyved on this side of the river in years, there were still men about who knew her face. She edged a slight way down the lane to get a better view up the high street. The alley met the broad thoroughfare at a fork, where a knot of hucksters peddled to passers-by going in both directions.

She soon spotted a grand company coming smartly up from the Thames, their jennets colourfully flounced for the occasion, the commoners parting at their approach. The younger of them ran alongside the horses, shouting for pennies. There were both lords and ladies but mostly ladies, perhaps twenty of them, veiled and bound for the palace and the Dunstan's Day feast. As the company passed the mouth of Pepper Alley two of the horses split off, with several guards falling in behind them. The guards wheeled round and allowed the two ladies to proceed up the alley about fifty feet, where they reined in their horses and pulled up their veils.

The powdered tip of a fine nose, then the face of Katherine

Swynford. Millicent had seen this nose only once before, during a mayor's show on Cat Street when she had stood proudly at Sir Humphrey ap-Roger's side, her knight pointing out the array of gentry in the crowd, though Millicent would have recognized it anywhere. Swynford wore a dress of silk brocade in white and blue, trimmed in furs of pured miniver dusting her fine neck.

'You're the prioress's girl?' Swynford said, her voice hard. Her companion gazed up at the tenements. The women looked strikingly alike.

'Yes, my lady,' Millicent said.

'My daughter tells me to trust the Reverend Mother.'

'Yes, my lady.'

'I agree,' said the other lady.

With a gloved finger, Swynford flicked a fly off her knee. 'Lancaster won't do a thing, of course,' she said to her companion. 'He doesn't credit for a minute that Richard would actually fall for this – this prophecy. Believe me, I considered telling him everything. But what would be the point?' She raised her chin. 'King Richard. Ugh! Staring off into space, making up little fantasies to amuse himself. As I've told John a hundred times, if that brat once gets it into his head that you're out to depose him, why – that's the end of the game, and we're all quartered for our troubles.'

'Surely, though,' said Millicent, hesitantly, 'the duke will not suspect your involvement, my lady. Won't you be handing the cloth off to the Countess of Kent before the feast?' This had been John Gower's suggestion, which the prioress had approved during his visit.

'It is more complicated than that, I'm afraid,' Swynford sighed. 'I have been asked for a round of Prince of Plums. By the Earl of Oxford himself.'

At Prince of Plums shall prelate oppose. The first line of the prophecy rang in Millicent's ears.

'Prince of Plums?' said Swynford's companion.

'Cards, Philippa,' said Swynford. 'It's a game of cards.'

The second woman was Philippa Chaucer, Millicent realized as the prophecy's words continued to echo in her mind. Swynford's sister, and the wife of a minor official in customs, though everyone knew the man was a long-time favourite with Gaunt. 'Why would you possibly front yourself in such a way?' she asked her sister. 'And at Oxford's bidding? What are you thinking, Katherine?'

'He approached me last week, all charm and baby fat. You know how the earl can be.'

Philippa turned away, her eyes closed.

'Everyone is speaking of this feast as a chance to make peace between Oxford and Lancaster, and Lancaster and the king,' she said, pleading her case. 'A moment of reconciliation, as the bishop is casting it, to unite us all before the renewal of the inevitable hostilities with France. Oxford believes the gesture will mean something to Duke John. That showing the duke's mistress in a favourable light may be met in kind, perhaps with a preferment by King Richard, or, I don't know—'

'Garter robes?' said Philippa.

Swynford ignored the jab. 'The chancellor has asked me to arrange the cards so that the game ends a certain way. In any case, the prioress assures me all is in hand. But if my duke suspects I'm part of this what will he do with me?'

'What Lancaster always does with you,' said Philippa, with a sad smile. 'Ignore you during the feast, make you leave by yourself, then order you to his bed once he's returned to the Savoy. He won't let a little prophecy get in the way of his prick.'

'This is different, Philippa. If there's to be an attempt on the king's life today—'

'Don't be indecisive, Katherine,' said Philippa. 'John is the great lover of your life, you have nothing to fear from him. It's Oxford who should terrify you.'

Swynford's thin brows knit in a deep frown. 'The earl is the king's favourite, and the king is the king. I just hope Prioress Isabel hasn't gone weak in the head.'

Philippa waved away a fly. Swynford looked down at Millicent, then extended a hand. 'Give it to me.'

Millicent handed up the cloth, folded into a neat roll and bound with a thong. As Swynford wordlessly turned her horse the animal's tail thwacked Millicent's cheeks. She stepped back right into a stopped gutter. Lifting her shoe out of the muck, she watched as the small company moved back up the alley, the guards falling in before and behind the mounted women. Soon they were gone.

Until a few weeks ago she would have given a painted fingernail for an audience with Katherine Swynford, even in such a miserable spot as Pepper Alley. Yet now she found herself longing instead for the simplicity of St Leonard's Bromley, where the food was plain and the dress plainer, the sisters quiet and, for the most part, kind. She shook her head, thinking of Agnes. What is happening to me? she wondered, not for the last time.

FORTY-EIGHT

Winchester Palace

The Bishop of London and the Duke of Lancaster sat on the dais, deep in discussion, both looking uncomfortably tense. The hall's long central tables were already set for the feast to follow Mass, the plate and glass filling the great chamber with a lustrous glow. At the west end the company had arranged itself around several trestle tables angled out to make room for games. Four men played dice off in the far corner, two went at Nine Men's Morris on a specially carved bench, and the remainder toyed at chess or engaged in idle conversation nearby.

There was a loud clap. Oxford had mounted a table. His hood, lined with ermine, was caught back from his hair in a way that framed a bashful smile. 'Good friends,' he called out to the company, 'I give you Lady Katherine Swynford.'

Oxford held out a hand. With a light step that I could only admire given the circumstances, Swynford joined the earl on the table. A smile as modest as she could manage warmed her face.

'Your ears, if you please.' Her voice was steady, though to me she seemed ill at ease.

On the dais Lancaster and Winchester had stopped talking, the bishop aghast at the sight of the duke's mistress calling for attention in his own hall. Gaunt wore that embarrassed but carnal smile he tended to show whenever he and Swynford appeared together in public. Oxford, I realized, had made a shrewd calculation: by recognizing Lancaster's mistress in this way he was granting her a certain unspoken status among the higher aristocracy, mimicking Lancaster's own habit of leading Swynford's horse on occasion. A friendly gesture on its face, in the conciliatory spirit of the day.

'For our amusement before the Mass,' Swynford said, 'we will have a game.'

'What game, Lady Katherine?' someone called from a bench.

'Prince of Plums.'

There were whispers as the guests decided whether to go along or turn away with courtly indifference.

'And the rules of this game, Lady Katherine?' the same voice inquired. It was Thomas Pinchbeak, the serjeant-at-law, lending his respectability to Swynford's provocation. It worked: she now had everyone's attention.

'There are seventy-four unique cards in this deck. Seventy-four guests will each take one card, and only one,' she said, her voice buoyed by Pinchbeak's approval – arranged, I felt certain, by Oxford. 'He must keep it with him all through our day, from the king's arrival through the feast after Mass. The single rule of the game is this: you may not look at your card, nor will I as I hand them out. Only at the departure of our king will each guest's card be revealed.'

'Let me take the first card, Lady Katherine,' said Pinchbeak, rising from the Morris bench and hobbling over. She handed him down a card, gave the second to Oxford, then the other guests formed a line, none of them wanting to be left out now that the serjeant-at-law and the earl were in. I secured a place in the line and watched the distribution. Once the cards were nearly gone Swynford, with a brazen disregard for propriety, approached the dais. In the silence she handed a card up to the bishop, who took it from her as if it were a live river rat to be held by the tail. Lancaster was more gracious, actually standing, bowing to his consort, and taking the card from her hand.

I looked from the dais to the far wall, across a sea of two hundred eager faces. One of the men in this great chamber carried the Five of Hawks, the fateful card named in the prophecy, though how Swynford's game would turn out was anyone's guess. With a studied indifference, I strolled out the buttery door and into the foreyard, where I stopped below a high wall that separated this small plot of grass from the kitchen gardens beyond. After a glance back over my shoulder, I discreetly removed my card, my eyes closed as I held it at my waist. Holding my breath, I looked.

Seven of Thistles.

I tucked the card away, strangely relieved. When I turned again, my aim to make my way back into the hall, a peculiar sight froze me in place. Through a long aperture formed by a rose arbour and the forked branches of a pear tree, I saw Ralph Strode, standing at the buttery door. From a distance of nearly eighty yards he was watching me across the lawn, dark pouches framing his sunken eyes, his hair lifted by the May breeze, his mouth a rigid line set in the great plane of his face. I raised a half smile, gave the common serjeant a nod. Yet Strode simply stared, a look of cold appraisal that I took as a silent intimation of my own blindness.

✣

Grimes's shop and yard on Cutter Lane were empty, as she knew they would be. Eleanor peered over the streetside fence, spying exactly what she had hoped to find: a row of clothes drying on the line. She vaulted the fence, took what she needed, and stripped off her dress, bunching it into her bag for later. She pulled on a pair of breeches and a one-piece shirt of the sort favoured by the butchers. An old pair of slaughter boots, found in the corner of the first barn, completed the outfit, though as Edgar left the yard he grabbed a stained apron from a hook and wrapped it around his middle. He roughed up his hair, put on a cap, smeared a bit of ash on his cheeks and brow, then left the butcher's precinct the way he had come, heading for the palace, and Gerald's fate.

FORTY-NINE

Winchester Palace

The thickening crowd flowed toward the gate facing New Rents. The palace yards were festooned with banners showing innumerable colours, England's heraldry on full display for the coming of King Richard. Winchester's gateyard was normally ankle-deep in muck and dung from the bishop's stables, and often it could be difficult to tell that the area was paved. Now the stones at my feet practically glistened, as if Wykeham had sent his entire household out for a week with brushes and vinegar. Even the scent was invigorating, with fresh juniper and rosemary underfoot. Over it all loomed Mark Blythe's pearl-and-oyster reliefs, tracing a pattern that summoned one of the clearest lines in the prophecy. *In palace of prelate with pearls appointed.* By the next bell, I brooded, King Richard could be dead.

I fell in place beside Thomas Pinchbeak, who was speaking earnestly to Sir Howard Payne. I listened in for a while, an interested smile fixed on my face, then moved to a spot off the gateyard's pavement to await the king's arrival from the hunting lodges at Easthampstead, feeling alone. The sky had darkened, hints of another May shower in the air. The moist breeze deadened voices, casting a clammy pall over the hushed conversations preceding the royal entrance.

Katherine Swynford, with Philippa at her side, took a position in the rearmost echelon of ladies; no cruel whispers that day, as the duchess was absent. In the faces of those closest to the gate – Wykeham, Gaunt, Oxford, Joan of Kent – I read a dark foreboding, as all seemed to be exchanging glances of secret knowledge and hidden intent. To my mind the entire assemblage felt taut, as if a bowstring had been pulled back to its limit, the archer's fingers on the verge of release.

If an attack on the king came, it would take place soon after his arrival. The bishop and his company were to greet the king and his court inside the palace's great gate. Together the two companies, the episcopal and the royal, would make their way to the pavilion to hear Mass. The singing of the processional hymn would begin upon the commingling of the companies, and conclude before the introit.

From outside the walls came the loud blasts of trumpets, the call of the chief herald, the roar of the Southwark commons. Hinges groaned, heads turned. Through the wide opening on to New Rents the royals appeared on foot, having dismounted before the gate. The king's guard had already clustered around Richard in a tight circle. Wykeham's own guards formed a solid line marching forward. The gate closed behind them.

The greeting was swift and simple. King Richard entered the palace grounds and came to a stop before Wykeham. The two exchanged bows, then the king took the bishop's hand and kissed his ring. Palm in palm, the two turned for the gardens as their retinues fell in behind them. With that the processional to St Dunstan began, the first stanza intoned by the Austin canons of St Mary Overey as the melody filled the courtyard.

Ave Dunstane, praesulum
Sidus decusque splendidum,

Lux vera gentis Anglicae,
Et ad Deum dux praevie.

The singing continued as the two companies turned to process to Mass. Those who knew the tune or words joined in with singing or humming, though in those agonizing moments I forced myself to keep my attention solely on the king.

Now the second stanza. My mind Englished the lines as I followed the king's progress. *In you do we place our trust, in your sight do we lift up our hands . . .* The crowd of guests started filling in behind as the magnates processed past the foreyard. I mouthed the next line, appropriate to the occasion: *Mucrone gentis barbarae,* 'the sword of a barbarous race'. I thought of Dunstan's famed role in prophesying the Danish invasions, of King Richard's present role in the holding off of France. As in the *De Mortibus* itself, past and present here collided with the force of a hurled stone on a palace wall.

I positioned myself at the front right edge of the crowd. Here my view of the central group was now somewhat obstructed. Looking around, I saw behind me the lip of an old, disused well, long since filled in. I stepped up on the stones. The extra height gave me a clear view of the king.

Richard and Wykeham had reached the entrance to the hall, which was standing open. The uppermost members of the company positioned themselves in a wide arc around the two magnates. Oxford stood just steps from the king. Behind him walked Sir Stephen Weldon, his palm on his swordhilt.

They turned at the passage to the kitchens, heading for the pavilion and Mass. All appeared well. No attack seemed to be forming, no apparent threats to the king that I could see. Would all this worry, all the trouble of these last months, be for nothing? I realized I had been holding my breath since the song's previous stanza. I started to exhale—

A flash of metal, in the darkened passage. *The butchers.* I looked around, but no one else seemed to have noticed the movement. I realized why: thanks to the well's stone lip, I alone stood at that particular angle to that corner of the passage.

Now the hymn's final verse, which extolled Dunstan's role in bringing hope, peace, and light to the world.

Per Te Pater spes unica . . .

Movement in the kitchen passage. Yes, the butchers, huddled in a bunch, assembled to rush the king. I was sure of it now, even from forty feet away. I looked around in a panic.

The voices of the Overey canons broke into harmony as they descanted on the second line.

Per Te Proles pax unica . . .

I stared in a cold horror even as my ears rang with the hopeful line. The butchers of Southwark were massed less than twenty feet from King Richard. Their leader was in front. He held a cleaver in one hand, a long knife in the other. Ten butchers at least, bristling with blades. Despite the king's guard how safe could Richard be?

'Your Highness!' I called out weakly over the din of the hymn, attracting annoyed looks from those nearby.

With no regard for propriety or my own fate, I started to push through the ranks, my gaze still fixed on the kitchen passage. The butchers crept forward in the shadows, still unnoticed by the crowd, all attention on the king. I pushed someone aside. 'What in—' Thomas Pinchbeak fell back as I passed, tripping over his stick.

Now an arm, and a leg – did no one else see them?

'Your Highness!' I was almost there. One of Richard's rear guards saw me coming. He reached for his sword.

The canons descanted the third line. I pushed toward the frontmost ranks, pointing madly back at the passage.

'Your Highness!' I yelled. I was shoved aside, by whom I would never know, and fell against a pavilion post.

> *Et Spiritus Lux—*
> *Spiritus!*

'Richard!' I cried as I came to my feet.

The singing stopped. Heads turned, including the king's.

'*For the commons!*' With a hoarse chorus of shouts the shadows came to life, and the butchers flew as one from the kitchen passage, twenty blades raised for the attack. For an awful moment all I saw was a tangle of arms bristling with blades, some grotesquely spiked machine of war hurtling toward the king. There was glee on their faces, a righteous madness bellowing from their opened mouths.

There was a scream. Wykeham leapt backwards. King Richard froze before his assailants.

Then, with a swift rush of air, the sky fell. A cascade of arrows took the butchers in their backs, necks, and chests. The entire group collapsed in place, most of them past agony before they hit the ground. I looked up. Royal archers, at least twenty of them, lined the inner roof on three sides, new arrows already notched.

I gaped at the spectacle. The butchers were dead or dying, pools of new blood glistening on the stone. A pile of corpses. Richard had been safe the entire time.

FIFTY

Winchester Palace

Edgar Rykener saw the shower of arrows before he saw his brother. At first he assumed Gerald was among the attackers, and the sight of his death was like an arrow in his own neck, so sudden and violent it was. Then he looked at the kitchen passage and saw Gerald's face, pale in the shadows. His eyes were wide, registering his boyish shock at what his fellow butchers had done. Edgar's heart soared. Gerald turned and fled.

As the crowd started to react to the attack Edgar dodged around a privet hedge and sprinted for the kitchen gate. Gerald was just disappearing through a second passageway toward the west courtyard. Edgar followed him as the shouts spread in their wake. The courtyard was deserted aside from an old horse and an empty wagon. Gerald sprinted across the space and dodged left at the wagon, angling for the west tower.

'Gerald!' Edgar called ahead before his brother disappeared. Gerald hesitated, turned.

'Edgar! What the—'

Gerald ran up to the next landing. It gave on to a poorly lit chamber above the bishop's lower gallery. He turned toward Edgar, kicking up dust.

Edgar embraced him, loving him for his defiance of Grimes, and felt his brother's hesitation before he returned the hug. 'He's gone now, Gerald. Grimes can't hurt you now.'

Gerald was trembling. 'Now I'll only be hanged,' he murmured.

Edgar didn't doubt it. He looked around, casting for a plan. The space was filled with old rugs and broken furniture, muffling the urgent shouts from below. 'Wykeham's probably rounding up all the kitchen folks as we stand here, seeing if others are part of it,' he said. 'You have to get out of the palace, and right soon.'

'How—how?'

Edgar looked at him in the darkness, asking himself the same question. Then he had it. From his side bag he removed the bundle of clothes and thrust them into Gerald's arms. Gerald looked down. He spread out the dress, then let out a cruel laugh.

'Oh, so now *I'm* to be the swerver?'

Edgar glared at him. 'You've a better thought?'

Gerald hesitated.

'It's the only way, Gerald,' said Edgar. 'Otherwise you're like to be caught and killed this very hour. Now, *put it on.*'

Reluctantly, Gerald eased himself out of his rough breeches, tunic, and apron then pulled the dress over his head. He tugged and smoothed until the garment, a one-piece woollen affair full of patches and stitching, sat more or less right.

Edgar stepped back and appraised him in the half light. He wet his fingertips to wipe some grime off his brother's cheeks, then teased the strands of hair pushing out of the plain coif he had tied around Gerald's head. His brother's voice hadn't yet cracked despite his age, no whiskers on him, and his thin-soled shoes could pass for a scullery maid's. He figured it would all do for the purpose. He walked to the top of the stairs and listened. Voices, two or three men approaching the tower. He turned back and pulled on Gerald's arm.

'Straight for the postern, Gerald. Then the Pricking Bishop on Rose Alley.' He handed him a few coins. 'Give these to that old sheath on the steps, and wait for me inside.'

Gerald looked at him, and Edgar wanted to laugh despite the danger. He put a hand to the back of his brother's head and pushed it down. 'Eyes to the ground and you'll be fine.'

Halfway down the stairs Edgar gave his brother a gentle push. Gerald didn't look back, but as he entered the west yard Edgar watched him through a narrow aperture along the tower wall. Gerald passed two guards but neither spared a glance for the ragged servingwoman coming from the tower. More guards in the yard now, searching out conspirators.

Now for his own escape. Edgar looked down at the courtyard, forming an idea. The horse-drawn cart was one of many in Southwark that doubled as a pageant wagon at festival time. Though the wagon itself was empty and wouldn't do, its undercarriage was obscured by the frayed cloths hanging over each side. He had to get to that wagon.

He waited for the last guard to disappear into one of the surrounding buildings. When he was gone Edgar climbed on to the stone sill, threw his legs over, hung for a moment, and dropped, meeting the courtyard pavers with a painful impact. He stood, ankles still sound. He darted for the wagon and slid beneath the cloths. Wedging himself between the clouts, he took his weight off his arms and tested the fit. It would work. He waited patiently, his mind on Gerald, until the cartman returned to the courtyard. After a word with the guards, he took the horse's reins. Edgar felt a lurch. The cart moved slowly toward the palace's back gate.

FIFTY-ONE

Winchester Palace

The king's guard had encircled Richard, swords drawn. The crowd, moments ago riven with cries of fright, had quieted itself to a low murmur. Most were huddled in small knots, watching ghoulishly as it became known that the danger had passed and a pile of bodies lay on the ground, and a search was on for any remaining conspirators. Hodge ordered the corpses hauled off, a swift task involving several handcarts and a dozen servants. Others brought out buckets of water and washed the blood off the pavers. The bishop spoke to the king, and it seemed the procession would continue to Mass when a loud voice filled the air.

'Your Highness,' said Robert de Vere, in a voice that carried through the assemblage.

'What is it, Oxford?' The king looked unsteady, sickened.

'With your leave, sire, I wish to speak.' The king nodded. The earl approached Richard with his right arm raised. He took a slow circle around the front of the pavilion, displaying something for all of us to see. 'Your eyes and ears, please,' he called out. The earl's hand clutched a book. A thin volume, with a simple, unembossed binding, and no clasps.

377

'What's the meaning of this, Oxford?' the king demanded.

'We have been preparing for this day with grim resolve, Your Highness,' said Oxford. 'In this book lies the key to this attempt on your life. The book is called the *Liber de Mortibus Regum Anglorum*. In our tongue, "The Book of the Deaths of English Kings".' The title sent a thrill through the guests. 'The work's author is named Lollius. A writer of ancient lineage, inking these prophecies during the reign of King William.'

Things had moved so quickly between the king's entrance and the death of the butchers that I had had little time to gather my thoughts. My first reaction to what had just happened was to assume that the plan to kill the king, whoever its instigator, had been thwarted, the prophecy proven false by a hail of arrows. Richard, after all, was alive and unharmed.

Yet now, with the disconcerting sight of the book in Oxford's hands, I was forced to wait as the ingenious machinery of the plot unfolded before my weak eyes. After so many weeks of ignorance I mistrusted my own reactions, and felt at the mercy of the many forces around me – beginning with the intimidating presence of Robert de Vere.

'Who was this Lollius?' asked the king. 'Was he an Englishman?'

'Little is known of him, Your Highness.' Oxford hesitated. 'Though his works are in favour with the followers of John Wycliffe.'

'Preposterous!' thundered John of Gaunt, who had been standing silent since the attack. 'Wycliffe's dissent was a theological one, Your Highness, not a political one.'

Oxford gave the duke a withering look. 'It is known that a copy of this work was made by Sir John Clanvowe, and that it has been circulated among Wycliffe's followers.' His cold eyes found me in the crowd. 'There are copies of this book being handed around in their conventicles, Your Highness.'

378

'You lie, Oxford,' Gaunt taunted him.

'Silence, Lancaster!' King Richard barked, causing a stir of frightened awe among the assembly. Despite their private disagreements, no one had ever seen the king dress down his uncle in public. This whole affair had just taken a dangerous new direction. I felt sick.

Gaunt stared in disbelief at his newly assertive nephew. King Richard turned to Oxford. 'Continue, Oxford.'

'As you wish, Your Highness,' said Oxford with a puerile sneer at Gaunt. 'We have recovered this book through the devices of Master Thomas Pinchbeak, appointed serjeant-at-law by good King Edward.'

'It is true, Your Highness.' Pinchbeak, having risen from his tumble, stepped forward and knelt gingerly before the king. King Richard looked at the powerful lawman: his leg lame from war, his back bent with compensation of his injury, the serjeant's stripes on his arm. Here was an unimpeachable source confirming Oxford's claims, a serjeant-at-law, appointed by patent of Richard himself.

'What is in these prophecies, Oxford?' asked the king. 'Tell us.'

'Certainly,' said Oxford. 'The prophecies, Your Highness, foretell the deaths of thirteen kings, beginning with the great William, Norman conqueror of the Saxons. Their deaths are related in detail and with an accuracy that matches the accounts set forth in our chronicles.' He went on to give several examples from the *De Mortibus*, all of them by now intimately familiar to me.

I watched the king's reaction to the earl's masterful discoursing. Richard was trying to remain impassive, though he was clearly affected by what he heard. By the time Oxford reached the death of the late King Edward, the crowd, I could tell, had been swayed. All that remained was for Oxford to convince the king that the final prophecy had been foiled.

'Yet it is the thirteenth prophecy, Your Highness, that most concerns us today.' Oxford's voice found a pitch that matched the insidious content of the matter. 'For in this final prophecy, your own death is shadowed forth in lines that leave little doubt concerning the day, place, and manner of the plot.'

'Read it, Robert,' Richard ordered, feigning a confidence belied by the deep blush that shot up his cheeks. Behind him, Bolingbroke looked similarly stricken.

The earl intoned the final prophecy:

> *'At Prince of Plums shall prelate oppose*
> *A faun of three feathers with flaunting of fur,*
> *Long castle will collar and cast out the core,*
> *His reign to fall ruin, mors regis to roar.*
> *By bank of a bishop shall butchers abide,*
> *To nest, by God's name, with knives in hand,*
> *Then springen in service at spiritus sung.*
> *In palace of prelate with pearls all appointed,*
> *By kingmaker's cunning a king to unking,*
> *A magnate whose majesty mingles with mort.*
> *By Half-ten of Hawks might shender be shown.'*

Oxford looked up at the king as he recited the final line.

> *'On day of Saint Dunstan shall Death have his doom.'*

The crowd erupted. During the reading of the prophecy more of the king's personal guard had stepped forward. Twenty powerful soldiers now surrounded the company of magnates, their intention to apprehend – and, I feared, likely to slay without thought – anyone named as a conspirator. I wondered how many of them were truly the king's men, and what portion fed from Oxford's trough.

King Richard, regaining some of his composure, stood

straight, a hand at his belt. 'Unravel this prophecy for us, Oxford,' he commanded.

'Yes, Your Highness.' Oxford looked around. 'I have consulted with men of Cambridge and Oxford, sire. Our wisest masters of theology. They have glossed this ancient prophecy, explaining its words, its symbols. I shall interpret it for you in turn, word for word – beginning with the "prelate", a great man of the realm who opposes the "faun of three feathers".'

'Three feathers,' King Richard repeated, slowly nodding. 'My father's crest?'

'The very same,' Oxford said with a brisk nod. 'Everyone knows the legend of your father at the Battle of Crécy, the ostrich feather seized from the crown of King John. You are the faun, sire, the offspring of Prince Edward.'

'What about this "flaunting of fur"?'

Oxford gave an exaggerated shrug. 'Like the three feathers, it must refer to heraldry. That part of a lord's livery consisting of animal fur.' He looked up and cast a meaningful glance over at Gaunt. 'Points of ermine, would be my best guess.'

The king slowly turned his head, staring at the band of ermine points on Gaunt's collar. Lancaster looked at Oxford with a searing hatred.

'Go on,' rattled the king.

'The next lines are clearer,' Vere continued. 'A "long castle" will collar and cast out the core. The core is the *cor*, Latin for "heart". You are the White Hart, Your Highness, to be cast out and your reign to "fall ruin". The Latin phrase *mors regis*, "death of a king", suggests that the deposition will come at the expense of your life.'

The king had gone pale.

'The prophecy even tells us the time, place, and manner of your death, Your Highness. The place: "by bank of a bishop", in the "palace of prelate with pearls all appointed". And here we all are, gathered at the palace of the Bishop of Winchester

381

on the banks of the Thames, with these fine carvings of pearls adorning the walls above our heads.' He spread his right hand, drawing all eyes up to Blythe's ornate pearl carvings.

'And the time,' said Oxford. 'We knew all along that the attack would take place on Dunstan's Day. Yet the prophecy is more specific than that. Our killers are to spring forth "in service" – during the Mass procession, Your Highness – "at *Spiritus* sung": in other words, at the singing of the word *spiritus*, a word which appears in the final verse of the processional proper to this day. And so it was: at the very moment this word was sung, your would-be assassins sprang forth to attack you.'

'Yes,' said King Richard, nodding weakly in the face of Oxford's relentless explication.

'And finally,' said the earl without a pause, 'we come to the killers themselves, and their weapons. Here the *De Mortibus* reads as follows: "By bank of a bishop shall butchers abide", with "knives in hand".' Oxford waved a hand toward the spot where the butchers had met their deaths, bloodied on the ground. 'You've seen our butchers, Your Highness. You've seen their knives.'

Finally, with a slow turn, he pointed to John of Gaunt. 'And here we have our "kingmaker", this cunning conspirator intent on seizing your crown – in the words of the prophecy, a magnate whose majesty mingles with *mort*. Your death, sire, and the death of England. Had we not discovered this conspiracy you would be dead, Your Highness. I give you the man thinly disguised in the prophecy as "long castle" – none other than your treacherous uncle, the Duke of Lancaster.'

John of Gaunt had few friends at Winchester Palace that day. The lawn and pavilion were shot through with an uneasy silence, as all present shared a common thought: What was to prevent the king's men from slaying Lancaster on the spot? With an assassination attempt foiled and the evidence of his uncle's guilt in hand, what would prevent King Richard from ordering his uncle's execution on the palace grounds? Such an order would be perfectly justified before all these witnesses – in fact, I reasoned, it would be much safer to kill Gaunt now rather than wait for a legal proceeding, which would give the forces loyal to Lancaster time and opportunity to redress Oxford's lethal accusation against the powerful duke.

King Richard looked from his uncle to Oxford to his guard, struggling within himself. I closed my eyes, waiting.

'Pray stay your hand, sire.'

A woman's voice, shattering the silence. I opened my eyes, and through the clearing blur saw that the speaker was Joan of Kent, mother of King Richard. The king turned with visible relief toward the countess as she stepped forward from the edge of the crowd.

'What is it, Countess?' he said in a quavering voice.

'Our Lord the Earl of Oxford has given us a remarkable performance,' said Joan with a tight smile. 'Why, he's almost convinced me that my husband's brother is behind this attempt on your life today. That it was Lancaster's hand guiding the men who nearly killed my son. Oxford's account is convincing, and you are right to take this dark prophecy with the utmost seriousness.'

She looked around and raised her voice. 'Yet there is one additional piece to this strange puzzle. As Lord Oxford knows very well, this book of prophecies has travelled from abroad wrapped in a cloth, a piece of embroidery fitted to the manuscript like a glove to a hand.'

Oxford looked delighted to have an unexpected ally. 'Your noble mother is correct, Your Highness. The book and the cloth have travelled together. The cloth went missing and hasn't been recovered.'

'The cloth has been found,' said Joan of Kent. Murmurs of surprise, and she held it bunched up above her head. Oxford looked at the embroidery like a dog at a cutlet. 'The cloth came to me, Your Highness, by the hand of the Mother Superior of St Leonard's Bromley, Prioress Isabel, who was brought the cloth by one of her former laysisters. It reveals with no room for doubt the identity of the agent behind this conspiracy.' She paused for effect. 'May I unfurl the cloth, Your Highness?'

'Please, Countess,' said Richard, almost pathetically grateful to have his moment of decision deferred.

'And with your consent, Lord Oxford?' The earl responded with a courtly nod.

With a flick of her shapely wrist, Joan snapped the cloth open. I craned my neck and smiled at the result of Millicent Fonteyn's handiwork. Where Lancaster's heraldry had once been embroidered into the cloth, there now appeared the arms of Robert de Vere, Earl of Oxford, emblazoned on a mounted knight, his sword thrust in the breast of an unarmed king bearing Richard's colours. A perfect substitution, and I found myself in a state of awe at the ingenuity of Bromley – and pleased that I had suggested the countess rather than Swynford as the agent of its revealing.

After the appropriate exclamations, everyone started speculating wildly. King Richard looked from his mother to the earl. 'What do you say to this, Oxford?' he demanded.

'This—' sputtered Oxford, as word and sight of the cloth spread quickly through the crowd, 'this is absurd, Your Highness! An outrage of the highest order!'

'Who could disagree?' Joan of Kent said. 'This cloth throws the whole of the prophecy into doubt, Your Highness. Many would say your close friendship with the Earl of Oxford renders the man half a king already, so the "kingmaker" could just as well point to him. And heaven knows that this "flaunting of fur", supposedly Lancaster's ermine points, could as easily refer to Robert de Vere, who ladies about wrapped in his fur-lined hood!'

There was scattered laughter as Oxford's hand went to his hood, lined in fox.

The countess was not finished. 'God Himself knows how

deeply I have despised my late husband's brother.' Lancaster said nothing. Joan approached her son and took his hand. 'But he loves you, Richard, as does his son.' A brief glance at Bolingbroke. 'You are the duke's liege lord, and he is your most loyal subject of all.'

Joan dropped the king's hand and looked around, matching Oxford's flourishes and volume with her steadiness and grace. 'The Duke of Lancaster has had many opportunities to take your life since your coronation, Your Highness. How often have you hunted together in Knaresburgh Forest, when a stray arrow might have taken you in the back? Instead he has protected you, Richard: from enemies, from slander, from treason. All of this while others conspire against you.'

'No, Your Highness!' Oxford protested. 'I beg you, sire, don't believe these words from your mother's false mo—' He caught himself before voicing the irrevocable insult, then straightened his back. 'The Countess of Kent has been fooled. This cloth is a false replica, Your Highness.'

'There are many false replicas in your kingdom,' said Joan to her son. 'False loyalties, false friends.' She looked at Oxford. 'And false lords.'

Oxford shook his head. 'The original embroidery is emblazoned with the arms of Lancaster, I swear it.'

'You have seen it, Robert?' the king demanded.

'Yes, Your Highness, though before it went missing.'

'Then why didn't you bring it to me earlier, along with this book, and tell me about this whole plot?' Richard sounded almost petulant; I winced for him.

Oxford hesitated. 'It was thought better to wait, Your Highness – to gauge the seriousness of the conspiracy, and allow us to reveal the perpetrators. As I believe we now have.'

'Indeed,' said Joan of Kent, her meaning lost on no one.

The earl's eyes brightened. 'There is one final token mentioned in the prophecy, Your Highness. One final sign of your betrayer.'

'And what is that, Oxford?' said the king, starting to lose patience.

'The Prince of Plums,' he said. 'The prophecy begins "At Prince of Plums" – a phrase everyone here will understand. Right now, Your Highness, we are in the middle of a game called Prince of Plums. Seventy-four of us, on our persons, carry a card from Lady Katherine Swynford's deck, a card to be revealed at some point during the feast.'

A number of the guests started patting themselves. Oxford raised a hand. 'Halt!' he shouted. 'Do not touch your card, under pain of seizure.' The guards spun round, warning the assembly against disobeying Oxford's orders. It was then that I realized what the earl had done. Somehow he had connived Swynford, Lancaster's mistress, into leading the guests in the card game – never revealing that its purpose would be to condemn the father of her children. I could only imagine what Oxford might have promised Gaunt's unknowing concubine in return. The Order of the Garter, perhaps?

'Each of the guests has been given one of the unique cards from Lady Katherine's stack, to carry on his person until the feast is done. According to the prophecy, your would-be killer will be known by the "Half-ten of Hawks". Whoever bears the Five of Hawks, then, is the agent behind this murderous plot.'

King Richard raised his chin. 'Hold your cards aloft, my good people,' he called to the crowd. 'We shall test the truth of Oxford's claim.' Numerous hands dug into pockets and folds, and soon dozens of cards were held overhead. Those without cards looked on in visible fear. Anything, it seemed, could happen now.

'Who holds the Five of Hawks?' Oxford demanded. He surveyed the elevated cards, walking about the crowd before coming to a position before Gaunt. The duke had not obeyed the king's orders. Instead he was staring with contempt at his card, which he held at waist height. 'Show us your card, Lancaster,' Oxford said to him.

Gaunt slowly turned his card toward the king and the earl. The Five of Hawks.

Oxford whirled toward the king. 'Do you see, Your Highness? "By Half-ten of Hawks might shender be shown." Lancaster's guilt is now beyond doubt.'

The king stared at the card in his uncle's hand, then slowly raised his eyes to meet the duke's.

'Now show us your card, Robert,' Gaunt said into the silence.

Robert de Vere scoffed.

'Yes, my Lord Oxford,' said Joan of Kent softly, looking intently at the earl. 'Show us your card.'

Vere shrugged and reached within his coat, pulling out a card without looking at it. The king stepped forward and took it from him.

King Richard looked down at the card. He audibly gasped. 'The Five of Hawks! Identical to Lancaster's card!'

As the gathering cooed astonishment I looked for Swynford, who had melted into the crowd behind the altar. Then I found her, standing between Ralph Strode and the Baron de la Pole. She had covered her mouth with a gloved hand, and I realized what she had done. Oxford must have requested the game of Prince of Plums from her well in advance of the feast, presenting it as an entertaining diversion and assuming she would go along with his plan to slip the Five of Hawks to her lover. But Swynford, as I knew from that appointment at La Neyte, possessed two identical decks, and an agility with the cards that would have made it an easy matter to place an extra Five of Hawks into the deck and slip it to Oxford. I was glad to see the familiar twinkle of amusement in her eye, and I wondered who had come up with the ingenious contrivance. Strode, I suspected, or perhaps the chancellor himself, each standing to one side of Lancaster's mistress as the spectacle unfolded.

'Again – again, Your Highness,' Oxford stammered, 'there has been a substitution of some kind, another attempt to deceive you. There is only one of each card in Lady Katherine's deck. The Duke of Lancaster has drawn the Five of Hawks, as we have all seen. That two Fives of Hawks have appeared in this game is—'

'A mysterious circumstance indeed, Your Highness,' said Lancaster quietly. 'Lady Katherine distributed the cards before your arrival. The Bishop of Winchester himself took one of them. He is no friend of mine, as you well know. But he will attest that there were no substitutions or trickery of any sort.'

King Richard looked at Wykeham, who said simply, 'His Lordship the Duke of Lancaster speaks the truth, Your Highness.'

The king stepped into the circle formed by his uncle, his mother, the earl, and the bishop. He looked small and wan. 'So here we are, then,' he said, spreading a sad look around the assemblage. 'The prophecy tells me that my uncle the Duke of Lancaster has betrayed me.' The king stared up at Gaunt. Lancaster's chin lifted; he would not meet his nephew's gaze. Richard then approached Oxford, who looked at him with a mix of deference and defiance. 'And yet this cloth, revealed to me by my own mother, suggests that another faction wishes me dead.' He placed a hand on Oxford's cheek. 'That Robert de Vere – friend, companion, loyal knight and earl – that it is you, Robert, who plots against me. Can it be true?'

'Of course not, Your Highness,' said Oxford hastily. 'The very thought is—'

'And yet if I am to credit these cards' – Richard held up the two fives – 'both of you want me gone, and soon.' The young king sighed, his shoulders sagging with the burden of indecision. 'So then. Whom should I believe? What is the solution to this awful dilemma?'

No one spoke as Richard weighed the consequences of all we had seen that day. The king's palm rested on the hilt of his sword, which, I feared, would be drawn at any moment and pointed at the man he decided was the guilty one. The moment stretched: the weightiest choice of King Richard's reign, an irrevocable decision that would alter the future in unimaginable ways. Whatever the king decided, whichever way he went, there would be heavy conflict, possibly all-out civil war. Richard's question hung in the air until a familiar voice sounded from the edge of the crowd.

'It is France, Your Highness.' One hundred heads swivelled toward the voice. It belonged to the Baron de la Pole, the Lord Chancellor.

'What's that?' The king peered through the throng. 'Who has spoken?'

At the far side of the pavilion the guests parted. The chancellor stepped into the tightened circle and took a knee before the king. Richard waved away his guard and bid the baron to stand. 'Explain yourself, Lord Chancellor.'

De la Pole came to his full, commanding height, dwarfing the king in stature and maturity. The baron had stood by King Edward's side for many years, a long history of dispassionate service to the realm evident in his bearing and the respect he was accorded by all. I remembered our last exchange, just outside St Lawrence Jewry, and wondered what he knew. 'Your Highness, we have learned that this book came into the realm through the agency of King Charles, aided by the Scots.'

Murmurs of concern. 'You're quite sure, Lord Chancellor?' asked the king.

'Indeed we are, Your Highness.' He held up a document. 'We have intercepted an encrypted dispatch, bought off a messenger in the service of Burgundy. As you know, sire, the truce has recently expired, and the French are eager to renew hostilities. According to this dispatch, which we managed to

389

decipher only yesterday, the admiral of France is to set sail from Sluys with a thousand lances, bound for Dunbar. The book and the cloth are part of a larger plot to destabilize the realm in advance of an invasion, as was the clumsy attack by the butchers of Southwark, cooked up by a Scottish priest in the pay of the French. Our archers were prepared for the attack, of course. Lord Oxford informed me of the prophecy nearly a week ago, and your royal life was never in jeopardy, though we had to let it go forward to test the reliability of our information. Now we know it is solid. This is good news, Your Highness.'

The King gaped. 'So you're saying all of this was the work of Charles? Who brought the book here, and who managed to deceive so many?'

'French spies, Your Highness, perhaps a whole nest of them.' I heard quite a few gasps as the assembly absorbed the news. The chancellor let them die down. 'Circulating copies of these foul prophecies, passing around cloths, trying to turn our highest noblemen against one another.' Here he paused again to bow to the duke and the earl, then did the same to the countess. 'If your lordships and your ladyship will pardon the expression, you have been played by the French. We all have, Your Highness. And they nearly succeeded in their aim.' The baron stared down Oxford, who looked about to protest but thought better of it.

When the noise had subsided, the king addressed his subjects in a voice cracking giddily with relief. 'Thanks be to God we have learned the source of this plot, and that through your good offices, Lord Chancellor, we have aborted it. A prophecy of my death, written as a poem and seeming to point a finger at no less than John of Gaunt, the Duke of Lancaster.' He laid a hand on his uncle's arm. 'A beautiful cloth, embroidered with the heraldry of one of the realm's greatest lords, Robert de Vere, the Earl of Oxford, tilting at his sovereign.' Another hand on Oxford's shoulder. 'And a game of cards incriminating both of you at once.' He hesitated for a moment, perhaps seeing a weakness in the chancellor's story, then deciding, like the rest of the assembly, to gloss over it in the interests of peace. 'Now it appears that we have been deceived, and by our common foe. Let us put it all behind us, and move forward in harmony, if we can.'

A wave of relief swept through the crowd.

'One last word, Your Highness,' said the chancellor, his voice stern but guarded.

'By all means, Baron,' said King Richard.

'I would appeal to the loyalty of this assembly in asking for discretion. It is imperative that no one speak of what has been heard and seen here today. Should word of this intercepted dispatch get to the French, they would know of our penetration of their networks, and our position would be greatly compromised.'

'Well spoken, Lord Chancellor,' said the king, nodding boyishly. 'By my command no one present may record or speak of what has happened here today. Your silence will be the test of your loyalty, to me and to this realm.'

Watching the effect of all this I marvelled at the chancellor's disingenuous appeal for circumspection. The servants were already whispering, and soon every detail of the exchange would cover London as rumours of Dido swyving Aeneas blanketed Carthage. It was the *performance* of discretion that counted, the useful fiction that we were all somehow privy to the clandestine workings of the military. The aristocracy has always loved such insider talk of espionage and coming war, and Michael de la Pole played to this fancy like a master.

'Uncle,' said Richard to Gaunt, 'take the arm of the Earl of Oxford.' With a reluctance lost on no one, though also with a visible relief, John of Gaunt and Robert de Vere joined arms and faced Richard. 'And now,' the king continued, 'if the Lord Bishop of Winchester will permit it, our Mass shall continue.'

The disordered crowd became an orderly congregation, the women finding their places to the rear of the assemblage. When the Mass was concluded I spent a while looking around the grounds for Chaucer, wanting to ask him the dozen questions rattling through my mind, though he was nowhere to be found. In the hall Wykeham sat alone on the dais, his guests of honour absent, a scowl and a napkined lip accompanying his every sip of wine. Though the feast was only beginning, it seemed that nearly everyone of importance had left the palace grounds: Lancaster, Swynford, Joan of Kent—

Though not Oxford. He had remained in the central courtyard and was leaning against one of the large posts holding up the pavilion, staring off into the distance with the copy of the *De Mortibus* still clutched in his hands. I approached him and waited until he turned to me.

'Give me the book, your lordship,' I murmured.

His lip curled. 'Why would I possibly do such a thing, Gower?'

'I know everything there is to know,' I lied, though fairly confident in my speculations. 'Hawkwood, Sir Stephen, the origin of the prophecies.'

He flinched. 'Who would believe *you*, of all people?'

'Belief is beside the point, my lord,' I said tiredly. 'Written proof? That is another matter.'

His eyes widened for a moment, then settled back into their familiar disdain. 'Your tricks don't intimidate me, Gower. You have nothing.'

I waited before I spoke, giving him a long moment to squirm. 'Are you quite sure, my lord? Simon is a thorough young man. You don't think he tracked Weldon's comings and goings, or thought to leave behind a record of some kind, perhaps a document or two in Sir Stephen's hand – or yours? I can show them to you, if you'd like.'

The earl shifted on his feet. I held his eyes, watching as

392

the weakness I had always sensed in this man crept slowly over his features. Finally he looked away, then down at the manuscript still in his hands, this book that had caused so much anguish, sought by half a kingdom and now seemingly worthless. The earl appeared to realize this as he gave a slight shrug and handed me the volume. I stuffed it in my bag.

'You have made a wise decision, your lordship.' I gave him a slight bow, allowing him to save face in case of any onlookers. 'We shouldn't need to speak of this again.'

He waved me off as he turned, calling angrily for his page and making for the main gates. The Earl of Oxford was still young, though his back was stooped as he walked away from me, his stride unconfident and self-conscious. This magnate would end the day a lesser man.

I was about to turn for the stable gate and home when I saw a movement to the earl's right. From the far side of the grange Sir Stephen Weldon emerged and stood in front of Oxford with his hands upraised, blocking his way. The two of them exchanged words. They were too far away to make anything out, but it was clear the knight was speaking angrily, even defiantly, to his lord, whose slouch now indicated the extent of his humiliation before the king. Oxford raised his fingers to his face, pinched his nose, wagged a hand. Not dismissing Weldon, I thought; it looked rather like a gesture of acquiescence.

Weldon spun on his heel and strode off, heading for the postern door farther down the wall. The earl watched him for a moment, then turned slowly back. I did nothing to conceal myself as I came into his line of vision. He looked unfazed by the evidence of my eavesdropping, which Weldon had not observed. The earl gave me a long look, then tilted his head slightly in the direction of the postern before turning for the main gate.

Weldon had already disappeared through the low door on

393

to New Rents, though the earl's message seemed clear enough. It would be in my interest to follow him, Oxford was telling me, wherever it led. I stood there for a moment, exhausted, wanting nothing more than a drink and a rest. Then, with a growing unease, I turned for the postern and the streets of Southwark.

FIFTY-TWO

New Rents, Southwark

An attack on the king?
In the midst of Mass.
But who done the thing?
And where can we find him to give our thanks?
Or a 'Better luck next time!'
Or a 'Richard? Why not Lancaster?'
None of that talk, now. Enough treason in the bishop's
liberties to go around.
Who done it, then?
Fishmonger, what I heard.
No, a butcher.
Butcher?
Whole scare of them, led by that cutter Grimes.
Ah! No surprise there.
Millicent hardly noticed the postern opening to her left,
rapt as she was by the news being shouted about at the gate.
The man who stepped through noticed her not at all, and
until he passed she gave him no more than a glance, assuming
that anyone exiting Winchester Palace by that door would be
a servant on an errand. As he walked past Millicent saw his

lower face, though his eyes were shadowed beneath a knight's hood. A scar traced a crescent-shaped path from his lip to the turn of his chin. Millicent knew that scar.

It came to her, finally. A hooked scar, white against sun-darkened skin. The ward watch, Eleanor said, had identified him as 'Sir Stephen' – and now she recalled his surname. He was Sir Stephen Weldon, a longtime member of Sir John Hawkwood's company, and a knight of Oxford's household. Sir Humphrey had pointed him out to her at a tournament, making an acerbic comment on the Italian style of his arms and raiment. 'Rides like a Visconti,' he'd said with disdain. 'Scarred like one, too.' Weldon was a badged man, sporting Oxford's livery proudly around his collar, and his own on the back of his surcoat. Quarterly or and gules, and there, in the first quarter, a mullet argent: the silver star of the Veres, plain as the moon.

Yet even as she watched his back recede down New Rents she heard another voice in her head. *It's the crochet. His face.* Some of her sister's last words, gasped from a bleeding mouth. Now she understood them. Sir Stephen Weldon, the man with the hook on his face.

The killer of Agnes.

Without thinking Millicent followed him down the alley beside the Overey churchyard and on to the crowded high street past the fishwives and the pillory. He jogged left on Pepper Alley, then into a narrower lane that led toward the mills on the river side of the palace wall. Millicent kept a safe distance, though never once did Weldon glance behind him.

As they neared the bankside she slowed her steps. Weldon's route had traced a full circle. He was now climbing a short but rough stairway built into the near embankment. He dis-appeared over the top. She took the steps slowly, stretching to peer over the dyke and down to the river. Just as she reached the uppermost step, she caught a glimpse of him on the near side of the wharf, keying open a low door set into

396

the embankment. With his foot the knight dragged a small stone to the opening, wedging the door open before disappearing within.

She descended the moist stair to the embankment and realized where he had gone: into the underpassage below the great chamber and almonry of Winchester Palace, where the bishop had his stores of drink delivered directly from the water. From this cellar the palace's river doors opened to the wharfage through a series of covered channels and ramps carved into the Thames bankside. Silently she pulled open the door, keeping the stone in place, and followed the knight into the dank passageway. She had been here before, though not since her childhood, when the palace environs had been a favourite destination for games of hide-and-tag with her many companions in the liberties. The cold river air felt distantly familiar, the splash of dripping water from the vaults summoning old memories as she walked away from the river and toward the palace undercroft. She heard voices.

'The garrison is encamped at Dartford, Sir Stephen, by the abbey mill, awaiting your orders.'

'There's been a change in plans.'

'A change in plans?'

'The men will need to stay in place for now.'

'For how long?'

There was a pause. Millicent edged around one of the great buttresses ascending to the undercroft's roof and beyond. She peered around and down a short stair into a wider chamber perhaps three feet below, awash in pale light from an opened trapdoor above. Weldon paced the chamber's width, giving orders to a nuncius wearing the king's colours.

'Next Friday is the feast of St Augustine, no?' the knight finally said, turning away with a hand to his mouth.

'And the third Ember Day.'

'They're to come up that day and camp at Mile End, on

397

the green. Their orders will come Trinity morning, likely by Tierce. Then it's up Aldgate Street as planned.'

'Anything else, Sir Stephen?'

'That's it for now. Keep me posted.'

'Yes, Sir Stephen.'

The man ducked through a low doorway. Millicent watched as the knight took a few slow turns around the dank chamber, one hand on his scarred chin, the other cupping his elbow. She thought about what she had heard, putting it together with the prophecies and the failed attempt on the king's life. It sounded as if Weldon had been planning to bring troops up from Dartford in the aftermath of the planned assassination. Who knew what else he had in store. She turned for the river door.

She slipped. She quickly recovered her footing, but not before a small fragment of stone, dislodged by her shoe, tumbled down the stairs. Weldon's head spun round. Frozen in terror, Millicent hesitated long enough for him to meet her gaze. His eyes widened, then narrowed in recognition. She knew that cold stare.

Rose Alley. Weldon had been the leader of the riders, the man challenged by St Cath at the porch of the Pricking Bishop. Looking for Millicent, and the book.

Millicent shot up the stairs. Through the door, over the dyke, down Pepper Alley. She looked back. Weldon was just making the turn.

She ducked between two tanners' stalls on the upper end. Rows of stretched hides gave some cover. An open door, at the end of the second yard. She sprinted through it. A tavern. Low ceiling, small crowd around a far table, the air sour with ale. She stepped from bench to bench and knocked several down on her way out, slowing Weldon a fraction. He stumbled, cursed. She heard his boots on the tables. The street door was also open.

The bankside again. She hesitated. Right, to the high street and the bridge? Or left, and into the stews? She went left.

The right decision, she knew as she sprinted past the mills. On the wide high street the knight would have had the advantage of speed. Here, among the dense and disconnected clusters of shops, houses, tenements, shacks, barns, yards and pens making up the bishop's liberties, she had the advantage of memory.

For though the neighbourhood had undergone many changes in the last ten years, it was all so familiar. Every corner, every turn, every gap between buildings came back to her. Narrow passageways appeared right where she expected to find them. Through the twists and turns of the liberties she ran, the very air before her seeming to shape itself into the form of a child leading her on. She was not alone.

The little girl ran wildly before her, golden hair in tangled streams. Dodging barrels, cornering barns, leaping ditches. *This way, Millie! Faster, Millie!* She never slowed as she led Millicent through the twisted byways of the stews. *I will catch you, Agnes, I will catch you!* The Southwark breeze chilled the tears on her face, as the unmapped warren of the liberties became an elaborate labyrinth through which only this little girl knew the way. Finally, nearing the mills again, the girl slowed. Turning back, her face shrouded in a blinding pool of light, she rose from the soil like a dove lifted by the wind.

With no breath left in her, Millicent squatted at the corner of a pighouse facing the eastern edge of the larger millpond, the phantasm still burning her eyes. She looked behind her. No Weldon.

Loud voices on Rose Alley, a woman's angry shout. Millicent peered around the corner of the low structure. Weldon stood at the door of the Pricking Bishop, having it out with St Cath. His head started to turn.

Millicent hurdled the fence. Squatting beside a great sow, clutching her dress tightly against the muck, she watched through the slats as Weldon looked down the narrow lane to the millpond. The deliberate sweep of his scarred chin, the jewelled scabbard at his side, the devilish gleam of his eyes: all these Millicent took in as she humbled herself with these Southwark pigs. The Overey bell rang None. The knight turned and struck St Cath with the flat of his sword. She collapsed against the doorway. Weldon spun on his heel and entered the Pricking Bishop.

Millicent hesitated, every part of her wanting to spring out and flee across the bridge, leaving Weldon to do what he wished. She thought of her mother, this woman who had never given her more than a bed to swyve on for her own profit. And why should I give her anything more in return? Then she thought of Prioress Isabel, and how the holy woman would answer this question. Finally she thought of Agnes, her sister's generous, selfless spirit, and it was then that she knew what must be done.

Millicent closed her eyes, said a prayer, and hopped back over the fence. With her fists clenched at her sides she strode down Rose Alley, wondering how on earth she might save her mother's life.

St Cath still lay on the stone, though she looked to be breathing. Millicent edged through the door and stood listening. She moved toward the rear of the building and heard the knight's heavy footsteps above, as he stomped around the upper floors, raising screams of terror from the maudlyns, a few indignant shouts from their unlucky jakes.

'Millicent.' She peered through the gloom. Bess Waller stood at the kitchen door, beckoning her forward. 'In here, girl,' she whispered.

Millicent dashed forward and had almost reached the kitchen when she tripped on the corner of a pallet. With a crash she fell into a deal table against the wall, knocking a brass ewer on to the floor. The *clang* resounded throughout the Bishop. The sound of the knight's boots above ceased, then began again with a renewed vigour as he crashed down the side stairs.

400

'Quickly,' said Bess Waller, pulling Millicent from the floor. In the kitchen the cellar door lay open to the stairs. It was all Millicent could do to stay on her feet as her mother pushed her toward the gaping hole in the floor. Once below she scurried down the steps. Her feet met the dirt floor. She looked back and caught a last glimpse of Bess Waller's face as the door slammed shut above, sealing her in darkness.

FIFTY-THREE

New Rents

Weldon was gone by the time I exited the palace through the postern and reached the market. I stepped up on a half-barrel and peered in both directions. Nothing. The knight had disappeared, absorbed into the thick crowd. A clutch of five street urchins were plucking at my hose, begging for coin. About to swat them away, I thought better of it and stepped off the half-barrel, reached into my purse, and knelt down, a handful of pennies clutched in my palm.

'One for each of you.' Three boys and two girls, their faces grimed in that way only a young Southwark face can be grimed, though they all seemed eager to earn despite the squalor. 'And another if you'll find someone for me.'

'Who, sir?'

'Who?'

'Who?'

'Who's it to find, good sir?'

'Man or woman, *I'll* find them, that's sure,' said the smallest of them, a girl of five or six.

'You know Sir Stephen Weldon?'

A few tentative nods, but the little girl shook her head truthfully.

'A knight with a curved scar, just here?' I traced it on her small chin.

'Hook on his face, bright as the moon!' crowed the little girl.

Nods all around. 'We know him, sir!'

'Find him for me, then,' I said. 'He left by the postern a little while ago. He can't have got far. First one back gets two pence.'

They sprinted off, getting underfoot of the merchants, pushing around the corners, spreading like a dropped sack of grain. It wasn't long before the first of them, the little girl, returned. Out of breath, she steadied herself on my leg then looked up in triumph.

'Saw him, sir, saw him I did.'

I knelt in the dirt. 'And where did you see him, my dear?'

'Past the millpond,' she said, 'on that Rose Alley. Going into the Pricking Bishop for a swyve, looked like.'

After paying the girl off I headed west past the Overey churchyard and toward the stews. Skirting the millpond I dodged a pighouse and entered Rose Alley. Few residents were about, all drawn to the palace, and no one looked my way as I walked beneath the low awnings and haphazard upper extensions lining the narrow lane. I was halfway up when I saw a figure leaning over a prostrate woman before the front door. Not Weldon, but a much younger man, slight, almost feminine. The old woman gave a gentle moan as he leaned her against the house's outer wall. He stroked her hair then turned for the door, which was unlatched and partially open. He turned, we locked eyes, then he disappeared into the Bishop. After peering up and down the lane I jogged to the house and followed him within.

⁌

Edgar heard the shouts from the back of the house, which he approached through the same front room he'd crossed weeks

403

ago, before taking the book. Reaching the kitchen door, he pressed his ear against the rough wood surface.

A man's voice. '. . . in the rancid stews of Southwark. Home of women and fish.'

Then Bess Waller: 'Get you gone from here, sir, there'll be no—'

'Where is she?' A few mumbles, then: 'So she *is* here, you lying whore.'

'No – no, sire, she's not, I'd swear it on—'

'On what?'

'On the blood of Mary, and the Maudlyn, and—'

'And your own?'

'Sire?'

'Or perhaps on the blood of your daughter. Not the one I've just chased through the stews, but the younger one. That pretty little thing over by Aldgate.'

Silence. Edgar closed his eyes, the sight of Agnes's body coming back to him with a wave of sadness. Then a groan of metal, a clap of wood, a shout.

'Leave her be!' Millicent's voice.

'Ah!' shouted the man. 'So *that's* where you were hiding, you snooping slut.'

Edgar pictured the kitchen. Bess Waller must have hidden Millicent in the cellar—the same dark space in which Edgar had trapped the bawd while searching for the book.

'You're the devil.' Millicent this time, her voice low with fury. Edgar braced himself against the door.

'Millicent, is it?' the man hissed. 'Former consort of the great Sir Humphrey ap-Roger, Humphrey the fat, Humphrey the codger, hmm? Your blood, perhaps?'

'Not her blood, false knight.' Bess's voice had steeled. 'Not Millicent's blood. I'll not have her harmed. Though this is Southwark there be laws in the bishop's liberties, and you're bound by them well as I. You leave her be.'

Edgar heard the swipe of the knight's sword. 'I'll leave neither of you be.' Another swipe, a splinter of glass.

'No.'

Edgar had heard enough. He looked about for a weapon of some kind. He pictured Weldon's short sword drawn, the point at Millicent's throat. His hand brushed a heavy candlestick. It would have to do. Calming himself with a deep breath, he grasped the latch.

A hand squeezed his arm. He turned in fright, ready to swing. *Gerald*. His brother had removed the dress and stood in his breeches, bare-chested and thin, though butcher's muscles were already outlined on his arms and torso. A knife was still at his belt.

'There another way in?' he asked. 'Through the alley, p'raps?'

Edgar thought about it, recalling his search through the kitchen. 'The walls be eight, nine feet deep on the wharf side. Door's bolted.' There had been so much flooding on this side of the Bishop's Wild that high berms had been built between the river and the lanes and alleys up from the shore, leaving the embankment vulnerable to severe erosion in the event of the river's swelling. 'There's a high window in there, you can get to it from the back. But you'd have to climb—'

He was already gone. Edgar watched his back for a moment, then turned to the kitchen door and pushed it open.

✜

The door swung wide. Millicent saw Edgar Rykener, in butcher's raiment and brandishing a candlestick. At his entrance Weldon spun and swiped the blade in an arc close to Edgar's face. With one step Edgar sprang toward Bess and Millicent. Now he stood with them, the candlestick held in front, the three of them huddled against the kitchen wall.

The high windows beneath the eaves, fully covered in parchment during the winter but now partially open to the air, let in enough light to catch the glint along the blade's embossed fullers. The same shafts brought out the scar on Weldon's chin, the jagged crescent Millicent couldn't help comparing

405

even in her fear to the hooks aligned above the hearth. She imagined being impaled on them, suspended before the knight's seething eyes, hooked iron in her brains.

She glanced sidelong at the garden door.

'Don't think of it,' said Weldon. 'I'll cut you before you reach the bolt.' He moved to the side. Pushed a table and a heavy cutting board against the door, blocking any hope of escape. He took a step toward them, waving his blade. Another step.

Millicent shrank back. Edgar raised the candlestick. He gave it a feeble swing. Weldon dodged it. With one slash Weldon sliced Edgar's hand. He dropped the candlestick. Millicent picked it up, then swung it through the air as hard as she could. The knight dodged this blow, too, with a deft step to the side. He raised his blade and plunged it into Bess Waller's chest.

Millicent screamed, then the inner door to the kitchen was filled with the faces of Bess's girls, drawn by the commotion. The moment stretched, and Millicent would always remember the three things that followed it. The first was a tearing sound from above, as the rolled parchment fell away and a figure leapt from the upper window. He landed on the knight's sword shoulder, disarming him with the force of the impact. The second was the rush of the maudlyns, five Southwark whores descending on the knight. The third was the aquamarine eyes of John Gower, the gentleman from St Leonard's. Now he was here, in her mother's kitchen. His features were the last thing she saw as her vision darkened and Bess Waller died in her arms.

⁜

I have witnessed many deaths. Hangings, quarterings, drownings, knifings on the Southwark streets. Once I watched at a tournament as a knight of the king's chamber was decapitated by a lance, his blood arcing toward the stands, his head falling to the earth with a gruesome finality as hundreds of England's highest of birth held their stomachs.

Yet nothing had quite prepared me for the grim work of these Southwark maudlyns as they swarmed toward Sir Stephen Weldon, covering him like a hill of ants meeting a honeyed bun. They gouged his eyes, bit his ears, pummelled his neck and his stomach. They stretched his arms and legs to their full length, tore off his clothing, and wrote their fury on his bare skin. They killed him with their fingers, their fists, their feet. They killed him with their teeth and their nails. The way his body was tossed among them they might have been a pack of dogs at a hart. I could almost feel sorry for Weldon, despite the private satisfaction I took in his death.

'Enough!' I shouted into the dim light. 'Enough!'

The fury slowed. The young man who had leapt from the window crawled toward the far wall, moaning with the pain of a broken leg. He made it to the side of the slight man I had seen on Rose Alley. The two embraced. Beside them was Millicent Fonteyn, the laysister from Bromley, holding her mother's outstretched body in her arms. The maudlyns circled their dead bawd, pawing at her bloody neck and chest. I stared at them, wondering at their peculiar courage.

A wheeze from the floor. I looked down with amazement at Weldon. Incredibly, the knight was alive, though clearly moments from his last breath. I knelt beside him, shielding his broken frame from view of the maudlyns, who were still crowded around their dead bawd.

He looked at me, blankly at first, then his sole remaining eye flashed recognition as the ragged edges of his lips lifted into a thin, cruel smile. 'Hawks,' he croaked, his windpipe nearly crushed. 'Hawks always strike twice, Gower.'

'What's that you say?' I hissed, shaking him, wondering what secrets would die with this man, wishing I could buy them all. I slapped his face. 'Who are the hawks, Weldon? When will they strike?'

'Always twice,' he said, then his eyes froze in death, the meaning of his final words lost in the slaked howling of the whores.

The fingers throb, the eyes weaken, the bent back aches. I have scraped these words throughout this long winter night, all the while picturing you in Rome, venturing out from the abitato to walk with the sheep among the ruins, clearing your fine head after a day of subterfuge at the papal curia.

Such pleasant thoughts must now be pushed aside, and this sad tale brought to an end.

✠

Simon Gower, no fool, had been watching us most carefully: our subtle looks, our secretive gestures, the wanton press of skin on skin as we made our greetings. He sensed the rising heat between us, our swelling need.

Jealousy is as fierce as the grave, the Song of Solomon teaches us, fuel of the truest fire and the fiercest flames.

It started, it must have started, with the cloth. My piece of youthful handiwork had hung in the gallery for over ten years, embroidered with the livery of Wales and Lancaster, both sons of old King Edward. The only distinction between their heraldry was in the labels: three points argent on Prince Edward's, three points ermine on Lancaster's.

As I recollect it now it seems so obvious, yet so darkly ingenious at the same time. With the death of Prince Edward, the royal arms passed to his son, then a child but now the king, who retained his father's label of three points argent. In every respect King Richard's arms match King Edward's. To anyone viewing the cloth in our day, the duke would appear to be attacking not Prince Edward, but King Richard.

Ermine against argent. Duke against king. Once a scene of noble rescue embroidered by a lost girl, the cloth now showed a spectacle of royal murder.

If the cloth inspired Simon Gower's betrayal, it was his envy of you, my heart, that guided his pen. 'Why, if Geoffrey Chaucer can fool his readers with counterfeited prophecies, so can I!'

409

But how did he do it? Let your thoughts take you back just four weeks, the day before your company's departure to Rome. You will remember your distress one morning at my father's house. 'My little book has gone missing from my rooms on the Via dei Calzaiuoli,' you whispered to me, your hand pushing through your thick hair. 'The quire is gone, and with it the prophecies I wrote for you.'

Yet your anguish seemed too great for such a trifle. Yes, you had written me an amusing poem, but its loss would hardly merit the fear I read on your face. There was more to this book, I suspected, something in it other than your clever prognostications.

It was Simon, of course, who stole your little book – stole it, copied it, then augmented your work with a poetical prophecy of his own. A thirteenth prophecy, added to your twelve, bringing the book's dark matter into the present time.

The victim?

England's young king.

The chief conspirator?

The king's uncle. The duke who saved my mother's life, and my own.

In the prophecy Lancaster is marked by his livery and his name, both disguised as they were in another poem you once shared with me. You called it an elegy, and you wrote it for the duke himself, on the death of his first wife. I can still recall the line, the company riding toward 'a long castle with white walls' as they pursue a white hart.

Lancaster, the White Hart: here again Il Critto chose carefully. His prophecy imputes the regicide to this same 'long castle,' a magnate and kingmaker whose identity the verses barely conceal. Still less do they disguise the alleged victim, young Richard, whose badge bears the white hart.

Nor do they obscure the identity of the author, despite your amusing effort to credit the work to your invented Lollius. Anyone familiar with your Book of the Duchess would easily detect your handiwork.

This, I believe, was Simon's hope. A master of deception, he used old parchment and disguised his hand to make the book take on greater antiquity. He then decorated the margins with plain but skilful drawings of the thistleflowers, plums, hawks, and swords that answered to the playing cards evoked in the prophecies.

Now it needed a final touch. Simon paid me a last visit on Epiphany Sunday, soon after your departure for Rome. Gone was the cavilling bitterness he had shown while the two of you were tilting for my attention. Instead he was all smiles and warmth. He expressed regret for his earlier behaviour, and we parted on the most pleasant terms.

The sole purpose of his visit, I know now, was to pilfer the cloth. He must have unpinned it from the tapestry while my attention was diverted, stuffed it away even as he lisped his pleasantries. It was then an easy matter to commission the embroidery of those simple shapes from Hawkwood's playing cards: plums, thistleflowers, hawks, and swords, surrounding the royal livery, tying the cloth inextricably to the book.

Now all that remained was to get the book into the hands of his master. 'By kingmaker's cunning a king to unking.' Simon wrote that line for Hawkwood. He knew this man, his grandiose designs, his thirst for new legitimacy in his homeland. To imagine himself as the kingmaker would feed his ambition and stoke his pride.

Yet to present the book directly to the great condottiero would have been unwise. Hawkwood is known to be changeable, and he might well have suspected a trap. So Simon arranged to have the prophecies made known to Hawkwood, dangled in front of the man like a riverbug before a pike.

Hawkwood, as Il Critto knew he would, bit.

You are asking yourself how I know all of this, by what means I gleaned this foul grain. There is a man in Hawkwood's inner circle, another Englishman. His name is Adam Scarlett. Though he has a less turbulent soul than his master's, his name is as respected as Hawkwood's, and nearly as feared.

Two evenings ago, a week after Simon's departure for England, Scarlett came to see my father. I heard their voices and walked over

411

to the far north corner of the gallery, where there is a squint down to the hall below. He was asking about Simon.

'Il Critto spent much time in this house,' said Scarlett. 'Tell me all you know about him.'

My father replied that he knew nothing of Simon's doings beyond the failed courtship of his daughter. Why, what else was there to know?

'Master Gower's departure was somewhat – abrupt,' Scarlett explained. 'Ser Giovanni sees no cause for concern in the matter. I am sure he is correct. But I am a thorough man.'

They went on like this for a while, as Scarlett plumbed my father's mind but found nothing. Then he asked a final question. 'Did Il Critto ever mention a book?'

'A book?'

Scarlett described the work to my father, explaining how it would abet Hawkwood's larger aims – aims for which we are all labouring, as he put it – and every word he spoke was a poisoned dart shot from his lips.

Prophecies.

The Duke of Lancaster.

The Earl of Oxford.

Sir Stephen Weldon.

St Dunstan's Day.

Treason.

Execution.

Rome.

France.

It was as if the thousand pieces of a shattered window reassembled themselves in an instant, and I saw it before me, in all its grim totality. Hawkwood, Scarlett, Simon, even my father: all of them in cruel confederation, striving for destruction. An intricate plot to destroy a duke, a king – an entire realm.

I dashed to the gallery. The cloth was gone. On the bench below the tapestry I saw Il Critto, or rather my memory of him. His eyes wide as he gaped at the cloth, his long limbs coiled tensely as he gazed with jealousy on our swelling love. I knew everything, and the knowledge boiled me with terror. For your life, for the life of the duke, for the blood of all England.

Now it is clear what must be done. Simon has been gone for over a week. Your prophetic book precedes him, augmented with his final prophecy and even now making its way overland to London, by the Rhineland roads. When you return to Florence in another fortnight, you shall find only these parchments waiting for you, sealed with my ring, and a very wet kiss – the only kiss you will receive for many months. For by then your bitter orange shall be gone.

Worry not for her safety, my poetical prince. There is still something of La Comadrejita in her, after all. She knows how to steal, how to stab, how to darn a gentleman's hose, wash a lord's pot, peel an earl's root. How to ask for a meal in a dozen tongues, yet garb herself as a peasant. How to barter like a tradesman's wife, yet mewl like a lady of the court. How to slit a man's throat. I dare say her life has equipped her for such a journey better than most.

She will act alone, her quest to find the book herself and prevent the fulfilment of Hawkwood's true aims. To find the book – or die trying. A long journey to England, then, by land and by sea. And when she finds the book, when this accursed volume is in her hands at last, she will burn it to finest ash.

I leave you with one last enigma, my only heart, in the spirit of our games of love and verse. May it goad and prick your mind as you follow our course to England.

Though faun escape the falcon's claws
    and crochet cut its snare,
When father, son, and ghost we sing,
    of city's blade beware.

413

I shall gloss it for you when our lips finally touch and the danger is well past, though I suspect you will have puzzled it out for yourself by then.

Until that blessed moment, I remain yours most faithfully—

Written at the Via dei Calzaiuoli,
by the Misericordia,
the Thursday next after Epiphany Sunday, by Seguina d'Orange

✥ ✥ ✥

FIFTY-FOUR

St Mary Overey, Southwark

On the third day following the deaths of Sir Stephen Weldon
and the butchers, as I dozed in the back garden, Will Cooper
appeared at my side. 'Master Chaucer for you, sir.'

We drank small ale beneath the arbour, with the heavy
scent of thirsty roses filling the air. Our talk was amiable,
though he sensed my reserve. He would hardly meet my eyes,
and he fidgeted on his chair.

'What's tickling your thoughts, Geoffrey?' I finally asked,
wanting to get to it.

Chaucer let out a breath. 'I have been avoiding this conversation, frankly.'

'I should think so,' I replied indifferently, though over the
following hours this indifference would yield by turns to
wonder, then outrage, then gnawing doubt.

He started with his arrival in Italy, and his introduction to
Seguina d'Orange. Simon had been courting her and was obviously in love, yet she used him to meet Chaucer. They developed
a quick intimacy and a ready attraction, meeting frequently
as they moved among the English residents of Florence.

'When you are newly in town, of course, everyone wants

to hear about doings at Westminster,' Chaucer said. 'The king's new wife, the buzz around Lancaster and the rivalries for the crown. Seguina's stepmother was an Englishwoman – a Londoner, in fact, the widow of one of Hawkwood's men. She had books and books of English romances, and Seguina herself spoke our language like a native. Her interest seemed only natural.'

He stared off over the priory walls, the line of his lips unbending. I stared at him in turn, wondering why I felt surprised at yet another example of Chaucer's baffling selfishness. A married man attempting to seduce a young woman nearly betrothed to the son of his closest friend.

'Seguina was a great story-teller,' he went on. 'The two of us swapped tales and enigmas like children trade river stones. Hers were fantastical, full of beasts and magic, caliphs and flying carpets, boiling oil, thieves visiting at night.'

'And the prophecies?'

'It started as a wager, really, a bit of a dare. I'll write a new work, I told her. Not my usual fare. Something darker, but tuned to the ears of the gullible. When I finished it I planned to read it to her. I showed up at her father's house, the draft in hand, quite pleased with myself.' He turned to me. 'Simon was there that morning, John. Come to pay a call, he said. Seguina invited him in, and together they listened to the prophecies as I read them aloud in the gallery.' Chaucer was measuring his words, trying to soften a coming blow. 'I suppose it was then that Simon saw his chance.'

'His chance? What are you talking about?'

He swallowed drily, his slender neck bobbing with the effort. 'A few weeks before my return to England I had to make a long-scheduled trip to Rome. I would be gone a month, perhaps more, before returning to Florence. The day before my departure, as I was packing my things, I realized it was missing.'

'What?'

'My little book.'

My little book. Chaucer's phrase for the leathern bifold he kept with him at all times, replacing the inner quire as needed. I recalled our meeting at the customhouse, the new red cover such a surprising replacement for the hand-worn skin he had carried for so many years.

Nothing here made sense. 'So you lose a book in Florence, and you ask me to find it in London?'

'Hardly,' he said, still hesitating. 'The book you were looking for was a copy of my own, made by . . . it was – it was Simon who stole my book—'

'As I suspected.'

'—who stole my book, copied out the *De Mortibus* word for word, line for line, and then—'

He stopped, a hand at his mouth as he looked sidelong at me.

'Then what, Geoffrey?'

'Then he added a final prophecy of his own.'

My vision blackened entirely, though only for a moment, and afterwards I felt a clarifying and melancholy sadness. Simon's involvement explained so much, and about everything. His return to England, his eagerness to mingle with the chancellor and official Westminster, that peculiar scene with Chaucer at Windsor. It was as if a piece of gauze had been torn suddenly from my lame and weakened eyes, even as a new weight settled around my heart. I wondered if anything Simon had said to me, anything at all, were true: his longing for home, his desire for a new intimacy with his father, his need to hear of Sarah's last days. All of it feigned?

'Simon wrote the thirteenth prophecy,' was all I could say.

'Out of spite, and simple jealousy,' said Chaucer. 'The jilted lover, revenging himself on the man who stole his lady's heart. One of the oldest stories there is, though in this case augmented by a reckless disregard for all the other lives affected, even the safety of the realm. With my little book in

417

hand he would have indisputable proof that I was involved in the *De Mortibus*, along with a host of other information he could peddle back in Westminster.'

'Information?'

'That quire was dangerous, true, but not only because of the prophecies, which, you must remember, I still regarded as nothing at the time. The book, you see, had all my jottings about what I had learned of Hawkwood's plans over my months in Italy. Troop movements, financing through bankers in Venice, plans for garrisoning and travel. While Simon was copying the prophecies he saw what was in front of him, and recognized it for what it was.'

'So why didn't you tell me all this earlier, Geoffrey? When we first spoke about it, or that day in the customhouse? Think of the time and trouble you might have spared me, and yourself.'

'Well, in my defence, I was almost as ignorant as you when we met at Monksblood's. I had suspected Simon of lifting my book but had no proof, nor even certain knowledge that he had returned to England. Then, once he showed himself, it became . . . personal, I suppose. I could see that you were taken with him, that the two of you were starting to reconcile after so many years.' He stopped, closing his eyes. 'And I have only just confirmed that Simon wrote the final prophecy.'

There was a large rose bush climbing an old trellis on the priory edge of the garden. My eyes had fixed on one stem heavy with newly opened buds, and as Chaucer pressed on I watched spots swimming in a field of cloying pink.

'It was Simon's peculiar mind that conjured the details that made the thing so damned convincing,' he said, as much to himself as to me. 'Wykeham has always had a feast on St Dunstan's Day, and Simon used to speak with such admiration about those pearls. You would show them to him when he was young, while Mark Blythe was carving them over the gates.'

Sunday strolls along the palace walls, admiring looks up at the reliefs. I recalled my visit to Newgate so many weeks ago, the feel of the mason's hands, rough with his labour. And of course the heraldry, the bit about the 'pearls all appointed', even the word *spiritus* from the processional, which Simon would have remembered from his years as a boy chorister.

'He made a fair copy of the prophecies, including his new verse, but used old parchment, masking the whole thing as an ancient manuscript written in the days of King William. He also drew thistleflowers, hawks, plums, and swords along the borders, to correspond to the symbols I had written into the prophecies.'

'From the cards,' I said, making another connection.

'Hawkwood had given me several decks as a gift my last time in Italy. I gave one of the decks to Swynford, simply as an amusement. But that was years ago, well before any of this. As for the verse, all that letter rhythm and so on?' He smiled, almost bashfully. 'I was amusing myself by writing in the rough style of other makers, like this William Langland or the poet of the green knight. *Rum, ram, ruf*, that dross. It was a simple thing to mimic, or misinterpret, as the case may be.' He hesitated. 'As was the heraldry on the cloth.'

'Not Simon's work, surely?'

The smile faded. 'Seguina's.'

'Peculiar,' I said, trying to make this piece fit. 'Why would Seguina participate in Simon's plan?'

'The cloth had nothing to do with the prophecies, not originally. Seguina had embroidered a cloth years before with the arms of Prince Edward and the Duke of Lancaster.'

'And Edward's arms passed to his son, now our king.'

'Precisely.'

'But how on earth did Seguina come to embroider the arms of Gaunt and Prince Edward?' The question, I would now learn, at the centre of it all.

Chaucer looked at me, his eyes lined with a sadness that,

for as long as he lived, would never entirely disappear. Over the following hours, as afternoon turned to dusk and dusk to evening, I listened to the saddest story I had ever heard. A story of Castile and Aragon, of Spain and Italy, of Moors and Christians. A story of two Spanish brothers, Pedro the Cruel and Henry of Trastámara, divided against themselves in war, and of Pedro's English allies: Prince Edward, eldest son of King Edward, and his brother, John of Gaunt, fighting on his behalf in Spain.

Yet most of all it was the story of a young woman. A daughter, a sister, a witness, a survivor, a beautiful girl who had seen her mother raped, her brother die, her noble father humiliated into the life of a mercenary. From the Castilian marches she had made her way to Lombardy and Milan, where her father hired himself and his men out to the great English *condottiero*. There, still a child, she learned to get by in the many languages spoken by Hawkwood's mercenary mélange: French, Italian, English, a smattering of Moorish, even Hebrew, all added to her native Castilian tongue. As she grew into a young woman, she learned to defend herself with fist, tooth, and knife, though she was saved from a life of savagery by her stepmother, a London gentlewoman living among the small English communities in Milan, then Florence. A skilful embroideress, her stepmother taught her this and other arts of womanhood: how to dress and care for her body, how to gesture and stand, how to feign interest in the conversation of men. She might be a lady herself someday, her stepmother told her, and it's best to be prepared. Yet through it all Seguina d'Orange never forgot the scene of her mother's violation, nor the English duke who had saved both their lives.

From the oratory came the distant drone of the office, the voices of the Austin canons carrying through the churchyard.

'Prince Edward, then,' I said into the cooling night. 'Edward was—'

'Her mother's ravisher. Picture our good Prince Edward,

420

heir to the English throne, abiding with Lancaster in Castile, waiting for Pedro the Cruel to pay his war debts. He never did. So Edward took it upon himself to extract them from the countryside and its people on his way back to Aquitaine. He was already falling ill, you know, and there were hints of concern about his mind. He'd learned his tactics from Pedro, and from his own long experience in the wars. He taught his men in turn to burn and rape their way through the land. He took what he wanted.'

'Prince Edward,' I whispered, my memories of the man already distant and opaque.

'The blackest prince who ever lived,' said Chaucer. 'They descended on the marches after the war, when her father was still absent, cleaning up with Pedro. She remembered the arms of her mother's rapist and her own saviour—'

'Gaunt.'

'—and pointed both of them into the cloth. When Simon saw it in her gallery it fired a connection in his mind with the prophecies I was reading them. The rest you already know.'

'Hawkwood must have been singing like a lark,' I said. 'Just as he's plotting a return to England, this falls into his lap, and gives him a covert means to get Lancaster out of the way.'

'I would put nothing past Hawkwood.' Chaucer sounded almost admiring of the man. 'He wears loyalty like a snake wears skin.'

'And Oxford?'

'Hawkwood's family has deep connections to the de Veres going back generations. John de Vere, the seventh earl, fought with Hawkwood's father in France.' He sighed. 'It was an ingenious plan, and might well have worked. Put the English king and his uncle at one another's throats, and bring down the House of Lancaster months before your own arrival with the French. Hawkwood values friendship and loyalty only when it suits his own purposes.'

421

I looked askance at him, incredulous at his lack of self-knowledge. He caught my glance and visibly winced.

'I know, I know. But put yourself in my place, John. You come home after a long absence, terrified for your lover, only to hear lines of your own poetry being whispered at court, along with rumours of a seditious prophecy on the death of King Richard. I suspected Simon was involved but had no idea how. That's why I had to meet with you as soon as I returned from Italy, and that's why I set you on the trail. I needed to find out what Simon knew, and where all of this was coming from.'

I recalled Chaucer's early suspicions at Monksblood's, testing my knowledge, more curious than concerned – then his shock when I confronted him at the customhouse.

'And I know you, John,' he continued, picking at a snag in his hose. 'Once you learned the nature of this book you would stop at nothing until you had it. What I didn't know, of course, was that there were two books all along.'

'Three, actually,' I said, thinking of Clanvowe's copy, now stowed with Oxford's manuscript in the wall of my house.

'And more, for all we know, given how quickly everyone seemed to be quoting from it.'

'Even Braybrooke's friars.'

'Yes. And it was Oxford, I gather, who started the ingenious rumours of interest in the prophecies among Wycliffe's followers. Then the book itself, with the cloth, was planted at La Neyte, and its contents hinted to a number of hermits in Gaunt's dependency, one of whom let it slip to me. The intention was to have it "discovered" at La Neyte by the king's guard, and Lancaster hauled away for conspiring treason well before St Dunstan's Day. The butchers, the card game, Oxford's speech at the bishop's palace – that all came later, once the book went missing.'

I frowned. 'So who stole the book from La Neyte?'

Chaucer said nothing, the moist curves of his eyes reflecting the low moon.

'Seguina d'Orange,' I said at last, as the chill of certainty swept my limbs. 'She was the girl murdered on the Moorfields.'

'She has to be one of the most resourceful women who has ever lived,' he said, his eyes flashing with admiration. 'When I learned she had left Florence I discovered that she used my contacts from the wool trade to arrange passage on a ship from Pisa, with a company of Genoese bankers bound for England. When she came to London, her aim was to find the book and the cloth. She had met Weldon in Florence and knew he was the go-between to Oxford. Once in London she must have followed him, learned the location of the book, recovered it, and fled with it through the city—'

'Pursued by Weldon—'

'Who caught her in the Moorfields—'

'After she handed the book to a maudlyn. After she handed the book to a maudlyn,' I said, filling in what he didn't know. I told him the rest: about Millicent Fonteyn, the murder of Bess Waller, the death of Sir Stephen Weldon. It was the knight's violent death that brought us back to Seguina's.

'That's how I see it.'

'But why?' I said. 'What motivated her to make such an impossible journey to England? Was it – was it merely love, a desire to protect Geoffrey Chaucer, her adulterous suitor, from bodily harm?'

'I think not,' Chaucer said wryly. 'That sort of sacrifice would have been predictable. Seguina was too great a woman for such a thing. Love was part of her motivation, I suppose. But remember, her life and her mother's had been saved by Lancaster – and it was Lancaster whose life she came here to save. I was incidental in the end. She wrote me a long letter explaining it all, then ordered a servant to deliver it to me upon my return from Rome.' He absently patted his breast. 'A story, really, and one for the ages.'

I looked at him, then guessed. 'You never found it.'

'Her servant would have been terrified of being found out

423

by one of Hawkwood's men. I went to visit Seguina when I returned, only to learn she had left Florence a week before, ostensibly to visit a cousin of her mother's. I distinctly recall the servant meeting me at the door, taking my bag while I waited for an audience with Seguina's father. The servant hid the letter in my bag, assuming I would find it in the folds of my little book. This one, in fact, which I had commissioned from a leatherworker in Rome.'

He tossed it to me, and I examined the construction. Aside from the colour and feel of the leather, it was an identical bifold to his old one, with matching vertical pockets on each inner cover, allowing the first and last folios of each new quire to be tucked inside. 'I found her letter two days ago. The morning after you confronted me at my Aldgate house, in fact. I was switching out quires, and there it was. The letter confirmed everything I had suspected but never knew – including Simon's authorship of the thirteenth prophecy.'

I thought for a moment. 'So you had Seguina's letter with you that day at Monksblood's?'

'But without knowing it.'

'Extraordinary.' I handed back his book, moved and shaken by the knowledge that Chaucer had just shared. The entire story of the last several months, carried on my old friend's person the entire time.

'When did Simon tell you of his involvement?' I asked him.

'At the St George's morrow feast at Windsor. That was the first time I had seen him since Florence, and he both admitted to stealing the book and confirmed Seguina's presence in England, though he swore he knew nothing about the last prophecy. Seguina had been dead for weeks by that point, and I was furious at him for all he had done – but also terrified of the implications. I thought he might well have killed her himself.'

'Was that you at the river inn that night, after the Garter feast?' A dog's bark, and Simon pissing from the landing, lying about his trip to the privy after that whispered encounter in the courtyard.

He looked confused.

'Simon told me he and Seguina were betrothed, you know,' I said quickly.

A bitter laugh. 'Another lie. A way of finding out if you knew anything about her.'

'Which I did not.' I recalled the look on Philippa Chaucer's face, the flash in Katherine Swynford's eyes at the mention of Seguina d'Orange. 'But Philippa did.'

'I'm not surprised,' he said. 'I wrote a ballade on her name, before I knew she had died. "To Seguina, My Orange, Wherever She May Dwell." Scribbled it on a scrap of banker's paper in our household account book. Philippa saw it when she was at our Aldgate house, and knew I had taken a lover in Italy.' He shook his head. 'Stupid, I know, to leave something like that lying around. But there it is.'

I smiled at him. 'You're remarkably careless with your poetry, Chaucer. And always have been.'

He spread his hands, then leaned forward and placed his hands on my knees. 'You know, John, despite everything, Simon could have betrayed me so easily once he was back in England with my first little book. Why, he could have taken it to Robert de Vere and proved that I wrote the prophecies even while trading on everything else he knew. No one would have noticed that the last prophecy wasn't there. My draft was just a draft, after all, scratched in my hand. For all anyone else knew I was in league with Lancaster against the king.'

It was a good point, though I still had many doubts. I found myself sifting every word and gesture, going back over every hurried meal and whisper of cloth, looking for the missed seed of Simon's mendacity.

Chaucer read my thoughts. 'Simon is confused, John. Brilliant and confused. He has been for years, despite that cock's face he wears. But confusion isn't a sin. What matters most is love. And Simon, for all his faults, loves you deeply.'

I let Chaucer's unmerited confidence hang in the priory air.

'There's one part I still don't understand,' he said. I tensed. 'At the end of her account Seguina left me an enigma, a puzzle of the sort we often invented for one another.' He pulled the letter out of his breast pocket and read it aloud.

> *'Though faun escape the falcon's claws*
> *and crochet cut its snare,*
> *When father, son, and ghost we sing,*
> *of city's blade beware.'*

He looked at me as he put the letter away. 'Have you heard this riddle, John, or read it yourself?'

'No,' I lied, recalling where I had seen those very words.

'A crochet, a city's blade. A bit threatening, wouldn't you say? Do you know what it means?'

'No,' I said, this time speaking the truth. *Hawks always strike twice.* Weldon's final words sounded again in my mind, the latest inkling of something missed. I said nothing to Chaucer. He had done enough, and I had no further patience for his manipulations. I felt almost gratified by his ignorance. For there had been something weak about his whole story, a subtle sense that his account was incomplete. That it failed to comprehend the full complexity of the aims motivating those he thought he knew best: Hawkwood and Weldon, Seguina and Simon. Especially Simon.

He was looking at me, waiting for some wisdom. I shrugged, covering my agitation. 'Likely just a lover's riddle. The butcher's blades did no harm, after all, and the king is alive. That's the important thing, I should think.'

There seemed nothing more to say. By the time Chaucer stretched and yawned I felt utterly drained, despite my inner turmoil at hearing Seguina's riddle. There was a twinge in my back. 'We are becoming old men, Geoffrey.'

He barked a laugh over the orchard as we rose. 'Old age is relative, John. It's writing that keeps us young. Or so I hope this summer will prove.'

Not for the first time I found myself wishing I saw my making as Chaucer experienced his. The man aged backwards, it seemed, accumulating youth with each fresh scratch of ink. For me every line of poetry is another grey hair, a defeat as much as a victory.

'So what will you write?' I said to his back, willing him to leave. I had a suspicion to confirm. He preceded me through the kitchen, the darkened lower gallery, the hall. We lingered outside my door, soft moonlight playing on the priory lane. 'This pilgrimage conceit, the miller and prioress and so on?'

His hand went to his chest again, and there was a whisper of parchment on his thumb. 'That comes later, after more thought. For now I have in mind the story of Cressida, told in that book of Boccaccio I gave to you. An old tragedy of war, and impossible love.' His dark eyes caught the flicker of the lanterns up by the gate. 'And a remarkable woman who learns to survive in the cruellest of worlds.' With that we parted, and Chaucer moved through the Southwark darkness, his lover's story still pressed to his heart.

FIFTY-FIVE

St Mary Overey

Ember Days. Penance and prayer, self-denial in all things, the mind focused on our faults and our tenuous hopes of salvation, so the priests instruct us. Chaucer swears that fasting clears the head like nothing else. Perfect for poets, he says, though his own abstinence is notoriously light. While Sarah was a pious observer of this Embers ritual, I tend to ignore it, as I do so many of the Church's more ascetic dogmas. I felt that week that I would have starved myself for a glimmer of discernment.

Over seven days had passed since Dunstan's Day. The maudlyns had snuck the corpse out of the Pricking Bishop that same night and abandoned it to the animals of Winchester's Wild. The king, the duke, and the earl had reached a tentative reconciliation, and in the aftermath of the palace affair it seemed that things had moved on. The king was resolved on a military expedition to the Scottish border, Gaunt was rumoured to be plotting his return to Castile with the help of Lisbon, and the Earl of Oxford had left London for Hall Place, the de Vere family manor at Earls Colne. A papal delegation from Rome was to arrive before Trinity Sunday, and the court had bigger things to think about than an expired prophecy.

The Friday after Pentecost found me in my study, wondering once more what I had missed. Weldon's dying words – *Hawks always strike twice* – carried a threat that would not leave my thoughts.

On the desk were the two copies of *De Mortibus Regum Anglorum* now in my possession. I knew every folio of Sir John Clanvowe's manuscript, written out in his neat, restrained hand, as I had studied it with great care in those weeks leading up to St Dunstan's Day. The copy in Simon's hand, the manuscript that had travelled from Italy and that I had taken from Robert de Vere, was different. The texts themselves were nearly identical, a few scribal errors here and there all that distinguished Clanvowe's text from the version he had copied from the more ornate manuscript. While Clanvowe's book was plain and undecorated, the margins of the Italian copy were decorated with the same four emblems found on Swynford's cards. Thistleflowers, hawks, swords, and plums, arrayed in an ascending pattern: one of each embellishing the first prophecy, two of each the second, and so on.

Yet there was something more. Seguina's couplet, composed in the common metre of the lays of Robin Hood or Sir Thopas, and scrawled beneath the last line of the final prophecy. I had dismissed the enigma's importance when Chaucer read it to me from her letter, had even lied to him about seeing it previously. Though I had read those scribbled lines after taking the manuscript from Oxford at Winchester Palace, once the dreadful events of St Dunstan's Day were past I had given them little thought. Yet to learn that the enigma had emerged from the mind of the woman at the middle of all this changed everything. That very night I had rushed inside after Chaucer's departure, opened the manuscript, and puzzled over the riddle's meaning, as I had done every day since. The lines were written not in Simon's neat hand, but in a thin and spidery script, scratched on the parchment with a charcoal nub and already fading.

> Though faun escape the falcon's claws and crochet
>   cut its snare,
> When father, son, and ghost we sing, of city's blade
>   beware.

The lines seemed meant to recast the imagery from the thirteenth prophecy while adding something darker to the mix. The 'faun', of course, was King Richard, and the 'crochet' had to be Sir Stephen Weldon, whose scar resembled nothing so much as a fishing hook. The falcon was surely Sir John Hawkwood, and the meaning of 'father, son, and ghost' seemed clear enough: the Holy Trinity. What continued to defeat me in this extra fragment of verse was the ominous evocation of the 'city's blade', which could refer to practically anyone in a city as large as London.

And who had written Seguina's peculiar couplet in the book? Perhaps Seguina herself, as she fled with the book from La Neyte, though it was hard to imagine her pausing to scribble a riddle in a manuscript while being pursued from Westminster and into the Moorfields. The lines did not appear in Clanvowe's copy, yet they carried a threat all the more ominous for their very uniqueness. Making a decision, I packed the two volumes in my bag and left the house.

✣

Westminster. In the great hall Sir Michael de la Pole was holding forth inside the priest's porch. When he saw me he gave a subtle nod, finished his business, then ushered me into his chambers. I spoke with the Lord Chancellor for over an hour, revealing nearly all I knew, even Simon's authorship of the thirteenth prophecy, though somehow he had already been made aware of that unpleasant fact. I showed him both books as well, making sure he understood the full implications of what I was telling him.

'You're saying there is to be a second attack on the king, then,' said the chancellor, sounding sceptical.

'Yes, my lord.' I repeated Sir Stephen Weldon's final words at the Pricking Bishop. '"Hawks always strike twice," he said. "Always twice." We all saw the first attack at Winchester's palace, how that turned out. And now the king's guard is down. I believe Seguina's lines are telling us the second attack is to come on Trinity Sunday.' I paused. 'Tomorrow, my lord.'

The chancellor still looked unconvinced. 'How can we know for certain that—'

'The thirteenth prophecy, the butchers, all of that – it was smoke,' I said, the words tumbling out of my mouth. 'Hawkwood's ruse, meant to turn suspicion on Lancaster, have him eliminated. And it nearly worked. But Lancaster was just the glaze on the bun. The real target is the king.'

'And you're basing all of this on this girl's two lines of doggerel? This chicken-scratch in your manuscript?'

'Not *my* manuscript, Lord Chancellor. This is the book from which Lord Oxford himself read on Dunstan's Day. The book we have all been tracking down for months.'

He gave me a strange look. 'Are you quite sure, Gower?'

'My lord?'

'You're quite sure this is the book we've all been looking for?'

He could see the confusion on my face. With a studied calm, the baron stood, walked to a book chest against the wall of his chamber, and fussed with the lock. He removed a small volume, no thicker than a short quire and covered in a skin of plain and weathered black. It looked familiar.

Back at his desk he opened it and spun it around. I recognized the hand immediately as Chaucer's. The quire was a messy jumble, the margins covered in notes and drawings:

431

tables, columns of figures, sketches, maps. I had struggled with Chaucer's shorthand before, and though I could make out little of his notation, I saw immediately that half of the quire was taken up with the *De Mortibus*. There was only one difference between this copy and the two on the chancellor's desk, I saw as I paged through to the end – a rather major difference.

The thirteenth prophecy was missing. Chaucer, then, had told me the truth. He had not written the prophecy of Richard's death.

'Three books,' I said, looking up.

'The one in your hands now is the original,' he said. 'Chaucer's draft, written in Florence, and covered with his notes and observations. Then came this one.' He tapped Oxford's copy, the book in my son's hand. 'Simon, when he wrote it, added the thirteenth prophecy.'

'Which Sir John copied along with the rest,' I said, indicating Clanvowe's manuscript.

'Though *before* your mysterious couplet was added. Otherwise Clanvowe would surely have copied that as well.'

I nodded absently. 'But how did you get Chaucer's original, my lord? Who gave it to you?'

A long pause. 'Your son.'

Of course. I thought of Simon waking me that night at Overey, the hole in my house's wall. It made a strange kind of sense, though the chancellor's subsequent account would leave me cold.

'As you know, Gower, King Richard made Sir John Hawkwood his ambassador to Rome just after the Rising,' he began. 'Not the most courtly envoy in the world, but Italy is a privy. We needed a strong presence there, a man flexible in his alliances. Hawkwood fit the bill like no one else. And he's one of us. An Englishman, yet with no ambition in his homeland.'

He settled his hands on his stomach. 'Or so we thought.

432

As we discovered about three years ago, Hawkwood has been buying up land and properties near his family seat. Nothing too substantial. Perhaps his wife was pregnant, and he was thinking about his legacy, was our thought. It happens. But then he started purchasing properties in other places. London, for one – a house here, a block of tenements there – as well as Essex. Gosfield, Sible Hedingham. It became clear that Hawkwood didn't want to simply retire. He wanted to come back here as a powerful man. Not just titled but garrisoned, it seemed. We tried to keep an eye on him from afar, but he was growing increasingly erratic. Envoys and letters were not enough.'

'You needed a spy,' I said.

'We wanted a man in Hawkwood's chancery, someone gifted with ciphers and scripts, who could tell us from abroad what he was up to, and get us the information we needed in a form we could trust. A forger, a cryptographer, a natural spy. We chose Simon.'

I frowned. 'You *chose* him? And how soon after his arrival in Florence was this?'

The baron looked chagrined. 'You don't understand, Gower. We sent him to Florence.'

'You *sent* him?' It hit me. 'What about the counterfeiting, the death of that man on the wharfage? Simon killed him. Chaucer cleaned it all up. That's why Simon went into Hawkwood's service in the first place.'

He gave a modest shrug. 'A charade, every bit of it. My man More set it up. The ward constable who was killed – and not by Simon, if that's any comfort – was an informant working for the French, lured to the wool wharf with the promise of an exchange. The watchmen were ours, paid from the royal treasury. It was a simple matter to get them swearing up and down they had watched a struggle and an accidental death at Simon's hands.'

'But Chaucer—'

433

'Chaucer had to be convinced it was all legitimate. That Simon had to leave London, and quickly, with the taint of scandal following him.'

I gaped at him.

'You have to see it our way,' he said, leaning forward. 'Chaucer and Hawkwood go back twenty, twenty-five years, since before Geoffrey was taken prisoner at Retters. It was Hawkwood who negotiated Chaucer's release on behalf of King Edward, you know, along with the others. After that they were together in Spain, France, Italy – getting up to God knows what. You've heard the stories.'

I admitted I had. Most of them I didn't believe, though the few that seemed credible could curdle milk. 'So you exploited Chaucer's long friendship with the man to get Simon placed down there,' I said. 'Then why did you send Chaucer back last year? Wasn't that something of a risk, given the circumstances?'

He grimaced. 'We needed to get a message to Simon, but couldn't risk having Hawkwood capture one of our messengers. So we sent Chaucer down there at the head of a diplomatic company, ostensibly to see about the wool.'

'Wool?'

'Nothing more complicated than that – nor more crucial to His Highness's treasury.'

'Wool, the goddess of the merchants,' I murmured, recalling one of my own French lines.

'Our greatest export,' said the chancellor, 'and the Genoese the only foreign shippers allowed to bypass Calais. Thousands of sacks a year from Southampton to Italy. Tens, maybe hundreds of thousands of pounds. We're always stepping in to sniff around for smuggling and evasion. Chaucer has been controller of the wool custom for some time, and he was only too happy to make a discreet trip south for a few months, get him away from Philippa. "We need some feathers smoothed," he was told.'

434

'He contacted Simon on your behalf, then, while in Tuscany?'

The baron scoffed. 'Hardly. We slipped one of our own men into his entourage.'

'Who?'

His look told me I didn't need to know. 'Simon got our message, did what we asked him to do. What he did next, though – copy Chaucer's book, pen a treasonous prophecy? That was all Simon, I'm afraid.'

He avoided my gaze, and I felt a sting of remorse, knowing what he must have been thinking. His father's son, apples falling close to trees. Everything I thought I knew about Simon had proved mistaken, as if my own son were a distant stranger, or one of Mandeville's monsters, a three-headed beast perched on the edge of the world. From a counterfeiting traitor to a loyal spy for the realm to a forger and cryptographer for a mercenary, in the space of a few days.

The chancellor looked at me, not unkindly. 'To be around a man like Hawkwood for that long, it has to rub off on you.' Thinking this would comfort me. 'Chaucer's company returned from Italy in early March. Simon had already been here for weeks, though without showing himself to anyone, including you.' I nodded vaguely, remembering Simon's appearance at St Mary Overey – exhausted after the long road from Italy, he had told me. 'Once I learned your son was back in London my intention was to bring him in, hold his feet to the fire. Make him tell us why he had left Florence without warning us.'

'When did you know he had returned?'

'You'll recall our chance meeting on Cat Street, that day you were searching out Strode's clerk. Ralph himself had just told me Simon was back.'

Strode had been feigning ignorance that day about Simon's return, then. Yet another deception. 'You covered well, my lord.'

He waved it off. 'When Simon came in that same week he

told me he had simply left Hawkwood's service a few months before. That he hadn't bothered writing in advance of his return but had done everything we asked of him, and more. Then he was overheard having a heated conversation with Chaucer during the Garter morrow feast out at Windsor, telling him he planned to sell his little book to the highest bidder, get him strung up for his treachery. It was only then that we began to suspect Simon's connection to these prophecies.'

'Was that one of Oxford's men, then, at the river inn?' This was the question that had confused Chaucer during our last conversation.

'No. It was my man More. He and Simon had arranged a meeting during the feast, supposedly in order for Simon to hand over the book and reveal everything he knew. They met in the courtyard. But Simon demanded money – lots of it – and claimed to have offered the book to the Earl of Oxford, with Sir Stephen Weldon acting as agent. I couldn't let that happen. Simon was speaking too freely about it all. I worried that the whole thing would explode in our faces. So, once More reported back to me, we decided to bring Simon in, press him harder this time.'

'Then he was taken.'

'Weldon got to him first. Plucked him right out of your house before your return from Oxford. Took him God knows where.'

'How did he escape?'

'Don't know. Don't know that he did escape, or that he was even under duress. But it was clear that Simon had been lying through his teeth, both to our man in Florence, to me at Westminster, probably to Hawkwood and Oxford as well. He's been playing us all against each other, and where his loyalties lie is anyone's guess. Chaucer confirmed as much.'

'I thought Chaucer was ignorant of it all.' Until he discovered Seguina's letter, at least – the one part of the whole story I had kept to myself.

'Of Simon's role, yes. But he learned more than he wanted

436

to about Hawkwood. It seems Chaucer was digging around in some Genoese shipping manifests, tracking sacks of English wool, when he discovered a large number of commissions from Hawkwood for transport of troops this upcoming summer. It gave him a glimmer of Hawkwood's plans. He never confronted Sir John about it.'

I considered this. 'Chaucer knows more than anyone what the man is capable of, I suppose. Hawkwood would torture his own leg if it was holding out on him.'

'Our man's dispatch reached us a week before his return, though none of us made the connection with the prophecies and Hawkwood's plot against Gaunt until much later. Only Simon knew all of that.' He looked at the three books, still opened on his desk. 'Now you're suggesting the king himself is the real target after all.'

'I believe so, my lord.'

'I'll admit the timing is – harrowing. France knows Richard is weak. The Scottish border needs defending. Word is King Richard will march up there this summer, leaving London and Westminster vulnerable.' He puffed his cheeks. 'You have to admire Hawkwood's audacity. Circulate a prophecy incriminating Lancaster, get him hanged, then go for the king. Once they're both out of the picture, swoop in and help install a new sovereign.'

'A kingmaker indeed,' I said, thinking of that line from the thirteenth prophecy, and marvelling at the cold ingenuity of Simon's poetry. I thought of Hawkwood in Florence, still believing all of this was unfolding hundreds of leagues to the north.

Then the chancellor dropped his last surprise. 'Though we won't have to worry about Hawkwood supporting an invasion, whatever happens after the truce expires.'

'My lord?'

'Simon left a little gift for Hawkwood a few days before his departure from Florence. An encrypted message, accusing one of his closest men of betraying his greater ambitions to us all along.'

'What man?'

'Adam Scarlett is his name. Hawkwood's chief lieutenant. A number of months ago we intercepted a rather shocking letter from Scarlett to one of his associates in Paris, boasting of Hawkwood's plans to join forces with the French following the truce. Simon was instructed to find some way of scuttling Hawkwood's plans. In the process, he believes, he will have turned the *condottiero* against his most loyal man.'

'I see,' I said, and I finally did. 'So that was the true purpose of last Autumn's diplomatic mission to Italy. Chaucer's mission.'

'Yes, though again, Chaucer was kept ignorant of Hawkwood's plans until he discovered them on his own. In any case, Simon believes the device he created will convince Hawkwood of Scarlett's disloyalty, and that its discovery will stem any further militant plans on Sir John's part toward England.'

I was incredulous. 'So Simon, despite all he's done, will stay in Hawkwood's good graces.'

'And in ours, to a point,' said the baron, with another of his pragmatic shrugs. 'Our business now must be the king.'

I thought for a moment, trying to push aside all the chancellor had told me in order to focus on the plot at hand. 'Can the festivities be cancelled, or abbreviated in some way? What if the cardinal were to process with the archbishop only rather than with the king and his retinue? I imagine you could come up with an excuse for the royal absence.'

He shook his head emphatically. 'Richard won't hear of it. He regards the abbey as his personal shrine, the embodiment of his invulnerability. You know the places his mind is taking him these days. By now he's convinced himself his survival on St Dunstan's Day was a miracle. That it was God's hand that shot the butchers.'

I pointed up. 'An angel's, perhaps?'

He scoffed. 'God, an angel, royal archers – all the same to His Highness. In any case, halting the procession and Mass is out of the question. We've just got through that whole

438

Dunstan's Day business. If Mars himself were to come hurtling at the king I couldn't get him to change course.'

'I understand, my lord,' I said. The chancellor had higher men to please.

He leaned forward, his face lined with concern. 'St Dunstan's Day was one thing. The attempt took place in the Bishop of Winchester's courtyard, a site easily contained and with a few hundred in attendance. But Westminster, between the abbey and the palace yard? With three or four *thousand* in the crowd – and our assassin any one of them, any *hundred* of them? That's another matter entirely.'

I agreed.

He stood, pacing the floor on the far side of his desk. 'We need to know where this originated, Gower. Does this last snatch of verse refer to a native plot, another bit of deception by Oxford and Weldon? And "city's blade" – what could that possibly mean? Are the mayor's men involved, the Guildhall? But that's unthinkable.'

He looked a bit desperate. I had never seen him in such a state. He said, 'The cardinal's delegation arrives from Windsor this evening, and the Mass is set for Sext tomorrow. We need more time. Or the answer to this damned riddle.'

I looked down at the book in question, still opened to the final prophecy and the scribbled verse. I thought of the manuscript's recent history. Where it had been, who had held it, stolen it, read from it, peddled it. As the chancellor had pointed out, the final couplet had to have been written into the book after Clanvowe copied from it – which meant what?

I felt a twinge of something. 'There may be another way, my lord.'

✤

The next morning I was at the gates of St Leonard's Bromley at first light, though I had to linger by the almonry until the Prime office had concluded before I could be escorted into

439

the prioress's apartments. Coals glowed on the small hearth, despite the rising heat outside. Eventually Prioress Isabel bustled in from the chapterhouse. The sight of me brought her up short. 'What is it?'

I told her, as quickly as I could, then she sent for Millicent Fonteyn. There was a sober cast to the young woman's face when she entered the parlour. Darkened eyes, nearly expressionless below the close-fitting bonnet worn by the order's laysisters. As I recalled from my prior visit, she was an extraordinary beauty, though I could see what a toll the deaths of her mother and sister had taken.

Wasting no time, I removed the book from my bag and opened it to the final prophecy. I turned it toward her and pointed to the peculiar couplet. 'Did you write these lines, madam?'

Her deep-set eyes widened at the sight of the page. She looked at the prioress, then at me. 'I did.'

'And why did you not tell me this before, when you showed me the cloth?' Not accusatory, but prodding.

'I confess I did not think it was important, Master Gower. With the prophecy of the butchers, the cloth, all the talk in the streets . . . these lines seemed a small nothing.'

'I understand why you might have regarded the verse as insignificant, in the light of everything else.' Nodding kindly, hoping to spur her memory. 'Where did you read these lines?'

She shook her head, the loose curls at her nape tossed by her vehemence. 'I never read them, sir. I only heard them, spoken by my sister.'

'Agnes,' I said, recalling the name, and her mother's sorrow. 'The one killed by Sir Stephen Weldon, up near Aldgate?'

'Aye, sir.'

'When I was here before St Dunstan's Day you told me your sister witnessed the murder in the Moorfields, yes?'

She blinked twice. 'She did, sir.'

'Is that where she heard these lines, on the Moorfields?'

440

She nodded.

'Tell me about it now.'

'The woman was kneeling in the dirt,' Agnes said, 'right in the clearing. The fire was going out. He asked her some questions. She didn't answer them, or Agnes didn't think she did. But she couldn't understand a word they were saying. Then he raised his hammer. That's when she screamed it.'

'Screamed what?'

'The verse, sir. The verse I wrote in the book. Agnes swore it was intended for her, that the girl knew she was still there. She couldn't get it out of her head. For weeks she repeated it, kept blurting it out at the oddest times. She felt sure it meant something, though to my mind we had enough trouble with the prophecies in the book, and they sounded like a minstrel's lines, and what could be the importance of that? I wrote them there on that final leaf, just to calm her down.' Millicent paused for a well-deserved breath.

Something about her account was odd. I closed my eyes, thought it all through, then looked at her again. 'You said the man was questioning the girl, but Agnes couldn't understand a word. And yet she understood this verse well enough to repeat it to *you* days later. How do you explain the discrepancy?'

She stared at me, confused, then her face relaxed into a sad smile. 'Pardon, Master Gower, I thought that part was clear. They weren't speaking English, you see.'

'French, then?'

'No, Agnes would have said. She'd had enough Calais jakes to ear out French, that's sure.'

'What tongue, then? Did she catch any snatches of it, any words that stood out?'

She thought for a moment, her brow knit. I felt my heart sink. Then her face brightened. 'Indeed she did, Master Gower. *Doovay leebro*.'

'*Doovay leebro*?' Something shifted inside me. 'You're sure?'

'*Doovay leebro*, is what Agnes said.' Feverish nods. '*Doovay leebro, doovay leebro*, like he was singing to her. Sounded like a lullaby, is what she said, and he kept at it until he killed her. *Doovay leebro*.'

Doovay leebro. And then, with a calm astonishment, I knew. 'Where is the cheese?' I whispered. The knowledge balanced me.

'Where is the *cheese*?' the prioress barked, her voice an incredulous smear. 'What on earth are you prattling about, Gower?'

'*Dov'è il formaggio*?' I said, the question a delicious taste on my tongue. The talgar at Monksblood's, a snatch of Italian, a girl killed for a book.

Millicent Fonteyn stared at me in a kind of rapt confusion. My vision, too, had a clarity it only rarely achieved, and she was in that moment the most beautiful thing I had ever seen. I could have kissed her; I could have kissed the prioress for that matter. Instead I bowed and took my leave, the life of King Richard hanging on the speed of my horse.

FIFTY-SIX

Westminster

Even if one avoids London altogether the ride from Stratford-at-Bowe to the city of Westminster is a hard and circuitous one, and as I splashed across the Lea it struck me that I might not make it in time for the procession, set to start shortly before Sext and the Mass of the day. Pushing the thought aside, I approached London on the Mile End Road at a swift gallop. Going through town, however direct the route, would slow me down considerably, so I branched off well before Aldgate and circled the city from afar, with the Moorfields to my left and the tower of Bethlem barely visible over a few low trees.

I came into Westminster from the west and posted my horse well up Orchard Street, going the rest of the way on foot at a jog, dodging around the crowds moving to the palace yard. The announcement of the papal delegation had stirred Westminster, London, even Southwark, hundreds of citizens boating up and walking over for a glimpse of the foreign officials. The crowd thickened as I neared the palace, then slowed as dozens crammed through the last feet of the lane.

The wide expanse between the palace yard and the abbey was a churning sea, a great plain of bobbing heads, lifted caps, shouts and cheers. The whole area had been cleared of hucksters and peddlers, all but a few of the fires extinguished. It appeared that the king and the cardinal had not yet left the palace, where a private service was being held in the St Stephen's upper chapel, though judging from the anticipation in the air the procession would begin at any moment.

The chancellor would be in his chambers off the hall. He avoided processions like the pestilence. My work, he would always say, is best done out of view, a sentiment I shared.

Two doors, then the lesser hall and the chancellor's rooms. My face must have registered my fear, for when he saw it, Sir Michael de la Pole, usually cool, stood at once. With him was Edward More, his secretary and fixer, a man I had dealt with many times. Broad-chested, commanding, with a head and beard of shining white, More had a reputation for ruthless partisanship and calm under pressure. 'What?' the chancellor demanded.

'It's Hawkwood,' I said breathlessly, my words barely a wheeze. 'He has a man, in the papal delegation.'

'How do you know this, Gower?'

'There's no time to explain, my lord.' A deep breath, holding my side. 'But believe me, my information is good.'

'Who is he, Gower?' More asked.

'We'll know him when we see him, I suspect. A trained assassin. Hawkwood wouldn't take any chances with a middling knife. One of the cardinal's guards, would be my guess.'

The chancellor went to a position by the outer door of his chambers, ducking his head to look out to the palace yard. 'We can't stop the procession. They just left the palace. We're too late.'

'Then we catch them,' said More, belting on his short sword. 'Even if it takes us to the abbey altar, we catch them.'

'Very well,' said the chancellor, arming himself as well. I followed them out of his chambers and across the hall, which was nearly empty as the procession got going from the palace. De la Pole summoned a clutch of pursuivants idling on the west porch, and we all sped together from the hall toward the royal procession, now making its slow way through the palace yard to meet the crowd still pouring in through the abbey gates, overwhelming the guards at the gatehouse.

As I saw immediately, the king and cardinal were on foot rather than mounted, as they would have been on the longer processions from the Tower, and it was nearly impossible to see them over the masses between their position and ours. The crowd was at least twenty ranks thick, all elbows and indignation as everyone fought for position. With the chancellor, Edward More, and the pursuivants we were ten men strong, though against so many moving hundreds we could hardly hope to force our way through. The noise was deafening, too, and our shouts could not be heard over the din. The pursuivants headed straight into the crowd, angling toward the king's position. I bobbed along behind the outermost rank of spectators, taking short leaps into the air, feeling useless, attempting to get a glimpse of the principals and those clustered around them.

I stopped for a moment and took in the scene from afar, imagining myself atop the Wardrobe Tower at the far corner of the yard, or the bell tower opposite, and picturing the next few minutes in my mind. I reasoned that the attack, when it came, would happen before the abbey's west entrance, where the procession would bottleneck to move through the great doors. If I could get well ahead of the principals I would have a better angle on any potential attacker, though it wasn't clear to me what I could do about it. I pushed my way toward the abbey and gave two boys a shilling apiece to give up their spot on a column base.

I was now elevated two feet above the yard, but that was enough. Pockets of commotion everywhere, hard to tell what represented danger and what did not. I saw More. He was leading the chancellor and the small wedge of pursuivants toward the rearmost line of the procession. His focus was on the cardinal's guards, a rank of ten Italian soldiers, dressed for the occasion in livery and flounce, with banners and flags held above as they marched. The guard had accompanied the prelate all the way from Rome. Despite the procession's gaudiness these were seasoned, well-armed men. Any one of them would be capable of assassinating the king without a thought.

Yet even the closest of them was nearly forty feet from Richard. It would take a great effort to clear the distance, especially with the royal rearguard positioned where they were. For the first time since leaving Bromley I felt a twinge of doubt.

My gaze moved forward, along the intermediate ranks between the cardinal's guard and the principals. Most of them were clergy, separated by order and office. In the rear walked monks of the abbey, a dozen of them in two close ranks. Next came the friars, six Franciscans and a lone Dominican, the seven of them forming a single rank. Before the friars marched five bishops: Wykeham, Braybrooke, William Courtenay the Archbishop of Canterbury, and two Italians, all of them grand with their caps and mitres in various bright hues.

In front of them, forming one rank behind Richard and the cardinal, walked the king's guard. Twelve hardened knights, a squat rectangle around the royal person and the papal delegate. Their heads swivelled at every step, looking for threats. My eyes swept back again, over the lines of clerics, back to the cardinal's guard, then forward once more, looking for something, anything that might indicate—

There. A face, standing out against the others. A friar. One of the Italian Franciscans – no, the Dominican, his black robe stark against the grey favoured by the other order. The balance of the clerics – canons, monks, friars, and bishops alike – had pious, beatific looks on their faces, all pretending not to be enjoying themselves as the citizens of Westminster and

London showered the company with spring flowers and words of praise.

The Dominican was different. His features hard, his frame lean, his stance taut as he walked, coiled, ready to spring. His eyes two slits of malice, measuring distances, reckoning angles. The ripple of his robes, loosely cinctured, obscured his hands, which seemed at the moment to be tucked behind him as he walked.

The procession was nearing the abbey door. The frontmost rank of guards would soon start to slow. I looked for More and the chancellor. The pursuivants were still too far away. I looked back at the friar. He was making his move. A flash of steel, and his knife was out, held against his chest, partially obscured by his hands. No one near him had noticed.

'*The friar!*' I shouted into the deafening roar, waving from my position at the column. '*More, More! It's the friar!*' The Dominican, oblivious of my shouted warnings, started to move, pushing gently through the row of bishops in front of him.

'*The friar!*' I shouted again. More didn't hear me either. I might as well have been screaming into a bucket sunk in the sea. But just as I had that thought the chancellor looked up at the abbey door and saw me pointing wildly. He pulled on the sleeve of the pursuivant immediately ahead of him. They both gaped at me. On an impulse I clasped my hands together, bowed my head in mock prayer, and pointed urgently to the cluster of friars pressed against the king's guard, which had now slowed to a near crawl. The abbot of Westminster prepared to welcome the king and cardinal at the abbey door, less than twenty feet in front of King Richard.

I mock-prayed again, pulled on an imaginary hood. The chancellor's eyes widened. He understood. *A friar*, I saw him mouth to the nearest pursuivants.

With a surge of forgotten strength the aged Lord Chancellor pushed ahead, taking Edward More and two pursuivants with him. They were fifteen feet from the friar, twelve, eight. Then, with a snake-like precision, the Dominican, sensing movement behind him, leapt forward, slashing at the necks of the king's guard, intent on his target. But one of the guards had heard More's and the chancellor's shouts. His sword was out. It slashed at the friar in a protective arc. The friar ducked, and it took another swipe to halt his lethal progress toward the king. Two of the chancellor's pursuivants had finally reached the spot. There was a brief but furious melee, arms and swords and knives flying about.

It ended quickly. By the time the king and the cardinal bothered to glance over their shoulders the threat had been neutralized, the friar sliced to a bleeding mess. The principals exchanged a few words with the abbot, received the blessings, and pressed forward through the doors, the seemingly minor nuisance behind them. Only the bishops looked somewhat flustered. Braybrooke, two ranks behind the king, gave me a dark look, which I returned with a low bow and a hidden smile.

The crowd surged against the abbey's west façade, all craning for a last glimpse of the king. The pursuivants dragged the friar against the tide of the commons, and few bothered to glance at them. Soon they had him hoisted on their shoulders, a trail of blood spattering the pavers in their wake. Walking behind the chancellor, Edward More turned to look back at me from the abbey's northwest corner. He gave me a small nod. The pursuivants, with the dying assassin, disappeared. More followed them.

Two groats to the abbey guard got me into the nave, where I watched the procession conclude before the altar. All was calm, disconcertingly normal after the madness outside. St Peter's nave glistened, gem-like, the clerestory windows casting mottled sun on a large crowd of nobles and clerics of all orders finding their places. The grand service began, an elaborate introit in five voices echoing to the vaults.

Not feeling prayerful I decided not to stay for Mass, angling instead up the nave and into the south transept along the narrow passage past the chapterhouse. There I paused for a moment before a painting of St Thomas I had always loved. Not St Thomas Becket, nor St Thomas Aquinas the philosopher, but St Thomas the Apostle. The great doubter, his unbelief perpetually etched in his face at that precise moment before he touches Jesus's side: his gaze cast down, his finger bent over his savior's open wound. This Thomas, I think, has always been my favourite occupant of the canon of saints. The patron saint of doubt and suspicion, of verifiable information, in whatever form it comes.

FIFTY-SEVEN

Priory of St Leonard's Bromley

'Prioress Isabel has asked me to remain at St Leonard's,' Millicent Fonteyn said to Eleanor Rykener. The sky was clear that afternoon, awash in a blue deeper than any in Millicent's memory. They sat in the small herb garden off the almonry, a promise of summer in the piney waft of rosemary from behind the bench. 'Says she'll take me in again as a laysister.'

Eleanor had begged a slab of tar from a ditcher along the walls. She had her shoe off, patching the leather. 'Will you stay, do you suppose?'

Millicent nodded. 'Not a sole doubt in my mind. Though maybe one small regret.'

'What's that?' Eleanor rubbed dirt over the tar, smoothing the patch with her palm.

Millicent smiled, thinking of John Gower. Widowed, tall, rich. 'Can I live my life without the touch of another man?'

Eleanor snorted. 'I'm touched by another man six, seven times a day. Can't say it's much to miss.'

'I suppose not,' said Millicent with a sigh. 'Though I'll miss my figs.'

'No figs at St Leonard's?'

'No figs, no money, no men.'

Eleanor slipped her shoe on. 'Nothing wrong with going figless, Millicent. Nor penniless, nor even cockless.'

'Millicent the Cockless,' she mused. 'I like it. And as Agnes used to goad me, I've always wanted a title.'

'Agnes,' said Eleanor wistfully.

Millicent regarded Eleanor Rykener with a stab of shame. Millicent had spent just a few years in her mother's service at the Bishop before seizing the opportunity to flee to St Leonard's and a new life. Eleanor Rykener had lived nearly ten years now on her stomach, enduring the gropes of monks, squires, and franklins, and all without a trace of the bitter self-pity that Millicent spoke like a second tongue.

She thought of the saints, that litany of suffering women whose works and lives the nuns of St Leonard's would intone in their offices. Of St Margaret, swallowed by the dragon, then standing triumphantly on its back. Of St Cecilia, her virtue threatened by a Roman despot, suffering three sword-strokes to her neck. Of the Blessed Maudlyn herself, lifted by Jesu from the bowels of the swyve. And here was Eleanor Rykener, enduring more trials of the flesh than all these sainted women put together. Yet no one would think to write Eleanor's life for an Austin canon to include in the *legendum*. No one would compose St Edgar Rykener a hymn, nor sing a collect in praise of St Eleanor the Swerver.

She had a sudden thought. 'Would you take up other work, do you suppose, if the opportunity came?'

Eleanor waved away a fly. Shrugged. 'Seems God suited me for swyving. There's not another line of work would let me be true to my mannish side, least that I can tell.' She smiled sadly. 'Imagine I'll keep with it till Gerald reaches his majority. Then we'll see.'

The next day Millicent visited the prioress in her apartments. All was arranged with a few words to Isabel.

'Your timing is propitious, Millicent,' the prioress told her.

'Bromley has received a generous endowment, in the neighbourhood of twenty pounds.'

'Twenty pounds?' Millicent marvelled at the sum. 'Who established this endowment, Reverend Mother?'

'Our benefactor has asked not to be named, though I can tell you he's a Southwark man. But the funds are not given freely.' She said this with a trace of disapproval. 'The endowment's terms are quite clear. It is to be employed in perpetuity for the benefit of the maudlyns of Southwark and London, with Bromley required to come to their aid and succour whenever possible. So it won't be difficult to budget ten shill a year for your Eleanor Rykener. Scullery work?'

Millicent nodded, delighted with the prioress's response. 'Or the animals, Reverend Mother. Whichever you think best.'

'She'll be your charge, Millicent, not mine,' said the prioress. 'But don't let me catch you running a flock of whores out of the gatehouse.' She went back to her book.

'No, Reverend Mother,' said Millicent with a hidden smile. She started to back out of the parlour.

'And, Millicent?'

She looked up. 'Yes, Reverend Mother?'

'Will Tewes, our yeoman cook, grows old,' said the prioress, her gaze still on the page. 'He's in need of a cutter, a young man good with a knife. See that one is found for him.'

FIFTY-EIGHT

San Donato a Torre

A knock at his opened door, then a boy's voice. 'Ser Giovanni invites you to dine with him, Master Scarlett.'

Adam Scarlett, annoyed at the interruption, turned from his desk with a frown. Not even a page at the door, but a boy from the villa's kitchens. He sighed, set down his pen, and closed the ledger. He followed the boy from his rooms and through the labyrinth of low hedges leading to the side door.

In the hall Hawkwood was bent over the central table, concentrating on a mess of papers. Two of his dogs, hunting hounds, all nose and tongue, were curled around his feet. The closer one licked Scarlett's hand as he sat.

A servant set a goblet of wine between them and a thick soup at Scarlett's place. At Hawkwood's inviting gesture he sipped contentedly until the *condottiero* looked up and joined him in the meal. Scarlett told him the news of the day – another letter from Carlo Visconti, a herd of poached sheep lost in transit from near Poggibonsi. Hawkwood nodded at the right places, asked a few questions; all seemed perfectly normal. Yet Scarlett could sense a certain tension in the air. There was a stiffness to Hawkwood's manner, a formality he rarely saw in the man when they were alone.

Finally Hawkwood leaned back, sighed, and put a hand on Scarlett's arm. 'Desilio has broken the final cipher,' he said, a note of longing in his voice.

Scarlett felt a leap of hope, though Hawkwood quickly dashed it. The *condottiero* lifted the topmost paper and read, his gravelled voice weighing the deciphered message with a heavy finality.

My Lord, know by this that our earlier suspicions are confirmed. John Hawkwood, false knight and traitor to the crown, plots against His Highness's rule. His brigades will sail from Spezia no later than the Feast of St Edmund, to join the French fleet off Sluys. Five thousand spears, with a thousand from Hawkwood, four from France. The coastal garrisons must be reinforced, the forts heavily manned, the artillery strengthened, and with all deliberate speed.

As Hawkwood recited the missive Scarlett felt his shoulders sink, all his fears realized. 'We are done, then. Betrayed, and by that snivelling runt.'

'So it seems,' said Hawkwood, patting Scarlett's arm. Scarlett grasped his master's hand, feeling the surge of disappointment through the rough skin.

They finished their meal in silence, the air heavy with regret and stifled ambition. When the service was cleared Hawkwood took a final swallow of wine, wiped his lips, and handed the goblet to Scarlett, who sipped once, then again – and his hand stopped in midair as three of Hawkwood's roughest men entered the hall from the direction of the main gallery. They positioned themselves in a shallow triangle around Scarlett's chair and stood, silent, as Hawkwood brought out his cards.

'My lord?' Scarlett said, hating the sudden fear in his voice.

'I'm learning, you know,' said the mercenary, placing down a first card. 'I've got my own set of signals now. "When I wipe my lips, enter the hall and surround the disloyal sack of shit." Not as sophisticated as Il Critto, perhaps, but it seems to work. And no need for a cipher.'

Scarlett said nothing, though his breathing grew shallower with each card Hawkwood arrayed on the table.

'Desilio came to me yesterday.' Another card. 'His face was pale, his hand shaking as he talked me through every step of the final code.' Four more cards, all face up. 'I was impatient at first, but he insisted that I work out the solution myself.' The third row complete. 'And he was right, for I would never have believed what I read had I not sifted through those pages myself, transcribed every letter in my own hand at his instruction. It wasn't difficult, really.' The last two cards, face up before Scarlett's hands.

From a bag at his side Hawkwood took out the scorched quire and went on, as if instructing a schoolboy in grammar. 'Each grouping of cards is a letter, you see. Start at the end and the beginning of the deck, excluding the trumps and taking the first and last cards as the letter *A*.' He pointed to the first pair he'd arranged. 'The second and the penultimate are *B*, the third and the antepenultimate *C*, and so on until you've exhausted the cards and the alphabet. Then you start over, with the second and the penultimate cards standing for *A* this time, the third and the antepenultimate for *B* – I won't go on. The suits must be ranked, of course, and it can get quite confusing if you forget which sequence you're on. There are as many as five different pairs standing for the letter *S* in this message alone. But Desilio took me through it, and eventually I was able to work out the message I've just read you.'

'I see,' said Scarlett, his uneasiness growing.

'What I didn't read you, though, was the last little bit. Do you mind if I do so now?'

'As you wish, Sir John,' said Scarlett stiffly, dreading to hear what came next. One of the dogs moved at his feet, nosing for a hand.

Hawkwood read.

To ensure its delivery to your hands, and to guard against the seizure of a messenger, we have sent this same information by land and by sea. Trust you in the truth of this, for Hawkwood himself has revealed all. Written at San Donato a Torre, by Firenze, the feast of Sts Perpetua and Felicitas, by your humble servant Adam Scarlett.

At the final words Hawkwood nodded up at his men, who descended on Scarlett as he sat frozen in his chair. He hardly noticed as his arms were thrust across the table, his wrists pinned in place by much stronger hands, his thumbs splayed to the sides as his palms were pressed against the wood's cool surface.

Hawkwood stood, took a heavy knife from one of the men, and brought it down on Scarlett's right thumb. Scarlett screamed, his legs quivering beneath him.

Yet even as his hand sang with an almost exquisite pain, his continuing screams now muffled by an oily cloth clamped over his mouth, he heard a sound that transcended agony. The crunch of bone, his bone, in the mouth of a dog.

At Hawkwood's signal the man behind him forced his head to the side, his eyes widening in terror as he watched the hound chew and spit, chew and spit, lick, then lip, then chew and spit again, the shards of his thumb now a moist bolus on the floor. Another flash of Hawkwood's knife, and the second dog had his treat. The men pressed vinegared cloths on Scarlett's fresh stubs, strumming his nerves even as they stanched the blood and kept him from passing out.

'Every lying finger, Adam,' said Hawkwood, his voice a calm promise of misery to come. 'Then every false toe. Then each treasonous ball, then your traitorous cock. After that

– well, after that we'll heal you up and get to work on your face.'

Scarlett closed his eyes, knowing it was useless to protest his loyalty to this man he would never have thought to betray. He was on the north downs, on Detling Hill after a walk from Maidstone. He had promised himself he would return there once back in England, and that his death, when it came, would not be in vain. So much for promises, and salvation.

'We'll keep you alive as long as we can, Adam Scarlett,' said Hawkwood. 'I wouldn't want you to miss a moment of the feast.'

FIFTY-NINE

St Paul's

On St Boniface's day, the fifth of June, I arranged an appointment at St Paul's with the bailiff of the Aldermen's Court. Nothing important, merely a glimpse at a recent deposition I had been wanting to see. But I suspected the chancellor would be at the cathedral that morning, and that he would be summoning me sooner or later in any case. While speaking with the bailiff I stood at a spot in the north transept by the passage to Minor Canons, where the baron would see me as he passed.

It did not take long. Once the bailiff had left I leaned on the doorway, composing a pair of couplets in my mind, until I felt a presence behind me.

'How did you do it, Gower?' I turned to see the baron, framed against the crossing. I bowed. 'How did you know?'

'They were speaking in Italian, my lord,' I said as we walked toward the less crowded south transept, our voices low. 'That night on the Moorfields. Weldon was interrogating her in Italian. That was the first clue.'

'So . . .?'

'So London had nothing to do with the "city's blade".

The girl was being questioned about the book, but she knew more. And that's what she revealed with her final words – in English, so that the maudlyn, Agnes Fonteyn, would understand and remember them. Weldon spent years with Hawkwood, and his Italian was as good as Chaucer's. He knew what he was doing. Recovering the book was crucial to keeping everyone focused on these elaborate prophecies and ignorant of Hawkwood's more direct plot against the king. The Trinity plot, like the book, originated with him.'

'"City's blade",' the chancellor mused. 'A city in Italy, then?'

'Florence, most obviously, though that wasn't quite it.' We had reached the opening to the chapel of St Katherine, empty but for a sole worshipper kneeling at the altar of Mary and Martha. 'But once Agnes's sister told me they were speaking Italian on the Moorfields it all came to me. London is to an Englishman what Rome is to an Italian: the principal city. After that it was a simple matter of translation. In Latin, the possessive of "city", *urbs*, is *urbis*.' I paused. 'She was making a pun, my lord.'

'The blade of Urban,' said the chancellor with a rueful smile.

'Pope Urban's blade,' I finished. And there it was, I explained. *When father, son, and ghost we sing, of city's blade beware.* The assassin – the true assassin of King Richard, not the bumbling company of butchers riled up by Weldon and Oxford and their skulking priest for St Dunstan's Day – would be a member of the papal delegation, scheduled to process with the king at the abbey on the morning of Trinity Sunday.

'The man was a professional and seasoned killer,' the baron said. 'Bernabò Visconti's deadliest knife, or so he claimed before we broke his neck. Planted by Hawkwood in the papal delegation. Had he not been stopped the king would surely be dead, taken with a blade in the ribs before his closest guard could blink.'

I silently wondered whether Oxford, in the thick of the plot against Gaunt, had known about the planned attempt on the king, despite the close friendship between the two young men. Weldon surely had, though this ugly knowledge had died with him. The foiled assassination would remain known only to a few, I observed, and lost to history.

'Just as well,' the chancellor said with an air of tired discretion. 'Though I do wish I could have met the girl, this Seguina d'Orange. Geoffrey Chaucer hardly deserved such a woman's love.'

'It wasn't all about his clever book in the end, my lord, let alone about him,' I said, speaking thoughts I had been mulling for days. 'There was a greater purpose to her sacrifice than saving the skin of a London poet.'

'That's why Seguina d'Orange came to England, then,' the baron mused. 'Not only to save Lancaster, or Chaucer, nor even to find the book, as important as that was.'

I peered into the chapel, at a high wall scorched with years of pious smoke. 'King Richard was the brother of her dead brother, and thus her own sibling, after a fashion. But he was also the son of her mother's ravisher – and yet she came here in part to save his life.'

'And she did it, didn't she, with her last words,' he said, his voice a soft coil of wonder.

'Though only just.' The close call before the abbey was still fresh in my mind.

'I was there, you know,' said the baron quietly.

'My lord?'

'The battle at Nájera, with Prince Edward and Lancaster, all those years ago.'

'You were in Edward's household,' I recalled, prompting a nod. 'During the Castile campaign for Pedro.'

'I wouldn't have been with them at that woman's castle. I

was with the Gascon encampment at Burgos during those weeks. But I remember Edward's illness after the battle, the fevers and the raging, this sense that the man was . . . detaching from himself, that his mind had bent somehow. Everyone agreed afterwards that Spain was the sad beginning of a long end for the prince. Seguina's mother wasn't the first woman he brutalized in those years, nor the last.'

We stood for a while longer, listening to the hurried murmurs of a priest from one of the chantries before the south porch. I think we both sensed a circle closing, though the machinations that had brought us here were clearly the beginning of something much larger. I thought of Hawkwood, spinning his sticky webs in Tuscany. Of Simon, fled for who knew where. Of Sarah, who had died knowing nothing of her son's chosen profession; a minor blessing.

'So what next?' I eventually asked him. 'Will you return the favour, have Hawkwood snipped?'

The chancellor let out a sigh, a slow wind of realism. 'We need Hawkwood, Gower, even more than Hawkwood needs England. I see a long war ahead of us. There's no reason to go stirring the pot over an unfortunate incident easily gotten past. This is how it works in the end. We pardon our second-worst enemies, make treaties with our former slaughterers. Overlook treason to win a battle.'

I told him I understood. He would get no objections from John Gower for choosing political expediency over moral purity. 'And Simon?' I asked neutrally. 'Will you pursue him further?'

'I will leave that in your hands.' He gave me a baronial look. 'The realm owes you a great debt, Gower. God knows your talents can create some peculiar twists. In this case, though, they've won the day.'

There was a rather uncomfortable pause. I knew what the chancellor expected me to say. He stood there, waiting for my demands. The Exchequer's books, a bishop's house on the

461

Strand. Even a knighting by the king was not out of the question.

I surprised myself by not asking for a single shilling.

⁘

The next morning, after one of the soundest sleeps of my life, I left the priory grounds on foot, crossing the bridge and walking beneath the outer arches of the St Thomas Chapel as the first glimmer of sun broke through low morning clouds. Once on the north bank I descended to the wharfage and the offices of the wool custom. Chaucer, so a clerk at the custom-house told me, was out of town. A difficulty at Hythe, rumours of illegal wool.

The clerk stepped out for a moment, giving me the opportunity to take a glimpse at Chaucer's desk. On it sat a small quire, weighted open to a page nearly empty of content: pen trials, a few doodles, some couplets. I leaned over and read.

> *Befell that in that season, on a day,*
> *In Southwark at the Tabard as I lay*
> *Ready to ride forth on my pilgrimage*
> *To Canterbury with full devout courage,*
> *At night was come into that hostelry*
> *Well nine and twenty in a company*
> *Of sundry folk, by adventure fallen*
> *In fellowship, and pilgrims were they all,*
> *That toward Canterbury would ride.*

I had to read the lines again. *In Southwark?* Chaucer was a London man, through and through, and as far as I knew had never gone on pilgrimage to Becket's shrine, or anywhere else, for that matter. If he travelled to Canterbury it would be for business or pleasure, not for faith. False prophecies, false pilgrimages: all the same to my slippery friend.

Outside the customhouse I stood on the wharfage, watching

462

the slow, careful movement of the Goose as it craned a pile of wool from the dock. On the decks of the trading vessels workers toiled at the crates and barrels of goods brought to London from around the earth, from the looms of Lyon, the vineyards of Alsace and Tuscany, the olive groves of al-Andalus, and there, on the river's edge of London, with the low bulk of Southwark rising before me, with the dense span of the bridge against the sky, I felt the unboundedness of it all. A history I would never fully understand had passed me by, these great machinations linking Florence, London, the marches of Aragon and Castile – and the narrow lanes of Southwark, and a dead woman on the moor.

We live in an immense world, whole universes of taste and touch and scent, of voices commingling in the light, and dying away with the common dread that stands at every man's door. Yet we perceive and remember this world only as it creates those single fragments of experience: moments of everyday kindness, or self-sacrificing love, or unthinkable brutality. I angled my face to the sun and blinked away a spot, then another, these dark blemishes floating in my sight, mottling my vision, more of them by the day. Yet behind and beyond them I could imagine, for a moment, the holy sheen of Sarah's skin, the faces of our children, the intricate gloss of some forgotten book, and I thought how simple it should be, to know and cherish the proper objects of our lives.

On the near end of the bridge I bought a bird pie. The pigeon was bad, I realized after the first bite – though thankfully before swallowing. I spat it out. I thought about returning to the pieman's booth though I would have to push back through the crowd, which had thickened with the unwelcome intrusion of aristocracy. A lower knight, mounted and shouting for space, passing over from the bankside. Then the catcalls, some trash dropped from the houses above, a few small missiles thrown, all done with that urban mix of defiance and cheer, the common resonance of this angry city I bafflingly loved.

It came to me then, the source of Chaucer's folly. A hostelry at night, a diverse company of pilgrims, a tale of fellowship and adventure, all beginning at the Tabard, of all places. A book for England's sake: stories within stories, and the stuff of life, encompassed by the one great story we all must share yet none of us will ever get to read. At the foot of the bridge I stumbled on a loose paver but recovered my footing as a flock of starlings whorled above, as the way widened into the teeming breadth of Southwark, like a narrow river finding the sea.

A Note to the Reader

One of the strange pleasures of writing *A Burnable Book* has been the discovery and partial correction of my own ignorance about much of medieval life. After half a career spent studying and teaching the literature of the Middle Ages, it came as a rude awakening to realize I couldn't answer a simple question posed by my younger son: 'Did they have forks?' (Yes, Malcolm, after a fashion, though not many of them, and mostly for serving, not eating.) Though I have drawn on many of the same sorts of sources I regularly consult in my academic work, fiction requires a more eclectic approach to research guided by the idiosyncrasies of story and character. As often as I have read around in the latest scholarship on aristocratic politics during the reign of Richard II, I have found myself consulting the work of nineteenth-century antiquarians on gutters and drainage in the Southwark stews.

I hope this note will guide readers in following up on any aspects of the historical setting that interest them, as well as help answer questions about the specific choices I have made in depicting a medieval world so familiar yet so foreign to our own. Readers will find occasional posts about setting and sources on my blog, *www.burnablebooks.com*, and I am happy to receive queries and corrections as they arise.

John Gower's London was three cities, not one, and much of its life and culture was shaped by the distinctive character of the two smaller suburbs lying outside the walled city itself (and beyond its jurisdiction). The history of London, Southwark, and Westminster in the decades following the Black Death has been the subject of considerable scholarship in recent years that has helped me flesh out the bones of a story set in a richly complex milieu. The works of urban history I have consulted most frequently include Caroline Barron's *London in the Later Middle Ages*, a magisterial study of the medieval city, its institutions, and its diverse population; Sheila Lindenbaum's numerous articles on everything from urban festivals to aristocratic tournaments; Robert Shepherd's *Westminster: A Biography*, with its rich appreciation for the historical contours and character of the royal city; Martha Carlin's *Medieval Southwark*, a thorough guide to the intricacies of life and politics in the small suburb across the bridge, where bishops and butchers, tanners and taverners lived side by side and elbowed for room; Barbara Hanawalt's *Growing Up in Medieval London*, with its inspiring recreations of individual lives of the young; the myth-busting scholarship of Judith Bennett, Marjorie McIntosh, Cordelia Beattie, Kim Phillips, and others on the lives, careers, and literacies of medieval singlewomen; the work of urban archaeologists on Winchester Palace, the customhouse near Billingsgate, and other medieval sites; and Frank Rexroth's *Deviance and Power in Late Medieval London*, a field guide of sorts to the underworld of urban grime and petty crime that surrounded Gower, Chaucer, and the other city-dwellers populating this story. I have also benefited from new work by Linne Mooney and Estelle Stubbs on the scribal culture of the London Guildhall, home to an urban bureaucracy that included the likes of Ralph Strode and Adam Pinkhurst – the latter, perhaps, Geoffrey Chaucer's most notable scribe. (The map included at the beginning of the book is based in part on the map of

466

late-medieval London included in Mooney and Stubbs' *Scribes and the City*, enhanced by the renderings in Carlin's *Medieval Southwark* and the wonderfully detailed maps created for the third volume of the British Atlas of Historic Towns.)

Other bureaucracies are also part of the story told in *A Burnable Book*, particularly the legal profession emerging during these years and the peculiar educational system that trained its members. The origins of the Inns of Court in the final decades of the fourteenth century are shrouded in obscurity. While the Inner and Middle Temples were organized well before 1385, the earliest written records from any of the four inns come from the 1420s; the exact nature of legal education and barrister culture in the fourteenth century is thus a matter of pure speculation (hence the raucous spectacle performed by the apprentices at Temple Hall, invented for this book). We do know something about the various personnel who defined the changing profession. The character of Thomas Pinchbeak, serjeant-at-law, is based on a real member of the Order of the Coif. The history of the order has been treated in great depth by J.H. Baker, whose many works have helped define the study of medieval English law and its institutions.

As one of my early readers helped me see, *A Burnable Book* is in part a story of town–crown conflict, with the novel's largely London-based narrative playing out against the political crisis that more broadly defined this period of English history. The year 1385 was a pivotal one for the nation's aristocratic classes, with the expiration in May of a truce with France, Scottish incursions along the northern border, and rising tensions between the uppermost factions in the realm. Just months after the events portrayed here, King Richard would create a number of new dukedoms and earldoms: John of Gaunt's brothers would become dukes, Michael de la Pole the Earl of Suffolk, and Robert de Vere the Duke of Ireland. While the machinations of magnates are only a small part of this story, they are an important backdrop to the intrigue

467

surrounding the book sought by Gower and others, and a domestic counterpart to equally pressing international affairs. Here I am indebted to studies of Richard II's reign by Nigel Saul, Chris Given-Wilson, Michael Bennett, and Anthony Goodman; to Jonathan Sumption's stirring history of the Hundred Years War, particularly his comments on the importance of spies; to biographies of the mercenary Sir John Hawkwood by William Caferro and Stephen Cooper; to Paul Strohm's many studies of literary culture and court politics; to books by W.H. Ormrod and Stephanie Trigg on the Order of the Garter; and to Alison Weir's *Mistress of the Monarchy*, a luminous re-evaluation of Katherine Swynford. The genealogical tables at the front are intended to bring out the close relationships between the upper English aristocracy and its foreign counterparts, including the crown of Castile and the Visconti of Milan.

The character of Eleanor/Edgar Rykener was inspired by an extraordinary document discovered by Sheila Lindenbaum in the Corporation of London Records Office. The document, subsequently transcribed and translated by David Lorenzo Boyd and Ruth Mazo Karras, was published in the first volume of the *Gay and Lesbian Quarterly* as 'The Interrogation of a Male Transvestite Prostitute in Fourteenth-Century London'. The work of Ruth Karras on medieval prostitution and the lives of those who practised it has been immensely helpful to me in imagining the denizens and cultures of Gropecunt Lane and Rose Alley, as has Carolyn Dinshaw's scholarship on medieval sexualities and gender.

Though the labours of modern scholars are an invaluable resource to any writer of historical fiction, they are no substitute for the primary sources in which medieval people speak to us in something like their own voices. I have consulted a wealth of sources attesting to the lives of the women and men of this era, always with an eye for unusual details. Coroners' rolls and bishops' registers, law cases and legal moots, memorandum books and conduct manuals: in these documents can be found the makings of countless medieval life stories whose contours appear only dimly to our modern eyes. Sources such as parish registers and household accounts have furnished given names and surnames (some of which I have altered for literary effect), while probate inventories, wills, and household account books show us glimpses of the objects, commodities, and habits that shaped the material world of late-medieval England. Readers wanting a taste of medieval London's documentary record for themselves might enjoy paging through the hundreds of examples collected and translated in Henry Thomas Riley's *Memorials of London and London Life in the XIIIth, XIVth, and XVth Centuries* or the *Liber Albus*, an immense compilation of rules and customs relating to city governance compiled in the early fifteenth century (both are freely available online). For a general guide to daily life and customs in the period, readers can do no better than Ian Mortimer's *Time Traveller's Guide to Medieval England*.

I have also consulted the writings of monastic and lay chroniclers of these fascinating years. The Westminster Chronicle details the tensions between John of Gaunt and King Richard over the first half of 1385, as well as contemporaneous events in Italy surrounding the Visconti and Sir John Hawkwood. The metrical chronicle of the Chandos Herald recounts the 1367 campaign of Edward the Black Prince in Castile and Aragon in the months surrounding the Battle of Nájera, providing the tragic background to the story of Seguina d'Orange.

The literature of medieval England, my own scholarly specialty, has been a constant source of reference, dialogue, and slang; readers familiar with the writings of Chaucer, Gower, William Langland, and others will find allusions and borrowings on nearly every page. The prophecies of the *De Mortibus Regum Anglorum* are modelled on the alliterative long lines of Langland and the Pearl poet. In addition to literary texts, innumerable historical and documentary sources are excerpted in the *Middle English Dictionary* and its compendium. As I always advise my students, the *MED* is far superior to the *OED* for anyone interested in early English wordings, first usages, and forms of address. (As the *MED* demonstrates, for example, words and phrases such as 'my lord' and 'sire' were ubiquitous in the period and used even within the household, despite the common assumption that they were reserved for aristocrats and kings.)

Finally, John Gower. Despite his prolific career, his adept use of three distinctive literary languages, and his featured role in Shakespeare's *Pericles*, Gower has always suffered by comparison to his more illustrious contemporary, Geoffrey Chaucer. Yet the two poets were close and perhaps life-long friends. We know about this friendship from several documentary sources, including one granting Gower power of attorney for the duration of Chaucer's 1378 trip to Italy (the later trip imagined here is my own invention). There are also several moments in which the two poets speak to one another within the lines of their verse. One of these, an apostrophe addressed by Chaucer to 'Moral Gower' near the end of *Troilus and Criseyde*, has largely shaped the critical perception of Gower's character.

The protagonist of *A Burnable Book* is a more . . . let's say *compromised* Gower. In exploring the darker sides of his character, his family, and his friendships, I have been guided above all by the poet's own writing: by the bleak, even nihilistic tone one often finds him adopting toward the many subjects he treats. For particular details of Gower's life and circumstances (including the encounter along the Thames with King Richard, based on the highly stylized account in the *Confessio Amantis*), I have relied on the scholarship of Robert F. Yeager, Derek Pearsall, Candace Barrington, John M. Bowers, Andrew Galloway, Jonathan Hsy, and Diane Watt, whose work sparked some of my initial thinking about the poet's shadier side. If the John Gower imagined here strikes specialists as untenable or overdone, I hope they will attribute this in part to the poet's own sense of our collective estrangement from the ever-changing world around us. As Gower puts it near the end of his greatest work, 'I know not how the world is went.'

Acknowledgments

G.K. Chesteron once called Geoffrey Chaucer a 'poet of gratitude,' a writer 'positively full of warm acknowledgment'. Of all the poet's qualities, this is perhaps the easiest to imitate. Over the years I have accumulated many debts to friends, colleagues, and correspondents who have leant support of various kinds, from careful readings to open ears and ready pints. They include Linda Blackford, Carol Blount, Heather Blurton, Andrew Cole, Edward Dusinberre, Mark Edmundson, Katherine Eggert, Dyan Elliott, David Gies, Jennifer Hershey, Jen Jahner, William Kuskin, Jana Mathews, Deborah McGrady, Christian McMillen, Howard Morhaim, John Parker, John Pepper, Caroline Preston, Patrick Pritchett, Myra Seaman, Lisa Russ Spaar, Emily Steiner, Beth Sutherland, John Stevenson, Michael Suarez, Christopher Tilghman, Cynthia Wall, and Mark Winokur. Paul Fox, chairman of the Heraldry Society, advised me on some of the finer points of royal heraldry in the Edwardian and Ricardian age. Amy Appleford shared her knowledge of burial practices for the poor of London. Paul Strohm, formerly the J.R.R. Tolkien Professor of Medieval Studies at Oxford and an endless reserve of knowledge about medieval London and its culture, read the manuscript in an early draft and made numerous suggestions about setting, chronology, and historical detail. Andrew Galloway and Claire Waters read the book meticulously and with careful attention to details of idiom and language.

As a teacher of medieval culture I am also indebted to the scholars whose formative teaching exposed me to the wonders of the medieval world—its history, its books, its literature, its music, its theology, and its art. Thanks to Teodolinda Barolini, Christopher Baswell, Marvin Becker, Caroline Walker Bynum, Rita Copeland, Consuelo Dutschke, Joan Ferrante, Carmela Franklin, Barbara Hanawalt, Robert Hanning, Ron Martinez, Linda Neagley, Susan Noakes, and David Wallace.

The editorial teams at HarperCollins (UK) and William Morrow (US) have shepherded this book through the complex and exciting process from contract to publication. I am deeply indebted to Julia Wisdom and Rachel Kahan, who acquired *A Burnable Book* and saw it through revisions and production, for their wisdom, support, and patience. Thanks also go to Emad Akhtar, Ben Bruton, Trish Daly, Jaime Frost, Tavia Kowalchuk, Ashley Marudas, Rachel Meyers, Anne O'Brien, Aja Pollock, and Kate Stephenson.

My marvelous agent, Helen Heller, plucked a manuscript out of her slush pile and took a chance on an unproven writer of turgid academic prose. She read multiple drafts of this book with her unique blend of patience and severity. Her support, dedication, and pep talks have meant the world to me (as have her unflinching critiques).

My parents, Sheila and Harry Holsinger, deserve endless gratitude for the selfless support they have given me over a lifetime; as do Carol Holsinger, Eric Holsinger, and Anna Jullien, my siblings, for their constancy and love; Betsy and Bob Brickhouse, my in-laws, for their warm friendship and encouragement; Campbell and Malcolm, my sons, for all the joy, energy, and soccer; and Anna Brickhouse, for love, brilliance—everything.

THE
FIFTH
WITNESS

THE
FIFTH
WITNESS

MICHAEL
CONNELLY

First published in Great Britain in 2011 by Orion Books,
an imprint of The Orion Publishing Group Ltd
Orion House, 5 Upper Saint Martin's Lane
London WC2H 9EA

An Hachette UK Company

1 3 5 7 9 10 8 6 4 2

A CIP catalogue record for this book is
available from the British Library.

ISBN (Hardback) 978 1 4091 1442 0
ISBN (Export Trade Paperback) 978 1 4091 1443 7

Printed in Great Britain by Clays Ltd, St Ives plc

The Orion Publishing Group's policy is to use papers that are natural,
renewable and recyclable products and made from wood grown in sustainable
forests. The logging and manufacturing processes are expected to
conform to the environmental regulations of the country of origin.

www.orionbooks.co.uk

This is for Dennis Wojciechowski,
with many thanks.

PART ONE

The Magic Words

One

Mrs. Pena looked across the seat at me and held her hands up in a beseeching manner. She spoke in a heavy accent, choosing English to make her final pitch directly to me.

"Please, you help me, Mr. Mickey?"

I looked at Rojas, who was turned around in the front seat even though I didn't need him to translate. I then looked past Mrs. Pena, over her shoulder and through the car window, to the home she desperately wanted to hold on to. It was a bleached pink, two-bedroom house with a hardscrabble yard behind a wire fence. The concrete step to the front stoop had graffiti sprayed across it, indecipherable except for the number 13. It wasn't the address. It was a pledge of allegiance.

My eyes finally came back to her. She was forty-four years old and attractive in a worn sort of way. She was the single mother of three teenage boys and had not paid her mortgage in nine months. Now the bank had foreclosed and was moving in to sell the house out from under her.

The auction would take place in three days. It didn't matter that the house was worth little or that it sat in a gang-infested neighborhood in South L.A. Somebody would buy it, and Mrs. Pena would become a renter instead of an owner — that is, if the new owner didn't evict her. For years she had relied on the protection of the Florencia 13. But times were different. No gang allegiance could help her now. She needed a lawyer. She needed me.

"Tell her I will try my best," I said. "Tell her I am pretty certain I will be able to stop the auction and challenge the validity of the foreclosure. It will at least slow things down. It will give us time to work up a long-range plan. Maybe get her back on her feet."

I nodded and waited while Rojas translated. I had been using Rojas as my driver and interpreter ever since I had bought the advertising package on the Spanish radio stations.

I felt the cell phone in my pocket vibrate. My upper thigh read this as a text message as opposed to an actual phone call, which had a longer vibration. Either way I ignored it. When Rojas completed the translation, I jumped in before Mrs. Pena could respond.

"Tell her that she has to understand that this isn't a solution to her problems. I can delay things and we can negotiate with her bank. But I am not promising that she won't lose the house. In fact, she's already lost the house. I'm going to get it back but then she'll still have to face the bank."

Rojas translated, making hand gestures where I had not. The truth was that Mrs. Pena would have to leave eventually. It was just a question of how far she wanted me to take it. Personal bankruptcy would tack another year onto foreclosure defense. But she didn't have to decide that now.

"Now tell her that I also need to be paid for my work. Give her the schedule. A thousand up front and the monthly payment plan."

"How much on the monthly and how long?"

I looked out at the house again. Mrs. Pena had invited me inside but I preferred meeting in the car. This was drive-by territory and I was in my Lincoln Town Car BPS. That stood for Ballistic Protection Series. I bought it used from the widow of a murdered enforcer with the Sinaloa cartel. There was armored plating in the doors, and the windows were constructed of three layers of laminated glass. They were bulletproof. The windows in Mrs. Pena's pink house were not. The lesson learned from the Sinaloa man was that you don't leave the car unless you have to.

Mrs. Pena had explained earlier that the mortgage payments she had stopped making nine months ago had been seven hundred a month. She would continue to withhold any payments to the bank while I worked the case. She would have a free ride for as long as I kept the bank at bay, so there was money to be made here.

"Make it two-fifty a month. I'll give her the cut-rate plan. Make sure she knows she's getting a deal and that she can never be late with the payments. We can take a credit card if she has one with any juice on it. Just make sure it doesn't expire until at least twenty twelve."

Rojas translated, with more gestures and many more words than I had used, while I pulled my phone. The text had come from Lorna Taylor.

CALL ME ASAP.

I'd have to get back to her after the client conference. A typical law practice would have an office manager and receptionist. But I didn't have an office other than the backseat of my Lincoln, so Lorna ran the business end of things and answered the phones at the West Hollywood condo she shared with my chief investigator.

My mother was Mexican born and I understood her native language better than I ever let on. When Mrs. Pena responded, I knew what she said—the gist of it, at least. But I let Rojas translate it all back to me anyway. She promised to go inside the house to get the thousand-dollar cash retainer and to dutifully make the monthly payments. To me, not the bank. I figured that if I could extend her stay in the house to a year my take would be four grand total. Not bad for what was entailed. I would probably never see Mrs. Pena again. I would file a suit challenging the foreclosure and stretch things out. The chances were I wouldn't even make a court appearance. My young associate would do the courthouse legwork. Mrs. Pena would be happy and so would I. Eventually, though, the hammer would come down. It always does.

I thought I had a workable case even though Mrs. Pena would not be a sympathetic client. Most of my clients stop making payments to the bank after losing a job or experiencing a medical catastrophe. Mrs. Pena stopped when her three sons went to jail for selling drugs and their weekly financial support abruptly ended. Not a lot of goodwill to be had with that story. But the bank had played dirty. I had looked up her file on my laptop. It was all there: a record of her being served with notices involving demands for payment and then foreclosure. Only Mrs. Pena said she had never received these notices. And I believed her. It wasn't the kind of neighborhood where process servers were known to roam freely. I suspected that the notifications had ended up in the trash and the server had simply lied about it. If I could make that case, then I could back the bank off Mrs. Pena with the leverage it would give me.

That would be my defense. That the poor woman was never given proper notice of the peril she was in. The bank took advantage of her, foreclosed on her without allowing her the opportunity to make up the arrears, and should be rebuked by the court for doing so.

"Okay, we have a deal," I said. "Tell her to go in and get her money while I print out a contract and receipt. We'll get going on this today."

I smiled and nodded at Mrs. Pena. Rojas translated and then jumped out of the car to go around and open her door.

Once Mrs. Pena left the car I opened the Spanish contract template on my laptop and typed in the necessary names and numbers. I sent it to the printer that sat on an electronics platform on the front passenger seat. I then went to work on the receipt for funds to be deposited into my client trust account. Everything was aboveboard. Always. It was the best way to keep the California Bar off my ass. I might have a bulletproof car but it was the bar I most often checked for over my shoulder.

It had been a rough year for Michael Haller and Associates, Attorneys-at-Law. Criminal defense had virtually dried up in the down economy. Of course crime wasn't down. In Los Angeles, crime marched on through any economy. But the paying customers were few and far between. It seemed as though nobody had money to pay a lawyer. Consequently, the public defender's office was busting at the seams with cases and clients while guys like me were left starving.

I had expenses and a fourteen-year-old kid in private school who talked about USC whenever the subject of colleges came up. I had to do something and so I did what I had once held as unthinkable. I went civil. The only growth industry in the law business was foreclosure defense. I attended a few bar seminars, got up to speed on it and started running new ads in two languages. I built a few websites and started buying the lists of foreclosure filings from the county clerk's office. That's how I got Mrs. Pena as a client. Direct mail. Her name was on the list and I had sent her a letter—in Spanish—offering my services. She told me that my letter happened to be the first indication she had ever received that she was in foreclosure.

The saying goes that if you build it, they will come. It was true. I was getting more work than I could handle—six more appointments after

Mrs. Pena today—and had even hired an actual associate to Michael Haller and Associates for the first time ever. The national epidemic of real estate foreclosure was slowing but by no means abating. In Los Angeles County I could be feeding at the trough for years to come.

The cases went for only four or five grand a pop but this was a quantity-over-quality period in my professional life. I currently had more than ninety foreclosure clients on my docket. No doubt my kid could start planning on USC. Hell, she could start thinking about staying for a master's degree.

There were those who believed I was part of the problem, that I was merely helping the deadbeats game the system while delaying the economic recovery of the whole. That description fit some of my clients for sure. But I viewed most of them as repeat victims. Initially scammed with the American dream of home ownership when lured into mortgages they had no business even qualifying for. And then victimized again when the bubble burst and unscrupulous lenders ran roughshod over them in the subsequent foreclosure frenzy. Most of these once-proud home owners didn't stand a chance under California's streamlined foreclosure regulations. A bank didn't even need a judge's approval to take away someone's house. The great financial minds thought this was the way to go. Just keep it moving. The sooner the crisis hit bottom, the sooner the recovery would begin. I say, Tell that to Mrs. Pena.

There was a theory out there that this was all part of a conspiracy among the top banks in the country to undermine property laws, sabotage the judicial system and create a perpetually cycling foreclosure industry that had them profiting from both ends of the process. Me, I wasn't exactly buying into that. But during my short time in this area of the law, I had seen enough predatory and unethical acts by so-called legitimate businessmen to make me miss good old-fashioned criminal law.

Rojas was waiting outside the car for Mrs. Pena to return with the money. I checked my watch and noted we were running late on my next appointment—a commercial foreclosure over in Compton. I tried to bunch my new client consultations geographically to save time and gas and mileage on the car. Today I worked the south end. Tomorrow I would hit East L.A. Two days a week I was in the car, signing up new clients. The rest of the time I worked the cases.

"Let's go, Mrs. Pena," I said. "We gotta roll."

I decided to use the waiting time to call Lorna. Three months earlier I had started blocking the ID on my phone. I never did that when I practiced criminal, but in my brave new world of foreclosure defense, I usually didn't want people having my direct number. And that included the lender attorneys as well as my own clients.

"Law offices of Michael Haller and Associates," Lorna said when she picked up. "How can I —"

"It's me. What's up?"

"Mickey, you have to get over to Van Nuys Division right away."

There was a strong urgency in her voice. Van Nuys Division was the LAPD's central command for operations in the sprawling San Fernando Valley, on the north side of the city.

"I'm working the south end today. What's going on?"

"They have Lisa Trammel there. She called."

Lisa Trammel was a client. In fact, my very first foreclosure client. I had kept her in her home for going on eight months and was confident I could take it at least another year further before we dropped the bankruptcy bomb. But she was consumed by the frustrations and inequities of her life and could not be calmed or controlled. She'd taken to marching in front of the bank with a placard decrying its fraudulent practices and heartless actions. That is, until the bank got a temporary restraining order against her.

"Did she violate the TRO? Are they holding her?"

"Mickey, they're holding her for murder."

That wasn't what I was expecting to hear.

"Murder? Who's the victim?"

"She said they're charging her with killing Mitchell Bondurant."

That gave me another great big pause. I looked out the window and saw Mrs. Pena coming out through her front door. She held a wad of cash in her hand.

"All right, get on the phone and reschedule the rest of today's appointments. And tell Cisco to head up to Van Nuys. I'll meet him there."

"You got it. Do you want Bullocks to take the afternoon appointments?"

"Bullocks" was what we called Jennifer Aronson, the associate I had hired out of Southwestern, a law school housed in the old Bullocks department store building on Wilshire.

"No, I don't want her doing intake. Just reschedule them. And listen, I think I have the Trammel file with me, but you have the call list. Track down her sister. Lisa's got a kid. He's probably in school and somebody's going to have to take him if Lisa can't."

We made every client fill out an extensive contact list because sometimes it was hard to find them for court hearings — and to get them to pay for my work.

"I'll start on that," Lorna said. "Good luck, Mickey."

"Same to you."

I closed the phone and thought about Lisa Trammel. Somehow I wasn't surprised that she had been arrested for killing the man who was trying to take her home away from her. It's not that I had thought it would come to this. Not even close. But deep down, I had known it was going to come to something.

TWO

I quickly took Mrs. Pena's cash and gave her a receipt. We both signed the contract and she got a copy for her own records. I took a credit card number from her and she promised it would withstand a $250-a-month hit while I was working for her. I then thanked her, shook her hand and had Rojas walk her back to her front door.

While he did that I popped the trunk with the remote I carried, and got out. The Lincoln's trunk was spacious enough to hold three cardboard file boxes as well as all my office supplies. I found the Trammel file in the third box and pulled it. I also grabbed the fancy briefcase I used for police station visits. When I closed the trunk I saw the stylized 13 spray-painted in silver on the lid's black paint.

"Son of a bitch."

I looked around. Three front yards down, a couple of kids were playing in the dirt but they looked too young to be graffiti artists. The rest of the street was deserted. I was baffled. Not only had I not heard or noticed the assault on my car that had taken place while I was having a client conference inside it, but it was barely past one and I knew most gangbangers didn't get up and embrace the day and all its possibilities until late afternoon. They were night creatures.

I headed back to my open door with the file. I noticed Rojas was standing at the front stoop, chatting with Mrs. Pena. I whistled and signaled him back to the car. We had to get going.

I got in. Message received, Rojas trotted back to the car and jumped in himself.

"Compton?" he asked.

"No, change of plans. We've got to get up to Van Nuys. Fast."

"Okay, Boss."

He pulled away from the curb and started making his way back to the 110 Freeway. There was no direct freeway route to Van Nuys. We would have to take the 110 into downtown where we'd pick up the 101 north. We couldn't have been starting off from a worse position in the city.

"What was she saying at the front door?" I asked Rojas.

"She was asking about you."

"What do you mean?"

"She said you looked like you shouldn't need a translator, you know?"

I nodded. I got that a lot. My mother's genes made me look more south of the border than north.

"She also wanted to know if you were married, Boss. I told her you were. But if you want to circle back and tap that, it'll be there. She'd probably want a discount on the fees, though."

"Thanks, Rojas," I said dryly. "She already got a discount but I'll keep it in mind."

Before opening the file I scrolled through the contacts list on my phone. I was looking for the name of someone in the Van Nuys detective squad who might share some information with me. But there was nobody. I was going in blind on a murder case. Not a good starting point either.

I closed the phone and put it into its charger, then opened the file. Lisa Trammel had become my client after responding to the generic letter I sent to the owners of all homes in foreclosure. I assumed I wasn't the only lawyer in Los Angeles who did this. But for some reason Lisa answered my letter and not theirs.

As an attorney in private practice you get to choose your own clients most of the time. Sometimes you choose wrong. Lisa was one of those times with me. I was eager to start the new line of work. I was looking for clients who were in jams or who had been taken advantage of. People who were too naive to know their rights or options. I was looking for underdogs and thought I had found one in Lisa. No doubt she fit the bill. She was losing her house because of a set of circumstances that had fallen like dominoes out of her control. And her lender had turned her case over to a foreclosure mill that had cut corners and even violated the rules. I signed Lisa up, put her on a payment plan and started to fight her fight. It was a good case and I was excited. It was only after this that Lisa became a nuisance client.

Lisa Trammel was thirty-five years old. She was the married mother of a nine-year-old boy named Tyler and their house was on Melba in Woodland Hills. At the time she and her husband, Jeffrey, bought the house in 2005, Lisa taught social studies at Grant High while Jeffrey sold BMWs at the dealership in Calabasas.

Their three-bedroom house carried a $750,000 mortgage against an appraised value of $900,000. The market was strong then and mortgages were plentiful and easy to get. They used an independent mortgage broker who shopped their file around and got them into a low-interest loan that carried a balloon payment at the five-year mark. The loan was then folded into an investment block of mortgages and reassigned twice before finding its permanent home at WestLand Financial, a subsidiary of WestLand National, the Los Angeles–based bank headquartered in Sherman Oaks.

All was well and good for the family of three until Jeff Trammel decided he didn't want to be a husband and father anymore. A few months before the $750,000 note on the house was due, Jeff took off, leaving his BMW M3 demo in the parking lot at Union Station and Lisa holding the balloon.

Down to a single income and a child to care for, Lisa looked at the reality of her situation and made choices. By now the economy had stalled out like a plane lumbering into the sky without enough airspeed. Given her teacher's income, no institution was going to refinance the balloon. She stopped making payments on the loan and ignored all communications from the bank. When the note came due, the property went into foreclosure and that was when I came onto the scene. I sent Jeff and Lisa a letter, not realizing Jeff was no longer in the picture.

Lisa answered it.

I define a nuisance client as one who does not understand the bounds of our relationship, even after I clearly and sometimes repeatedly delineate them. Lisa came to me with her first notice of foreclosure. I took the case and told her to sit back and wait while I went to work. But Lisa couldn't sit back. She couldn't wait. She called me every day. After I filed a lawsuit putting the foreclosure before a judge, she showed up at court for routine filings and continuances. She had to be there and she had to know every move I made, see every letter I sent and be summarized on every call I received. She often called me and yelled when she perceived that I was not giving her case my fullest attention. I began to understand why her husband had hightailed it. He had to get away from her.

I began to wonder about Lisa's mental health and suspected a bipolar affliction. The incessant calls and activities were cyclical. There were weeks when I heard nothing, alternating with weeks where she would call daily and repeatedly until she got me on the line.

Three months into the case she told me she had lost her job with the L.A. County School District because of unexcused absences. It was then that she talked about seeking damages from the bank that was foreclosing on her home. A sense of entitlement moved into the discourse. The bank was responsible for everything: the abandonment by her husband, the loss of her job, the taking of her home.

I made a mistake in revealing to her some of my case intelligence and strategy. I did it to appease her, to get her off the line. Our examination of the loan record had turned up inconsistencies and issues in the mortgage's repeated reassignment to various holding companies. There were indications of fraud that I thought I could use to swing leverage to Lisa's side when it came time to negotiate an out.

But the information only galvanized Lisa's belief in her victimization at the hands of the bank. Never did she acknowledge the fact that she had signed for a loan and was obliged to repay it. She saw the bank only as the source of her woes.

The first thing she did was register a website. She used www .californiaforeclosurefighters.com to launch an organization called Foreclosure Litigants Against Greed. It worked better as an acronym—FLAG— and she effectively made use of the American flag on her protest signs. The message being that fighting foreclosure was as American as apple pie.

She then took to marching in front of WestLand's corporate headquarters on Ventura Boulevard. Sometimes by herself, sometimes with her young son, and sometimes with people she had attracted to the cause. She carried signs that decried the bank's involvement in illegal foreclosures and in putting families out of their homes and onto the streets.

Lisa was quick to alert local media outlets to her activities. She got on TV repeatedly and was always ready with a sound bite that gave voice to people in her situation, casting them as victims of the foreclosure epidemic, not garden-variety deadbeats. I had noticed that on Channel 5 she had even become part of the stock footage thrown up on the screen whenever there was an update on nationwide foreclosure issues or statistics. California was the third leading state in the country for foreclosures and Los Angeles was the hotbed. As these facts were reported, there would be Lisa and her group on the screen carrying their signs — DON'T TAKE MY HOME! STOP ILLEGAL FORECLOSURE NOW!

Alleging that her protests were illegal gatherings that impeded traffic and endangered pedestrians, WestLand sought and received a restraining order that kept Lisa one hundred yards from any bank facility and its employees. Undaunted, she took her signs and her fellow protestors to the county courthouse, where foreclosures were fought every day.

Mitchell Bondurant was a senior vice president at WestLand. He headed up the mortgage loan division. His name was on the loan documents relating to Lisa Trammel's house. As such his name was on all of my filings. I had also written him a letter, outlining what I described as indications of fraudulent practices by the foreclosure mill WestLand had contracted with to carry out the dirty work of taking the homes and other properties of their default customers.

Lisa was entitled to see all documents arising from her case. She was copied on the letter and everything else. Despite being the human face of the effort to take her home away, Bondurant remained above the fray, hiding behind the bank's legal team. He never responded to my letter and I never met him. I had no knowledge that Lisa Trammel had ever met or spoken with him either. But now he was dead and the police had Lisa in custody.

We exited the 101 at Van Nuys Boulevard and headed north. The civic center was a plaza surrounded by two courthouses, a library, City Hall North and the Valley Bureau police complex, which included the Van Nuys Division. Various other government agencies and buildings

were clustered around the main grouping. Parking was always a problem but it wasn't my worry. I pulled my phone and called my investigator, Dennis Wojciechowski.

"Cisco, it's me. You close?"

In his early years Wojciechowski was associated with the Road Saints
motorcycle club but there was already a member named Dennis. Nobody
could pronounce Wojciechowski so they called him the Cisco Kid
because of his dark looks and mustache. The mustache was now gone
but the name had stuck.

"Already here. I'll meet you on the bench by the front stairs to the PD."

"I'll be there in five. Have you talked to anyone yet? I've got nothing."

"Yeah, your old pal Kurlen's running lead on this. The victim, Mitchell Bondurant, was found in the parking garage at WestLand's headquarters on Ventura about nine this morning. He was on the ground between
two cars. Not clear how long he was down but he was dead on scene."

"Do we know the cause yet?"

"There it gets a little hinky. At first they put out that he'd been shot
because an employee who was on another level of the garage told
responding police she had heard two popping sounds, like shots. But
when they examined the body on the scene it looked like he had been
beaten to death. Hit with something."

"Was Lisa Trammel arrested there?"

"No, from what I understand, she was picked up at her home in
Woodland Hills. I still have some calls out but that's about the extent of
what I've got so far. Sorry, Mick."

"Don't worry about it. We'll know everything soon enough. Is
Kurlen at the scene or with the suspect?"

"I was told he and his partner picked up Trammel and took her in.
The partner's a female named Cynthia Longstreth. She's a D-one. I've
never heard of her."

I had never heard of her either but since she was a detective one, my
guess was that she was new to the homicide beat and paired with the
veteran Kurlen, a D-3, to get some seasoning. I looked out the window.
We were passing a BMW dealership and it made me think of the missing husband who had sold Beemers before pulling the plug on the marriage and disappearing. I wondered if Jeff Trammel would show up now

that his wife was arrested for murder. Would he take custody of the son he had abandoned?

"You want me to get Valenzuela over here?" Cisco asked. "He's only a block away."

Fernando Valenzuela was a bail bondsman I used on Valley cases. But I knew he wouldn't be needed this time.

"I'd wait on that. If they've tagged her with murder she isn't going to make bail."

"Right, yeah."

"Do you know if a DA's been assigned yet?"

I was thinking about my ex-wife who worked for the district attorney's office in Van Nuys. She might be a useful source of back-channel information—unless she had been put on the case. Then there would be a conflict of interest. It had happened before. Maggie McPherson wouldn't like that.

"I've got nothing on that."

I considered what little we knew and what might be the best way to proceed. My feeling was that once the police understood what they had in this case—a murder that could draw wide attention to one of the great financial catastrophes of the time—they would quickly go to lockdown, putting a lid on all sources of information. The time to make moves was now.

"Cisco, I changed my mind. Don't wait for me. Go over to the scene and see what you can find out. Talk to people before they get locked down."

"You sure?"

"Yeah. I'll handle the PD and I'll call if I need anything."

"Got it. Good luck."

"You too."

I closed the phone and looked at the back of my driver's head.

"Rojas, turn right at Delano and take me up Sylmar."

"No problem."

"I don't know how long I'll be. I want you to drop me and then go back up Van Nuys Boulevard and find a body shop. See if they can get the paint off the back of the car."

Rojas looked at me in the rearview mirror.

"What paint?"

Three

The Van Nuys police building is a four-story structure serving many purposes. It houses the Van Nuys police division as well as the Valley Bureau command offices and the main jail facility serving the northern part of the city. I had been here before on cases and knew that as with most LAPD stations large or small, there would be multiple obstacles standing between my client and me.

I have always had the suspicion that officers assigned to front desk duty were chosen by cunning supervisors because of their skills in obfuscation and disinformation. If you doubt this, walk into any police station in the city and tell the desk officer who greets you that you wish to make a complaint against a police officer. See how long it takes him to find the proper form. Desk cops are usually young and dumb and unintentionally ignorant, or old and obdurate and completely deliberate in their actions.

At the front desk at Van Nuys station I was met by an officer with the name CRIMMINS printed on his crisp uniform. He was a silver-haired veteran and therefore highly accomplished when it came to the dead-eyed stare. He showed this to me when I identified myself as a defense attorney with a client waiting to see me in the detective squad. His response consisted of pursing his lips and pointing to a row of plastic chairs where I was supposed to meekly go to wait until he deemed it time to call upstairs.

Guys like Crimmins are used to a cowering public: people who do

17

exactly as he says because they are too intimidated to do anything else. I wasn't part of that public.

"No, that's not how this works," I said.

Crimmins squinted. He hadn't been challenged by anybody all day, let alone a criminal defense attorney — emphasis on *criminal*. His first move was to fire up the sarcasm responders.

"Is that right?"

"Yes, that's right. So pick up the phone and call upstairs to Detective Kurlen. Tell him Mickey Haller is on the way up and that if I don't see my client in the next ten minutes I'll just walk across the plaza to the courthouse and go see Judge Mills."

I paused to let the name register.

"I'm sure you know of Judge Roger Mills. Lucky for me, he used to be a criminal defense attorney before he got elected to the bench. He didn't like being jacked around by the police back then and doesn't like it much when he hears about it now. He'll drag both you and Kurlen into court and make you explain why you were playing this same old game of stopping a citizen from exercising her constitutional rights to consult an attorney. Last time it went down like that Judge Mills didn't like the answers he got and fined the guy who was sitting where you are five hundred bucks."

Crimmins looked like he'd had a hard time following my words. He was a short-sentence man, I guessed. He blinked twice and reached for the phone. I heard him confer directly with Kurlen. He then hung up.

"You know the way, smart guy?"

"I know the way. Thank you for your help, Officer Crimmins."

"Catch you later."

He pointed his finger at me like it was a gun, getting the last shot in so he could tell himself that he had handled that son-of-a-bitch lawyer. I left the desk and headed into the nearby alcove where I knew the elevator was located.

On the third floor Detective Howard Kurlen was waiting for me with a smile on his face. It wasn't a friendly smile. He looked like the cat who just ate the canary.

"Have fun down there, Counselor?"

"Oh, yeah."

"Well, you're too late up here."

"How's that? You booked her?"

He spread his hands in a phony *Sorry about that* gesture.

"It's funny. My partner took her out of here just before I got the call from downstairs."

"Wow, what a coincidence. I still want to talk to her."

"You'll have to go through the jail."

This would probably take me an extra hour of waiting. And this was why Kurlen was smiling.

"You sure you can't have your partner turn around and bring her down? I won't be long with her."

I said it even though I thought I was spitting into the wind. But Kurlen surprised me and pulled his phone off his belt. He hit a speed-dial button. It was either an elaborate hoax or he was actually doing what I asked. Kurlen and I had a history. We had squared off against each other on prior cases. I had attempted on more than one occasion to destroy his credibility on the witness stand. I was never very successful at it but the experience still made it hard to be cordial afterward. But now he was doing me a good turn and I wasn't sure why.

"It's me," Kurlen said into the phone. "Bring her back here."

He listened for a moment.

"Because I told you to. Now bring her back."

He closed the phone without another word to his partner and looked at me.

"You owe me one, Haller. I could've hung you up for a couple hours. In the old days, I would've."

"I know. I appreciate it."

He headed back toward the squad room and signaled me to follow. He spoke casually as he walked.

"So, when she told us to call you she said you were handling her foreclosure."

"That's right."

"My sister got divorced and now she's in a mess like that."

There it was. The quid pro quo.

"You want me to talk to her?"

"No, I just want to know if it's best to fight these things or just get it over with."

The squad room looked like it was in a time warp. It was vintage 1970s, with a linoleum floor, two-tone yellow walls and gray government-issue desks with rubber stripping around the edges. Kurlen remained standing while waiting for his partner to come back with my client.

I pulled a card out of my pocket and handed it to him.

"You're talking to a fighter, so that's my answer. I couldn't handle her case because of conflict of interest between you and me. But have her call the office and we'll get her hooked up with somebody good. Make sure she mentions your name."

Kurlen nodded and picked a DVD case off his desk and handed it to me.

"Might as well give you this now."

I looked at the disc.

"What's this?"

"Our interview with your client. You will clearly see that we stopped talking to her as soon as she said the magic words: I want a lawyer."

"I'll be sure to check that out, Detective. You want to tell me why she's your suspect?"

"Sure. She's our suspect and we're charging her because she did it and she made admissions about it before asking to call her lawyer. Sorry about that, Counselor, but we played by the rules."

I held the disc up as if it were my client.

"You're telling me she admitted killing Bondurant?"

"Not in so many words. But she made admissions and contradictions. I'll leave it at that."

"Did she by any chance say in so many words why she did it?"

"She didn't have to. The victim was in the process of taking away her house. That's plenty enough motive right there. We're as good as gold on motive."

I could've told him that he had that wrong, that I was in the process of stopping the foreclosure. But I kept my mouth shut about that. My job was to gather information here, not give it away.

"What else you got, Detective?"

"Nothing that I care to share with you at the moment. You'll have to wait to get the rest through discovery."

"I'll do that. Has a DA been assigned yet?"

"Not that I heard."

Kurlen nodded toward the back of the room and I turned to see Lisa Trammel being walked toward the door of an interrogation room. She had the classic deer-in-the-headlights look in her eyes.

"You've got fifteen minutes," Kurlen said. "And that's only because I'm being nice. I figure there's no need to start a war."

Not yet, at least, I thought as I headed toward the interrogation room.

"Hey, wait a minute," Kurlen called to my back. "I have to check the briefcase. Rules, you know."

He was referring to the leather-over-aluminum attaché I was carrying. I could've made an argument about the search infringing on attorney-client privilege but I wanted to talk to my client. I stepped back toward him and swung the case up onto a counter, then popped it open. All it contained was the Lisa Trammel file, a fresh legal pad and the new contracts and power-of-attorney form I had printed out while driving up. I figured I needed Lisa to re-sign since my representation was crossing from civil to criminal.

Kurlen gave it a quick once-over and signaled me to close it.

"Hand-tooled Italian leather," he said. "Looks like a fancy drug dealer's case. You haven't been associating with the wrong people, have you, Haller?"

He put on that canary smile again. Cop humor was truly unique in all the world.

"As a matter of fact, it did belong to a courier," I said. "A client. But where he was going he wasn't going to need it anymore so I took it in trade. You want to see the secret compartment? It's kind of a pain to open."

"I think I'll pass. You're good."

I closed the case and headed back to the interrogation room.

"And it's Colombian leather," I said.

Kurlen's partner was waiting at the room's door. I didn't know her but didn't bother to introduce myself. We were never going to be friendly and I guessed she would be the type to stiff me on the handshake in order to impress Kurlen.

She held the door open and I stopped at the threshold.

"All listening and recording devices in this room are off, correct?"

21

"You got it."

"If they're not that would be a violation of my client's—"

"We know the drill."

"Yeah, but sometimes you conveniently forget it, don't you?"

"You've got fourteen minutes now, sir. You want to talk to her or keep talking to me?"

"Right."

I went in and the door was closed behind me. It was a nine-by-six room. I looked at Lisa and put a finger to my lips.

"What?" she asked.

"That means don't say a word, Lisa, until I tell you to."

Her response was to break down in a cascade of tears and a loud and long wail that tailed off into a sentence that was completely unintelligible. She was sitting at a square table with a chair opposite her. I quickly took the open chair and put my case up on the table. I knew she would be positioned to face the room's hidden camera, so I didn't bother to look around for it. I snapped open the case and pulled it close to my body, hoping that my back would act as a blind to the camera. I had to assume that Kurlen and his partner were listening and watching. One more reason for his being "nice."

While one by one I took out the legal pad and documents with my right hand, I used the left to open the case's secret compartment. I hit the engage button on the Paquin 2000 acoustic jammer. The device emitted a low-frequency RF signal that clogged any listening device within twenty-five feet with electronic disinformation. If Kurlen and his partner were illegally listening in, they were now hearing white noise.

The case and its hidden device were almost ten years old and as far as I knew, the original owner was still in federal prison. I'd taken it in trade at least seven years ago, back when drug cases were my bread and butter. I knew law enforcement was always trying to build a better mousetrap, and in ten years the electronic eavesdropping business must have undergone at least two revolutions. So I was not completely put at ease. I would still need to exercise caution in what I said and hoped my client would as well.

"Lisa, we're not going to talk a whole lot here because we don't know who may be listening. You understand?"

"I think so. But what is happening here? I don't understand what's *happening!*"

Her voice had risen progressively through the sentence until she was screaming the last word. This was an emotional speaking pattern she had used several times on the phone with me when I was handling only her foreclosure. Now the stakes were higher and I had to draw the line.

"None of that, Lisa," I said firmly. "You do not scream at me. You understand? If I'm going to represent you on this you do not scream at me."

"Okay, sorry, but they're saying I did something I didn't do."

"I know and we're going to fight it. But no screaming."

Because they had pulled her back before the booking process had begun, Lisa was still in her own clothes. She was wearing a white T-shirt with a flower pattern on the front. I saw no blood on it or anywhere else. Her face was streaked with tears and her brown curly hair was unkempt. She was a small woman and seemed even more so in the harsh light of the room.

"I need to ask you some questions," I said. "Where were you when the police found you?"

"I was home. *Why are they doing this to me?*"

"Lisa, listen to me. You have to calm down and let me ask the questions. This is very important."

"But what's going on? No one tells me anything. They said I was under arrest for murdering Mitchell Bondurant. When? How? I didn't go near that man. I didn't break the TRO."

I realized that it would have been better if I had viewed Kurlen's DVD before speaking with her. But it was par for the course to come into a case at a disadvantage.

"Lisa, you are indeed under arrest for the murder of Mitchell Bondurant. Detective Kurlen — he's the older one — told me that you made admissions to them in re—"

She shrieked and brought her hands to her face. I saw that she was cuffed at the wrists. A new round of tears started.

"I didn't admit anything! *I didn't do anything!*"

"Calm down, Lisa. That's why I'm here. To defend you. But we don't have a lot of time right now. They're giving me ten minutes and then they're going to book you. I need to—"

"I'm going to jail?"

I nodded reluctantly.

"Well, what about bail?"

"It is very hard to get bail on a murder charge. And even if I could get something set, you don't have the—"

Another piercing wail filled the tiny room. I lost my patience.

"*Lisa! Stop doing that!* Now listen, your life is at stake here, okay? You have to calm down and listen to me. I am your attorney and I will do my best to get you out of here but it's going to take some time. Now listen to my questions and answer them without all the—"

"What about my son? What about Tyler?"

"Someone from my office is making contact with your sister and we will arrange for him to be with her until we can get you out."

I was very careful not to introduce a hard time line for her release. *Until we can get you out.* As far as I was concerned, that might be days, weeks or even years. It might never happen. But I did not need to get specific.

Lisa nodded as if there was some relief in knowing her son would be with her sister.

"What about your husband? You have a contact number for him?"

"No, I don't know where he is and I don't want you contacting him anyway."

"Not even for your son?"

"Especially not for my son. My sister will take care of him."

I nodded and let it go. Now was not the time to ask about her failed marriage.

"Okay, calmly now, let's talk about this morning. I have the disc from the detectives but I want to go over this myself. You said you were home when Detective Kurlen and his partner arrived. What were you doing?"

"I was...I was on the computer. I was sending e-mails."

"Okay, to who?"

"To my friends. To people in FLAG. I was telling them that we were going to meet tomorrow at the courthouse at ten and to bring the placards."

"Okay, and when the detectives showed up, what exactly did they say?"

"The man did all the talking. He —"

"Kurlen."

"Yes. They came in and he asked me some things. Then he asked if I wouldn't mind coming to the station to answer questions. I said about what and he said Mitch Bondurant. He didn't say anything about him being dead or killed. So I said yes. I thought maybe they were finally investigating him. I didn't know they were investigating me."

"Well, did he tell you that you had certain rights not to speak to him and to contact a lawyer?"

"Yes, like on TV. He told me my rights."

"When exactly?"

"When we were already here, when he said I was under arrest."

"Did you ride with him here?"

"Yes."

"And did you speak in the car?"

"No, he was on his cell phone almost the whole time. I heard him say things like 'I have her with me' and like that."

"Were you handcuffed?"

"In the car? No."

Smart Kurlen. He risked riding in the car with an uncuffed murder suspect in order to keep her suspicions down and to lull her into agreeing to speak with him. You can't build a better mousetrap than that. It would also allow the prosecution to argue that Lisa was not under arrest yet and therefore her statements were voluntary.

"So you were brought here and you agreed to talk to him?"

"Yes. I had no idea they were going to arrest me. I thought I was helping them with a case."

"But Kurlen didn't say what the case was."

"No, never. Not until he said I was under arrest and that I could make a call. And that's when they handcuffed me, too."

Kurlen had used some of the oldest tricks in the book but they were still in the book because they worked. I had to watch the DVD to know exactly what Lisa had admitted to, if anything. Asking her about it while she was upset was not the best use of my limited time. As if to underscore this, there was a sudden and sharp knock on the door followed by a muffled voice saying I had two minutes.

"Okay, I am going to go to work on this, Lisa. I need you to sign a couple of documents first, though. This first one is a new contract that covers criminal defense."

I slid the one-page document over to her and put a pen on top of it. She started to scan it.

"All these fees," she said. "A hundred fifty thousand dollars for a trial? I can't pay you this. I don't have it."

"That's a standard fee and that's only if we go to trial. And as far as what you can pay, that's what these other documents are for. This one gives me your power of attorney, allowing me to solicit book and movie deals, things like that, coming from the case. I have an agent I work with on this stuff. If there's a deal out there he'll get it. The last document puts a lien on any of those funds so that the defense gets paid first."

I knew this case was going to draw attention. The foreclosure epidemic was the country's biggest ongoing financial catastrophe. There could be a book in this, maybe even a film, and I could end up getting paid.

She picked up the pen and signed the documents without reading further. I took them back and put them away.

"Okay, Lisa, what I am about to tell you now is the most important piece of advice in the world. So I want you to listen and then tell me you understand."

"Okay."

"Do not talk about this case with anyone other than me. Do not talk to detectives, jailers, other jail inmates, don't even talk to your sister or son about it. Whenever anyone asks — and believe me, they will — you simply tell them that you cannot talk about your case."

"But I didn't do anything wrong. I'm innocent! It's people who are guilty who don't talk."

I held my finger up to admonish her.

"No, you're wrong, and it sounds to me like you are not taking what I say seriously, Lisa."

"No, I am, I am."

"Then do what I am telling you. Talk to no one. And that includes the phone in the jail. All calls are recorded, Lisa. Don't talk on the phone about your case, even to me."

"Okay, okay. I got it."

"If it makes you feel any better, you can answer all questions by saying 'I am innocent of the charges but on the advice of my attorney I am not going to talk about the case.' Okay, how's that?"

"Good, I guess."

The door opened and Kurlen was standing there. He was giving me the squint of suspicion, which told me it was a good thing I had brought the Paquin jammer with me. I looked back at Lisa.

"Okay, Lisa, it gets bad before it gets good. Hang in there and remember the golden rule. Talk to no one."

I stood up.

"The next time you'll see me will be at first appearance and we'll be able to talk then. Now go with Detective Kurlen."

Four

The following morning Lisa Trammel made her first appearance in Los Angeles Superior Court on charges of first-degree murder. A special circumstances count of lying in wait was added by the district attorney's office, which made her eligible for a sentence of life without parole and even for the death penalty. It was a bargaining chip for the prosecution. I could see the DA wanting this case to go away with a plea agreement before public sympathy swung behind the defendant. What better way to get that result than to hold LWOP or the death penalty over the defendant's head?

The courtroom was crowded to standing room only with members of the media as well as FLAG recruits and sympathizers. Overnight the story had grown exponentially as word spread about the police and prosecution's theory that a home foreclosure may have spawned the murder of a banker. It put a blood-and-guts twist on the nationwide financial plague and that, in turn, packed the house.

Lisa had calmed considerably after almost twenty-four hours in jail. She stood zombie-like in the custody pen awaiting her two-minute hearing. I assured her first that her son was safe in the loving hands of her sister and second that Haller and Associates would do all that was possible to provide her with the best and most rigorous defense. Her immediate concern was in getting out of jail to take care of her son and to assist her legal team.

Though the first-appearance hearing was primarily just an official acknowledgment of the charges and the starting point of the judicial process, there would also be an opportunity to request and argue for bail. I was planning to do just that as my general philosophy was to leave no stone unturned and no issue un-argued. But I was pessimistic about the outcome. By law, bail would be set. But in reality, bail in murder cases was usually set in the millions, thereby making it unattainable for the common man. My client was an unemployed single mother with a house in foreclosure. A seven-figure bail meant Lisa wouldn't be getting out of jail.

Judge Stephen Fluharty pushed the Trammel case to the top of the docket in an effort to accommodate the media. Andrea Freeman, the prosecutor assigned to the case, read the charges and the judge scheduled the arraignment for the following week. Trammel would not enter a plea until then. These routine procedures were dispensed with quickly. Fluharty was about to call a short recess so the media could pack up equipment and leave en masse when I interrupted and made a motion requesting him to set bail for my client. The second reason for doing this was to see how the prosecution responded. Every now and then I got lucky and the prosecutor revealed evidence or strategy while arguing for a high bail amount.

But Freeman was too cagey to make such a slip. She argued that Lisa Trammel was a danger to the community and should continue to be held without bail until further into the proceedings of the case. She noted that the victim of the crime was not the only individual involved in foreclosing on Lisa's place of residence, but only one link in a chain. Other people and institutions in that chain could be endangered if Trammel was set free.

There was no big reveal there. It seemed obvious from the start that the prosecution would use the foreclosure as the motive for the murder of Mitchell Bondurant. Freeman had said just enough to make a convincing argument against bail, but had mentioned little about the murder case she was building. She was good and we had faced each other on cases before. As far as I remembered, I had lost them all.

When it was my turn, I argued that there was no indication, let alone evidence, that Trammel was either a danger to the community or a flight risk. Barring such evidence, the judge could not deny the defendant bail.

Fluharty split his decision right down the middle, giving the defense a victory by ruling that bail should be set, and giving the prosecution a win by setting it at two million dollars. The upshot was that Lisa wasn't going anywhere. She would need two million in collateral or a bail bondsman. A ten percent bond would cost her $200,000 in cash and that was out of the question. She was staying in jail.

The judge finally called for the recess and that gave me a few more minutes with Lisa before she was removed by the courtroom deputies. As the media filed out I quickly admonished her one more time to keep her mouth shut.

"It's even more important now, Lisa, with all of the media on this case. They may try to get to you in the jail — either directly or through other inmates or visitors you think you can trust. So, remember —"

"Talk to no one. I get it."

"Good. Now, I also want you to know that my entire staff is meeting this afternoon to review the case and set some strategies. Can you think of anything you want brought up or discussed? Anything that can help us?"

"I just have a question and it's for you."

"What is it?"

"How come you haven't asked me if I did it?"

I saw one of the courtroom deputies enter the pen and come up behind Lisa, ready to take her back.

"I don't need to ask you, Lisa," I said. "I don't need to know the answer to do my job."

"Then ours is a pitiful system. I am not sure I can have a lawyer defending me who doesn't believe in me."

"Well, it's certainly your choice and I'm sure there would be a line of lawyers out the door of the courthouse who would love to have this case. But nobody knows the circumstances of this case or the foreclosure like I do, and just because somebody says they believe you, it doesn't mean they really do. With me, you don't get that bullshit, Lisa. With me, it's don't ask, don't tell. And that goes both ways. Don't ask me if I believe you, and I won't tell you."

I paused to see if she wanted to respond. She didn't.

"So are we good? I don't want to be spinning my wheels on this if you're going to be looking for a believer to take my place."

"We're good, I guess."

"All right, then I'll be by to see you tomorrow to discuss the case and what direction we are going to be moving in. I am hoping that my investigator will have a preliminary take on what the evidence is showing by then. He's —"

"Can I ask you a question, Mickey?"

"Of course you can."

"Could you lend me the money for the bail?"

I was not taken aback. I long ago lost track of how many clients hit me up for bail money. This might have been the highest amount so far, but I doubted it would be the last time I was asked.

"I can't do that, Lisa. Number one, I don't have that kind of money, and number two, it's a conflict of interest for an attorney to provide bail for his own client. So I can't help you there. What I think you need to do is get used to the idea that you are going to be incarcerated at least through your trial. The bail is set at two million and that means you would need at least two hundred thousand just to get a bond. It's a lot of money, Lisa, and if you had it, I'd want half of it to pay for the defense. So either way you'd still be in jail."

I smiled but she didn't see any humor in what I was telling her.

"When you put up a bond like that, do you get it back after the trial?" she asked.

"No, that goes to the bail bondsman to cover his risk because he'd be the one on the hook for the whole two million if you were to flee."

Lisa looked incensed.

"I'm not going to flee! I am going to stay right here and fight this thing. I just want to be with my son. He needs his mother."

"Lisa, I was not referring to you specifically. I was just telling you how bail and bonds work. Anyway, the deputy behind you has been very patient. You need to go with him and I need to get back to work on your defense. We'll talk tomorrow."

I nodded to the deputy and he moved in to take Lisa back to the courthouse lockup. As they went through the steel door off the side of the custody pen Lisa looked back at me with scared eyes. There was no way she could know what lay ahead, that this was only the start of what would be the most harrowing ordeal of her life.

Andrea Freeman had stopped to talk with a fellow prosecutor

and that allowed me to catch up with her as she was leaving the courtroom.

"Do you want to grab a cup of coffee and talk?" I asked as I came up beside her.

"Don't you need to talk to your people?"

"My people?"

"All the people with cameras. They'll be lined up outside the door."

"I'd rather talk to you and we could even discuss media guidelines if you would like."

"I think I can spare a few minutes. You want to go down to the basement or come back with me to the office for some DA coffee?"

"Let's hit the basement. I'd be looking over my shoulder too much in your office."

"Your ex-wife?"

"Her and others, though my ex and I are in a good phase right now."

"Glad to hear it."

"You know Maggie?"

There were at least eighty deputy DAs working out of Van Nuys.

"In passing."

We left the courtroom and stood side by side in front of the assembled media to announce that we would not be commenting on the case at this early stage. As we headed to the elevators at least six reporters, most of them from out of town, shoved business cards into my hand — *New York Times*, CNN, *Dateline*, *Salon*, and the holy grail of them all, *60 Minutes*. In less than twenty-four hours I had gone from scrounging $250-a-month foreclosure cases in South L.A. to being lead defense attorney on a case that threatened to be the signature story of this financial epoch.

And I liked it.

"They're gone," Freeman said once we were on the elevator. "You can wipe the shit-eating grin off your face."

I looked at her and really smiled.

"That obvious, huh?"

"Oh, yeah. All I can say is, enjoy it while you can."

That was a not-so-subtle reminder of what I was facing with this case. Freeman was an up-and-comer in the DA's office and some said she would someday run for the top job herself. The conventional wisdom was to attribute her rise and rep in the prosecutor's office to her skin color and to internal politics. To suggest she got the good cases because she was a minority who was the protégée of another minority. But I knew this was a deadly mistake. Andrea Freeman was damn good at what she did and I had the winless record against her to prove it. When I got the word the night before that she had been assigned the Trammel case, I had felt it like a poke in the ribs. It hurt but there was nothing I could do about it.

In the basement cafeteria we poured cups of coffee from the urns and found a table in a quiet corner. She took the seat that allowed her to see the entrance. It was a law enforcement thing that extended from patrol officers to detectives to prosecutors. Never turn your back on a potential point of attack.

"So...," I said. "Here we are. You're in the position of having to prosecute a potential American hero."

Freeman laughed like I was insane.

"Yeah, right. Last I heard, we don't make heroes out of murderers."

I could think of an infamous case prosecuted locally that might challenge that statement but I let it go.

"Maybe that is overreaching a bit," I said. "Let's just say that I think public sympathy is going to be running high on the defendant's side of the aisle on this one. I think fanning the media flames will only heighten it."

"For now, sure. But as the evidence gets out there and the details become known, I don't think public sympathy is going to be an issue. At least not from my standpoint. But what are you saying, Haller? You want to talk about a plea before the case is even a day old?"

I shook my head.

"No, not at all. I don't want to talk about anything like that. My client says she is innocent. I brought up the sympathy angle because of the attention the case is already getting. I just picked up a card from a producer at *Sixty Minutes*. So I'd like to set up some guidelines and agreements on how we proceed with the media. You just mentioned the evidence and how it gets out there into the public domain. I hope you are talking about evidence presented in court and not selectively fed to the *L.A. Times* or anybody else in the fourth estate."

"Hey, I'd be happy to call it a no-fly zone right now. Nobody talks to the media under any circumstances."

I frowned.

"I'm not ready to go that far yet."

She gave me the knowing nod.

"I didn't think so. So all I'll say then is be careful. Both of us. I for one won't hesitate to go to the judge if I think you're trying to taint the jury pool."

"Then same here."

"Good. Then that's settled for now. What else?"

"When am I going to start seeing some discovery?"

She took a long draw on her coffee before answering.

"You know from prior cases how I work. I'm not into *I'll show you mine if you show me yours.* That's always a one-way street because the defense doesn't show dick. So I like to keep it nice and tight."

"I think we need to come to an accommodation, Counselor."

"Well, when we get a judge you can talk to the judge. But I'm not playing nice with a murderer, no matter who her lawyer is. And just so you know, I already came down hard on your buddy Kurlen for giving you that disc yesterday. That should not have happened and he's lucky I didn't have him removed from the case. Consider it a gift from the prosecution. But it's the only one you'll be getting...Counselor."

It was the answer I was expecting. Freeman was a damn good prosecutor but in my view she didn't play fair. A trial was supposed to be a spirited contesting of facts and evidence. Both sides with equal footing in the law and the rules of the game. But using the rules to hide or withhold facts and evidence was the routine with Freeman. She liked a tilted game. She didn't carry the light. She didn't even see the light.

"Andrea, come on. The cops took my client's computer and all her paperwork. It's her stuff and I need it to even start to build the defense. You can't treat that like discovery."

Freeman scrunched her mouth to the side and posed as though she was actually considering a compromise. I should've seen it for the act it was.

"I'll tell you what," she said. "As soon as we are assigned to a judge, you go in and ask about that. If a judge tells me to turn it over, I'll turn it all over. Otherwise, it's mine and I ain't sharing."

"Thanks a lot."

She smiled.

"You're welcome."

Her response to my request for cooperation and her smiling way of delivering it only served to underline a thought I had growing in the back of my mind since I had gotten word she was on the case. I had to find a way to make Freeman see the light.

Five

Michael Haller and Associates had a full staff meeting that afternoon in the living room of Lorna Taylor's condo in West Hollywood. Attending were Lorna, of course, as well as my investigator, Cisco Wojciechowski — it was his living room, too — and the junior associate of the firm, Jennifer Aronson. I noticed that Aronson looked uncomfortable in the surroundings and I had to admit it was unprofessional. I had rented a temporary office the year before when I was engaged in the Jason Jessup case and it had worked out well. I knew that it would be best to have a real office, instead of two staff members' living room, for the Trammel case. The only problem was it would add another expense I would have to eat until I manufactured fees out of the movie and book rights of the case — if I managed to make that happen. This had made me reluctant to pull the trigger, but seeing Aronson's disappointment made the decision for me.

"Okay, let's start," I said after Lorna had served everybody soda or iced tea. "I know this is not the most professional way to run a law firm and we'll be looking into getting some office space as soon as we can. In the mean—"

"Really?" Lorna said, clearly surprised by this information.

"Yes, I just sort of decided that."

"Oh, well, I'm glad you like my place so much."

"It's not that, Lorna. I've just been thinking lately, you know, with taking on Bullocks here, it's like we've got a real firm now and maybe we

36

should have a legit address. You know, so clients can come in instead of us always going to them."

"Fine with me. As long as I don't have to open shop till ten and I can wear my bedroom slippers to work. I'm kind of used to that."

I could tell I had insulted her. We had been married once for a short time and I knew the signs. But I would have to deal with it later. It was time to put the focus on the Lisa Trammel defense.

"So anyway, let's talk about Lisa Trammel. I had my first sit-down with the prosecutor after first appearance this morning and it didn't go so well. I've done the dance with Andrea Freeman before and she's a give-no-quarter kind of prosecutor. If it's something that can be argued then she's going to argue it. If it's discoverable material that she can sit on until the judge orders her to give it up, then she'll do that, too. In a way, I admire her but not when we're on the same case. The bottom line is that getting discovery out of her is going to be like pulling teeth."

"Well, is there even going to be a trial?" Lorna asked.

"We have to assume so," I answered. "In my brief discussions with our client she has expressed only a desire to fight this thing. She says she didn't do it. So for now that means no plea agreement. We plan on a trial but remain open to other possibilities."

"Wait a minute," Aronson said. "You e-mailed me last night saying you wanted me to look at the video you got of the interrogation. That's discovery. Didn't that come from the prosecution?"

Aronson was a petite twenty-five-year-old with short hair that was carefully made to look stylishly unkempt. She wore retro-style glasses that partially hid brilliant green eyes. She came from a law school that didn't turn any heads in the silk-stocking firms downtown but when I interviewed her I sensed that she had a drive that was fueled by negative motivation. She was out to prove those silk-stocking assholes wrong. I hired her on the spot.

"The video disc came from the lead detective, and the prosecutor wasn't happy about it at all. So don't be expecting anything else. We want something, we go to the judge or we go out and get it ourselves. Which brings us to Cisco. Tell us what you've got so far, Big Man."

All eyes turned to my investigator, who sat on a leather swivel chair next to a fireplace that was filled with potted plants. He was dressed up today, meaning he had sleeves on his T-shirt. Still, the shirt did little to hide the tats and the gun show. His bulging biceps made him look more like a strip club bouncer than a seasoned investigator with a lot of finesse in his kit.

It had taken me a long time to get over the idea of this giant beef dish being my replacement with Lorna. But I had worked through it and, besides, I knew of no better defense investigator. Early in his life, when he was cruising with the Road Saints, the cops had tried to set him up twice on drug raps. It built a lasting distrust of the police in him. Most people give the police the benefit of the doubt. Cisco didn't and that made him very good at what he did.

"Okay, I am going to break this into two reports," he said. "The crime scene and the client's house, which was searched by police for several hours yesterday. First the crime scene."

Without using any notes, he proceeded to detail all of his findings from WestLand National's headquarters. Mitchell Bondurant had been surprised by his attacker while getting out of his car to report for work. He was struck at least twice on the head with an unknown object. Most likely attacked from behind. There were no defensive wounds on his hands or arms, indicating he was incapacitated almost immediately. A spilled cup of Joe's Joe coffee was found on the ground next to him along with his briefcase, which was open, beside the back tire of his car.

"So what about the gunshots somebody said they heard?" I asked.

Cisco shrugged.

"I think they're looking at that as car backfire."

"Two backfires?"

"Or one and an echo. Either way, there was no gunplay involved."

He went back to his report. The autopsy results were not yet in but Cisco was betting on blunt-force trauma being the cause of death. At the moment, time of death was listed as between 8:30 and 8:50 A.M. There was a receipt in Bondurant's pocket from a Joe's Joe four blocks away. It was time-stamped 8:21 A.M. and investigators figured the fastest he could have gotten from the coffee shop to his parking space in the bank garage was nine minutes. The 911 call from the bank employee who found his body was logged at 8:52 A.M.

So estimated time of death had an approximate twenty-minute

swing. It wasn't a lot of time but when it came to things like documenting a defendant's movements for the purpose of alibi, it was an eternity.

Police interviewed everyone who was parking on the same level as
well as all of those who worked in Bondurant's department at the bank.
Lisa Trammel's name came up early and often during these interviews.
She was named as an individual Bondurant had reportedly felt threatened by. His department kept a threat-assessment file and she was number one on the list. As we all knew, she had been served with a restraining
order keeping her away from the bank.

The police hit the jackpot when one bank employee reported seeing
Lisa Trammel walking away from the bank on Ventura Boulevard
within minutes of the murder.

"Who is this witness?" I asked, zeroing in on the most damaging
part of his report.

"Her name is Margo Schafer. She's a bank teller. According to my
sources she's never had contact with Trammel. She works in the bank,
not the loan operation. But Trammel's photo was circulated to staff after
they got the TRO against her. Everybody was told to be aware of her and
to report it if she was seen. So she recognized her."

"And was this on bank property?"

"No, it was on the sidewalk a half block away. She was supposedly
walking east on Ventura, away from the bank."

"Do we know anything about this Margo Schafer?"

"Not now, but we will. I'm on it."

I nodded. It usually wasn't necessary for me to tell Cisco what to
investigate. He moved on to the second part of his report, the search of
Lisa Trammel's house. This time he referred to a document he pulled
from a file.

"Lisa Trammel volunteered — their word — to accompany detectives to Van Nuys Division about two hours after the murder. They're
claiming she was not placed under arrest until the conclusion of an interview at the station. Using statements made during that interview as well
as the eyewitness account of Margo Schafer, the detectives obtained a
search warrant for Trammel's home. They spent about six hours there
looking for evidence, including a possible murder weapon as well as digital and hard-copy documentation of a plan to kill Bondurant."

Search warrants designate a specific window of time during which the search must take place. Afterward, police must in a timely manner file a document with the court called a search-warrant return that lists exactly what was seized. It is then the judge's responsibility to review the seizure to make sure that the police acted within the parameters of the warrant. Cisco said the detectives Kurlen and Longstreth had filed the return that morning and he had obtained a copy through the clerk's office. It was a key part of the case at this point because the police and prosecution weren't sharing information with the defense. Andrea Freeman had shut that down. But the search-warrant request and return were public records. Freeman could not stop their release. And they gave me the best look at how the state was building its case.

"Give us the highlights," I said. "But then I want a copy of the whole thing."

"This is your copy here," Cisco said. "As far as —"

"May I please get a copy, too?" Aronson asked.

Cisco looked at me for permission. It was awkward. He was silently asking if she was truly a member of the team and not just a client handholder I had brought in from the department-store law school.

"Absolutely," I said.

"You got it," Cisco said. "Now, the highlights. As far as the weapon goes, it looks like the detectives went into the garage and took every handheld tool they could find off the workbench."

"So they don't know what the murder weapon was," I said.

"No autopsy yet," Cisco said. "They'll have to make wound comparisons. That will take time but I've got the medical examiner's office wired. When they know it, I'll know it."

"Okay, what else?"

"They took her laptop, a three-year-old MacBook Pro, and various and sundry documents relating to the foreclosure of the home on Melba. This is where they might piss the judge off. They do not specifically list the documents, probably because there were too many. They mention just three files. They are marked FLAG, FORECLOSURE ONE and FORECLOSURE TWO."

I assumed that any foreclosure documents Lisa had at home were documents I had given her. The FLAG file as well as the computer could hold names of the members of Lisa's group, an indication that the police were possibly looking for co-conspirators.

"Okay, what else?"

"They took her cell phone, one pair of shoes from the garage and here's the kicker. They seized a personal journal. They don't describe it beyond that or say what was in it. But I'm thinking that if it's got her ranting against the bank or the victim in particular, then we'll have a problem."

"I'll ask her about it when I visit her tomorrow," I said. "Back up for a second. The cell phone. Was it specifically stated in the warrant application that they wanted her phone? Are they suggesting a conspiracy, that she had help killing Bondurant?"

"No, nothing about co-conspirators in the application. They're probably just making sure they cover all possibilities."

I nodded. Seeing the moves the investigators were making against my client was very helpful.

"They've probably filed a separate search warrant seeking call records from her service provider," I said.

"I'll check into it," Cisco said.

"Okay, anything else on the warrant?"

"The shoes. The return lists one pair of shoes taken from the garage. Doesn't say why, just says that they were gardening shoes. They were a woman's shoes."

"No other shoes taken?"

"Not that they're taking credit for. Just these."

"You've got nothing about shoe prints at the crime scene, right?"

"I've got nothing on that."

"Okay."

I was sure the reason for the seizure of the shoes would become apparent soon enough. On a search warrant police throw as wide a net as the court allows. It's better to seize as much as possible than leave anything behind. Sometimes that means seizing items that ultimately have nothing to do with the case.

"By the way," Cisco said, "if you get the chance, the application makes interesting reading if you can get past the misspellings and grammar issues. They used her interview extensively but we already saw all of that on the disc Kurlen gave you."

"Yes, her so-called admissions and his exaggerations."

I stood up and started pacing in the middle of the room. Lorna also got up and took the search warrant from Cisco so she could make a copy. She disappeared into a nearby den where she had her office and where there was a copier.

I waited for her to come back and hand a copy of the documents to Aronson before I began.

"Okay, this is how we are going to do this. First thing is we need to get moving on getting a real office. Some place close to the Van Nuys courthouse where we can set up our command post."

"You want me on that, Mick?" Lorna asked.

"Yes, I do."

"I'll make sure there's parking and good food nearby."

"It would be nice to be able to just walk to court."

"You got it. Short-term lease?"

I paused. I liked working out of the backseat of the Lincoln. It had a freedom to it that was conducive to my thought processes.

"We'll take it for a year. See what happens."

I looked at Aronson next. She had her head down and was writing notes on a legal pad.

"Bullocks, I need you to hand-hold our current clients and respond with the basics to new callers. The radio ads run through the month so we can expect no downturn in business. I also need you to help out on Trammel."

She looked up at me and her eyes brightened at the prospect of being on a murder case less than a year after being admitted to the bar.

"Don't get too excited," I said. "I'm not giving you second chair just yet. You'll be doing a lot of the grunt work. How were you on probable cause back at the department-store school?"

"I was the best in my class."

"Of course you were. Well, you see that document in your hand? I want you to take that search warrant and break it down and tear it apart. We're looking for omissions and misrepresentations, anything that can be used in a motion to suppress. I want all evidence taken from Lisa Trammel's house thrown out."

Aronson visibly gulped. This was because I was issuing a tall order.

And it was more than grunt work because the task would probably mean a lot of effort for little return. It was rare that evidence was kicked wholesale from a case. I was simply covering all the bases and using Aronson on one of them. She was smart enough to see that and it was one reason I had hired her.

"Remember, you're working on a murder case," I said. "How many of your classmates can say they've done that yet?"

"Probably none."

"Damn right. So next I want you to take the disc of Lisa's police interview and do the same thing. Look for any false move by the cops, anything we can use to get that knocked out as well. I think there might be something here in light of the Supreme Court's ruling last year. Are you familiar with it?"

"Uh...this is my first criminal case."

"Then get familiar with it. Kurlen went out of his way to make it look like she came in for a voluntary interview. But if we can show he had her in his control, cuffs or not, we can make a case for her being under arrest from the start. We do that and everything she said before Miranda goes bye-bye."

"Okay."

Aronson didn't look up from her writing.

"Do you understand your assignments?"

"Yes."

"Good, then go to it, but don't forget about the rest of the clients. They're paying the bills around here. For now."

I turned back to Lorna.

"Which reminds me, Lorna, I need you to make contact with Joel Gotler and get something rolling on this story. This whole thing might go away if there's a plea agreement, so let's try to get a deal now. Tell him we're willing to go low on the back end for some decent up-front cash. We need to fund the defense."

Gotler was the Hollywood agent who represented me. I used him whenever Hollywood came calling. This time we were going to go calling on Hollywood and proactively try to get a deal.

"Sell him on it," I told Lorna. "I've got a business card in the car from a producer at *Sixty Minutes*. That's how big this is getting."

"I'll call Joel," she said. "I know what to say."

I stopped pacing to consider what was left and what my role was going to be. I looked at Cisco.

"You want me on the witness?" he asked.

"That's right. And the victim, too. I want the full picture on both of them."

My order was punctuated by a sharp buzzing sound from an intercom speaker on the wall next to the kitchen door.

"Sorry, that's the front gate," Lorna said.

She made no move to go to the intercom.

"You want to answer it?" I asked.

"No, I'm not expecting anyone and all the delivery guys know the combination. It's probably a solicitor. They walk this neighborhood like zombies."

"Okay," I said, "then let's move on. The next thing we need to be thinking about is the alternate killer."

That drew everyone's undivided attention.

"We need a setup man," I said. "If we take this thing to trial it's not going to be good enough to just potshot the state's case. We are going to need an aggressive defense. We have to point the jury in a direction away from Lisa. To do that, we need an alternate theory."

I was aware of Aronson watching me as I spoke. I felt like a teacher in law school.

"What we need is a hypothesis of innocence. If we build that, we win the case."

The gate buzzer went off again. It was then followed by two more long and insistent buzzes.

"What the hell?" Lorna said.

Annoyed, she got up and walked to the intercom. She pushed the communication button.

"Yes, who is it?"

"Is this the law offices of Mickey Haller?"

It was a woman's voice and it sounded familiar but I couldn't immediately place it. The speaker was tinny and the volume turned low. Lorna looked back at us and shook her head as though she was confused. Her address was not on any of our advertising. How did this person get to the front gate?

"Yes, but it is by appointment only," Lorna responded. "I can give you the number to call if you want to set up a consultation with Mr. Haller."

"Please! I need to speak to him now. This is Lisa Trammel and I'm already a client. I need to speak with him as soon as possible."

I stared at the intercom speaker as though I believed it to be a direct pipeline to the Van Nuys women's jail — where Lisa was supposed to be. Then I looked at Lorna.

"I guess you'd better open the gate."

Six

L isa Trammel was not alone. When Lorna answered her front door my client walked through in the company of a man I recognized as having been in court during Lisa's first appearance. He had been in the front row of the gallery and stood out to me because he didn't look like a lawyer or journalist. He looked Hollywood. And not the glitzy, confident Hollywood. The other one. The Hollywood on the make. Either a toupee or amateur dye job on the hair, requisite matching fringe on the chin, wattled throat... he looked like a sixty-year-old trying without a lot of success to pass for forty. He wore a black leather sport coat over a maroon turtleneck. A gold chain with a peace sign on it hung from his neck. Whoever he was, I had to suspect he was the reason Lisa was walking free.

"Well, you either escaped from Van Nuys jail or you made bail," I said. "I'm thinking that somehow, someway, it's the latter."

"Smart man," Lisa said. "Everyone, this is Herbert Dahl, my friend and benefactor."

"That's D-A-H-L," said the smiling benefactor.

"Benefactor?" I asked. "Does that mean you put up Lisa's bail?"

"A bond, actually," Dahl said.

"Who did you use?"

"A guy named Valenzuela. His place is right by the jail. Very convenient and he said he knew you."

"Right."

46

I paused for a moment, wondering how to proceed, and Lisa filled in the space.

"Herb is a true hero, rescuing me from that horrible place," she said. "Now I'm out and free to help our team fight these false charges."

Lisa had worked previously with Aronson but not directly with Lorna or Cisco. She stepped over and put her hand out to them, introducing herself and shaking hands as if this was all part of a routine day and it was time to get down to business. Cisco glanced over at me and gave me a look that said *What the hell is this?* I shrugged. I didn't know.

Lisa had never mentioned Herb Dahl to me, a dear enough friend and "benefactor" that he was willing to drop 200K on a bond. This, and the fact that she hadn't tapped his largesse to pay for her defense, did not surprise me. Her barging in all bluster and business, ready to be part of the team, didn't either. I believed that with strangers Lisa was very skilled at keeping her personal and emotional issues beneath the surface. She could charm the stripes off a tiger and I wondered if Herb Dahl knew what he was getting into. I assumed he was working an angle, but he might not understand that he was being worked as well.

"Lisa," I said, "can we step back here into Lorna's office and speak privately for a moment?"

"I think Herb should hear whatever it is you have to say. He's going to be documenting the case."

"Well, he's not going to document our conversations because communications between you and your attorney are private and privileged. He can be compelled to testify in court about anything he hears or sees."

"Oh...well, isn't there a way of deputizing him or something to make him part of the legal team?"

"Lisa, just come back here for a few minutes."

I pointed toward the den and Lisa finally started moving in that direction.

"Lorna, why don't you get Mr. Dahl something to drink?"

I followed Lisa into the den and closed the door. There were two desks. One for Lorna and one for Cisco. I pulled a side chair over in front of Lorna's and told Lisa to sit down. I then went behind the desk and sat down to face her.

"This is a strange law office," she said. "It feels like somebody's home or something."

"It's temporary. Let's talk about your hero out there, Lisa. How long have you known him?"

"Just a couple months or so."

"How did you meet him?"

"On the courthouse steps. He came to one of the FLAG protests. He said he was interested in us from a filmmaker's perspective."

"Really? So he's a filmmaker? Where's his camera?"

"Well, he actually puts things together. He's very successful. He does, like, book deals and movies. He's going to handle all of that. This case is going to get massive attention, Mickey. At the jail they told me I had interview requests from thirty-six reporters. Of course they didn't let me speak to them, only Herb."

"Herb got to you in the jail, did he? He must be relentless."

"He said that when he sees a story he stops at nothing. Remember that little girl who lived for a week on the side of the mountain with her dead father after he crashed off the road? He got her a TV movie."

"That's impressive."

"I know. He's very successful."

"Yes, you said that. So did you make some sort of agreement with him?"

"Yes. He'll put all the deals together and we split everything fifty-fifty after his expenses and he gets the bail money back. I mean, that's only fair. But he's talking about a lot of money. I might be able to save my house, Mickey!"

"Did you sign something? A contract or any sort of agreement?"

"Oh, yes, it's all legal and binding. He has to give me my share."

"You know that because you showed it to your lawyer?"

"Uh...no, but Herb said it was standard boilerplate. You know, legal mumbo-jumbo. But I read it."

Sure she did. Just like when she signed the contracts with me.

"Can I see the contract, Lisa?"

"Herb kept it. You can ask him."

"I will. Now did you happen to tell him about our agreements?"

"Our agreements?"

"Yes, you signed contracts with me yesterday at the police station, remember? One was for me to represent you criminally and the others granted me power of attorney to represent you and negotiate any sale of story rights so that we can fund your defense. You remember that you signed a lien?"

She didn't answer.

"Did you see I have three people out there, Lisa? We're all working on your case. And you haven't paid us a penny so far. So that means I have to come up with all their salaries, all their expenses. Every week. That's why in the agreements you signed yesterday you were giving me the authority to make book and film deals."

"Oh...I didn't read that part."

"Let me ask you something. Which is more important to you, Lisa, that you have the best defense possible and try to defy the odds and win this case, or that you have a book or movie deal?"

Lisa put a pouting look on her face, and then promptly deflected the question.

"But you don't understand. I'm innocent. I didn't—"

"No, you don't understand. Whether you're innocent or not has nothing to do with this equation. It's what we can prove or disprove in court. And when I say 'we' I really mean 'me,' Lisa. *Me.* I'm your hero, not Herb Dahl out there in the leather jacket and Hollywood piece sign. And I mean that as in piece of the pie."

She paused for a long moment before responding.

"I can't, Mickey. He just bailed me out. It cost him two hundred thousand dollars. He has to make that back."

"While your defense team goes hungry."

"No, you're going to get paid, Mickey. I promise. I get half of everything. I'll pay you."

"After he gets his two hundred grand back, plus expenses. Expenses that could be anything, it sounds like."

"He said he got a half a million for one of Michael Jackson's doctors. And that was just for a tabloid story. We might get a movie!"

I was on the verge of losing it with her. Lorna had a stress-release squeeze toy on the desk. It was a small judge's gavel, a sample of a give-away she was considering for marketing and promotional purposes. The name and number of the firm could be printed on the side. I grabbed it and squeezed hard on the barrel, thinking of it as Herb Dahl's windpipe. After a few moments the anger eased. The thing actually worked. I made a mental note to tell Lorna to go ahead with the purchase. We'd give them out at bail bond offices and street fairs.

"Okay," I said. "We'll talk about this later. We're going to go back out there now. You are still going to send Herb home because we are going to talk about your case and we do not do that in front of people who are not in the circle of privilege. Later, you are going to call him and tell him he is not to make any deal or move without my approval. Do you understand, Lisa?"

"Yes."

She sounded chastised and meek.

"Do you want me to tell him to leave or do you want to handle it?"

"Can you handle it, Mickey?"

"No problem. I think we're done here."

We stepped back into the living room and caught Dahl as he was finishing a story.

"...and that was before he made *Titanic*!"

He laughed at the kicker but the others in the room failed to show the same sense of Hollywood humor.

"Okay, Herb, we're going to get back to work on the case and we need to talk with Lisa," I said. "I'm going to walk you out now."

"But how will she get home?"

"I have a driver. We can handle that."

He hesitated and looked to Lisa to save him.

"It's okay, Herb," she said. "We need to talk about the case. I'll call you as soon as I get home."

"Promise?"

"Promise."

"Mick, I can walk him out," Lorna offered.

"No, that's okay. I have to go to the car anyway."

Everyone said goodbye to the man with the peace sign, and Dahl and I left the condo. Each unit in the building had an exterior exit. We walked down a pathway to the front gate on Kings Road. I saw a delivery of phone books underneath the mailbox and used one stack to prop the gate open so I could get back in.

We walked out to my car, which was parked against a red curb in front. Rojas was leaning on the front fender, smoking a cigarette. I had left my remote in the cup holder, so I called to him.

"Rojas, the trunk."

He pulled his keys and popped the rear lid. I told Dahl there was something I wanted to give him and he followed me over.

"You're not going to stuff me in there, are you?"

"Not quite, Herb. I just want to give you something."

We went behind the car and I pushed the trunk all the way open.

"Jeez, you got it all set up back here," he said when he saw the file boxes.

I didn't respond. I grabbed the contracts file and pulled out the agreements Lisa had signed the day before. I moved around the car and copied it on the multipurpose machine on the front seat. I handed the copies to Dahl and kept the originals.

"There, read that stuff when you have a few minutes."

"What is it?"

"It is my representation contract with Lisa. Standard boilerplate. There's also a power of attorney and a lien on any and all income derived from her case. You'll notice that she signed and dated them all yesterday. That means they supersede your contract, Herb. Check the small print. It gives me control of all story rights — books, movies, TV, everything."

I saw his eyes harden.

"Wait just a —"

"No, Herb, you wait a minute. I know you just shelled out two hundred big ones on the bond, plus whatever you paid to get to her in the jail. I get it, you've got a huge investment riding on this. I'll see that you get it back. Eventually. But you're in second position here, buddy. Accept it and step the fuck back. You make no moves or deals without talking to me first."

I tapped the contract he was staring at.

"You don't listen to me and you're going to need a lawyer. A good one. I'll tie you up for two years and you won't ever see a dime of that two hundred back."

I slammed the car door to punctuate the point.

"Have a nice day."

I left him there and went to the trunk to return the originals to the file. When I closed the lid I noticed that I could still see the shadow of the graffiti. The spray paint had been removed but it had permanently marred the gloss of the car's finish. The Florencia 13 still had its mark on me. I looked down at the license plate on the bumper.

IWALKEM

That was going to be easier said than done this time. I passed by Dahl, who was still standing on the sidewalk looking at the contracts. Back at the condo gate, I picked a phone book off the stack that was propping it open. I thumbed the corner back on a random page. My ad was there. My smiling face on the corner.

SAVE YOUR HOME!
DON'T LET THEM FORECLOSE WITHOUT A FIGHT
Michael Haller & Associates, Attorneys-at-Law
CALL:
323-988-0761
OR VISIT:
www.stopfinancialruin.com
Se Habla Español

I checked a few other pages to make sure the ad was on every page, which I had paid for, and then dropped the book back onto the stack. I wasn't even sure who still used phone books, but my message was there just in case.

The others were waiting silently for me when I got back to the condo. Lisa's arrival with her benefactor had put an awkward spin on things. I tried to get the meeting restarted in a way that would promote team unity.

"Okay, so everybody's met everybody. Lisa, we were in the middle of discussions about how we are going to proceed and what we need to know as we go forward. We didn't have the advantage of having you here because, frankly, I was pretty sure you weren't going to be getting out of jail until we got the not-guilty verdict at the end. But now you're here and I certainly want to include you in our strategies. Do you have anything you want to say to the group?"

I felt like I was leading a group therapy session at The Oaks. But Lisa lit up at the chance to hold the floor.

"Yes, I first wanted to say that I am very grateful for all of your efforts on my behalf. I know that in the law things like guilt and innocence don't really matter. It's what you can prove. I understand that but I thought it might be good for you to hear it, even if it is only this one time. I am innocent of these charges. I did not kill Mr. Bondurant. I hope that you believe me and that at trial we prove it. I have a little boy and he badly needs to be with his mother."

No one spoke but everybody nodded somberly.

"Okay," I said, "before your arrival we were going through the division of labor. Who is in charge of what, who needs to do what, that sort of thing. I'd like to include you in the assignments as well."

"Whatever I can do."

She was sitting bolt upright on the edge of her chair.

"The police spent several hours in your house after your arrest. They searched it top to bottom and, subject to the authority the search warrant gave them, they took several items that might be evidence in the case. We have a list, which you are welcome to look at. Included are your laptop and three files marked FLAG and FORECLOSURE ONE and TWO. This is where you come in. The minute we are assigned a courtroom and a judge, we will file a motion asking to be immediately allowed to examine the laptop and the files, but until then I need you to list as best you can what was in the files and on the computer. In other words, Lisa, what is in these documents that would make the cops seize them? Do you understand?"

"Of course, and yes, I can do this. I'll start on it tonight."

"Thank you. There is one other thing I want to ask you about. You see, if this thing goes to trial, then I don't want any loose ends. I don't want anybody showing up out of the woodwork or —"

"Why do you say *if*?"

"Excuse me?"

"You said if. If this thing goes to trial. There are no ifs."

"Sorry. Slip of the tongue. But just so you know, a good attorney will always listen to an offer from the prosecution. Because many times these negotiations allow you a sneak peek into the state's case. So if I tell you that I am talking to the prosecution about a deal, remember that I have an ulterior motive, okay?"

"Okay, but I am telling you now, I won't plead guilty to anything I haven't done. There's a killer out there walking free while they try to do this to me. Last night I couldn't sleep in that terrible place. I kept thinking about my son...I could never face him if I pleaded guilty to something I'm not guilty of."

I thought she was about to turn on the faucet but she held back.

"I understand," I said softly. "Now, Lisa, this other thing I want to talk about is your husband."

"Why?"

I immediately saw the warning flags go up. We were crossing into difficult terrain.

"He's a loose end. When was the last time you heard from him? Is he going to show up and cause us a problem? Could he testify about you, about any prior acts of retribution or revenge? We need to know what is out there, Lisa. Whether it ever materializes doesn't matter. If there is a threat, I need to know about it."

"I thought a spouse could not testify against a partner."

"There is a privilege that you get to invoke but it can be a gray area, especially with you two no longer living together. So I want to tie up the loose end. Do you have any idea where your husband is at this time?"

I wasn't being fully accurate on the law but I needed to get to the husband to further understand the dynamic of their marriage and how it might or might not play into the defense. Estranged spouses were wild cards. You might be able to prevent them from testifying against your client but that didn't mean you could keep them from cooperating with the state outside the courtroom.

"No, none," she answered. "But I assume he will show up sooner or later."

"Why?"

Lisa turned her palms up as if to show the answer was easy.

"There's money to be made. If he is anywhere near a TV or a newspaper and he gets wind of what's going on, he'll show up. You can count on it."

It seemed like an odd answer, as though there was a history of her husband being a money grubber, when I knew that wherever he was, he was spending very little of it.

"You told me he maxed out your credit card in Mexico."

"That's right. Rosarito Beach. He put forty-four hundred on the Visa and exceeded the limit. I had to cancel it and that was the only card we had left. But I didn't realize that by canceling it I would lose the ability to track him. So the answer is, I don't know where he is now."

Cisco cleared his throat and entered the interview.

"What about contact? Any phone calls, e-mails, texts?"

"There were a few e-mails at first. Then nothing until he called on our son's birthday. That was six weeks ago."

"Did your son ask him where he was?"

Lisa hesitated and then said no. She wasn't a good liar. I could tell there was something more there.

"What is it, Lisa?" I asked.

She paused and then relented.

"You'll all think I'm a terrible mother but I didn't let him talk to Tyler. We got into an argument and I just...hung up on him. Later I felt bad but I couldn't call back because the number had been blocked."

"But he does have a cell phone?" I asked.

"No. He did but that number's been out of service for a while. He didn't call on his phone. He either borrowed a phone or got a new number, which he hasn't given me."

"Could've been a throwaway," Cisco said. "They sell them in every convenience store."

I nodded. The story of marital disintegration left everyone somber. Finally, I spoke up.

"Lisa, if he makes new contact, you let me know right away."

"I will."

I looked from her to my investigator. We locked eyes and in the silent transmission I told him to check out everything he could about Lisa's wandering husband. I didn't want him popping up in the middle of trial.

Cisco gave me the nod. He was on it.

"A couple other things, Lisa, and we'll have enough to get started."

"Okay."

"When the police searched your house yesterday they took some other things we haven't talked about. One was described as a journal. Do you know what this was?"

"Yes, I was writing a book. A book about my journey."

"Your journey?"

"Yes, the journey to finding myself in this cause. The movement. Helping people fight to save their homes."

"Okay, so it was like a diary of the protests and things like that?"

"That's right."

"Do you remember if you ever put Mitchell Bondurant's name in the journal?"

She looked down as she searched her memory.

"I don't think so. But I may have mentioned him. You know, said that he was the man behind everything."

"Nothing about hurting him?"

"No, nothing like that. And I didn't hurt him! I didn't do this!"

"I'm not asking you that, Lisa. I am trying to figure out what evidence they have against you. So you're saying that this journal is not going to be a problem for us, correct?"

"That's right. It will be no problem. There's nothing bad in there."

"Okay, good."

I looked at the other members of my staff. The verbal sparring with Lisa had made me forget the next question. Cisco prompted me.

"The witness?"

"Right. Lisa, yesterday morning at the time of the murder, were you anywhere near the WestLand National building in Sherman Oaks?"

She didn't answer right away, which told me we had a problem.

"Lisa?"

"My son goes to school in Sherman Oaks. I take him in the mornings and I drive right by that building."

"That's okay. So you drove by yesterday. What time would that have been?"

"Um, about seven forty-five."

"That was taking him to school, right?"

"Right."

"What about after you drop him off? Do you go back the same way?"

"Yes, most days."

"What about yesterday? We're talking about yesterday. Did you drive back by?"

"I think so, yes."

"You don't remember?"

"No, I did. I take Ventura to Van Nuys and then up to the freeway."

"So did you go back by after dropping off Tyler or did you do something else?"

"I stopped to get coffee and then I went home. I drove by then."

"What time?"

"I'm not sure. I wasn't watching the clock. I think it was around eight thirty."

"Did you ever get out of your car in the vicinity of WestLand National?"

"No, of course not."

"You are sure?"

"Of course I'm sure. I would remember that, don't you think?"

"Okay. Where did you stop to get your coffee?"

"At the Joe's Joe on Ventura by Woodman. I always go there."

I paused. I looked at Cisco and then at Aronson. Cisco had previously reported that Mitchell Bondurant had been carrying a cup of Joe's Joe when attacked. I decided not to ask the obvious question yet about whether Lisa had seen or interacted with Bondurant at the coffee shop. As Lisa's defense attorney I would be bound by what I knew. I could never assist in perjury. If Lisa was to tell me that she had seen Bondurant and even exchanged words with him then I would not be allowed to have her spin a different story at trial if she was to testify.

I had to be careful about soliciting information that would constrain me this early in the case. I knew this was a contradiction. My mission was to know all I could and yet there were things I didn't want to know right now. Sometimes knowing things limits you. Not knowing them gives you more latitude in crafting a defense.

Aronson was staring at me, obviously wondering why I wasn't asking the follow-up question. I just gave her a quick head shake. I would explain my reasons to her later — one more lesson they didn't teach her in law school.

I stood up.

"Lisa, I think that's enough for today. You've given us a lot of information and we'll go to work on it. I'll have my driver take you home now."

Seven

She was fourteen years old and still liked to eat pancakes for dinner. My daughter and I had a booth at the Du-par's in Studio City. Our Wednesday night ritual. I picked her up from her mother's and we stopped for pancakes on the way back to my place. She did her homework and I did my casework. It was my most treasured routine.

The official custody arrangement was that I had Hayley every Wednesday night and then every other weekend. We alternated Christmases and Thanksgivings and I also had her for two weeks in the summer. But that was just the official arrangement. Things had been going well over the past year and often the three of us did things together. On Christmas we had dinner as a family. Sometimes my ex-wife even joined us for pancakes. And that was worth treasuring, too.

But on this night it was just Hayley and me. My casework involved my review of the protocol from the autopsy of Mitchell Bondurant. It included photos of the procedure as well as the body where it was found in the bank's garage. So I was leaning back in the booth and trying to make sure neither Hayley nor anybody else in the restaurant saw the gruesome images. They wouldn't go well with pancakes.

Meantime, Hayley was doing her science homework, studying changes in matter and the elements of combustion.

Cisco had been right. The autopsy concluded that Bondurant had died from brain hemorrhaging caused by multiple points of blunt-force trauma to the head.

Three points exactly. The protocol contained a line drawing of the top of the victim's head. Three points of impact were delineated on the crown in a grouping so tight that all three could have been covered with a teacup.

Seeing this drawing got me excited. I flipped to the front page of the protocol where the body being examined was described. Mitchell Bondurant was described as six foot one and 180 pounds. I did not have Lisa Trammel's dimensions handy so I called the number of the cell phone Cisco had dropped off to her that morning—since her own phone had been seized by the police. It was always a priority to make sure a client could be contacted at any time.

"Lisa, it's Mickey. Real quick, how tall are you?"

"What? Mickey, I'm in the middle of dinner with—"

"Just tell me how tall you are and I'll let you go. Don't lie. What's it say on your driver's license?"

"Um, five three, I think."

"Is that accurate?"

"Yes. What is—"

"Okay, that's all I needed. You can go back to dinner. Have a good night."

"What—"

I hung up and wrote her height on the legal pad I had on the table. Next to it I wrote Bondurant's height. The exciting point was that he had ten inches on his suspected killer and yet the impacts that punctured his skull and killed him were delivered to the crown of his head. This raised what I called a question of physics. The kind of question a jury can puzzle over and decide for themselves. The kind of question a good defense attorney can make something with. This was if-the-glove-doesn't-fit-you-must-acquit stuff. The question here was, how did diminutive Lisa Trammel hit six-foot-one Mitchell Bondurant on the top of the head?

Of course, the answer depended on the dimensions of the weapon as well as a few other things, such as the victim's position. If he was on the ground when attacked then none of this would matter. But it was something to grab on to at the moment. I quickly went to one of the files on the table and pulled out the search-warrant return.

"Who was that you called?" Hayley asked.

"My client. I had to find out how tall she was."

"How come?"

"Because it might have something to do with whether she could do what they're saying she did."

I checked the list of items seized. As Cisco had reported, only one pair of shoes was on it and they were described as gardening shoes taken from the garage. No high heels, no platform sandals or any other footwear. Of course, the detectives conducted the search prior to the autopsy and before they knew its findings. I considered all of this and concluded that gardening shoes probably didn't have much of a heel on them. If they were suggesting the shoes were worn during the killing then Bondurant still probably had ten inches on my client — if he was standing when attacked.

This was good. I underlined the notes on heights three times on my legal pad. But then I also started thinking about the seizure of only one pair of shoes. The search-warrant return did not say why the gardening shoes were taken but the warrant gave the police authority to seize anything that could have been used in the commission of the crime. They had zeroed in on the gardening shoes and I was at a loss to explain why.

"Mom said you have a really big case now."

I looked at my daughter. She rarely talked to me about my work. I believed that this was because at her young age she still saw things as black and white and without any gray areas. People were either good or bad, and I represented the bad ones for a living. So there was nothing to talk about.

"Did she? Yeah, well, it's getting a lot of attention."

"It's the lady who killed the man taking away her house, right? Was that her you just talked to?"

"She's *accused* of killing the man. She hasn't been convicted of anything. But, yes, that was her."

"How come you need to know how tall she is?"

"You really want to know?"

"Uh-huh."

"Well, they're saying she killed a man who was a lot taller than her by hitting him on the top of the head with some kind of a tool or something. So I'm just wondering if she's tall enough to have done it."

"So Andy will have to prove that she was, right?"

"Andy?"

"Mom's friend. She's the prosecutor on your case, Mom said."

"You mean Andrea Freeman? Tall black lady with real short hair?"

"Yeah."

So it was "Andy" now, I thought. Andy who said she knew my ex-wife *only in passing*.

"So she and Mom are pretty good friends? I didn't know that."

"They do yoga and sometimes Andy comes by when I have Gina and they go out. She lives in Sherman Oaks, too."

Gina was the sitter my ex used when I wasn't available or when she didn't want me to know about her social activities. Or when we went out together.

"Well, do me a favor, Hay. Don't tell anybody what we are talking about or what you heard me saying on the phone. It's sort of private stuff and I don't want it getting back to Andy. I probably shouldn't have made that call in front of you."

"Okay, I won't."

"Thanks, sweetie."

I waited to see if she would say more about the case but she went back to the science workbook.

I turned back to the autopsy protocol and the photos of the fatal wounds on Bondurant's head. The medical examiner had shaved the victim's head in the vicinity of the wounds. A ruler had been placed in the photo to give dimension. On the skin the impacts were pinkish and circular. The skin was broken but the blood had been washed away to show the wounds. Two overlapped and the third was only an inch away.

The circular shape of the weapon's impact surface led me to think that Bondurant had been attacked with a hammer. I'm not much of a home fix-it man but I know my way around a toolbox and I knew that the striking surface of many hammers was circular, sometimes ovoid. I was sure this would be confirmed by the coroner's tool-mark expert, but it was always good to be a step ahead and anticipate their moves. I noticed that there was a small V-shaped notch in each of the impact marks and wasn't sure what it meant.

I checked the search-warrant return again and saw that the police had not listed a hammer among the tools seized from Lisa Trammel's garage. This was curious because so many other, less common, tools were seized. Again, it may have been because the search was carried out before the autopsy was conducted and such facts were known. The police took all tools rather than a specific tool. It still left the question, though.

Where was the hammer?

Was there a hammer?

This, of course, was the case's first double-edged sword. The prosecution would hold that the lack of a hammer in a fully stocked workbench was an indication of culpability. The defendant used the hammer to strike and kill the victim, then discarded it to hide her involvement in the crime.

The defense's side of that argument was that the missing hammer was exculpatory. You have no murder weapon, you have no connection to the defendant, you have no case.

On paper, it should be a wash. But not always. Jurors typically leaned toward the prosecution in such questions. Call it the home-field advantage. The prosecution is always the home team.

Still, I made a note to tell Cisco to chase down the hammer as best he could. Talk to Lisa Trammel, see what she knew. Track down her husband, if only to ask if there ever was a hammer and what had happened to it.

The next photos from the autopsy were of the shattered skull itself after the scalp had been pulled back over the cranium. The damage was extensive, the skull having been punctured by all three of the blows and fractured in almost wavelike patterns emanating from the impact areas. The wounds were described as unsurvivable and the photos completely backed this conclusion.

The autopsy listed several other lacerations and abrasions on the body and even a fracture as well as three broken teeth, but the examiner interpreted all of these as injuries sustained when Bondurant fell face forward to the ground during the attack. He was unconscious if not already dead before he hit the garage floor. There were no defensive wounds listed.

Part of the autopsy protocol contained color photocopies of the crime scene photos provided to the examiner by the LAPD. It was not a complete set but just six shots that showed the body's orientation in situ — meaning situated as it had been found. I would've rather had a full set of prints of the actual photographs, but I wouldn't get those until I got a judge to ease the discovery embargo placed on the case by *Andy* Freeman.

The crime scene photos showed Bondurant's body from numerous angles. It was sprawled between two cars in the garage. The driver's side door of a Lexus SUV was open. There was a Joe's Joe coffee cup on the ground and a pool of spilled coffee. Nearby was an open briefcase.

Bondurant was facedown on the ground, the back and top of his head matted with blood. His eyes were open and appeared to be staring at concrete.

In the photos there were evidence markers next to blood drips on the concrete. There was no analysis to determine if this was blood spatter from the attack itself or drippings from the murder weapon.

I found the briefcase to be a curious thing. Why was it open? Had anything been taken? Had the murderer taken the time to rifle through the case after killing Bondurant? If so, this would seem to be a cold and calculated move. The garage was filling with employees coming to work at the bank. To take the time to go through a briefcase while the body of your victim lies nearby seemed like an extreme risk but not the sort of move a killer fueled by emotion and vengeance would make. It was not the move of an amateur.

I wrote a few more notes in regard to these questions and then a final reminder. I would have Cisco find out if there was assigned parking in the garage. Did Bondurant have his name on the wall at the front of the stall? The lying-in-wait tag added to the murder charge indicated the prosecution believed Trammel knew where Bondurant would be, and when. They would have to prove that at trial.

I closed the Trammel files and wrapped a rubber band around them and the legal pad.

"You doing okay?" I asked Hayley.

"Sure."

"Are you almost finished?"

"My food or my homework?"

"Both."

"I'm finished eating but I still have social studies and English. But we can go if you want."

"I still have a few other files to look at. I have court tomorrow."

"For the murder case?"

"No, other cases."

"Like where you're trying to let people stay in their houses?"

"That's right."

"How come there are so many cases like that?"

Out of the mouths of babes.

"Greed, honey. It all comes down to greed on everybody's part."

I looked at her to see if that would suffice but she didn't go back to her homework. She looked at me expecting more, a fourteen-year-old who was interested in what most of the country was not.

"Well, what happens is that it takes a lot of money to buy a house or a condo most of the time. That's why so many people rent their homes instead. Most people who buy a home put down a big chunk of money, but they almost never have enough to buy the whole house, so they go to the bank for a loan. The bank decides if they have enough money and make enough money to pay back the loan, which is called a mortgage. So if everything looks good, they buy the home they want and pay back the mortgage with monthly payments for many years. Does this make sense?"

"You mean like they pay rent to the bank."

"Sort of. But when you rent from a landlord you don't get any ownership. There is supposed to be ownership involved when you have a mortgage. It is your home and they say the American dream is to own your own home."

"Do you own yours?"

"I do. And your mom owns hers."

She nodded but I wasn't so sure we were talking at a level understandable to a fourteen-year-old. She didn't see much of the American dream in her parents having separate mortgages to go with their separate addresses.

"Okay, so a while back they started making it easier to buy a home. And soon practically anybody who walked into a bank or went to see a mortgage broker was being given a loan on a home. There was a lot of fraud and corruption and there were a lot of loans given to people who shouldn't have been given them. Some people lied to get loans and sometimes it was the loan makers who lied. We're talking about millions of loans, Hay, and when you have that much going on, there are not enough people or rules to control it all."

"Was it like nobody made anybody pay?"

"There was some of that but it was mostly that people were taking on more than they could handle. And these loans had interest rates that changed. These rates dictated how much the home owner had to pay each month and they could go up by a lot. Sometimes they had what's called a balloon payment where you have to pay it all back at the end of five years. To make a long and complicated story short, the country's economy went down and the values of the homes went down with it. It became a crisis because millions of people in the country couldn't pay for the houses they bought and they couldn't sell them because they were worth less than what was owed on them. But the banks and other lenders and these investment syndicates that held all the mortgages didn't really care about that. They just wanted their money back. So when people couldn't pay they started taking their houses."

"So those people hire you."

"Some of them do. But there are millions of foreclosures going on. These lenders all want their money back and so some of them do bad things and some of them hire people to do bad things. They lie and cheat and they take away people's houses without doing it fairly or under the law. And that's where I come in."

I looked at her. I had probably lost her already. I pulled over the second stack of files I had on the table and opened the top one. I spoke as I read.

"Okay, now here's one. This family bought a house six years ago and the monthly payment was nine hundred dollars. Two years later when the shit started to hit the—"

"Dad!"

"Sorry. Two years later when things started going wrong in this country their interest rate went up and so did their payment. At the same time, the husband lost his job as a school bus driver because he had an accident. So the husband and wife went to the bank and said, 'Hey, we have a problem. Can we change or restructure our loan so we can still pay for our house?' This is called loan modification and it's pretty much a joke. These people did the right thing, going in like that, but the bank led them on and said, 'Yes, we'll work with you. You keep paying what you can while we go to work on this.' So they paid what they could but it wasn't enough. They waited and waited but they never heard anything from the bank. That is, until they got the notice in the mail that they were being foreclosed on. So it's this kind of stuff that is wrong and I try to do something about it. It's David and Goliath stuff, Hay. The giant financial institutions are running roughshod over people and they don't have too many guys like me standing up for them."

It was during my explanation to my young daughter that I finally realized why I had been drawn to this particular practice of law. Yes, some of my clients were just gaming the system. They were charlatans no better than the banks they were taking on. But some of my clients were the downtrodden and disadvantaged. They were the true under-dogs in society and I wanted to stand for them and keep them in their homes for as long as I possibly could.

Hayley had raised her pencil and was itching to go back to work as soon as I dismissed her. She was polite that way and must have gotten it from her mother.

"Anyway, that's what it's all about. You can go back to work now. You want something else to drink or a dessert?"

"Dad, pancakes are like dessert."

She had braces and had chosen lime green bands. When she spoke my attention was constantly drawn to her teeth.

"Oh, right, yeah. Then what about something else to drink? More milk?"

"No, I'm fine."

"Okay."

I went back to work too and separated the three foreclosure files in front of me. I had been getting so much business off the radio ads that we had been bundling court appearances. That is, trying to schedule together hearings and appearances on all cases that I had before a par-ticular judge. In the morning I had three hearings before Judge Alfred Byrne in the downtown county courthouse. All three were defenses based on claims of wrongful foreclosure and fraud perpetrated by the lender or the loan-servicing agent employed by the lender.

In each of the cases I had stayed foreclosure with my court filings.

My clients were in their homes and not required to make their monthly payments. The other side viewed this as a scam equal in size to the foreclosure epidemic. I was despised by opposing counsel for perpetuating fraud myself and only delaying an inevitable outcome.

That was okay by me. When you come from the criminal defense bar, you are used to being despised.

"Am I too late for pancakes?"

I looked up to see my ex-wife slide into the booth next to our daughter. She landed a kiss on Hayley's cheek before the girl could go on the defensive. She was at that age. I wished Maggie had slid into my side of the booth and planted one on me. But I could wait.

I smiled at her as I started pulling all the files off the table to make room.

"It's never too late for pancakes," I said.

Eight

Lisa Trammel was formally arraigned in Van Nuys the following Tuesday. It was a routine hearing intended to put her plea on record and to start the clock in order to meet the state's speedy-trial requirement. However, because my client was free on bail, we would likely be waiving speedy trial. There was no reason to hurry as long as she was breathing free air. The case would slowly build momentum like a summer storm and begin when the defense was fully prepared.

But the arraignment did serve the purpose of putting Lisa's forthright and emphatic "not guilty" on the court record as well as on video for the gathered media. Though attendance was lower than it was at her first appearance (the national media tends to retreat from the ongoing mundane processes of a case as it passes through the justice system), the local media still showed in force and the fifteen-minute hearing was well documented.

The case had been assigned to Superior Court Judge Dario Morales for arraignment and preliminary hearing. The latter would be a perfunctory rubber-stamping of the charges. Lisa would undoubtedly be held to answer and the case would then be assigned to another judge for the main event, the trial.

Though I had talked to her on the phone almost daily since her arrest, I had not seen Lisa in more than a week. She had declined my invitations to meet in person and now I knew why. She looked like a different woman when she showed up in court. Her hair had been cut into a stylish wave and her face looked both excessively pink and smooth. Whispers in the courtroom hinted that Lisa had had a Botox facial treatment in order to become more visually appealing.

I believed these physical changes, as well as the smart new suit Lisa was wearing, were the work of Herb Dahl. He and Lisa seemed inseparable and Dahl's involvement was becoming more and more troubling. He had begun incessantly referring producers and screenwriters to my office number. This left Lorna constantly deflecting their attempts to secure a piece of the Lisa Trammel story. Quick checks of the Internet Movie Database usually revealed these Herb Dahl referrals to be Hollywood hacks and bottom-feeders of the lowest caliber. It wasn't that we couldn't use a nice big infusion of Hollywood cash to defray our mounting costs, but these were all deal-now-pay-later people and that wouldn't do. Meantime, my own agent was out there trying to sew up a deal with an up-front fee that would cover a few salaries and the rent on an office and still leave enough to pay back Dahl and make him go away.

With almost any court hearing, the most important information and actions are not what ends up on the record. So, too, with Lisa's arraignment. After her plea was routinely put on record and Morales scheduled a status hearing for two weeks later, I told the judge that the defense had a number of motions to submit to the court for consideration. He welcomed them and I stepped forward and handed his clerk five separate motions. I gave Andrea Freeman copies as well.

The first three motions had been prepared by Aronson after her in-depth review of the LAPD's search-warrant application, the video of Detective Kurlen interviewing Lisa Trammel, and the questions regarding Miranda and when Lisa was actually placed under arrest. Aronson had found inconsistencies, procedural errors and exaggerations of fact. She drew up motions to suppress, asking that the taped interview be disallowed in the case and that all evidence gathered from the search of the defendant's home be excluded as well.

The motions were well thought out and cogently written. I was proud of Aronson and pleased with myself for seeing her as a diamond in the rough when her résumé had crossed my desk. But the truth was I knew her motions didn't stand much of a chance. No judge elected to the bench wants to throw out the evidence in a murder case. Not if he wants the voting public to keep him on the bench. So the jurist will look for ways to maintain status quo and get the decisions on evidence before a jury.

Nevertheless, Aronson's motions played an important role in the defense strategy. Because accompanying them were two other motions. One sought to jump-start the discovery process by requesting defense access to all records and internal memoranda pertaining to Lisa Trammel and Mitchell Bondurant held by WestLand Financial. The other was a motion compelling the prosecution to allow the defense to examine Trammel's laptop computer, cell phone and all personal documents seized in the search of her home.

Since Morales would want to act equitably toward both defense and prosecution, my strategy was to push the judge toward a Solomonic solution. Split the baby. Dismiss the motions to suppress but give the defense the access requested in the other two motions.

Of course, both Morales and Freeman had been around the block a few times and would see this strategy coming from a mile away. Still, just because they knew what I was doing didn't mean they could stop it. Besides that, I had a sixth motion in my pocket that I had not yet filed with the court and it was going to be my ace in the hole.

Morales gave Freeman ten days to respond to the motions and adjourned the hearing, quickly moving on to his next case. A good judge always keeps the cases moving. I turned to Lisa and told her to wait for me in the hallway because I was going to speak to the prosecutor. I noticed Dahl waiting for her at the gate. He would be more than happy to escort her out. I decided to deal with him later and went over to the prosecution table. Freeman had her head down and was writing a note on a legal pad.

"Hey, Andy?"

She looked up at me. She had just begun to smile, expecting to see some friend who typically called her Andy. When she saw it was me the smile disappeared in an instant. I placed the sixth motion down on the table in front of her.

"Take a look at that when you have a minute. I'm going to file it tomorrow morning. Didn't want to inundate the court with a blizzard of paper today, you know? Tomorrow morning should be fine but I thought I'd give you a heads-up since it involves you."

"Me? What are you talking about?"

I didn't answer. I left her there and made my way through the gate and out of the courtroom. As I stepped through the double doors I saw my client and Herb Dahl already holding court in front of a deep semi-circle of reporters and cameras. I quickly walked up behind Lisa, took her by the arm and pulled her away while she was in midsentence.

"Th-th-th-that's all, folks!" I said in my best Porky Pig.

Lisa struggled against my pull but I still managed to get her away from the pack and start walking her down the hallway.

"What are you doing?" she protested. "You are embarrassing me!"

"Embarrassing you? Lisa, you are embarrassing yourself with that guy. I told you to drop him. Now, look at you, all done up like you're some kind of movie star. This is a trial, Lisa, not *Entertainment Tonight*."

"I was telling them my story."

I stopped walking when we were far enough away from the crowd not to be overheard.

"Lisa, you can't talk openly to the media like that. It can come back to bite you on the ass."

"What are you talking about? It was a perfect opportunity to give my side of this. I'm being railroaded here and it's time to speak out. I told you, it's guilty people who don't speak."

"The problem is the DA has a media unit and they copy and record every story about you that is printed and aired. Everything you say, they have a copy of it. And if you ever change your story even slightly from one statement to the next then they've got you. They'll crucify you with it in front of a jury. What I'm trying to say is it's not worth the risk, Lisa. You should let me do the talking for you. But if you can't do that and really want to put out your story yourself then we'll prepare and rehearse you and plan it with strategic hits in the media."

"But that's where Herb comes in. He was making sure I didn't—"

"Let me explain it again to you, Lisa. Herb Dahl is not your attorney and does not have your best interests as his priority. He has Herb Dahl's. Okay? I can't seem to get the message through to you. You have to cut him loose. He—"

"No! I can't! I won't! He's the only one who truly cares."

"Oh, that's really breaking my heart, Lisa. If he's the only one who cares about you what's he doing still talking to those people?"

I pointed to the knot of reporters and photographers. Sure enough, Dahl was still holding forth, feeding them whatever they needed.

"What is he saying to them, Lisa? Do you know? Because I sure as shit don't and that's sort of funny because you're the defendant and I'm the defense attorney. Who's he?"

"He can speak for me," Lisa said.

As we watched Dahl pointing his finger to call on reporters, I saw the door to the courtroom we had just left swing open. Andrea Freeman strode out, holding my sixth motion in her hand, her eyes scanning the hallway. At first she zeroed in on the media knot but then she saw it was not me at the center of it. When her radar picked me up, she corrected her course and made a beeline right toward me. A few of the reporters called to her but she sharply waved them off with the document.

"Lisa, go over to one of those benches and sit down and wait for me. And don't talk to any reporters."

"What about—"

"Just do it."

As Lisa walked away Freeman came up on me. She was mad and I could see the fire in her eyes.

"What is this shit, Haller?"

She held up the paper. I maintained a calm demeanor even as she stepped right into my personal space.

"Well," I said, "I think it's pretty obvious what it is. It's a motion to have you dismissed from the case because you have a conflict of interest."

"*I* have a conflict of interest? What conflict?"

"Look, Andy—I can call you Andy, right? I mean my daughter does so I should, too, don't you think?"

"Cut the shit, Haller."

"Sure, I can do that. The conflict that I am objecting to is that you've been discussing this case with my ex-wife and—"

"Who happens to be a prosecutor working in the same office as me."

"That's true but these discussions haven't taken place in the office exclusively. In fact, they've taken place at yoga and in front of my daughter and probably all over the Valley, as far as I know."

"Oh, come on. This is such bullshit."

"Really? Then why did you lie to me?"

"I've never lied. What are you—"

"I asked you if you knew my ex-wife and you said *in passing.* That's not really the truth, is it?"

"I just didn't want to get into it with you."

"So you lied. I didn't mention that in the motion but I could add it before I file it. The judge could decide if it is important."

She blew out her breath in agitated surrender.

"What do you want?"

I looked around. No one could hear us.

"What do I want? I want to show you that I can play it your way, too. You want to be a hard-ass with me, I can be one with you."

"Meaning what, Haller? What's the quid pro quo?"

I nodded. We were getting down to the deal now.

"You know if I file this tomorrow you are history. The judge will err on the side of the defense. He'll avoid anything that might have any chance of getting him reversed. Besides, he knows there are three hundred able-bodied prosecutors in the DA's office. They can just send in a replacement."

I pointed to the gaggle of reporters assembled in the hall, most of them still surrounding Herb Dahl.

"You see all of those reporters and all that attention? All of that will go away. Probably the biggest case of your career and it all goes away. No press conferences, no headlines, no spotlight. It all goes to whoever they send in to take your place."

"First of all I will fight this thing and it is not a given that Judge Morales will fall for your bullshit. I will tell him exactly what you are doing. Trying to DA-shop. Trying to get rid of a prosecutor you are flat-out scared of."

"You can tell him all you like but you'll still have to tell the judge—in open court—how it is that my fourteen-year-old daughter was reciting facts of this case back to me at dinner last week."

"That is bullshit. You should be ashamed of using your—"

"What, are you saying that I'm the liar or my daughter is the liar? Because we can bring her into court, too. I'm not so sure your bosses are going to like the spectacle this will cause—or the headlines. You know, DA grills fourteen-year-old, calls the kid a liar. Kind of tawdry, don't you think?"

Freeman turned her back and took a step to walk away from me but then stopped. I knew I had her. She should walk away from me and the case, but she couldn't. She wanted the case and all that it could bring her.

She turned back to me. She looked at me as though I were not even there, as if I were dead.

"Again, what do you want?"

"I'd rather not file this tomorrow. I'd rather just withdraw the motions I had to make to get my client's property back and to see the WestLand documents. All I want is cooperation. A friendly give-and-take on discovery. I want it to start flowing now, not later. I don't want to go to the judge every time I want something I'm entitled to."

"I could complain to the bar about you."

"Good, we can make cross-complaints. They'll investigate both of us and find that only you acted inappropriately by discussing the case with defense counsel's ex-wife and daughter."

"I didn't discuss it with your daughter. She was just there."

"I'm sure the bar will make that distinction."

I let her twist for a moment. It was her move but she needed one final push.

"Oh, and by the way, if I file the motion tomorrow I'll be sure to drop a dime to the *Times*. Who's their court reporter? Salters? I think she'd find this to be an interesting little side story. A nice exclusive."

She nodded as though her predicament had just become crystal clear in front of her.

"Withdraw your motions," she said. "You will have everything you asked for by the end of the day Friday."

"Tomorrow."

"That's not enough time. I have to pull it together and get it copied. The copy shop is always backed up."

"Then Thursday by noon or I file the motion."

"Fine, asshole."

"Good. Once I go through it all, maybe we can start talking about a plea. Thank you, Andy."

"Fuck you, Haller. And there isn't going to be a plea. We've got her nailed and I'm going to be looking at you, not her, when the verdict comes in."

She pivoted and started to walk away, but then turned right back to me.

"And don't call me Andy. You don't get to call me that."

She marched away then, moving in long, angry strides toward the elevator lobby, totally ignoring a reporter who trotted up to her and tried to get a quote.

I knew there would be no plea agreement. My client wouldn't allow it. But I gave Freeman the opening so she could throw it back in my face. I wanted her to go away angry but not that angry. I wanted her to think she had salvaged something. It would make her easier to deal with.

I looked around and saw Lisa waiting dutifully on the bench I had earlier pointed her to. I signaled her to get up.

"Okay, Lisa, let's get out of here."

"But what about Herb? I drove in with him."

"Your car or his?"

"His."

"Then he's fine. My guy will drive you home."

We walked into the elevator alcove. Thankfully, Andrea Freeman had already caught a ride down to the DA's office on the second floor. I pushed the button but the elevator didn't come soon enough. We were joined by Dahl.

"What, were you leaving without me?"

I didn't respond to his question and quickly dispensed with any guise of civility.

"You know, you're fucking me up by talking to the media like that. You think you're helping the cause but you're not—unless Herbert Dahl is the cause."

"Whoa, what's with the language? We're in a courthouse."

"I don't care where we are. Do *not* speak for my client. Do you understand? If you do it again I'm going to call a press conference and you're not going to like what I have to say about you."

"Fine. That was it. My last press conference. But now I got a question. What's goin' on with all these people I've been sending your way? Some of them called me back and said they were treated pretty rudely by your staff."

"Yeah, you keep sending them and we'll keep treating them that way."

"Hey, I know the business and these are legitimate people."

"*The Grind Side.*"

Dahl looked confused. He looked at Lisa and then back at me.

"What's that mean?"

"*The Grind Side.* Come on, you mean you haven't heard of *The Grind Side?*"

"You mean *The Blind Side?* The movie about the lady who adopts the football player?"

"No, I mean *The Grind Side.* The movie made by one of the producers you sent over to us. It's about this lady who adopts a football player and then has sex with him three or four times a day. Then when that gets boring she invites the whole football team over. I don't think it made as much money as *The Blind Side.*"

Lisa was turning pale. I got the feeling that what I was saying about Dahl's Hollywood connections wasn't matching up with what Dahl had been putting in her ears for weeks.

"Yeah, this is what he's doing for you, Lisa. These are the kind of people he wants to put you with."

"Look," Dahl said, "do you have any idea how hard it is to get something going in this town? A project? There are those who can and those who can't. I don't care what the guy made before as long as he can get something going now. You understand? These are legitimate people and I have a lot of money on the line here, Haller."

An elevator finally arrived. I directed Lisa onto it but then put my hand on Dahl's chest and slowly pushed him away from the door.

"Just back off, Dahl. You'll get your money and then some. But you just back off."

I stepped into the elevator and turned to make sure Dahl didn't attempt to jump on at the last moment. He didn't try it, but he didn't move either. I held his hateful stare until the doors closed on it.

Nine

We moved into our new offices on Saturday morning. It was a three-room suite in a building at Victory and Van Nuys Boulevards. The place was even called the Victory Building, which I liked. It was also fully furnished and only two blocks from the courthouse where Lisa Trammel would face trial.

All hands were on deck to help with the move. Including Rojas, who wore a T-shirt and baggies, showing off the tattoos that completely covered his arms and legs. I didn't know which was more shocking, seeing the tattoos or seeing Rojas in anything other than the suit he always wore while driving me.

The setup in the new place was that I got my own office while Cisco and Aronson shared the other, larger office and Lorna anchored the reception area in between. Going from the backseat of a Lincoln to an office with ten-foot ceilings, a full desk and a nap couch was a big change. The first thing I did upon settling in was to use the open space and polished wood floor to spread out the eight-hundred-plus pages of discovery documents I had received from Andrea Freeman.

Most of it was from WestLand and a lot of it was filler. It was Freeman's passive-aggressive response to being maneuvered by the defense. There were dozens of pages and packets on bank policy and procedures and other forms I didn't need. These all went into one pile. There were also copies of all communications that went directly to Lisa Trammel, most of which I already had and was familiar with. These went into a

77

second pile. And finally, there were copies of internal bank communications as well as communications between the victim, Mitchell Bondurant, and the outside company the bank used to carry out its foreclosures.

This company was called ALOFT and I was already quite familiar with it because it was my adversary on at least a third of my foreclosure cases. ALOFT was a mill, a company that filed and tracked all documents required in the lengthy foreclosure process. It was a go-between that allowed bankers and other lenders to keep their hands clean in the dirty business of taking people's homes away from them. Companies like ALOFT got the job done without the bank's so much as having to send a letter to the customer faced with foreclosure.

It was this stack of correspondence that I was most interested in, and it was here that I found the document that would change the course of the case.

I moved behind my desk, sat down and studied the phone. There were more buttons on it than I would ever have use for. I finally found the intercom button for the other office and pushed it.

"Hello?"

Nothing. I pushed it again.

"Cisco? Bullocks? Are you there?"

Nothing. I got up and started toward the door, intent on communicating with my staff the old-fashioned way, when a response finally came over the phone's speaker.

"Mickey, is that you?"

It was Cisco's voice. I hurried back to the desk and pushed the button.

"Yeah, it's me. Can you come in here? And bring Bullocks."

"Roger and out."

A few minutes later my investigator and associate counsel entered.

"Hey, Boss?" Cisco asked, looking at the stacks of documents on the floor. "The point of the office is to put stuff in drawers and file cabinets and up on shelves."

"I'll get around to it," I said. "Shut the door and have a seat."

Once we were all in place, I looked at them across my big rented desk and laughed.

"This is weird," I said.

"I could get used to it, having an office," Cisco said. "But Bullocks doesn't know from nothing."

"Yes, I do," Aronson protested. "Last summer I interned at Shandler, Massey and Ortiz and I had my *own* office."

"Well, maybe next time you get your own with us," I said. "So now, down to business. Cisco, did you get the laptop to your guy?"

"Yeah, dropped it off yesterday morning. I told him it was a rush job."

We were talking about Lisa's laptop, which had been returned by the DA's office along with her cell phone and the four boxes of documents.

"And he's going to be able to tell us what the DA was looking at?"

"He said he'll be able to provide a list of the files they opened and how long they were opened. From that we should be able to get an idea of what they paid attention to. But don't get your hopes up."

"Why?"

"Because Freeman gave in on this way too easily. I don't think she would've given us back the computer if it was that important to her."

"Maybe."

Neither he nor Aronson was aware of the deal I made with Freeman or the leverage I had used. I turned my attention to Aronson. After she completed the motions to suppress earlier in the week I had put her on backgrounding the victim. This came after Cisco had picked up some preliminary indications in his investigations that all was not well in Mitchell Bondurant's personal world.

"Bullocks, what've you got on our victim?"

"Well, there's still a lot I need to check out, but there's no doubt that he was heading over the falls. Financially, that is."

"How so?"

"Well, when the going was good and the financing came easy, he was a definite player in the real estate market. Between oh-two and oh-seven he bought and flipped twenty-one properties, mostly residential real estate. Made good money and plowed it back into bigger deals. Then the economy tanked and he was caught holding the bag."

"He was upside-down?"

"Exactly. At the time of his death he owned five large properties that suddenly weren't worth what he paid for them. It looks like he had been trying to sell them for more than a year. No takers. And three of them had balloons that were going to pop this year. It added up to over two million dollars he would owe."

I stood up and came around the desk. I started pacing. Aronson's report was exciting. I didn't know exactly how it fit in but I was confident I could make it fit. We just had to talk it out.

"Okay, so Bondurant, the senior vice president in charge of the home loan side of WestLand, was falling victim to the same sort of situation as many of the people he was foreclosing on. When the money was flowing he took mortgages with five-year balloon notes, thinking like everybody else that he'd turn the properties over or remortgage long before the five years were up."

"Except the economy goes into the toilet," Aronson said. "He can't sell them and he can't remortgage them because they aren't worth what he paid for them. No bank would touch his paper, not even his own."

Aronson had a glum look on her face.

"This is all good work, Bullocks. What's wrong?"

"Well, I'm just wondering what all this has to do with the murder?"

"Maybe nothing. Maybe everything."

I went back to the desk and sat down. I handed her the three-page document I had found in the volumes the prosecution had provided. She took it and held it so she and Cisco could both look at it.

"What's this?" she asked.

"I think it's our smoking gun."

"I forgot my glasses in the other office," Cisco said.

"Read it, Bullocks."

"It's a copy of a certified letter from Bondurant to Louis Opparizio at A. Louis Opparizio Financial Technologies, or ALOFT, for short. It says, 'Dear Louis, Attached you will find correspondence from an attorney named Michael Haller who is representing the home owner in one of the foreclosure cases you are handling for WestLand.' It gives Lisa's name, loan number and the address of the house. Then it goes, 'In his letter Mr. Haller makes allegations that the file is replete with fraudulent actions perpetrated in the case. You will note that he gives specific instances, all of which were carried out by ALOFT. As you know and we have discussed, there have been other complaints. These new allegations against ALOFT, if true, have put WestLand in a vulnerable position, especially considering the government's recent interest in this aspect of the mortgage business. Unless we come to some sort of arrangement and understanding in regard to this I will be recommending to the board that WestLand withdraw from its contract with your company for cause and any ongoing business be terminated. This action would also require the bank to file an SAR with appropriate authorities. Please contact me at your earliest convenience to further discuss these matters.' That's it. A copy of your original letter is attached and a copy of the return card from the post office. The letter was signed for by someone named Natalie and I can't read the last name. Begins with an *L*."

I leaned back in my leather executive chair and smiled at them while rolling a paper clip over my fingers like a magician. Aronson, eager to impress, jumped in first.

"So, Bondurant was covering his ass. He had to have known what ALOFT was doing. The banks have a wink-wink relationship with all these foreclosure mills. They don't care how it's done, they just want it done. But by sending this letter he was distancing himself from ALOFT and the underhanded practices."

I shrugged as if to say *maybe*.

" 'Arrangement and understanding,' " I said.

They both looked at me blankly.

"That's what he said in the letter. 'Unless we come to some sort of arrangement and understanding...' "

"Okay, what's it mean?" Aronson asked.

"Read between the lines. I don't think he was distancing himself. I think the letter was a threat. I think it means he wanted a piece of ALOFT's action. He wanted in *and* he was covering his ass, yes, by sending the letter, but I think there was another message. He wanted some of the action or he was going to take it away from Opparizio. He was even threatening to file an SAR."

"What exactly is an SAR?" Aronson asked.

"Suspicious activity report," Cisco said. "A routine form. The banks file them over anything."

"With who?"

"Federal trade, FBI, Secret Service, whoever they want to, really."

I could tell I had not sold them on anything yet.

"Do you have any idea what sort of money ALOFT is raking in?" I asked. "It's easily involved in a third of our cases. I know it's unscientific but if you take that out across the board and ALOFT's got a third of the cases in L.A. County then you are talking about millions and millions in fees from this one county. They say that in California alone there will be three million foreclosures before this plays out over the next few years."

"Plus, there's the acquisition."

"What acquisition?" Aronson asked.

"You gotta read the papers. Opparizio is in the process of selling ALOFT to a big investment fund, a company called LeMure. It's publicly traded and any sort of controversy regarding one of its satellite acquisitions could affect the deal as well as the stock price. So don't kid yourself. If Bondurant was desperate enough, he could make some waves. He may have made more than he was counting on."

Cisco nodded, the first to tumble to my theory.

"Okay, so we have Bondurant facing personal financial disaster," he said. "Three balloons about to pop. So he turns around and tries to muscle in on Opparizio, the LeMure deal and the whole foreclosure gravy train. And it gets him killed?"

"That's right."

Cisco was sold. I now swiveled in my chair so that I was looking directly at Aronson.

"I don't know," she said. "It's a big jump. And it's going to be hard to prove."

"Who says we have to prove it? We just have to figure out how to get it before the jury."

The reality was we didn't need to prove a damn thing. We only had to suggest it and let a jury do the rest. I just had to plant the seeds of reasonable doubt. To build the hypothesis of innocence. I leaned forward across my big wooden desk and looked at my team.

"This is our defense theory. Opparizio is our straw man. He's the guy we paint as guilty. The jury points the finger at him and our client walks."

I looked at both their faces and got no reaction. I kept going.

"Cisco, I want you to focus on Louis Opparizio and his company. Get me everything that's out there. History, known associates, everything. All the details of the merger. I want to know more about that deal and this guy than even he knows. By the end of next week I want to subpoena records from ALOFT. They'll fight it but it ought to stir things up a bit."

Aronson shook her head.

"But wait a minute," she said. "Are you saying this is all bullshit? Just a defense gambit and this guy Opparizio didn't really do it? What if we're right about Opparizio and they're wrong about Lisa Trammel? What if she's innocent?"

She looked at me with eyes full of naive hope. I smiled and looked at Cisco.

"Tell her."

My investigator turned to face my young associate.

"Kid, you're new at this so you get a pass. But we never ask that question. It doesn't matter if our clients are guilty or innocent. They all get the same bang for the buck."

"Yes, but..."

"There are no buts," I said. "We are talking about avenues of defense here. Ways to provide our client with the best defense possible. These are strategies we will follow regardless of guilt or innocence. You want to do criminal defense, this is what you have to understand. You never ask your client if he did it. Yes or no, the answer is only a distraction. So you don't need to know."

She tightened her lips into a thin, straight line.

"How are you on Tennyson?" I asked. "'The Charge of the Light Brigade'?"

"What does—"

"'Theirs not to reason why, theirs but to do or die.' We're the Light Brigade, Bullocks. We go up against an army that has more people, more weapons, more everything. Most of the time it amounts to little more than a suicide run. No chance of survival. No chance of winning. But sometimes you get a case where you have a shot. It might be a long shot, but it's a shot nonetheless. So you take it. You charge... and you don't ask questions like that."

"Actually, I think it's 'do *and* die.' That was the point of the poem. They didn't have the choice to do or die. They had to do and die."

"So you know your Tennyson. I like 'do or die' better. The point is, did Lisa Trammel kill Mitchell Bondurant? I really don't know. She says she didn't and that's good enough for me. If it's not good enough for you, then I'll take you off this one and put you back on foreclosures full-time."

"No," Aronson said quickly. "I want to stay. I'm in."

"That's good. Not many lawyers get to sit second chair on a murder case ten months out of law school."

She looked at me, eyes wide.

"Second chair?"

I nodded.

"You deserve it. You've done some really good work on this."

But the light quickly faded.

"What?"

"I just don't know why you can't have it both ways. You know, give unbridled effort in your defense but be conscientious about your work. Try for the best outcome."

"The best outcome for who? Your client? Society? Or for yourself? Your responsibility is to your client and the law, Bullocks. That's it."

I gave her a long stare before continuing.

"Don't go growing a conscience on me," I said. "I've been down that road. It doesn't lead you to anything good."

Ten

After spending most of the day setting up the office I didn't get home till almost eight. I found my ex-wife sitting on the steps leading up to the front deck. Our daughter wasn't with her. In the past year there had been several encounters between us that did not include Hayley and I was thrilled by the prospect of another. I was dog-tired from the day's mental and physical work but I could easily rally for Maggie McFierce.

"Hey, Mags. You forget the key?"

She got up, and just from her stiff posture and the way she dusted off the backside of her jeans all businesslike I knew something wasn't right. When I got to the top step I moved in for a kiss — just on the cheek. But she immediately made an evasive maneuver and my suspicion was confirmed.

"That's where Hayley gets it," I said. "The old duck and roll when I give her a kiss."

"Well, I'm not here for that, Haller. I didn't use my key because I thought you might consider it some sort of conflict of interest if you found a prosecutor in your house."

Now I got it.

"Yoga today? You saw Andrea Freeman?"

"That's right."

Suddenly, I didn't feel the strength to rally anymore. I unlocked the door like a prisoner punished with the indignity of letting himself into the room where they give you the needle.

"Come on in. I guess we'll get this over with."

She came in quickly, my last comment throwing another log on her fire.

"What you did was despicable. Using our daughter in such an under-handed way."

I wheeled around on her.

"Using our daughter? I did no such thing. Our daughter was put in the middle of this thing and I learned of it only by accident."

"It doesn't matter. You're disgusting."

"No, I'm a defense lawyer. And your good pal Andy was discussing me and my case with my ex-wife in front of my daughter. And then she outright lied to me."

"What are you talking about? She doesn't lie."

"I'm not talking about Hayley. I'm talking about *Andy*. I asked her on the first day she was on the case if she knew you and she said she knew you only in passing. I think we can agree that that is not the case. And I don't know for sure but I would guess that if we described this situation to ten different judges that maybe *ten* would consider it a conflict."

"Look, we weren't discussing you or the case. It came up when we were having lunch. Hayley happened to be there. What am I supposed to do, disavow my friends because of you? It doesn't work that way."

"If it was no big deal, why did she lie to me?"

"It wasn't a direct lie. It's not like we're best friends or anything. Besides, she probably didn't want you to get into it like you have anyway."

"So now we're qualifying lies on a sliding scale. Some are indirect and no big deal. Don't worry about those lies."

"Haller, don't be an asshole."

"Look, you want something to drink?"

"I don't want anything. I came to tell you that you not only embarrassed me and your daughter, but yourself. It was low, Haller. You used something innocent from your own daughter to get an edge. It was really low."

I was still holding my briefcase. I put it down on the table in the din-ing alcove. I put my hands on the top of one of the chairs and leaned down on it as I thought out my comeback.

"Come on," Maggie said, baiting me. "You always have a quick answer for everything. The great defender. Let's hear it this time."

I laughed and shook my head. She was so damn beautiful when she was mad. It was disarming. And the bad part was I think she knew it.

"Oh, so this is funny. You threaten to ruin someone's career and then can laugh about it."

"I didn't threaten to ruin her career. I threatened to kick her off the case. And no, it's not funny. It's just that..."

"What, Haller? It's just that what? I've been sitting out there for two hours wondering if you were going to show up because I want to know how you could do this."

I stepped away from the table and went on the offensive, moving toward her as I spoke. Making her step back and then crowding her into a corner, ending my words with my finger pointing inches from her chest.

"I did it because I'm a defense attorney and as a defense attorney I have taken an oath to defend my clients to the best of my ability. So, yes, I saw an advantage here. Your good pal *Andy*—and you—clearly crossed a line. Sure, no harm was done—as far as I know. But that doesn't mean the line wasn't crossed. If you jump a fence with a sign on it that says NO TRESPASSING then you are still trespassing even if you jump right back across. So I became aware of this trespass and I used it to my advantage to get something I need to defend my client. Something I should've been given as a matter of course but which your friend was holding back simply because she could.

"Was she within the rules? Yes. Was it fair? No. And one reason you are all hot and bothered about it is that you know it wasn't fair and that I made the right move. It was something you would have done yourself."

"Never in a million years. I would never stoop so low."

"Bullshit."

I turned away from her. She stayed in the corner.

"What are you doing here, Maggie?"

"What do you mean? I just told you why I'm here."

"Yeah, but you could've picked up a phone or sent me an e-mail. Why did you come here?"

"I wanted to see your face when you gave an explanation."

I turned back to her. This whole thing was a sideshow. I moved in on her and put my hand on the wall right next to her head.

"It was bullshit arguments like this that wrecked our marriage," I said.

"I know."

"You know it's been eight years? We've been divorced as long as we were married."

Eight years and I still couldn't shake her.

"Eight years and here we are."

"Yes, here we are."

"You know, you're the trespasser, Haller. You jump over everybody's fences. Come in and out of our lives whenever you want. And we just let you."

I slowly leaned in closer until we were breathing the same air. I kissed her lightly and then harder when she tried to say something. I didn't want to hear any more words. I was finished with words.

PART TWO

The Hypothesis
of Innocence

Eleven

The office was closed and locked for the evening but I was still in place at my desk, prepping for the preliminary hearing. It was a Tuesday in early March and I wished I could have opened a window to let in the cool evening breeze. But the office was hermetically sealed with vertical windows that did not open. Lorna hadn't noticed that when she'd inspected the place and signed the lease. It made me miss working out of the backseat of the Lincoln, where I could slide a window down and catch the breeze whenever I wanted.

The preliminary hearing was a week away. By prepping, I mean I was trying to anticipate what my opponent Andrea Freeman would be willing to part with when she put her case before the judge.

A preliminary hearing is a routine step on the way to a trial. It is one hundred percent the prosecution's show. The state is charged with presenting its case to the court and the judge then rules on whether there is sufficient evidence to take it forward to a jury trial. This isn't the reasonable doubt threshold. Not even close. The judge only has to decide if a preponderance of the evidence supports the charges. If so, then the next stop is a full-blown trial.

The trick for Freeman would be to parcel out just enough evidence to cross that preponderance line and get the judge's nod of approval without giving away the whole store. Because she knew that I would be going to school on whatever she presented.

There is no doubt that the prosecution's burden is no burden at all.

Though the idea of a preliminary hearing is to provide a check on the system and to make sure the government does not run roughshod over the individual, it is still a fixed game. The California state assembly saw to that.

Frustrated by the seemingly interminable duration of criminal cases as they slowly wound through the justice system, the politicians in Sacramento took action. The prevailing view was that justice delayed was justice denied, never mind that this sentiment conflicted with a basic component of the adversarial system — a strong and vigorous defense. The assembly sidestepped that minor inconvenience and voted for change, installing measures that streamlined the process. The preliminary hearing went from a full airing of the prosecution's evidence to what is essentially a game of hide-and-seek. Few witnesses had to be called besides the lead investigator, hearsay was approved rather than discouraged and the prosecution need not offer even half of its evidence. Just enough to get by.

The result was that it was beyond rare that a case did not measure up to the level of preponderance and the preliminary hearing became a routine rubber-stamping of the charges on the way to trial.

Still, there was a value for the defense in the proceedings. I still got a peek at what was to come and an opportunity to raise questions about what witnesses and evidence were presented. And therein was the prep work. I needed to anticipate which cards Freeman would show and decide how I would play against them.

We were way past any notion of a plea agreement. Freeman still wasn't giving on that end and my client still wasn't taking. We were on a direct course toward a trial in April or May and I can't say I was unhappy about it. We had a legitimate shot and if Lisa Trammel wanted to go for it I was going to be ready.

In recent weeks we had gotten some good news as well as bad on the evidence front. As expected, Judge Morales ruled against our motions to suppress the police interview and the search of Lisa's home. This cleared the way for the prosecution to build its case around the pillars of motivation, opportunity and the single eyewitness account. They had the foreclosure action. They had Lisa's history of protest against the bank. They had her incriminating admissions during her interview. And most of all, they had the eyewitness, Margo Schafer, who claimed to have seen Lisa just a block from the bank and only minutes after the killing.

But we were building a defense case that attacked these pillars and contained much evidence that was indeed exculpatory.

No murder weapon had been identified or found yet, and the state's zeal to prove that a tiny blemish of blood found on a pipe wrench taken from the tool bench in Lisa's garage had backfired when testing concluded it was not Mitchell Bondurant's blood. Of course, the prosecution would not bring this up at the preliminary hearing or the trial, but I could and would. It is the defense's job to take the miscues and mistakes of the investigation and ram them down the state's throat. I would not hold back.

Additionally, my investigator had gathered information that would put into question the observations of the state's key witness, even though we would not get that shot until trial. And we also had the hypothesis of innocence. The alternate theory was building nicely. We had served subpoenas on Louis Opparizio and his company ALOFT, the foreclosure mill at the center of the defense strategy.

I anticipated that no defense tactics or evidence would come up during the preliminary hearing. Freeman would put Detective Kurlen on the stand and he would walk the judge through the entire case, making sure to sidestep any weaknesses in the evidence. She would also put on the medical examiner and possibly a forensic analyst.

Schafer, the witness, was the only question. My first thought was that Freeman would hold her back. She could rely on Kurlen to present information from his interview with her, thereby bringing out what Schafer would eventually testify to at trial. No more was needed for a prelim. On the other hand, Freeman might put Schafer on the stand in a bid to see what I had. If I revealed during cross-examination how I planned to handle the witness, it would help Freeman prepare for what was ahead at trial.

It was all strategy and games at this point and I had to admit it was the best part of a trial. The moves made outside the courtroom were always more significant than those made inside. The inside moves were all prepped and choreographed. I preferred the improvisation done away from the courtroom.

I was underlining the name Schafer on my legal pad when I heard the phone ring in the reception area. I could have taken it on my set but didn't bother. It was well after hours and I knew the number on the phone-book ad had been forwarded to the new office number. Anybody calling this late was probably looking for foreclosure advice. They could leave a message.

I pulled the blood analysis file to front and center on the desk. It contained the DNA comparison report that had been run on blood extracted from a crevice in the handle of the pipe wrench from Lisa's tool bench. It had been a rush job, the prosecution popping for an expensive analysis from an outside firm rather than wait for the regional lab to do it. I imagined the disappointment Freeman must have felt when the report came in negative. Not Mitchell Bondurant's blood. Not only was it a setback for the prosecution—a match would have killed any chance Lisa had at an acquittal and forced her into a plea agreement. But now Freeman knew I could wave the report in front of the jury and say, "See, their case is full of wrong turns and wrong evidence."

We also scored when footage from video cameras in the bank building and garage entrance failed to show Lisa Trammel during the time before and after the killing. The cameras did not cover the entire facility but that was beside the point. It was exculpatory evidence.

Now my cell phone started to vibrate. I pulled it out of my pocket and looked at the ID. It was my agent, Joel Gotler, calling. I hesitated but then took the call.

"You're working late," I said by way of answering.

"Yeah, don't you read your e-mails?" Gotler said. "I've been trying to reach you."

"Sorry, my computer's right here but I've been busy. What's going on?"

"We've got a big problem. Do you read *Deadline Hollywood*?"

"No, what's that?"

"It's a blog. Look it up on your computer."

"Now?"

"Yeah, now. Do it."

I closed the blood file and slid it aside. I pulled my laptop over and opened it. I went online and navigated to the *Deadline Hollywood* site. I started scrolling. It looked like a list of short reports on Hollywood deals, box office estimates and studio comings and goings. Who bought and sold what, who left what agency, who was going down and who was going up, that sort of thing.

"Okay, what am I looking for here?"

"Scroll down to three forty-five this afternoon."

The posts on the blog were time-stamped. I did as instructed and came to the late afternoon post Gotler wanted me to see. The headline alone kicked me in the nuts.

Archway Grabs Real-Life Murder Mystery
> Dahl/McReynolds to produce
> Sources tell me that Archway Pictures has anted up six figures against a seven-figure backend to acquire rights to the foreclosure-revenge case currently twisting its way through the justice system here in LaLaLand. The accused, Lisa Trammel, was represented by Herb Dahl in the deal and he will produce alongside Archway's Clegg McReynolds. The multitiered deal includes TV and documentary rights. The ending of the story, however, has yet to be written as Trammel still faces trial in the murder of the banker who was trying to foreclose on her house. In a press release McReynolds said Trammel's story will be used to put a magnifying glass on the foreclosure epidemic that has swept across the country in recent years. She is expected to go to trial in two months.

"That motherfucker," I said.

"Yeah, that's about right," Gotler said. "What the hell is going on? I'm out there trying to sell this thing and was very close to a deal with Lakeshore and then I read this! Are you kidding me, Haller? You stab me in the back like this?"

"Look, I don't know exactly what is going on here but I have a contract with Lisa Trammel and—"

"Do you know this guy Dahl? I do and he's a complete sleaze."

"I know, I know. He tried to make a move and I shut his ass down. He got Lisa to sign something but—"

"Ah, jeez, she signed with this guy?"

"No. I mean yes, but after she signed with me. I have a contract. I have first po—"

I stopped right there. The contracts. I remembered making copies and giving them to Dahl. I then put the originals back in the file in the trunk of the Lincoln. Dahl saw the whole thing.

"Son of a bitch!"

"What is it?"

I looked at the stack of files on the corner of my desk. They had all been generated by the Lisa Trammel case. But I had not brought in the files from the trunk of the Lincoln because I had been lazy. I figured they were all old contracts and old cases and maybe I wasn't sure how I would ultimately like working out of a bricks-and-mortar office. The contracts file was still in the trunk.

"Joel, I'll call you right back."

"Hey, what is—"

I closed the phone and headed to the door. The Victory Building had its own two-level garage but it was not attached. I had to leave the building and walk to the garage next door. I trotted up the ramp and on the second level headed to my car, popping the trunk with the remote as I approached. My Lincoln was the only vehicle left on the upper level. I pulled the contracts file and leaned under the light from the trunk lid to look for the agreement Lisa Trammel had signed.

It wasn't there.

To say I was angry was an understatement. I shoved the file back into its slot and slammed the lid. I pulled my phone and called Lisa as I headed back to the ramp. The call went to message.

"Lisa, this is your attorney. I thought we agreed that when I called you, you would answer. No matter what time, no matter what you were doing. But here I am calling and you're not answering. Call...me... back. I want to talk to you about your little friend Herb and the deal he just made. I am sure you are aware of it. But what you may not be aware of is that I am going to be suing his ass for this stunt. I'm going to put him under the earth, Lisa. So call me back! Now!"

I closed the phone and squeezed it as I headed down the ramp. I barely noticed the two men walking up the ramp until one of them called to me.

"Hey, you're that guy, right?"

I stopped, confused by the question, my mind still firmly wrapped around Herb Dahl and Lisa Trammel.

"Excuse me?"

"The lawyer. You're the famous lawyer from TV."

They both moved toward me. They were young guys in bomber jackets, hands in their pockets. I didn't want to stop to make small talk.

"Uh, no, I think you've got the wrong—"

"No, man, that's you. I seen you on the TV, right?"

I gave up.

"Yeah, I have a case. It gets me on TV."

"Right, right, right...and what's your name again?"

"Mickey Haller."

As soon as I said my name I saw the silent one take his hands out of his jacket pockets and square his shoulders toward me. He was wearing black fingerless gloves. It wasn't cool enough for gloves and in that moment I realized that, since there were no other cars up on the second level, these guys hadn't been going up there. They had been looking for me.

"What's this all—"

The silent man swung a left fist into my midsection. I doubled over just in time to feel his right fist crush three of my left ribs. I remembered dropping my phone at that point but little else. I know I tried to run but the talker blocked my way and then turned me around, pinning my elbows at my sides.

He was wearing black gloves, too.

Twelve

They left my face alone, but that was about the only thing that didn't feel bruised or broken when I woke up in ICU at Holy Cross. The final tally included thirty-eight stitches in my scalp, nine fractured ribs, four broken fingers, two bruised kidneys and one testicle that had been twisted 180 degrees before the surgeons straightened it. My torso was the color of a grape Popsicle and my urine the dark hue of Coca-Cola.

The last time I had stayed in a hospital I got hooked on oxycodone, an addiction that nearly cost me my child and career. This time I told them I'd gut it out without the chemical help. And this of course was a painful mistake. Two hours after taking my stand I was pleading with the nurses, the orderlies and anyone who would listen to give me the drip. It finally took care of the pain but left me floating too close to the ceiling. It took them a couple days to find the right equilibrium of pain relief and consciousness. That was when I started accepting visitors.

Two of the first were a pair of detectives from the Van Nuys Division CAPs Unit. Their names were Stilwell and Eyman. They asked me basic questions so that they could complete their paperwork. They had about as much interest in determining who had attacked me as they did in the idea of working through lunch. I was, after all, the defense counsel to an alleged murderer their colleagues down the hall had popped. In other words, they weren't going to get their own balls in a twist over this one.

When Stilwell closed his notebook I knew the interview — and the investigation—was over. He told me they would check back if anything came up.

"You forgot something, didn't you?" I said.

I spoke without moving my jaw because somehow moving my jaw set off the pain receptors in my rib cage.

"What's that?" Stilwell asked.

"You never asked me to describe my attackers. You didn't even ask what color they were."

"We can get all of that on our next visit. The doctor told us you need your rest."

"You want to make an appointment for the next visit?"

Neither detective answered. They wouldn't be coming back.

"I didn't think so," I said. "Goodbye, Detectives. I'm glad the Crimes Against Persons Unit is on this. Makes me feel safe."

"Look," Stilwell said. "Likely this was a random thing. Two muggers looking for an easy mark. The chances of us—"

"They knew who I was."

"You said they recognized you from the TV and the newspapers."

"I didn't say that. I said they recognized me and made it appear as though it was from TV or something. If you really cared about this you would've made that distinction."

"Are you accusing us of not caring about a random act of violence in this community?"

"Pretty much, yeah. And who says it was random?"

"You said you didn't know or recognize the assailants. So unless you are changing your mind about that, there is no evidence that this was anything other than a random act. Or at best a lawyer hate crime. They recognized you and didn't like that you defend murderers and scumbags and decided to relieve their frustrations on your body. Could've been a lot of things."

My entire body throbbed with pain ignited by their indifference. But I was also tired and wanted them gone.

"Never mind, Detectives," I said. "Go on back to Crimes Against Persons and fill out your paperwork. You can forget about this one. I'll take it from here."

I closed my eyes on them then. It was the only thing I could do.

*   *   *

The next time my lids came open I saw Cisco sitting in a chair in the corner of the room, staring at me.

"Hey, Boss," he said gently, as if his usual booming voice might hurt me. "How's it hanging?"

I coughed as I came fully awake and that set off a paroxysm of pain in my testicles.

"Feels like it's still about a hundred eighty degrees to the left."

He smiled because he thought I was delirious. But I was lucid enough to know that this was his second visit and that I had asked him to do some sleuthing when he had come the first time.

"What time is it? I'm losing track, sleeping so much."

"Ten after ten."

"Thursday?"

"No, Friday morning, Mick."

I'd been sleeping more than I realized. I tried to sit up but the movement set off a burning wave of pain across my left side.

"Jesus Christ!"

"You okay, Boss?"

"Whadaya got for me, Cisco?"

He stood up and came to the side of the bed.

"Not a whole lot but I'm still working it out. I got a look at the police report, however. Not a lot there but it did say that you were found by the night cleaning crew that came in about nine o'clock to work in the building. They found you out cold on the garage ramp and called it in."

"Nine o'clock wasn't too long after. Did they see anything else?"

"No, they didn't. According to the report. I plan to be there tonight to interview them myself."

"Good. What about the office?"

"Me and Lorna checked as best we could. It doesn't look like anybody was in there. Nothing missing, as far as we can tell. And it was left unlocked the whole night. I think you were the target, Mick. Not the office."

The medication drip worked on a regulated feed system that parceled out the sweet juice of relief according to impulses sent from a computer in another room and programmed by someone I had never met. But at that moment that computer nerd was my hero. I felt the cold trickle of a boost moving through my arm and into my chest. I was silent as I waited for my screaming nerve endings to be calmed.

"What are you thinking, Mick?"

"My mind's a blank. I told you I didn't recognize them."

"I'm not talking about them. I'm talking about who sent them. What's your gut tell you? Opparizio?"

"It would certainly be the choice. He knows we're coming for him. I mean, who else?"

"What about Dahl?"

I shook my head.

"What for? He already stole my contract and made the deal. Why beat me up after?"

"Maybe just to slow you down. Maybe to add intrigue to the project. This adds another dimension. It's part of the story."

"Seems like a stretch. I like Opparizio better."

"But why would he do it?"

"Same thing. To slow me down. Warn me off. He doesn't want to be a witness and he doesn't want to be dragged through the shit he knows I have on him."

Cisco shrugged.

"Still not sure I'm buying it."

"Well, whoever it was doesn't matter. This isn't going to slow me down."

"What exactly are you going to do about Dahl? He stole the contract."

"I'm working on it. I'll have a plan for that douche bag by the time I get out of here."

"When's that supposed to be?"

"They're waiting to see if I'm healing all right. If not, they might take off my left nut."

Cisco cringed as though I was talking about his left nut.

"Yeah, I try not to think about it," I said.

"Okay then, moving on. What about the two men? I've got two white guys, early thirties, leather bomber jackets and gloves. You remember anything else this time?"

"Nope."

"No regional or foreign accents?"

"Not that I can remember."

"Scars, limps or tattoos?"

"None that I remember. It went down pretty quick."

"I know. You think you could pick them out of a six-pack?"

He was talking about a photo spread of mug shots.

"One of them I could. The one who did all the talking. I didn't look at the other one too much. Once he hit me I wasn't seeing anything."

"Right. Well, I'll keep working on it."

"What else, Cisco? I'm getting tired."

I closed my eyes to accentuate the point.

"Well, I was supposed to call Maggie as soon as you were awake. Her timing's been off. Every time she's been in here with Hayley you've been out."

"You can call her. Just tell her to wake me up if I'm asleep. I want to see my kid."

"Okay, I'll tell her to bring her after school. Meantime, Bullocks wants to bring by the motion for a continuance for your approval and signature before filing it by the end of the day."

I opened my eyes. Cisco had moved to the other side of the bed.

"What continuance?"

"For the prelim. She's going to ask the judge to put it back a few weeks in light of your hospitalization."

"No."

"Mick, it's Friday. The prelim's Tuesday. Even if they let you out of here by then you're not going to be in any kind of condition to—"

"She can handle it."

"Who, Bullocks?"

"Yes. She's good. She can handle it."

"She's good but green. Are you sure you want somebody just out of law school handling a prelim for a murder trial?"

"It's a prelim. Trammel's going to be bound over for trial whether I'm there or not. The best we can hope for is a little peek at the prosecution's case strategy and Aronson will be able to report back on that."

"You think the judge is going to allow it? He might see it as a move to set up an ineffective-counsel beef if there's ultimately a conviction."

"If Lisa signs off on it, we'll be okay. I'll call her and tell her it's part of the case strategy. Bullocks can spend some time here with me over the weekend and I'll prep her."

"But what is the case strategy, Mick? Why not just wait till you're healthy?"

"Because I want them to think they succeeded."

"Who?"

"Opparizio. Whoever did this to me. Let them think I'm incapacitated or running scared. Whatever. Aronson handles the prelim and then we push this thing to trial."

Cisco nodded.

"Got it."

"Good. You go now and call Maggie. Tell her to wake me up no matter what the nurses say, especially if she comes with Hayley."

"Will do, Boss. But, uh, there's one more thing."

"What?"

"Rojas is sitting out there in the waiting room. He wanted to visit but I told him to wait out there. He came yesterday, too, but you were sleeping."

I nodded. Rojas.

"Did you check the car's trunk?"

"I did. I didn't see any evidence of a pick. No scratches on the tumblers."

"Okay. When you go out, send him in."

"You want to see him alone?"

"Yeah. Alone."

"You got it."

He left then and I grabbed the bed's remote. I slowly and painfully raised the bed to about forty-five degrees so I was half sitting up for my next visitor. The adjustment ignited another run of searing pain that burned across my rib cage like an August brushfire.

Rojas tentatively entered the room, waving and nodding at me.

"Hey, Mr. Haller, how you doin'?"

"I've had better days, Rojas. How are you doing?"

"I'm good, I'm good. I just wanted to stop by and say hello and all."

He was as nervous as a feral cat. And I thought I knew why.

"It was nice of you to come by. Why don't you sit in that chair over there."

"Okay."

He took the chair in the corner. This allowed me a full view of him. I would be able to pick up all body movements as I tried to read him. He was already displaying some of the classic tells of a dissembler — avoidance of eye contact, inappropriate smiling, constant hand movement.

"Did the doctors tell you how long you have to stay here?" he asked.

"A few more days, I think. At least until I stop pissing blood."

"Man, that's bad shit! They going to catch who did it?"

"They don't seem to be working too hard on it."

Rojas nodded. I said nothing else. Silence is often a very useful interview tool. My driver then rubbed his palms up and down his thighs a few times and stood up.

"Well, I didn't want to interrupt you. You probably have to get your sleep or something."

"No, I'm up for the day, Rojas. It hurts too much to sleep. You can stay. What's the hurry? You're not driving somebody else now, are you?"

"Oh, no, no, nothing like that."

He reluctantly sat down again. Rojas had been a client before he was my driver. He'd been popped on a possession-of-stolen-property beef and had a prior conviction to go with it. The prosecution wanted jail time but I was able to get him probation. He owed me three grand for my efforts but had lost his job since his employer was also the victim of the theft. I told him he could work it off by driving and translating for me and he took the job. I started out paying him $500 a week and counted an additional $250 against the debt. After three months the debt was cleared but he stayed on, collecting the whole $750 now. I thought he was happy and on the straight and narrow path, but maybe once a thief, always a thief.

"I just want you to know, Mr. Haller, that once you get out of here, I'm on call for you twenty-four hours a day. I don't want you driving nowhere. If you even have to go down the hill to the Starbucks, I'll be there to take you."

"Thank you, Rojas. After all, I guess it's the least you can do, right?"

"Uh..."

He looked confused but not that confused. He knew where this was headed. I decided not to dance around it any longer.

"How much did he pay you?"

He fidgeted in the seat.

"Who? For what?"

"Come on, Rojas. Don't play it this way. It's embarrassing."

"I really don't know what you're talking about. Maybe I should go after all."

He stood up.

"We don't have an agreement, Rojas. We don't have a contract, no verbal promises, nothing. You walk out of this room and I fire you and that's it. Is that what you want here?"

"Doesn't matter if there's an agreement. You can't just fire me for no reason."

"But I have the reason, Rojas. Herb Dahl told me all about it. You should know there's no honor among thieves. He said you called him up and told him you'd get him whatever he needs."

The bluff worked. I saw the rage explode in Rojas's eyes. I had my finger on the nurse-call button just in case.

"That greasy little shit eater!"

I nodded.

"Good description. How —"

"I didn't call his ass up. The fucker came to me. He said he just wanted fifteen seconds in the trunk. I shoulda known this would blow up on me."

"I thought you were smarter than that, Rojas. How much did he pay you?"

"Four bills."

"Not even a week's pay and now you're not going to have any pay."

Rojas came close to the bedside. I held my finger on the call button. I figured he was going to either attack me or ask me for a deal.

"Mr. Haller...I...need this job. My kids..."

"This is like last time, Rojas. Didn't you learn a lesson about ripping off your employer?"

"Yes, sir, I did. Dahl told me he just wanted to look at something but then he took it and when I tried to stop him he said, 'What are you going to do about it?' He had me. I couldn't stop him."

"You still have the four hundred?"

"Yes, I didn't spend a thing. Four hundred-dollar bills. And they looked real to me."

I pointed him back to the chair. I didn't want him so close.

"Okay, time to make a choice, Rojas. You can walk out that door with your four hundred and I'll never see you again. Or I can give you a second—"

"I want the second chance. Please, I'm sorry."

"Well, you're going to have to earn it. You're going to have to help me make right what you did. I am going to sue Dahl for taking that document and I am going to need you to be the witness who explains exactly what happened."

"I'll do it but who will believe me?"

"That's where your four hundred-dollar bills come in. I want you to go home or to wherever they are and—"

"I have them right here. In my wallet."

He jumped up from the seat and pulled his wallet.

"Take them out like this."

I held my finger and thumb close together.

"They can get fingerprints off money?"

"They sure can and if we can get Dahl's off those then it doesn't matter what he says about you. He's nailed."

I opened a drawer of the little table to the side of my bed. A plastic Ziploc bag containing my wallet and keys and loose change and currency was there. It had all been bagged by the paramedics who had been called to the garage of the Victory Building. Cisco had secured it and had only just given it back. I dumped the contents into the drawer and then handed the bag to Rojas.

"Okay, put the money in there and seal it."

He did as instructed and then I waved him over to give me the bag. The hundreds looked crisp and new. Less prior handling of the currency would mean a better shot at pulling prints.

"Cisco will take it from here. I'll call him and tell him to come back and pick these up. At some point he'll need your prints."

"Uh…"

Rojas's eyes were on the bag and the money.

"What?"

"Will I get that money back?"

I put the bag in the drawer and slammed it shut.

"Jesus Christ, Rojas, get out of here before I change my mind and fire your ass."

"Okay, okay, I'm sorry, you know?"

"You're sorry you got caught and that's all. Just go! I can't believe I just gave you a second chance. I must be a fucking idiot."

Rojas retreated like a dog with its tail between its legs. After he was gone I slowly lowered the bed and tried not to think about his betrayal or who had sent the two men in black gloves or anything else to do with the case. I looked up at the bag of clear liquid hanging up there overhead and waited for the blessed boost that would make at least some of the pain go away.

Thirteen

As expected, Lisa Trammel was held to answer and ordered to stand trial for murder by Judge Dario Morales at the end of a daylong preliminary hearing in Van Nuys Superior Court. Using Detective Howard Kurlen as her primary carrier of evidence, Prosecutor Andrea Freeman deftly presented a net of circumstantial evidence that quickly enclosed Lisa. Freeman took the case across the preponderance threshold like a hundred-meter sprinter and the judge was equally swift in rendering his ruling. It was routine. Matter-of-fact. Chop-chop and Lisa was held to answer.

My client was there at the defense table for the hearing but I was not. Jennifer Aronson held forth for the defense as best she could in a one-sided game. The judge had allowed the hearing to proceed only after questioning Lisa exhaustively to assure himself that her decision to go forward without me there was knowing, voluntary and strategic. Lisa acknowledged in open court that she was aware of Aronson's lack of courtroom experience and waived any claim to the argument of ineffective counsel as grounds for an appeal of the judge's eventual determination.

I watched most of it from the confines of my home where I was continuing to recover from my injuries. KTLA Channel 5 had carried the morning session live in lieu of other local programming before flipping back to the usual slate of insipid afternoon talk shows. This meant I missed only the last two hours of the hearing. But that was okay because by that point I knew how it would go. There were no surprises and the only disappointment was in not getting any sort of new read on how the prosecution would unfurl the flag at trial, when it all counted.

As decided during our prep sessions in my room at Holy Cross, Aronson presented no witnesses or any affirmative defense. We chose to reserve any indication of our hypothesis of innocence for trial, when the threshold of guilt beyond a reasonable doubt raised the game to almost an even match. Aronson used cross-examination of the state's witnesses sparingly. These were all seasoned veterans of courtroom testimony — Kurlen, a forensic expert and the medical examiner among them. Freeman chose not to put Margo Schafer on the stand, using Kurlen to recount his interview with the eyewitness who placed Lisa Trammel a block from the murder. There wasn't much to get from the state's lineup and so our strategy was to observe and wait. To bide our time. We would simply go at them at trial where we stood the best chance.

At the end of the hearing Lisa was ordered to stand trial before Judge Coleman Perry on the sixth floor of the courthouse. Perry was yet another judge I had never stood before. But since I knew his courtroom was one of four possible destinations for my client, I had done some checking with other members of the defense bar. The overall report I got was that Perry was a straight shooter with a short temper. He was fair until you crossed him and then he was prone to hold a grudge that might last an entire trial. It was good knowledge to have as the case progressed to its final stage.

Two days later, I finally felt ready to return to the fray. My broken fingers were bound tightly in a form-fitted plaster cast and my bruised torso was losing the shadings of deep blue and purple for a sickly tone of yellow. My scalp stitches had been removed and I was able to delicately comb my hair back over the shaved wound as if I was hiding a bald spot.

Best of all, my formerly twisted testicle, which the doctor had ultimately chosen not to remove, was improving a little bit every day, according to the doctor and his powers of observation and palpation. It was left to see whether it would resume normal activity and function, or die on the vine like an unpicked Roma tomato.

By previous arrangement, Rojas had the Lincoln at the bottom of the front steps at eleven o'clock sharp. I slowly made my way down, walking cane firmly in hand. Rojas was there to help me get into the back of the car. We moved carefully and soon I was in my usual place, ready to roll. Rojas jumped behind the wheel and we jerked forward and down the hill.

"Easy, Rojas. It hurts too much for me to wear a seat belt. So don't send me into the front seat."

"Sorry, Boss. I'll do better. Where are we going today? The office?"

He had gotten that Boss stuff from Cisco. I hated being called a boss, even though I knew that was what I was.

"The office is later. First we go to Archway Pictures on Melrose."

"You got it."

Archway was a second-tier studio across Melrose from one of the behemoths, Paramount Pictures. Started as a studio lot to handle the overflow demand for soundstages and equipment, it grew into a self-sustaining studio under the guidance of the late Walter Elliot. It now made its own slate of films each year and created its own overflow demand. Coincidentally, Elliot happened to be a client of mine at one time.

It took Rojas twenty minutes to get from my house above Laurel Canyon to the studio. He pulled up to the security booth at the signature arch that spanned the studio's entrance. I lowered the window and told the security man who approached me that I was there to see Clegg McReynolds. He asked for my name and ID and I gave him my driver's license. He retreated to the booth and consulted a computer screen. He frowned.

"I'm sorry, sir, but you're not on the drive-on list. Do you have an appointment?"

"No appointment but he'll want to see me."

I hadn't wanted to give McReynolds too much advance notice.

"Well, I can't let you in without an appointment."

"Can you call him and tell him I'm here? He'll want to see me. You know who he is, right?"

The implication was clear. This was one you didn't want to screw up.

The guard slid the door shut while he made the call to McReynolds. Through the glass I saw him talking. He had a live one on the line. Then he slid the door open and extended the phone to me. It was on a long cord. I took it and then raised the window on the guard. Tit for tat.

"This is Michael Haller. Is this Mr. McReynolds?"

"No, this is Mr. McReynolds's personal assistant. How can I help you, Mr. Haller? I see no appointment here in the book and, frankly, I don't know who you are."

The voice was female, young and confident.

"I'm the guy who is going to make your boss's life miserable if you don't get him on the line."

There was a bubble of silence before the voice responded.

"I don't think I like your threatening manner. Mr. McReynolds is on the set and —"

"It was not a threat. I don't make threats. I just speak the truth. Where's the set?"

"I'm not telling you that. You're not getting anywhere near Clegg until I know what this is about."

I noted that she was on a first-name basis with the boss. A horn blared from behind me. The cars were stacking up. The guard rapped his knuckles on my window, then bent down to try to see in through the smoked glass. I ignored him. A second horn honked from the rear.

"This is about your saving your boss a lot of grief. Are you familiar with the deal he announced last week regarding the woman accused of killing the banker foreclosing on her home?"

"Yes, I am."

"Well, your boss acquired those rights illegally. I'm assuming this was through no fault or knowledge of his own. If I'm right, he's the victim of a scam and I'm here to make it right for him. This is a one-time opportunity. After this, Clegg McReynolds gets pulled down into the quicksand."

The final threat was punctuated with another long blast from the car directly behind me and a sharp rap on the window.

"Talk to the guard," I said. "Tell him yea or nay."

I lowered the window and handed the phone out to the angry guard. He held it to his ear.

"What's it going to be? I've got a line of cars out to Melrose here."

He listened and then stepped back into his booth and hung up the phone. Then he looked at me as he pushed the button that opened the gate.

"Stage nine," he said. "Straight ahead and left at the end. You can't miss it."

I threw him a told-you-so smile as I raised the window and Rojas drove under the rising gate.

Stage 9 was a soundstage big enough to house an aircraft carrier. It was surrounded by equipment trucks, star wagons and craft services vans. Four stretch limos were parked end to end along one side, their engines running and drivers waiting for filming to end and the anointed to exit.

It looked like a major production but I wasn't going to get the chance to see what it was about. Walking down the middle of the driveway between Buildings 9 and 10 were an older man and a younger woman. The woman wore a headset, which I assumed made her a PA. She pointed a finger at my approaching car.

"Okay, let me out here."

Rojas stopped and as I was opening the door my phone rang. I pulled it and looked at the screen.

ID UNAVAILABLE

It said that on the calls I used to get from my clients in the drug trade. They used cheap throw-away phones to avoid wiretaps and record searches. I ignored the call and left the phone on the seat. You want me to answer your call, you gotta tell me who you are.

I slowly got out, leaving the cane behind as well. Why advertise a weakness, my father, the great lawyer, always said. I slowly walked toward the producer and his assistant.

"You're Haller?" the man called out.

"That's me."

"I want you to know that this production you just pulled me out of is running a quarter million dollars an hour. They went ahead and shut down inside just so I could come outside to deal with you."

"I appreciate that and I'll make it quick."

"Good. Now what the fuck is this about me being scammed? Nobody scams me!"

I looked at him and waited and said nothing. It only took McReynolds five more seconds to blow another gasket.

"Well, are you going to tell me or not? I don't have all day here."

I looked at his personal assistant and then back at him. He got the message.

"Uh-uh, I'm going to have a witness to anything that's said here. The girl stays."

I shrugged and pulled a compact recorder out of my pocket and turned it on. I held it up, its red light glowing.

"Then I'll make sure I have a record, too."

McReynolds looked down at the device and I could see the concern in his eyes. His voice, his words preserved on tape. That could be dangerous in a place like Hollywood. Visions of Mel Gibson danced in his head.

"Okay, turn that off and Jenny goes."

"Clegg!" Jenny protested.

McReynolds reached down and spanked her hard on the rump.

"I said go."

Humiliated, the young woman hurried off like a schoolgirl.

"Sometimes you have to treat 'em that way," McReynolds explained.

"And I'm sure they learn from it."

McReynolds nodded in agreement, not picking up on the sarcasm in my voice.

"So again, Haller, what's this about?"

"It's about you, Clegg, being played for a sucker by Herb Dahl, your partner on the Lisa Trammel deal."

McReynolds emphatically shook his head.

"No way. Legal's all over that deal. It's squeaky clean. Even the woman signed off. Trammel. I could make her a three-hundred-pound whore who likes black dick in the movie and she couldn't do a thing about it. That deal is perfect."

"Yeah, well, what Legal's missed is the part about neither one of them having the rights to the story to sell you in the first place. Those rights happen to reside here with me. Trammel signed them over to me before Dahl came along and took second position. He thought he could move up one by stealing the original contracts out of my files. Only that's not going to work. I've got a witness to the theft and Dahl's fingerprints. He's going to go down on fraud and theft charges and your choice here is to decide whether you want to go down with him, Clegg."

"Are you threatening me? Is this some sort of shakedown? Nobody shakes me down."

"No, no shakedown. I just want what's mine. So you can either stick with Dahl as your partner or you can have the same deal with me."

"It's too late. I signed. We all signed. The deal is done."

He turned to walk away.

"Have you paid him?"

He turned back to me.

"Are you kidding? This is Hollywood."

"And you probably only signed deal memos, right?"

"That's right. Contracts in four weeks."

"Then your deal is announced but not done. That's how you do it in Hollywood. But if you want to make a change, you can. If you want to find a deal killer, you can."

"I don't want to do any of that. I like the project. Dahl brought it to me. I made the deal with him."

I nodded like I understood his dilemma.

"Suit yourself. But I go to the police tomorrow morning and file the suit in the afternoon. You'll be named as a defendant. As someone who colluded in the perpetration of the fraud."

"I did no such thing! I didn't even know about all of this until you told me."

"That's right. I told you and you did nothing. You chose to move forward with a thief despite knowing the facts. That's collusion and that makes my case."

I reached into my pocket and pulled the tape recorder out. I held it up so he could see the red light was still on.

"I'm going to tie this movie up so long, the girl whose ass you just slapped will be running this place by the time it's done."

This time I walked away and he called me back.

"Wait a minute, Haller."

I turned around. He looked off to the north, toward the sign high on the mountain that drew everybody here.

"What do I need to do?" he asked.

"You need to make the same deal with me. I'll take care of Dahl. He deserves something and he'll get it."

"I need a phone number to give Legal."

I pulled a card and gave it to him.

"Remember, I have to hear something today."

"You will."

"By the way, what are the numbers on the deal?"

"Two-fifty against a million. Another quarter to produce."

I nodded. A quarter million dollars up front would certainly fund Lisa Trammel's defense. There might even be a piece left over for Herb Dahl. It all depended on how I wanted to handle this and how fair I wanted to be to a thief. Realistically, I'd have liked to put the guy in the ground, but then again he did find the project a legitimate home.

"Tell you what, I'm the only guy in town who will ever say this, but I don't want to produce. You keep that part of the deal with Dahl. That's his end."

"As long as he's not in jail."

"Put a character clause in the contract."

"That'll be something new around here. I hope Legal can handle it."

"Pleasure doing business with you, Clegg."

Once more I turned and headed back toward my car. This time Clegg came up alongside me and walked with me.

"We'll be able to reach you, right? We'll need you as a technical advisor. Especially on the screenplay."

"You have my card."

I got to the Lincoln and Rojas had the door open for me. Once again I carefully slipped in, nice and easy on the *cojones,* and then looked back at McReynolds.

"One more thing," the producer said. "I was thinking of going to Matthew McConaughey with this. He'd be excellent. But who do *you* think could play you?"

I smiled at him and reached for the door handle.

"You're looking at him, Clegg."

I pulled the door closed and through the smoked glass watched the confusion spread on his face.

I told Rojas to head toward Van Nuys.

Fourteen

Rojas told me that my phone had been ringing repeatedly while I was talking to McReynolds. I checked it and found no messages. I then opened the call record and saw that a total of four calls from a line with an unavailable ID had come in during the ten minutes I was out of the car. The time intervals were too disparate for it to have been an errant fax call on a repeat dialer. Someone had been trying to reach me but apparently it wasn't urgent enough to warrant leaving a message.

I called Lorna and told her I was on the way in. I filled her in about the deal I had made with McReynolds and said to expect a call from the Archway legal department before the end of the day. She was excited about the prospect of money coming in on the case instead of going out only.

"What else?"

"Andrea Freeman's called twice."

I thought about the four calls on my cell.

"You give her my cell?"

"I did."

"I think I just missed her but she didn't leave a message. Something must be up."

Lorna gave me the number Andrea had left with her.

"Maybe you can reach her if you call right back. I'll let you go."

"Okay, but where's everybody at right now, in or out?"

"Jennifer's here in her office and I just heard from Cisco. He's heading back from some field work."

"What field work?"

"He didn't say."

"Okay, then I'll see everybody when I get there."

I disconnected and called the number for Freeman. I had not heard from her since I'd been attacked by the black-gloved boys. Even Kurlen had come by to visit and check on me. But not even a get-well-soon card from my worthy opponent. Now six calls in one morning but no messages. I was certainly curious.

She answered after one ring and got right down to business.

"When can you come in?" she said. "I'd like to float something by you before we hit the gas and go."

It was her way of saying she was open to the possibility of ending this case with a plea agreement before the whole machinery of a trial started to crank to life.

"I thought you said there wasn't going to be an offer."

"Well, let's just say cooler heads have prevailed. I'm not stepping back from what I think of your moves on this case, but I don't see why your client should pay for your actions."

Something was going on. I could sense it. Some sort of problem with her case had come up. A piece of evidence lost or a witness had changed stories. I thought of Margo Schafer. Maybe there was a problem with the eyewitness. After all, Freeman hadn't trotted her out during the prelim.

"I don't want to come into the DA's office. You can come to my office or we meet on neutral ground."

"I'm not afraid to enter the enemy's camp. Where's your office?"

I gave her the address and we agreed to meet in an hour. I disconnected the call and tried to zero in on what could have gone wrong with the state's case at this point in the game. I came back to Schafer again. It had to be her.

My phone vibrated in my hand and I looked down at the screen.

ID UNAVAILABLE

Freeman was calling me back, probably to cancel the meeting and reveal that the whole thing was a charade, just another maneuver out of the prosecutorial psych-ops manual. I pushed the button and connected.

"Yes?"

Silence.

"Hello?"

"Is this Michael Haller?"

A male voice, one I didn't recognize.

"Yes, who is this?"

"Jeff Trammel."

For some reason it took me a moment to place the name, and then it came through to me big time. The prodigal husband.

"Jeff Trammel, yes, how are you?"

"I'm good, I guess."

"How did you get this number?"

"I was talking to Lisa this morning. I checked in. She told me I should call you."

"Well, I'm glad you did. Jeff, are you aware of the situation your wife is in?"

"Yes, she told me."

"You didn't see it on the news?"

"There's no TV or anything here. I can't read Spanish."

"Where exactly are you, Jeff?"

"I'd rather not say. You'd probably tell Lisa and I'd rather she didn't have that information right now."

"Will you be coming back for the trial?"

"I don't know. I don't have any money."

"We could get you some money for travel. You could come back here and be with your wife and son during this difficult time. You could also testify, Jeff. Testify about the house and the bank and all the pressures."

"Um...no, I couldn't. I don't want to put myself out like that, Mr. Haller. My failings. That wouldn't feel right."

"Not even to save your wife?"

"More like my ex-wife. We just haven't made it all legal."

"Jeff, what do you want? Do you want money?"

There was a long pause. Now we would get down to it. But then he surprised me.

"I don't want anything, Mr. Haller."

"Are you sure about that?"

"I just want to be left out of it. It's not my life anymore."

"Where are you, Jeff? Where is your life now?"

"I'm not telling you that."

I shook my head in frustration. I wanted to keep him on the phone like a cop trying for a trace, only there was no trace.

"Look, Jeff, I hate to bring this up but it's my job to cover all the bases, you know what I mean? And if we lose this case and there's a conviction, then Lisa will be sentenced. There will be a time when her loved ones and her friends will be able to address the court and say good things about her. We will be able to bring up what we consider to be mitigating factors. Her fight to keep the house, for example. I would want to be able to count on you to come in and testify."

"Then you think you're going to lose?"

"No, I think we have a damn good chance of winning this thing. I really do. It's an entirely circumstantial case with a witness I think we can blow out of the water. But I have to be prepared for the opposite result. Are you sure you can't tell me where you are, Jeff? I can keep it confidential. I mean, I'll need to know where you are if we're going to send you money."

"I need to go now."

"What about the money, Jeff?"

"I'll call you back."

"Jeff?"

He was gone.

"I almost had him, Rojas."

"Sorry, Boss."

I put the phone down on the armrest for a moment and looked out to see where we were. The 101 through the Cahuenga Pass. I was still another twenty minutes out.

Jeff Trammel hadn't said no to the money the last time I mentioned it.

My next call was to my client. When she answered I heard TV noise in the background.

"Lisa, it's Mickey. We need to talk."

"Okay."

"Can you turn that TV off?"

"Oh, sure. Sorry."

I waited and soon her end was silent.

"Okay."

"First of all, your husband just called me. You gave him my number?"

"Yes, you told me to, remember?"

"Yes, that's fine. I was just checking. It didn't go well. It sounds like he wants to stay away."

"That's what he told me."

"Did he tell you where he is? If I knew that I could send Cisco to convince him to help us."

"He wouldn't tell me."

"I think he might still be in Mexico. He said he had no money."

"He said the same to me. He wants me to send him some of the movie money."

"You told him about that?"

"There's going to be a movie, Mickey. He should know."

Or maybe she meant that he should have his nose rubbed in it.

"Where were you going to send the money?"

"He said I could just deposit it in Western Union and he could access it from any of their offices."

I knew there were Western Union offices all over Tijuana and points south. I'd sent money to clients before. We could send the money and then narrow things down by seeing which office Jeff Trammel went into to get the cash. But if he was smart he wouldn't go to the office closest to where he was living and we'd be back to square one.

"Okay," I said. "We'll think about Jeff later. I also wanted to tell you that the deal Herb Dahl made with Archway has changed."

"How so?"

"It's with me now. I just left Archway. Herb can still produce if they ever make a movie. And he gets to stay out of jail. So he comes out ahead. You come out ahead because your defense team will now be paid for their work and you'll get the rest, which by the way will be much more than you were ever going to see from Herb."

"Mickey, you can't do that! He made that deal!"

"I just unmade it, Lisa. Clegg McReynolds wasn't interested in being entangled in the legal net I was about to throw over Herb's head. You can tell Herb or you can have him call me if he wants."

She was silent.

"There's one more thing and this is important. You listening?"

"Yes, I'm here."

"I'm going to the office where I'm going to meet with the prosecutor. She called the meeting. I think something's up. Something's gone wrong for their side. She wants to talk about a deal and she would have never agreed to come to my office if she didn't have to. I just wanted you to know. I'll call you after the meeting."

"No deals, Mickey, unless she's offering to stand on the steps of the courthouse and announce to CNN and Fox and all the others that I'm innocent."

I felt the car swerve from course and looked out the window. Rojas was bailing off the freeway early because of traffic.

"Well, I don't think that's what she's coming over to offer, but it is my duty to keep you informed of your choices. I don't want you to become some sort of martyr for this... this cause of yours. You should listen to all offers, Lisa."

"I'm not pleading guilty. Period. Is there anything else you want to talk about?"

"I'm good for now. I will call you later."

I put the phone down on the armrest. Enough talk for now. I closed my eyes to rest for a few minutes. I tried to wiggle my fingers in the plaster and the effort hurt but was successful. The doctor who studied the X-rays said he believed the damage had occurred when someone stomped on my hand after I was on the ground and already unconscious. Lucky for me, I guess. He predicted full recovery for the fingers.

In the dark world behind my eyelids I saw the men in black gloves moving toward me. It played in a repetitive loop. I saw the dispassionate look in their eyes as they approached me. It was just a piece of business for them. Nothing else on the line. For me it was four decades of confidence and self-esteem shattered like small bones on the pavement.

After a while I heard Rojas from the front seat.

"Hey, Boss, we're here."

Fifteen

As I entered the reception area Lorna waved a hand in warning from behind the desk. She then pointed toward the door to my office. She was telling me that Andrea Freeman was already in there waiting. I made a quick detour to the other office, knocked once and opened the door. Cisco and Bullocks were behind their desks. I went to Cisco's and put my phone down in front of him.

"Lisa's husband called. In fact he called several times. Unavailable ID. Can you see what you can do?"

He rubbed a finger across his mouth as he considered the request.

"Our carrier has a threat-trace service. I give the exact time of the calls and they'll see what they can find. Takes a few days but all they'll be able to do is identify the number, not the location. You need law enforcement if you are going to try to triangulate this guy's location."

"I just want the number. Next time I want to call him instead of the other way around."

"You got it."

As I turned to leave I looked at Aronson.

"Bullocks, you want to come in and see what the district attorney's office has to say?"

"Love to."

We moved through the suite to my office. Freeman was sitting in a chair in front of my desk, reading e-mail on her phone. She was in non-court clothes. Blue jeans and a pullover sweater. It must've been all inside work today. I closed the door and she looked up.

"Andrea, can I get you something to drink?"

"No, I'm fine."

"And you know Jennifer from the prelim."

"Silent Jennifer, of course. Didn't make a peep at the prelim."

As I came around my desk I checked Aronson and saw her face and neck start to color with embarrassment. I tried to throw her a line.

"Oh, she wanted to make a peep or two but she had her orders from me. Strategy, you know. Jennifer, pull that chair over."

Aronson dragged a side chair toward the desk and sat down.

"So, here we are," I said. "What brings the DA's office to my humble place of work?"

"Well, we're getting close and I thought, you know. I figured you work the whole county and might not be as familiar with Judge Perry as I am."

"That's an understatement. I've never even been in front of him."

"Well, he likes to keep a clean docket. He doesn't care about headlines and hoopla. He'll just want to know that there was a vigorous effort to end this matter through disposition. So I thought maybe we could have one more discussion about it before we get down to a full-blown trial."

"One more? I don't remember the first discussion."

"Do you want to talk about it or not?"

I leaned back and swiveled in my chair as if mulling the question over. This was all a little dance and we both knew it. Freeman wasn't acting out of some desire to please Judge Perry. There was something else unseen in the room. Something had gone wrong and there was an opportunity for the defense. I wiggled my fingers in the cast, trying to relieve an itch on my palm.

"Well...," I said. "I'm not sure what you're thinking. Every time I bring up a plea with my client she tells me to pound sand. She wants a trial. Of course, I've seen this before. The old no deal, no deal, no deal, yes deal scenario."

"Right."

"But my hands are sort of tied here, Andrea. My client has twice forbidden me from approaching your office with a tender. She won't allow me to initiate. So here we are, you've come to me, so that works. But you have to open negotiations. You tell me what you're thinking."

Freeman nodded.

"Fair enough. I did make the call after all. Are we in agreement that this is off the record? Nothing leaves this room if no agreement is eventually struck."

"Sure."

Aronson nodded along with me.

"Okay then, this is what we are thinking. And this already has approval from on high. We drop down to man and recommend the mid-level."

I nodded, projecting my lower lip in a manner that suggested that it was an offer with merit. But I knew that if she opened with manslaughter with a mid-range sentence recommendation, it could only get better for my client. I also knew that my instincts were right. There was no way the DA would float an offer like this unless something was seriously wrong. By my estimation their case was weak from the moment they put the cuffs on my client. But now something had fallen out of place. Something big, and I had to find out what that was.

"That's a good offer," I said.

"You're damn right. We're coming down off premeditated and lying in wait."

"I'm assuming we're talking voluntary manslaughter?"

"It would be hard even for you to make a case for involuntary. It's not like she just happened to be in that garage. Do you think she'll take it?"

"I don't know. She's said since the start no deals. She wants a trial. I can try to sell it. It's just that..."

"Just that what?"

"I'm curious, you know? Why such a nice offer? Why are you coming down to this? What's gone wrong inside your case that makes you feel you need to cut and run?"

"This is not cutting and running. She'll still go to prison and there will still be justice. There's nothing wrong with our case but trials are expensive and long. Across the board the DA's office is trying for dispositions over trials. But dispositions that make sense. This is one of those times. You don't want it, I'm ready to go."

I held my hands up in surrender. I could see her focus on the plaster cast on my left hand.

"It's not whether I want it. It's my client's choice and I have to give her all the information I can, that's all. I've been in this position before. Usually a deal this good is too good to be true. You take it and you end up finding out later that the main witness was going to flake out or the prosecution just picked up a nice piece of exculpatory evidence you would've gotten in discovery if you'd hung on just a little bit longer."

"Yeah, well, not this time. It is what it is. You have twenty-four hours and then it comes off the table."

"What about going with the low range?"

"*What?*"

It was almost a shriek.

"Come on, you didn't come in here and give me your last, best offer. No one works that way. You have one more give and we both know it. Voluntary manslaughter, low-range sentencing recommendation. She'll do five to seven tops."

"You're killing me. The press will eat me alive."

"Maybe, but I know your boss didn't send you over here with one offer, Andrea."

She leaned back and looked at Aronson and then around the rest of the room, her eyes trailing over the shelves of books that came with the office.

I waited. I glanced at Aronson and winked. I knew what was coming.

"I'm sorry about your hand," Freeman said. "That must've hurt."

"Actually, it didn't. I was already down for the count when they did it. I never felt a thing."

I held up my hand again and wiggled my fingers, their tips moving along the top edge of the cast.

"I can already move them pretty good."

"Okay, low range. I still need to hear back in twenty-four hours. And this is all off the record. Other than to your client, this is not to be revealed outside of this room if it doesn't go."

"We already agreed to that."

"Okay, then I guess that's it. I'll be heading back."

She stood up and Aronson and I followed. We dropped into the sort of small talk that often follows a meeting of great importance.

"So who's going to be the next DA?" I asked.

"Your guess is as good as mine," Freeman said. "There's no front-runner yet, that's for sure."

The office was currently operating with an interim district attorney following the appointment of its former holder to a top job in the U.S. Attorney General's Office in Washington, D.C. A special election would be held in the fall to fill the slot and so far the field of candidates was uninspiring.

Finished with the pleasantries, we shook hands and Freeman left the office. Sitting back down, I looked at Aronson.

"So what do you think?"

"I think you're right. The offer was too good and then she made it even better. Something's gone wrong in her case."

"Yeah, but what? We can't exploit it if we don't know what it is."

I leaned forward to the phone and pushed the intercom. I told Cisco to come in. I swiveled in silence while we waited. Cisco entered, put my cell phone down on the desk and then took the seat where Freeman had sat.

"I have the trace underway. I'd give it three days. They don't move that quickly."

"Thanks."

"So what's up with the prosecutor?"

"She's running scared and we don't know why. I know you've vetted everything she's given us and checked out the witnesses. I want to do it again. Something's changed. Something they thought they had, they no longer have. We have to find out what it is."

"Margo Schafer, probably."

"How so?"

Cisco shrugged.

"Just speaking from experience. Eyewitnesses are unreliable. Schafer is a big part of a very circumstantial case. They lose her or she turns up shaky and they have a big problem. We already know it's going to be tough to convince a jury that she saw what she claims she saw."

"But we still haven't talked to her?"

"She refused to be interviewed and is under no obligation to do so."

I opened the middle drawer of the desk and pulled out a pencil. I pushed its point into the top opening of the cast and down between two fingers, then maneuvered the pencil back and forth to scratch my palm.

"What are you doing?" Cisco asked.

"What's it look like? Itching my palm. It was driving me crazy the whole meeting."

"You know what they say about itchy palms," Aronson said.

I looked at her, wondering if there was some sort of sexual innuendo to the answer.

"No, what?"

"If it's your right hand you are going to come into money. If it's your left then you are going to pay out money. If you scratch them, you stop it from happening."

"They teach you that in law school, Bullocks?"

"No, my mother always said it. She was superstitious. She thought it was true."

"Well, if it is, I just saved us a bunch of money."

I pulled the pencil out and put it back in the drawer.

"Cisco, take another run at Schafer. Try to catch her off guard. Show up somewhere she'd never expect it. See how she reacts. See if she talks."

"You got it."

"If she doesn't talk, take another run at her background. Maybe there's a connection we don't know about."

"If there is I'll find it."

"That's what I'm counting on."

Sixteen

As I had expected, Lisa Trammel wanted no part in a plea agreement that would put her in prison for as long as seven years, even though she faced the possibility of four times that amount if convicted at trial. She chose to take her chances on an acquittal and I couldn't blame her. While I remained at a loss to explain the state's change of heart, the offer of a defense-friendly disposition made me think the prosecution was running scared and that we had a legitimate fighting chance. If my client was willing to roll the dice, then so was I. It wasn't my freedom at stake.

I was cruising home at the end of work the next day when I called Andrea Freeman to give her the news. She had left several messages early in the day and I had strategically not returned them, hoping to make her sweat. It turned out she was anything but feeling the heat. When I told her my client was passing on the offer she simply laughed.

"Uh, Haller, you might want to start returning your messages a little sooner. I tried several times this morning to get to you. That offer was permanently taken off the table at ten o'clock. She should've accepted it last night and it probably would have saved her about twenty years in prison."

"Who pulled the offer, your boss?"

"I did. I changed my mind and that's that."

I couldn't think of what could have caused such a dramatic change in less than twenty-four hours. The only activity on the case that morning that I knew of was Louis Opparizio's attorney filing a motion to quash the subpoena we had served on him. But I didn't see the connection to Freeman's abrupt change in direction on the plea.

When I didn't respond, Freeman moved to end the call.

"So, Counselor, I guess I'll see you in court."

"Yeah, and just so you know, I'm going to find it, Andrea."

"Find what?"

"Whatever it is you're hiding. The thing that went wrong yesterday, that made you bring me that offer. Doesn't matter if you think it's all fixed now, I'm going to find it. And when we get to trial, I'll have it in my back pocket."

She laughed into the phone in a way that immediately undercut the confidence I'd had in my statement.

"Like I said, I'll see you in court," she said.

"Yeah, I'll be there," I said.

I put the phone down on the armrest and tried to intuit what was going on. Then it struck me. I might already be carrying Freeman's secret in my back pocket.

The letter from Bondurant to Opparizio had been hidden in the haystack of documents Freeman had turned over. Maybe she had found it only recently herself and realized what I could do with it, how I could build a defense case around it. It happens sometimes. A prosecutor gets a case with what seems like overwhelming evidence, and hubris sets in. You go with what you've got and other potential evidence goes undiscovered until late. Sometimes too late.

I became convinced. It had to be the letter. A day ago she was running scared because of the letter. Now she was confident. Why? The only difference between yesterday and today was the motion to quash the Opparizio subpoena. All at once I understood her strategy. The prosecution would support the dismissal of the subpoena. If Opparizio didn't testify I might not be able to get the letter before the jury.

If I had it right, then there could be a severe setback for the defense at the hearing on the motion. I now knew I had to be prepared to fight as though my case depended on it. Because it did.

I decided to put the phone in my pocket. No more calls. It was Friday evening. I would put the case aside and take it all up again in the morning. Everything could wait until then.

"Rojas, put on some music. It's the weekend, man!"

Rojas hit the button on the dash to play the CD. I had forgotten what I had in there but soon identified the song as Ry Cooder singing "Teardrops Will Fall," a cover of the 1960s classic on his anthology disc. It sounded good and it sounded right. A song about love lost and being left alone.

The trial would start in less than three weeks. Whether or not we figured out what Freeman was hiding, the defense team was locked and loaded and ready to go. We still had some outstanding subpoenas to serve but otherwise we were fit for battle and I was growing more confident every day.

The following Monday I would hole up in my office and start choreographing the defense case. The hypothesis of innocence would be carefully revealed piece by piece and witness by witness until it all came together in a crushing wave of reasonable doubt.

But I still had a weekend to fill before that and I wanted to put as much distance as I could between me and Lisa Trammel and everything else. Cooder was now on to "Poor Man's Shangri-La," the one about the UFOs and space *vatos* in Chávez Ravine before they took it away from the people and put up Dodger Stadium.

> *What's that sound, what's that light?*
> *Streaking down through the night*

I told Rojas to turn it up. I lowered the back windows and let the wind and music blow through my hair and ears.

> *UFO got a radio*
> *Little Julian singing soft and low*
> *Los Angeles down below*
> *DJ says, we gotta go*
> *To El Monte, to El Monte, pa El Monte*
> *Na, na, na, na, na*
> *Livin' in a poor man's Shangri-La*

I closed my eyes as we cruised.

Seventeen

Rojas dropped me at the steps of my home and I slowly made my way up while he put the Lincoln in the garage. His own car was parked on the street. He'd take it home and come back Monday, the usual routine.

Before opening the door I stepped to the far end of the deck and looked out at the city. The sun still had a couple hours of work ahead, then would set on another week. From up here the city had a certain sound that was as identifiable as a train whistle. The low hiss of a million dreams in competition.

"You all right?"

I turned around. It was Rojas at the top of the steps.

"Yeah, fine. What's the matter?"

"I don't know. I saw you standing up here and thought maybe something was wrong, like you were locked out or something."

"No, I was just checking out the city."

I went over to the door, pulling out my house key.

"Have a good weekend, Rojas."

"You too, Boss."

"You know, you should probably stop calling me Boss."

"Okay, Boss."

"Whatever."

I turned the lock and pushed the door open. I was immediately greeted with a sharp and multivoiced cheer of "Surprise!"

I once got shot in the gut after opening the same door. This surprise was a lot better. My daughter rushed forward and hugged me and I hugged her back. I looked around the room and saw everybody: Cisco, Lorna, Bullocks. My half brother Harry Bosch and his daughter, Maddie. And Maggie was there, too. She came up next to Hayley and kissed me on the cheek.

"Uh," I said, "I've got some bad news. Today is not my birthday. I am afraid you've all been led astray by someone with some sort of devious plan to get cake."

Maggie punched me on the shoulder.

"Your birthday's Monday. Not a good day for a surprise party."

"Yeah, exactly as I had planned it."

"Come on, get out of the door and let Rojas in. Nobody's staying that long. We just wanted to say happy birthday."

I leaned forward and kissed her cheek and whispered in her ear.

"What about you? You're not staying long either?"

"We'll see about that."

She escorted me in through a gauntlet of handshakes, kisses and back pats. It was nice and totally unexpected. I was placed in the seat of honor and handed a lemonade.

The party lasted another hour and I got time to visit with all my guests. I hadn't seen Harry Bosch in a few months. I had heard he'd come by the hospital but I wasn't awake for the visit. We had worked a case the year before, with me as a special prosecutor. It had been nice being on the same side and I had thought the experience would keep us close. But it hadn't really worked out that way. Bosch remained as distant as ever and I remained as saddened about it as ever.

When I saw the opportunity I moved toward him and we stood side by side in front of the window that gave the best view of the city.

"From this angle it's hard not to love it, isn't it?" he asked.

I turned from the view to him and then back. He was drinking a lemonade, too. He had told me he'd stopped drinking when his teenage daughter had come to live with him.

"I know what you mean," I said.

He drained his glass and thanked me for the party. I told him he could leave Maddie with us if she wanted to visit Hayley longer. But he said that he already had plans to take her to a shooting range in the morning.

"A shooting range? You're taking your daughter to a shooting range?"

"I've got guns in the house. She should know how to use them."

I shrugged. I guessed there was a logic in it.

Bosch and his daughter were the first to leave and soon afterward the party ended. Everybody left except for Maggie and Hayley. They had decided to stay the night.

Exhausted by the day and the week and the month, I took a long shower and then got into bed early. Soon Maggie came in, after talking Hayley to sleep in her room. She closed the door and that was when I knew my real birthday present was coming.

She hadn't brought any nightclothes with her. Lying on my back, I watched her get undressed and then slip under the covers with me.

"You know, you're a piece of work, Haller," she whispered.

"What did I do this time?"

"You just trespassed all over the place."

She moved in close and then over on top of me. She bent down, tenting my face with her hair. She kissed me and started slowly moving her hips, then put her lips against my ear.

"So," she said. "Normal function and activity, that's what the doctor told you, right?"

"That's what he said."

"We'll see."

PART THREE
Boléro

Eighteen

L ouis Opparizio was a man who did not want to be served. As an attorney he knew that the only way he could be dragged into the Lisa Trammel trial was to be served with a subpoena to testify. Avoiding service meant avoiding testimony. Whether he had been tipped to the defense strategy or simply was smart enough to understand it on his own, he seemingly disappeared just at the time we began looking for him. His whereabouts became unknown and all the routine tricks of the trade to track him and draw him out had failed. We did not know if Opparizio was in the country, let alone in Los Angeles.

Opparizio had one very big thing going for him in his effort to hide. Money. With enough money you can hide from anybody in this world and Opparizio knew it. He owned numerous homes in numerous states, multiple vehicles and even a private jet to help him connect quickly to all his dots. When he moved, whether it was from state to state or from Beverly Hills home to Beverly Hills office, he traveled behind a phalanx of security men.

He also had one thing going against him. Money. The vast wealth he had accumulated by carrying out the bidding of banks and other lenders had also given him an Achilles' heel. He had acquired the tastes and desires of the super rich.

And that was how we eventually got him.

In the course of his efforts to locate Opparizio, Cisco Wojciechowski amassed a tremendous amount of information about his quarry's profile.

From this data a trap was carefully planned and executed to perfection. A glossy presentation package announcing the closed-bid auction of an Aldo Tinto painting was sent to Opparizio's office in Beverly Hills. The package said the painting would be on view for interested bidders for only two hours beginning at 7 P.M. two nights hence in Studio Z at Bergamot Station in Santa Monica. Bids would then be accepted until midnight.

The presentation looked professional and legitimate. The depiction of the painting had been lifted from an online art catalog that displayed private collections. We knew from a two-year-old profile of Opparizio in a bar journal that he had become a collector of second-tier painters and that the late Italian master Tinto was his obsession. When a man called the phone number on the portfolio, identified himself as a representative of Louis Opparizio and booked a private viewing of the painting, we had him.

At precisely the appointed time, the Opparizio entourage entered the old Red Car trolley station, which had been turned into an upscale gallery complex. While three sunglassed security men fanned out across the grounds, two more swept Gallery Z before giving the all-clear signal. Only then did Opparizio emerge from the stretch Mercedes.

Inside the gallery Opparizio was met by two women who disarmed him with their smiles and excitement about the arts and the painting he was about to see. One woman handed him a glass flute of Cristal to celebrate the moment. The other gave him a thick folded packet of documents on the painting's pedigree and exhibition history. Because he held the champagne in one hand he could not open the documents. He was told he could read it all later because he must see the painting now before the next appointment. He was led into the viewing room where the piece sat on an ornate easel covered with a satin drape. A lone spotlight lit the center of the room. The women told him he could remove the drape himself and one of them took his glass of champagne. She wore long gloves.

Opparizio stepped forward, his hand raised in anticipation. He carefully pulled the satin off the frame. And there pinned to the board was the subpoena. Confused, he leaned forward to look, perhaps thinking this was still the Italian master's work.

"You've been served, Mr. Opparizio," Jennifer Aronson said. "You have the original in your hand."

"I don't understand," he said, but he did.

"And the whole thing from the moment you drove in is on video-tape," said Lorna.

She stepped to the wall and hit the switch, bathing the entire room in light. She pointed to the two overhead cameras. Jennifer lifted the champagne flute as if giving a toast.

"We have your prints, too, if needed."

She turned and raised a toast to one of the cameras.

"No," Opparizio said.

"Yes," Lorna said.

"We'll see you in court," Jennifer said.

The women headed to the side door of the gallery where a Lincoln driven by Cisco was waiting. Their job was done.

That was then, this was now. I sat in the Honorable Coleman Perry's courtroom preparing to defend the service and validity of the Opparizio subpoena and the very heart of the defense's case. My co-counsel, Jennifer Aronson, sat next to me at the defense table and next to her was our client, Lisa Trammel. At the opposing table sat Louis Opparizio and his two attorneys, Martin Zimmer and Landon Cross. Andrea Freeman was in a seat located back against the rail. As the prosecutor of the criminal case out of which this hearing arose, she was an interested party but this wasn't her cause of action. Additionally, Detective Kurlen was in the courtroom, sitting three rows back in the gallery. His presence was a mystery to me.

The cause of action was Opparizio's. He and his legal crew were out to quash the subpoena and prevent his participation in the trial. In strategizing how to do so they had thought it prudent to tip Freeman to the hearing in case the prosecution also saw merit in keeping Opparizio from the jury. Though largely there as a bystander, Freeman could step into the fray whenever she wanted and she knew that whether she joined in or not, the hearing would likely offer her a good look at the defense's trial strategy.

It was the first time I saw Opparizio in person. He was a block of a man who somehow appeared as wide as he was tall. The skin on his face had been stretched tight by the scalpel or by years of anger. By the cut of his hair and of his suit, he looked like money. And he seemed to me to be the perfect straw man because he also looked like a man who could kill, or at least give the order to kill.

Opparizio's lawyers had asked the judge to hold the hearing *in camera* — behind closed doors in his chambers — so that the details revealed would not reach the media and therefore possibly taint the jury pool that would assemble the following day. But everybody in the room knew that his lawyers were not being altruistic. A closed hearing guarded against details about Opparizio leaking to the press and informing something much larger than the jury pool. Public opinion.

I argued vigorously against closing the proceedings. I warned that such a move would cause public suspicion about the subsequent trial and this outweighed any possible taint of the jury pool. Elected to the bench, Perry was ever mindful of public perception. He agreed with me and declared the hearing open to the public. Score a big one for me. My prevailing on that one argument probably saved the entire case for the defense.

Not a lot of the media was there but there was enough for what I needed. Reporters from the *Los Angeles Business Journal* and the *L.A. Times* were in the front row. A freelance video man who sold footage to all the networks was in the empty jury box with his camera. I had tipped him to the hearing and told him to be there. I figured that between the print media and the lone TV camera, there would be enough pressure on Opparizio to force the outcome I was looking for.

After dispensing with the request to hide behind closed doors, the judge got down to business.

"Mr. Zimmer, you have filed a motion to quash the subpoena of Louis Opparizio in the matter of *California versus Trammel*. Why don't you state your case, sir?"

Zimmer looked like a lawyer who had been around the block a few times and usually got to carry his enemies home in his briefcase. He stood to respond to the judge.

"We would love to address the court on this matter, Your Honor. I am going to speak first to the facts of the service of the subpoena itself and then my colleague, Mr. Cross, will discuss the other issue for which we seek relief."

Zimmer then proceeded to claim that my office had engaged in mail fraud in laying the trap that resulted in Opparizio being served a subpoena. He said that the glossy brochure that had baited his client was an instrument of fraud and its placement in the U.S. mail constituted a felony that invalidated any action that followed, such as service of the subpoena. He further asked that the defense be penalized by being disallowed from any subsequent effort to subpoena Opparizio to testify.

I didn't even have to stand up for this one — which was a good thing because the simple acts of standing and sitting still set off flares of pain across my chest. The judge raised his hand in my direction to hold me in check and then tersely dismissed Zimmer's argument, calling it novel but ridiculous and without merit.

"Come on, Mr. Zimmer, this is the big league," Perry said. "You have anything with some meat on the bone?"

Properly cowed, Zimmer deferred to his colleague and sat down. Landon Cross stood up next to face the judge.

"Your Honor," he said, "Louis Opparizio is a man of means and standing in this community. He has had nothing to do with this crime or this trial and objects to his name and reputation being sullied by his inclusion in it. Let me emphatically repeat, he had nothing to do with this crime, is not a suspect and has no knowledge of it. He has no probative or exculpatory information to provide. He objects to defense counsel's putting him on the witness stand to conduct a fishing expedition and he objects to counsel's using him as a deflection from the case at hand. Let Mr. Haller fish for red herrings in a different pond."

Cross turned and gestured to Andrea Freeman.

"I might add, Your Honor, that the prosecution joins me in this motion to quash for the same reasons mentioned."

The judge swiveled on his seat and looked at me.

"Mr. Haller, you want to respond to all of that?"

I stood up. Slowly. I was holding the foam gavel from my desk, working it with my fingers, which were newly freed from plaster but still stiff.

"Yes, Your Honor. I would first like to say that Mr. Cross makes a good point about the fishing expedition. Mr. Opparizio's testimony at trial, if allowed to proceed, would include a fair amount of fishing. Not all of it, mind you, but I would like to drop a line in the water. But this is only, Your Honor, because Mr. Opparizio and his defensive front have made it darn near impossible for the defense to conduct a thorough investigation of the murder of Mitchell Bondurant. Mr. Opparizio and his henchmen have thwarted all—"

Zimmer was up on his feet objecting loudly.

"Your Honor! I mean, really! Henchmen? Counsel is clearly engaged in playing to the media in the courtroom at Mr. Opparizio's expense. I once again urge you to move these proceedings to chambers before we continue."

"We're staying put," Perry said. "But Mr. Haller, I'm not going to allow you to call this witness just to let you grandstand for the jury. What's his connection? What's he got?"

I nodded like I was ready with an obvious answer.

"Mr. Opparizio founded and operates a company that acts as a middleman in the foreclosure process. When the victim in this case decided to foreclose on the home of the defendant, he went to Mr. Opparizio to get it done. That, to me, Your Honor, puts Mr. Opparizio on the front line of this case and I would like to ask him about this because the prosecution has stated to the media that the foreclosure is the motive for the murder."

Zimmer jumped in before the judge could respond.

"That is a ridiculous assertion! Mr. Opparizio's company has a hundred eighty-five employees. It is housed in a three-level office building. To—"

"Foreclosing on people's homes is big business," I interjected.

"Counsel," the judge warned.

"Mr. Opparizio had nothing whatsoever to do with the defendant's foreclosure other than the fact that it was handled by his company along with about a hundred thousand other such cases this year," Zimmer said.

"A hundred thousand cases, Mr. Zimmer?" the judge asked.

"That's right, Judge. On average the company has been handling two thousand foreclosures a week for more than two years. This would include the defendant's foreclosure case. Mr. Opparizio has no specific knowledge of her case. It was one of many and was never on his radar."

The judge dropped deep into thought and looked like he had heard enough. I had hoped not to have to reveal my ace in the hole, especially in front of the prosecutor. But I had to assume Freeman was already aware of the Bondurant letter and its value.

I reached down to the file in front of me on the table and flipped it open. There were the letter and four copies, ready to go.

"Mr. Haller, I'm inclined to —"

"Your Honor, if the court would indulge me, I would like to be allowed to ask Mr. Opparizio the name of his personal secretary."

That gave Perry another pause and he screwed his mouth up in confusion.

"You want to know who his secretary is?"

"His personal secretary, yes."

"Why would you want to know that, sir?"

"I am asking the court to indulge me."

"Very well. Mr. Opparizio? Mr. Haller would like the name of your personal secretary."

Opparizio leaned forward and looked at Zimmer as if needing his approval. Zimmer signaled him to go on and answer the question.

"Uh, Judge, I actually have two. One is Carmen Esposito and the other is Natalie Lazarra."

He then leaned back. The judge looked at me. It was time to play the ace.

"Judge, I have here copies of a certified letter that was written by Mitchell Bondurant, the murder victim, and sent to Mr. Opparizio. It was received and signed for by his personal secretary Natalie Lazarra. The letter was turned over to me in discovery by the prosecution. I would like Mr. Opparizio to testify in court so that I can question him about it."

"Let's take a look," Perry said.

I stepped away from the table and delivered copies of the letter to the judge and then to Zimmer. On my way back I swung by Freeman and offered her a copy.

"No, thanks. I already have it."

I nodded and went back to the table but stayed standing.

"Your Honor?" Zimmer said. "Can we have a short recess to look this over? We haven't seen it before."

"Fifteen minutes," Perry said.

The judge stepped down from the bench and went through the door to his chambers. I waited to see if the Opparizio team would take it out into the hall. When they didn't move, I didn't. I wanted them to worry that I might overhear something.

I huddled with Aronson and Trammel.

"What are they doing?" Aronson whispered. "They had to have known about the letter already."

"I am sure the prosecution gave them a copy," I said. "Opparizio acts like he's the smartest guy in the room. Now we're going to see if he *is* the smartest guy in the room."

"What do you mean?"

"We've got him between a rock and a hard place. He knows he should tell the judge that if I ask about that letter he will take the Fifth and therefore the subpoena should be kicked. But he knows if he takes the Fifth in front of the media here, he's in trouble. That puts blood in the water."

"So what do you think he'll do?" Trammel asked.

"Act like the smartest guy."

I pushed back from the table and stood up. I nonchalantly started to pace behind the tables. Zimmer looked over his shoulder at me and then leaned in closer to his client. Eventually, I came back to Freeman, still in her chair.

"When do you wade in?"

"Oh, I'm thinking I might not have to."

"They already had the letter, didn't they? You gave it to them."

She shrugged her shoulders but didn't answer. I looked past her to Kurlen sitting three rows back.

"What's Kurlen doing here?"

"Oh... he might be needed."

That was a lot of help.

"Last week when you made the offer, that was because you had found the letter, wasn't it? You thought your case was in real trouble."

She looked up at me and smiled, not giving anything away.

"What changed? Why'd you pull the offer back?"

Again she didn't answer.

"You think he's going to take the Fifth, don't you?"

The shrug again.

"I would," I said. "But him...?"

"We'll know soon enough," she said, dismissively.

I went back to the table and sat down. Trammel whispered to me that she still wasn't clear on what was going on.

"We want Opparizio to testify at trial. He doesn't want to but the only way the judge will let him out of the subpoena is if he says he'll invoke his Fifth Amendment protection against self-incrimination. If he does that, we're dead. He's our straw man. We need to get him on the stand."

"Do you think he will take the Fifth?"

"I'm betting no. Too much at stake with the media here. He's putting the finishing touches on a big merger and knows if he takes the nickel the media will be all over him. I think he's just smart enough to think he can talk his way out of it on the stand. That's what I'm counting on. Him thinking he's smarter than everybody else."

"What if—"

She was cut off by the return of the judge to the bench. He quickly went back on record and Zimmer asked to address the court.

"Your Honor, I would like the record to reflect that against the advice of counsel my client has instructed me to withdraw the motion to quash."

The judge nodded and pursed his lips. He looked at Opparizio.

"So your client will testify in front of the jury?" he asked.

"Yes, Your Honor," Zimmer said. "He has made that decision."

"You sure about this, Mr. Opparizio? You have a lot of experience sitting with you at that table."

"Yes, Your Honor," Opparizio said. "I'm sure."

"Then motion withdrawn. Any other business before the court before we begin jury selection tomorrow morning?"

Perry looked past the tables to Freeman. It was a tell. He knew there was further business to discuss. Freeman stood up, file in hand.

"Yes, Your Honor, may I approach?"

"Please do, Ms. Freeman."

Freeman stepped forward but then waited for the Opparizio team to finish packing and move off the prosecution's table. The judge waited patiently. Finally, she took her place at the table, remaining standing.

"Let me guess," Perry said. "You want to talk about Mr. Haller's updated witness list."

"Yes, Judge, I do. I also have an evidentiary issue to bring up. Which would you like to hear first?"

Evidentiary issue. I suddenly knew why Kurlen was in the courtroom.

"Let's go with the witness list first," the judge said. "I saw that one coming."

"Yes, Your Honor. Mr. Haller has put his co-counsel down on the witness list and I think, first of all, he needs to choose between having Ms. Aronson as second chair and having her as a witness. But second, and more important, Ms. Aronson has already handled the preliminary hearing for the defense as well as other duties, and so the state objects to this sudden move to make her a witness in the trial."

Freeman sat down and the judge looked over at me.

"Sort of late in the game, isn't it, Mr. Haller?"

I stood.

"Yes, Your Honor, except for the fact that it is no game and it's my client's freedom at stake here. The defense would ask the court for wide latitude in this regard. Ms. Aronson was intimately involved in the defense against the foreclosure proceedings against my client and the defense has come to the conclusion that she will be needed to explain to jurors what the background was and what was happening at the time of the murder of Mr. Bondurant."

"And is it your plan to have her do double duty, both witness and defense counsel? That's not going to happen in my courtroom, sir."

"Your Honor, I assumed when I put Ms. Aronson's name on the final list that we would have this discussion with Ms. Freeman. The defense is open to the court's decision in regard to this."

Perry looked at Freeman to see if she had further argument. She held still.

"Very well then," he said. "You just lost your second chair, Mr. Haller. I will allow Ms. Aronson to remain on the witness list but tomorrow when we start picking the jury, you're on your own. Ms. Aronson stays clear of my courtroom until she comes in to testify."

"Thank you, Your Honor," I said. "Will she be able to join me as second chair after her testimony is concluded?"

"I don't see that as a problem." Perry asked, "Ms. Freeman, you had a second issue for the court?"

Freeman stood back up. I sat down and leaned forward with my pen, ready to take notes. The movement caused a searing pain to cross my torso and I almost groaned out loud.

"Your Honor, the state wants to head off an objection and protest I am sure will come from counsel. Late yesterday, we received a return on DNA analysis of a very small blood trace found on a shoe belonging to the defendant and seized during the search of her house and garage on the day of the murder."

I felt an invisible punch in my stomach that made my rib pain disappear quickly. I instinctively knew this was going to be a game changer.

"The analysis matches the blood from the shoe to the victim, Mitchell Bondurant. Before counsel protests, I must inform the court that analysis of the blood was delayed because of the backup in the lab and because the sample being worked with was rather minute. The difficulty was accentuated by the need to preserve a portion of the sample for the defense."

I flipped my pen up into the air. It bounced onto the table and then clattered to the floor. I stood up.

"Your Honor, this is just outrageous. On the eve of jury selection? To pull this now? And boy oh boy, that was sure nice of them to leave some for the defense. We'll just run out and get it analyzed before jury selection starts tomorrow. You know, this is just—"

"Point well taken, Counsel," the judge interrupted. "It troubles me as well. Ms. Freeman, you've had this evidence since the inception of the case. How can it be that it conveniently lands the day before jury selection?"

"Your Honor," Freeman said, "I have a full understanding of the burden this places on the defense and the court. But it is what it is. I was informed of the findings at eight o'clock this morning when I received the report from the lab. This is the first opportunity I've had to bring it before the court. As to the reason for its coming in now, well, there are a few. I am sure the court is aware of the backup for DNA analysis at the lab at Cal State. There are thousands of cases. While homicide investigations certainly get a priority it is not to the exclusion of all other cases. We elected not to go to a private lab that could have turned it around faster because of the concern over the size of the sample. We knew if anything went wrong with an outside vendor then we would have completely lost the opportunity to test the blood — and hold a portion for the defense."

I shook my head in frustration while waiting for the chance to speak again. This was indeed a game changer. It had been a completely circumstantial case. Now it was a case involving direct evidence connecting the defendant to the crime.

"Mr. Haller?" the judge said. "You want to respond?"

"I sure do, Judge. I think this goes beyond being sandbagged and I don't for a moment believe the timing here is happenstance. I would ask that the court tell the prosecution that it is too late to spring this now. I move that this so-called evidence be excluded from the trial."

"What about delaying the trial?" the judge said. "What if you were given the time to get the analysis done and get up to speed on this?"

"Get up to speed? Judge, this isn't just about getting our own analysis done. This is about changing the entire defense strategy. The prosecution is seeking to change this from a circumstantial case to a science-based case on the eve of trial. I don't only need time to do DNA testing. After two months, I now need to rethink the entire case. This is devastating, Your Honor, and it should not be allowed under the basic idea of fair play."

Freeman wanted a comeback but the judge didn't allow it. I took that as a good sign until I saw him looking at the calendar hanging on the wall behind the clerk's corral. That told me he was only willing to ameliorate the situation with time. He was going to allow the DNA into evidence and would just give me extra time to prepare for it.

I sat back down in defeat. Lisa Trammel leaned toward me and desperately whispered, "Mickey, this can't be. It's a setup. There's no way his blood could be on those shoes. You have to believe me."

I put my hand up to cut her off. I didn't have to believe a word out of her mouth and that was all beside the point. The reality was that the case was shifting. No wonder Freeman had all her confidence back.

Suddenly I realized something. I quickly stood back up. Too quickly. Pain shot down my torso into my groin and I bent over the defense table.

"Your … Honor?"

"Are you all right, Mr. Haller?"

I slowly straightened up.

"Yes, Your Honor, but I need to add something to the record, if I may."

"Go ahead."

"Your Honor, the defense questions the veracity of the prosecution's claim of learning about this DNA result only this morning. Three weeks ago Ms. Freeman offered my client a very attractive disposition, giving Ms. Trammel twenty-four hours to think it over. Then—"

"Your Honor?" Freeman said.

"Don't interrupt," the judge commanded. "Continue, Mr. Haller."

I had no qualms about breaking my agreement with Freeman not to reveal the disposition negotiations. The gloves were off at this point.

"Thank you, Your Honor. So we get the offer on a Thursday night and then on Friday morning Ms. Freeman mysteriously yanks it right back off the table without explanation. Well, I think we now have that explanation, Judge. She knew back then—three weeks ago—about this supposed DNA evidence but decided to sit on it in order to surprise the defense with it on the eve of trial. And I—"

"Thank you, Mr. Haller. What about that, Ms. Freeman?"

I could see the skin around the judge's eyes had drawn tight. He was upset. What I had just revealed had the ring of truth to it.

"Your Honor," Freeman said indignantly. "Nothing could be further from the truth. I have with me in the gallery here Detective Kurlen who will be happy to testify under oath that the DNA report was delivered over the weekend to his office and opened by him shortly after his arrival at seven thirty this morning. He then called me and I brought it to court. The district attorney's office has not sat on anything and I resent the aspersion directed at me personally by counsel."

The judge glanced out to the rows of seats and spotted Kurlen, then looked back at Freeman.

"Why did you withdraw the offer a day after making it?" he asked.

The million-dollar question. Freeman seemed unsettled that the judge would carry the inquiry any further.

"Judge, that decision involved internal issues perhaps better not aired in court."

"I want to understand this, Counsel. If you want this evidence then you better allay my concerns, internal issues or not."

Freeman nodded.

"Yes, Your Honor. As you know, there is an interim district attorney since Mr. Williams joined the U.S. Attorney General's Office in Washington. This has resulted in a situation where we don't always have clear lines of communication and direction. Suffice it to say that on that Thursday I had a supervisor's approval for the offer I made to Mr. Haller. But on Friday morning I learned from a higher authority in the office that the offer was not approved internally and so I withdrew it."

It was a load of crap but she had delivered it well and I had nothing that contradicted it. But when she told me the offer was gone that Friday I knew by the tone of her voice that she had something new, something else, and her decision had nothing to do with internal communication and direction.

The judge made his ruling.

"I am going to put back jury selection ten court days. This should give the defense time to have DNA testing of the evidence completed if it chooses to do so. It also allows ample time to consider what strategic change will come with this information. I will hold the state responsible for being totally cooperative in this matter and in getting the biological material to the defense without delay. All parties will be prepared to begin jury selection two weeks from today. Court is adjourned."

The judge quickly left the bench. I looked down at the empty page on my legal pad. I had just been eviscerated.

Slowly I started packing my briefcase.

"What do we do?" Aronson asked.

"I don't know yet," I said.

"Run the test," Lisa Trammel said urgently. "They've got it wrong. It can't be his blood on my shoes. This is unreal."

I looked at her. Her brown eyes fervent and believable.

"Don't worry. I'll figure something out."

The optimism tasted sour in my mouth. I glanced over at Freeman. She was looking through files in her briefcase. I sauntered over and she gave me a dismissive look. She wasn't interested in hearing my tale of woe.

"You look like things just went exactly the way you wanted them to go," I said.

She showed nothing. She closed her case and headed toward the gate. Before pushing through she looked back at me.

"You want to play hardball, Haller?" she said. "Then you have to be ready to catch."

Nineteen

The next two weeks went by quickly but not without progress. The defense rethought and retooled. I had an independent lab confirm the state's DNA findings—at a rush cost of four grand—and then assimilated the devastating evidence into a view of the case that allowed for the science to be correct as well as my client's innocence to be possible, if not probable. The classic setup defense. It would be an additional and natural dimension to the straw-man gambit. I began to believe it could work and my confidence began to rebuild. By the time delayed jury selection finally started, I had some momentum going and rolled it into the effort, actively looking for the jurors who might lend themselves to believing the new story I was going to spin for them.

It wasn't until the fourth day of jury selection that yet one more Free-man fastball came whistling at my head. We were nearing completion of the panel and it was one of those rare times when both prosecution and defense were happy with the jury's makeup, but for different reasons. The panel was well stocked with working-class men and women. Home owners who came from two-income households. Few had college diplomas and none had advanced degrees. Real salt-of-the-earth people and this was a perfect composition for me. I was going for people who lived close to the edge in the tough economy, who felt the threat of foreclosure at all times, and would have a hard time looking at a banker as a sympathetic victim.

On the other hand, the prosecution asked detailed financial questions of each prospective juror and was looking for hard workers who wouldn't see someone who stopped paying her mortgage as a victim, either. The result, until the morning of the fourth day, was a panel full of jurors neither side objected to and who we each thought we could mold into our own soldiers of justice.

The fastball came when Judge Perry called for the midmorning break. Freeman immediately stood up and asked the judge if counsel could meet in chambers during the break to discuss an evidentiary issue that had just come up. She asked if Detective Kurlen could join the meeting. Perry granted the request and doubled the break time to a half hour. I then followed Freeman, who followed the court reporter and the judge into chambers. Kurlen came in last and I noticed that he was carrying a large manila envelope with red evidence tape on it. It was bulky and appeared to have something heavy inside. The paper envelope was the real giveaway, though. Biological evidence was always wrapped in paper. Plastic evidence bags trapped air and humidity and could damage biologicals. So I knew going in that Freeman was about to drop another DNA bomb on me.

"Here we go again," I said under my breath as I entered the chambers.

The judge moved behind his desk and sat down, his back to a window that looked south toward the hills over Sherman Oaks. Freeman and I took side-by-side seats opposite the desk. Kurlen pulled a chair over from a nearby table and the court reporter sat on a stool to the judge's right. Her steno machine was on a tripod in front of her.

"We're on the record here," the judge said. "Ms. Freeman?"

"Judge, I wanted to meet with you and counsel for the defense as soon as possible because I am anticipating that once again Mr. Haller will howl at the moon when he hears what I have to say and what I have to show."

"Then let's get on with it," Perry said.

Freeman nodded to Kurlen and he started peeling back the tape on the evidence envelope. I said nothing. I noticed that he had a rubber glove on his right hand.

"The prosecution has come into possession of the murder weapon," Freeman stated matter-of-factly, "and plans to introduce it as evidence as well as make it available to the defense for examination."

Kurlen opened the envelope, reached in and brought out a hammer. It was a claw hammer with a brushed steel head and a circular striking surface. It had a polished redwood handle tipped in black rubber at the end. I saw a notch at twelve o'clock on the strike face and knew it likely corresponded with the skull impressions cataloged during the autopsy.

I stood up angrily and walked away from the desk.

"Oh, come on," I said in full outrage. "Are you kidding me?"

I looked at the wall of shelved codebooks Perry had at the far side of the room, put my hands on my hips in indignation and then turned back to the desk.

"Judge, excuse my language, but this is bullshit. She can't do this again. To spring this—what, four days into jury selection and a day before opening statements? We have most of the box already picked, we are possibly going to start tomorrow and she's suddenly laying the sup- posed *murder weapon* on me?"

The judge leaned back in his seat as if distancing himself from the hammer Kurlen was holding.

"You better have a good and convincing story, Ms. Freeman," he said.

"I do, Judge. I could not bring this forward until this morning and I am more than willing to explain why if—"

"You allowed this!" I said, interrupting and pointing a finger at the judge.

"Excuse me, Mr. Haller, but don't you dare point your finger at me," he said with restraint.

"I'm sorry, Judge, but this is your fault. You let her get away with the bullshit DNA story and after that there's no reason for her not to—"

"*Excuse me,* sir, but you had better proceed cautiously. You are about five seconds away from seeing the inside of my holding cell. You do not point your finger or address a superior court judge as you have. Do you understand me?"

I turned back to the codebooks and took a deep breath. I knew I had to get something out of this. I had to come out of this room with the judge owing me something.

"I understand," I finally said.

"Good," Perry said. "Now come back over here and take a seat. Let's hear what Ms. Freeman and Detective Kurlen have to say and it better be good."

Reluctantly, I returned like a chastised child and dropped into my seat.

"Ms. Freeman, let's hear it."

"Yes, Your Honor. The weapon was turned in to us late Monday afternoon. A land—"

"Great!" I said. "I knew it. So you wait until four days into jury selection before you decide to—"

"*Mr. Haller!*" the judge barked. "I have lost all patience with you. Do not interrupt again. Continue, Ms. Freeman. Please."

"Of course, Your Honor. As I said, we received this at the LAPD's Van Nuys Division late Monday afternoon. I think it would be best if Detective Kurlen runs you through the chain of custody."

Perry gestured to the detective to begin.

"What happened was that a landscaper working in a yard on Dickens Street near Kester Avenue found it that morning, lodged in a hedge near the front of his client's house. This is in the street that runs behind WestLand National. The house is approximately two blocks from the rear of the bank. The landscaper who found the hammer is from Gardenia and had no idea about the murder. But thinking the tool belonged to his client, he left it on the porch for him. The home owner, a man named Donald Meyers, didn't see it until he came home from work about five o'clock that afternoon. He was confused because he knew it was not his hammer. However, he then remembered reading articles about the Bondurant murder, at least one of which indicated the murder weapon might be a hammer and that it had not been found yet. He called his landscaper and got his story, then he called the police."

"Well, you've told us how you got it," Perry said. "You haven't explained why we're hearing about it three days later."

Freeman nodded. She was ready for this and took over the narrative.

"Judge, we obviously had to confirm what we had and the chain of custody. We immediately turned it over to the Scientific Investigation Division for processing and only received the lab reports yesterday evening after court."

"And what do those reports conclude?"

"The only fingerprints on the weapon belonged to—"

"Wait a minute," I said, risking the judge's ire again. "Can we just refer to it as the hammer? Calling it 'the weapon' on the record is a bit presumptuous at this point."

"Fine," Freeman said before the judge could respond. "The hammer. The only fingerprints on *the hammer* belonged to Mr. Meyers and his landscaper, Antonio Ladera. However, two things tie it solidly into the case. A small spot of blood found on the neck of the hammer has been conclusively matched through DNA testing to Mitchell Bondurant. We rushed this test with an outside vendor because of the protest counsel made over the precautions taken with the other test. The hammer was also turned over to the medical examiner's office for comparison to the wound patterns on the victim. Again, we have a match. Mr. Haller, you can refer to it as the hammer or the tool or whatever you want. But I'm calling it the murder weapon. And I have copies of the lab reports to turn over to you at this time."

She reached into the manila envelope, removed two paper-clipped documents and handed them to me with a satisfied smile on her face.

"Well, that's nice of you," I said in full sarcasm. "Thank you very much."

"Oh, and there's also this."

She reached into the envelope again and withdrew two eight-by-ten photos, giving one to the judge and one to me. It was a photo of a workbench with tools hung on a pegboard on the wall behind it. I knew it was the workbench from Lisa Trammel's garage. I had been there.

"This is from Lisa Trammel's garage. It was taken on the day of the murder during the search of the premises under the authority of a court-ordered search warrant. You will notice that one tool is missing from the pegboard's hooks. The open space created by this corresponds to the dimensions of a claw hammer."

"This is crazy."

"SID has identified the recovered hammer as a Craftsman model manufactured by Sears. This particular hammer is not sold separately. It comes only in the two-hundred-thirty-nine-piece Carpenter's Tool Package. From this photograph we have identified more than a hundred other tools from that package. But no hammer. It's not there because

Lisa Trammel threw it into the bushes after leaving the scene of the crime."

My mind was racing. Even with a defense based on the theory that the defendant was set up, there was a law of diminishing returns. Explaining away the blood drop on the shoe was one thing. Explaining away your client's ownership of and connection to the murder weapon was not just a second thing. There was an exponential increase in the odds against setup as each piece of evidence is revealed. For the second time in three weeks the defense had been handed a devastating blow and I was left almost speechless. The judge turned to me. It was time to respond but I had no comeback that was worthy.

"This is very compelling evidence, Mr. Haller," he prompted. "You have anything to say?"

I had nothing but I picked myself up off the mat before he reached the ten count.

"Your Honor, this so-called evidence that just sort of conveniently dropped from heaven should have been announced to the court and the defense the moment it was brought forward. Not three days later, not even a day later. If only to allow the defense to properly inspect the evidence, conduct its own tests and observe those of the prosecution. It was supposedly in the bushes undiscovered for what, three months at this point? And yet—*voilà!*—we have DNA to match to the victim. This whole thing stinks of a setup. And it's too damn late, Your Honor. The train has left the station. We might have opening statements as early as tomorrow. The prosecution has had all week to think about how to drop the hammer into hers. What am I supposed to do at this point?"

"Were you planning to give your statement at the beginning or reserve until the defense phase?" the judge asked.

"I was planning on giving it tomorrow." I lied. "I already have it written. But this is also information I could have used while picking the jurors we already have in the box. Judge, this whole thing—look, all I know is that five weeks ago the prosecution was desperate. Ms. Freeman came to *my* office to offer my client a deal. Whether she'll admit it or not, she was running scared and she gave me everything I asked for. And then suddenly, we have the DNA on the shoe. Now, lo and behold, the hammer turns up and, of course, nobody's talking about a disposition anymore. The coincidence of all of this puts it all to doubt. But the malfeasance in how it was handled should alone lead you to refuse to allow it into evidence."

"Your Honor," Freeman said as soon as I was finished. "May I respond to Mr. Haller's allegation of mal—"

"No need to, Ms. Freeman. As I already said, this is compelling evidence. It comes in at an inopportune time but it is clearly evidence the jury should consider. I will allow it but I will also once again allow the defense extra time to prepare for it. We're going to go back out there now and finish picking a jury. Then I am going to give them a long weekend and bring them back Monday for opening statements and the start of the trial. That gives you three extra days to prepare your opener, Mr. Haller. That should be enough time. Meanwhile, your staff, including that young go-getter you hired out of my alma mater, can work on assembling whatever experts and testing you'll need on the hammer."

I shook my head. It wasn't good enough. I was going down fast here.

"Your Honor, I move that the trial be stayed while I take this matter up on appeal."

"You can take it up on appeal, Mr. Haller. That's your right. But it's not going to stop the trial. We go on Monday."

He gave me a little nod that I took as a threat. I take him up on appeal and he won't forget it during trial.

"Do we have anything else to discuss?" Perry asked.

"I'm good," Freeman said.

"Mr. Haller?"

I shook my head as my voice deserted me.

"Then let's go out there and finish picking a jury."

Lisa Trammel was pensively waiting for me at the defense table.

"What happened?" she asked in an urgent whisper.

"What happened was that we just got our asses handed to us again. This time it's over."

"What do you mean?"

"I mean they found the fucking hammer you threw in the bushes after you killed Mitchell Bondurant."

"That's crazy. I—"

"No, you're crazy. They can tie it directly to Bondurant and they can tie it to you. It's right off your fucking workbench. I don't know how you could've been so stupid but that's beside the point. It actually makes keeping the bloody shoes seem like a smart choice in comparison. Now I have to figure out a way to get a deal out of Freeman when she has absolutely no need to make a deal. She's got a slam-bang case so why cut a deal?"

Lisa reached over with one hand and grabbed the left side of my jacket collar. She pulled me closer. Now she whispered through clenched teeth.

"You listen to yourself. How could I have been so stupid? That's the question and the answer is I wasn't. You know if anything I'm not stupid. I've told you from day one, this is a setup. They wanted to get rid of me and this is what they did. But I didn't do this. You've had it right all along. Louis Opparizio. He needed to get rid of Mitchell Bondurant and he used me as the fall guy. Bondurant sent him your letter. That started everything. I didn't—"

She faltered as the tears started to flood her eyes. I put my hand over hers as if to calm her and detached it from my collar. I was aware that the jury was filing into the box and didn't want them to see any attorney-client discord.

"I didn't do this," she said. "You hear me? I don't want any deal. I won't say I did something I didn't do. If that's your best shot then I want a new attorney."

I looked away from her to the bench. Judge Perry was watching us.

"Ready to proceed, Mr. Haller?"

I looked at my client and then back at the judge.

"Yes, Your Honor. Ready to proceed."

Twenty

I t was like being in the losing locker room but we had yet to play the game. It was Sunday afternoon, eighteen hours before opening statements to the jury, and I huddled with my crew, already conceding defeat. It was the bitter end before the trial had even begun.

"I don't understand," Aronson said into the void of silence that had enveloped my office. "You said we needed a hypothesis of innocence. An alternate theory. We have that with Opparizio. We have it in spades. Where is the problem?"

I looked over at Cisco Wojciechowski. It was just the three of us. I was in shorts and a T-shirt. Cisco was in his riding clothes, an army-green tank top over black jeans. And Aronson was dressed for a day in court. She hadn't gotten the memo about it being Sunday.

"The problem is, we're not going to get Opparizio into the trial," I said.

"He withdrew the motion to quash," Aronson protested.

"That doesn't matter. The trial is about the state's evidence against Trammel. It's not about who else might have committed the crime. Might'ves don't count. I can put Opparizio on the stand as the expert on Trammel's foreclosure and the foreclosure epidemic. But I'm not going to get near him as an alternate suspect. The judge won't let me unless I can prove relevance. So we've come all this way and we still don't have relevancy. We still don't have that one thing that pulls Opparizio all the way in."

Aronson was determined not to give up.

"The Fourteenth Amendment guarantees Trammel a 'meaningful opportunity to present a complete defense.' An alternate theory is part of a complete defense."

So she could quote the Constitution. She was book smart but experience poor.

"*California versus Hall,* nineteen eighty-six. Look it up."

I pointed to her laptop, which was open on the corner of my desk. She leaned over and started typing.

"Do you know the citation?"

"Try forty-one."

She typed it in, got the ruling on her screen and started scanning. I looked over at Cisco, who had no idea what I was doing.

"Read it out loud," I said. "The pertinent parts."

"Uh... 'Evidence that another person had motive or opportunity to commit the charged crime, or had some remote connection to the victim or crime scene, is insufficient to raise the requisite reasonable doubt... Evidence of alternate party culpability is relevant and admissible only if it links the alternate party to the actual perpetration of the crime...' Okay, we're screwed."

I nodded.

"If we can't put Opparizio or one of his goons in that parking garage, then we are indeed screwed."

"The letter doesn't do it?" Cisco asked.

"Nope," I said. "There's no way. Freeman will kick my ass if I say the letter opens the door. It gives Opparizio a motive, yes. But it doesn't link him directly to the crime."

"Shit."

"That's about right. Right now, we don't have it. So we don't have a defense. And the DNA and the hammer... well, that nails it all down nicely for the state. No pun intended."

"Our lab reports say there is no biological connection to Lisa," Aronson said. "I also have a Craftsman expert who will testify it is impossible to say that the hammer in evidence came from her specific set of tools. Plus, we know the garage door was unlocked. Even if it is her hammer, anyone could've taken it. And anyone could have planted the blood on the shoes."

"Yeah, yeah, I know all of that. It's not enough to say what could've happened. We're going to have to say this *is* what happened and we're going to have to back it up. If we can't, we won't even get it in. Opparizio is the key. We need to be able to go at him without Freeman standing up on every question and saying, 'What's the relevance?'"

Aronson wouldn't give it up.

"There must be something," she said.

"There's always something. We just haven't found it yet."

I swiveled on my chair until I was looking directly at Cisco. He frowned and nodded. He knew what was coming.

"On you, man," I said. "You've got to find me something. Freeman's going to take about a week to present the state's case. That's how much time you have. But if I stand up tomorrow and throw the dice, saying I'm going to prove somebody else did it, then I have to deliver."

"I'll start over," Cisco said. "Ground up. I'll find you something. You do what you have to do tomorrow."

I nodded, more in thanks than in faith that he would come through. I didn't really believe there was anything out there to get. I had a guilty client and justice was going to prevail. End of story.

I looked down at my desk. Spread across it were crime scene photos and reports. I held up the eight-by-ten of the victim's briefcase lying open on the garage's concrete floor. It was the thing that had stuck with me since the beginning, had given me hope that maybe my client didn't do it. That is, until the last two evidentiary rulings by the judge.

"So still no report on the briefcase contents and if anything was missing?" I asked.

"Not that we've gotten," Aronson said.

I had put her in charge of the first review of discovery materials as they had come in.

"So the guy's briefcase was left wide open and they never tried to see if there was anything missing?"

"They inventoried the contents. We have that. I just don't think they made a report on what was possibly *not* in it. Kurlen's cagey. He wasn't going to create an opening for us."

"Yeah, well, he might be walking around with that briefcase shoved up his ass after I'm through with him on the stand."

Aronson blushed. I pointed at my investigator.

"Cisco, the briefcase. We've got the list of contents. Talk to Bondurant's secretary. Find out if anything was taken."

"I already tried. She wouldn't talk to me."

"Try again. Give her the gun show. Win her over."

He flexed his arms. Aronson continued to blush. I stood up.

"I'm going home to work on my opener."

"You sure you want to give it tomorrow?" Aronson asked. "If you defer until the defense phase you'll know what Cisco's been able to find."

I shook my head.

"I got the weekend because I told the judge I want to give it at the start of the trial. I go back on that and he's going to blame me for losing Friday. He's already a judge with a grudge because I lost it in chambers with him."

I moved around from behind the desk. I handed the photo of the briefcase to Cisco.

"Make sure you guys lock up."

No Rojas on Sundays. I drove the Lincoln home alone. There was light traffic and I got back quickly, even stopping to pick up a pizza at the little Italian joint under the market at the bottom of Laurel Canyon. When I got to the house I didn't bother edging the big Lincoln into the garage next to its fleet twin. I parked at the bottom of the steps, locked it and went on up to the front door. It wasn't until I got up to the deck that I saw that I had someone waiting for me.

Unfortunately, it wasn't Maggie McFierce. Rather, a man I had never seen before sat in one of the director's chairs at the far end of the deck. He was slightly built and disheveled, a week's worth of beard on his cheeks. His eyes were closed and his head tilted back. He was asleep.

I wasn't concerned for my safety. He was alone and he wasn't wearing black gloves. Still, I quietly put the key into the lock and opened the door without a sound. I stepped in, closed the door silently and put the pizza down on the kitchen counter. I then moved back to my bedroom and into the walk-in closet. Off the upper shelf—too high for my daughter to get to—I took down the wooden box that held the Colt Woodsman I'd inherited from my father. It had a tragic history and I hoped not to add to it now. I loaded a full magazine of ammunition into it, then headed back to the front door.

I took the other director's chair and moved it over until it faced the sleeping man. Only after I sat down, holding the gun casually in my lap, did I reach out with my foot and tap him on the knee.

He startled awake, his eyes wide and darting about until they finally landed on my face then dropped to the gun.

"Whoa, wait a minute, man!"

"No, you wait a minute. Who are you and what do you want?"

I didn't point the gun. I kept things casual. He raised his hands, palms out in surrender.

"Mr. Haller, right? I'm Jeff, man. Jeff Trammel. We talked on the phone, remember?"

I stared at him for a moment and realized I had not recognized him because I had never seen a photograph of him. During the times I had been in Lisa Trammel's home there were no framed photos of him. She had excised his presence from the house after he had chosen to hightail it.

Now here he was. Haunted eyes and hangdog look. I thought I knew just what he was looking for.

"How did you know where I live? Who told you to come here?"

"Nobody told me. I just came. I looked your name up on the California Bar website. There was no office listed but this was the correspondence address. I came and saw it was a house and figured you live here. I didn't mean nothing by it. I need to talk to you."

"You could've called."

"That phone ran out of juice. I gotta buy another one."

I decided to run a little test on Jeff Trammel.

"That time you called me, where were you?"

He shrugged like it was no big deal to give up the information now.

"Down in Rosarito. I been staying down there."

That was a lie. Cisco had gotten the trace back on his call. I had the number of the phone and the originating cell tower. The call had come from Venice Beach, about two hundred miles from Rosarito Beach in Mexico.

"What did you want to talk to me about, Jeff?"

"I can help you, man."

"Help me? How?"

"I was talking to Lisa. She told me about the hammer they found. It's not hers—I mean, ours. I can tell you where ours is. Lead you right to it."

"Okay, then where is it?"

He nodded and looked off to the right and at the city down below. The never-ending hiss of traffic filtered up to us.

"That's the thing, Mr. Haller. I need some money. I want to go back to Mexico. You don't need a lot down there but you need a start, if you know what I mean."

"So how much of a start do you want?"

He turned and looked directly at me now because I was speaking his language.

"Just ten grand, man. You got all that movie money coming in and ten won't hurt you too bad. You give me that and I give you the hammer."

"And that's it?"

"Yeah, man, I'll be out of your hair."

"What about testifying on Lisa's behalf at the trial? Remember, we talked about that?"

He shook his head.

"No, I can't do that. I'm not the testifying type. But I can help you on the outside like this. You know, lead you to the hammer, stuff like that. Herb said the hammer is their biggest evidence and it's bullshit because I know where the real one is."

"So you're talking to Herb Dahl, too."

I could tell by the grimace that he'd made a slip. He was supposed to keep Herb Dahl out of the conversation.

"Uh, no, no, it was what Lisa said he said. I don't even know him."

"Let me ask you something, Jeff. How am I going to know this is the real hammer and not some replacement you've cooked up with Lisa and Herb?"

"Because I'm telling you. I know. I was the one who left it where it is. Me!"

"But you're not going to testify, so all I'm left with is a hammer and no story. Do you know what 'fungible' means, Jeff?"

"Fun — uh, no."

"It means mutually interchangeable. An item is fungible in the law if it can be replaced by an identical item. And that's what we have here, Jeff. Your hammer is useless to me without the story attached. If it is your story then you have to testify to it. If you won't testify, then it doesn't matter."

"Huh..."

He seemed crestfallen.

"Where's the hammer, Jeff?"

"I'm not telling you. It's all I have."

"I'm not paying you a cent for it, Jeff. Even if I believed there was a hammer — the real hammer — I wouldn't pay you a cent. That's not how it works. So you think things over and you let me know, okay?"

"Okay."

"Now get off my porch."

I carried the gun down at my side and stepped back into the house, locking the door behind me. I grabbed the car keys off the pizza box and hurried through the house to the back door. I went through and then slipped along the side of the house to a wooden gate that opened onto the street. I opened it a crack and looked for Jeff Trammel.

I didn't see him but I heard a car engine roar to life. I waited and soon a car moved by. I went through the gate and tried to get a look at the plate but I was too late. The car coasted down the hill. It was a blue sedan but I was too consumed with the plate to identify the make and model. As soon as it took the first curve I hurried up the street to my own car.

If I was to follow him, I would have to get down the hill in time to see if he turned left or right on Laurel Canyon Boulevard. Otherwise it was a fifty-fifty chance of losing him.

But I was too late. By the time the Lincoln negotiated the sharp turns and the intersection at Laurel Canyon came into sight, the blue sedan was gone. I pulled up to the stop sign and didn't hesitate. I turned right, heading north toward the Valley. Cisco had traced Jeff Trammel's call to Venice but everything else about the case was in the Valley. I headed that way.

It was a single lane on the northbound ascent of the roadway that cut over the Hollywood Hills. It then opened to two lanes on the down slope into the Valley. But I never caught up to Trammel and soon realized I had chosen the wrong way. Venice. I should've turned south.

Not being a fan of cold or reheated pizza I pulled off to eat at the Daily Grill at Laurel and Ventura. I parked in the underground garage and was halfway to the escalator when I realized I had the Woodsman tucked into the back of my pants. Not good. I returned to the car and put it under the seat, then double-checked to make sure the car was locked.

It was early but nonetheless crowded in the restaurant. I sat at the bar rather than wait for a table and ordered an iced tea and a chicken pot pie. I then opened my phone and called my client. She answered right away.

"Lisa, it's your attorney. Did you send your husband over to speak to me?"

"Well, I told him he should see you, yes."

"And was that your idea or Herb Dahl's?"

"No, mine. I mean Herb was here but it was my idea. Did you talk to him?"

"I did."

"Did he lead you to the hammer?"

"No, he didn't. He wanted ten thousand dollars to do that."

There was a pause but I waited.

"Mickey, it doesn't seem like a lot to ask for something that will destroy the state's evidence."

"You don't pay for evidence, Lisa. If you do, you lose. Where is your husband staying these days?"

"He wouldn't tell me."

"Did you talk to him in person?"

"Yes, he came here. He looked like something the cat dragged in."

"I need to find him so I can subpoena him. Do you have any —"

"He won't testify. He told me. No matter what. He just wants money and to see me in pain. He doesn't even care about his own son. He didn't even ask to see him when he came by."

My meal was placed down in front of me and the bartender topped off my tea. I sliced into the top crust with my fork, just to let some of the steam out. It would be a good ten minutes before the dish would be cool enough to eat.

"Lisa, listen to me, this is important. Do you have any idea where he could be living or staying?"

"No. He said he came up from Mexico."

"That's a lie. He's been here all the time."

She seemed taken aback.

"How do you know that?"

"Phone records. Look, it doesn't matter. If he calls you or comes by, find out where he is staying. Promise him there's money coming or whatever you need to do but get me a location. If we can get him into court he'll have to tell us about the hammer."

"I'll try."

"Don't try, Lisa. Do it. This is your life we're talking about here."

"Okay, okay."

"Now did he drop any hint about the hammer at all when he spoke to you?"

"Not really. He just said, 'Remember how I used to keep the hammer in my car when I was on repo duty?' When he was at the dealership he had to repossess cars sometimes. They took turns. I think he kept the hammer for protection or in case they had to break into a car or something."

"So he was saying the original hammer from your garage tool set was kept in his car?"

"I guess so. The Beemer. But that car was taken away after he abandoned it and disappeared."

I nodded. I could put Cisco on it, have him try to confirm the story by seeing if a hammer was found in the trunk of the BMW left behind by Jeff Trammel.

"Okay, Lisa, who are Jeff's friends? Up here in the city."

"I don't know. He had friends at the dealership but nobody that he brought around. We didn't really have friends."

"Do you have any names of those people from the dealership?"

"Not really."

"Lisa, you're not helping me here."

"I'm sorry. I can't think. I didn't like his friends. I told him to keep them away."

I shook my head and then thought of myself. Who were my friends outside of work? Could Maggie answer these same questions about me?

"All right, Lisa, enough of this for now. I want you thinking about tomorrow. Remember what we talked about. How you act and react in front of the jury. A lot will ride on it."

"I know. I'm ready."

Good, I thought. I wish I was.

Twenty-one

Judge Perry wanted to make up for some of the court time lost the Friday before, so on Monday morning he arbitrarily limited opening statements to the jury to thirty minutes apiece. This ruling came even though both the prosecution and the defense had ostensibly been laboring through the weekend on statements previously scheduled to be an hour long. The truth was, the edict was fine by me. I doubted I would even take ten minutes. The more you say on the defense side, the more the prosecution has to aim at in closing arguments. Less is always more when it comes to the defense. However, the capriciousness of the judge's ruling was something else to consider. It clearly sent a message. The judge was telling us mere lawyers that he was firmly in charge of the courtroom and the trial. We were just visitors.

Freeman went first and as is my usual practice, I never took my eyes off the jury as the prosecutor spoke. I listened closely, ready to object on a moment's notice, but I never once looked at her. I wanted to see how the jurors' eyes took Freeman in. I wanted to see if my hunches about them were going to pay off.

Freeman spoke clearly and eloquently. No histrionics, no flash. It was straightforward eyes-on-the-prize stuff.

"We're here today about one thing," she said, standing firmly in the center of the well, the open space directly in front of the jury box. "We are here because of one person's anger. One person's need to lash out in frustration over her own failures and betrayals."

170

Of course, she spent most of her time warning the jurors off what she called the defense's smoke and mirrors. Confident in her own case, she sought to tear down mine.

"The defense is going to try to sell you a bill of goods. Big conspiracies and high drama. This murder is big but the story is simple. Don't be led astray. Watch closely. Listen closely. Make sure that whatever is said here today is backed during the trial with evidence. Real evidence.

"This was a well-planned crime. The killer knew Mitchell Bondurant's routines. The killer stalked Mitchell Bondurant. The killer was lying in wait for Mitchell Bondurant and then attacked swiftly and with the ultimate malice. That killer is Lisa Trammel and during this trial she will be brought to justice."

Freeman pointed the accusatory finger at my client. Lisa, as previously instructed by me, stared back at her without blinking.

I zeroed in on juror number three who sat in the middle of the front row of the box. Leander Lee Furlong Jr. was my ace in the hole. He was my hanger, the one juror I was counting on to vote my way all the way. Even if it hung the jury.

About a half hour before the jury selection process had begun, the court clerk gave me the list of eighty names composing the first jury pool. I turned the list over to my investigator, who stepped out into the hallway, opened his laptop and went to work.

The Internet provides many avenues for researching the backgrounds of potential jurors, particularly when the trial will revolve around a financial transaction such as a foreclosure. Every person in the jury pool filled out a questionnaire, answering basic questions: Have you or anyone in your immediate family been involved in a foreclosure? Have you ever had a car repossessed? Have you ever filed for bankruptcy? These were weed-out questions. Anyone who answered yes to these questions would be dismissed by either the judge or the prosecutor. A person answering yes would be deemed biased and unable to fairly weigh evidence.

But the weed-outs were very general and there were gray areas and room between the lines. That's where Cisco came in. By the time the judge had sat the first panel of twelve prospective jurors and gone over their questionnaires, Cisco was back to me with background notes on seventeen of the eighty. I was looking for people with bad experiences with and maybe even grudges against banks or government institutions. The seventeen ran the gamut from people who had outright lied on their questionnaires about bankruptcies or repossessions, to plaintiffs in civil claims against banks, to Leander Furlong.

Leander Lee Furlong Jr. was a twenty-nine-year-old assistant manager at the Ralph's supermarket in Chatsworth. He had answered no to the question about foreclosure. In Cisco's digital background search he went the extra mile and searched some national data sites. He came up with a reference to a 1994 foreclosure auction of property in Nashville, Tennessee, on which Leander Lee Furlong was listed as the owner. The petitioner in the action was the First National Bank of Tennessee.

The name seemed unique and the two instances had to be related. My prospective juror would have been thirteen at the time of the foreclosure. I assumed it was his father who lost the property to the bank. And Leander Lee Furlong Jr. had left mention of it off his questionnaire.

As jury selection progressed over two days, I nervously waited for Furlong to be randomly selected and moved into the box for questioning by the judge and attorneys. Along the way I passed up a handful of good prospects, using my peremptory challenges to clear spaces in the box.

Finally on the fourth morning Furlong's number came up and he was seated for questioning. When I heard him speak with a southern accent I knew I had my hanger. He had to carry a grudge against the bank that took away his parents' property. He was hiding it to get on the jury.

Furlong passed the judge's and prosecutor's questions with flying colors, saying just the right things and presenting himself as a God-fearing, hardworking man who had conservative values and an open mind. When it was my turn I hung back and asked a few general questions, then hit him with a zinger. I needed him to appear acceptable to me. I asked him if he thought people in foreclosure should be looked down upon or if it was possible that there were legitimate reasons why people sometimes could not pay for their home. In his southern twang, Furlong said that each case was different and it would be wrong to generalize about all people in foreclosure.

A few minutes and few more questions later, Freeman punched his ticket and I concurred. He was on the jury. Now I just had to hope his family history wasn't discovered by the prosecution. If so he would be removed from the jury faster than a Crip from a Bloods holding cell.

Was I being unethical or breaking the rules by not reporting Furlong's secret to the court? It depends on your definition of *immediate*—as in immediate family. The meaning of who and what constitutes your immediate family changes as you move through life. Furlong's sheet said he was married and had a young son. His wife and child were his immediate family now. For all I knew, his father might not even be alive. The question asked was, "Have you or anyone in your immediate family been involved in a foreclosure?" The word *ever* was not in that sentence.

So it was a gray area and I felt I was under no obligation to help the prosecution by pointing out what was omitted from the question. Freeman had the same list of names and the power of the district attorney's office and the LAPD at her immediate disposal. There had to be someone in those two bureaucracies as smart as my investigator. Let them look and find for themselves. If not, it was their loss.

I watched Furlong as Freeman started listing the building blocks of her case: the murder weapon, the eyewitness, the blood on the defendant's shoe and her history of targeting the bank with her anger. He sat with both elbows on the armrests of his chair, his fingers steepled in front of his mouth. It was like he was hiding his face, peeking over his hands at her. It was a posture that told me I had read him right. He was my hanger, for sure.

Freeman began to lose steam as she hurried through a truncated recitation of how all the evidence fit together as guilt beyond a reasonable doubt. This was where she had obviously chopped content out of her opener in deference to the judge's arbitrary time constraint. She knew she could tie it all up in closing arguments so she skipped a lot of it here and got to her conclusion.

"Ladies and gentlemen, blood will tell," she said. "Follow the evidence and it will lead you, without a doubt, to Lisa Trammel. She took Mitchell Bondurant's life. She took everything he had. And now it's time to bring her to justice."

She thanked the jurors and returned to her seat. It was my turn now. I put my hand down below the table to check my zipper. You have to stand before a jury only once with your fly open and it will never happen again.

I got up and took the same spot in the well where Freeman had stood. I once again tried to show no sign of my still-healing injuries. And I began.

"Ladies and gentlemen, I want to start with a couple of introductions. My name is Michael Haller. I am counsel for the defense. It is my job to defend Lisa Trammel against these very serious charges. Our Constitution ensures that anyone accused of a crime in this country is entitled to a full and vigorous defense, and that is exactly what I intend to provide during the course of this trial. If I rub some of you the wrong way as I do this, then let me apologize up front. But please remember, my actions should not reflect on Lisa."

I turned to the defense table and raised my hand as if welcoming Trammel to the trial.

"Lisa, would you please stand for a moment?"

Trammel stood up and turned slightly to the jury, her eyes slowly scanning the twelve faces. She looked resolute, unbroken. Just the way I told her to be.

"And this is Lisa Trammel, the defendant. Ms. Freeman wants you to believe she committed this crime. She is five foot three in height, weighs a hundred nine pounds soaking wet and is a schoolteacher. Thank you, Lisa. You can sit down now."

Trammel took her seat and I turned back to the jury, keeping my eyes moving from face to face as I spoke.

"We agree with Ms. Freeman that this crime was brutal and violent and cold-blooded. No one should have taken Mitchell Bondurant's life and whoever did should be brought to justice. But there should never be a rush to judgment. And that's what the evidence will prove happened here. The investigators on this case saw the little picture and the easy fit. They missed the big picture. They missed the real murderer."

From behind me I heard Freeman's voice.

"Your Honor, can we please approach for a sidebar?"

Perry frowned but then signaled us up. I followed Freeman to the side of the bench, already formulating my response to what I knew she was going to object to. The judge flipped on a sound distortion fan so the jurors wouldn't hear anything they shouldn't and we huddled at the side of the bench.

"Judge," Freeman began, "I hate interrupting an opening statement but this doesn't sound like an opening statement. Is defense counsel going to hit us with the facts his defense case will prove and the evidence he has, or is he just going to talk in generalities about some mysterious killer that everybody else missed?"

The judge looked at me for a response. I looked at my watch.

"Judge, I object to the objection. I am less than five minutes into a thirty-minute allotment and she's already objecting because I haven't put anything on the board? Come on, Judge, she's trying to show me up in front of the jury and I request that you take a continuing objection from her and not allow her to interrupt again."

"I think he's right, Ms. Freeman," the judge said. "Way too early to object. I'll carry it now as a running objection and will step in myself if I need to. You go back to the prosecution table and sit tight."

He flipped the fan off and rolled his chair back to the center of the bench. Freeman and I returned to our positions.

"As I was saying before being interrupted, there is a big picture to this case and the defense is going to show it to you. The prosecution would like you to believe that this is a simple case of vengeance. But murder is never simple and if you look for shortcuts in an investigation or a prosecution then you are going to miss things. Including a killer. Lisa Trammel did not even know Mitchell Bondurant. Had never met him before. She had no motive to kill him because the motive the prosecution will tell you about was false. They'll say she killed Mitchell Bondurant because he was going to take away her house. The truth was, he wasn't going to get the house and we will prove that. A motive is like a rudder on a boat. You take it away and the boat moves at the whim of the wind. And that's what the prosecution's case is. A lot of wind."

I put my hands in my pockets and looked down at my feet. I counted to three in my head and when I looked up I was staring directly at Furlong.

"What this case is really about is money. It's about the epidemic of foreclosure that has swept across our country. This was not a simple act of vengeance. This was the cold and calculated murder of a man who was threatening to expose the corruption of our banks and their agents of foreclosure. This is about money and those who have it and will not part with it at any cost—even murder."

I paused again, shifting my stance and moving my eyes across the whole panel. They came to a female juror named Esther Marks and held. I knew she was a single mother who worked as an office manager in the garment district. She probably made less than the men doing the same job and I had her pegged as someone who would be sympathetic to my client.

"Lisa Trammel was set up for a murder she did not commit. She was the patsy. The fall guy. She protested the bank's harsh and fraudulent foreclosure practices. She fought against them and for that she was kept away with a restraining order. The very things that made her a suspect to lazy investigators were what made her a perfect patsy. And we're going to prove it to you."

All their eyes were on me. I'd captured their complete attention.

"The state's evidence won't stand," I said. "Piece by piece we'll knock it down. The measure by which you are charged to make your decision here is guilt beyond a reasonable doubt. I urge you to pay close attention and to think for yourself. You do that and I guarantee that you'll have more reasonable doubt than you'll know what to do with. And you'll be left with only one question. Why? Why was this woman charged with this crime? Why was she put through this?"

One final pause and then I nodded and thanked them for their attention. I quickly moved back to my seat and sat down. Lisa reached over and put her hand on my arm as if to thank me for standing for her. It was one of our choreographed moves. I knew it was an act but it still felt good.

The judge called for a fifteen-minute break before the start of testimony. As the courtroom emptied, I stayed in place at the defense table. My opener had continued my sense of momentum. The prosecution would hold sway over the next few days but Freeman was now on notice that I was coming after her.

"Thank you, Mickey," Lisa Trammel said as she got up to go out into the hall with Herb Dahl, who had come through the gate to collect her.

I looked at him and then I looked at her.

"Don't thank me yet," I said.

Twenty-two

After the break, Andrea Freeman came out of the gate with what I called the prosecution's scene-setter witnesses. Their testimony was often dramatic but did not get to the guilt or innocence of the defendant. They were merely called as part of the architecture of the state's case, to set the stage for the evidence that would come later.

The trial's first witness was a bank receptionist named Riki Sanchez. She was the woman who found the victim's body in the parking garage. Her value was in helping to set a time of death and in bringing the shock of murder to the everyday people on the jury.

Sanchez commuted to work from the Santa Clarita Valley and therefore had a morning routine that she strictly adhered to. She testified that she regularly pulled into the bank garage at 8:45 A.M., which gave her ten minutes to park, get to the employee entrance and be at her desk by 8:55 to prepare for the bank's doors to open to the public at 9.

She testified that on the day of the murder she had followed her routine and found an unassigned parking slot approximately ten spaces from Mitchell Bondurant's assigned space. After leaving and locking her car, she walked toward the bridge that connected the garage to the bank building. It was then that she discovered the body. She first saw the spilled coffee, then the open briefcase on the ground, and finally Mitchell Bondurant lying facedown and bloodied.

Sanchez knelt next to the body and checked for signs of life, then pulled her cell phone out of her purse and called 911.

It's rare to score defense points off a scene-setter witness. Their testimony is usually very prescribed and rarely contributes to the question of guilt or innocence. Still, you never know. On cross-examination I stood and threw a few questions at Sanchez just to see what might pop loose.

"Now, Ms. Sanchez, you described your very precise morning routine here but there really is no routine once you drive into the bank's garage, correct?"

"I'm not sure what you mean."

"I mean that you do not have an assigned parking space so there is no routine when it comes to that. You get into the garage and have to start hunting for a space, right?"

"Well, sort of. The bank isn't open yet so there are always plenty of spaces. I usually go up to the second floor and park in the area where I did that day."

"All right. In the past, had you walked into work with Mr. Bondurant?"

"No, he was usually in earlier than me."

"Now on the day that you found Mr. Bondurant's body, where was it that you saw the defendant, Lisa Trammel, in the garage?"

She paused as if it was a trick question. It was.

"I don't—I mean, I didn't see her."

"Thank you, Ms. Sanchez."

Next up on the stand was the 911 operator who took the 8:52 A.M. emergency call from Sanchez. Her name was LeShonda Gaines and her testimony was used primarily to introduce the tape of the call from Sanchez. Playing the tape was an overly dramatic and unneeded maneuver but the judge had allowed it over a pretrial objection from me. Freeman played forty seconds of the tape after handing out transcripts to the jurors as well as to the judge and the defense.

GAINES: Nine-one-one, what is your emergency?

SANCHEZ: There's a man here. I think he's dead! He's all bloody and he won't move.

GAINES: What is your name, ma'am?

SANCHEZ: Riki Sanchez. I'm in the parking garage at WestLand National in Sherman Oaks.

(pause)

GAINES: Is that the Ventura Boulevard location?

SANCHEZ: Yes, are you sending someone?

GAINES: Police and paramedics have been dispatched.

SANCHEZ: I think he's already dead. There's a lot of blood.

GAINES: Do you know who he is?

SANCHEZ: I think it's Mr. Bondurant but I'm not sure. Do you want me to turn him over?

GAINES: No, just wait for the police. Are you in any danger, Ms. Sanchez?

(pause)

SANCHEZ: Uh, I don't think so. I don't see anybody around.

GAINES: Okay, wait for the police and keep this line open.

I didn't bother asking any questions on cross-examination. There was nothing to be gained for the defense.

Freeman threw her first curveball after Gaines was excused. I expected her to go with the first responding officer next. Have him testify about arriving and securing the scene, and get the crime scene photos to the jury. But instead she called Margo Schafer, the eyewitness who put Trammel close to the crime scene. I immediately saw the strategy Freeman was employing. Instead of sending the jury to lunch with crime scene photos in their minds, send them out with the first *ah-ha* moment of the trial. The first piece of testimony that connected Trammel to the crime.

It was a good plan but Freeman didn't know what I knew about her witness. I just hoped I got to her before lunch.

Schafer was a petite woman who looked nervous and pale as she took the witness stand. She had to pull the stemmed microphone down from the position Gaines had left it in.

Under direct questioning, Freeman drew from Schafer that she was a bank teller who had returned to work four years earlier after raising a family. She had no corporate aspirations. She just enjoyed the responsibility that came with the job and the interaction with the public.

After a few more personal questions designed to create a rapport between Schafer and the jury, Freeman moved on to the meat of her testimony, asking the witness about the morning of the murder.

"I was running late," Schafer said. "I am supposed to be in place at my window at nine. I first go to get my bank out of the vault and sign it out. So usually I am there by quarter of. But on that day I hit traffic on Ventura Boulevard because of an accident and was very late."

"Do you remember exactly how late, Ms. Schafer?" Freeman asked.

"Yes, ten minutes exactly. I kept looking at the clock on the dashboard. I was running exactly ten minutes behind schedule."

"Okay, and when you got close to the bank did you see anything out of the ordinary or that caused you concern?"

"Yes, I did."

"And what was that?"

"I saw Lisa Trammel on the sidewalk walking away from the bank."

I stood and objected, saying that the witness would have no idea where the person she claimed was Trammel was walking from. The judge agreed and sustained.

"What direction was Ms. Trammel walking in?" Freeman asked.

"East."

"And where was she in relation to the bank?"

"She was a half a block east of the bank, also walking east."

"So she was walking in a direction away from the bank, correct?"

"Yes, correct."

"And how close were you when you saw her?"

"I was going west on Ventura and was in the left lane so that I could move into the turning lane to turn into the entrance to the bank's garage. So she was three lanes across from me."

"You had your eyes on the road, though, didn't you?"

"No, I was stopped at a traffic light when I first saw her."

"So was she at a right angle to you when you saw her?"

"Yes, directly across the street from me."

"And how was it that you knew this woman to be the defendant, Lisa Trammel?"

"Because her photo is posted in the employee lounge and in the vault. Plus her photo was shown to bank employees about three months before."

"Why was that done?"

"Because the bank had been granted a restraining order prohibiting her from coming within a hundred feet of the bank. We were shown her photo and told to immediately report to our supervisors any sighting of her on bank property."

"Can you tell the jury what time it was when you saw Lisa Trammel walking east on the sidewalk?"

"Yes, I know exactly what time it was because I was running late. It was eight fifty-five."

"So at eight fifty-five, Lisa Trammel was walking east in a direction that was moving away from the bank, correct?"

"Yes, correct."

Freeman asked a few more questions designed to elicit answers that indicated that Lisa Trammel was only a half block from the bank within a few minutes of the 911 call reporting the murder. She finally finished with the witness at 11:30 and the judge asked if I wanted to take an early lunch and begin my cross-examination afterward.

"Judge, I think it's only going to take me a half hour to handle this. I'd rather go now. I'm ready."

"Very well then, Mr. Haller. Proceed."

I stood up and went to the lectern located between the prosecution table and the jury box. I carried a legal pad with me and two display boards. I held these so that their displays faced each other and could not be seen. I leaned them against the side of the lectern.

"Good morning, Ms. Schafer."

"Good morning."

"You mentioned in your testimony that you were running late because of a traffic accident, correct?"

"Yes."

"Did you happen to come upon the accident site while making the commute?"

"Yes, it was just west of Van Nuys Boulevard. Once I got past it, I started to move smoothly."

"Which side of Ventura was it on?"

"That was the thing. It was in the eastbound lanes but everybody on my side had to slow down to gawk."

I made a note on my legal pad and changed direction.

"Ms. Schafer, I noticed that the prosecutor forgot to ask you if Ms.

Trammel was carrying a hammer when you saw her. You didn't see anything like that, did you?"

"No, I didn't. But she was carrying a large shopping bag that was more than big enough for a hammer."

This was the first I had heard about a shopping bag. It had not been mentioned in the discovery materials. Schafer, the ever-helpful witness, was introducing new material. Or so I thought.

"A shopping bag? Did you happen to mention this shopping bag during any of your interviews with the police or the prosecutor on this case?"

Schafer gave it some thought.

"I'm not sure. I may not have."

"So as far as you remember, the police didn't even ask if the defendant was carrying anything."

"I think that's correct."

I didn't know what that meant or if it meant anything at all. But I decided to stay away from the shopping bag for the moment and to steer once again in a new direction. You never wanted the witness to know where you were going.

"Now, Ms. Schafer, when you testified just a few minutes ago that you were three lanes from the sidewalk where you supposedly saw the defendant, you miscounted, didn't you?"

The second abrupt change of subject matter and the question gave her a momentary pause.

"Uh...no, I did not."

"Well, what cross street were you at when you saw her?"

"Cedros Avenue."

"There are two lanes of eastbound traffic on Ventura there, aren't there?"

"Yes."

"And then you have a turn lane onto Cedros, right?"

"Yes, that's right. That makes three."

"What about the lane of curbside parking?"

She made an *Oh, come on* face.

"That's not a real lane."

"Well, it's space between you and the woman you claim was Lisa Trammel, isn't it?"

"If you say so. I think that's being picky."

"Really? I think it's just being accurate, wouldn't you say?"

"I believe most people would say there were three lanes of traffic between me and her."

"Well, the parking zone, let's call it, is at least a car-length wide and actually wider, correct?"

"Okay, if you want to nitpick. Call it a fourth lane. My mistake."

It was a grudging if not bitter concession and I was sure that the jury was seeing who the real nitpicker was.

"So then you are now saying that when you supposedly saw Ms. Trammel you would've been about four lanes away from her, not the three you previously testified to, correct?"

"Correct. I said, my mistake."

I made a notation on my legal pad that really didn't mean anything but that I hoped would look to the jurors as though I was keeping some sort of score. I then reached down to my display boards, separated them and chose one.

"Your Honor, I would like to display for the witness a photograph of the location we are talking about here."

"Has the prosecution seen it?"

"Judge, it was contained on the exhibits CD turned over in discovery. I did not specifically provide the board to Ms. Freeman and she did not ask to see it."

Freeman made no objection and the judge told me to carry on, calling the first board Defense Exhibit 1A. I set up a folding easel in an open area between the jury box and the witness stand. The prosecution planned to use the overhead screens to present exhibits and later I would as well, but for this demonstration I wanted to go the old-fashioned way. I put the display board up and then returned to the lectern.

"Ms. Schafer, do you recognize the photograph I have put on the easel?"

It was a thirty-by-fifty-inch aerial view of the two-block stretch of Ventura Boulevard in question. Bullocks had gotten it off Google Earth and all it cost us was the price of the blowup and the mounting on the board.

"Yes. It looks like a top view of Ventura Boulevard and you can see the bank and also the intersection with Cedros Avenue about a block away."

"Yes, an aerial view. Can you please step down and use the marker on the easel's ledge to circle the spot where you believe you saw Lisa Trammel?"

Schafer looked at the judge as if to seek permission. He nodded his approval and she stepped down. She took the black marker from the ledge and circled an area on the sidewalk, a half block from the bank's entrance.

"Thank you, Ms. Schafer. Can you now mark for the jury where your car was located when you looked out the window and supposedly saw Lisa Trammel?"

She marked a spot in the middle lane that appeared to be at least three car lengths from the crosswalk.

"Thank you, Ms. Schafer. You can return to the witness stand now."

Schafer put the marker back on the ledge and moved back to her seat.

"So how many cars were in front of you at the light, would you say?"

"At least two. Maybe three."

"What about the turn lane to your immediate left, were there any cars there waiting to turn?"

She was ready for that one and wasn't going to let me trick her.

"No, I had a clear view of the sidewalk."

"So it was rush hour and you're telling us there was nobody waiting in the turn lane to get to work."

"Not next to me but I was two or three cars back. There could've been someone waiting to turn, just not next to me."

I asked the judge if I could put the second board, Defense Exhibit 1B, on the easel now and he told me to go ahead. This was another photo blowup, but it was from ground level. It was a photo that Cisco had taken from a car window while sitting at the traffic light in the middle west-bound lane of Ventura Boulevard at Cedros Avenue at 8:55 A.M. on a Monday a month after the murder. There was a time imprint on the bottom right corner of the image.

Back at the lectern, I asked Schafer to describe what she saw.

"It's a photo of that same block, from the ground. There's Danny's Deli. We go there sometimes at lunch."

"Yes, and do you know if Danny's is open for breakfast?"

"Yes, it is."

"Have you ever been there for breakfast?"

Freeman stood to object.

"Judge, I hardly see what this has to do with the witness's testimony or the elements of this trial."

Perry looked at me.

"If Your Honor would give me a moment the relevance will become quite clear."

"Carry on, but make it quick."

I refocused on Schafer.

"Have you had occasion to have breakfast at Danny's, Ms. Schafer?"

"No, not breakfast."

"But you do know that it is popular at breakfast, correct?"

"I really wouldn't know."

It wasn't the answer I wanted but it was helpful. It was the first time Schafer was being clearly evasive, purposely avoiding the obvious confession. Jurors who picked up on this would begin to see someone who wasn't being an impartial witness, but a woman who refused to stray from the prosecution's line.

"Then let me ask you this. What other businesses on this block are open before nine o'clock in the morning?"

"Mostly there are stores that wouldn't be open. You can see the signs in the picture."

"Then what do you think accounts for the fact that every metered space in this photo is taken? Would it be customers of the deli?"

Freeman objected again, saying the witness was hardly qualified to answer the question. The judge agreed and sustained the objection, telling me to move on.

"On the Monday morning at eight fifty-five when you claim you saw Ms. Trammel from four lanes away, do you recall how many cars were parked in front of the deli and along the curb?"

"No, I don't."

"You testified just a few moments ago, and I can have it read back to you if you wish, that you had a clear view of Lisa Trammel. Is it your testimony that there were no vehicles in the parking lane?"

"There may have been some cars there but I saw her clearly."

"What about the traffic lanes, they were clear, too?"

"Yes. I could see her."

"You said you were running late because westbound traffic was moving very slowly because of an accident, correct?"

"Yes."

"An accident in the eastbound lanes, right?"

"Yes."

"So how far was traffic backed up in the eastbound lanes if the westbound lanes were backed up enough to make you ten minutes late for work?"

"I don't really recall."

Perfect answer. For me. A dissembling witness always scores points for the D.

"Isn't it true, Ms. Schafer, that you had to look across two lanes of backed-up traffic, plus a full parking lane, in order to see the defendant on the sidewalk?"

"All I know is that I saw her. She was there."

"And she was even carrying a big shopping bag, you say, correct?"

"That's right."

"What kind of shopping bag?"

"The kind with handles, the kind you get in a department store."

"What color was it?"

"It was red."

"And could you tell if it was full or empty?"

"I couldn't tell."

"And she carried this down at her side or in front of her?"

"Down at her side. With one hand."

"You seem to have a good sense of this bag. Were you looking at the bag or the face of the woman who was carrying it?"

"I had time to look at both."

I shook my head as I looked at my notes.

"Ms. Schafer, do you know how tall Ms. Trammel is?"

I turned to my client and signaled her to stand up. I probably should have asked the judge's permission first but I was on a roll and didn't want to hit any speed bumps. Perry said nothing.

"I have no idea," Schafer said.

"Would it surprise you to know she is only five foot three?"

I nodded to Lisa and she sat back down.

"No, I don't think that would surprise me."

"Five foot three and you still picked her out across four lanes packed with cars."

Freeman objected as I knew she would. Perry sustained the objection but I didn't need an answer for the point to be made. I checked my watch and saw it was two minutes before noon. I fired my final torpedo.

"Ms. Schafer, can you look at the photograph and point to where you see the defendant on the sidewalk?"

All eyes moved to the photo blowup. Because of the line of cars in the parking lane, the pedestrians on the sidewalk were unidentifiable in the image. Freeman leapt to her feet and objected, claiming the defense was trying to sandbag the witness and the court. Perry called us to a sidebar. When we got there, he had stern words for me.

"Mr. Haller, yes or no, is the defendant in the photo?"

"No, Your Honor."

"Then you're engaged in attempting to trick the witness. That will not happen in my courtroom. Take your photo down."

"Judge, I'm not trying to trick anyone. She could simply say that the defendant is not in the photo. But she clearly can't see the pedestrians on the other side of the traffic and I am trying to make that clear to—"

"I don't care what you're trying to do. Take your photo down and if you try another move like that you're going to find yourself in a contempt hearing at the close of business. Understood?"

"Yes, sir."

"Your Honor," Freeman said. "The jury should be told that the defendant is not in the photo."

"I agree. Go back."

On my way back to the lectern I took the display boards off the easel.

"Ladies and gentlemen," the judge said. "Let it be noted that the defendant was not in the photo that defense counsel put on display."

The jury instruction was fine with me. I still made my point. The fact that the jurors had to be told that Lisa was not in the photo underlined how hard it would have been to see and identify someone on the sidewalk.

The judge told me to continue my cross-examination and I leaned to the microphone.

"No further questions."

I sat down and put the photo boards on the floor under the table. They had served me well. I took the hit from the judge but it was worth it. It's always worth it if you make your point.

Twenty-three

L isa Trammel was ecstatic about my cross-examination of Margo Schafer. Even Herb Dahl couldn't hold back from congratulating me as the trial was recessed for lunch. I counseled them not to get overly excited. It was early in the trial and eyewitnesses like Schafer were usually the easiest to handle and damage on the stand. There were still tough witnesses and tougher days ahead. They could count on that.

"I don't care," Lisa said. "You were marvelous and that lying bitch got just what she deserved."

The invective was dripping with hate and it made me pause for a moment before responding.

"The prosecutor is still going to have a chance to rehabilitate her on redirect after lunch."

"And then you can destroy her again on re-cross."

"Well...I don't know about destroying anybody. That's not what—"

"Can you join us for lunch, Mickey?"

She punctuated the request by swinging her arm around Dahl, clearly showing what I had been assuming, that they were together in more than just business.

"There is nothing good around here," she continued. "We're going down to Ventura Boulevard to find a place. We might even try Danny's Deli."

"Thank you but no. I need to get back to the office and meet with my crew. They're not here because they can't be. They're working and I need to check in."

Lisa gave me a look that told me she didn't believe me. It didn't much matter to me. I represented her in court. It didn't mean I had to eat with her and the man I was still sure was scheming to rip her off, no matter the romantic entanglement—if it even was romantic. I headed out on my own and walked back to my office in the Victory Building.

Lorna had already gone to the competing and far better Jerry's Famous Deli in Studio City and picked up turkey and coleslaw sandwiches. I ate at my desk while telling Cisco and Bullocks what had happened that morning in court. Despite my reserve with my client, I felt pretty good about my cross with Schafer. I thanked Bullocks for the display board, which I believed had impressed the jury. Nothing like a visual aid to help throw doubt on a supposed eyewitness.

When I finished recounting the trial testimony I asked them what they had been working on. Cisco said he was still reviewing the police investigation, looking for errors and assumptions made by the detectives that could be turned against Kurlen during cross-examination.

"Good, I need all the ammo I can get," I said. "Bullocks, anything from your end?"

"I pretty much spent the morning with the foreclosure file. I want to be bulletproof when it's my turn."

"Okay, good, but you've got some time there. My guess is the defense won't start until next week. Freeman looks like she's trying to keep a certain rhythm and momentum going, but she's got a lot of witnesses on her list and it doesn't look like a lot of smoke."

Often prosecutors and defense attorneys pad their witness lists to keep the other side guessing as to who would actually get called and who was important in terms of testimony. It didn't appear to me that Freeman had engaged in this sort of subterfuge. Her list was lean and every name on it had something to bring to the case.

I dipped my sandwich into some Thousand Island dressing that had dripped onto the paper wrapper. Aronson pointed to one of the display boards I had brought back with me from court. It was the ground-level shot I had tried to fool Margo Schafer with.

"Wasn't that risky? What if Freeman hadn't objected?"

"I knew she would. And if she didn't the judge would have. They don't like you trying to trick witnesses like that."

"Yeah, but then the jury knows you're lying."

"I wasn't lying. I asked the witness a question. Could she point out where Lisa was in the photo? I didn't say Lisa was in the photo. If she had been given the opportunity to answer, the answer would have been no. That's all."

Aronson frowned.

"Remember what I said, Bullocks. Don't grow a conscience. We're playing hardball here. I played Freeman and she's trying to play me. Maybe she already has played me in some way and I don't even know it. I took a risk and got a little hand-slap from the judge. But every person on that jury was looking at that photo while we were at sidebar and every one of them was thinking how hard it would have been for Margo Schafer to see what she claimed she saw. That's how it works. It's cold and calculating. Sometimes you win a point but most times you don't."

"I know," she said dismissively. "It doesn't mean I have to like it."

"No, you don't."

Twenty-four

Freeman surprised me after lunch by not calling Margo Schafer back to the stand to try to repair the damage I had inflicted on cross. My guess was that she had something else planned for later that would help salvage the Schafer testimony. Instead, she called LAPD Sergeant David Covington, who was the first officer to respond to WestLand National after the 911 call from Riki Sanchez was logged.

Covington was a seasoned veteran and a solid witness for the prosecution. In the precise if not droll delivery of someone who has seen more dead bodies and testified about them more times than he can remember, he described arriving on scene and determining that the victim was dead by means of foul play. He then described closing access to the entire garage, corralling Riki Sanchez and other possible witnesses, and cordoning off the second-floor area where the body was located.

Through Covington the crime scene photographs were introduced and displayed in all their bloody glory on the two overhead flat screens. These more than any testimony from Covington established the crime of murder, a requirement for conviction.

I'd had marginal success during a pretrial skirmish involving the crime scene photos. I had objected to their introduction, particularly the prosecution's plan to display three-by-three blowups on easels in front of the jury box. I had argued that that they were prejudicial to my client. Photos of real victims of murder are always shocking and provoke strong emotions. It is human nature to want to harshly punish those responsible. Photos can easily turn a jury against the accused, regardless of what evidence connects the accused to the crime. Perry tried to split the baby. He limited the number of photos the prosecution could introduce to four and told Freeman she had to use the overhead screens, thus limiting the size of the photos. I had won a few points but knew that the judge's order would not limit the visceral response of the jurors. It was still a victory for the prosecution.

Freeman chose the four photos that showed the most blood and the pitiful angle at which Bondurant had dropped face-first onto the concrete floor of the garage.

On cross-examination I zeroed in on one photo and tried to get the jury thinking about something other than avenging the dead. The best way to do that is to plant questions. If they are left with questions but no answers then I have done my job on cross.

With the judge's permission, I used the projection remote to eliminate three of the photos on the screens, leaving only one remaining.

"Sergeant Covington, I want to draw your attention to the photo I've left on display. I believe it is marked People's Exhibit Three. Can you tell me what that is in the foreground of the photo?"

"Yes, that is an open briefcase."

"Okay, and is that how you found it when you arrived at the scene?"

"Yes, it is."

"It was sitting there open like that?"

"Yes."

"Okay, and did you make any inquiry of any witness or anyone else to determine if someone had opened it after the victim was discovered?"

"I asked the woman who had called nine-one-one if she had opened it and she said she had not. That was the extent of my inquiry on it. I left it for the detectives."

"Okay, and you've testified here that you have been working patrol for your entire career of twenty-two years, correct?"

"Yes, that's correct."

"You have responded to a lot of nine-one-one calls?"

"Yes."

"What did seeing that open briefcase mean to you?"

"Nothing really. It was just part of the crime scene."

"Did your experience cause you to think there may have been a robbery involved in this murder?"

"Not really. I'm not a detective."

"If robbery was not a motive in this crime, why would the killer take the time to open the victim's briefcase?"

Freeman objected before Covington could answer. She said that the question was beyond the witness's scope of expertise and experience.

"Sergeant Covington has spent his entire career working patrol. He is not a detective. He has never investigated a robbery."

The judge nodded.

"I tend to agree with Ms. Freeman, Mr. Haller."

"Your Honor, Sergeant Covington may not have ever been a detective but I think it is safe to say he has responded to robbery calls and conducted preliminary investigations. I think he can certainly answer a question about his initial impressions of the crime scene."

"I'm still going to sustain the objection. Ask your next question."

Defeated on that point, I looked down at the notes I had previously worked up for Covington. I felt confident that I had firmly planted the question about robbery and the motive for the murder in the jurors' minds, but I didn't want to leave it at that. I decided to try a bluff.

"Sergeant, after you arrived in response to the nine-one-one call and surveyed the crime scene, did you call for investigators and medical examiners and crime scene experts?"

"Yes, I contacted the com center, confirming that we had a homicide and requesting the usual response of investigators from Van Nuys Division."

"And you maintained control of the crime scene until those people arrived?"

"Yes, that is how it works. I transferred custody of the scene to the investigators. Detective Kurlen to be exact."

"Okay, and at any time during this process, did you discuss with Kurlen or any other law enforcement officer the possibility that the murder had come out of a robbery attempt?"

"No, I did not."

"Are you sure, Sergeant?"

"Quite sure."

I wrote something on my legal pad. It was a meaningless scribble done for the jury.

"I have no further questions."

Covington was excused and one of the paramedics who had responded to the nine-one-one call testified about confirming that the victim was dead at the scene. He was on and off the stand in five minutes, as Freeman was interested only in confirming death and I had nothing to gain from cross-examination.

Next up was the victim's brother, Nathan Bondurant. He was used to confirm identification of the victim, another requirement for conviction. Freeman also used him much as she did the crime scene photos, to stir emotions in the jury. He tearfully described being taken by detectives to the medical examiner's office where he identified his younger brother's body. Freeman asked him when he had last seen his brother alive and his answer brought another torrent of tears as he described attending a Lakers basketball game together just a week before the murder.

It's a rule of thumb to leave a crying man alone. There usually isn't anything to be gained from cross-examining a victim's loved one, but Freeman had opened a door and I decided to step through it. The risk I ran was that jurors might view me as cruel if I went too far in questioning the bereaved family member.

"Mr. Bondurant, I am sorry for your family's loss. I have only a few quick questions. You mentioned that you and your brother went to the Lakers game a week before this horrible crime occurred. What did you talk about during that outing?"

"Uh, we talked about a lot of things. It would be hard to remember everything right now."

"Only sports and Lakers?"

"No, of course not. We were brothers. We talked about a lot of things. He asked about my kids. I asked if he was seeing anyone. Things like that."

"Was he seeing anyone?"

"No, not at the time. He said he was too busy with work."

"What else did he say about work?"

"He just said it was busy. He was in charge of home loans and it was a bad time. A lot of foreclosures and all of that sort of stuff. He didn't really get into it."

"Did he talk about his own real estate holdings and what was happening with them?"

Freeman objected on relevance. I asked for a sidebar and it was granted. At the bench I argued that I had already put the jury on notice that I would not only be debunking the state's case but putting forward a defense case that included evidence of an alternate theory of the crime.

"This is that alternate theory, Judge. That Bondurant was in trouble financially and his efforts to get out of the hole brought about his demise. I should be given the latitude to pursue this with any witness the prosecution puts before the jury."

"Judge," Freeman countered, "just because counsel says something is relevant doesn't mean it is. The victim's brother has no direct knowledge of Mitchell Bondurant's financial or investment situation."

"If that's the case, Judge, Nathan Bondurant can say so and I'll move on."

"Very well, overruled. Ask your question, Mr. Haller."

Back at the lectern I asked the witness the question again.

"He spoke very briefly and without going into detail about it," the witness replied.

"What exactly did he say?"

"He just said that he was upside-down on his investment properties. He didn't say how many that was or how much was involved. That was all he said."

"What did that mean to you when he said he was upside-down?"

"That he owed more on his properties than they were worth."

"Did he say he was trying to sell them?"

"He said he couldn't sell them without taking a bath."

"Thank you, Mr. Bondurant. I have no further questions."

Freeman completed her tour of minor players by calling a witness named Gladys Pickett, who identified herself on the stand as the head teller at WestLand National's main branch in Sherman Oaks. After eliciting from Pickett what her duties were at the bank Freeman got right down to the salient testimony.

"As the person in charge of the tellers at the bank, you have how many people reporting to you, Mrs. Pickett?"

"About forty altogether."

"Is one of those people a teller named Margo Schafer?"

"Yes, Margo is one of my tellers."

"I would like to draw your attention back to the morning of Mitchell Bondurant's murder. Did Margo Schafer come to you with a particular concern?"

"Yes, she did."

"Can you please tell the jury what Ms. Schafer was concerned about?"

"She came to me and reported that she had seen Lisa Trammel just a half block from the bank, walking down the sidewalk and moving in a direction away from the bank."

"Why was this a concern?"

"Well, we have Lisa Trammel's photograph up in the employees' lounge and inside our vault and we have been instructed to report any sighting of Lisa Trammel to our supervisors."

"Do you know why this instruction was put in place?"

"Yes, the bank has a restraining order keeping her away from the property."

"Can you tell the jury what time it was when Margo Schafer told you about seeing Ms. Trammel near the bank?"

"Yes, it was as soon as she came into work that day. It was the first thing she did."

"Now do you keep a record of when tellers arrive at work?"

"I keep a checkout list in the vault on which the time is posted."

"This is when tellers come into the vault and get their money boxes to take to their stations?"

"Yes, that's right."

"On the day in question, at what time do you show Margo Schafer's name being checked off?"

"It was nine oh-nine. She was the last one checked in. She was late."

"And would that have been when she told you about seeing Lisa Trammel?"

"Yes, precisely."

"Now, at that time, did you know that Mitchell Bondurant had been murdered in the bank's garage?"

"No, no one knew that yet because Riki Sanchez had stayed in the garage until the police came and then they kept her there for questioning. We didn't know what was going on."

"So the idea that Margo Schafer would have concocted the story about seeing Lisa Trammel after hearing about Mr. Bondurant's murder is not possible, correct?"

"Correct. She told me about seeing her before she or I or anybody in the bank knew about Mr. Bondurant."

"So at what point did you learn of Mr. Bondurant's murder in the garage and offer the information you had received from Margo Schafer?"

"That was about a half hour later. That's when we heard and I obviously thought the police needed to know that this woman had been seen nearby."

"Thank you, Mrs. Pickett. I have no further questions."

It was Freeman's biggest hit so far. Pickett had successfully undone much of what I had been able to accomplish with Schafer on the stand. Now I had to decide whether to leave it alone or risk making things worse.

I decided to cut my losses and move on. They say never ask a question you don't already know the answer to. The rule applied here. Pickett had refused to talk to my investigator. Freeman could be setting a trap, leaving her up there with one more piece of information I might stumble into with an ill-advised question.

"I have no questions for this witness," I said from my place at the defense table.

Judge Perry excused Pickett and called for the afternoon break of fifteen minutes. As people stood to leave the courtroom, my client leaned into me at the table.

"Why didn't you go after her?" she whispered.

"Who? Pickett? I didn't want to make it worse by asking the wrong thing."

"Are you kidding me? You needed to destroy her like you did Schafer."

"The difference was I had something to work with on Schafer. I didn't have it on Pickett and going after somebody with nothing to go after her with is potential disaster. I left it alone."

I could see anger darkening her eyes.

"Well, you should've gotten something on her."

It came out as a hiss through what I believed were clenched teeth.

"Look, Lisa, I'm your attorney and I decide—"

"Never mind. I have to go."

She stood up and hurried through the gate and toward the courtroom exit. I glanced over to Freeman to see if she had caught the display of attorney-client disagreement. She gave me a knowing smile, indicating she had.

I decided to go out into the hall to see why my client had so abruptly needed to leave. I stepped out and was immediately drawn by the cameras to one of the benches that ran along the hallway between courtroom doors. The focus was on Lisa, who was sitting on the bench hugging her son, Tyler. The boy looked extremely uncomfortable in the camera lights.

"Jesus Christ," I whispered.

I saw Lisa's sister standing on the periphery of the group and walked over.

"What is this, Jodie? She knows the judge ruled she can't have the kid in court."

"I know. He's not going into the courtroom. He had a half day at school and she wanted me to bring him by. She thought if the media saw her with Ty that it might help things, I guess."

"Yeah, well, the media's got nothing to do with this. Don't bring him back. I don't care what she says, don't bring him back."

I looked around for Herb Dahl. This had to be his move and I wanted to deliver the same message to him. But there was no sign of the erstwhile Hollywood player. He had probably been smart enough to stay clear of me.

I headed back into the courtroom. I still had ten minutes of the break left and planned to use it brooding about working for a client I didn't like and was beginning to despise.

Twenty-five

After the break Freeman moved on to what I call the hunter-gatherer stage of the prosecution's case. The crime scene technicians. Their testimony would be the platform on which she would present Detective Howard Kurlen, the lead investigator.

The first hunter-gatherer was a coroner's investigator named William Abbott who had responded to the crime scene and was charged with the body's documentation and transport to the medical examiner's office, where the autopsy would be conducted.

His testimony covered his observations of the crime scene, the head wounds sustained by the victim and the personal property found on the body. This included Bondurant's wallet, watch, loose change and a money clip containing $183 in currency. There was also the receipt from the Joe's Joe franchise that had helped investigators set the time of death.

Abbott, like Covington before him, was very matter-of-fact in his testimony. Being at the scene of a violent crime was routine for him. When it was my turn to ask the questions, I zeroed in on this.

"Mr. Abbott, how long have you been a coroner's investigator?"

"I'm going on twenty-nine years now."

"All with L.A. County?"

"That's right."

"How many murder scenes do you estimate you have been to in that time?"

"Oh, gee, probably a couple thousand. A lot."

"I bet. And I assume many were scenes where great violence was involved."

"That's the nature of the beast."

"What about this scene? You examined and photographed the wounds on the victim, correct?"

"Yes, I did. That is part of the protocol we follow before transporting the body."

"You have a crime scene report in front of you that was admitted into evidence by pretrial agreement. Could you read the second paragraph of the summary to the jury?"

Abbott turned the page on his report and found the paragraph.

"'There are three distinct impact wounds on the crown of the head noted for their violence and damage. Positioning of the body indicates immediate loss of consciousness before impact on the ground.' Then in parentheses I have the word 'overkill.'"

"Yes, I'm curious about that. What did you mean by putting 'overkill' in the summary?"

"Just that it looked to me like any one of these impacts would've done the job. The victim was unconscious and possibly even dead before he hit the ground. The first blow did that. This would indicate that two of the impacts came after he was facedown on the ground. It was overkill. Somebody was very angry at him is the way I was looking at it."

Abbott probably thought he was smartly giving me the answer I most didn't want to hear. Freeman, too. But they were wrong.

"So you are indicating in your summary that you detected there was some sort of emotional involvement in this murder, correct?"

"Yes, that is what I was thinking."

"What kind of training do you have in terms of homicide investigation?"

"Well, I trained for six months before starting the job way back thirty years ago. And we have ongoing in-service training a couple of times a year. We're taught the latest investigative techniques and so forth."

"Is this specific to homicide investigation?"

"Not all of it but a lot of it is."

"Isn't it a basic tenet of homicide that a crime of overkill usually indicates that the victim knew his or her killer? That there was a personal relationship?"

"Uh..."

Freeman finally got it. She stood and objected, saying that Abbott was not a homicide investigator and the question called for expertise he did not have. I didn't have to argue. The judge held his hand up to stop me from speaking and told Freeman that I had just walked Abbott down the path without objection from the state. The investigator had testified to his experience and training in the area of homicide without a peep from Freeman.

"You gambled, Ms. Freeman. You thought it was going to cut your way. You can't back out now. The witness will answer the question."

"Go ahead, Mr. Abbott," I said.

Abbott stalled by asking for the question to be read to him by the court stenographer. He then had to be prompted again by the judge.

"There is that consideration," he finally said.

"Consideration?" I asked. "What does that mean?"

"When you have a crime of high violence it should be considered that the victim personally knew his attacker. His killer."

"When you say crime of high violence, do you mean overkill?"

"That could be part of it, yes."

"Thank you, Mr. Abbott. Now, what about other observations you made at the crime scene? Did you form any opinion in regard to the kind of power it took to make these three brutal strikes on the top of Mr. Bondurant's head?"

Freeman objected again, stating that Abbott was not a medical examiner and did not have the expertise to answer the question. This time Perry sustained the objection, giving her a small victory.

I decided to take what I had gotten and be happy with it.

"No further questions," I said.

Next up was Paul Roberts, who was the senior criminalist in the three-member LAPD crime scene unit that processed the scene. His testimony was less eventful than Abbott's because Freeman kept him on a short leash. He spoke only of procedures and what he collected at the scene and processed later in the SID lab. On cross I was able to use the paucity of physical evidence to my client's advantage.

"Can you tell the jury the locations of the fingerprints you collected from the scene that were later matched to the defendant?"

"There were none that we found."

"Can you tell the jury what samples of blood collected at the scene came from the defendant?"

"There was none that we found."

"Well, then what about hair and fiber evidence? Surely you connected the defendant to the crime scene through hair and fiber evidence, correct?"

"We did not."

I took a few steps away from the lectern as if walking off my frustration and then came back.

"Mr. Haller," the judge said. "Let's skip the playacting."

"Thank you, Your Honor," Freeman said.

"I wasn't addressing you, Ms. Freeman."

I looked at the jury for a long moment before asking my next and final question.

"In summary, sir, did you and your team gather a single shred of evidence in that garage that connects Lisa Trammel to the crime scene?"

"In the garage? No, we didn't."

"Thank you, then I have nothing further."

I knew that Freeman could hit back hard on redirect by asking Roberts about the hammer with Bondurant's blood on it and the shoe with the same blood on it found in my client's garage. He was part of the crime scene crews that handled both places. But I was guessing she wouldn't do it. She had choreographed the delivery of her case to the last piece of evidence and to change things now would be to knock the case out of rhythm, threatening her momentum and the ultimate impact when all things came together. She was too good to risk that. She would take her lumps now, knowing that she would eventually deliver the knockout punch later in the trial.

"Ms. Freeman, redirect?" the judge asked, once I had returned to my seat.

"No, Your Honor. No redirect."

"The witness may step down."

I had Freeman's witness list stapled to the inside flap of a case file on the table in front of me. I drew a line through the names Abbott and

Roberts and scanned the names that were left. The first day of trial wasn't even quite over and she had already put a sizable dent into the list. I scanned the remaining names and determined that Detective Kurlen was most likely the next witness up. But this presented a bit of a problem for the prosecutor. I checked my watch. It was 4:25 and court was scheduled to end at 5. If Freeman put Kurlen on the stand she would just be getting started when the judge recessed for the day. It was possible she could lead him toward a revelation that would be nice to have the jury considering overnight, but this might entail shuffling the delivery of his testimony and again I didn't think Freeman would consider it a worthy trade.

I scanned the list again to see if she had a floater, a witness who could be dropped in anywhere in the prosecution's case. I didn't see one and looked across the aisle at the prosecutor, unsure what move she would make.

"Ms. Freeman," the judge prompted. "Call your next witness, please."

Freeman rose from her seat and addressed Perry.

"Your Honor, it is expected that the witness I planned to call next will be providing lengthy testimony on both direct and cross-examination. I would like to ask for the court's indulgence and allow me to call the witness first thing in the morning so that the jury will not feel a disruption in testimony."

The judge looked over Freeman's head at the clock on the rear wall of the courtroom. He slowly shook his head.

"No," he said. "No, we're not going to do that. We have more than a half hour of court time left and we are going to use it. Call your next witness, Ms. Freeman."

"Yes, Your Honor," Freeman said. "The People call Gilbert Modesto."

I had been wrong about the floater. Modesto was head of corporate security at WestLand National and Freeman must have believed his testimony could be dropped into the trial at any point and not be detrimental to momentum and flow.

After being sworn in and taking his seat on the stand, Modesto proceeded to outline his experience in law enforcement and his current duties at WestLand National. Freeman then brought the questioning around to his actions on the morning of Mitchell Bondurant's slaying.

"When I heard it was Mitch, the first thing I did was pull the threat file to give to the police," he said.

"What is the threat file?" Freeman asked.

"It's a file we keep that contains every mailed or e-mailed threat to the bank or bank personnel. It also contains notes on any other kind of threat that comes in through phone or third party or the police. We have a protocol for weighing the severity of the threat and we have names that we flag and so forth."

"How familiar are you personally with the threat file?"

"Very familiar. I study it. It's my job."

"How many names were in that file on the morning of Mitchell Bondurant's murder?"

"I didn't count but I would say a couple dozen."

"And these were all considered legitimate threats to the bank and its employees?"

"No, our rule is that if we get a threat it goes into the file. Doesn't matter how legitimate it is. It goes into the file. So most of them are not considered serious, just somebody blowing off steam or a little frustration."

"In the file that morning, what name was on the top of the list in terms of seriousness of the threat?"

"The defendant, Lisa Trammel."

Freeman paused for effect. I studied the jury. Almost all eyes looked toward my client.

"Why is that, Mr. Modesto? Did she make a specific threat against the bank or any bank employee?"

"No, she didn't. But she was engaged in a foreclosure fight with the bank and had a history of protesting outside the bank until our lawyers got a temporary restraining order keeping her away. It was her actions that were perceived as a threat and it looks like we were right about that."

I jumped up and objected, asking the judge to strike the end of Modesto's answer as being inflammatory and prejudicial. The judge agreed and admonished Modesto to keep such opinions to himself.

"Do you know, Mr. Modesto," Freeman said, "whether Lisa Trammel had made a direct threat against anyone at the bank, including Mitchell Bondurant?"

Rule number one was to turn all weaknesses into advantages. Freeman was asking my questions now, robbing me of the chance to inflect them with my own outrage.

"No, not specifically. But it was our feeling in terms of threat assessment that she was someone we should keep an eye out for."

"Thank you, Mr. Modesto. Who did you give this file to within the LAPD?"

"Detective Kurlen, who was heading up the investigation. I went directly to him with it."

"And did you have occasion to speak to Detective Kurlen again later in the day?"

"Well, we spoke a few times as the investigation was progressing. He had questions about the surveillance cameras in the garage and other things."

"Was there a second time when you contacted him?"

"Yes, when it came to my attention that one of our employees, a teller, had reported to her supervisor that she believed she had seen Lisa Trammel either near or on the bank property that morning. I thought that was information the police needed to have so I called Detective Kurlen and set up an interview for him with the teller."

"And was that Margo Schafer?"

"Yes, it was."

Freeman ended her direct examination there and turned the witness over to me. I decided it would be best to get in and out, sow a few seeds and come back to harvest later.

"Mr. Modesto, as chief of corporate security at WestLand, did you have access to the foreclosure action the bank was taking against Lisa Trammel?"

Modesto emphatically shook his head.

"No, that was a legal case and as such I was not privy to it."

"So when you gave Detective Kurlen that file with Lisa Trammel's name at the top of the list, you wouldn't have known if she was about to lose her house or not, correct?"

"That is correct."

"You wouldn't have known if the bank was in the process of backing off her foreclosure because it had employed a company engaged in fraudulent activities, am I—"

"Objection!" Freeman shrieked. "Assumes facts not in evidence."

"Sustained," Perry said. "Mr. Haller, be careful here."

"Yes, Your Honor. Mr. Modesto, at the time you gave the threat file to Detective Kurlen, did you mention Lisa Trammel specifically or did you just hand him the file and let him go through it on his own?"

"I told him she was on the top of our list."

"Did he ask you why?"

"I don't really recall. I just remember telling him about her but I can't say for sure whether that was volunteered by me or whether he asked me specifically."

"And at the time you spoke to Detective Kurlen about Lisa Trammel as being a threat, you had no idea what the status of her foreclosure case was, correct?"

"Yes, that is correct."

"So Detective Kurlen didn't have that information either, am I right?"

"I can't speak for Detective Kurlen. You would have to ask him."

"Don't worry, I will. I have no further questions at this time."

I checked the back wall as I returned to my seat. It was five minutes before five and I knew we were finished for the day. There was always so much that went into prepping for a trial. The end of the first day usually was accompanied by a wave of fatigue. I was just feeling it start to hit me.

The judge admonished the jurors to keep an open mind about what they had heard and seen during the day. He told them to avoid media reports on the trial and not to discuss the case among themselves or with others. He then sent them home.

My client went off with Herb Dahl, who had returned to the courthouse, and I followed Freeman through the gate.

"Nice start," I said to her.

"Not bad yourself."

"Well, we both know you get to pick off the low-hanging fruit at the beginning of a trial. Then it's gone and it gets tough."

"Yes, it's going to get tough. Good luck, Haller."

Once in the hallway we went our separate ways. Freeman down the stairs to the DA's office and me to the elevator and then back to my office. It didn't matter how tired I was. I still had work to do. Kurlen would likely be on the stand all day the next day. I was going to be ready.

Twenty-six

The People call Detective Howard Kurlen."

Andrea Freeman turned from the prosecution table where she stood and smiled at the detective as he walked down the aisle, two impressively thick blue binders known as murder books under his arm. He came through the gate and headed toward the witness stand. He looked at ease. This was routine for him. He put the murder books down on the shelf in front of the witness chair and raised his hand to take the oath. He shot me a sideways look at that point. Outwardly, Kurlen looked cool, calm and collected, but we had done this dance before and he had to be wondering what I would be bringing this time.

Kurlen wore a sharply cut navy blue suit with a bright orange tie. Detectives always put on their best look to testify. Then I realized something. There was no gray in Kurlen's hair. He was closing in on sixty and had no gray. He had dyed it for the TV cameras.

Vanity. I wondered if it was something I could use as an edge when it was my turn to ask him questions.

After Kurlen was sworn in, he took the witness seat and made himself comfortable. He'd probably be there the whole day and maybe longer. He poured himself a glass of water from the pitcher set up by the judge's clerk, took a sip and looked at Freeman. He was ready to go.

"Good morning, Detective Kurlen. I would like to start this morning with you telling the jury a little bit about your experience and history."

"I'd be glad to," Kurlen said with a warm smile. "I am fifty-six years

208

old and I joined the LAPD twenty-four years ago after spending ten years in the marines. I have been a homicide detective assigned to the Van Nuys Division for the past nine years. Before that I spent three years working homicides at the Foothill Division."

"How many homicide investigations have you worked?"

"This case is my sixty-first homicide. I was a detective assigned to investigations of other crimes — robbery, burglary and auto theft — for six years before moving to homicide."

Freeman was standing at the lectern. She flipped back a page on a legal pad, ready to move on to what mattered.

"Detective, let's begin on the morning of the murder of Mitchell Bondurant. Can you walk us through the initial stages of the case?"

Smart move saying "us," implying that the jury and prosecutor were part of the same team. I had no doubts about Freeman's skills and she would be at her sharpest with her lead detective on the stand. She knew that if I could damage Kurlen, the whole thing might come tumbling down.

"I was at my desk at about nine fifteen when the detective lieutenant came to me and my partner, Detective Cynthia Longstreth, and said a homicide had occurred in the parking garage of the WestLand National headquarters on Ventura Boulevard. Detective Longstreth and I immediately rolled on it."

"You went to the scene?"

"Yes, immediately. We arrived at nine thirty and took control of the scene."

"What did that entail?"

"Well, the first priority is to preserve and collect the evidence from the crime scene. The patrol officers had already taped off the area and were keeping people away. Once we were satisfied that everything was covered there, we divvied up responsibilities. I left my partner in charge of overseeing the crime scene investigation and I would conduct preliminary interviews of the witnesses the patrol officers were holding for questioning."

"Detective Longstreth is a less experienced detective than you, correct?"

"Yes, she has been working homicide investigations with me for three years."

"Why did you give the junior member of your team the very important job of overseeing the crime scene investigation?"

"I did it that way because I knew that the crime scene people and the coroner's investigator who were on scene were all veterans with many years on the job and that Cynthia would be with good experienced hands."

Freeman then led Kurlen through a series of questions about his interviews with the gathered witnesses, starting with Riki Sanchez, who had discovered the body and called 911. Kurlen was at ease on the stand and almost folksy in his delivery. The word that came to mind was *charming*.

I didn't like charming but I had to bide my time. I knew it might be the end of the day before I got the chance to go after Kurlen. In the meantime I had to hope that by then the jury hadn't fallen completely in love with him.

Freeman was smart enough to know you can't keep a jury's attention with charm alone. Eventually, she moved out of the scene-setting preliminaries and started to deliver the case against Lisa Trammel.

"Detective, was there a time during the investigation when the defendant's name became known to you?"

"Yes, there was. The bank's head of security came to the garage and asked to see me or my partner. I spoke to him briefly and then accompanied him to his office, where we reviewed video from the cameras located at the vehicle entrance and exits to the garage and in the elevators."

"And did the review of those videos provide you with any investigative leads?"

"Nothing initially. I saw no one carrying a weapon or acting in a suspicious way before or after the approximate time of the murder. Nobody running from the garage. There was nothing suspicious about the vehicles going in and out. Of course, we would run every license plate. But there was nothing on video upon that initial viewing that helped us and, of course, the actual murder itself was not captured by any camera. That was another detail that the perpetrator of the crime seemed to be aware of."

I rose and objected to Kurlen's last line and the judge struck it from the record and told the jury to ignore it.

"Detective," Freeman prompted, "I believe you were going to tell us how Lisa Trammel's name first came up in the investigation."

"Yes, right. Well, Mr. Modesto, the bank security chief, also provided me with a file. What he called the threat-assessment file. He turned that over to me and it contained several names, including the name of the defendant. Then, just a short while later, Mr. Modesto called me and informed me that Lisa Trammel, one of the people listed in the file, happened to be seen that morning in close proximity to the bank."

"The defendant. And so this was how her name came up in the investigation, correct?"

"Correct."

"What did you do with this information, Detective?"

"I first returned to the crime scene. I then sent my partner to interview the witness who said she saw Lisa Trammel near the bank. It was important that we confirm that sighting and get the details. I then began to go through the threat-assessment file to study all of the names and the details of the perceived threats."

"And did you draw any immediate conclusions?"

"I didn't believe there was any individual listed who would immediately jump to the level of a person of interest based solely on what was reported in the file about them and their disputes with the bank. Obviously, they would all have to be looked at carefully. However, Lisa Trammel did rise to the level of being a person of interest because I knew from Mr. Modesto that she had allegedly been seen in the vicinity of the bank at the time of the murder."

"So Lisa Trammel's time and geographic proximity to the murder was key to your thinking at this point?"

"Yes, because proximity could mean access. It appeared from the crime scene that someone had been waiting for the victim. He had an assigned parking space with his name on the wall. There was a large support column next to the space. Our initial theory was that the killer had hidden behind the column and waited for Mr. Bondurant to pull in and park. It appeared that he was struck the first time from behind, just as he left his car."

"Thank you, Detective."

Freeman led her witness through a few more of the steps taken at the crime scene before bringing the focus back to Lisa Trammel.

"Did your partner return to the crime scene at some point to report back about her interview with the bank employee who claimed to have seen Lisa Trammel near the bank?"

"Yes, she did. My partner and I felt that the identification made by the witness was solid. We then discussed Lisa Trammel and the need for us to speak to her quickly."

"But, Detective, you had a crime scene investigation under way and a file full of the names of people who had made threats against the bank or its employees. Why the urgency involving Lisa Trammel?"

Kurlen leaned back in his witness chair and adopted the pose of a wise and wily old veteran.

"Well, there were a couple things that gave us a sense of urgency in regard to Ms. Trammel. First of all, her dispute with the bank was over the foreclosure of her property. That put her dispute specifically in the home loan division. The victim, Mr. Bondurant, was a senior vice president directly in charge of the home loan division. So we were looking at that connection. Additionally, and more importantly—"

"Let me interrupt you there, Detective. You called that a connection. Did you know if the victim and Lisa Trammel knew each other?"

"Not at that point, no. What we knew was that Ms. Trammel had a history of protesting the foreclosure of her home and that the foreclosure action was initiated by Mr. Bondurant, the victim. But we did not know at that time whether these two people knew each other or had ever even met."

It was a smooth move, bringing out the deficiencies in her case to the jury before I did. It made it harder for the defense to make its case.

"Okay, Detective," Freeman said. "I interrupted you when you were going to tell us a second reason for having some urgency in regard to Ms. Trammel."

"What I wanted to explain is that a murder investigation is a fluid situation. You must move carefully and cautiously, but at the same time you must go where the case takes you. If you don't, then evidence could be at risk — and possibly other victims. We felt there was a need to make contact with Lisa Trammel at this point in the investigation. We couldn't wait. We could not give her time to destroy evidence or harm other persons. We had to move."

I checked the jury. Kurlen was giving one of his best performances ever. He held every eye in the jury box. If Clegg McReynolds ever made a movie, maybe Kurlen should play himself.

"So what did you do, Detective?"

"We ran a check on Lisa Trammel's driver's license, got her address in Woodland Hills and proceeded to her home."

"Who was left at the crime scene?"

"Several people. Our coordinator and all the SID techs and the coroner's people. They still had a lot to do and we were waiting on them anyway. Going to Lisa Trammel's house in no way compromised the scene or the investigation."

"Your coordinator? Who's that?"

"The detective-three in charge of the homicide unit. Jack Newsome. He was the supervisor on scene."

"I see. So what happened when you got to Ms. Trammel's home? Was she there?"

"Yes, she was. We knocked and she answered."

"Can you take us through what happened next?"

"We identified ourselves and said we were conducting an investigation of a crime. Didn't say what it was, just said it was serious. We asked if we could come inside to ask her a few questions. She said yes, so we entered."

I felt a vibration in my pocket and knew I had received a text on my cell phone. I slipped it out of my pocket and held it down below the table so the judge would not see it. The message was from Cisco.

Need to talk, show you something.

I texted back and we had a quick digital conversation:

You verify the letter?

No, something else. Still working the letter.

Then after court. Get me the letter.

I put the phone away and went back to watching Freeman's direct examination. The letter in question had come in the afternoon before in the mail to my P.O. box. It came anonymously but if its contents could be confirmed by Cisco I would have a new weapon. A powerful weapon.

"What was Ms. Trammel's demeanor when you met her?" Freeman asked.

"She seemed pretty calm to me," Kurlen said. "She didn't seem particularly curious about why we wanted to talk to her or what the crime was. She was nonchalant about the whole thing."

"Where did you and your partner speak to her?"

"She walked us into the kitchen where there was a table and she invited us to sit down. She asked if we wanted water or coffee and we both said no."

"And you started asking her questions then?"

"Yes, we started by asking if she had been in the house all morning. She said she had been except for when she drove her son to school in Sherman Oaks at eight. I asked if she had made any other stops on the way home and she said no."

"And what did that mean to you?"

"Well, that somebody was lying. We had the witness who put her near the bank at close to nine. So somebody was wrong or somebody was lying."

"What did you do at that point?"

"I asked if she would be willing to come with us to the police station where she would be interviewed and asked to look at some photographs. She said yes and we took her to Van Nuys."

"Did you first apprise her of her constitutional rights not to speak to you without an attorney present?"

"Not at that time. She was not a suspect at this point. She was simply a person of interest whose name had come to the surface. I didn't believe that we needed to give her the rights warning until we crossed that threshold. We weren't close to being there yet. We had a discrepancy between what she told us and what a witness had told us. We needed to explore that further before anybody became a suspect."

Freeman was at it again. Trying to patch holes before I could tear them open. It was frustrating but there was nothing I could do about it. I was busy writing down questions I would later ask Kurlen, ones that Freeman wouldn't anticipate.

Skillfully Freeman led Kurlen back to Van Nuys station and the interview room where he had sat with my client. She used him to introduce the video of the session. It was played for the jury on two overhead screens. Aronson had ably argued against showing the interview but to no avail. Judge Perry had allowed it. We could appeal after conviction but success there was a long shot. I had to turn things now. I had to find a way to make the jury see it as an unfair process, a trap into which my innocent client had stumbled.

The video was shot from an overhead angle and the defense scored a minor point right off the bat because Howard Kurlen was a big man and Lisa Trammel was small. Sitting across a table from Trammel, Kurlen looked like he was crowding her, cornering her, even bullying her. This was good. This was part of a theme I planned to put into my cross-examination.

The audio was clear and the sound crisp. Over my objection, the jurors as well as the other players in the trial had been given transcripts with which to read along. I had objected because I didn't want the jurors reading. I wanted them watching. I wanted them to see the big man bullying the little woman. There was sympathy to be gained there, but not in the words on the page.

Kurlen started casually, announcing the names of those in the room and asking Trammel if she was there voluntarily. My client said that she was but the starkness and angle of the video belied her words. She looked like she was being held in a prison.

"Why don't we start with you telling us about your movements today?" Kurlen asked next.

"Starting when?" Trammel responded.

"How about with the moment you woke up?"

Trammel outlined her early morning routine of waking and preparing her son for school, then driving him there. The boy attended a private school and the drive usually ranged from twenty to forty minutes depending on traffic. She said she stopped after the drop-off to get coffee and then she went back home.

"You told us at your home you didn't make any stops. Now you stopped for coffee?"

"I guess I forgot."

"Where?"

"A place called Joe's Joe on Ventura."

A veteran interrogator, Kurlen abruptly went in a new direction, keeping his quarry off guard.

"Did you go by WestLand National this morning?"

"No. Is that what this is about?"

"So if someone said they saw you there, they would be lying?"

"Yes, who said that? I have not violated the order. You—"

"Do you know Mitchell Bondurant?"

"Know him? No. I know of him. I know who he is. But I don't know him."

"Did you see him today?"

Trammel paused here and this was detrimental to her cause. On the video, you could see the wheels working. She was considering whether to tell the truth. I glanced at the jury. I didn't see one face that wasn't turned up toward the screens.

"Yes, I saw him."

"But you just said you didn't go on WestLand property."

"I didn't. Look, I don't know who told you they saw me at the bank. And if it was him then he's a liar. I wasn't there. I saw him, yes, but that was at the coffee shop, not the—"

"Why didn't you tell us that this morning at your home?"

"Tell you what? You didn't ask."

"Have you changed clothes since this morning?"

"What?"

"Did you change clothes this morning after you got back home?"

"Look, what is this? You asked me to come down to talk and this is some sort of setup. I have not violated the order. I—"

"Did you attack Mitchell Bondurant?"

"What?"

Kurlen didn't answer. He just stared at Trammel as her mouth came open in a perfect O. I checked the jury. All eyes were still on the screens. I hoped they saw what I saw. Genuine shock on my client's face.

"Is that—Mitchell Bondurant was attacked? Is he all right?"

"No, actually, he's dead. And at this point I want to advise you of your constitutional rights."

Kurlen read Trammel the Miranda rights warning and Trammel said the magic words, the smartest four words to ever come out of her mouth.

"I want my attorney."

That ended the interview and the video concluded with Kurlen placing Trammel under arrest for murder. And that was how Freeman ended Kurlen's testimony. She surprised me by abruptly saying she was finished with the witness and then sitting down. She still had the search of my client's house to cover with the jury. And the hammer. But it looked like she wouldn't be using Kurlen for these.

It was 11:45 and the judge broke for an early lunch. That gave me an hour and fifteen minutes to make final preparations for Kurlen. Once more we were about to do the jury dance.

Twenty-seven

I stepped over to the lectern carrying two thick files and my trusty legal pad. The files were superfluous to my cross-examination but my hope was that they would make an impressive prop. I took my time organizing everything on top of the lectern. I wanted Kurlen to dangle. My plan was to treat him in the same manner he had treated my client. Bobbing and weaving, jabbing with the left when he was expecting the right, a hit-and-run mission.

Freeman had made the smart play, breaking up the testimony between the partners. I wouldn't get the chance to make a cohesive attack on the case through just Kurlen. I would have to deal with him now and his partner Longstreth much later. Case choreography was one of Freeman's strong points and she was showing it here.

"Anytime, Mr. Haller," the judge prompted.

"Yes, Your Honor. Just getting my notes in order. Good afternoon, Detective Kurlen. I wonder if we could start by going back to the crime scene. Did you —"

"Whatever you want."

"Yes, thank you. How long were you and your partner at the crime scene before you went off to chase down Lisa Trammel?"

"Well, I wouldn't call it chasing her down. We —"

"Is that because she wasn't a suspect?"

"That's one of the reasons."

"She was just a person of interest, is that what you call it?"

"That's right."

"So then how long were you at the crime scene before you left to find this woman who was not a suspect but only a person of interest?"

Kurlen referred to his notes.

"My partner and I arrived at the crime scene at nine twenty-seven and one or both of us were there until we left together at ten thirty-nine."

"That's...an hour and twelve minutes. You spent only seventy-two minutes at the crime scene before feeling the need to leave to pick up a woman who was not even a suspect. Do I have that right?"

"It's one way to look at it."

"How did you look at it, Detective?"

"First of all, leaving the crime scene was not an issue because the crime scene was under the control and direction of the homicide squad coordinator. Several technicians from the Scientific Investigation Division were also on hand. Our job was not the crime scene. Our job was to follow the leads wherever they took us and they led us at that point to Lisa Trammel. She wasn't a suspect when we went to see her but she became one when she started giving inconsistent and contradictory statements during the interview."

"You're talking about the interview back at Van Nuys Division, yes?"

"That's correct."

"Okay, then what were the inconsistent and contradictory statements you just mentioned?"

"At her house she said she made no stops after dropping the kid off. At the station she suddenly remembers getting coffee and seeing the victim there. She says she wasn't near the bank but we had a witness who put her a half a block away. That was the big one right there."

I smiled and shook my head like I was dealing with a simpleton.

"Detective, you're kidding us, right?"

Kurlen gave me the first look of annoyance. It was just what I wanted. If it was perceived as arrogance it would be all the better when I humiliated him.

"No, I am not kidding," Kurlen said. "I take my job very seriously."

I asked the judge to allow me to replay a portion of the Trammel interview. Permission granted, I fast-forwarded the playback, keeping my eye on the time code at the bottom. I slowed it to normal play just in time for the jury to watch the exchange centering on Trammel's denial of being near WestLand National.

"Did you go by WestLand National this morning?"

"No. Is that what this is about?"

"So if someone said they saw you there, they would be lying?"

"Yes, who said that? I have not violated the order. You—"

"Do you know Mitchell Bondurant?"

"Know him? No. I know of him. I know who he is. But I don't know him."

"Did you see him today?"

"Yes, I saw him."

"But you just said you didn't go on WestLand property."

"I didn't. Look, I don't know who told you they saw me at the bank. And if it was him then he's a liar. I wasn't there. I saw him, yes, but that was at the coffee shop, not the—"

"Why didn't you tell us that this morning at your home?"

"Tell you what? You didn't ask."

I stopped the video and looked at Kurlen.

"Detective, where is it that Lisa Trammel contradicts herself?"

"She says right there that she wasn't near the bank and we have a witness who says she was."

"So you have a contradiction between two statements by different people, but Lisa Trammel did not contradict herself, correct?"

"You are talking semantics."

"Can you answer the question, Detective?"

"Yes, right, a contradiction between two statements."

Kurlen didn't consider the distinction important but I hoped the jury would.

"Isn't it true, Detective, that Lisa Trammel has never contradicted her statement that she was not near the bank on the day of the murder?"

"I wouldn't know. I am not privy to everything she has ever said since then."

Now he was just being churlish, which was fine by me.

"Okay, then as far as you know, Detective, has she ever contradicted that very first statement to you that she was not near the bank?"

"No."

"Thank you, Detective."

I asked the judge if I could replay another segment of the video and was granted permission. I moved the video back to a time spot early in the interview and froze it. I then asked the judge if I could put one of the prosecution's crime scene photos on one of the overhead screens while leaving the video on the other. The judge gave me the go-ahead.

The crime scene photo I put up was a wide-angle shot that took in almost the entire crime scene. The tableau included Bondurant's body as well as his car, the open briefcase and the spilled cup of coffee on the ground.

"Detective, let me draw your attention to the crime scene photo marked People's Exhibit Three. Can you describe what you see in the foreground?"

"You mean the briefcase or the body?"

"What else, Detective?"

"You've got the spilled coffee, and the evidence marker on the left is where they found a tissue fragment later identified as coming from the victim's scalp. You can't really see that in the photo."

I asked the judge to strike the part of the answer concerning the tissue fragment as nonresponsive. I had asked Kurlen to describe what he could see in the photo, not what he couldn't see. The judge didn't agree and let the whole answer stand. I shook it off and tried again.

"Detective, can you read what it says on the side of the coffee cup?"

"Yes, it says Joe's Joe. It's a gourmet coffee shop about four blocks from the bank."

"Very good, Detective. Your eyes are better than mine."

"Maybe because they look for the truth."

I looked at the judge and spread my hands like a baseball manager who just saw a fastball down the pipe called a ball. Before I could verbally react the judge was all over Kurlen.

"Detective!" Perry barked. "You know better than that."

"I'm sorry, Your Honor," Kurlen said contritely, his eyes holding on mine. "Mr. Haller somehow always seems to bring out the worst in me."

"That's no excuse. Another one like that and you and I are going to have a serious problem."

"It won't happen again, Judge. I promise."

"The jury will disregard the witness's comment. Mr. Haller, proceed and take us away from this."

"Thank you, Your Honor. I'll do my best. Detective, when you were at the crime scene for seventy-two minutes before leaving to question Ms. Trammel, did you determine whose coffee cup that was?"

"Well, we later found out that—"

"No, no, no, I didn't ask you what you *later* found out, Detective. I asked you about those first seventy-two minutes when you were at the crime scene. During that time, before you went to Lisa Trammel's house in Woodland Hills, did you know whose coffee that was?"

"No, we had not determined that yet."

"Okay, so you didn't know who dropped that coffee at the crime scene, correct?"

"Objection, asked and answered," Freeman said.

It was a useless objection but she had to do something to try to knock me out of rhythm.

"I'll allow it," the judge said before I could respond. "You can answer the question, Detective. Did you know who dropped that cup of coffee at the crime scene?"

"Not at that time."

I went back to the video and played the segment I had cued and ready to go. It was from the early part of the interview, when Trammel was recounting her routine activities during the morning of the murder.

"You stopped for coffee?"

"I guess I forgot."

"Where did you stop to get the coffee?"

"A place called Joe's Joe. It's on Van Nuys Boulevard right by the intersection with Ventura."

"Do you remember, did you get a large or small cup?"

"Large. I drink a lot of coffee."

I stopped the video.

"Tell me something now, Detective. Why did you ask what size coffee she got at Joe's Joe?"

"You throw out a big net. You go for as many details as you can."

"Was it not because you believed the coffee cup found at the scene of the murder might have been Lisa Trammel's?"

"That was one possibility at that point."

"Did you count this as one of those admissions from Lisa Trammel?"

"I thought it was significant at that point in the conversation. I wouldn't call it an admission."

"But then, under further questioning, she told you she saw the victim at the coffee shop, correct?"

"Correct."

"So didn't that change your thinking on the coffee cup at the scene?"

"It was just additional information to consider. It was very early in the investigation. We had no independent information that the victim had been in the coffee shop. We had this one person's statement but it was inconsistent with the statement of a witness we had already spoken to. So we had Lisa Trammel saying she saw Mitchell Bondurant at the coffee shop but that didn't make it a fact. We still needed to confirm that. And later we did."

"But do you see where what you considered an inconsistency early in the interview turned out to be totally consistent with the facts later?"

"In this one instance."

Kurlen would give no quarter. He knew I was trying to back him up to the edge of a cliff. His job was to keep from going over.

"In fact, Detective, wouldn't you say that when all was said and done, the only thing inconsistent about the interview with Lisa Trammel was that she said she wasn't near the bank and you had a witness who claimed she was?"

"It's always easy to look back with twenty-twenty vision. But that one inconsistency was and is pretty important. A reliable witness put her close to the scene of the crime at the time of the crime. That hasn't changed since day one."

"A reliable witness. Based on one short interview with Margo Schafer she was deemed a reliable witness?"

I put the proper mix of outrage and confusion in my voice. Freeman objected, saying that I was simply badgering the witness because I was not getting the answers I wanted. The judge overruled but it was a good message for her to get to the jury — the idea that I wasn't getting what I wanted. Because, in fact, I was.

"The first interview with Margo Schafer was short," Kurlen said. "But she was reinterviewed several times by several investigators. Her observations on that day have not changed one iota. I believe she saw what she said she saw."

"Good for you, Detective," I said. "Let's go back to the coffee cup. Did there come a time that you came to a conclusion as to whose coffee was spilled and left at the crime scene?"

"Yes. We found a Joe's Joe receipt in the victim's pocket for a large cup of coffee purchased that morning at eight twenty-one. Once we found that, we believed that the coffee cup at the crime scene was his. This was later confirmed by fingerprint analysis. He got out of the car with it and dropped it when he was attacked from behind."

I nodded, making sure the jury understood that I was indeed getting the answers I wanted.

"What time was it when that receipt was found in the victim's pocket?"

Kurlen checked his notes and didn't find an answer.

"I am not sure because the receipt was found by the coroner's investigator who was in charge of checking the victim's pockets and securing all property that had been on the victim's person. This would have been done before the body was transported to the coroner's office."

"But it was well after you and your partner took off in pursuit of Lisa Trammel, correct?"

"We didn't take off in pursuit of Trammel, but the discovery of the receipt would have been after we left to talk to Trammel."

"Did the coroner's investigator call you and tell you about the receipt?"

"No."

"Did you find out about the receipt before or after you arrested Lisa Trammel for murder?"

"After. But there was other evidence in support of —"

"Thank you, Detective. Just answer the question I ask, if you don't mind."

"I don't mind telling the truth."

"Good. That's what we're here for. Now, wouldn't you agree that you arrested Lisa Trammel on the basis of inconsistent and contradictory statements that later turned out to be, in fact, consistent and not in contradiction with the evidence and the facts of the case?"

Kurlen answered as if by rote.

"We had the witness who placed her near the scene of the crime at the time of the crime."

"And that's all you had, correct?"

"There was other evidence tying her to the murder. We have her hammer and—"

"I'm talking about at the time of her arrest!" I yelled. "Please answer the question I ask you, Detective!"

"Hey!" the judge exclaimed. "There's only one person who's going to be allowed to raise their voice in my courtroom, and, Mr. Haller, you aren't that person."

"I'm sorry, Your Honor. Could you please instruct the witness to answer the questions he is asked and not those that are not asked?"

"Consider the witness so advised. Proceed, Mr. Haller."

I paused for a moment to collect myself and swept my eyes across the jury. I was looking for sympathetic reactions but I didn't see any. Not even from Furlong, who didn't meet my eyes with his. I looked back at Kurlen.

"You just mentioned the hammer. The defendant's hammer. This was evidence you didn't have at the time of the arrest, correct?"

"That's correct."

"Isn't it true that once you made the arrest and realized that the inconsistent statements you relied upon were not actually inconsistent, you began looking for evidence to fit your theory of the case?"

"Not true at all. We had the witness but we still kept a wide-open view of this thing. We weren't wearing blinders. I would've been happy to drop the charges against the defendant. But the investigation was ongoing and the evidence that we started accumulating and evaluating did not cut her way."

"Not only that but you had motive, too, didn't you?"

"The victim was foreclosing on the defendant's house. As far as motive went, that looked pretty strong to me."

"But you were not privy to the details of that foreclosure, only that there was a foreclosure in process, correct?"

"Yes, and that there was a temporary restraining order against her, too."

"You mean you are saying that the restraining order itself was a motive to kill Mitchell Bondurant?"

"No, that's not what I'm saying and not what I mean. I'm just saying it was part of the whole picture."

"The whole picture adding up at that point to a rush to judgment, correct, Detective?"

Freeman jumped up and objected and the judge sustained it. That was okay. I wasn't interested in Kurlen's answer to the question. I was only interested in putting the question in each juror's mind.

I checked the rear wall of the courtroom and saw that it was three thirty. I told the judge that I was going to move in a new direction with my cross-examination and that it might be a good time to take the afternoon break. The judge agreed and dismissed the jury for fifteen minutes.

I sat back down at the defense table and my client reached over and squeezed my forearm with a powerful grip.

"You're doing so good!" she whispered.

"We'll see. There's still a long way to go."

She pushed her chair back to get up.

"Are you going for coffee?" she asked.

"No, I need to make a call. You go. Just remember, no talking to the media. Don't talk to anybody."

"I know, Mickey. Loose lips sink ships."

"You got it."

She left the table then and I watched her head out of the courtroom. I didn't see her constant companion, Herb Dahl, anywhere.

I pulled my phone and called Cisco's cell number. He answered right away.

"I'm out of time, Cisco. I need the letter."

"You got it."

"What do you mean, it's confirmed?"

"Totally legit."

"We're lucky we're talking on the phone."

"Why's that, Boss?"

"Because I might have to kiss you for this."

"Uh, that won't be necessary."

Twenty-eight

I used the last few minutes of the break to prepare the second part of my cross-examination of Kurlen. Cisco's news was going to send a wave through the whole trial. How I handled the new information with Kurlen would impact the rest of the trial. Soon everyone was back in the courtroom and I was at the lectern and ready to go. I had one last item on my list to hit before I got to the letter.

"Detective Kurlen, let's go back to the crime scene photo you see on the screen. Did you identify the ownership of the briefcase that was found open next to the victim's body?"

"Yes, it had the victim's property in it and his initials engraved on the brass locking plate. It was his."

"And when you arrived at the crime scene and saw the open briefcase next to the body, what were your initial impressions of it?"

"None. I try to keep an open mind about everything, especially when I first come into a case."

"Did you think the open briefcase could mean that robbery was a motive for the murder?"

"Among many possibilities, yes."

"Did you think, Here is a banker dead and an open briefcase next to him. I wonder what the killer was after?"

"I had to think of that as a possible scenario. But as I said it was—"

"Thank you, Detective."

Freeman objected, saying I was not giving the witness time to fully answer the question. The judge agreed and let Kurlen finish.

"I was just saying that the possibility of this being a robbery was just one scenario. Leaving the briefcase open could just as easily have been a move to make it look like a robbery when it wasn't."

I pushed on without losing a beat.

"Did you determine what was taken from the briefcase?"

"As far as we knew then and know now, nothing was taken from it. But there was no inventory as to what should have been in the briefcase. We had Mr. Bondurant's secretary look at his files and work product to see if she could determine if anything was missing, like a file or something. She found nothing missing."

"Then do you have any explanation for why it was left open?"

"As I said before, it could have been done as misdirection. But we also believe there is a good chance that the case sprung open when it was dropped on the concrete during the attack."

I put my incredulous look on.

"And how did you come to that determination, sir?"

"The briefcase has a faulty locking mechanism. Any sort of jarring of the case could lead to its release. We conducted experiments with the case and found that when it was dropped to a hard surface from a height of three feet or more, it sprung open about one out of every three times."

I nodded and acted like I was computing this information for the first time even though I already had it from one of the investigative reports received in discovery.

"So what you're saying is that there was a one in three chance that the briefcase came open on its own when Mr. Bondurant dropped it."

"That's correct."

"And you called that a good chance, correct?"

"A solid chance."

"And of course there was a greater chance that that was not how the briefcase came open, right?"

"You can look at it that way."

"There is a greater chance that someone opened the briefcase, correct?"

"Again, you can look at it that way. But we determined that nothing was missing from the briefcase so there was no apparent reason for it to have been opened except to create a misdirection of some kind. Our working theory was that it sprung open when it was dropped."

"Do you notice in the crime scene photograph, Detective, that none of the contents of the case have fallen out and onto the pavement?"

"That's correct."

"Do you have an inventory of the briefcase in your binder there that you can read to us?"

Kurlen took his time finding it and then read it to the jury. The briefcase contained six files, five pens, an iPad, a calculator, an address book and two blank notebooks.

"When you conducted your tests in which you dropped the briefcase to the ground to see about the possibility of it popping open, did the case have the same contents?"

"It had similar contents, yes."

"And on the times that the case popped open, how often did all the contents remain inside it?"

"Not every time but most of the time. It definitely could have happened."

"Was that the scientific conclusion to your scientific experiment, Detective?"

"It was done in the lab. It wasn't my experiment."

With a pen and a noticeable wrist flourish, I made several check marks on my legal pad. I then moved on to the most important avenue of my cross-examination.

"Detective," I said, "you told us earlier today that you received a threat-assessment file from WestLand National and that it contained information about the defendant. Did you ever check out any of the other names in the file?"

"We reviewed the file several times and did some limited follow-up. But as evidence came in against the defendant, we saw less and less of a need to."

"You weren't going to go chasing rainbows when you had your suspect already in hand, is that it?"

"I wouldn't put it that way. Our investigation was thorough and exhaustive."

"Did this thorough and exhaustive investigation include pursuing any other leads at any time that did not involve Lisa Trammel as a suspect?"

"Of course. That's what the job involves."

"Did you review Mr. Bondurant's work product and look for any leads unrelated to Lisa Trammel?"

"Yes, we did."

"You have testified about investigating threats made against the victim in this case. Did you investigate any threats he might have made against others?"

"Where the victim threatened someone else? Not that I recall."

I asked the court's permission to approach the witness with Defense Exhibit 2. I handed copies to all parties. Freeman objected but she was simply going through the motions. The issue regarding Bondurant's letter of complaint to Louis Opparizio had already been decided during pretrial arguments. Perry was allowing it, if only to even the score for allowing the state to enter the hammer and the DNA. He overruled Freeman's objection and told me I could proceed.

"Detective Kurlen, you hold a letter sent by certified mail from Mitchell Bondurant, the victim, to Louis Opparizio, president of ALOFT, a contracted vendor to WestLand National. Could you please read the letter to the jury?"

Kurlen stared at the page I gave him for a long moment before reading.

"'Dear Louis, Attached you will find correspondence from an attorney named Michael Haller who is representing the home owner in one of the foreclosure cases you are handling for WestLand. Her name is Lisa Trammel and the loan number is oh-four-oh-nine-seven-one-nine. The mortgage is jointly held by Jeffrey and Lisa Trammel. In his letter Mr. Haller makes allegations that the file is replete with fraudulent actions perpetrated in the case. You will note that he gives specific instances, all of which were carried out by ALOFT. As you know and we have discussed, there have been other complaints. These new allegations against ALOFT, if true, have put WestLand in a vulnerable position, especially considering the government's recent interest in this aspect of the mortgage business. Unless we come to some sort of arrangement and understanding in regard to this I will be recommending to the board that WestLand withdraw from its contract with your company for cause and any ongoing business be terminated. This action would also require the bank to file an SAR with appropriate authorities. Please contact me at your earliest convenience to further discuss these matters.'"

Kurlen held the letter out to me as if he was finished with it. I ignored the gesture.

"Thank you, Detective. Now the letter mentions the filing of an SAR. Do you know what that is?"

"A suspicious activity report. All banks are required to file them with the Federal Trade Commission if such activity comes to their attention."

"Have you ever before seen the letter you hold, Detective?"

"Yes, I have."

"When?"

"While reviewing the victim's work product. I noticed it then."

"Can you give me a date when this happened?"

"Not an exact date. I would say I became aware of this letter about two weeks into the investigation."

"And that would have been two weeks after Lisa Trammel was already arrested for the murder. Did you investigate further upon becoming aware of this letter, maybe talk to Louis Opparizio?"

"At some point I made inquiries and learned that Mr. Opparizio had a solid alibi for the time of the killing. I left it at that."

"What about the people working for Opparizio? Did they all have alibis?"

"I don't know."

"You don't know?"

"That's right. I did not pursue this because it appeared to be a business dispute and not a legitimate motive for murder. I do not view this letter as a threat."

"You did not consider it unusual that in this day of instant communication the victim chose to send a certified letter instead of an e-mail or a text or a fax?"

"Not really. There were several other copies of letters sent by certified mail. It seemed to be a way of doing business and keeping a record of it."

I nodded. Fair enough.

"Do you know if Mr. Bondurant ever filed a suspicious activity report in regard to Louis Opparizio or his company?"

"I checked with the Federal Trade Commission. He did not."

"Did you check with any other government agency to see if Louis Opparizio or his company were the subject of an investigation?"

"As best I could. There was nothing."

"As best you could . . . and so this whole thing was a dead end to you, correct?"

"That's correct."

"You checked with the FTC and you ran down a man's alibi, but then dropped it. You already had a suspect and the case against her was easy and just fell right into place for you, correct?"

"A murder case is never easy. You have to be thorough. You can leave no stone unturned."

"What about the U.S. Secret Service? Did you leave that stone unturned?"

"The Secret Service? I'm not sure what you mean."

"Did you have any interaction with the U.S. Secret Service during this investigation?"

"No, I didn't."

"How about the U.S. Attorney's Office in Los Angeles?"

"I did not. I can't speak for my partner or other colleagues who worked the case."

It was a good answer but not good enough. In my peripheral vision I could see that Freeman had moved to the edge of her seat, ready for the right moment to object to my line of questioning.

"Detective Kurlen, do you know what a federal target letter is?"

Freeman leapt to her feet before Kurlen could respond. She objected and asked for a sidebar.

"I think we'd better step back into chambers for this," the judge said. "I want the jury and court personnel to stay in place while I confer with counsel. Mr. Haller, Ms. Freeman, let's go."

I pulled a document and the attached envelope from one of my files and followed Freeman toward the door that led to the judge's chambers. I was confident that I was about to tilt the case in the defense's direction or I was headed to jail for contempt.

Twenty-nine

Judge Perry was not a happy jurist. He didn't even bother to go behind his desk and sit down. We entered his chambers and he immediately turned on me and folded his arms across his chest. He stared hard at me and waited for his court reporter to take a seat and set up her machine before he spoke.

"Okay, Mr. Haller, Ms. Freeman is objecting because my guess is that this is the first she's heard about the Secret Service and the U.S. Attorney's Office and a federal target letter and what it all may or may not have to do with this case. I'm objecting myself because it's the first I remember any mention of the federal government and I'm not going to allow you to go on a federal fishing trip in front of the jury. Now if you have something, I want an offer of proof on it right now, and then I want to know why Ms. Freeman doesn't know anything about it."

"Thank you, Judge," Freeman said indignantly, hands on her hips.

I tried to defuse the situation a bit by casually stepping away from our tight grouping and moving toward the window with the view that rolled up the side of the Santa Monica Mountains. I could see the cantilevered homes along the crest. They looked like matchboxes ready to drop with the next earthquake. I knew what that was like, clinging to the edge.

"Your Honor, my office received an anonymously sent envelope in the mail that contained a copy of a federal target letter addressed to Louis Opparizio and ALOFT. It informed him that he and his company

233

were the target of an investigation into fraudulent foreclosure practices undertaken on behalf of his client banks."

I held up the document and envelope.

"I have the letter right here. It is dated two weeks before the murder and just eight days after the letter of complaint Bondurant sent to Opparizio."

"When did you receive this supposedly anonymous envelope?" Freeman asked, her voice dripping with skepticism.

"It turned up yesterday in my P.O. box but wasn't opened until last night. If counsel does not believe me I will have my office manager come over and you can ask her any question you like. She's the one who went to the box."

"Let me see it," the judge demanded.

I handed Perry the letter and envelope. Freeman moved in close to him to read it as well. It was a short letter and he soon gave it back to me without asking Freeman if she was finished reading.

"You should've brought this up this morning," the judge said. "At the very least you should have provided a copy to opposing counsel and told her you planned to introduce it."

"Judge, I would have but it's obviously a photocopy and it came in the mail. I've been sandbagged before. We probably all have. I needed to verify the document and make sure it was legitimate before I told anyone. I didn't get that confirmation until less than an hour ago during the afternoon break."

"What was the source of the confirmation?" Freeman asked before the judge could.

"I don't know the exact details. My investigator simply told me that the letter was confirmed by the feds as legitimate. If you want further detail, I can also call in my investigator."

"That won't be necessary because I am sure Ms. Freeman will want to do her own due diligence. But bringing it up in cross-examination was far out of line, Mr. Haller. You should have informed the court this morning that you had received something in the mail that you were in the process of checking out and planned to introduce in court. You blindsided the state *and* the court."

"I apologize, Your Honor. My intention was to handle it properly. I guess it was a learned behavior, seeing how the state has blindsided me at least twice so far with surprise evidence and questions about timing and chain of custody."

Perry gave me a hard look but I knew he got the point. Ultimately, I believed he was a fair judge and would act accordingly. He knew the letter was legitimate and vital to the defense's case. Basic fairness held that I be allowed to pursue it. Freeman read the same thing I did and tried to head the judge off.

"Your Honor, it's four fifteen. I request that court be adjourned for the day so that the prosecution can digest this new material and be adequately prepared to proceed in the morning."

Perry shook his head.

"I don't like losing court time," he said.

"I don't either, Judge," Freeman responded. "But no doubt, as you just said, I've been blindsided here. Counsel should have brought this information forward this morning. You cannot allow him to just proceed with it without the prosecution being prepared and conducting its own confirmation and due diligence as to the context of this information. I am asking for forty-five minutes, Judge. Surely, the state is entitled to that."

The judge looked at me for opposing argument. I held my hands wide.

"Doesn't matter to me, Judge. She can take all the time in the world but it doesn't change the fact that Opparizio was and is under federal investigation for his dealings with WestLand among other banks. That would make the victim in this case a potential witness against him — the letter we introduced earlier makes that clear. The police and prosecution completely missed this aspect of the case and now Ms. Freeman wants to blame the messenger for their shallow invest—"

"Okay, Mr. Haller, we're not in front of the jury here," Perry said, cutting me off. "I understand your point. I'm going to adjourn early today but we'll start at nine sharp tomorrow and I expect all parties to be prepared and for there to be no further delays."

"Thank you, Your Honor," Freeman said.

"Let's go back," Perry said.

And we did.

*   *   *

My client was clinging to me as we left the courthouse. She wanted to know what other details I had about the federal investigation. Herb Dahl trailed behind us like the tail on a kite. I was uncomfortable speaking to both of them.

"Look, I don't know what it means, Lisa. That's one reason why the judge broke early today. So both the defense and the prosecution can do some work on it. You have to just back off for a bit and let me and my staff handle it."

"But this could be it, right, Mickey?"

"What do you mean, 'it'?"

"The evidence that shows it wasn't me—that proves it!"

I stopped and turned to her. Her eyes were searching my face for any sign of affirmation. Something about her desperation made me think for the first time that she may have truly been framed for Bondurant's murder.

But that wasn't like me, to believe in innocence.

"Look, Lisa, I am hoping that it will very clearly demonstrate to the jury that there is a strong alternate possibility, complete with motive and opportunity. But you need to calm down and recognize that it might not be evidence of anything. I expect that the prosecution is going to come in tomorrow with an argument to keep it away from the jury. We have to be prepared to fend that off as well as to proceed without it. So I have a lot—"

"They can't just do that! This is evidence!"

"Lisa, they can argue anything they want. And the judge will decide. The good thing is he owes us one. In fact, he owes us two for the hammer and the DNA dropping out of the sky. So I hope he'll do the right thing here and we'll get it in. That's why you have to let me go now. I need to get back to the office and get to work on this."

She reached up and patted down my tie and adjusted the collar on my suit coat.

"Okay, I get it. You do what you have to do, but call me tonight, okay? I want to know where things stand at the end of the day."

"If there's time, Lisa. If I'm not too tired, I will call."

I looked over her shoulder at Dahl, who stood two feet behind her. I actually needed the guy at the moment.

"Herb, take care of her. Get her home so I can go back to work."

"I've got her," he said. "No worries."

Right, no worries. I had the whole case to worry about and I couldn't help but worry about my client going off with the man I just sent her with. Was Dahl for real or was he just protecting his investment? I watched them head off across the plaza toward the parking garage. I then walked past the library and north toward my office. I was probably more excited about the possibilities that had dropped into my lap than Lisa was. I just wasn't showing it. You never show your cards unless your opponent has called the final bet.

When I got back to the office I was still floating on adrenaline. The pure, high-octane form that comes with the unexpected twist in your favor. Cisco and Bullocks were waiting for me when I entered. They both started talking at once and I had to raise my hands to cut them both off.

"Hold on, hold on," I said. "One at a time and I go first. Perry adjourned early so the state could jump on the target letter. We need to be ready for their best shot in the morning because I want to get it before the jury. Cisco, now you, what've you got? Tell me about the letter."

My momentum, carried all the way from the courthouse, took us into my office and I went behind the desk. The seat was warm and I could tell someone had been working there all afternoon.

"Okay," Cisco said. "We confirmed the letter was legit. The U.S. Attorney's Office wouldn't talk to us, but I found out that the Secret Service agent who's named in the letter, Charles Vasquez, is assigned to a joint task force with the FBI that is looking into all angles of mortgage fraud in the Southern California district. Remember last year when all the big banks temporarily halted foreclosures and everybody in Congress said they would investigate?"

"Yeah, I thought I was going out of business. Until the banks started foreclosing again."

"Yeah, well, one of the investigations that did get going was right here. Lattimore put together this task force."

Reggie Lattimore was the U.S. attorney assigned to the district. I knew him years ago when he was a public defender. He later switched sides and became a federal prosecutor and we moved in different orbits. I tried to stay away from the federal courthouse. I saw him from time to time at lunch counters downtown.

"Okay, he won't talk to us. What about Vasquez?"

"I tried him, too. I got him on the line, but as soon as he knew what it was about he had no comment. I called back a second time and he just hung up on me. I think if we want to talk to him we're going to have to paper him."

I knew from experience that trying to serve a subpoena on a federal agent could be like fishing without a hook on the end of your line. If they don't want to be papered they'll be able to avoid it.

"We might not have to," I said. "The judge adjourned early so the prosecution could run the letter down. My guess is she'll bring either Lattimore or Vasquez in and put him on before we can do it. Then she can try to spin it her way."

"She won't want this to blow up in her face during the defense phase," Aronson added, like the seasoned trial veteran she was not. "And the best way to guard against that is to bring Vasquez in as a witness herself."

"What do we know about this task force?" I asked.

"I don't have anybody inside," Cisco said. "But I've got someone close enough to know what is going on. The task force is obviously very political. The thinking was that there is so much fraud out there, it would be like shooting fish and they could grab headlines and look like they were doing something on their end about the whole mess. Opparizio is a perfect target: rich, arrogant and Republican. Whatever they are working in regard to him, it's just starting and hasn't gone very deep."

"Doesn't matter," I said. "The target letter is all we need. It will make Bondurant's letter look like a legitimate threat."

"Do you really think this is what happened or are we just using this coincidence to deflect the jury's attention?" Aronson asked.

She was still standing even though Cisco and I had sat down. There was something symbolic about it. As if by not sitting down with us as we schemed this out, she was not buying in or selling her soul.

"It doesn't matter, Bullocks," I said. "We have one job here and that's to put a not guilty on the scoreboard. How we get there..."

I didn't need to finish. I could see in her face that she was continuing to have difficulty with the lessons taught outside the classroom. I turned back to Cisco.

"So who leaked the letter to us?"

"That I don't know," he said. "I kind of doubt it was Vasquez. He acted too surprised and edgy on the phone. I'm thinking somebody in the U.S. Attorney's Office."

I agreed.

"Maybe Lattimore himself. If we're lucky enough to get Opparizio on the stand, it might actually help the feds to have him locked into some sworn testimony."

Cisco nodded. It was as good a possibility as anything else. I moved on.

"Cisco," I said, "the text you sent me in the courtroom said you had something unrelated to this to tell me."

"To show you. We need to take a ride when we're finished here."

"Where?"

"I'd rather just show you."

I could tell by the way his face froze that he wasn't going to talk in front of Bullocks. It didn't matter that she was a trusted part of the team. I got the message and turned back to her.

"Bullocks, you wanted to say something when I first came in?"

"Uh, no, I just wanted to talk about my testimony. But we have a few days before we need to touch base. I guess we should just stay in the moment."

"You sure? I can talk."

"No, go with Cisco. Maybe we'll get some time tomorrow."

I could tell that something in the initial conversation was bothering her. I let it go and got up from my desk. I felt sympathy for her but not too much. Idealism dies hard with everybody.

Thirty

I drove the Lincoln because Cisco had ridden his motorcycle to work. He directed me north on Van Nuys Boulevard.

"Is this about Lisa's husband?" I asked. "You found him?"

"Uh, no, not about that. It's about the two guys in the garage, Boss."

"The guys who attacked me? You connected them to Opparizio?"

"Yes and no. It's about them, but it's not connected to Opparizio."

"Then who the hell sent them after me?"

"Herb Dahl."

"What? You gotta be shitting me."

"I wish."

I looked over at my investigator. I completely trusted him but wasn't seeing the logic in Dahl's putting the two goons on me. We'd had the dispute over movie control and money, but how would busting my ribs and twisting my nuts help him in that regard? At the time of the attack, I had just found out he had made the deal with McReynolds. I got mugged before I could even register a protest.

"You better run this down for me, Cisco."

"I can't really do that yet. That's why we're in the car."

"Then talk to me. What's going on? I'm in the middle of trial here."

"Okay, you told me you didn't trust Dahl and that I should check him out. I did. I also had a couple of my guys start to keep an eye on him."

"By your guys you mean Saints?"

"That's right."

Once upon a time, long before he married Lorna, Cisco was with the Road Saints, a motorcycle club that was somewhere on the spectrum between the Hell's Angels and the Shriners' clowns on wheels. He managed to retire from membership without a criminal record and now maintained an association with the club. For a long time I did, too, serving as house counsel and handling various traffic, brawling and drug offenses that distracted the membership. That was how I had first met Cisco. He was running security investigations for the club and I started using him on the criminal cases that came up. The rest was history.

On more than one occasion over the years Cisco had enlisted the Saints on my behalf. I even credit them with saving my family from potential harm when I was involved in the Louis Roulet case. So it was not a surprise to me that he had called on them again, except that he hadn't bothered to clue me in.

"Why didn't you tell me this?"

"I didn't want to complicate things for you. You had the case to worry about. I was handling the two dirtbags who messed you up."

By messed up he meant more than physically. He was keeping me out of things because he knew that sometimes the psychological beating you take is worse than the physical. He didn't want me distracted or looking over my shoulder.

"Okay, I get it," I said.

Cisco reached inside his black-leather riding vest and pulled out a folded photograph. He handed it to me and I waited until I stopped at the light at Roscoe before I looked. I unfolded it and saw a picture of Herb Dahl getting into a car with the two black-gloved assailants who had so expertly put me down on the floor of the parking garage by the Victory Building.

"Recognize them?" Cisco asked.

"Yeah, it's them," I said, anger rising in my throat. "Fucking Dahl, I'm going to kick his fucking ass."

"Maybe. Turn left here. We're going to the compound."

I looked over my shoulder and squeezed the car into the turning lane just as the light changed and I got the signal. We headed west and I had to flip down the visor against the dropping sun. By compound I knew he meant the Saints' clubhouse, which was near the brewery on the other side of the 405 Freeway. It had been a while since I had been there.

"When was that photo taken?" I asked.

"While you were in the hospital. They didn't—"

"You've been sitting on this since then?"

"Relax. I wasn't checking with my guys every day, okay? They also didn't know about your ass getting kicked. So they saw Dahl with these guys, took a couple of pictures and never showed them to me because they didn't print them out for more than a month. It was a fuckup, I know, but these guys aren't pros. They're lazy. I take responsibility for it. So if you need to blame someone, blame me. I saw the photo for the first time last night. The other thing is my guys told me they didn't get it with the camera but they also saw Dahl give both of these assholes a roll of cash. So I think it's pretty clear. He hired them to kick your ass, Mick."

"Son of a bitch."

I was seized with the same sense of helplessness I had felt when one of the assailants had pinned my arms and held me while the other one hit me with his gloved fists. I felt sweat popping on my scalp. And sympathetic pain throbbed in my ribs and testicles.

"If I ever get a chance to—"

I stopped and looked across the seat at Cisco. He had a slight smile playing on his face.

"Is that what this is? You have these two guys at the clubhouse?"

He didn't answer but he kept the smile.

"Cisco, I'm in the middle of a trial and now you're telling me the guy who has his fingers in my client's pie is the one who set me up for that . . . that assault? I don't have time for this, man. I have too much—"

"They want to talk."

That shut my protest down quick.

"Did you interview them?"

"Nope. Waiting for you. Thought you should get first crack at them."

I drove in silence the rest of the way, pondering what lay ahead. Soon we pulled to a stop in front of a compound on the east side of the brewery. Cisco got out to open the gate and the car immediately became infected with the sour smell of the brewery.

The compound was surrounded by a chain-link fence with a twist of razor wire running along top. The concrete-block clubhouse, which sat in the middle of the hardscrabble lot, looked unimpressive in comparison to the gleaming row of machines parked out front. Harleys and Triumphs only. No rice rockets for this crew.

We entered the clubhouse, took a moment to let our eyes adjust and then I saw Cisco walk up to a serve-yourself bar where two other men in leather vests sat on stools.

"Ready to do this?" he said.

The two men spun off their stools and stood up. Both of them went an easy six foot four and three hundred pounds. They were enforcers. Cisco introduced them to me as Tommy Guns and Bam Bam.

"They're back here," said Tommy Guns.

The two men led us down a hallway behind the bar. They were so big they had to walk in single file. There were doors on either side. Bam Bam opened a door midway down the right side and we entered a windowless room with the walls and ceiling painted black and a single bulb hanging from above. In the dim light I could see sketches painted on the walls. Men with beards and long hair. I realized this was like a dark chapel where the fallen Saints were memorialized. My first thought as I looked about was *Pulp Fiction*. My second was that I didn't want to be here. Two men were lying on the floor hog-tied, with their arms and feet up behind their backs. They had black bags over their heads.

Bam Bam leaned down and started to pull the bags off. This started a chorus of groans and fearful sounds from the two men.

"Wait a minute," I said. "Cisco, I can't be here. You're bringing me into—"

"Is it them?" Cisco said, not waiting for me to finish my protest. "Look closely. You don't want to make a mistake."

"Me? It's not my mistake! I didn't ask you to do this!"

"Calm down. You're here, so just look. Is it them?"

"Jesus Christ!"

Both men were gagged with duct tape wrapped completely around their heads. Their faces were distorted further by the swelling and bruising already forming around their eyes. They had been beaten. The features didn't match with what I remembered from the Victory Building garage or even the photograph Cisco had showed me earlier. I bent down to look closer. Both men looked up at me, complete fear in their eyes.

"I can't tell," I said.

"It's a yes-or-no question, Mick."

"Yeah, but they weren't scared shitless when they beat the crap out of me and they weren't gagged."

"Take off the tape," Cisco ordered.

Bam Bam moved in, springing a switchblade open and roughly cutting through the tape on the first man. He then tore it off, taking chunks of neck hair with it. The man yelped in pain.

"Shut the fuck up!" Tommy Guns yelled.

The second man learned from his friend's example. He took the harsh tape-removal process without making a sound. Bam Bam threw the gag to the side of the room and then moved behind the men. He grabbed the nexus of the rope that tied the arms and legs together and knocked each man onto his side so I could see his face better.

"Please don't kill us," one of the men said, desperation tightening his voice. "It wasn't personal. We were paid to do a job. We coulda killed you but we didn't."

I suddenly recognized him as the one who did all the talking in the garage.

"It's them," I said, pointing down. "He did the talking and he did the punching. Who are they?"

Cisco nodded as though the confirmation was only a formality.

"They're brothers. The talker is Joey Mack. The puncher is, get this, Angel Mack."

"Listen, we don't even know what it was about," the Talker yelled out. "Please! We made a mistake. We—"

"You're fucking-A right you made a mistake!" Cisco yelled, his voice coming down on both of them like the wrath of God. "And now you pay. Who wants to go first?"

The Puncher started to whimper. Cisco walked over to a card table where there was a spread of tools and weapons, plus the roll of tape. He chose a pipe wrench and a set of pliers and turned back. I thought and hoped it was all an act. But if it was, Cisco was turning in an Oscar-caliber performance. I put my hand on his shoulder and held him from approaching the two men. I didn't have to say anything but the message was clear. Let me have a shot at them.

I took the wrench from Cisco and squatted like a baseball catcher in front of the captives. I hefted the heavy tool in my hand for a few seconds, getting a good feel for its weight, before speaking.

"Who hired you to hurt me?"

The Talker answered immediately. He wasn't interested in protecting anybody but himself and his brother.

"A guy named Dahl. He told us to hit you hard but not kill you. You can't do this, man."

"I think we can do whatever we want. How do you know Dahl?"

"We don't. But we had a mutual connection."

"And who was that?"

No answer. I didn't have to wait long before Bam Bam lived up to his moniker and leaned down and hit them both with pistonlike punches to the jaw. The Talker was spitting blood when he gave me the name.

"Jerry Castille."

"And who's Jerry Castille?"

"Look, you can't tell anybody this."

"You're not in a position to tell me what I can or can't do. Who's Jerry Castille?"

"He's the west coast representative."

I waited but that was it.

"I don't have all night, man. West coast representative of what?"

The bloodied man nodded like he knew there was only one way to go here.

"Of a certain east-coast organization. You get it?"

I looked at Cisco. Herb Dahl had ties to east-coast organized crime? It seemed far-fetched.

"No, you don't get it," I said. "I'm a lawyer. I want a direct answer. Which organization? You have exactly five seconds until—"

"He works for Joey Giordano outta Brooklyn, okay? Now you've sealed the deal on us anyway. So go fuck yourself."

He reared back and spit blood at me. I had left my suit coat and tie at the office. I looked down at my white shirt and saw a bloodstain just outside the area that would be covered by a tie.

"This is a monogrammed shirt, you shit head."

Tommy Guns suddenly moved between us and I heard the brutal impact of fist on face but didn't see it because of Tommy's massive size. He then stepped back and I could see the Talker was now spitting out teeth.

"Monogrammed shirt, man," Tommy Guns said, as if offering an explanation for his vicious action.

I stood up.

"Okay, cut them loose," I said.

Cisco and the two Saints turned to look at me.

"Cut 'em loose," I said again.

"You sure?" Cisco said. "They'll probably go running back to this fucker Castille and tell him we know."

I looked down at the two men on the floor and shook my head.

"No, they won't. They tell him that they talked and they'll probably end up dead. So cut them loose and it's like this never happened. They'll drop out of sight until the bruises go away. And that will be the end of it."

I bent down to get close to the two captives.

"I have that right, right?"

"Yeah," said the Talker, a bulge the size of a marble forming on his upper lip.

I looked at his brother.

"Is that right? I want to hear it from both of you."

"Yeah, yeah, right," the Puncher said.

I looked at Cisco. We were finished here. He gave the order.

"Okay, Guns, listen up. You wait till dark. You leave them in here and wait till dark. Then you bag 'em and take 'em back to wherever they want to go. You drop them off but you leave 'em alone. You got it?"

"Yeah, I got it."

Poor Tommy Guns. He truly looked disappointed.

I took one last look at the bloodied men on the floor. And they looked up at me. The feeling of holding their lives in my hands sent an electric jolt through me. Cisco tapped me on the back and I followed him from the room, closing the door behind me. We started down the hall but I put my hand on my investigator's arm and stopped him.

"You shouldn't have done that. You shouldn't have brought me here."

"Are you kidding? I had to bring you here."

"What are you talking about? Why?"

"Because they did something to you. Inside. You lost something, Mick, and if you don't get it back you aren't going to be much good to yourself or anybody else."

I stared at him for a long moment and then nodded.

"I got it back."

"Good. Now we never have to talk about this again. Can you take me back to the office so I can pick up my bike?"

"Yeah. I can do that."

Thirty-one

Driving by myself after dropping Cisco in the garage, I thought about the law of the land and the law of the streets and the differences between them. I stood in courtrooms and insisted that the law of the land be applied fairly and appropriately. There was nothing that had been fair and appropriate about what I had just been party to in the black room.

Still, it didn't bother me. Cisco had been right. I needed to gain the upper hand inside my own soul before I could gain it in court or anywhere else. I felt renewed as I drove. I opened all the Lincoln's windows and let the evening air course through the car as I came down Laurel Canyon toward home.

This time Maggie had used her key. She was already inside when I got there, an unexpected but pleasant surprise. The refrigerator door was open and she was leaning down and looking in.

"I really came because you always used to stock up before a trial. Your refrigerator was like going down the cold aisle at Gelson's. But what happened? There's nothing here."

I dropped my keys on the table. She had been to her own home from work first and had changed. She wore faded denim jeans, a peasant shirt and sandals with thick cork heels. She knew I liked that outfit.

"I guess I didn't get around to it this time."

"Well, I wish I'd known. Might've considered going somewhere else on my one night this week with a sitter."

She smiled slyly. I couldn't figure out why we weren't still living together.

"How about we go down to Dan's?"

"Dan Tana's? I thought you went there only when you won a case. You already counting your chickens, Haller?"

I smiled and shook my head.

"No, no way. But if I went there only when I won then I'd hardly ever get to eat there."

She pointed a finger at me and smiled. It was a dance and we were both well used to it. She closed the fridge and walked through the kitchen door and then right past me without so much as a kiss.

"Dan Tana's is open late," she said.

I watched her walk down the hallway toward the master bedroom. She pulled the peasant blouse up over her head just as she disappeared into the room.

We didn't really make love. Something about what I had seen and felt in the black room at the Saints was still with me. Call it residual aggression or the release of the impotent anger I had felt. Whatever it was, it informed all my moves with her. I pulled and pushed too hard. I bit her lip and held her wrists together above her head. I controlled her and I knew what it was all about while I did it. Maggie went with it at first. The newness of it was probably interesting. But curiosity eventually turned to concern and she turned her face from mine and struggled to free her hands. I held her wrists tighter. Finally, I saw tears well in her eyes.

"What?" I whispered into her ear, my nose pressing hard into her hair.

"Just finish," she said.

All aggression and drive and desire went down the psychic drain after that. Her tears and telling me to finish made me unable to. I pulled out and off, rolling to the side of the bed. I put a forearm across my eyes but still could feel her watching me.

"What?"

"What is with you tonight? Is this something to do with Andrea? Getting me back for what's going on in court or something?"

I felt her move off the bed.

"Maggie, of course not! Court's got nothing to do with it."

"Then what?"

But the bathroom door had closed before I could answer and the shower immediately was turned on, cutting off the exchange.

"I'll tell you at dinner," I said, even though I knew she couldn't hear me.

Dan Tana's was packed but Christian came through and got us quickly into a booth in the left corner. Maggie and I had not spoken during the fifteen-minute ride into West Hollywood. I had tried some small talk about our daughter but Maggie had been unresponsive so I let it go. I thought that I would try again in the restaurant.

We both ordered the Steak Helen with pasta on the side. Alfredo for Maggie and Bolognese for me. Maggie picked an Italian red for herself and I ordered a bottle of fizzy water. After the waiter left I reached across the table and put my hand on her wrist, gently this time.

"I'm sorry, Maggie. Let's start over."

She pulled her arm away from me.

"You still owe me an explanation, Haller. That wasn't making love. I don't know what's going on with you. I don't think you should treat any-one that way, but especially not me."

"Maggie, I think you're overdoing it a bit. For a while there you liked it and you know it."

"And then you started to hurt me."

"I'm sorry. I never want to hurt you."

"And don't try to act like it was a passing thing. If you ever want to be with me again you'd better start telling me what is happening with you."

I shook my head and looked out at the crowded room. The Lakers were on the overhead TV in the bar that divided the place. People were crowded three deep behind the lucky patrons who had the stools. The waiter brought our drinks and that bought me some more time. But as soon as he left the table, Maggie was on me.

"Talk to me, Michael, or I'm taking my dinner to go. I'll take a cab."

I took a long drink of water and then looked at her.

"It has nothing to do with court or Andrea Freeman or anybody or anything else you know, okay?"

"No, not okay. Talk to me."

I put my glass down and folded my arms on the table.

"Cisco found the two guys who attacked me."

"Where? Who are they?"

"That doesn't matter. He didn't call the police, he didn't turn them in."

"You mean he just let them go?"

I laughed and shook my head.

"No, he held them. Him and two of his associates from the Saints. For me. In this place they have. To do what I wanted. Whatever I wanted. He said I needed it."

She reached across the checked tablecloth and put her hand on my forearm.

"Haller, what did you do?"

I held her eyes for a moment.

"Nothing. I questioned them and then told Cisco to let them go. I know who hired them."

"Who?"

"I'm not going to get into that. It's not important. But you know what, Maggie? When I was in the hospital waiting to find out if they were going to be able to save my twisted nut, all I could think about were these violent images of me getting those two guys back. I mean, Hieronymus Bosch torture stuff. Medieval shit. I wanted to hurt them so bad. Then I get my chance, and believe me these guys would have just disappeared after, and I let it go... and then I'm with you and..."

She leaned back in the booth. She stared off into space, a mixture of sadness and resignation on her face.

"Pretty fucked up, huh?"

"I wish you hadn't told me all of that."

"You mean as a prosecutor?"

"There's that."

"Well, you kept asking. I guess I should've made up a story about being mad at Andrea Freeman. That would've been okay with you, right? If it was about men and women, you could understand that."

She looked back at me.

"Don't patronize me."

"Sorry."

We sat in silence and watched the activities in the bar. People drinking, being happy. At least outwardly. The waiters in tuxedos moving about and squeezing between the crowded tables.

When our food came I was no longer particularly hungry even though the best steak in town was on the plate in front of me.

"Can I ask you one final thing about it?" Maggie asked.

I shrugged. I didn't see the point in talking about it anymore but relented.

"Ask away."

"How do you know for sure that Cisco and his associates let those two men go?"

I cut into my steak and blood oozed onto the plate. It was undercooked. I looked up at Maggie.

"I guess I don't know for sure."

I went back to my steak and in my peripheral vision I saw Maggie wave down the busboy.

"I'm going to take this to go and try to grab a cab out front. Can you bring it out to me?"

"Of course. Right away."

He hustled off with the plate.

"Maggie," I said.

"I just need some time to think about all of this."

She slid out of the booth.

"I can drive you."

"No, I'll be fine."

She stood next to the table, opening her purse.

"Don't worry about it. I've got it."

"You sure?"

"If there's no cab out there, look down the street at the Palm. There might be one there."

"Okay, thanks."

She left then to wait for her food outside. I pushed my plate a few inches back and contemplated the half-full glass of wine she left behind. Five minutes later I was still considering it when Maggie suddenly appeared, the to-go bag in her hand.

"They had to call a cab," she said. "It should be here any minute."

She picked up her glass and sipped from it.

"Let's talk after your trial," she said.

"Okay."

She put the glass down, leaned over and kissed me on the cheek. Then she left. I sat there for a while thinking about things. I thought maybe that last kiss had saved my life.

Thirty-two

This time in his chambers Judge Perry sat down. It was 9:05 Wednesday morning and I was there along with Andrea Freeman and the court reporter. Before resuming trial the judge had agreed with Freeman's request for one more conference out of the public eye. Perry waited for us to settle in our seats, then checked that his reporter's fingers were poised over the keys of her steno machine.

"Okay, we're on the record here in *California versus Trammel*," he said. "Ms. Freeman, you called for an *in camera* conference. I hope you're not going to tell me you need more time to pursue the issue involving the federal target letter."

Freeman moved to the front edge of her seat.

"Not at all, Your Honor. There is nothing worth pursuing. The issue has been thoroughly vetted but full knowledge of what is going on with the federal agencies involved does not comfort me. I believe it is clear from what I know now that Mr. Haller is going to attempt to push this trial off the rails with issues that are definitely irrelevant to the matter before the jury."

I cleared my throat but the judge stepped in first.

"We handled the issue of third-party guilt in pretrial, Ms. Freeman. I am allowing the defense the leeway to pursue it to a point. But you have to give me something here. Just because you don't want Mr. Haller to pursue this target letter doesn't make it irrelevant."

"I understand that, Judge. But what—"

"Excuse me," I said. "Do I get a turn here? I'd like the chance to respond to the insinuation that I'm pushing—"

"Let Ms. Freeman finish and then you'll get a good long tug, Mr. Haller. I promise you that. Ms. Freeman?"

"Thank you, Your Honor. What I'm trying to say is that a federal target letter essentially means almost nothing. It is a notice of a *pending* investigation. It is not a charge. It's not even an allegation. It doesn't mean that they have found something or will find something. It is simply a tool used by the feds to say, 'Hey, we heard something and we're going to look into it.' But in Mr. Haller's hands in front of the jury, he's going to spin this into the harbinger of doom and attach it to someone not even on trial here. Lisa Trammel is the one on trial and this whole thing about federal target letters is not even remotely relevant to the material issues. I would ask that you disallow Mr. Haller from making any further inquiry of Detective Kurlen in this regard."

The judge was leaning back with his hands in front of his chest, the fingers of each hand pressed against each other. He swiveled to face me. Finally, my cue.

"Judge, if I were in Your Honor's position, I think that I would ask counsel, since she says she thoroughly vetted this letter and its origin, if there is a sitting federal grand jury looking into foreclosure fraud in Southern California. And then I would ask how she has concluded that a federal target letter amounts to 'almost nothing.' Because I don't think the court is getting a very accurate assessment of what the letter means or what its impact is on this case."

The judge swiveled back to Freeman and broke one of his fingers free to point in her direction.

"What about that, Ms. Freeman? Is there a grand jury?"

"Judge, you are putting me in an awkward position here. Grand juries work in secret and—"

"We're all friends here, Ms. Freeman," the judge said sternly. "Is there a grand jury?"

She hesitated and then nodded.

"There is a grand jury, Your Honor, but it has not heard any testimony in regard to Louis Opparizio. As I said, the target letter is nothing more than a notice of a pending investigation. It's hearsay, Judge, and it doesn't fit into any exception that would speak to its admissibility in this trial. Though the letter was signed by the U.S. attorney for this district, it was actually authored by a Secret Service agent handling the inquiry. I have the agent waiting downstairs in my office. If the court wishes, I can have him in chambers in ten minutes to tell you exactly what I just did. That this is a lot of smoke and mirrors on Mr. Haller's part. At the time of Mr. Bondurant's death there was no active investigation yet and no connection between the two. There was just the letter."

That was a mistake. By revealing that Vasquez, the Secret Service agent who penned the target letter, was in the building, Freeman had put the judge into a difficult position. That the agent was nearby and easily accessible would make it harder for the judge to dismiss the issue out of hand. I stepped in before the judge could respond.

"Judge Perry? I would suggest that, since counsel says she has the federal agent who wrote the letter right here in the courthouse, she simply put him on the stand to counter anything that I might draw from Detective Kurlen on cross-examination. If Ms. Freeman is so sure the agent will say the target letter he wrote amounts to nothing, then let him tell the jury that. Let him blow me out of the water. I remind the court that we've already dipped our toes into these waters. I asked Kurlen about the letter yesterday. To simply go back out there and not mention it again or have you tell the jurors to un-ring the bell and dismiss it from memory... that could be more damaging to our collective cause than a full airing of this issue."

Perry answered without hesitation.

"I tend to think that you are correct about this, Mr. Haller. I don't like the idea of leaving the jury all night with this mysterious target letter to ponder and then pulling the rug out from under them this morning."

"Your Honor," Freeman said quickly. "May I be heard once more?"

"No, I don't think that is necessary. We need to stop wasting time in here and get the trial started."

"But, Your Honor, there is one other exigent issue the court has not even considered."

The judge looked frustrated.

"And what is that, Ms. Freeman? My patience is drawing thin."

"Allowing testimony about a target letter directed at the defense's key witness will likely complicate that witness's previous decision not to invoke his Fifth Amendment rights during testimony in this case. Louis Opparizio and his legal counsel may well reconsider that decision once this target letter is introduced and discussed publicly. Therefore, Mr. Haller may be building a defense case that ultimately results in his key witness and straw man, if you will, refusing to testify. I want it on record now that if Mr. Haller plays this game he must abide by the consequences. When Opparizio decides next week that it's in his best interest not to testify and asks for a new hearing on the subpoena, I don't want defense counsel crying to the court for a do-over. No do-overs, Judge."

The judge nodded, agreeing with her.

"I guess that would be tantamount to the man who killed his parents asking the court to show mercy on him because he's an orphan. I'm in agreement, Mr. Haller. You are on notice that if you play it this way you must be prepared to shoulder the consequences."

"I understand, Judge," I said. "And I will make sure my client does as well. I only have one point of argument and that is counsel's labeling of Louis Opparizio as a straw man. He's no straw man and we'll prove it."

"Well," the judge said, "at least you'll get a chance to. Now time is wasting. Let's get back into the courtroom."

I followed Freeman out, leaving the judge behind while he put on his robe. I expected her to hit me with a verbal assault but I got the opposite.

"Well played, Counselor," she said.

"Thanks, I think."

"Who do you think sent you the letter?"

"I wish I knew."

"Have the feds contacted you? My guess is they're going to want to find out who's leaking sensitive and confidential documents to the public."

"Nobody's said jack yet. Maybe it was the feds who leaked it. If I get Opparizio on the stand he's stuck with his testimony. Maybe I'm just an instrument of the federal government here. Ever think of that?"

The suggestion seemed to put a pause in her step. As I passed her I smiled.

As we entered the courtroom I saw Herb Dahl in the front row of the gallery behind the defense table. I suppressed the urge to pull him over the rail and pound his face into the stone floor. Freeman and I took our positions at our respective tables and in a whisper I filled my client in on what had happened in chambers. The judge entered and brought the jury in.

The last piece of the picture was filled in when Detective Kurlen returned to the witness stand. I grabbed my files and legal pad and went back to the lectern. It seemed like a week since my cross-examination had been interrupted but it had been less than a day. I acted as though it had been less than a minute.

"Now, Detective Kurlen, when we left off yesterday I had just asked you if you knew what a federal target letter is. Can you answer that question now?"

"My understanding is that when a federal agency is interested in gathering information from an individual or company, they sometimes send out a letter that tells that individual or company that they want to talk. It's sort of a letter that says, 'Come on in and let's talk about this so there's no misunderstanding.'"

"And that's it?"

"I'm not a federal agent."

"Well, do you think it's a serious matter to receive a letter from the federal government telling you that you are the target of an investigation?"

"It could be, I guess. I would assume that it depends on the crime they're looking into."

I asked the judge for permission to approach the witness with a document. Freeman objected for the record, citing relevance. The judge overruled without comment and told me I could give the document to the witness.

After handing the document to Kurlen I returned to the lectern and asked the judge to mark the document as Defense Exhibit 3. I then told Kurlen to read the letter.

"'Dear Mr. Opparizio, This letter is to inform —'"

"Wait," I interrupted. "Could you first read and describe what is at the top of the letter? The letterhead?"

"It says 'Office of the United States Attorney, Los Angeles' and it's got a picture of an eagle on one side and the U.S. flag on the other. Should I read the letter part now?"

"Yes, please do."

"'Dear Mr. Opparizio, This letter is to inform you that A. Louis Opparizio Financial Technologies—known as ALOFT—and you, individually, are among the targets of a multi-agency task force investigating all levels of mortgage fraud in Southern California. Receipt of this letter puts you on notice not to remove or destroy any documents or work materials related to the business of your company. Should you wish to discuss this investigation and cooperate with members of the task force, please do not hesitate to call or have your legal counsel make contact with me or Charles Vasquez, of the U.S. Secret Service, who has been assigned to the ALOFT investigation as case agent. We will make every effort to meet with you to discuss this matter. If you do not wish to cooperate, you can be assured that you will be contacted shortly by agents of the task force. I once again have to remind you not to destroy or remove any documents or work product from your offices or associated premises. To do so after receiving this notice would be to commit a serious crime against the United States of America. Sincerely, Reginald Lattimore, U.S. Attorney, Los Angeles.' That's it, except it gives everybody's phone numbers at the bottom."

A low murmur went through the courtroom. I was sure most of the general citizenry was unaware of things like federal target letters. It was law enforcement in the new era. I was sure the so-called task force amounted to token contributions of agents from a handful of agencies and no budget. Instead of mounting expensive investigations, it would take a shot at scaring people into coming in and begging for mercy. A design to pick the low-hanging fruit, grab a few headlines and call it a day. Someone like Opparizio probably used the original letter received via certified mail as toilet paper. But that didn't matter to me. My plan was to use the letter to help keep my client out of prison.

"Thank you, Detective Kurlen. Now, can you tell us, is the letter dated?"

Kurlen checked the copy before answering.

"It's dated January eighteenth of this year."

"Now, Detective, had you seen that letter before yesterday?"

"No, why should I have seen it? It's got nothing to do with—"

"Move to strike as unresponsive," I said quickly. "Your Honor, the question was simply whether he had seen the letter before."

The judge instructed Kurlen to answer only the question asked.

"I had not seen this letter before yesterday."

"Thank you, Detective. And now let's go back to the other letter I asked you to read yesterday, from the victim, Mitchell Bondurant, to the same Louis Opparizio who is addressed in the federal target letter. Do you have that handy there in your binder?"

"If I could have a moment."

"Please."

Kurlen found the letter in the binder, removed it and held it up.

"Good. Can you tell us the date of that letter, please?"

"January tenth, this year."

"And that letter was delivered to Mr. Opparizio by certified mail, correct?"

"It was sent certified. I cannot tell you if Mr. Opparizio received it or ever saw it. It has someone else's name listed as signing for it."

"But no matter who signed for it, it is a certainty that it was sent on January tenth, correct?"

"I think that's correct."

"And the second letter we've talked about here, the target letter from the Secret Service agent, was sent by certified mail as well, am I right?"

"That's right."

"So the date of January eighteenth is certified as to when it was mailed."

"Correct."

"So let me see if I have this right. Mr. Bondurant sends Louis Opparizio a certified letter that threatens to expose alleged fraudulent practices in his company and then eight days later a federal task force sends Mr. Opparizio another certified letter, this one saying he is the target of an investigation into foreclosure fraud. Do I have this time line right, Detective Kurlen?"

"As far as I know, yes."

"And then less than two weeks later Mr. Bondurant is brutally murdered in the garage at WestLand, right?"

"That's right."

I paused and rubbed my chin like a deep thinker. I really wanted to hold the jury with this. I wanted to look at their faces but knew it would reveal my play. So I went with the deep thinker pose.

"Detective, you have testified about your wealth of experience as a homicide detective, correct?"

"I have a lot of experience, yes."

"Hypothetically speaking, do you wish you knew then what you know now?"

Kurlen squinted like he was confused, even though he knew exactly what I was doing and where I was going.

"I'm not sure I understand," he said.

"Put it this way, would it have been good for you to have those letters in hand on the first day of the murder investigation?"

"Sure, why not? I'd take all evidence and information on the first day anytime. But that never happens."

"Hypothetically speaking, if you knew that your victim, Mitchell Bondurant, had sent a letter threatening to expose another man's criminal behavior just eight days before that man learned he was the target of a criminal investigation, wouldn't that be a significant avenue of investigation for you?"

"It is hard to say."

Now I looked at the jury. Kurlen was waffling, refusing to acknowledge what common sense dictated he should own up to. You didn't need to be a detective to understand that.

"Hard to say? Are you saying that if you had this information and these letters on the day of the murder it would be hard to say if you would follow up on them as a significant lead?"

"I'm saying that we don't have all the details so it is hard to say how significant it was or wasn't. But as a general answer, all leads are followed up. It's as simple as that."

"As simple as that, yet you never pursued this angle of investigation, did you?"

"I didn't have this letter. How could I have followed it up?"

"You had the victim's letter and you did nothing with it, did you?"

"Not true at all. I checked it out and determined it had nothing to do with the murder."

"But isn't it true that by that time you already had your supposed murderer and you weren't going to let anything change your mind or make you deviate from that path?"

"No, not true. Not true at all."

I stared at Kurlen for a long time, hoping that my face showed my disgust.

"No further questions at this time," I finally said.

Thirty-three

Freeman kept Kurlen on the stand for another fifteen minutes of redirect and did her best to resculpt his account of the investigation into a sterling effort of crime fighting. When she was through I passed on another crack at him because I was convinced that I was already ahead on Kurlen. My effort had been to sell the investigation as an exercise in tunnel vision and I believed I had succeeded.

Freeman apparently felt that the need to address the federal target letter was urgent. Her next witness was the Secret Service agent, Charles Vasquez. He had not even been known to her twenty-four hours earlier but had now been interjected into her carefully orchestrated lineup of witnesses and evidence. I could have objected to his testimony on the grounds that I had not had the opportunity to question or prepare for Vasquez but I thought that would be pushing it with Judge Perry. I decided to at least see what the agent had to say on direct before I'd go that far.

Vasquez was about forty, with a dark complexion and hair to match. During the preliminaries he said he had formerly been a DEA agent before shifting to the Secret Service. He went from chasing drug dealers to chasing counterfeiters until the opportunity came to join the foreclosure task force. He said the task force had a supervisor and ten agents coming from the Secret Service, FBI, the Postal Service and the IRS. An assistant U.S. attorney oversaw their work but the agents, assigned to pairs, largely worked autonomously, with freedom to pursue targets of their choice.

"Agent Vasquez, on January eighteenth of this year you authored a so-called target letter to a man named Louis Opparizio and it was signed by U.S. Attorney Reginald Lattimore. Do you recall that?"

"Yes, I do."

"Before we get into that specific letter, can you tell the jury exactly what a target letter is?"

"It's a tool we use to smoke out suspects and offenders."

"How so?"

"We basically inform them that we are looking into their affairs, their business practices and actions they have taken. A target letter always invites the recipient to come in to discuss the situation with the agents. A high percentage of the time the recipients do just that. Sometimes it leads to cases, sometimes it leads to other investigations. It's become a useful tool because investigations cost a lot. We don't have the budget. If a letter can result in charges being filed or a witness cooperating or a solid investigative lead then it's a good deal for us."

"So in regard to the letter to Louis Opparizio, what made you send him a target letter?"

"Well, my partner and I were very familiar with his name because it came up often in other cases we were working. Not necessarily in a bad way, just that Opparizio's company is what we call a foreclosure mill. It handles all the paperwork and filing on foreclosures for many of the banks operating in Southern California. Thousands of cases. So we kept seeing the company—ALOFT—and sometimes there were complaints about the methods the company was using. My partner and I decided to take a closer look. We sent out the letter to see what sort of response we'd get."

"Does that mean you were fishing for a reaction?"

"It was more than fishing. As I said, there was quite a lot of smoke from this place. We were looking for fire and sometimes the reaction we get from a target letter dictates what our next moves will be."

"At the time you authored and sent the target letter, had you gathered any evidence of criminal wrongdoing on the part of Louis Opparizio or his company?"

"Not at that point, no."

"What happened after you sent the letter?"

"Nothing so far."

"Has Louis Opparizio responded to the letter?"

"We got a response from an attorney saying that Mr. Opparizio welcomed the investigation because it would give him the opportunity to show he ran a clean business."

"Have you availed yourself of that welcome and investigated Mr. Opparizio or his company further?"

"No, there hasn't been time. We have several other ongoing investigations that appear to be more fruitful."

Freeman checked her notes before finishing.

"Finally, Agent Vasquez, is Louis Opparizio or ALOFT currently under investigation by your task force?"

"Technically, no. But we plan to follow up on the letter."

"So the answer is no?"

"Correct."

"Thank you, Agent Vasquez."

Freeman sat down. She was beaming and obviously pleased with the testimony she had drawn from the agent. I stood up and took my legal pad back to the lectern. I had written down a few questions off the direct examination.

"Agent Vasquez, are you telling the jury that an individual who does not respond to your target letter by immediately coming in and confessing must be innocent of any wrongdoing?"

"No, I'm not."

"Because Louis Opparizio did not do so, do you consider him to be in the clear now?"

"No, I don't."

"Do you make it a practice to send target letters to individuals you believe are innocent of any criminal activity?"

"No, I don't."

"Then what is the threshold, Agent Vasquez? What does one need to do to receive a target letter?"

"Basically, if you come across my radar in any sort of suspicious way, then I'll do some preliminary checking and that may lead to the letter. We're not sending these out scattershot. We know what we're doing."

"Did you or your partner or anyone from the task force speak with Mitchell Bondurant in regard to the practices of ALOFT?"

"No, we didn't. Nobody did."

"Would he have been someone you would've talked to?"

Freeman objected, calling the question vague. The judge sustained the objection. I decided to leave the question floating out there unanswered in front of the jury.

"Thank you, Agent Vasquez."

Freeman went back to her scheduled rollout of the case after Vasquez, calling the gardener who found the hammer in the bushes of the home a block and a half from the scene of the murder. His testimony was quick and uneventful, by itself unimportant until it would be tied in later with testimony from the state's forensic witnesses. I did score a minor point by getting the gardener to acknowledge that he had worked in and around the bushes at least twelve different times before he found the hammer. It was a little seed to plant for the jury, the idea that maybe the hammer itself had been planted long after the murder.

After the gardener, the prosecution followed with a few quick hits of testimony from the home owner and the cops who carried the chain of custody of the hammer to the forensic lab. I didn't even bother with cross-examination. I was not going to contest chain of custody or the fact that the hammer was the murder weapon. My plan was to agree not only that it was the weapon that killed Mitchell Bondurant but also that it belonged to Lisa Trammel.

It would be an unexpected move, but the only one that worked with the defense theory of a setup. The lead through Jeff Trammel that the hammer might be in the back of the BMW he'd left behind when he disappeared to Mexico didn't pan out. Cisco was able to locate that car, still in use at the dealership where Jeff Trammel had worked, but there was no hammer in the trunk and the man in charge of fleet management said there never was. I dismissed Jeff Trammel's story as an effort to get paid off for information that might be helpful to his estranged wife's case.

The murder weapon sequence brought us to lunch, and the judge, as was beginning to be his custom, broke fifteen minutes early. I turned to my client and invited her to go to lunch with me.

"What about Herb?" she said. "I promised him I would go to lunch with him."

"Herb can come, too."

"Really?"

"Sure, why not?"

"Because I thought you didn't... Never mind, I'll tell him."

"Good. I'll drive."

I had Rojas pick us up and we went down Van Nuys to the Hamlet near Ventura. The place had been there for decades and while it had classed itself up since the days it was called Hamburger Hamlet, the food was just the same. Because the judge had gotten us out early, we avoided the noon lineup and were immediately shown to a booth.

"I love this place," Dahl said. "But I haven't been here in ages."

I sat across from Dahl and my client. I didn't respond to his enthusiasm for the restaurant. I was too busy working out how I was going to play the lunch.

We ordered quickly because even with the early start our time window was small. Our conversation was focused on the case and how Lisa perceived things to be going. She was pleased so far.

"You get something that helps me from every witness," she said. "It's quite remarkable."

"But the question is, do I get enough?" I responded. "And what you have to remember is that the mountain gets steeper with each witness. Do you know the piece *Boléro*? It's classical music. I think it was composed by Ravel."

Lisa gave me a blank stare.

"Bo Derek, in *Ten*," Dahl said. "Love it!"

"Right. Anyway, the point is it's a long piece, maybe fifteen minutes or so, and it starts off slow with just a few quiet instruments and then it gathers momentum and builds and builds into a crescendo, a big finish with all the instruments in the orchestra coming in together. And at the same time, the emotions of the listeners build and come together at the same moment. And that's what the prosecutor is doing here. She's building sound and momentum. Her best stuff is still to come because she's going to bring everything together with drums and strings and horns by the time she's finished. You understand, Lisa?"

She nodded reluctantly.

"I'm not trying to knock you down. You are excited and hopeful and righteous and I want you to stay that way. Because the jury picks up on it and it helps just as much as anything I do in there. But you have to remember, the mountain is getting steeper. She's got the science still to come and juries love science because it gives them a way out, a way of deferring. People think they want to be on jury duty. You get out of work, you sit front row on an interesting case, real-life drama in front of you instead of on the tube at home. But eventually they have to go back into that room and look at each other and decide. They have to decide somebody's life. Believe me, not too many people want to do that. The science makes it easier. 'Oh, well, if the DNA matches then it can't be wrong. Guilty as charged.' You see? This is what we still face, Lisa, and I don't want there to be any illusions about it."

Dahl gallantly put his hand on her arm, which leaned on the table. He gave it a comforting squeeze.

"Well, what will we do about their DNA?" Trammel asked.

"Nothing," I said. "There's nothing I can do. I told you before trial we had our own people test it and we got the same answers. It's legit."

Her eyes were cast down in defeat and I saw the start of tears, which was what I wanted. The waitress chose that moment to show up with our lunch plates. I waited until we were left alone before continuing.

"Cheer up, Lisa. The DNA is just window dressing."

She looked up at me in confusion.

"I thought you just said it's legit."

"It is. But that doesn't mean there isn't an explanation for it. I'll handle the DNA. Like you said when we sat down, my job here is to drop a doubt into each piece of their puzzle. Then we hope when all their pieces are in place and they hold the picture up to the jury that all the little seeds of doubt we have sown have grown into something that changes that picture. If we do that, then we get tan."

"What's that mean?"

"We go home. We go to the beach and we get tan."

I smiled at her and she smiled back. Her tearing up had smeared the intricate makeup work she had performed that morning.

The rest of lunch was punctuated by small talk and uninformed or inane observations of the criminal justice system by my client and her paramour. This was a common thing I had observed in my clients. They don't know the law but are quick to tell me what is wrong with it. I waited until Trammel forked the last bite of salad into her mouth.

"Lisa, your mascara got a little smeared during the first part of our conversation. It's very important that you stay strong and look strong. I want you to go into the restroom and make yourself look strong, okay?"

"Can I just do it at the courthouse?"

"No, because we might be going in at the same time as some of the jurors or the reporters. You never know who will see you. I don't want anyone thinking you're spending your lunch hour crying, okay? I want you to do it now. And I'll call Rojas to come pick us up."

"It might take me a few minutes."

I checked my watch.

"Okay, take your time. I'll wait a little bit on Rojas."

Dahl got up so she could slide out of the booth. Then we were left alone. I had pushed my plate to the side and had my elbows on the table. I had my hands clasped together in front of my mouth, like a poker player holding up his cards to help hide his face. At heart a good lawyer was a negotiator. And now it was time to negotiate Herb Dahl's exit.

"So Herb... it's time for you to go."

He gave me a small smile of misunderstanding.

"What do you mean? We all came together."

"No, I mean from the case. From Lisa. It's time for you to disappear."

He kept the *I don't understand* demeanor going.

"I'm not going anywhere. Lisa and me... we're close. And I have a lot of money tied up in this thing."

"Well, your money's gone. And as far as Lisa goes, that's a charade that is coming to an end right now."

I reached into the inside pocket of my coat and pulled out the photo of Herb with the brothers Mack that Cisco had given me the night before. I handed it across the table to him. He gave it a quick look and then laughed uneasily.

"Okay, I'll bite. Who are they?"

"The Mack brothers. The men you hired to work me over."

He shook his head and glanced over his shoulder at the rear hallway that led to the restrooms. He then turned back to me.

"Sorry, Mickey, but I don't know what you're talking about. I think you have to remember here that you and I have a deal on the movie. A deal involving circumstances I am sure the California Bar would be interested in reviewing, but other than that..."

"Are you threatening me, Dahl? Because if you are you're making a mistake."

"No, no threat. I'm just trying to figure out where you're coming from."

"I'm coming from a dark room where I had an interesting conversation with the Mack brothers."

Dahl refolded the photo and handed it back to me.

"These two? They were asking me for directions, that's all."

"Directions, huh? Are you sure it wasn't money they were asking for? Because we have photos of that, too."

"I might've given them a few bucks. They asked for help and seemed nice enough."

Now I had to smile.

"You know, you're good, Herb, but I got their story. So let's just skip all the bullshit and get down to the play."

He shrugged.

"Okay, this is your show. What's the play?"

"The play is what I said at the top. You're gone, Herb. You kiss Lisa goodbye. You kiss the movie deal goodbye. You kiss your money goodbye."

"That's a lot of kissing. What do I get for all that?"

"You get to stay out of prison, that's what you get."

He shook his head and glanced over his shoulder again.

"Doesn't work that way, Mick. You see, that wasn't my money. It didn't come from me."

"Who'd it come from, Jerry Castille?"

His eyes made a quick movement and then settled. The name had hit him like an invisible punch. He now knew that the Mack brothers had caved and talked.

"Yeah, I know about Jerry and I know about Joey in New York, too. No honor among thugs, Herb. The Mack brothers are ready to start singing like Sonny and Cher. And the song is 'I've Got You, Babe.' I've got you all wrapped up in a nice little package and unless you slink on out of Lisa's life and my life today, I'm going to drop it off at the DA's office where I happen to have an ex-wife who's a prosecutor and who was very distressed by that attack on me.

"I figure she'll sail this one through the grand jury in a single morning and you, asshole, will go down for aggravated assault with GBH. That means 'with great bodily harm.' It's called a charging enhancement. It will get you an extra three years on the sentence. And as the victim I'm going to insist on that. That's for my twisted nut. I'd say that all told with gain time you're looking at four years inside, Herb. And there's one thing you should know. They don't let you wear no fucking peace sign in Soledad."

Dahl put his elbows on the table and leaned forward. For the first time I could see desperation enter his eyes.

"You don't know what the fuck you're doing. You don't know who you're dealing with."

"Listen, asshole—can I call you asshole?—I don't give a rat's ass who I'm dealing with. I'm looking at you and I want you away from me and this case and—"

"No, no, you don't get it. I can help you. You think you know what's going on in this case? You don't know shit. But I can school you, Haller. I can help you reach the beach and we can all get tan."

I leaned back away from him, my arm up on the booth's padded backrest. Now I was puzzled. I flicked a wrist like this was a complete waste of time.

"So school me."

"You think I just showed up on her picket line and said, 'Let's make a movie'? You dumb fuck! I was sent there. Before Bondurant was even put down, I was getting close to Lisa. You think that was happenstance?"

"Sent by who?"

"Who do you think?"

I stared at him and felt the coalescing of all aspects of the case, like streams to the river. The hypothesis of innocence was not a hypothesis. The setup was real.

"Opparizio."

He made one slight nod in confirmation. And at that moment I saw Lisa come through the back hallway, heading toward us, her eyes shiny and bright again for court. I looked back at Dahl. I wanted to ask many questions but we were out of time.

"Seven o'clock tonight. Be at my office. Alone. You tell me about Opparizio then. You tell me about everything . . . or I go to the DA."

"The one thing is I'll never testify to anything. Never."

"Seven o'clock."

"I'm supposed to have dinner with Lisa."

"Yeah, well, change of plans. Think of something. You just be there. Now let's go."

I started to slide out of the booth as Lisa arrived. I pulled my phone and called Rojas.

"We're ready," I said. "Pick us up out front."

Thirty-four

After court reconvened the prosecution called Detective Cynthia Longstreth to the witness stand. By going with Kurlen's partner as her next witness Freeman was confirming what had been my growing assumption: that her version of *Boléro* climaxed with the science. It was the smart play. Go with what can't be questioned or denied. Lay out the investigation through Kurlen and Longstreth and then bring it all together with the forensics. She would finish out the case with the medical examiner and the DNA evidence. A nice tight package.

Detective Longstreth did not look as tough and as severe as she did the first day of the case when I had met her at Van Nuys Division. First of all, she was wearing a dress that made her look more like a schoolteacher than a detective. I had seen this sort of transformation before and it always bothered me. Whether it was at the instruction of the prosecutor or by the detective's own wiles, many a time I had been faced with a female police witness who had transformed herself to be softer and more pleasing to the jury. But if I dared point this out to the judge, or anybody for that matter, I ran the risk of being slapped down as a misogynist.

So most times I just had to grin and eat it.

Freeman was using Longstreth to outline the second half of the investigation. Her testimony would be primarily about the search of the Trammel house and its findings. I was expecting no surprises here. After Freeman got her witness's bona fides on the record, she went right to it.

"Did you obtain a search warrant from a judge granting you access to Lisa Trammel's home?" Freeman asked.

"Yes, I did."

"What is that process? How do you get a judge to issue such an order?"

"You make a request that contains a probable cause statement, which lists the facts and evidence that have led you to the point of needing to search the premises. I did that here, using the statement of the witness who saw the suspect in the vicinity of the bank as well as the suspect's own inconsistent statements during the interview. The warrant was signed and issued by Judge Companioni and we proceeded to the house in Woodland Hills."

"Who is 'we,' Detective?"

"My partner, Detective Kurlen and I, and we decided to bring a videographer and a crime scene team with us to process anything we might find during the search."

"So the whole search was put on video?"

"Well, I would not say it was the whole search. My partner and I split up to make things move faster. But there was only one cameraman and he couldn't be with both of us at once. The way we worked it was that when we found something that looked like evidence or something we wanted to take into custody for examination, we would call for the camera."

"I see. And did you bring the video with you today?"

"I did and it has been placed in the player and is ready to go."

"Perfect."

The jury was then treated to a ninety-minute video accompanied by Longstreth's narration. The camera followed the police team as they arrived at the house and made a complete circuit around it before entering. While the view was in the backyard, Longstreth made sure to point out to jurors an herb garden stepped with railroad ties and freshly turned soil. It was what the great filmmakers would call foreshadowing. Its meaning would become apparent later, once the camera was inside the garage.

I was having trouble concentrating on the testimony. Dahl had dropped a bomb when he revealed the connection to Opparizio. I kept thinking about the possible scenario and what it could mean to the case. I wanted court to be over and for it to be seven o'clock.

On the video, a key taken from Lisa Trammel's belongings following her arrest was used to gain entrance to the house without damaging the property. Once inside, the team began a systematic search of the premises that seemed to follow a protocol born of experience. The shower and bathtub drains were examined for blood evidence. The washer and dryer as well. The longest part of the search took place in the closets, where every shoe and piece of clothing was carefully examined and subjected to chemical and lighting treatments designed to draw attention to blood evidence.

The camera eventually followed Longstreth as she left a side door to the house and crossed a small portico to another door. This door was unlocked and she went through it, bringing the camera into the garage. Freeman stopped the video here. Like an expert Hollywood craftsman, she had built her viewers' anticipation and now came the big tease.

"What was found in the garage became very important to the investigation, correct, Detective?"

"Yes, it did."

"What did you find?"

"Well, in one incidence, it was what we didn't find."

"Can you explain what you mean by that?"

"Yes. There was a tool bench that ran along the back wall of the garage. It appeared to be fully stocked with tools. Most of them were hanging on hooks attached to a pegboard installed above the bench and along the wall. The different locations for hanging the tools were marked with the name of the tool. Everything had its place on the board."

"Okay, can you show us?"

The video was restarted and soon it came to a head-on view of the workbench. At this point Freeman froze the image on the overhead screens.

"Okay, so this is the workbench, correct?"

"Yes."

"We see the tools hanging on the pegboard. Is there anything missing?"

"Yes, the hammer is missing."

Freeman asked the judge for permission for Longstreth to step down and use a laser pointer to show on the screens where the spot for the hammer was on the pegboard. The judge allowed it. Longstreth pointed it out on both screens and then returned to the witness stand.

"Now, Detective, was that spot specifically marked as being for a hammer?"

"Yes, it was."

"So the hammer was missing."

"It was not found anywhere in the garage or the house."

"And did there come a time when you identified the make and model of the tools that were on the pegboard?"

"Yes, by using the tools that were still there we were able to determine that the Trammels had a set of Craftsman tools that came in a specific package. It was a two-hundred-thirty-nine-piece set called the Carpenter's Tool Package."

"And was the hammer from this package available outside of this set?"

"No, it was not. There was a specific hammer that came from this particular set of tools."

"And it was missing from the tool set in Lisa Trammel's garage."

"That is correct."

"Now, did there come a time during the investigation that a hammer was turned in to police that had been found near the scene of the murder of Mitchell Bondurant?"

"Yes, a hammer was found by a gardener in some bushes a block and a half from the garage where the murder took place."

"Did you examine this hammer?"

"I examined it briefly before turning it over to the Scientific Investigation Division for analysis."

"What kind of hammer was it?"

"It was a claw hammer."

"And do you know who manufactured the hammer?"

"It was produced by Sears Craftsman."

Freeman paused as though she was expecting the jury to collectively gasp at the revelation when everybody in the courtroom had known exactly what was coming. She then stepped over to the prosecution table and opened a brown evidence bag. From it she pulled out a hammer that was encased in a clear plastic bag. Holding the hammer aloft she returned to the lectern.

"Your Honor, may I approach the witness with an exhibit?"

"You may."

She walked the hammer to Longstreth and handed it to her.

"Detective, I ask you to identify the hammer you are holding."

"This is the hammer that was found and turned over to me. My initials and badge number are on this evidence bag."

Freeman retrieved the hammer from her and asked that it be marked as state's evidence. Judge Perry gave his approval. After returning the hammer to the prosecution table, Freeman went back to the lectern and proceeded with her examination.

"You testified that the hammer was turned over to SID for forensic examination, correct?"

"Yes, correct."

"And subsequent to that did you get a forensics report on the tool?"

"Yes, and I have it here."

"What were their findings?"

"Two things of note. One was that they identified the hammer as being made exclusively for the Craftsman Carpenter's Tool Package."

"The same set that was found in the defendant's garage?"

"Yes."

"But minus the hammer?"

"Correct."

"And the other forensic finding of note was what?"

"They found blood on the hammer's handle."

"Even though it had been found in the bushes and been there for several weeks?"

I stood and objected, arguing that no testimony or evidence established how long the hammer had been in the bushes.

"Your Honor," Freeman responded. "The hammer was found several weeks after the murder occurred. It only stands to reason that it was in the bushes during that time."

Before the judge could make a ruling I quickly countered.

"Again, Judge, the state has introduced nothing in the way of evidence or testimony that concludes the hammer was in that bush for that long a time. In fact, the man who found it testified he had worked in and around those bushes at least twelve times since the murder and didn't see it until the morning he actually found it. The hammer could have easily been planted the night before it was—"

"Objection, Your Honor!" Freeman shouted. "Counsel is using his objection to put forth the defense's case because he knows it will—"

"Enough!" the judge bellowed. "From both of you. The objection is sustained. Ms. Freeman, you need to reword your question so that it does not assume facts not in evidence."

Freeman looked down at her notes, calming herself.

"Detective, did you see blood on the hammer when it was turned in to you?"

"No, I did not."

"Then how much blood was actually on the hammer?"

"It is described in the report as trace blood. A minute amount that was beneath the upper part of the rubber grip that encases the wood handle."

"Okay, so what did you do after receiving the report?"

"I arranged for the blood from the hammer to be tested at a private DNA lab in Santa Monica."

"Why didn't you use the regional crime lab at Cal State? Isn't that normal procedure?"

"It is normal procedure but we wanted to put a rush on this. We had the money in the budget so we thought we should move quickly with it. I had the results reviewed by our lab."

Freeman paused there and asked the judge to include the forensic report on the hammer as a prosecution exhibit. I didn't object and the judge approved. Freeman then changed course, leaving the DNA revelation for the DNA expert who would come in at the end of the prosecution's case.

"Let's go back to the garage now, Detective. Were there any other significant findings?"

I objected again, this time to the form of the question, which assumed that there had been a significant finding when in fact none had been testified to. It was a cheap shot but I took it because the last skirmish over an objection had knocked down Freeman's momentum. I wanted to keep trying to do that. The judge told her to rephrase the question and she did.

"Detective, you have testified about what you didn't find in the garage. The hammer. What can you tell us that you did find?"

Freeman turned to me after asking it as if to get my approval. I nodded at her and smiled. The fact that she would even acknowledge me was a sign I had gotten to her with the last two objections.

"We found a pair of gardening shoes and got a positive reaction for blood when we conducted a Luminol test."

"Luminol being one of the agents that reacts to blood under ultraviolet lighting, correct?"

"That's correct. It is used to detect locations where blood has been cleaned or wiped away."

"Where was the blood found here?"

"On the shoelace of the left shoe."

"Why were these particular shoes tested with Luminol?"

"First of all, it is routine to test all shoes and clothing when you are looking for the possibility of blood evidence. There was blood at the scene of the crime so you work under the assumption that some must have gotten on the assailant. Secondly, we had noticed in the backyard that the garden had been recently worked. The soil had been overturned and yet these shoes were very clean."

"Well, wouldn't someone clean their gardening shoes before going into the house?"

"Possibly, but we weren't in the house. We were in the garage and the shoes were in a cardboard box that contained a lot of loose dirt, presumably from the garden, and yet the shoes were quite clean. It drew our attention."

Freeman forwarded the video to the point where the shoes were shown. They were sitting side by side in a box that said COCA-COLA. They were on a shelf under the workbench. Not hidden by any means. Just in the spot where they were probably routinely stored.

"Are these the shoes?"

"Yes. You can see one of the forensic techs collecting them there."

"So you are saying that the fact that they were so clean but stored in a dirty box made them suspicious?"

I objected, stating she was leading the witness. I won the point but the message got to the jury. Freeman moved on.

"What made you think the shoes were Lisa Trammel's?"

"Because they were small, obviously a woman's shoes, and because we found a framed photograph in the house that depicted Lisa working in the garden. She was wearing the shoes."

"Thank you, Detective. What became of the shoes and the spot on the one shoelace that initially tested as showing blood?"

"The shoelace was turned over to the regional crime lab at Cal State for DNA testing."

"Why didn't you use the private lab for this?"

"The sample of blood was quite small. We decided not to risk that we might lose the sample in an outside lab. My partner and I actually hand-delivered it to the Cal State lab. We also sent along other exemplars for comparison."

"Other exemplars for comparison—what does that mean?"

"Blood from the victim was sent under separate delivery to the lab as well so that it could be compared to what was found on the shoe."

"Why separate delivery?"

"So there would be no chance of cross-contamination."

"Thank you, Detective Longstreth. I have no further questions at this time."

The judge called for the mid-afternoon break before cross-examination would begin. My client, unaware of the true purpose of my lunch invitation, invited me to join her and Dahl for coffee. I declined, saying I had to write out my questions for cross. The truth was I already had my questions ready. While before the trial I had thought Freeman would use Kurlen to introduce and testify about the hammer, the shoes and the search of Lisa Trammel's home, I was nonetheless ready because the direct examination had gone exactly as I had expected it would.

Instead, I spent the break on the phone with Cisco, preparing him for the meeting with Dahl at seven. I told him to clue in Bullocks and have Tommy Guns and Bam Bam outside the Victory Building for security. I wasn't sure whether Dahl was going to play it straight or not, but I was going to be ready either way.

Thirty-five

After the break, Detective Longstreth retook the stand and the judge turned it over to me. I threw no softballs and got right to the points I wanted to make in front of the jury. Primarily, this was testimony that informed the jury that the neighborhood surrounding WestLand was searched by police on the day of the murder. This included the house and presumably the landscaping where the hammer was eventually found.

"Detective," I asked, "did it trouble you that this hammer was found so long after the murder and yet so close to the murder scene and in a spot that was inside a rather intense search perimeter?"

"No, not really. After the hammer was found I went out and looked at the bushes in front of that house. They were big and very dense. It didn't surprise me or trouble me at all that a hammer could have been in there all that time. In fact, I thought we had been pretty lucky that it had been found at all."

Good answer. I was beginning to see why Freeman had broken things up between Kurlen and Longstreth. Longstreth was damn good on the stand, maybe even better than her veteran partner. I moved on. One of the rules of the game was to distance yourself from mistakes. Don't compound things by dwelling.

"Okay, let's move to the house in Woodland Hills now. Detective, wouldn't you agree that the search of the house was a bust?"

"A bust? I'm not sure I would call it a bust. I—"

"Did you find the defendant's bloody clothes?"

"No, we did not."

"Did you find the victim's blood in the shower or bathtub drains?"

"No, we did not."

"What about in the washing machine?"

"No."

"What evidence has the state presented during this trial that was obtained from inside the defendant's home? I am not talking about the garage. Just the home."

It took Longstreth a few long moments of silence as she conducted an internal inventory. Finally, she shook her head.

"I can't recall anything at the moment. But that still doesn't mean the search was a bust. Sometimes not finding evidence is just as useful as finding it."

I paused. She was baiting me. She wanted me to ask her to explain. But if I did that I had no idea where she would go. I decided to pull back, not take the bait and move on.

"Okay, but the real treasure—the evidence you did find—was found in the garage, right? The evidence that *has* been or will be brought to court in this trial."

"I would think so, yes."

"We're talking about the shoe with the blood on it and the tool set missing the hammer, correct?"

"That is correct."

"Am I missing something else?"

"I don't think so."

"Okay, then let me show you something here on the overhead screens."

I grabbed the remote, which Freeman had conveniently left on the lectern. I reversed the search video, keeping my eyes on the rewinding images. I ran it right by the images I wanted and stopped it, then moved forward to the right spot and paused.

"Okay, can you tell the jury what is happening at this point in the video?"

I hit the play button and the image on the screen started to move. It showed Longstreth and one of the forensic techs leaving the main house and crossing the portico to the door that led to the garage.

"Uh, this is when we go into the garage," Longstreth said.

Then her voice came from the recording.

"We might need the key from Kurlen," she said.

But on the video she reached a gloved hand to the doorknob and it turned.

"Never mind, it's open."

I let the video run until Longstreth and the forensic tech had entered the garage and turned on the lights. I then paused it again.

"Was this the first time you had entered the garage, Detective?"

"Yes."

"I see you turned on the lights here. Had anybody else from the search team entered the garage before you?"

"No, they had not."

I slowly backed up the video to the point where she had opened the door to enter. I started the playback again and asked my questions as it played.

"I notice you don't use a key to enter the garage, Detective. Why is that?"

"I tried the door, as you can see here, and it was unlocked."

"Do you know why?"

"No, it was just unlocked."

"Was anybody at the home when the search team arrived?"

"No, the house was empty."

"And the door to the house itself was locked, correct?"

"Yes, Ms. Trammel had locked it when she agreed to accompany us to Van Nuys."

"Did she want to lock it or did you have to tell her?"

"No, she wanted to lock up."

"So at the time that she locked the house she left the outside door that led into the garage unlocked, correct?"

"It would appear so."

"It's safe to say that it was unlocked at the time you and the others arrived with the search warrant, correct?"

"That is correct."

"Meaning anyone could have entered the garage while its owner, Lisa Trammel, was in police custody, correct?"

"I guess it's possible, yes."

"By the way, when you and Detective Kurlen left the house with Ms. Trammel that morning, did you leave a police officer on post at the house to sort of watch over it, make sure nothing was disturbed or taken from inside?"

"No, we did not."

"Didn't you think that would be prudent, considering that the house might contain evidence in a murder investigation?"

"At the time she was not a suspect. She was just someone we wanted to talk to."

I almost smiled and Longstreth almost smiled. She had tiptoed past a trap I had set for her. She was good.

"Ah," I said. "Not a suspect, that's right. So how long, would you say, was that side door left unlocked and the garage available for anyone to enter?"

"That would be impossible for me to tell. I don't know when it was left unlocked in the first place. It's possible she never locked the garage."

I nodded and put a pause under her answer.

"Did you or Detective Kurlen instruct the forensics team to see if there were any fingerprints on the door leading to the garage?"

"No, we did not."

"Why not, Detective?"

"We didn't think it was necessary. We were searching the house, not holding it as a crime scene."

"Let me ask you hypothetically, Detective. Do you think that someone who has carefully planned and carried out a murder would then leave a pair of bloody shoes in their unlocked garage? Especially after taking the time to get rid of the murder weapon?"

Freeman objected, citing the compound nature of the question and arguing that it assumed facts not in evidence. I didn't care. The question hadn't been for Longstreth to consider. It had been directed at the jury.

"Your Honor, I withdraw the question," I announced. "And I have nothing further for this witness."

I moved away from the lectern and sat down. I stared pointedly at the jurors, my eyes sweeping across one row of them and then the other. Finally, I held them on Furlong in the three spot. He held my stare and didn't look away. I took that as a very good sign.

Thirty-six

Herb Dahl came alone. Cisco met him at the door of the office suite and escorted him into my office, where I was waiting. Bullocks sat to my left and we had an empty seat for Dahl right in front of my desk. Cisco stayed standing, which was by design. I wanted Cisco pacing and pensive. I wanted Dahl to feel unease, that the wrong word spoken could unleash the big man in the tight black T-shirt.

I didn't offer Dahl coffee, soda or water. I didn't start with any platitudes or efforts to mend our strained relationship. I simply got down to business.

"What we're going to do here, Herb, is find out exactly what you've done, what your involvement with Louis Opparizio has been and what we're going to do about it. As far as I know, I'm not needed anywhere until nine o'clock tomorrow morning, so we've got all night if that's what it takes."

"Before we start I want to know that we have a deal if I cooperate," Dahl said.

"I told you at lunch the deal is you stay out of prison. In exchange, you tell me what you know. Beyond that, no promises."

"I won't testify to anything. This is informational only. Besides, I have something better for you than my testifying."

"We'll see about that. But right now why don't we start at the beginning? You said today that you were told to go on Lisa Trammel's picket line. Start there."

Dahl nodded but then disagreed.

"I think I have to start before that. This goes back to the beginning of last year."

I raised two open hands.

"Have at it. We've got all night."

Dahl then proceeded to tell a long story about a movie he produced a year earlier called *Blood Racer*. It was a warm family movie about a girl who is given a horse named Chester. She finds a tattooed number inside the animal's lower lip that indicates he was once a thoroughbred racehorse thought to have been killed in a barn fire years before.

"So she and her pop do some more investigating and—"

"Look," I interrupted. "It sounds like a nice story but can we talk about Louis Opparizio? I may have all night but let's stay on point anyway."

"That is the point. This movie. It was supposed to be low budget all the way but I love horses. Ever since I was a little kid. And I really thought I could get out of the racks with this one."

"The racks?"

"The straight-to-DVD dreck you see out there. I was thinking this story was a diamond in the rough and if we did it right we could get a major theatrical release. But to get that you need production value and to get that you need money."

It always comes down to money.

"You borrowed the money?"

"I borrowed the money and put it into the flick. Stupid, I know. And this was on top of the investor money I took at the start. But the director was this perfectionist freak from Spain. Guy barely spoke English but we hired him. He did take after take on every setup—thirty takes at a frickin' snack bar scene! Bottom line is we ran out of money and I needed a quarter mill minimum just to finish the film. I had already been all over town and everybody was tapped. But I loved this flick. To me it was like the little movie that could, you know?"

"You got the money on the street," Cisco said from a position behind Dahl's chair.

Dahl twisted around to look up at him and nodded.

"Yeah, from a guy I know. A bent-nose guy."

"What's his name?" I asked.

"We don't need his name in this," Dahl said.

"Yes, we do. What is his name?"

"Danny Greene."

"I thought you said —"

"Yeah, I know. He's with them but his name's Greene — what can I say? It's 'Green' with an 'e' at the end."

I gave Cisco a look. He would need to check this out.

"Okay, so you took a quarter million from Danny Greene and what happened?"

Dahl raised his palms in a gesture indicating frustration.

"That's just it, nothing happened. I finished the flick but I couldn't sell it. I took it to every frickin' festival in North America and nobody wanted it. I took it to the American Film Market, rented a frickin' suite at the Loews in Santa Monica and only sold it to Spain. Of course, the one country that was interested was where my asshole director was from."

"So Danny Greene wasn't too happy, was he?"

"Nope, he wasn't. I mean, I had been keeping up with the payments but it was a six-month loan and he called it in. I couldn't pay it all. I gave him the Spanish money but most of that was on the come. They gotta dub it and all that shit and I won't see most of that cash till the end of *this* year when the movie comes out over there. So I was seriously fucked."

"What happened?"

"Well, one day Danny comes to me. I mean, he just shows up and I'm thinking he's here to break my legs. But instead he says they need me to do something. It's like a long-term job and if I do it they'll restructure my loan and I can even lay off a good chunk of the remaining principal. So, man, I'm sitting there, I've got no choice. What'm I going to do, tell Danny Greene no? Uh-uh, doesn't work that way."

"So you said yes."

"That's right. I said yes."

"And what was the job?"

"To get close to these people who were agitating and protesting about all the foreclosures. This organization called FLAG. He wanted me to get inside their camp if I could. So I did and that's how I met Lisa. She was the top agitator."

This sounded crazy but I played along with it.

"Were you told why?"

"Not really. I was just told there was a guy out there who was sort of paranoid and he wanted to know what she was up to. He had some kind of deal going and didn't want these people to mess it up. So if Lisa was planning a protest or something, then I was supposed to tell Danny where it would be and who the target was and like that."

The story was starting to have the ring of truth to it. I thought about the LeMure deal. Opparizio had been in the process of setting up the sale of ALOFT to the publicly traded company. It was prudent business practice to keep tabs on any potential threats to the deal before it was finished in February. That could even include Lisa Trammel. Bad publicity could hinder the sale. Stockholders always want squeaky-clean acquisitions.

"Okay, what else?"

"Not a whole lot else. Just intelligence gathering. I got close to Lisa but then like a month later she got popped for the murder. Danny came back then. I thought he was going to say deal's off because she was in jail. But he said he wanted me to put up the money and get her out. He gave me the money in a bag — two hundred thou. Then when I got her out I was supposed to do the same thing again, only with you people. Get inside the defense camp, see what was going on and report back."

I looked over at Cisco. His pensive moves were no longer an act. We both knew that Dahl could be the tip of an iceberg that would tear the bottom out of the prosecution's case and sink it. We also knew we might have a client in Lisa Trammel who was completely unlikable but innocent.

And if she was innocent...

"Where does Opparizio come into this?" I asked.

"Well, he sort of doesn't — at least, not directly. But when I call Danny to check in he always wants to know what you've got on Opparizio. That's how he says it, 'What do they have on Opparizio?' He asks that every time. So I'm thinking, maybe he's the guy I'm really doing this work for, you know?"

I didn't respond at first. I swiveled in my chair, thinking the story over.

"You know what I don't get and what isn't in your story, Dahl?" Cisco said.

"What?"

"The part about you hiring those two guys to go after Mick. You left that part out, asshole."

"What about that?" I added.

Dahl raised his hands in surrender to show his innocence.

"Hey, they told me to do it. They sent me those two guys."

"Why beat me up? What did that do?"

"It slowed you down, didn't it? They want Lisa to go down for this and they started thinking you were too good. They wanted to slow you down."

Dahl avoided eye contact by brushing imaginary lint off his thigh as he spoke. It made me think he might be lying about the reason behind the attack on me. It was the first false note I had picked up during the confession. My guess was that Dahl had been freelancing on the attack, that maybe he was the one who wanted me hurt.

I looked at Bullocks and then at Cisco. My quibble with Dahl's last answer aside, we had an opportunity here. I knew what Dahl was going to offer next. Himself as a double agent. We'd reach the beach with him feeding Opparizio false intelligence.

I had to think about this. I could easily give Dahl misleading information to take back to Danny Greene. But it would be a risky maneuver, not to mention the ethical considerations.

I stood up and signaled Cisco toward the door.

"Everybody sit tight for a minute. I want to talk to my investigator out here."

We stepped into the reception area and I closed the door behind me. I walked over to Lorna's desk.

"You know what this means?" I asked.

"It means we're going to win this fucking case."

I opened the middle drawer of Lorna's desk and took out the stack of delivery menus for local restaurants and fast-food chains.

"No, it means those two guys at the clubhouse? They might've been Bondurant's killers and we fucked things up with that little play in the back room."

"I don't know about that, Boss."

"Yeah, what did your two associates do with them?"

"Exactly what I told them to do, drop them off. They told me later that both of them wanted to be left off at some bottle club in downtown. That was it. I mean it, Mick."

"It's still fucked up."

With the menus in my hand, I headed toward the door to my office. Cisco spoke to my back.

"Do you believe Dahl?"

I looked back at him before opening the door.

"To a point."

I went into the office and put the menus down in the middle of the desk. I took my seat again and looked at Dahl. He was a weasel always on the make. And I was about to go down the path with him.

"We shouldn't do it," Bullocks said.

I looked at her.

"Do what?"

"Use him to feed bad intel back to Opparizio. We should put him on the stand and make him tell the story to the jury."

Dahl immediately protested.

"I'm not testifying! Who the fuck is she, saying how this—"

I raised my hands in a calming gesture.

"You're not testifying," I said. "Even if I wanted you to I couldn't get you on the stand. You have nothing that directly connects Opparizio to this. Have you ever even met the man?"

"No."

"Have you ever seen him before?"

"Yeah, in the court."

"Before that."

"No, and I had never even heard his name until Danny asked me about him."

I looked at Bullocks and shook my head.

"They're too smart to leave a direct link out there. The judge wouldn't let him anywhere near the stand."

"Then what about Danny Greene? We put him on the stand."

"And what do we use to compel him to testify? He'd take the Fifth before we even got to his name. There is only one thing to do here."

I waited for further protest but Bullocks was finally and sullenly silent. I looked back at Dahl. I disliked the man intensely and trusted him about as much as I trusted that he had his own hair. But that didn't stop me from taking the next step.

"Dahl, how is contact initiated with Danny Greene?"

"I usually call him about ten."

"Every night?"

"Yeah, during the trial it's been that way. He always wants to hear from me. Most nights he answers and if not he calls me back pretty quick."

"Okay, let's dig in and order some takeout. Tonight you make the call from here."

"What am I going to say?"

"We're going to work that out between now and ten when you make the call. But essentially I think you are going to tell Danny Greene that Louis Opparizio doesn't have a thing to worry about when he takes the stand. You're going to tell him that we've got nothing, that we've been bluffing and that the coast is clear."

Thirty-seven

Thursday was supposed to be the day when all the orchestral elements came together in a crescendo for the prosecution. Since Monday morning Andrea Freeman had carefully rolled out her case, easily handling the variables and unknowns, like the potshots I had taken and the intrusion of the federal target letter, in a strategic buildup that gathered momentum and led inalterably to this day. Thursday was the science day, the day that all elements of evidence and testimony would be tied together with the unbreakable bindings of scientific fact.

It was a good strategy but this is where I intended to turn her plans upside-down. In the courtroom there are three things for the lawyer to always consider: the knowns, the known unknowns and the unknown unknowns. Whether at the prosecution or defense table, it is the lawyer's job to master the first two and always be prepared for the third. On Thursday I intended to be one of the unknown unknowns. I had seen Andrea Freeman's strategy from a mile away. She would not see mine until she had stepped into it like quicksand and it silenced her crescendo.

Her first witness was Dr. Joachim Gutierrez, the assistant medical examiner who performed the autopsy on Mitchell Bondurant's body. Using a morbid slide show that I had halfheartedly and unsuccessfully objected to, the doctor took the jury on a magical mystery tour of the victim's body, cataloging every bruise, abrasion and broken tooth. Of course, he spent the most time describing and showing on the screens the damage created by the three impacts of the murder weapon. He pointed out which had been the first blow and why it was fatal. He called the second two strikes, delivered when the victim was facedown on the ground, overkill and testified that in his experience overkill was equated with an emotional context. The three brutal strikes revealed that the killer had personal animosity toward the victim. I could have objected to both the question and answer but they played nicely into a question I would later ask.

"Doctor," Freeman asked at one point, "you have three brutal strikes on the top of the head, all within a circle with a four-inch diameter. How is it that you can tell which one came first and which one was the fatal blow?"

"It is a painstaking process yet a very simple one. The blows to the skull created two fracture patterns. The immediate and most damaging impact was in the contact area where each strike of the weapon created what is termed a depressed calvarial fracture, which is really just a fancy way of saying it created a depression in the skull or a dent."

"A dent?"

"You see, all bone has a certain elasticity. With injuries like this—a forceful, traumatic impact—the skull bone depresses in the shape of the striking instrument and two things happen. You get parallel break lines on the surface—these are called terraced fractures—and on the interior, you get a deep depression fracture—the dent. On the inside of the skull this depression causes a fracture that we call a pyramid splinter. This splinter projects through the dura, which is the interior lining, and directly into the brain. Often, and as was found in this case, the splinter breaks and is propelled deep into the brain tissue like a bullet. It instantly causes the termination of brain function and death."

"Like a bullet, you said. So these three impacts on the victim's head were so forceful that it was literally tantamount to him being shot three times in the head?"

"Yes, that is correct. But it only took one of these splinters to kill him. The first one."

"Which brings me back to my initial question. How can you tell which impact was the first one?"

"Can I demonstrate this?"

The judge gave permission for Gutierrez to put a diagram of a skull on the video screens. It was an overhead view and it showed the three impact spots where the hammer had struck. These points were drawn in blue. Other fractures were drawn in red.

"To determine the sequence of blows in a multiple-trauma situation we go to the secondary fractures. Those are the fractures in red. I called these parallel breaks terraced fractures because, as I said earlier, they are like steps moving away from the impact point. A fracture or crack like this can extend completely across the bone and here you see that with this victim these fracture lines stretch across the parietal-temporal region. But such fractures always end when they reach an already-existing fracture. The energy is simply absorbed by the existing fracture. Therefore, by studying the victim's skull and tracing the terraced fractures it becomes possible to determine which of these fractures came first. And then of course you trace these back to the impact point and you can easily see the order of the blows."

On the drawing on the screen the numbers 1, 2 and 3 were in place, depicting the order of blows that rained down on Mitchell Bondurant's head. The first blow — the fatal impact — had been to the very top of his head.

Freeman moved on from there and spent most of the morning milking the testimony, finally reaching a point where she was belaboring the obvious in many areas with too many questions that were repetitive or not germane. Twice the judge asked her to move along to other areas of testimony. And I began to believe she was trying to stall. She had to keep the witness going through the morning because her next witness was possibly not on hand and may have even flaked out on her.

But if she was nervous about some problem, Freeman didn't show it. She kept her focus on Gutierrez and steadfastly walked him through his testimony, finishing with what was most important — tying the Craftsman hammer found in the bushes to the wounds on the victim's head.

To do this she brought out the props. Following the Bondurant autopsy, Gutierrez had made a mold of the victim's skull. He also took a series of photos of the scalp and had prints made that depicted the wounds in one-to-one size.

Presented with the hammer that had been entered into evidence,

Gutierrez removed it from its plastic bag and began a demonstration that showed how its flat, circular face fit the wounds and skull indentations perfectly. The hammer also had a notch on the top edge of its facing that could be used to hold a nail. This notch was clearly seen in the depression left on the skull. It all fit together in a perfect prosecutorial puzzle. Freeman was beaming as she saw a key element of proof solidify in front of the jury.

"Doctor, do you have any hesitation in telling the jury that this tool could have created the fatal injury to the victim?"

"None."

"You realize that this tool is not unique, correct?"

"Of course. I am not saying that this specific hammer caused these injuries. I am saying it was either this hammer or one that came out of the same mold. I can't be more specific than that."

"Thank you, Doctor. Now let's talk about the notch on the strike surface of the hammer. What can you tell about the position of the notch in the wound pattern?"

Gutierrez held up the hammer and pointed to the notch.

"The notch is on the top edge. This area is magnetized. You put the nail in place here, the hammer holds it and then you drive the nail into the surface of the material you are working with. Because we know the notch is on the top edge we can then look at the wounds and see which direction they came from."

"And what direction is that?"

"From the rear. The victim was struck from behind."

"So he may have never even seen his assailant coming."

"That is correct."

"Thank you, Dr. Gutierrez. I have no further questions at this time."

The judge turned the witness over to me and as I passed Freeman on the way to the lectern she gave me a deadpan look that transmitted the message: Take your best shot, asshole.

I intended to. I put my legal pad down on the lectern, tightened my tie and shot my cuffs, then looked at the witness. Before I sat down again, I wanted to own him.

"Around the medical examiner's office, they call you Dr. Guts, don't they, sir?"

It was a good out-of-the-gate question. It would make the witness wonder what other inside information I knew and could possibly spring on him.

"Uh, sometimes, yes. Informally, you might say."

"Why is that, Doctor?"

Freeman objected on relevance and it got the judge's attention.

"Do you want to tell me how this ties into the reason we are here today, Mr. Haller?" he asked.

"Your Honor, I think if allowed to respond, the answer Dr. Gutierrez will give will reveal that he has an expertise in pathology that is not in the area of tool patterns and head wounds."

Perry mulled things over and then nodded.

"The witness will answer."

I turned my focus back to Gutierrez.

"Doctor, you can answer the question. Why are you called Dr. Guts?"

"It is because as you said I have an expertise in identifying diseases of the gastrointestinal tract—the guts—and it also goes with the name, especially when it is pronounced incorrectly."

"Thank you, Doctor. Now can you tell us how many times you have had a case in which you matched a hammer to the wounds on a victim's skull?"

"This would be the first one."

I nodded to underline the point.

"So you're sort of a rookie when it comes to a killing with a hammer."

"That's right, but my comparison was painstaking and cautious. My conclusions are not wrong."

Play to his superiority complex. I am a doctor, I am not wrong.

"Have you ever been wrong before in giving court testimony as a witness?"

"Everyone makes mistakes. I am sure I have."

"What about the Stoneridge case?"

Freeman quickly objected as I knew she would. She asked for a sidebar and the judge waved us up. I knew this would go no further but I had gotten it out in front of the jury. They knew from what little had just been said that somewhere in his past Gutierrez had testified and been wrong. That was all I needed.

"Judge, we both know where counsel is going and not only is it not relevant to this matter, but Stoneridge is still under investigation and there has been no official conclusion. What could—"

"I withdraw it."

She looked at me with searing hostility in her eyes.

"No problem. I have another question."

"Oh, as long as the jury hears the question you don't care what the answer is. Judge, I want an instruction on this because what he is doing is not right."

"I'll take care of it. Go back. And Mr. Haller? You watch yourself."

"Thank you, Your Honor."

The judge instructed the jurors to disregard my question and reminded them that it would be unfair of them to consider anything outside of the evidence and testimony while later conducting their deliberations. He then told me to proceed and I went in a new direction.

"Doctor, let's zero in on the fatal wound and get a little more detailed. You called this a depression fracture, correct?"

"Actually, I called it a depressed calvarial fracture."

I always loved it when the prosecution's witnesses corrected me.

"Okay, so the depression or dent that was left by this traumatic impact, did you measure it?"

"Measure it in what way?"

"How about its depth? Did you measure that?"

"Yes, I did. May I refer to my notes?"

"You sure can, Doctor."

Gutierrez checked his copy of the autopsy protocol.

"Yes, we called the fatal impact wound one-A. And, yes, indeed, I did measure the definitions of the wound pattern. Shall I give you those measurements?"

"My next question. Please tell us, Doctor, how did it measure out?"

Gutierrez looked at his report while speaking.

"Measurements were taken at four points of the circular impact location. Using a clockface, the measurements were at three, six, nine and twelve. The twelve being where the notch on the surface was located."

"And what did the measurements tell you?"

"There was very little play in these numbers. Less than a quarter of a centimeter separated the four measurements. They averaged out to seven millimeters in depth, which is approximately a quarter of an inch."

He looked up from his notes. I was writing his numbers down even though I had already gotten them off the autopsy protocol. I glanced over at the box and saw a few jurors writing in their notebooks. A good sign.

"So, Doctor, I noticed that this part of your work didn't come up on direct examination by Ms. Freeman. What did these measurements mean to you in terms of the angle of impact of the weapon?"

Gutierrez shrugged. He stole a glance at Freeman and got the message. Be careful here.

"There is nothing really to conclude from these numbers."

"Really? Wouldn't the fact that the impression in the bone—the dent, as you called it—left by the hammer was almost even at all measurable points indicate to you that the hammer struck the victim evenly on the top of the head?"

Gutierrez looked down at his notes. He was a man of science. I had just asked him a science-based question and he knew how to answer it. But he also knew he had somehow strayed into a minefield. He didn't know how or why, only that the prosecutor sitting fifteen feet from him was nervous.

"Doctor? Do you want me to repeat the question?"

"No, that is not necessary. You must remember that in science one-tenth of a centimeter can mean quite a difference."

"Are you saying that the hammer did not strike Mr. Bondurant evenly, sir?"

"No!" he said in an annoyed tone. "I am just saying that it is not as cut and dried as people think. Yes, it appears that the hammer struck the victim flush, if you will."

"Thank you, Doctor. And when you look at your wound-depth measurements on the second and third strikes, they are not as even, correct?"

"Yes, that is correct. In both of these impacts the deviation ranges up to three millimeters in each."

I had him now. I was rolling. I stepped back from the lectern and started to wander to my left, into the open space between the lectern and the jury box. I put my hands in my pockets and adopted a pose of a completely confident man.

"And so, Doctor, you have the fatal blow delivered clean and flush to the top of the head. The next two, not the same way. What would account for this difference?"

"The orientation of the skull. The first strike stopped brain function within a second. The abrasions and other injuries to the body — the broken teeth, for example — indicate an immediate dead fall from a standing position. It is likely that the second and third strikes occurred after he was down."

"You just said the other injuries indicate 'an immediate dead fall from a standing position.' Why are you sure the victim was standing when attacked from behind?"

"The abrasions to both knees are indicative of this."

"So he could not have been kneeling when attacked?"

"It seems unlikely. The abrasions on the knees indicate otherwise."

"What about crouching, like a baseball catcher?"

"Again, not possible when you look at the damage to his knees. Deep abrasions and a fracture to the left patella. The kneecap, as it is more commonly called."

"So no doubt in your mind that he was standing when struck with the fatal blow?"

"None."

It was perhaps the most important answer to any question in the whole trial, but I glided on like it was just part of the routine.

"Thank you, Doctor. Now let's go back to the skull for a moment. How strong would you say the skull is in the area where the fatal impact occurred?"

"Depends on the age of the subject. Our skulls grow thicker as we age."

"Our subject is Mitchell Bondurant, Doctor. How thick was his skull? Did you measure it?"

"I did. It was point eight centimeters thick in the impact region. About one-third of an inch."

"And have you conducted any sort of study or test to determine what kind of force it would have taken for a hammer to create the fatal dent fracture in this case?"

"I have not, no."

"Are you aware of any such studies of this question in general?"

"There are studies in the area. The conclusions are very broad. I happen to think each case is unique. You can't go by general studies."

"Isn't it widely held that the threshold measurement of pressure needed to create a depression fracture is one thousand pounds of pressure per square inch?"

Freeman stood and objected. She said that I was asking questions outside the scope of Dr. Gutierrez's expertise as a witness.

"Mr. Haller himself was quick to point out in his cross-examination that the witness's expertise is in diseases of the GI tract, not bone elasticity and depression."

It was a no-win situation for her and she had chosen the lesser of two evils: burning her witness or allowing me to continue to ask him questions that he didn't know the answers to.

"Sustained," the judge said. "Let's move on, Mr. Haller. Ask your next question."

"Yes, Your Honor."

I flipped a few pages on my pad and acted like I was reading. It would buy me a few moments while I considered the next move. I then turned and looked at the clock on the back wall of the courtroom. It was fifteen minutes till lunch. If I wanted to send the jury out with a final bit of food for thought, I needed to act now.

"Doctor," I said. "Did you record the height of the victim?"

Gutierrez checked his notes.

"Mr. Bondurant was six feet, one inch tall at the time of his death."

"So this area at the crown of the head would be six feet and one inch high. Is that fair to say, Doctor?"

"Yes, it is."

"Actually, with Mr. Bondurant wearing shoes he would have been even taller, correct?"

"Yes, maybe an inch and a half to account for the heels."

"Okay, so knowing the victim's height and knowing that the fatal wound came in flush on the top of his head, what does that tell us about the angle of attack?"

"I am not sure what you mean by angle of attack."

"Are you sure about that, Doctor? I am talking about the angle the hammer was at in relation to the impact area."

"But this would be impossible to know because we don't know the posture of the victim or whether he was ducking from the blow or what the exact situation was when he was struck."

Gutierrez ended his answer with a nod, as though proud of the way he had handled the challenge.

"But Doctor, didn't you testify during direct examination from Ms. Freeman that it appeared to you, at least, that Mr. Bondurant was struck from behind in a surprise attack?"

"I did."

"Doesn't that contradict what you just said about ducking from the blow? Which is it, Doctor?"

Feeling cornered, Gutierrez reacted in the way most cornered men do. With arrogance.

"My testimony is that we do not know exactly what happened in that garage or what posture the victim was in or what the orientation of his skull was when he was struck with the fatal blow. To be minutely guessing and second-guessing at this point is a fool's errand."

"You are saying it is foolish to attempt to understand what happened in the garage?"

"No! I am not saying that at all. You are taking the words and twisting them."

Freeman had to do something. She stood and objected and said I was badgering the witness. I wasn't and the judge said as much, but the little interruption was enough for Gutierrez to collect himself and resume his calm and superior demeanor. I decided to wrap things up. I had largely been using Dr. Guts as a setup man for my own expert, who would testify during the defense phase. I believed I was almost there.

"Doctor, would you agree that if we *could* determine the victim's posture and the orientation of his skull at the time of that first, fatal blow, then we would have insight as to the angle at which the murder weapon was held?"

Gutierrez considered the question for longer than it had taken me to ask it, then reluctantly nodded.

"Yes, it would give us some insight. But it is imposs—"

"Thank you, Doctor. My next question is if we knew all of these things—the posture, the orientation, the angle of the weapon—wouldn't we then be able to make some assumptions about the height of the attacker?"

"It doesn't make sense. We can't know these things."

He held both his hands up in frustration and turned to look at the judge for help. He got none.

"Doctor, you are not answering the question. Let me ask you again. If we did indeed know all of these factors, could we then make assumptions about the attacker's height?"

He dropped his hands in an *I give up* gesture.

"Of course, of course. But we do not know these factors."

"'We,' Doctor? Don't you mean *you* don't know these factors because you didn't look for them?"

"No, I—"

"Don't you mean you didn't want to know these factors because they would reveal that it was physically impossible for the defendant, at five foot three, to have ever committed—"

"Objection!"

"—this crime against a man ten inches taller than her?"

Luckily they no longer used gavels in California courtrooms. Perry would have smashed his through the bench.

"Sustained! Sustained! Sustained!"

I picked up my pad and flipped over all the folded back pages in a show of frustration and finality.

"I have nothing further for—"

"Mr. Haller," the judge barked, "I have warned you repeatedly about acting out in front of the jury. Consider this your last warning. Next time, there will be consequences."

"Noted, Your Honor. Thank you."

"The jury will disregard the last exchange between counsel and the witness. It is stricken from the record."

I sat down, not daring to glance at the jury box. But that was okay, I felt the vibe. Their eyes were on me. They were riding with me.

Not all of them, but enough.

Thirty-eight

I spent the lunch hour schooling Lisa Trammel on what to expect during the afternoon session of court. Herb Dahl was not present, having been dispatched on a phony errand so I could be alone with my client. As best I could, I tried to explain to her the risks we would be taking as the prosecution's case wound down and the defense took center stage. She was scared, but she trusted me and that's about all you can ask from a client. The truth? No. But trust? Yes.

Once court reconvened Freeman called Dr. Henrietta Stanley to the witness stand. She identified herself as a supervising biologist for the Los Angeles Regional Crime Laboratory at Cal State L.A. My guess was that she would be the last witness for the prosecution and her testimony would have two parts of major significance. She would confirm that DNA testing of the blood found on the recovered hammer matched Mitchell Bondurant's DNA perfectly and that the blood found on Lisa Trammel's gardening shoe also matched the victim's.

The scientific testimony would bring the case full circle, with blood being the link. My only intention was to rob the prosecution of the moment.

"Dr. Stanley," Freeman began. "You either conducted or supervised all DNA analysis that came from the investigation of Mitchell Bondurant's death, did you not?"

"I supervised and reconfirmed one analysis conducted by an outside vendor. The other analysis I handled myself. But I must add that I have two assistants in the lab who help me and they do a good portion of the work under my supervision."

"At one point in the investigation you were asked to have a small amount of blood that had been found on a hammer analyzed for a DNA comparison to the victim, were you not?"

"We used an outside vendor on that analysis because time was of the essence. I supervised that process and later confirmed the findings."

"Your Honor?"

I was standing at the defense table. The judge looked annoyed with me for interrupting Freeman's examination.

"What is it, Mr. Haller?"

"To save the court's time and the jury from going through a long-drawn-out explanation of DNA analysis and matching, the defense stipulates."

"Stipulates to what, Mr. Haller?"

"That the blood on the hammer came from Mitchell Bondurant."

The judge didn't miss a beat. The chance to jump the trial forward an hour or more was welcomed — with caution.

"Very well, Mr. Haller, but you will not get the opportunity to challenge this during the defense phase. You know that, right?"

"I know it, Judge. There will be no need to challenge it."

"And your client does not object to this tactic?"

I turned my body slightly toward Lisa Trammel and gestured to her.

"She is perfectly aware of this tactic and agrees. She is also willing to go on record, if you wish to ask her directly."

"I don't think that is necessary. How does the state feel about this?"

Freeman looked suspicious, like she was looking for the trap.

"Judge," she said, "I want it clear that the defendant is acknowledging that the blood found on the hammer was indeed Mitchell Bondurant's blood. And I want a waiver on ineffective counsel."

"I don't think a waiver is necessary," Perry said. "But I will get the stipulation directly from the defendant."

He then asked Lisa questions that confirmed she was on board with the stipulation.

Once Freeman said she was satisfied Perry turned his chair and rolled to the end of the bench so he could address the jury.

"Ladies and gentlemen, the witness was going to take you through an explanation of the science of DNA typing and matching, leading you to testimony in regard to lab tests matching blood found on the hammer that is in evidence to that of our victim, Mitchell Bondurant. By stipulating, the defense is saying they agree with those findings and will not object to them. So what you take from this is that the blood found on the handle of the hammer found in the bushes near the bank did indeed come from the victim, Mitchell Bondurant. This is now stipulated as a proven fact and I will have that in writing for you when you begin your deliberations."

He nodded once and then rolled back into place where he told Freeman to proceed. Knocked out of rhythm by my unexpected move, she asked the judge for a few moments while she got her bearings and found the place from which to restart her examination. Finally, she looked up at her witness.

"Okay, Dr. Stanley, the blood from the hammer was not the only sample of blood from this case that you were asked to have analyzed, correct?"

"That is correct. We were also given a separate sample of blood discovered on a shoe found on the defendant's premises. In the garage, I believe. We typed—"

"Your Honor," I said as I rose from my seat again, "once more the defense wishes to stipulate."

This time the move brought complete silence to the courtroom. Nobody was whispering in the gallery, the bailiff wasn't using his hand to muffle his voice on his telephone, the court reporter's fingers were held steady over the keys. Complete silence.

The judge had been sitting with the fingers of both hands knitted together beneath his chin. He held his pose for a long moment before using both hands to signal Freeman and me forward to the bench.

"Come on up here, Counsel."

Freeman and I stood side by side in front of the bench. The judge whispered.

"Mr. Haller, your reputation preceded you when you came into my courtroom on this case. I was told by more than one source that you were a damn fine lawyer and a tireless advocate. I need to ask, however, if you know what you're doing here. You want to stipulate to the prosecution's contention that the victim's blood was found on your client's own shoe? Are you sure about that, Mr. Haller?"

I nodded as if to concede that he had made a good point in questioning my trial strategy.

"Judge, we did the analysis ourselves and it came back as a match. The science doesn't lie and the defense is not interested in trying to mislead the court or the jury. If a trial is a search for truth then let the truth come out. The defense stipulates. We will prove later that the blood was planted on the shoe. That is where the real truth lies, not with whether or not it was his blood. We acknowledge that it was and we're ready to move on."

"Your Honor, may I be heard?" Freeman said.

"Go ahead, Ms. Freeman."

"The state objects to the stipulation."

She had finally caught on. The judge looked aghast.

"I don't understand, Ms. Freeman. You get what you want. The victim's blood on the defendant's shoes."

"Your Honor, Dr. Stanley is my last witness. Counsel is seeking to undercut the state's case by robbing me of the ability to present evidence in the way I wish to present it. This witness's testimony is devastating to the defense. He just wants to stipulate to lessen its impact on the jury. But a stipulation must be agreed to by both parties. I made a mistake taking the stipulation on the hammer, but not this time. Not on the shoes. The state objects to this."

The judge was undaunted. He saw a savings of at least a half day of court time and he wasn't going to let it go.

"Counsel, understand that the court can overrule your objection in the cause of judicial economy. I'd rather not do that."

He was telling her not to go against him on this. To accept the stipulation.

"I'm sorry, Your Honor, but the state still objects."

"Overruled. You can step back."

And so it went. As with the hammer, the judge relayed the stipulation to the jury and promised they would receive a document outlining the evidence and facts agreed to by the start of deliberations. I had successfully silenced the crescendo of the prosecution's case. Instead of going out with the crashing of cymbals, drums and evidence that screamed

SHE DID IT! SHE DID IT! SHE DID IT!, the prosecution went out with a whimper. Freeman was seething. She knew how important the payoff was to the gradual buildup. You don't listen to *Boléro* for ten minutes and turn it off with the final two minutes to go.

Not only did the truncating of her case hurt, but I had effectively turned her last and most important witness into the first witness for the defense. By stipulating, I had made it seem as if the DNA returns were the initial building blocks of my case. And there was nothing Freeman could do. She had put the whole case out and had nothing left. After excusing Stanley from the witness stand, she sat at the prosecution table, turning through her notes, probably thinking about whether she should put Kurlen or Longstreth back on the stand to finish the case with a detective's roundup of all the evidence. But there were risks to that. She had rehearsed their testimony before. But not this time.

"Ms. Freeman?" the judge finally asked. "Do you have another witness?"

Freeman looked over at the jury box. She had to believe she had the verdict. So what if the evidence wasn't delivered according to the plan she had choreographed? The evidence was still there and in the record. The vic's blood on the hammer and on the defendant's shoes. It was more than enough. She *had* the verdict in her pocket.

She slowly rose, still looking at the jurors. Then she turned and addressed the judge.

"Your Honor, the People rest."

It was a solemn moment and again the courtroom turned still and silent, this time for almost a whole minute.

"Very well," the judge finally said. "I don't think any of us thought we would be at this place so soon. Mr. Haller, are you ready to proceed with the presentation of the defense's case?"

I stood.

"Your Honor, the defense is ready to proceed."

The judge nodded. He still seemed a bit shell-shocked by the defense's decision to acknowledge and accept as evidence the victim's blood on the defendant's shoes.

"Then we'll take our afternoon break a little early," he said. "And when we come back, the defense phase will begin."

PART FOUR

The Fifth Witness

Thirty-nine

I f the defense tactics during the latter stages of the prosecution's case
were surprising, the first step out of the corner during the defense phase
did nothing to lessen some observers' doubts as to the competence of
counsel. Once everyone was back in place following the afternoon break,
I went to the lectern and threw another *What the hell?* move into the trial.

"The defense calls the defendant, Lisa Trammel."

The judge asked for quiet as my client stood and made her way to the
stand. That she was called at all was shocking and caused a roll of whispers and chatter in the courtroom. As a general rule, defense attorneys
don't like to put a client on the witness stand. In a risk-to-reward ratio this
tactic ranks quite low. You can never be sure what your client will say
because you can never fully believe anything she has told you. And to be
caught in a single lie while under oath and on the stand in front of the
twelve people determining your guilt or innocence is devastating.

But this time and this case were different. Lisa Trammel had never
wavered in her claim to innocence. She had never once waffled in her
response to the evidence against her. And she had never once been
remotely interested in any sort of deal. Given this, and the developments
regarding the Herb Dahl–Louis Opparizio connection, I was viewing
her differently than I had at the start of the trial. She had insisted on having a chance to tell the jury she was innocent and it occurred to me the
night before that she should be given the opportunity the very moment it
became available. She would be the first witness.

The defendant took the oath with a slight smile on her face. It may have seemed out of place to some. After she was seated and her name was in the record, I jumped right on it.

"Lisa, I just saw you smiling a little bit when you were taking the oath to tell the truth. Why were you smiling?"

"Oh, you know, nervousness. And relief."

"Relief?"

"Yes, relief. I finally get the chance to tell my side. To tell the truth."

It started out well. From there I quickly took her through the standard list of basic questions about who she was, what she did for a living and the state of her marriage, as well as touching on the state of her home ownership.

"Did you know the victim of this terrible crime, Mitchell Bondurant?"

"Know him, no. Know of him, yes."

"What do you mean by that?"

"Well, over the past year or so, when I started to get in trouble with the mortgage, I had seen him. I went to the bank a couple times to plead my case to him. They never let me talk to him, but I saw him back there in his office. The wall of his office was completely made of glass, which was a joke. Like you could see him but not talk to him."

I checked the jury. I didn't see any outright head nods, but I thought the answer and the image my client had conjured were perfect. The banker hiding behind a wall of glass while the downtrodden and disadvantaged are kept away.

"Did you ever see him anywhere else?"

"On the morning of the murder. I saw him at the coffee shop I stop at. He was two people behind me in line. That's why I was confused when I was talking to the detectives. They were asking about Mr. Bondurant and I had just seen him that morning. I didn't know he was dead. I didn't realize they were investigating me for a murder I didn't know had even been committed."

So far, so good. She was playing it as we had discussed and rehearsed, right down to always referring to the victim with complete respect if not sympathy.

"Did you talk to Mr. Bondurant that morning?"

"No, I didn't. I was afraid he might think I was stalking him or something and take me to court. Also, I had been warned by you to avoid any encounter or confrontation with people from the bank. So I quickly got my coffee and left."

"Lisa, did you kill Mr. Bondurant?"

"No! Of course not!"

"Did you sneak up behind him with a hammer from your garage and hit him on the head so hard that he was dead before he hit the ground?"

"No, I did not!"

"Did you hit him two more times when he was on the ground?"

"No!"

I paused as if to study my notes. I wanted her denials to echo in the courtroom and in each juror's mind.

"Lisa, you made quite a name for yourself fighting the foreclosure of your home, didn't you?"

"It wasn't my intention. I just wanted to keep my home for myself and my son. I did what I thought was right. It ended up getting a lot of attention."

"It wasn't good attention for the bank, was it?"

Freeman objected, arguing that I was asking Trammel a question she would not have the knowledge to answer. The judge agreed and told me to ask something else.

"There came a time when the bank sought to stop your protests and other activities, correct?"

"Yes, they took me to court and got a restraining order against me. I couldn't have any more protests at the bank. So I had them at the courthouse."

"And did people join your cause?"

"Yes, I started a website and hundreds of people — a lot of them like me, losing their homes — joined in."

"You became quite visible as the leader of this group, didn't you?"

"I guess so. But it was never about getting attention for myself. It was about what they were doing, the frauds they were committing when they took away people's houses and condos and everything."

"How many times do you think you were on the television news or in the newspaper?"

"I didn't keep count but a few times I went national. I was on CNN and Fox."

"By the way, speaking of going national, Lisa, on the morning of the murder, did you walk by WestLand National in Sherman Oaks?"

"No, I didn't."

"That wasn't you on the sidewalk, just a half block away?"

"No, it was not."

"So the woman who testified she saw you was lying under oath?"

"I don't want to call anyone a liar but it wasn't me. Maybe she just made a mistake."

"Thank you, Lisa."

I looked down at my notes and shifted direction. By seemingly keeping my own client off guard with changing subjects and questions I was in effect keeping the jury off guard, which is what I wanted to do. I didn't want them thinking ahead of me. I wanted their undivided attention and I wanted to feed them the story in pieces and in an order of my choosing.

"Do you normally keep your garage door locked?" I asked.

"Yes, always."

"Why is that?"

"Well, it's not attached to the house. You have to go outside the house to go into the garage. So I always have the door locked. I have mostly junk in there but some stuff is valuable. My husband always treated the tools like they were precious and I have the helium tank for balloons and parties and I don't want any of the older kids in the neighborhood to get into that. And, well, I once read about somebody who had a detached garage like mine and she never locked her door. And then one day she went into the garage and a man was in there stealing stuff. He raped her. So I always keep the door locked."

"Do you have any idea why it was unlocked when the police searched your home on the day of the murder?"

"No, I always kept it locked."

"When was the last time before this trial that you saw the hammer from your workbench in its place in the garage?"

"I don't remember ever seeing it. My husband was the one who had all the tools set up in there. I'm not really good with tools."

"What about gardening tools?"

"Well, I take that back if you mean tools like that. I do the gardening and those are my tools."

"Do you have any idea how a micro-dot of blood from Mr. Bondurant ended up on one of your gardening shoes?"

Lisa stared forward with a troubled look on her face. Her chin wavered slightly as she spoke.

"I don't know. There's no explanation. I hadn't worn those shoes in a long time and I didn't kill Mr. Bondurant."

Her last line was spoken almost as a plea. It carried a sense of desperation and truth. I paused to savor it and hoped the jurors had noted it as well.

After that I spent another half hour with her, working mostly the same themes and denials. I got into more detail about her coffee-shop encounter with Bondurant as well as the foreclosure process and the hopes she had of winning the case.

Her purpose in the defense case was threefold. I needed her denial and explanations on record. I needed her personality to engender sympathy from the jury and put a human face on a case about murder. And finally, I needed to have the jurors start to wonder if this diminutive and seemingly fragile woman could lie in wait and then forcefully swing a hammer at a man's head. Three times.

By the time I came to the end of the direct examination, I felt I had gone a long way toward accomplishing all three of these goals. I tried to go out with a little crescendo of my own.

"Did you hate Mitchell Bondurant?" I asked.

"I hated what he and his bank were doing to me and others like me. But I didn't hate him personally. I didn't even know him."

"But you had lost your marriage and you had lost your job and now you were in danger of losing your house. Didn't you wish to lash out at the forces you believed were hurting you?"

"I was already lashing out. I was protesting my mistreatment. I had hired a lawyer and was fighting the foreclosure. Yes, I was angry. But I wasn't violent. I am not a violent person. I'm a schoolteacher. I was lashing out, if you have to use those words, in the only way I knew. Peacefully protesting something that was wrong. Very definitely wrong."

I glanced at the jury and thought I caught a woman in the back row wiping away a tear. I hoped to God she was. I turned back to my client and moved in for the big closing.

"I ask you once again, Lisa, did you kill Mitchell Bondurant?"

"No, I didn't."

"Did you take a hammer and strike him with it in the garage at the bank?"

"No, I wasn't there. It wasn't me."

"Then how was the hammer from your garage used to kill him?"

"I don't know."

"How was his blood found on your shoes?"

"I don't know! I didn't do it. I was *set up!*"

I paused for a moment and calmed my voice before finishing.

"One last question, Lisa. How tall are you?"

She looked confused, like a rag doll that had been pulled one way and then the other.

"What do you mean?"

"Just tell us how tall you are."

"I'm five three."

"Thank you, Lisa. I have nothing further."

Freeman had her work cut out for her. Lisa Trammel had been a solid witness and the prosecutor wasn't going to break her. She tried in a few places to get contradictory responses but Lisa more than held her own. After a half hour of Freeman trying to break down a door with a tooth-pick I began to think my client was going to sail through. But it never pays to think you're safe until your client is off the stand and sitting next to you. Freeman had at least one card up her sleeve and she eventually played it.

"When Mr. Haller asked you a little while ago if you had committed this crime, you said you were not violent. You said you were a school-teacher and that you weren't violent, do you remember that?"

"Yes, it's true."

"But isn't it true that you were forced to change schools and undergo anger-management treatment four years ago when you struck a student with a three-sided ruler?"

I quickly stood and objected and asked for a sidebar. The judge allowed us to approach.

"Judge," I whispered before Perry even asked, "there's nothing in any of the discovery about a three-sided ruler. Where's this coming from?"

"Judge," Freeman whispered before Perry even asked, "it's new information that just came to us late last week. We had to verify it."

"Oh, come on," I said. "You're going to say you didn't have her full teaching record from the get-go? You expect us to believe that?"

"You can believe whatever you want," Freeman responded. "We didn't offer it in discovery because I had no intention of bringing it up until your client started testifying about her nonviolent history. This obviously puts a lie to that and has become fair game."

I turned my attention back to Perry.

"Judge, her excuse doesn't matter. She's not playing by the rules of discovery. The question should be stricken and she should not be allowed to pursue this line of questioning."

"Judge, this is —"

"Counsel is right, Ms. Freeman. You can save it for rebuttal, provided you come up with the witnesses, but you're not going to bring it in here. It should have been part of discovery."

We returned to our positions. I would now have to put Cisco on the incident because no doubt Freeman would be bringing it up again later. This annoyed me because one of the first assignments I had given Cisco when we got the case was to completely vet our client. This event had somehow been missed.

The judge instructed the jury to disregard the prosecutor's question and then told Freeman to proceed with a different line of questioning. But I knew that bell had been rung loud and clear for the jury. The question might have been wiped from the record but not from their minds.

Freeman went on with her cross-examination, potshotting Trammel here and there but not penetrating the armor of her direct testimony. My client could not be shaken from her contention that she was not walking near WestLand National on the morning of the murder. With the exception of the three-sided ruler, it was a damn good start because it put the jury on immediate notice that we were engaged in an affirmative defense. We would not be going down without a fight.

The prosecutor took it right on up to five o'clock, thus preserving the ability to come up with something overnight and hit Trammel with it in the morning. The judge recessed for the evening and everybody was sent home. Except for me. I was heading back to the office. There was still more to do.

Before leaving the courtroom I huddled with my client at the defense table and whispered angrily to her.

"Thanks for telling me about the three-sided ruler. What else don't I know?"

"Nothing, that was stupid."

"What was stupid? That you hit a kid with a ruler or that you didn't tell me?"

"It was four years ago and he deserved it. That's all I'm going to say about it."

"It's not going to be your choice. Freeman can still bring it up on rebuttal, so you better start thinking about what you're going to say."

A look of concern creased her face.

"How can she? The judge told the jury to forget it was brought up."

"She can't bring it up on cross but she'll find a way to bring it up later. There are different rules about rebuttal. So you'd better tell me all about it and anything else I should know but you've neglected to tell me."

She glanced over my shoulder and I knew she was looking for Herb Dahl. She had no idea what Dahl had revealed to me or about the double-agent work he was doing.

"Dahl isn't here," I said. "Talk to me, Lisa. What else should I know?"

When I got back to the office I found Cisco in the reception area, hands in his pockets and chatting up Lorna, who was behind the front desk.

"What going on?" I demanded. "I thought you were going to the airport to get Shami."

"I sent Bullocks," Cisco said. "She got her and is on the way back."

"She should have stayed here preparing for her testimony, which will probably come tomorrow. You're the investigator, you should've gone to the airport. Both of them together probably can't carry the dummy."

"Relax, Boss, they got it covered. And they're fine together. Bullocks just called from the road. So you keep your cool and we'll do the rest."

I stared hard at him. I didn't care if he was six inches taller and seventy-five more pounds of muscle. I'd had it. I'd been carrying everything and I'd had it.

"You want me to relax? You want me to be cool? Fuck you, Cisco. We just started the defense and the problem is we don't have a defense. I have a lot of talk and a dummy. The problem is, unless you get your hands out of your fucking pockets and find me something, I'm the one who is going to look like the dummy. So don't tell me to be cool, okay? I'm the one who's standing in front of the jury every fucking day."

First Lorna burst out laughing and soon Cisco followed.

"You think this is funny?" I said in full outrage. "It's not funny. What the fuck makes it so fucking funny?"

Cisco held up his hands in a calming gesture until he could contain himself.

"Sorry, Boss, it's just that when you get yourself worked up...and that thing about the dummy."

This made Lorna start another cycle of laughter. I made a mental note to fire her after the trial. In fact, I'd fire them both. That would really be funny.

"Look," Cisco said, apparently sensing I wasn't picking up on the humor of the situation. "Go into your office, take your tie off and sit down in the big chair. I'll go get my stuff and I'll show you what I've got working. I've been dealing with Sacramento all day so the going is slow but I'm getting close."

"Sacramento? The state crime lab?"

"No, corporate records. Bureaucrats, Mickey. That's why it's taking forever. But you don't have to worry. You do your job and I'll do mine."

"Kind of hard to do my job when I'm waiting on you to do yours."

I headed toward my office. I threw a baleful look at Lorna as I went by. It only served to make her laugh again.

Forty

I was uninvited and unexpected. But having not seen my daughter in a week—I'd had to cancel Wednesday night pancakes because of the trial—and leaving things last time on a rough note with Maggie, I felt compelled to drop by the home they shared in Sherman Oaks. Maggie opened the door with a frown, apparently after seeing me through the peephole.

"Bad night for surprise visitors, Haller," she said.

"Well, I'll just visit Hayley for a bit, if that's okay."

"She's the one having the bad night."

She stepped back and to the side to allow me to enter.

"Really?" I said. "What's the problem?"

"She's got a ton of homework and she doesn't want to be bothered by anyone, even me."

I looked from the entry area into the living room but didn't see my daughter.

"She's in her room with the door closed. Good luck. I'll be cleaning up in the kitchen."

She left me there and I looked up the stairs. Hayley's bedroom was up there and all at once the climb looked forbidding. My daughter was a teenager and subject to all the mood swings that come with that designation. You never knew what you were going to get.

I made the journey anyway and my polite knock on her bedroom door was greeted with a *"What?"*

"It's Dad. Can I come in?"

"Dad, I have a ton of homework!"

"So that means I can't come in?"

"Whatever."

I opened the door and stepped in. She was in the bed and under the covers. She was surrounded by binders, books and a laptop.

"And you can't kiss me. I have zit cream on."

I came to the side of the bed and leaned down. I managed to kiss her on the top of the head before the arm came up to push me away.

"How much more have you got?"

"I told you, tons."

The math book was open and facedown so she wouldn't lose her place. I picked it up to see what the lesson was.

"Don't lose my spot!"

Sheer panic, end-of-the-world angst in her voice.

"Don't worry. I've been handling books going on forty years now."

As far as I could tell, the lesson was about equations assigning values to X and Y and I was completely lost. They were teaching her things beyond my reach. It was too bad it was stuff she'd never use.

"Boy, I couldn't help you even if I wanted to."

"I know, neither can Mom. I'm all alone in the world."

"Aren't we all."

I realized that she hadn't looked up at me once since I'd been in the room. It was depressing.

"Well, I just wanted to say hi. I'll leave now."

"Bye. I love you."

Still no eye contact.

"Good night."

I closed the door behind me and went down to the kitchen. The other female who seemed to be able to control my mood at her whim was sitting on a stool at the breakfast counter. She had a glass of chardonnay in front of her and an open file.

She at least looked up at me. She didn't smile but she made eye contact and I took that as a victory in this home. Her eyes then went back to the file.

"What are you working on?"

"Oh, just refreshing. I have a prelim tomorrow on a strong arm and I haven't really looked at it since I filed it."

The usual grind of the justice system. She didn't offer me a glass of wine because she knew I didn't drink. I leaned against the counter opposite the breakfast bar.

"So I'm thinking of running for district attorney," I said.

Her head shot up and she looked at me.

"What?"

"Nothing, just trying to get somebody's attention around here."

"Sorry, but it's a busy night. I've got to work."

"Yeah, well, I'll go. Your pal Andy's probably burning the oil, too."

"I think so. I was supposed to meet her for a drink after work but she canceled. What did you do to her, Haller?"

"Oh, I clipped her wings a little bit at the end of her case, then came out on mine like gangbusters. She's probably trying to figure out how to counter."

"Probably."

She went back to her file. I was clearly being wordlessly dismissed. First my daughter, now the ex-wife I still loved. I did not want to go gentle into that good night.

"So what about us?" I asked.

"What do you mean?"

"You and me. Things didn't end so good the other night at Dan Tana's."

She closed the file, slid it aside and looked up at me. Finally.

"Some nights are like that. It doesn't change anything."

I pushed off the counter and came to the breakfast bar. I leaned down on two elbows. We were eye to eye.

"So if nothing's changed, then what about us? What are we doing?"

She shrugged.

"I want to try again. I still love you, Mags. You know that."

"I also know that it didn't work before. We are the kind of people who bring home what we do. It wasn't good."

"I'm beginning to think my client is innocent and that she was set up and that even with all of that I still might not be able to get her off. How would you like to bring that home with you?"

"If it bothers you so much then maybe you should run for DA. The job's open, you know."

"Yeah, maybe I just will."

"Haller for the People."

"Yeah."

I hung around for a few minutes after that but could tell I wasn't making any headway with Maggie. She had a skill for freezing you out and making you feel it.

I told her I was going and to tell Hayley I said good night. There was no rush to bar the door before I could exit. But Maggie did call one thing after me that made me feel good.

"Just give it time, Michael."

I turned back to her.

"What are you talking about?"

"Not what, who. Hayley...and me."

I nodded and said I would.

Driving back to my place I let the accomplishments of the court day boost my spirits. I started thinking about the next witness I planned to put on the stand after Lisa. The task ahead was still formidable but it didn't help to think that far in advance. You start with a day's momentum and go from there.

I took Beverly Glen up to the top, then drove Mulholland east toward Laurel Canyon. I got glimpses of the city lights both to the north and the south. Los Angeles spread out like a shimmering ocean. I kept the music off and the windows down. I let the chill air work like loneliness into my bones.

Forty-one

All that had been won the day before was lost in a span of twenty minutes Friday morning when Andrea Freeman continued her cross-examination of Lisa Trammel. Being sandbagged by the prosecution in the midst of trial is certainly never a good thing, but in many ways it is acceptable as part of the game. It's one of the unknown unknowns. But being sandbagged by your own client is the worst thing that can happen. One of the unknown unknowns should never be the person you are defending.

With Trammel in place on the witness stand, Freeman went to the lectern carrying a thick document with crisp edges and one pink Post-it sticking out of the pages. I thought it was a prop, designed to distract me, and paid it no mind. She started things off with what I call setup questions. These were designed to get a witness's answers on the record before they were proven false. I could see the trap forming but wasn't sure where the net was going to fall.

"Now, you testified yesterday that you did not know Mitchell Bondurant, is that correct?"

"Yes, correct."

"You never met him?"

"Never."

"Never spoke to him?"

"Never."

"But you tried to meet him and speak to him, right?"

"Yes, I went to the bank twice to try to meet him to talk about my home, but he wouldn't see me."

"Do you remember when you made those efforts?"

"They were last year. But I don't remember the exact dates."

Freeman then seemed to shift directions, but I knew it was all part of a careful plan.

She asked Trammel a series of seemingly innocuous questions about her FLAG organization and its purpose. Much of this had already been touched on during my direct examination. I still couldn't see the play. I glanced over at the document with the bright pink Post-it and started to believe it was no prop. Maggie had told me yesterday that Freeman was working the night shift. Now I knew why. She had obviously found something. I leaned across the defense table in the direction of the witness stand, as if being closer to the source would speed the arrival of understanding.

"And you have a website that you use to support the efforts of FLAG, don't you?" Freeman asked.

"Yes," Trammel replied. "California Foreclosure Fighters dot com."

"And you are also on Facebook, aren't you?"

"Yes."

I could tell by the timid, cautious way in which my client said that one word that this was where the trap was set. It was the first I'd heard of Lisa on Facebook.

"For those on the jury who might not know, what exactly is Facebook, Ms. Trammel?"

I leaned back in my chair and surreptitiously pulled my phone. I quickly tapped out a text to Bullocks telling her to drop whatever she was doing and see what she could find out about Lisa's Facebook page. See what's there, I said.

"Well, it's a networking site and it lets me stay in touch with people involved in FLAG. I post updates on what is happening. I tell them where we are going to meet or march, things like that. People can set it up so they get automatic notifications on their phone or computer whenever I put a post on there. It has been very useful in our organizing."

"You can post on your Facebook page right from your phone, too, correct?"

"Yes, I can."

"And this digital location where you make these posts is called your 'wall,' correct?"

"Yes."

"And you have used your wall to do more than just send out messages about protest marches, haven't you?"

"Sometimes."

"You gave regular updates on your own foreclosure case as well, didn't you?"

"Yes, I wanted it to be like a personal journal of a foreclosure."

"Did you also use Facebook to alert the media to your activities?"

"Yes, that too."

"So in order to receive this information someone would have to sign up as a friend, correct?"

"Yes, that's how it works. People who want to friend me make the request, I accept them and then they have access to my wall."

"How many friends do you have?"

I didn't know where this was going but I knew it wasn't going to be good. I stood and objected, telling the judge that it appeared we were on a fishing expedition with no defined purpose or relevance. Freeman promised that relevance would become clear very soon and Perry let her go on.

"You can answer the question," he said to Trammel.

"Um, I think... well, last time I checked I had over a thousand."

"When did you first join Facebook?"

"Last year. I think it was in July or August when I filed papers for FLAG and started the website. I did it all at once."

"So let's make this very clear. As far as the website goes, anybody with a computer and the Internet has access, correct?"

"Right."

"But your Facebook page is a little more private and personal. To gain access a person has to be accepted by you as a friend. Is that correct?"

"Yes, but I generally friend anybody who asks. I don't know them all because there are too many. I just assume they've heard about our good work and are interested. I don't turn anybody down. That's how I got to a thousand in less than a year."

"Okay, and you have been making regular posts on your wall since you joined Facebook, correct?"

"Pretty regular, yes."

"In fact you've posted updates on this trial, have you not?"

"Yes, just my opinion of things."

I could feel my temperature rising. My suit was beginning to feel like it was made of plastic and was trapping my body heat inside. I wanted to loosen my tie but knew if a juror saw such a move during this questioning, it would send a disastrous signal.

"Now, can anyone go on the page and post a message under your name?"

"No, just me. People can respond and make their own posts, but not under my name."

"How many posts would you say you've put on your wall since last summer?"

"I have no idea. A lot."

Freeman held up the thick document with the Post-it sticking out.

"Would you believe that you have posted more than twelve hundred times on your wall?"

"I don't know."

"Well, I do. I have every one of your posts printed right here. Your Honor, may I approach the witness with this document?"

Before the judge could respond I asked for a sidebar. Perry waved us up. Freeman brought the thick document with her.

"Your Honor, what's going on?" I said. "I have the same objection I did yesterday to the prosecution's deliberate avoidance of discovery. There has been nothing about this previously, and now she wants to introduce twelve hundred Facebook posts? Come on, Judge, this isn't right."

"There has been nothing in discovery because this Facebook account was unknown until last night."

"Judge, if you believe that, I have some property west of Malibu I'd like to sell you."

"Judge, yesterday afternoon my office came into possession of a printout of all posts made by the defendant to her Facebook page. I was pointed to a set of posts from last September that are relevant to this case and the defendant's own testimony. If I can be allowed to proceed this will become very obvious, even to counsel."

"'Came into possession'?" I said. "What's that mean? Judge, you have to be an invited friend to see my client's Facebook wall. If the government engaged in subter—"

"It was given to me by a member of the media who is friends with the defendant on Facebook," Freeman interjected. "There was no subterfuge. But its source should not be at issue here. *Res ipsa loquitur*—the document speaks for itself, Judge, and I am sure the defendant can identify her own Facebook posts for the jury. Counsel is simply engaged in trying to prevent the jurors from seeing what he knows is evidence of his client's—"

"Judge, I have no idea what she's even talking about. The first I heard about a Facebook page was during her cross. Counsel's view of—"

"Very well, Ms. Freeman," Perry interrupted. "Give her the document but get to the point quickly."

"Thank you, Your Honor."

As I sat back down I felt my phone vibrate in my pocket. I pulled it and read the text under the table and out of the judge's view. It was from Bullocks and she simply said she had access to Lisa's Facebook wall and was working on my request. I typed with one hand, telling her to check the posts from September, then pocketed the phone.

Freeman gave Trammel the printout and had her verify the most recent posts as coming from her Facebook wall.

"Thank you, Ms. Trammel. Could you now go to the page I have marked with the Post-it?"

Lisa reluctantly did as instructed.

"You will see that I have highlighted a series of three of your posts from last September seventh. Could you please read the first one to the jury, including the time of the posting?"

"Um, one forty-six. 'I am heading into WestLand to see Bondurant. This time I'm not taking no for an answer.'"

"Now, you just pronounced the name Bondurant but it is misspelled, is it not, in the post?"

"Yes."

"How is it spelled in your post?"

"B-O-N-D-U-R-U-N-T."

"Bondurunt. I notice that the name is spelled that way on all posts in which he is mentioned. Was that intentional or a mistake?"

"He was taking away my house."

"Could you please answer the question?"

"Yes, it was intentional. I called him Bondurunt because he was not a good man."

I could feel the sweat moving through my hair. The hidden Lisa was about to come out.

"Could you please read the next highlighted post? With the time."

"Two eighteen. 'They wouldn't let me see him again. So unfair.'"

"And now please read the next post and time?"

"Two twenty-one. 'Found his spot. I'm going to wait for him in the garage.'"

The quiet in the courtroom was as loud as a train.

"Ms. Trammel, did you wait for Mitchell Bondurant in the parking garage at WestLand National on September seventh of last year?"

"Yes, but not that long. I realized it was dumb and he wouldn't even be out until the end of the day. So I left."

"Did you go back to that garage and wait for him on the morning of his murder?"

"No, I didn't! I wasn't there."

"You saw him in the coffee shop, you became enraged and knew just where he would be, didn't you? You went to the garage and waited for him and then —"

"Objection!" I yelled.

"— you killed him with the hammer, didn't you?"

"No! No! No!" Trammel yelled. "I didn't do it!"

She burst into tears, loudly moaning like some kind of cornered animal.

"Your Honor, objection! She's badgering the —"

Perry seemed to snap out of some reverie as he watched Trammel.

"Sustained!"

Freeman stopped. The courtroom was again silent except for the sound of my client sobbing. The courtroom deputy came over with a box of tissues and Lisa's tears finally subsided.

"Thank you, Your Honor," Freeman finally said. "I have no further questions."

I asked for an early morning break so my client could compose herself and I'd have time to decide whether to continue on redirect. The judge granted the request, probably because he felt sorry for me.

Lisa's tears did not undercut the fact that Freeman had been masterful in setting her trap. But all was not lost. The best thing about a setup defense is that almost every piece of damning evidence or testimony — even when it comes from your own client — can become part of the setup.

After the jury was led out I walked up to the witness stand to console my client. I pulled two tissues out of the box and handed them to her. She took them and started dabbing her eyes. I cupped my hand over the microphone to avoid broadcasting our conversation across the courtroom. I tried my best to control my tone.

"Lisa, why the hell am I finding out about Facebook now? Do you have any idea what this could do to our case?"

"I thought you knew! I friended Jennifer."

"My Jennifer?"

"Yes!"

Nothing like having both your junior associate and your client know more than you.

"But what about these posts from September? Do you know how damaging they are?"

"I'm sorry! I totally forgot about them. They were so long ago."

It looked like another cascade of tears was coming. I tried to head it off.

"Well, we're lucky. We might be able to make this work for us."

She stopped dabbing at her face with the tissue and looked at me.

"Really?"

"Maybe. But I need to go outside and call Bullocks."

"Who's Bullocks?"

"Sorry, it's what we call Jennifer. You sit tight and pull yourself together."

"Am I going to be asked more questions?"

"Yes. I want to do some redirect."

"Then can I go fix my face?"

"That's a good idea. Just don't take long."

I finally got out to the hallway and called Bullocks at the office.

"Did you see the entries on September seventh?" I asked by way of a greeting.

"Just saw them. If Freeman——"

"She already did."

"Shit!"

"Yeah, well, it was bad but there might be a way out. Lisa said you're her friend on Facebook?"

"Yes, and I'm sorry. I knew she had a page. It never occurred to me to go back and look at previous posts on her wall."

"We'll talk about it later. Right now, I need to know if you have access to her list of friends."

"I'm looking at it right now."

"Okay, first I want you to print out all the names, give them to Lorna and have Rojas drive her over here with them. Right away. Then I want you and Cisco to start working the names yourselves, find out who these people are."

"There's more than a thousand. You want us to run them *all* down?"

"If you have to. I'm looking for a connection to Opparizio."

"Opparizio? Why would——"

"Trammel was a threat to him, just like she was a threat to the bank. She was protesting fraud in foreclosure. The fraud was being committed by Opparizio's company. We know through Herb Dahl that she was on Opparizio's radar. It stands to reason that somebody in that company was checking on her through Facebook. Lisa just testified that she accepted anybody who asked to friend her. Maybe we'll get lucky and find a name we know."

There was a silence and then Bullocks tumbled to what I was thinking.

"By tracking her on Facebook they would know what she was up to."

"And they could have known that at one time she waited for Bondurant in the garage."

"And then they could have constructed his murder around that record."

"Bullocks, I hate to tell you this but you're thinking like a defense lawyer."

"We'll get right on this."

I could hear the urgency in her voice.

"Good, but first print that list and get it over to me. I start redirect in about fifteen minutes. Tell Lorna to walk it right in to me. Then if you and Cisco find something, text it to me right away."

"You got it."

Forty-two

Freeman was still swelling with pride over her morning victory when I got back to the courtroom. She sauntered over, folded her arms and leaned her hip against the defense table.

"Haller, tell me that was just an act, you not knowing about the Facebook page."

"Sorry, I can't tell you that."

She rolled her eyes.

"Uh-oh, sounds like somebody needs a client who isn't hiding things ... or maybe a new investigator who can find them."

I ignored the taunt, hoping she would stop gloating and go back to her table. I started flipping through the pages of a legal pad, pretending I was looking for something.

"That was like manna from heaven last night when I got that print-out and read those posts."

"You must've been very pleased with yourself. Which asshole reporter gave it to you?"

"Wouldn't you like to know."

"I will know. Whichever one breaks out the next exclusive from the DA's office will be the one who helped you out. They'll never get so much as a 'no comment' from me."

She chuckled. My threat had nothing to do with her. She had gotten the posts out before the jury and nothing else mattered. I finally looked up at her and squinted.

"You don't get it, do you?"

"Get what? That the jury now knows your client was previously at the scene of the crime — proving that she had knowledge of where to find the victim? No, I completely get that."

I looked away and shook my head.

"You'll see. Excuse me."

I stood up and headed toward the witness stand. Lisa Trammel had just returned from the restroom. She had redrawn the makeup on her eyes. When she started to speak, I cupped the microphone again.

"What were you doing talking to that bitch? She's a horrible person," she said.

A bit stunned by the unbridled anger, I looked back at Freeman, now sitting at the prosecution table.

"She's not horrible and she's not a bitch, okay? She's just doing —"

"Yes, she is. You don't know."

I leaned close to her and whispered.

"And what, you do? Look, Lisa, don't go bipolar on me. You've got less than a half hour of testimony still to go. Let's just get through it without cluing the jury in to your issues. Okay?"

"I don't know what you're talking about but it's very hurtful."

"Well, I'm sorry about that. I'm trying to defend you and it doesn't help me to have to find out about things like Facebook when you're being cross-examined by the prosecution."

"I told you, I'm sorry. But your associate knew."

"Yeah, well, I didn't."

"Look, you said before that you might be able to make this work in our favor. How?"

"Simple. If someone was going to set you up, this Facebook page would have been a damn good place to start."

Talk about manna from heaven. Her eyes looked upward and pure relief colored her face as she came to understand the tactic I was about to employ. The anger that had darkened her expression only a minute before was now completely gone. It was just then that the judge entered the courtroom, ready to go. I nodded to my client and went back to the defense table as the judge instructed the deputy to bring in the jury.

Once everyone was situated the judge asked if I wished to question my client on redirect examination. I jumped up from my seat like I had been waiting ten years for the opportunity. It cost me. A jolt of pain moved like lightning across my torso. The ribs may have mended but the wrong move still lit me up.

Just as I walked to the lectern the rear door of the courtroom opened and Lorna came in. Perfect timing. Carrying a file and a motorcycle helmet, she walked swiftly down the center aisle to the gate.

"Your Honor, could I have a moment with my associate?"

"Make it fast, please."

I met Lorna at the gate and she handed over the file.

"That's the list of all her Facebook friends, but as of when I left, Dennis and Jennifer hadn't found any connection to you know who."

It was strange hearing Cisco and Bullocks referred to by their real names. I looked down at the helmet she carried. I whispered.

"You rode Cisco's motorcycle over here?"

"You wanted it quick and I knew I could park up close."

"Where's Rojas?"

"I don't know. He didn't answer his cell."

"Great. Listen, I want you to leave Cisco's bike where it is and walk back to the office. I don't want you riding that suicide machine."

"I'm not your wife anymore. I'm his."

Just as she whispered this I looked over her shoulder and saw Maggie McPherson sitting in the gallery. I wondered if she was there for me or for Freeman.

"Look," I said. "That's got nothing to do with—"

"Mr. Haller?" the judge intoned from behind me. "We're waiting."

"Yes, Your Honor," I said loudly without turning around. Then in a whisper to Lorna, I said, "Walk back."

I returned to the lectern, opening the file. It contained nothing more than raw data—a thousand-plus names, listed in two columns per page—but I looked at it as if I had just been given the Holy Grail.

"Okay, Lisa, let's talk about your Facebook page. You testified earlier that you have more than a thousand friends. Are all of these people personally known to you?"

"No, not at all. Because so many people know about me through

FLAG, I just assume that when someone wants to friend me, they are supportive of that cause. I just accept them."

"So then the posts on your wall are open to a significant number of people who are Facebook friends but in reality complete strangers to you. Is that right?"

"Yes, that's correct."

I felt my phone vibrate in my pocket.

"So any one of these strangers who was interested in your movements, past or present, could just go to your Facebook page and see the posts on your wall, am I right?"

"Yes, that's right."

"For example, someone could go to that page right now and scroll through your updates and see that back in September of last year you hung out in the garage at WestLand, waiting for Mitchell Bondurant, correct?"

"Yes, they could."

I pulled my phone out of my pocket and, using the lectern as a blind, brought it up and put it down on the work surface. While leafing through the printout of names with one hand, I used the other to open the text I had just received. The message was from Bullocks.

3rd page, right column, 5th from bottom — Don Driscoll. We have a Donald Driscoll as former ALOFT in IT. We're working it.

Bingo. Now I had something I could hit out of the park.

"Your Honor, I would like to show the witness this document. It is a printout of the names of people who have friended Lisa Trammel on Facebook."

Freeman, seeing her victorious morning in jeopardy, objected but the judge overruled without argument from me, saying Freeman had opened this door herself. I gave my client the list and returned to the lectern.

"Can you please go to the third page of the printout and read the name that is fifth up from the bottom in the right-side column?"

Freeman objected again, stating that the list was unverified. The judge advised her to challenge it on re-cross if she thought I was introducing a bogus exhibit. I told Lisa she could read the name.

"Don Driscoll."

"Thank you. Now is that name familiar to you?"

"Not really, no."

"But he is one of your Facebook friends."

"I know but like I said, I don't know everybody who friends me. There are too many."

"Well, do you recall if Don Driscoll ever contacted you directly and identified himself as working for a company called ALOFT?"

Freeman objected and asked for a sidebar. We were called to the bench.

"Judge, what's going on here? Counsel can't just throw names around. I want an offer of proof that he isn't just throwing darts at the list and picking out a name."

Perry nodded thoughtfully.

"I agree, Mr. Haller."

My phone was still on the lectern. If I had gotten any updates from Bullocks they weren't going to help me now.

"Judge, we could go into chambers and get my investigator on the phone, if you wish. But I would ask the court for some leeway here. The prosecution opened up this Facebook issue just this morning and I am trying to respond. We can hold things up for an offer of proof or we can wait until the defense calls Don Driscoll to the stand and Ms. Freeman can have at him and see if I am mischaracterizing who he is."

"You are going to call him?"

"I don't think I have any choice in light of the state's decision to pursue my client's old Facebook posts."

"Very well, we'll wait for Mr. Driscoll to testify. Don't disappoint me, Mr. Haller, and come into court and say you changed your mind. I won't be happy if that happens."

"Yes, Your Honor."

We returned to our places and I asked Lisa the question again.

"Did Don Driscoll ever contact you on Facebook or anywhere else and say he worked for ALOFT?"

"No, he didn't."

"Are you familiar with ALOFT?"

"Yes. That is the name of the foreclosure mill that banks like West-Land use to file all the paperwork on their foreclosures."

"Was this company involved in the foreclosure of your home?"

"Yes, totally."

"Is ALOFT an acronym? Do you know what it stands for?"

"A. Louis Opparizio Financial Technologies. That's the name of the company."

"Now, what would it mean to you if this person Donald Driscoll, who was one of your friends on Facebook, was employed by ALOFT?"

"It would mean that somebody from ALOFT was getting all my posts."

"So, essentially, this person Driscoll would know where you've been and where you're going, correct?"

"That's correct."

"He would have been privy to your posts from last September that said you had found Mr. Bondurant's parking spot at the bank and that you were going to wait for him, correct?"

"Yes, correct."

"Thank you, Lisa. I have nothing further."

On my way back to my seat I had to steal a glance at Freeman. She was no longer beaming. She was staring straight ahead. I then looked out into the gallery for Maggie, but she was gone.

Forty-three

The afternoon belonged to Shamiram Arslanian, my forensics expert from New York. I had used Shami to great effect in previous trials and that was again the plan here. She had degrees from Harvard, MIT and John Jay, was currently a research fellow at the latter, and had a winning and telegenic personality. On top of that she had an integrity that shone through on the witness stand with every word of testimony. She was a defense lawyer's dream. No doubt, she was a gun for hire but she took the job only if she believed in the science and in what she was going to say on the stand. What's more, there was a bonus for me in this case. She was the exact same height as my client.

During the lunch break Arslanian had set up a mannequin in front of the jury box. It was a male figure standing exactly six foot two and a half inches tall, the same height as Mitchell Bondurant in his shoes. It wore a suit similar to the one Bondurant was wearing on the morning of his murder and the exact same shoes. The mannequin had joints that allowed for a full range of natural human motion.

After court resumed and my witness took the stand, I took my time going through her voluminous bona fides. I wanted the jurors to understand this woman's accomplishments and to like her offhand manner of answering questions. I also wanted them to realize that her skills and knowledge put her on a different plane than the state's forensic witnesses. A higher plane.

Once the impression had been made I got down to the business of the mannequin.

"Now, Dr. Arslanian, I asked you to review aspects of the murder of Mitchell Bondurant, is that true?"

"Yes, you did."

"And in particular I wanted to examine the physics of the crime, true?"

"Yes, you basically asked me to find out if your client could've actually done the crime in the way the police said she did."

"And did you conclude that she could have?"

"Well, yes and no. I determined that yes, she could have done it but it wouldn't have been in the manner the detectives out here were saying."

"Can you explain your conclusion?"

"I would rather demonstrate, using myself in the place of your client."

"How tall are you, Dr. Arslanian?"

"I'm five foot three in my stocking feet, same height that I was told Lisa Trammel is."

"And did I send you a hammer that was a duplicate of the hammer recovered by police and declared to be the murder weapon?"

"Yes, you did. And I brought it with me."

She held the duplicate hammer up from the shelf at the front of the witness box.

"And did you get photos from me depicting the gardening shoes that were seized from the defendant's unlocked garage and later found to have the victim's blood on them?"

"Yes, you did that, too, and I was able to procure an exact duplicate pair on the Internet. I'm wearing them now."

She kicked one leg out from the side of the witness box, showing off the waterproof shoe. There was a polite round of laughter in the courtroom. I asked the judge to allow my witness to conduct the demonstration of her findings and he agreed over objection from the prosecution.

Arslanian left the witness box with the hammer and proceeded with her demonstration.

"The question I was asking myself was, could a woman the defendant's height, which is five foot three like mine, have struck the fatal blow on the crown of the head of a man who is six foot two and a half in his work shoes? Now the hammer, which adds about an extra ten inches in reach, is helpful in this regard, but is it enough? That was my question."

"Doctor, if I can interrupt, can you tell us about your mannequin and how you prepared it for your testimony?"

"Of course. Everybody, this is Manny and I use him all the time when I testify in trials and when I conduct tests in my lab back at John Jay. He has all the joints like a real human being and he comes apart if I need him to and the best thing is he never talks back or says I look fat in my jeans."

Again she scored some polite laughter.

"Thank you, Doctor," I said quickly before the judge could tell her to keep it serious. "If you could go on with your demonstration."

"Sure. Well, what I did was use the autopsy report and the photos and drawings to exactly locate the spot on the skull of the mannequin where the fatal blow was struck. Now we know because of the notch in the striking face that Mr. Bondurant was struck from behind. We also know by the even depth of the depression fracture to the skull that he was struck evenly on the top of the head. So by attaching the hammer at a flush angle like so..."

Climbing onto a short stepladder next to Manny, she was able to place the strike face of the hammer against the crown of the skull and then hold it in place with two bands that went under the faceless mannequin's chin. She then stepped down and gestured to the hammer and its handle, which was extending at a right angle and parallel to the floor.

"So as you can see, this doesn't work. I'm five four in these shoes, the defendant is five four in these shoes, and the handle is way up here."

She reached up to the hammer. It was impossible for her to grasp it properly.

"What this tells us is that the fatal blow could not have been struck by the defendant with the victim in this position — standing up straight, head level. Now, what other positions are available that do work with what we know? We know the attack was from behind so if the victim was leaning forward — say he dropped his keys or something — you see that it still doesn't work because I can't reach the hammer over his back."

As she spoke she manipulated the mannequin, bending it over at the waist, and then reaching toward the hammer's handle from the rear.

"No, doesn't work. Now for two days, between classes, I looked for other ways to strike the blow, but the only way I could make it work was if the victim was on his knees or crouched down for some reason, or if he happened to be looking up at the ceiling."

She manipulated the mannequin again and stood it up straight. She then bent the head back at the neck and the handle came down. She grasped it and the position looked comfortable, but the mannequin was looking almost straight up.

"Now, according to the autopsy there were significant abrasions on both knees and one even had a cracked patella. These were described as impact injuries coming from Mr. Bondurant's fall to the ground after he was struck. He dropped to his knees first and then fell forward, face-first. What we call a dead fall. So with that kind of injury to the knees, I rule out that he was kneeling or crouched close to the ground. That leaves only this."

She gestured toward the mannequin's head, angled sharply back with the faceplate up. I checked the jury. Everybody was watching intently. It was like show-and-tell in first grade.

"Okay, Doctor, if you put the angle of the head back to even or just slightly elevated, did you come up with a range of heights for the real perpetrator of this crime?"

Freeman jumped up and objected in a tone of complete exasperation.

"Your Honor, this isn't science. This is junk science. The whole thing is smoke and mirrors, and now he's asking her to give the height of someone who *could* have done it? It is impossible to know exactly what posture or neck angle the victim of this horrible —"

"Your Honor, closing arguments are not till next week," I interjected. "If the state has an objection then counsel should state it to the court instead of speaking to the jury and trying to sell —"

"All right," the judge said. "Both of you, stop it. Mr. Haller, you've been given wide latitude with this witness. But I was beginning to agree with Ms. Freeman until she got on her soapbox. Objection sustained."

"Thank you, Your Honor," Freeman said as though she had just been rescued from abandonment in a desert.

I composed myself, looked at my witness and her mannequin, then checked my notes and finally nodded. I'd gotten what I could.

"I have no further questions," I said.

Freeman did have questions but try as she might to shake Shami Arslanian from her direct testimony and conclusions, the veteran prosecutor never got the veteran witness to concede an inch. Freeman worked her on cross for nearly forty minutes but the closest she got to scoring a point for the prosecution was to get Arslanian to acknowledge that there was no way of knowing for sure what happened in the garage when Bondurant was murdered. The judge had announced earlier in the week that Friday would be a short day because of a districtwide judges' meeting planned for late in the afternoon. So there was no afternoon break and we worked until almost four before Perry recessed the trial for the weekend. We moved into the two-day break with me feeling like I had the upper hand. We had weathered the state's case by potshotting much of the evidence, then closed out the week with Lisa Trammel's denial and claim to be the victim of a setup, and my forensic witness's supposition that it was physically impossible for the defendant to commit the crime. Unless, of course, she happened to strike the fatal blow to the victim while he was looking straight up at the ceiling of the parking garage.

I believed these were powerful seeds of doubt. Things felt good to me and when I finished packing my briefcase, I lingered at the defense table, looking through a file for something that wasn't really there. I was half expecting Freeman to come over and beg me to sell my client a plea bargain.

But it didn't happen. When I looked up from my phony busywork she was gone.

I took the elevator down to two. The judges might all be getting off early for a meeting on the eroding rules of courtroom decorum, but I figured the DA's office was still working until five. I asked at the counter for Maggie McPherson and was allowed back. She shared an office with another deputy DA but luckily he was on vacation. We were alone. I pulled the missing man's chair away from his desk and sat down in front of Maggie.

"I came by court a couple times today," she said. "Watched some of your direct with the lady from John Jay. She's a good witness."

"Yeah, she's good. And I saw you there. I didn't know who you were there for — me or Freeman."

She smiled.

"Maybe I was there for myself. I still learn things from you, Haller."

Now I smiled.

"Maggie McFierce learning from me? Really?"

"Well—"

"No, don't answer that."

We both laughed.

"Either way, I'm glad you came by," I said. "What's going on this weekend with you and Hay?"

"I don't know. We'll be around. You have to work, I guess."

I nodded.

"We have to track somebody down, I think. And Monday and Tuesday are going to be the biggest days of the trial. But maybe we can do a movie or something."

"Sure."

We were silent for a few moments. I had just come off one of my best days in court ever, yet I felt pierced by a growing sense of loss and sadness. I looked at my ex-wife.

"We're never going to get back together, are we, Maggie?"

"What?"

"It just kind of hit me. You want it the way it is now. There when one of us really needs it, but never what it was. You won't ever give me that."

"Why do you want to talk about this now, Michael? You're in the middle of a trial. You have—"

"I'm in the middle of my life, Mags. I just wish there was a way to make you and Hayley proud of me."

She leaned forward and reached out. She put her hand against my cheek for a moment and then pulled it back.

"I think Hayley is proud of you."

"Yeah? What about you?"

She smiled but it was sort of in a sad way.

"I think you should go home and not think about this or the trial or anything else just for tonight. Let your mind clear of the clutter. Relax."

I shook my head.

"Can't. I have a meeting at five with a snitch."

"On the Trammel case? What snitch?"

344

"Never mind, and you're just trying to change the subject. You'll never completely forgive and forget, will you? It's not in you and maybe it's what makes you such a good prosecutor."

"Oh, I'm so good all right. That's why I'm stuck out here in Van Nuys filing armed robberies."

"That's politics. Has nothing to do with skills and dedication."

"It doesn't matter and I can't have this conversation now. I'm still on the clock and you need to go see your snitch. Why don't you call me tomorrow if you want to take Hayley to a movie. I'll probably let you take her while I run errands or something."

I stood up. I knew a losing cause when I saw one.

"Okay, I'm leaving. I'll call you tomorrow. But I hope you'll come with us to the movie."

"We'll see."

"Right."

I took the stairs down for a quick exit. I crossed the plaza and headed north on Sylmar toward Victory. I soon came to a motorcycle parked at the curb. I recognized it as Cisco's. A prized '63 H-D panhead with a black pearl tank and matching fenders. I chuckled. Lorna, my second ex-wife, had actually done what I had told her to do. It was a first.

She had left the bike unlocked, probably figuring it was safe in front of the courthouse and adjoining police station. I steered it away from the curb and walked it down Sylmar. I must've been quite a sight, a man in his nicest Corneliani suit pushing a Harley down the street, briefcase propped on the handlebars.

When I finally got back to the office it was only four thirty, a half hour before Herb Dahl was scheduled to come in for a briefing. I called for a staff meeting and tried plugging back into the case as a means of pushing out thoughts about the conversation with Maggie. I told Cisco where I had parked his bike and I asked for an update on the list of our client's Facebook friends.

"First of all, why the hell didn't I know about her Facebook account?" I asked.

"It's my fault," Aronson said quickly. "Like I told you earlier, I knew about it and even accepted her friend request. I just didn't realize the significance of it."

"I missed it, too," Cisco said. "She friended me, too. I looked and didn't see anything. I should've looked harder."

"Me, too," Lorna added.

I looked at their faces. It was a unified front.

"Great," I said. "I guess all four of us missed it and our client didn't bother to tell us. So the bunch of us, I guess we're all fired."

I paused for effect.

"Now, what about this name you came up with? This Don Driscoll, where did that come from and do we know anything more? Freeman could've unwittingly dropped the key to the whole case in our laps this morning, people. What've we got?"

Bullocks looked at Cisco, deferring.

"As you know," he said, "ALOFT was sold in February to the LeMure Fund with Opparizio still in place to run it. Because LeMure is a publicly traded company, everything about the deal was monitored by the Federal Trade Commission and made public to shareholders. Including a list of employees that would remain at ALOFT following the transition. I have the list, dated December fifteenth."

"So we started cross-referencing the ALOFT employees to the list of Lisa's Facebook friends," Bullocks said. "Luckily Donald Driscoll was early in the alphabet. We came up with him pretty quickly."

I nodded, impressed.

"So who is Driscoll?"

"In the FTC docs his name was in a group listed under information technology," Cisco said. "So what the hell, I called IT at ALOFT and asked for him. I was told that Donald Driscoll used to work there but his employment contract expired on February first and it wasn't extended. He's gone."

"You've started the trace?" I asked.

"We have. But it's a common name and that's slowing us down. As soon as we have something, you'll be the first to know."

Running names from the private sector always took time. It wasn't as easy as being a cop and simply typing a name into one of the many law enforcement databases.

"Don't let up," I said. "This could be the whole game right here."

"Don't worry, Boss," Cisco said. "Nobody's letting up."

Forty-four

Donald Driscoll, thirty-one, formerly employed by ALOFT, lived in the Belmont Shore area of Long Beach. On Sunday morning I rode down with Cisco to tag Driscoll with a subpoena, the hope being that he would talk to me before I had to put him on the witness stand blind.

Rojas agreed to work on his day off to help make up for his misdeeds. He drove the Lincoln and we sat in the back, Cisco updating me on his conclusions regarding his latest investigations of the Bondurant murder. There was no doubt that the defense case was coming together and Driscoll just might be the witness who could cap it all off.

"You know," I said, "we could actually win this thing if Driscoll cooperates and says what I think he's going to say."

"That's a big if," Cisco replied. "And look, we have to be prepared for anything with this guy. For all we know, he could *be* the guy. Do you know how tall he is? Six four. Has it on his driver's license."

I looked over at him.

"Which I wasn't supposed to see but happened to get access to," he said.

"Don't tell me about any crimes, Cisco."

"I'm just saying I saw the info on his license, that's all."

"Fine. Leave it at that. So what do you suggest we do when we get down there? I thought we were just going to knock on the door."

"We are. But you still have to be careful."

"I'll be standing behind you."

"Yeah, you're a true friend."

"I am. And by the way, if I put you on the stand tomorrow you're going to have to come up with a shirt that has sleeves *and* a collar. Make yourself presentable, man. I don't know how Lorna puts up with your shit."

"So far she's put up with it longer than she ever put up with yours."

"Yeah, I guess that's true."

I turned and looked out the window. I had two ex-wives who were probably also my two best friends. But it didn't go past that. I'd had them but couldn't hold them. What did that say about me? I lived in a daydream that one day Maggie, my daughter and I would live together again as a family. The reality was, it was never going to happen.

"You all right, Boss?"

I turned back to Cisco.

"Yeah, why?"

"I don't know. You're looking a little shaky there. Why don't you let me go knock on the door and if he'll talk I'll give you a bump on the cell and you come in."

"No, we do it together."

"You're the boss."

"Yeah, I'm the boss."

But I felt like the loser. I decided right at that moment that I was going to change things and find a way to redeem myself. Right after the trial.

Belmont Shore had the feel of a rustic beach town even though it was part of Long Beach. Driscoll's residence was a two-story, 1950s-style apartment building of aqua blue and white off Bayshore near the pier.

Driscoll's place was on the second floor where an exterior walkway ran along the front of the building. Apartment 24 was halfway down. Cisco knocked and then took a position to the side of the door, leaving me standing there.

"Are you kidding?" I asked.

He just looked at me. He wasn't.

I took a step to the side. We waited but nobody answered even though it was before ten on a Sunday morning. Cisco looked at me and raised his eyes as if to ask *What do you want to do?*

I didn't answer. I turned to the railing and looked down at the parking lot in front. I saw some empty spaces and they were numbered. I pointed.

"Let's find twenty-four and see if his car is here."

"You go," Cisco said. "I'll check around up here."

"What?"

I didn't see anything to check around for. We were on a five-foot-wide walkway that ran in front of every second-floor apartment. No furniture, no bikes, just concrete.

"Just go check the parking lot."

I headed back downstairs. After ducking to look under the front of three cars to get the number painted on the curb, I realized that the parking slot numbers did not correspond to the apartment numbers. It was a twelve-unit building, apartments 1 through 6 on the bottom and 21 through 26 up top. But the parking lot spaces were numbered 1 through 16. I took a guess that under that number scheme Driscoll had number 10 if each apartment got one space, which stood to reason since there were only sixteen spots and I saw that two were labeled as guest parking and two were marked for handicapped parking.

I was in the middle of turning these numbers in my head and looking at the ten-year-old BMW parked in slot 10 when Cisco called my name from the walkway above. I looked and he waved me up.

When I got back up there he was standing in the open door of apartment 24. He waved me in.

"He was asleep but he finally answered."

I walked in and saw a disheveled man sitting on a couch in a sparsely furnished living room. His hair was sticking up in frozen curls and knots on the right side. He huddled with a blanket around his shoulders. Even so, I could tell he matched a photo Cisco had pulled off Donald Driscoll's own Facebook account.

"That's a lie," he said. "I didn't invite him in. He *broke* in."

"No, you invited me," Cisco said. "I have a witness."

He pointed to me. The bleary-eyed man followed the finger and looked at me for the first time. I could see recognition in his eyes. I knew then that it was Driscoll and that we were on to something here.

"Hey, look, I don't know what this—"

"Are you Donald Driscoll?" I asked.

"I'm not telling you shit, man. You can't just break—"

"*Hey!*" Cisco yelled loudly.

The man jumped in his seat. Even I startled, not having expected Cisco's new interviewing tactic.

"Just answer the question," Cisco continued in a calmer voice. "Are you Donald Driscoll?"

"Who wants to know?"

"You know who wants to know," I said. "You recognized me the moment you looked at me. And you know why we're here, Donald, don't you?"

I walked across the room, pulling the subpoena out of my windbreaker. Driscoll was tall but slightly built and vampire white, which was strange for a guy living a block from the beach. I dropped the folded document in his lap.

"What is this?" he said, slapping it onto the floor without even unfolding it.

"It's a subpoena and you can throw it on the floor and choose not to read it but that doesn't matter. You've been served, Donald. I have a witness and I am an officer of the court. You don't show up tomorrow at nine to testify and you'll be in jail on a charge of contempt by lunchtime."

Driscoll reached down and grabbed the subpoena.

"Are you fucking kidding me? You're going to get me killed."

I glanced over at Cisco. We were definitely on to something.

"What are you talking about?"

"I'm talking about that I can't testify! If I come anywhere near that courthouse they'll kill me. They're probably watching this place right fucking now!"

I looked again at Cisco and then back down at the man on the couch.

"Who is going to kill you, Donald?"

"I'm not saying. Who the fuck do you think?"

He threw the subpoena at me and it bounced off my chest and fluttered to the ground. He jumped from the couch and started to break for the open door. The blanket fell and I saw he was wearing only gym shorts and a T-shirt. Before he made it three strides Cisco hit him with his body like an outside linebacker. Driscoll caromed into the wall and fell to the floor. A framed poster of a girl on a surfboard slid down the wall and the frame broke on the floor next to him.

Cisco calmly bent down, pulled Driscoll up and walked him right back to the couch. I stepped over to the door and closed it, just in case the wall banging brought out a curious neighbor. I then came back to the living room.

"You can't run from this, Donald," I said. "You tell us what you know and what you did and we can help you."

"Help me get killed, you assholes. And I think you fucking broke my shoulder."

He started working his arm and shoulder like he was warming up to pitch nine innings. He grimaced.

"How's it feel?" I said.

"I told you, it feels broken. I felt something give."

"You wouldn't be able to move it," Cisco said.

Cisco's voice had a threatening tone to it, as if there would be further consequences if the shoulder actually was broken. When I spoke, my voice was calm and welcoming.

"What do you know, Donald? What would make you a danger to Opparizio?"

"I don't know anything and I didn't say that name—you did."

"You have to understand something. You have been served with a valid subpoena. You show up and you testify or you stay in jail until you do. But think about this, Donald. If you testify about what you know about ALOFT and what you did, then you're protected. Nobody will make a move against you because it would be obvious where it came from. It's your only move here."

He shook his head.

"Yeah, obvious if they did it now. What about in ten years when nobody remembers your stupid-ass trial and they can still hide behind all the money in the world?"

I didn't really have an answer to that one.

"Look, I've got a client on trial for what amounts to her life. She's got a little boy and they're trying to take everything away from her. I'm not going to—"

"Fuck off, man, she probably did it. We're talking about two different things here. I can't help her. I have no evidence. I've got nothing. Just leave me the hell alone, would you? What about *my* life? I want to have a life, too."

I looked at him and sadly shook my head.

"I can't leave you alone. I'm putting you on the stand tomorrow. You can refuse to answer questions. You can even take the Fifth if you've committed crimes. But you'll be there and they'll be there. They'll know they've got a continuing problem with you. Your best bet is to spill it all, Donald. Put it out there and be protected. Five years, ten years, they'll never be able to do a damn thing to you because there will be a record."

Driscoll was staring at an ashtray full of coins on the coffee table, but he was seeing something else.

"Maybe I should get an attorney," he said.

I gave Cisco a look. This was exactly what I didn't want to have happen. A witness with his own attorney was never a good thing.

"Sure, fine, if you've got a lawyer, bring him. But a lawyer is not going to stop the forward progress of this trial. That subpoena is bullet-proof, Donald. A lawyer will charge you a grand to try to knock it down but it won't work. It will only make the judge mad at you for making him take time out of the trial."

My phone started to buzz in my pocket. It was early enough on a Sunday to be unusual. I pulled it out to check the display. Maggie McPherson.

"Think about what I said, Donald. I have to take this but I'll be quick."

As I answered I walked into the kitchen.

"Maggie? Everything all right?"

"Sure, why not?"

"I don't know. It's kind of early for a Sunday. Is Hayley still asleep?"

Sunday was always my daughter's catch-up day. She could easily sleep past noon if not roused.

"Of course. I'm just calling because we didn't hear from you yesterday so I guess that makes today movie day."

"Uh..."

I vaguely remembered promising a movie outing when I had been in Maggie's office Friday afternoon.

"You're busy."

The Tone had entered her voice. The judgmental you-are-full-of-shit Tone.

"I am at the moment. I'm down in Long Beach talking to a wit."

"So, no movie? Is that what I should tell her?"

I could hear both Cisco's and Driscoll's voices from the living room but was too distracted to hear what was said.

"No, Maggie, don't tell her that. I'm just not sure when I'm going to be out of here. Let me finish here and I'll call you back. Before she even wakes up, okay?"

"Fine, we'll wait on you."

Before I could respond she disconnected. I put the phone away and then looked around. It appeared that the kitchen was the least used room in the apartment.

I went back to the living room. Driscoll was still on the couch and Cisco was still standing close enough to prevent another escape attempt.

"Donald was just telling me how he wanted to testify," Cisco said.

"Is that right? How come you changed your mind, Donald?"

I moved past Cisco so that I stood right in front of Driscoll. He looked up at me and shrugged, then nodded in Cisco's direction.

"He said you've never lost a witness and that if it comes down to it he knows people who can handle their people without breaking a sweat. I kind of believe him."

I nodded and momentarily had a vision from the dark room at the Saints' clubhouse. I quickly shut it out.

"Yeah, well, he's right," I said. "So you are saying you want to cooperate?"

"Yeah. I'll tell you everything I know."

"Good. Then why don't we start right now?"

Forty-five

At the start of the trial Andrea Freeman had successfully kept my associate, Jennifer Aronson, off the defense table as my second chair by challenging her listing as a defense witness as well. On Monday morning, when it was time for Aronson to testify, the prosecutor sought to prevent her testimony, challenging it as irrelevant to the charges. I couldn't prevent the first challenge from succeeding but felt I had the legal gods on my side for the second. I also had a judge who still owed me after toeing the prosecution's line on two critical decisions earlier in the trial.

"Your Honor," I said, "this can't really be a sincere objection by counsel. The state has set before the jury a motive for the defendant's supposedly having committed this crime. The victim was engaged in taking her house away. She was angry and frustrated, and she killed. That's their case in its entirety. So now to object to a witness who will provide the details of that inciting action, the foreclosure, on grounds of relevance is specious at best and at worst pure hypocrisy."

The judge wasted no time in his response and ruling.

"Objection to the witness is overruled. We will now bring in the jury."

Once the jury was in place and Aronson was in the witness's seat, I proceeded with my direct examination, starting with a clarification of why she was the defense expert on the foreclosure of Lisa Trammel's home.

"Now Ms. Aronson, you were not counsel of record on the Trammel foreclosure, were you?"

"No, I was associate counsel to you."

I nodded.

"As such, you really did all the work while my name was on the pleadings, correct?"

"Yes, correct. Most of the documents in the foreclosure file were prepared by me. I was intimately involved in the case."

"Such is the life of a first-year associate, correct?"

"I guess so."

We shared a smile. From there I walked her step by step through the foreclosure proceedings. I don't ever say you have to talk down to a jury but you do have to talk in ways that are universally understandable. From stockbrokers to soccer moms, there are twelve minds on the jury and they've all been marinated in different life experiences. You have to tell them all the same story. And you only get one chance. That's the trick. Twelve minds, one story. It's got to be a story that speaks to each of them.

Once I established the financial and legal issues my client was facing, I moved on to how the game was played by WestLand and its representative, ALOFT.

"So when you were given the file on this matter, what was the first thing you did?"

"Well, you had told me to make a practice of checking all the dates and details. You said to make sure with every case that the petitioner actually has standing, meaning that we needed to make sure that the institution making the claim of foreclosure actually had standing to make such a claim."

"But wouldn't that have been obvious in this case since the Trammels had been making mortgage payments to WestLand for almost four years before their financial difficulties changed things?"

"Not necessarily, because what we were finding was that the mortgage business exploded in the middle of the decade. So many mortgages were made and then repackaged and resold that in many instances the conveyances were never completed. It didn't really matter in this case who the Trammels made their mortgage payments to. What mattered was what entity legitimately held the mortgage."

"Okay, so what did you find when you checked dates and details on the Trammel foreclosure?"

Freeman objected again on relevance and she was again overruled. I didn't need to ask Aronson the question again.

"When I reviewed the dates and details I found discrepancies and indications of fraud."

"Can you describe these indications?"

"Yes. There was irrefutable evidence that conveyance documents were forged, giving WestLand false standing to seek the foreclosure."

"Do you have those documents, Ms. Aronson?"

"Yes, I do and we are able to display them in our PowerPoint presentation."

"Please do."

Aronson opened a laptop on the shelf in front of her and started the program. The document in question appeared on the overhead screens and I sought further explanation from Aronson.

"What are we looking at here, Ms. Aronson?"

"If I could explain, six years ago Lisa and Jeff Trammel bought their house, obtaining a mortgage through a broker called CityPro Home Loans. CityPro then grouped their mortgage in a portfolio with fifty-nine other mortgages of similar value. The entire portfolio was bought by WestLand. It was up to WestLand at that point to make sure the mortgage for each of those properties was properly conveyed through legal documentation to the bank. But that never happened. The assignment of mortgage in the case of the Trammel home was not done."

"How do you know that? Isn't this the conveyance right here in front of us?"

I stepped out from behind the lectern and gestured toward the overhead screens.

Aronson continued. "This document purports to be the assignment of mortgage but if you go to the last page…"

She hit the down arrow button on her computer and flipped through the document to the final page. It was the signing page, with the signatures of an officer of the bank and a notary as well as the notary's required state seal.

"Two things here," Aronson said. "According to the notarization you see that the document was purportedly signed on March sixth, two thousand seven. This would have been shortly after WestLand bought the mortgage portfolio from CityPro. The signing officer listed here is Michelle Monet. We have so far been unable to find a Michelle Monet who is or was an employee of WestLand National in any capacity at any bank branch or location. The second issue is if you look at the notary seal the expiration date is clearly seen here as two thousand fourteen."

She stopped there, just as we had rehearsed, as if the fraud involving the notary seal was obvious to all. I held a long moment as if waiting for more.

"Okay, what's wrong with the expiration being two thousand fourteen?"

"In the state of California notary licenses are awarded for five years. This would mean that this notary's seal was issued in two thousand nine, yet the date being notarized on this document is March sixth, two thousand seven. This notary seal had not been issued in two thousand seven. This means that this document was created to falsely convey the mortgage note on the Trammel property to WestLand National."

I stepped back to the lectern to check my notes and let Aronson's testimony float in front of the jury a little longer. I stole a quick glance at the box and noticed several of the jurors were still staring up at the screens. This was good.

"So what did this tell you when you discovered this fraud?"

"That we could challenge WestLand's right to foreclose on the Trammel property. WestLand was not the legitimate holder of the mortgage. It still remained with CityPro."

"Did you inform Lisa Trammel of this discovery?"

"On December seventeenth of last year we had a client meeting which was attended by Lisa, you and myself. She was informed then that we had clear and convincing evidence of fraud in the foreclosure filing. We also told her that we would use the evidence as leverage to negotiate a positive outcome to her situation."

"How did she react to this?"

Freeman objected, saying I was asking a question requiring a hearsay answer. I argued that I was allowed to establish the defendant's state of mind at the time of the murder. The judge agreed and Aronson was allowed to answer.

"She was very happy and positive. She said it was an early Christmas present, knowing that she wasn't going to lose her house anytime soon."

"Thank you. Now did there come a time when you wrote a letter to WestLand National for my signature?"

"Yes, I wrote a letter for your signature that outlined these findings of fraud. It was addressed to Mitchell Bondurant."

"And what was the purpose of this letter?"

"This was part of the negotiation we told Lisa Trammel about. The idea was to inform Mr. Bondurant of what ALOFT was doing in the bank's name. We believed that if Mr. Bondurant was concerned about the bank's exposure on this, it would help facilitate a negotiation beneficial to our client."

"When you wrote that letter for my signature, did you know or intend that Mr. Bondurant would forward it to Louis Opparizio at ALOFT?"

"No, I did not."

"Thank you, Ms. Aronson. I have no further questions."

The judge called for the morning break and Aronson took the defendant's seat when Lisa and Herb Dahl left to stretch their legs in the hallway.

"Finally, I get to sit here," she said.

"Don't worry, after today, you're there. You did great, Bullocks. Now comes the hard part."

I glanced over at Freeman, who was staying at the prosecution table during the break, finishing her plan for the cross-examination.

"Just remember, you are entitled to take your time. When she asks the tough ones, you just take a breath, compose yourself and then answer if you know the answer."

She looked at me as if questioning whether I really meant it: *You mean tell the truth?*

I nodded.

"You'll do fine."

After the break, Freeman went to the lectern and spread open a file containing notes and her written questions. It was just a show for the most part. She did what she could but it is always a challenge to cross-examine an attorney, even a new one. For nearly an hour she tried to shake Aronson on her direct testimony but to no avail.

Eventually, she went in a different direction, using sarcasm whenever possible. A sure sign that she was frustrated.

"So, after that wonderful, happy client conference you had before Christmas, when was the next time you saw your client?"

Aronson had to think for a long moment before answering.

"It would have been after she was arrested."

"Well, what about phone calls? After the client conference, when was the next time you talked to her on the phone?"

"I am pretty sure she spoke to Mr. Haller a number of times but I did not speak to her again until after her arrest."

"So during the time between the meeting and the murder, you would have no idea what sort of state of mind your client was in?"

As instructed, my young associate took her time before answering.

"If there had been a change in her view of the case and how it was going I think I would have been informed of it by her directly or through Mr. Haller. But nothing like that occurred."

"I'm sorry but I didn't ask what you think. I asked what you directly know. Are you telling this jury that based on your meeting in December, you know what your client's state of mind was a whole month later?"

"No, I'm not."

"So you can't sit there and tell us what Lisa Trammel's state of mind was on the morning of the murder, can you?"

"I can tell you only what I know from our meeting."

"And can you tell us what she was thinking when she saw Mitchell Bondurant, the man who was trying to take away her home, that morning at the coffee shop?"

"No, I can't."

Freeman looked down at her notes and seemed to hesitate. I knew why. She had a tough decision to make. She knew she had just scored some solid points with the jury and now had to decide whether to try to scrape up a few more or let it end on the high note.

She finally decided she'd gotten enough and folded her file.

"I have nothing further, Your Honor."

Cisco was scheduled to come up next but the judge broke for an early lunch. I took my team over to Jerry's Famous Deli in Studio City. Lorna was waiting there in a booth near the door that led to the bowling alley behind the restaurant. I sat next to Jennifer and across from Lorna and Cisco.

"So, how did it go this morning?" Lorna asked.

"Good, I think," I answered. "Freeman scored some points on cross but I think overall we came out ahead. Jennifer did very well."

I don't know if anybody had noticed but I had decided I would no longer be calling her Bullocks. In my estimation she had outgrown the nickname with her performance on the witness stand. She was no longer the young lawyer from the department-store school. She had made her bones on this case with her work in and out of the courtroom.

"And now she gets to sit at the big table!" I added.

Lorna cheered and clapped.

"And now it's Cisco's turn," Aronson said, clearly uncomfortable with the attention.

"Maybe not," I said. "I think I need to go to Driscoll next."

"How come?" Aronson said.

"Because this morning in chambers I informed the court and the prosecution of his existence and his addition to my wit list. Freeman objected but she was the one who brought up Facebook so the judge called Driscoll fair game. So now I'm thinking that the faster I get to him the less time Freeman will have to prepare. If I stick with the plan and put Cisco on, Freeman can work him all afternoon while her investigators are running down Driscoll."

Only Lorna nodded at my reasoning. But that was good enough for me.

"Shit, and I got all dressed up," Cisco exclaimed.

It was true. My investigator was wearing a long-sleeved collared shirt that looked like it would burst at the seams if he flexed his muscles. I had seen it before, though. It was his testifying shirt.

I ignored his complaint.

"Speaking of Driscoll, what's his status, Cisco?"

"My guys picked him up this morning and brought him up. Last I heard, he was shooting pool at the club."

I stared at my investigator.

"They're not giving him alcohol, right?"

"Course not."

"That's all I need, a drunk witness on the stand."

"Don't worry. I told them no alcohol."

"Well, call your guys. Have them deliver Driscoll to the courthouse by one. He's next."

It was too loud in the restaurant for a phone call. Cisco slipped out of the booth and headed toward the door while pulling his cell. We watched him go.

"You know, he looks good in a real shirt like that," Aronson said.

"Really?" Lorna responded. "I don't like the sleeves."

Forty-six

I almost didn't recognize Donald Driscoll with his hair combed and a suit on. Cisco had placed him in a witness room down the hall from the courtroom. When I stepped in he looked up at me from the table with scared eyes.

"How was the Saints club?" I asked.

"I would've rather been somewhere else," he said.

I nodded in false sympathy.

"Are you ready for this?"

"No, but I'm here."

"Okay, in a few minutes Cisco will come get you and bring you to the courtroom."

"Whatever."

"Look, I know it doesn't seem like it now, but you're doing the right thing."

"You're right... about it not seeming like it now."

I didn't know what to say to that.

"All right, I'll see you in there."

I left the room and signaled to Cisco, who was standing in the hallway with the two men who had been minding Driscoll. I pointed down the hall toward the courtroom and Cisco nodded. I proceeded on and entered the courtroom to find Jennifer Aronson and Lisa Trammel at the defense table. I sat down but before I could say anything to either one of them, the judge entered the courtroom and took the bench. He called for the jury and we quickly went back on the record. I called Donald Driscoll to the stand. After he was sworn in, I got right down to business.

"Mr. Driscoll, what is your profession?"

"I'm in IT."

"And what does IT mean?"

"Information technology. It means I work with computers, the Internet. I find the best way to use new technologies to gather information for the client or employer or whoever it may be."

"You are a former employee of ALOFT, correct?"

"Yes, I worked there for ten months until earlier this year."

"In IT?"

"Yes."

"What exactly did you do in IT for ALOFT?"

"I had several duties. It's a very computer-reliant business. A lot of employees and a great need for access to information through the Internet."

"And you helped them get it."

"Yes."

"Now, do you know the defendant, Lisa Trammel?"

"I've never met her. I know of her."

"You know of her from this case?"

"Yeah, but also from before."

"From before. How so?"

"One of my duties at ALOFT was to try to keep tabs on Lisa Trammel."

"Why?"

"I don't know why. I was just told to do it and I did it."

"Who told you to keep tabs on Lisa Trammel?"

"Mr. Borden, my supervisor."

"Did he tell you to keep tabs on anybody else?"

"Yes, a bunch of other people."

"How many is a bunch?"

"I guess there were about ten."

"Who were they?"

"Other mortgage protestors like Trammel. Plus employees of some of the banks we did business with."

"Like who?"

"The man who was killed. Mr. Bondurant."

I checked my notes for a while and let that percolate with the jury.

"Now, by keeping tabs, what did that mean?"

"I was to look for whatever I could find on these people online."

"Did Mr. Borden ever tell you why you had this assignment?"

"I asked him once and he said because Mr. Opparizio wants the information."

"Is that Louis Opparizio, founder and president of ALOFT?"

"Yes."

"Now were there any specific instructions from Mr. Borden in regard to Lisa Trammel?"

"No, it was just sort of see what you can find out there."

"And when did this become your assignment?"

"It was last year. I started working at ALOFT in April and so it would have been a few months after that."

"Could it have been July or August?"

"Yeah, right about then."

"Did you give the information you got to Mr. Borden?"

"Yes, I did."

"Did there come a time that you became aware that Lisa Trammel was on Facebook?"

"Yes, it was sort of an obvious thing to check."

"Did you become her friend on Facebook?"

"Yes."

"And this put you in a position to monitor her posts about the FLAG organization and the foreclosure of her home, correct?"

"Yes."

"Did you tell your supervisor about this specifically?"

"I told him that she was on Facebook and was fairly active, and that it was a good spot for monitoring what she was doing and planning for FLAG."

"How did he respond?"

"He told me to monitor it and then summarize everything once a week in an e-mail. So that's what I did."

"And did you use your own name when you sent Lisa Trammel your friend request?"

"Yes. I was already on Facebook as, you know, myself. So I didn't hide it. I mean, I doubted she knew who I was anyway."

"What sort of reports did you give Mr. Borden?"

"You know, like if her group was planning a protest somewhere I would tell them the date and time, that sort of stuff."

"You just said 'them.' Were you giving these reports to someone other than Mr. Borden?"

"No, but I knew he was forwarding them to Mr. Opparizio because Mr. O. would send me e-mails every now and then about the stuff I sent Mr. Borden. So I knew he was seeing the reports."

"In all of this, did you do anything illegal while snooping around for Borden and Opparizio?"

"No, sir."

"Now did one of your weekly summaries of Lisa Trammel's activities ever include reference to her posts about being in the garage at West-Land National and waiting to talk to Mitchell Bondurant?"

"Yes, there was one. WestLand was one of the company's biggest clients and I thought maybe Mr. Bondurant should know, if he didn't already, that this woman had waited for him out there."

"So you gave Mr. Borden the details of how Lisa Trammel had found Mr. Bondurant's parking spot and waited for him?"

"Yes."

"And he said thanks?"

"Yes."

"And this was all in e-mails?"

"Yes."

"Did you keep a copy of the e-mail you sent Mr. Borden?"

"Yes, I did."

"Why did you do that?"

"It's just kind of a general practice of mine, to keep copies, especially when dealing with important people."

"Did you happen to bring a copy of that e-mail with you today?"

"I did."

Freeman objected and asked for a sidebar. At the bench she success-fully argued that there was no way of legitimizing what purported to be a printout of an old e-mail. The judge wouldn't let me introduce it, say-ing I would have to stick with Driscoll's recollections.

Returning to the lectern, I decided I had made it clear to the jury that Borden knew Trammel had previously been in the garage and that Borden was a conduit to Opparizio. The elements of a setup were right there. The prosecution would have them believe that the first time Lisa was in the garage was a dry run for the murder she would later commit. I would have them believe that whoever set Trammel up had all he needed to know, thanks to Facebook.

I moved on.

"Mr. Driscoll, you said that Mitchell Bondurant was one of the peo-ple you were asked to gather information on, is that correct?"

"Yes."

"What information did you gather on him?"

"Mostly about his personal real estate holdings. What properties he owned, when he bought them and for how much. Who held the mort-gages. That sort of thing."

"So you supplied to Mr. Borden a financial snapshot."

"That's right."

"Did you come across any liens against Mr. Bondurant or his properties?"

"Yes, there were several. He owed money around."

"And all of this information went to Borden?"

"Yes, it did."

I decided to leave it there on Bondurant. I didn't want the jury stray-ing too far from the main point of Driscoll's testimony: that ALOFT had been watching Lisa and had all the information needed to set her up for murder. Driscoll had been effective and I would now close out his testimony with a bang.

"Mr. Driscoll, when did you leave your position at ALOFT?"

"February first."

"Was it your choice or were you fired?"

"I told them I was quitting so they fired me."

"Why did you want to quit?"

"Because Mr. Bondurant had gotten murdered in the parking garage and I didn't know whether the lady who got arrested, Lisa Trammel, did it or if there was something else going on. I saw Mr. Opparizio in the elevator the day after it was in the news and everybody in the office knew about it. We were going up but when we got to my floor he held my arm while everybody else got off. We went up to his floor alone and he didn't say anything until the doors opened. Then he said, 'Keep your fucking mouth shut,' and got off. And the doors closed."

"Those were his words, 'Keep your fucking mouth shut'?"

"Yes."

"Did he say anything else?"

"No."

"So this led you to quit your job?"

"Yes, about an hour later I gave two weeks' notice. But about ten minutes after I did that Mr. Borden came to my desk and told me I was out. Fired. He had a box for my personal stuff and he had a security guard come watch me while I packed up. Then they walked me out."

"Did they give you a severance package?"

"As I was leaving Mr. Borden gave me an envelope. It had a check in it for a year's salary."

"That was pretty generous, giving you a year's salary, considering you hadn't even worked there a full year and you had said you were quitting, don't you think?"

Freeman objected on relevance and it was sustained.

"I have nothing further for this witness."

Freeman took my place, arriving at the lectern with her trusty file, which she spread open. I had not put Driscoll on my witness list until that morning but his name had come up during Friday's testimony. I was sure Freeman had done some prep work. I was about to find out how much.

"Mr. Driscoll, you don't have a college degree, do you?"

"Uh, no."

"But you attended UCLA, did you not?"

"Yes."

"Why didn't you graduate?"

I stood and objected, saying her questions were going way outside the scope of Driscoll's direct testimony. But the judge said I opened the door when I asked the witness about his credentials and experience in IT. He told Driscoll to answer the question.

"I didn't graduate because I was expelled."

"For what?"

"Cheating. I hacked into a teacher's computer and downloaded an exam the night before it was given."

Driscoll said it with an almost bored tone to his voice. Like he knew this was going to come out. I knew this was in his background. I told him that if it came out he had only one choice, to be absolutely honest. Otherwise, he would be inviting disaster.

"So you are a cheater and a thief, correct?"

"I was, and that was more than ten years ago. I don't cheat anymore. There's nothing to cheat for."

"Really? And what about stealing?"

"Same thing. I don't steal."

"Isn't it true that your employment at ALOFT was severed abruptly when it was discovered that you were systematically stealing from the company?"

"That is a lie. I told them I was quitting and then they canned me."

"Aren't you the one who is lying here?"

"No, I'm telling the truth. You think I could just make this stuff up?"

Driscoll made a desperate glance toward me and I wished he hadn't. It could be interpreted as collusion between us. Driscoll was on his own up there. I couldn't help him.

"As a matter of fact I do, Mr. Driscoll," Freeman said. "Isn't it true that you had quite a little business for yourself running out of ALOFT?"

"No."

Driscoll demonstrably shook his head in support of his denial. I read him as lying right there and I realized I was in deep trouble. The severance package, I thought. The year's pay. They don't fire people and give them a year's pay if they've been stealing. Bring up the severance package!

"Were you not using ALOFT as a front to order expensive software, then break the security codes and sell bootleg copies over the Internet?"

"That's not true. I knew this would happen if I told anyone what I know."

This time he did more than look at me. He pointed at me.

"I told you this would happen. I told you these people don't—"

"Mr. Driscoll!" the judge boomed. "You answer the question posed to you by counsel. You do *not* talk to defense counsel or anyone else."

Trying to keep her momentum, Freeman swooped in for the kill.

"Your Honor, may I approach the witness with a document?"

"You may. Are you going to mark it?"

"People's Exhibit Nine, Your Honor."

She had copies for everybody. I leaned close to Aronson so we could read it together. It was a copy of an internal investigation report from ALOFT.

"Did you know about any of this?" Aronson whispered.

"Of course not," I whispered back.

I leaned forward to focus on the examination. I didn't want a first-year lawyer *tsk-tsk*ing me over a gigantic vetting failure.

"What is that document, Mr. Driscoll?" Freeman asked.

"I don't know," the witness responded. "I've never seen it before."

"It is an internal investigation summary from ALOFT, isn't it?"

"If you say so."

"When is it dated?"

"February first."

"That was your last day of work at ALOFT, wasn't it?"

"Yes, it was. That morning I gave my supervisor two weeks' notice and then they erased my login and fired me."

"For cause."

"For no cause. Why do you think they gave me the big check at the door? I knew things and they were trying to shut me up."

Freeman looked up at the judge.

"Your Honor, could you instruct the witness to refrain from answering my questions with his own questions."

Perry nodded.

"The witness will answer questions, not pose them."

It didn't matter, I thought. He had gotten it out there.

"Mr. Driscoll, could you please read the paragraph of the report I have highlighted in yellow?"

I objected, stating that the report was not in evidence. The judge overruled, allowing the reading to proceed subject to a later evidentiary ruling.

Driscoll read the paragraph to himself and then shook his head.

"Out loud, Mr. Driscoll," the judge prompted.

"But this is all complete lies. This is what they do to—"

"Mr. Driscoll," the judge intoned grumpily. "Read the paragraph aloud, please."

Driscoll hesitated one last time and then finally read.

"'The employee admitted that he had purchased the software packages with a company requisition and then returned them after copying the copyrighted materials. The employee admitted he has been selling counterfeit copies of the software over the Internet, using company computers to facilitate this business. The employee admitted earning more than one hundred thousand—'"

Driscoll suddenly crushed the document with both hands into a ball and threw it across the courtroom.

Right at me.

"You did this!" he yelled at me, following his pitch with a pointed finger. "I was fine in the world till you showed up!"

Once again Judge Perry could've used a gavel. He called for order and for the jury to return to the deliberations room. They quickly filed out of the courtroom as if being chased by Driscoll himself. Once the door was closed the judge took further action, signaling the courtroom deputy forward.

"Jimmy, take the witness to the holding cell while counsel and I discuss this in chambers."

He got up and stepped off the bench and quickly slipped through the door to his chambers before I could mount a protest over how my witness was being treated.

Freeman followed and I detoured to the witness stand.

"Just go and I'll get this over. You'll be right back out."

"You fucking liar," he said, anger jumping in his eyes. "You said it would be easy and safe and now look at this. The whole world thinks I'm a fucking software thief! You think I'll ever find work again?"

"Well, if I had known you were hijacking software I probably wouldn't have put you on the stand."

"Fuck you, Haller. You better hope this is over because if I have to come back here, I'm going to make up some shit about you."

The deputy was leading him toward the door that led to the holding cell next to the courtroom. As he went I noticed Aronson standing at the defense table. Her face told the story. All her good work of the morning possibly undone.

"Mr. Haller?" the court clerk said from her corral. "The judge is waiting."

"Yeah," I said. "I'm coming."

I headed toward the door.

Forty-seven

Four Green Fields was always dead on Monday nights. It was a bar that catered to the legal crowd and it usually wasn't until a few days into the week that lawyers started to need alcohol to dampen the burdens of conscience. We could've had our pick of the place but we took to the bar, Aronson sitting between me and Cisco.

We ordered a beer, a cosmo and a vodka tonic with lime and without the vodka. Still smarting from the Donald Driscoll fiasco, I had called the after-hours meeting to talk about Tuesday. And because I thought my two associates could use a drink.

There was a basketball game on the TV but I didn't even bother to check who was playing or what the score was. I didn't care and couldn't see much further than the Driscoll disaster. His testimony had ended after the blowup and finger pointing. In chambers the judge had worked out a curative address to the jurors, telling them that both the prosecution and defense had agreed that he would be dismissed from giving further testimony. Driscoll at best had been a wash. His direct testimony certainly set up the defense contention that Louis Opparizio had brought about the demise of Mitchell Bondurant. But his credibility had been undermined during cross-examination and his volatile behavior and enmity toward me didn't help. Plus, the judge was obviously holding me responsible for the spectacle and that would probably end up hurting the defense.

"So," Aronson said after her first sip of cosmo. "What do we do now?"

"We keep fighting, is what we do. We had one bad witness, one fiasco. Every trial has a moment like this."

I pointed up to the TV.

"You a football fan, Jennifer?"

I knew she had gone to UC–Santa Barbara for her undergraduate degree, then Southwestern. Not much in the way of collegiate football powers.

"That's not football. That's basketball."

"Yeah, I know, but do you like football?"

"I like the Raiders."

"I knew it!" Cisco said gleefully. "A girl after my own heart."

"Well," I said. "When you're a defense lawyer you have to be like a cornerback. You know you're going to get burned from time to time. It's just part of the game. So when it happens you have to pick yourself up, dust yourself off and forget about it because they're about to snap the ball again. We gave them a touchdown today—*I* gave them a touchdown. But the game's not over, Jennifer. Not by a long shot."

"Right, so what do we do?"

"What we've planned to do all along. Go after Opparizio. It comes down to him. I've got to push him to the edge. I think Cisco's given me the firepower to do it and hopefully his guard will be down because we've had Dahl telling him it's going to be a walk in the park. Realistically, right now, I think the score is tied. Even with Driscoll blowing up, I'd say we're either tied or maybe the prosecution's got a few points up on us. I've got to change that tomorrow. If I don't, we lose."

A somber silence followed until Aronson asked another question.

"What about Driscoll, Mickey?"

"What about him? We're done with Driscoll."

"Yeah, but did you believe him about all the software stuff? Do you think Opparizio's people set him up? Was all of that about him stealing software made-up lies? Because now it's out in front of the media."

"I don't know. Freeman did a smart thing. She coupled it with something he wouldn't or couldn't deny—stealing the test. So it all sort of flowed together. Anyway, it doesn't matter what I believe. It's what the jury believes."

"I think you're wrong. I think that what you believe is always important."

I nodded.

"Maybe so, Jennifer."

I took a long sip of my anemic drink. Aronson then went in a new direction.

"How come you stopped calling me Bullocks?"

I looked at her and then looked back at my drink. I shrugged.

"Because you did so well today. It's like you're all grown up or something and you shouldn't be called by a nickname."

I looked past her at Cisco and pointed.

"But him? With a name like Wojciechowski, he's got his nickname for life. And that's just the way it is."

We all laughed and it seemed to relieve some of the pressure. I knew alcohol could help with that but it had been two years now and I was strong. I wouldn't slip.

"What did you tell Dahl to go back with today?" Cisco asked.

I shrugged again.

"The defense is in disarray, they lost their best shot with Driscoll when Freeman destroyed him. Then the usual, we don't have anything on Opparizio and testifying will be like cutting butter left out on the counter. He's supposed to call me after he talks to his handler."

Cisco nodded. I continued in another direction.

"I'm thinking Opparizio is the way to end it. If I can get what Cisco has gotten for me to the jury in questions and his answers, and I push him to the nickel, then I think I'll just end it there and Cisco, you won't testify."

Aronson frowned like she wasn't sure that would be a good move.

"Good," Cisco said. "I won't have to wear the monkey suit tomorrow."

He tugged at his collar like it was made of sandpaper.

"No, you have to wear it again, just in case. You have another shirt like that, don't you?"

"Not really. I guess I'll have to wash this tonight."

"Are you kidding me? You only—"

Cisco made a low whistling sound and nodded toward the door

behind me. I turned just as Maggie McPherson slipped onto the open stool next to me.

"There you are."

"Maggie McFierce."

She pointed to my drink.

"That better not be what I think it is."

"Don't worry, it's not."

"Good."

She ordered a real vodka tonic from Randy the bartender, probably just to rub it in.

"So, drowning your sorrows without the drown. I did hear it was a good day for the good guys."

Meaning the prosecution. Always.

"Maybe. You hired a sitter for a Monday night?"

"No, the sitter offered to sit tonight. I take it when I can get it because she's got a boyfriend now so I've probably seen my last Friday and Saturday nights out on the town."

"Okay, so you get her tonight and you go out to the bar by yourself?"

"Maybe I was looking for you, Haller. Ever think of that?"

I turned on my stool so my back was to Aronson and I was directly facing Maggie.

"Really?"

"Maybe. I thought you could use some company. You're not answering your cell."

"I forgot. It's still off from court."

I pulled the phone and turned it on. No wonder I hadn't gotten the call from Herb Dahl.

"You want to go to your place?" she asked.

I looked at her for a long moment before answering.

"Tomorrow's going to be the most important day of the trial. I should—"

"I have till midnight."

I took a deep breath but more air went out than came in. I leaned toward her and then tilted so that our heads were touching, sort of like how they touch sabers before a fencing match. I whispered in her ear.

"I can't keep doing things this way. We have to go forward or be done."

She put her hand on my chest and pushed me back. I was afraid of what my life would be like with her completely gone from it. I regretted the ultimatum I had just set out because I knew that if forced to make a choice she would pick the latter.

"What do you say we just worry about tonight, Haller?"

"Okay," I said so quickly that we both started laughing.

I had dodged a bullet I had fired at myself. For now.

"I still have to get some work done at some point."

"Yeah, we'll see about that."

She reached to the bar for her drink but took mine by mistake. Or maybe not by mistake. She sipped and then screwed up her face in disgust.

"That tastes just awful without vodka. What's the point?"

"I know. Was that some sort of test?"

"No, just a mistake."

"Sure."

She drank from her own glass now. I turned slightly and looked back at Cisco and Aronson. They were leaning toward each other, engaged in a conversation and ignoring me. I turned back to Maggie.

"Marry me again, Maggie. I'm going to change everything after this case."

"I've heard that before. The second part."

"Yeah, but this time it's going to happen. It already is."

"Do I have to answer right now? Is it a one-time thing or can I think about it?"

"Sure, take a few minutes. I'm going to hit the head and then I'll be back."

We laughed again and then I leaned forward and kissed her and held my face in her hair. I whispered again.

"I can't think of being with anybody else."

She turned in to me and kissed my neck, then pulled back.

"I hate public displays of affection, especially in bars. Seems so cheap."

"Sorry."

"Let's go now."

She slid off the stool. And took a last sip of her drink while standing.

I pulled my cash and peeled off enough to cover everybody, including the bartender. I told Cisco and Aronson I was going.

"I thought we were still talking about Opparizio," Aronson protested.

I saw Cisco surreptitiously touch her arm in a *not now* signal. I appreciated that.

"You know what?" I said. "It's been a long day. Sometimes not thinking about something is the best way to prepare for it. I'll be in the office early tomorrow before going to court. If you want to come by. Otherwise, I'll see you in court at nine."

We said our goodbyes and I walked out with my ex-wife.

"You want to leave a car here or what?" I asked.

"No, too dangerous to come back here after dinner and being in bed with you. I'll want to go in for one last drink and then it might not be the last. I have the sitter to relieve and work tomorrow, too."

"Is that how you view it? Just dinner and sex and getting home by midnight?"

She could've really hurt me then, said I was whining like a woman complaining about men. But she didn't.

"No," she said. "I actually view it as the best night of the week."

I raised my hand and clasped the back of her neck as we walked to our cars. She always liked that. Even if it was a public display of affection.

Forty-eight

You could feel the tension rise with each step as Louis Opparizio made his way to the witness stand on Tuesday morning. He wore a light tan suit with a blue shirt and maroon tie. He looked dignified in a way that bespoke money and power. And it was clear that he looked at me through contemptuous eyes. He was my witness but obviously there was no love lost here. Since the start of the trial I had pointed the finger of guilt at someone other than my client. I had pointed at Opparizio and now he sat before me. This was the main event and as such it had drawn the biggest crowd — both media and onlookers — of the trial.

I started things out cordially but wasn't planning to continue that way. I had one goal here and the verdict was riding on whether I achieved it. I had to push the man in the witness box to the limit. He was there only because he had been cornered by his own avarice and vanity. He had ignored legal counsel, declined to hide behind the Fifth Amendment and accepted the challenge of going one-on-one with me in front of a packed house. My job was to make him regret those decisions. My job was to make him take the Fifth in front of the jury. If he did that, then Lisa Trammel would walk. There could be no stronger reasonable doubt than to have the straw man you've been pointing at all trial long hide behind the Fifth, to refuse to answer questions on the grounds that he would incriminate himself. How could any honest juror vote guilty beyond a reasonable doubt after that?

"Good morning, Mr. Opparizio. How are you?"

"I'd rather be somewhere else. How are you?"

I smiled. He was feisty from the start.

"I'll tell you that in a few hours," I answered. "Thank you for being here today. I noticed a bit of a northeastern accent. Are you not from Los Angeles?"

"I was born in Brooklyn fifty-one years ago. I moved out here for law school and never left."

"You and your company have been mentioned here during the trial more than a few times. It seems to hold the lion's share of foreclosure work in at least this county. I was—"

"Your Honor?" Freeman interrupted from her seat. "Is there going to be a question here?"

Perry looked down at her for a moment.

"Is that an objection, Ms. Freeman?"

She realized she had not stood. The judge had instructed us in pre-trial meetings that we must stand to make an objection. She quickly stood up.

"Yes, Your Honor."

"Ask a question, Mr. Haller."

"I was about to, Your Honor. Mr. Opparizio, could you tell us in your words what it is that ALOFT does?"

Opparizio cleared his throat and turned directly toward the jurors when he answered. He was a polished and proficient witness. I had my work cut out for me.

"I'd be happy to. Essentially, ALOFT is a processing firm. Large loan servicers such as WestLand National pay my company to handle property foreclosures from start to finish. We handle everything from drawing up the paperwork to serving notices to appearing in court as necessary. All for one all-inclusive fee. Nobody likes to hear about fore-closures. We all struggle on some level to pay our bills and try to keep our homes. But sometimes it doesn't work out and foreclosure is required. That's where we come in."

"You say 'but sometimes it doesn't work out.' Over the past few years it has been working out pretty good for you, though, hasn't it?"

"Our business has seen tremendous growth in the past four years and it has only now finally started to level off."

"You mentioned WestLand National as a client. WestLand was a significant client, correct?"

"It was and still is."

"About how many foreclosures do you handle for WestLand in a year?"

"I wouldn't know off the top of my head. But I think it's safe to say that with all of their locations in the western United States, we get close to ten thousand files from them in a year."

"Would you believe that over the past four years you have averaged over sixteen thousand cases a year referred by WestLand? It's in the bank's annual report."

I held it up for all to see.

"Yes, I would believe that. Annual reports don't lie."

"What is the fee that ALOFT charges per foreclosure?"

"On residential we charge twenty-five hundred dollars and that's for everything, even if we have to go to court on the matter."

"So doing the math, your company takes in forty million dollars a year from WestLand alone, correct?"

"If the figures you used are correct, that sounds right."

"I take it, then, that the WestLand account was very big at ALOFT."

"Yes, but all our clients are important."

"So you must have known Mitchell Bondurant, the victim in this case, pretty well, correct?"

"Of course I knew him well and I think it's a terrible shame about what happened to him. He was a good man, trying to do a good job."

"I am sure we all appreciate your sympathy. But at the time of his death, you weren't very happy with Mr. Bondurant, were you?"

"I'm not sure what you mean. We were business associates. We had minor disputes from time to time but that always happens in the natural course of business."

"Well, I'm not talking about minor disputes or the natural course of business. I'm asking you about a letter Mr. Bondurant sent to you shortly before his murder that threatened to expose fraudulent practices within your company. The certified letter was signed for by your personal secretary. Did you read it?"

"I skimmed it. It indicated to me that one of my hundred eighty-five employees had taken a shortcut. This was a minor dispute and nothing about it was threatening, as you say. I told the person who had that particular file to fix it. That's all, Mr. Haller."

But that wasn't all I had to say about the letter. I made Opparizio read it to the jury and for the next half hour I asked increasingly specific and uncomfortable questions about its allegations. I then moved on to the federal target letter and made the witness read that as well. But again Opparizio was unflappable, dismissing the federal letter as a shot in the dark.

"I welcomed them with open arms," he said. "But you know what? Nobody's come in. All this time later and not a word from Mr. Lattimore or Agent Vasquez or any other federal agent. Because their letter didn't pay off. I didn't run, I didn't sweat, I didn't cry foul or hide behind a lawyer. I said I know you've got a job to do, come on in and check us out. Our doors are open and we've got absolutely nothing to hide."

It was a good and well-rehearsed answer and Opparizio was clearly winning the early rounds. But that was okay because I was saving my best punches. I wanted him to feel confident and in control. Through Herb Dahl he had been fed a steady diet of no worries. He had been led to believe I had nothing but a few desperate hints of conspiracy that he could easily swat away as he was doing right now. His confidence was growing. But when he got too confident and complacent, I was going to move in and go for the knockout. This fight wouldn't go fifteen rounds. It couldn't.

"Now at the time these letters were coming in you were engaged in a secret negotiation, were you not?"

Opparizio paused for the first time since I had begun asking him questions.

"I was engaged at the time in private business discussions, as I am at almost all times. I would not use the word 'secret' because of the connotation. Secrecy being wrong when in fact keeping one's business private is a matter of course."

"Okay, then this private discussion was actually a negotiation to sell your company ALOFT to a publicly traded company, correct?"

"Yes, that is so."

"A company called LeMure?"

"Yes, correct."

"This deal would be worth a lot of money to you, would it not?"

Freeman stood and asked for a sidebar. We approached and she stated her objection in a forceful whisper.

"How is this relevant? Where are we going with this? He now has us on Wall Street and that has nothing to do with Lisa Trammel and the evidence against her."

"Your Honor," I said quickly, before he could cut me off. "The relevance will become apparent soon. Ms. Freeman knows exactly where this is headed and she just doesn't want to go there. But the court has given me the latitude to put forth a defense involving third-party guilt. Well, this is it, Judge. This is where it comes together and so I ask for the court's continued indulgence."

Perry didn't have to think too long before answering.

"Mr. Haller, you may proceed but I want you to land this plane soon."

"Thank you, Judge."

We returned to our positions and I decided to move things along at a quicker pace.

"Mr. Opparizio, back in January, when you were in the midst of these negotiations with LeMure, you knew you stood to make a great deal of money if this deal went through, did you not?"

"I would be generously compensated for the years I spent growing the company."

"But if you lost one of your biggest clients—to the tune of forty million in annual revenues—that deal would have been in peril, correct?"

"There was no threat from any client to leave."

"I draw your attention back to the letter Mr. Bondurant sent you, sir. Wouldn't you say that there is a clear threat from Mr. Bondurant to take WestLand's business away from you? I believe you still have a copy of the letter there in front of you, if you want to refer to it."

"I don't need to look at the letter. There was no threat to me whatsoever. Mitch sent me the letter and I took care of the problem."

"Like the way you took care of Donald Driscoll?"

"Objection," Freeman said. "Argumentative."

"I'll withdraw it. Mr. Opparizio, you received this letter smack-dab in the middle of your deal making with LeMure, correct?"

"It was during negotiations, yes."

"And at the time you received this letter from Mr. Bondurant, you knew he was in financial straits himself, correct?"

"I knew nothing about Mr. Bondurant's personal financial situation."

"Did you not have an employee of your company do financial background searches on Mr. Bondurant and other bankers you dealt with?"

"No, that's ridiculous. Whoever said that is a liar."

It was time for me to test Herb Dahl's work as a double agent.

"At the time Mr. Bondurant sent you that letter, was he aware of your secret dealings with LeMure?"

Opparizio's answer should have been "I don't know." But I had told Dahl to send back word through his handler that the Trammel legal team had found nothing on this key part of the defense strategy.

"He knew nothing about it," Opparizio said. "I had kept all of our client banks in the dark while negotiations were ongoing."

"Who is LeMure's chief financial officer?"

Opparizio seemed momentarily nonplussed by the question and the seeming change in direction.

"That would be Syd Jenkins. Sydney Jenkins."

"And was he the leader of the acquisition team you dealt with on the LeMure deal?"

Freeman objected and asked where this was going. I told the judge he would know shortly and he allowed me to continue, telling Opparizio to answer the question.

"Yes, I dealt with Syd Jenkins on the acquisition."

I opened a file and removed a document while asking the judge for permission to approach the witness with it. As expected, Freeman objected and we had a spirited sidebar over the admissibility of the document. But just as Freeman had won the battle over presenting Driscoll with the internal investigation report from ALOFT, Judge Perry evened the score, allowing me to introduce the document subject to his later ruling.

Permission granted, I handed a copy to the witness.

"Mr. Opparizio, can you tell the jury what that document is?"

"I can't tell for sure."

"Is it not a printout from a digital daybook?"

"If you say so."

"And what name is on the top of the sheet there."

"Mitchell Bondurant."

"And what is the date on the page?"

"December thirteenth."

"Can you read the appointment entry for ten o'clock?"

Freeman asked for a sidebar and once more we stood in front of the judge.

"Your Honor, Lisa Trammel is on trial here. Not Louis Opparizio or Mitchell Bondurant. This is what happens when someone takes advantage of the court's goodwill when given leeway. I object to this line of questioning. Counsel is taking us far afield of the matter this jury must decide."

"Judge," I said. "Again this goes to third-party guilt. This is a page from the digital diary turned over to the defense in discovery. The answer to this question will make it clear to the jury that the victim in this case was involved in subtly extorting the witness. And that is a motive for murder."

"Judge, this—"

"That's enough, Ms. Freeman. I will allow it."

We returned to our places and the judge told Opparizio to answer the question. I repeated it for the sake of the jury.

"What is listed on Mr. Bondurant's calendar for ten o'clock on December thirteenth?"

"It says 'Sydney Jenkins, LeMure.'"

"So would you not take from that log line that Mr. Bondurant became aware of the ALOFT-LeMure deal in December of last year?"

"I couldn't begin to know what was said at that meeting or if it even took place."

"What reason would the man leading the acquisition of ALOFT have for meeting with one of ALOFT's most important bank clients?"

"You would have to ask Mr. Jenkins that."

"Perhaps I will."

Opparizio had developed a scowl in the course of the questioning. The Herb Dahl plant had worked well. I moved on.

"When did the deal on the sale of ALOFT to LeMure close?"

"The deal closed in late February."

"How much was it sold for?"

"I'd rather not say."

"LeMure is a publicly traded company, sir. The information is out there. Could you save us the time and —"

"Ninety-six million dollars."

"Most of which, as sole owner, went to you, correct?"

"A good portion of it, yes."

"And you got stock in LeMure as well, correct?"

"That's right."

"And you remain president of ALOFT, don't you?"

"Yes. I still run the company. I just have bosses now."

He tried a smile but most of the working stiffs in the courtroom didn't see the humor in the comment, considering the millions he had taken out of the deal.

"So you are still intimately involved in the day-to-day operations of the company?"

"Yes, sir, I am."

"Mr. Opparizio, was your personal take in the sale of ALOFT sixty-one million dollars, as reported by the *Wall Street Journal*?"

"They got that wrong."

"How so?"

"My deal was worth that amount, but it didn't come to me all at once."

"You get deferred payments?"

"Something along those lines but I don't really see what this has to do with who killed Mitch Bondurant, Mr. Haller. Why am I here? I had nothing to —"

"Your Honor?"

"Hold on a moment, Mr. Opparizio," the judge said.

He then leaned forward over the bench and paused as if to contemplate something.

"We're going to take our morning break now and counsel will join me in chambers. The court is in recess."

Once more we followed the judge back into chambers. Once more I was going to be the one put on the spot. But I was so angry at Perry that I went on the offensive. I stayed standing while both he and Freeman took seats.

"Your Honor, with all due respect, I had a certain momentum going out there and taking the morning break early is killing it."

"Mr. Haller, you may have had plenty of momentum but it was taking you far away from this case. I have bent over backward to allow you to present a third-party defense but I am beginning to feel I've been had."

"Judge, I was four questions away from bringing it all back home to this case but you just stopped me."

"You stopped yourself, Counsel. I can't sit up there and let this go on. Ms. Freeman's been objecting, now even the witness is objecting. And I'm looking like a fool. You're fishing. You told me and you told those jurors that you would not only prove that your client didn't commit the crime, but that you would prove who did. But we are now five witnesses into the defense case and you are still fishing."

"Your Honor, I can't believe—look, I am not fishing here. I am proving. Bondurant had threatened to cost that man out there sixty-one million dollars. It is obvious and anyone with common sense sees this. And if that is not motive for a murder then I guess I—"

"Motive isn't proof," Freeman said. "It's not evidence and you obviously don't have any. The defense's whole case is a charade. What's next, you name everybody Bondurant was foreclosing on as a suspect?"

I pointed down at her in the chair.

"That wouldn't be a bad idea. But the fact is the defense case is not a charade and if allowed to continue my examination of the witness I will get to the evidence very quickly."

"Sit down, Mr. Haller, and please watch your tone when you are addressing me."

"Yes, Your Honor. I apologize."

I sat down and waited while Perry brooded over the situation. Finally, he spoke.

"Ms. Freeman, anything else?"

"I think the court is well aware of how the prosecution views what Mr. Haller has been allowed to do. I warned early and often that he would create a sideshow that had nothing to do with the case at hand. We are well past that point now and I have to agree with the court's assessment that all of this makes the court look foolish and manipulated."

She had gone too far. I could see the skin around Perry's eyes tighten as she stated that he looked like a fool. I think she'd had him in her hand but then lost him.

"Well, thank you very much, Ms. Freeman. I think at this time I'm inclined to go back out and give Mr. Haller one final chance to tie it all in. Do you understand what I mean by *final* chance, Mr. Haller?"

"Yes, Your Honor. I will comply."

"You'd better, sir, because the court's patience has drawn thin. Let's go back now."

Out at the defense table I saw Aronson waiting by herself and realized she hadn't followed me into chambers. I sat down wearily.

"Where's Lisa?"

"In the hallway with Dahl. What happened?"

"I've got one more chance. I have to move things up and go in for the kill now."

"Can you do it?"

"We'll see. I've got to run out to the facilities before we start again. Why didn't you come into chambers?"

"No one asked me to, and I didn't know if I should just follow you in."

"Next time follow me in."

Courthouse designs are good at separating parties. Jurors have their own assembly and deliberation rooms, and there are aisles and gates to separate opposing parties and supporters. But the restrooms are the great equalizers. You step into one of these and you never know who you will encounter. I pushed through the inner door of the men's room and almost walked right into Opparizio, who was washing his hands at the sink. He was bent over and looked up at me in the mirror.

"Well, Counselor, did the judge slap your hands a little bit?"

"That's none of your business. I'll find another restroom."

I turned around to leave but Opparizio stopped me.

"Don't bother. I'm leaving."

He shook his wet hands off and moved toward the door, coming very close to me and then suddenly stopping.

"You are despicable, Haller," he said. "Your client is a murderer and you have the balls to try to cast the blame on me. How do you look at yourself in the mirror?"

He turned and gestured toward the line of urinals.

"This is where you belong," he said. "In the toilet."

Forty-nine

It all came down to the next half hour—maybe an hour at the most. I sat at the defense table, composing my thoughts and waiting. Everyone was in place except for the judge, who remained in chambers, and Opparizio, who was smugly conferring with his two attorneys in the first row of the gallery where they had reserved seats. My client leaned toward me and whispered, so that not even Aronson could hear.

"You have more, right?"

"Excuse me?"

"You have more, don't you, Mickey? More to go after him with?"

Even she knew that what I had already trotted out was not enough. I whispered back.

"We'll know before lunch. We'll either be drinking champagne or crying in our soup."

The door to the judge's chambers opened and Perry emerged. He called for the jury and the witness to return to the stand before he was even seated on the bench. A few minutes later I was back at the lectern, staring down Opparizio. The restroom confrontation seemed to give him renewed confidence. He adopted a relaxed posture that announced to the world that he was home free. I decided that there was no sense in waiting. It was time to start swinging.

"Now then, Mr. Opparizio, continuing our discussion from before, you have not been completely truthful in your testimony today, have you?"

"I have been completely honest and I resent the question."

"You lied from the start, didn't you, sir? Giving a false name when sworn in by the clerk."

"My name was legally changed thirty-one years ago. I did not lie and it has nothing to do with this."

"What is the name that is on your birth certificate?"

Opparizio paused and I think I saw the first inkling or recognition of where I was going with this.

"My birth name was Antonio Luigi Apparizio. Like now but spelled with an *A*. Growing up, people called me Lou or Louie because there were a lot of Anthonys and Antonios in the neighborhood. I decided to go with Louis. I legally changed my name to Anthony Louis Opparizio. I Americanized it. That's it."

"But why did you change the spelling of your last name too?"

"There was a professional baseball player at the time named Luis Aparicio. I thought the names were too close. Louis Apparizio and Luis Aparicio. I didn't want to have a name so close to a famous person's so I changed the spelling. Is that okay with you, Mr. Haller?"

The judge admonished Opparizio to simply answer the questions and not ask them.

"Do you know when Luis Aparicio retired from professional baseball?" I asked.

I glanced at the judge after asking the question. If his patience was being stretched before, it was now probably as thin as the piece of paper a contempt citation would be printed on.

"No, I don't know when he retired."

"Does it surprise you to learn that it was eight years before you changed your name?"

"No, it doesn't surprise me."

"But you expect the jury to believe that you changed your name to avoid a match to a baseball player long out of the game?"

Opparizio shrugged.

"It's what happened."

"Isn't it true that you changed your name from Apparizio to *Opparizio* because you were an ambitious young man and wanted to at least outwardly distance yourself from your family?"

"No, untrue. I did want to have a more American-sounding name, but I wasn't distancing myself from anyone."

I saw Opparizio's eyes make a quick dart in the direction of his attorneys.

"You were originally named after your uncle, were you not?" I asked.

"No, that's not true," Opparizio answered quickly. "I wasn't named after anyone."

"You had an uncle named Antonio Luigi Apparizio, the same name as on your birth certificate, and you are saying it was just coincidence?"

Realizing his mistake in lying, Opparizio tried to recover but only made it worse.

"My parents never told me who I was named after or even if I was named after someone."

"And a bright person like you didn't put it together?"

"I never thought about it. When I was twenty-one I came west and was not close to my family anymore."

"You mean geographically?"

"In any way. I started a new life. I stayed out here."

"Your father and your uncle were involved in organized crime, were they not?"

Freeman quickly objected and asked for a sidebar. When we got there she did everything but roll her eyes back into her head as she tried to communicate her frustration.

"Your Honor, enough is enough. Counsel may show no shame in besmirching the reputations of his own witnesses, but this has to end. This is a trial, Judge, not a deep-sea fishing trip."

"Your Honor, you told me to move quickly and that is what I am doing. I have an offer of proof that clearly shows this is no fishing trip."

"Well, what is it, Mr. Haller?"

I handed the judge a thick bound document I had carried to the sidebar. There were several Post-its of different colors protruding from its pages.

"That is the U.S. Attorney General's 'Report to Congress on Organized Crime.' It's dated nineteen eighty-six and the AG at the time was Edwin Meese. If you go to the yellow Post-it and open the page, the highlighted paragraph is my offer of proof."

The judge read the passage and then turned the book around so Freeman could read it. Before she was finished he ruled on the objection.

"Ask your questions, Mr. Haller, but I'm giving you about ten minutes to connect the dots. If you don't do it by then, I'm going to shut you down."

"Thank you, Judge."

I went back to the lectern and asked the question again, but in a different way.

"Mr. Opparizio, were you aware that your father and your uncle were members of an organized crime group known as the Gambino family?"

Opparizio had seen me offer the bound book to the judge. He knew I had something to back my question. Rather than throw out a full denial he went with the vague response.

"As I said, I left my family behind when I went off to school. I didn't know about them after that. And I was told nothing before."

It was time to be relentless, to back Opparizio to the edge of the cliff.

"Wasn't your uncle known as Anthony 'The Ape' Apparizio because of his reputation for brutality and violence?"

"I wouldn't know."

"Didn't your uncle act as a father figure in your life while your own father spent most of your teenage years in prison for extortion?"

"My uncle took care of us financially but he was not a father figure."

"When you moved out west at age twenty-one was it to distance yourself from your family or to extend your family's business opportunities to the west coast?"

"Now that's a lie! I came out here for law school. I had nothing and brought nothing with me. Including family connections."

"Are you familiar with the term 'sleeper' as it is applied in organized crime investigations?"

"I don't know what you're talking about."

"Would it surprise you to learn that the FBI, starting in the 1980s, believed that the mob was attempting to move into legitimate areas of business by sending its next generation of members to schools and other locales so that they could sink roots and start businesses, and that these people were called sleepers?"

"I am a *legitimate* businessman. No one sent me anywhere and I put myself through law school working for a process server."

I nodded as though I expected the answer.

"Speaking of process servers, you own several companies, don't you, sir?"

"I don't understand."

"Let me rephrase. When you sold ALOFT to the LeMure Fund you kept ownership of a variety of companies that contracted with ALOFT, correct?"

Opparizio took his time thinking about an answer. He made another furtive glance toward his attorneys. It was a *Get me out of this* look. He knew where I was going and he knew I couldn't be allowed to get there. But he was on the witness stand and there was only one way out.

"I have ownership and part ownership in a variety of different enterprises. All of them legal, all of them aboveboard and legitimate."

It was a good answer but it was not going to be good enough.

"What kind of companies? What services do they provide?"

"You mentioned process serving, that's one of them. I have a paralegal referral and placement company. There's an office staffing company and an office furniture supply entity. There's—"

"Do you own a courier service?"

The witness paused before answering. He was trying to think two questions ahead and I wasn't staying in a rhythm he could pick up on.

"I'm an investor. I'm not the sole owner."

"Let's talk about the courier service. First of all, what's it called?"

"Wing Nuts Courier Services."

"And is that a Los Angeles–based company?"

"Based here but with offices in seven cities. It operates all over this state and Nevada."

"Exactly how much of Wing Nuts do you own?"

"I am a partial participant. I believe I own forty percent of it."

"And who are some of the other participants?"

"Well, there are several. Some aren't people, they're other companies."

"Like AA-Best Consultants of Brooklyn, New York, which is listed on corporate records in Sacramento as part owner of Wing Nuts?"

Opparizio was again slow to answer. This time he seemed lost in a dark thought until the judge prompted him.

"Yes, I believe that is one of the investors."

"Now, corporation documents held by the state of New York show that the majority owner of AA-Best is one Dominic Capelli. Are you familiar with him?"

"No, I am not."

"You are saying that you are unfamiliar with one of your partners in Wing Nuts, sir?"

"AA-Best invested. I invested. I don't know all the individuals involved."

Freeman stood. It was about time. I had been waiting for her to object for at least four questions. I was spinning my wheels waiting.

"Your Honor, is there a point to all of this?" she asked.

"I was beginning to wonder about that myself," Perry said. "You want to enlighten us, Mr. Haller?"

"Three more questions, Your Honor, and I think the relevance here will be crystal clear to everyone," I said. "I beg the court's indulgence for just three more questions."

I had stared at Opparizio the whole time I'd said it. I was sending the message. Pull the plug now or your secrets will be put out there in the world. LeMure will know. Your stockholders will know. The U.S. Attorney's Office will know. Everyone will know.

"Very well, Mr. Haller."

"Thank you, Your Honor."

I looked down at my notes. Now was the time. If I had Opparizio right, now was the time. I looked back up at him.

"Mr. Opparizio, would it surprise you to learn that Dominic Capelli, the partner you claim not to know, is listed by the New York —"

"Your Honor?"

It was Opparizio. He had cut me off.

"On advice of counsel and pursuant to my Fifth Amendment rights and privileges granted by the Constitution of the United States and the state of California, I respectfully decline to answer this or further questions."

There.

I stood totally still but that was only on the outside. Energy flooded through me like a scream. I was barely aware of the rumble of whispers that went through the courtroom. Then from behind me a voice firmly addressed the court.

"Your Honor, may I address the court please?"

I turned and saw it was one of Opparizio's attorneys, Martin Zimmer.

Then I heard Freeman, her voice high and tight, calling an objection and asking for a sidebar.

But I knew a sidebar wasn't going to do it this time. And so did Perry.

"Mr. Zimmer, you may sit down. We are going to break now for lunch and I expect all parties to be back in court at one o'clock this afternoon. The jury is directed not to discuss the case with one another or to draw any conclusions from the testimony and request of this witness."

Court broke loudly after that, with the members of the media talking among themselves. As the last juror was going through the door I stepped away from the lectern and leaned down to the defense table to whisper in Aronson's ear.

"You might want to come back to chambers this time."

She was about to ask what I meant when Perry made it official.

"I want counsel to join me in chambers. Immediately. Mr. Opparizio, I want you to stay right there. You can consult with your counsel, but don't leave the courtroom."

With that the judge got up and headed back.

I followed.

Fifty

By now I was intimately getting to know the wall hangings and furnishings and everything else in the judge's chambers. But I expected that this would be my last visit, and probably the most difficult. As we entered, the judge stripped off his robe and threw it haphazardly over the hat rack in the corner rather than carefully put it on a hanger as he had for prior *in camera* meetings. He then dropped into his seat and loudly exhaled. He leaned far back and looked up at the ceiling. He had a petulant look on his face, as though his concerns over what would be decided here were more about his own reputation as a jurist than about justice for a murder victim.

"Mr. Haller," he said as though he was releasing a great burden.

"Yes, Your Honor?"

The judge rubbed his face.

"Please tell me that it was not your plan all along, and from the beginning, to force Mr. Opparizio into taking the Fifth in front of the jury."

"Judge," I said, "I had no idea he was going to take the Fifth. After the motion to quash hearing we had, I thought there was no way he would. I was pushing him, sure, but I wanted the answers to my questions."

Freeman shook her head.

"You have something to add, Ms. Freeman?"

"Your Honor, I think defense counsel has treated the court and the justice system with nothing but contempt from the start of this trial. He didn't even answer your question just now. He didn't say it wasn't his plan,

Your Honor. He just said he had no idea. Those are two separate things and they underline the fact that defense counsel is sneaky and has tried to sabotage this trial from the start. He has now succeeded. All along Opparizio was a Fifth witness—a straw man he could set up in front of the jury and then knock down when he took the Fifth. That was the plan and if that is not a subverting of the adversarial system, then I don't know what is."

I glanced at Aronson. She looked mortified and maybe even swayed by Freeman's statement.

"Judge," I said calmly, "I can only say one thing to Ms. Freeman. Prove it. If she's so sure this was some kind of master plan then she can try to prove it. The truth is, and my young, idealistic colleague here can back me on this, we did not even become aware of Opparizio's organized crime connections until just recently. My investigator literally stumbled across them while tracking back all of Opparizio's holdings as listed in his SEC filings. The police and prosecution had the opportunity to do this but either chose to ignore it or came up short of the mark. I think counsel's upset largely extends from that, not what tactics I employ in court."

The judge, who was still leaning back and looking at the ceiling, made a waving gesture with his hand. I didn't know what it meant.

"Judge?"

Perry swung the chair around and leaned forward, addressing all three of us.

"So what do we do about this?"

He looked at me first. I glanced at Aronson to see if she had something to offer but she looked frozen in place. I turned back to the judge.

"I don't think there is anything that can be done. The witness invoked the Fifth. He's done testifying. We can't go on with him selectively using the Fifth whenever or wherever he wants. He invoked, he's done. Next witness. I have one more and then I'm done, too. I'll be ready to give my closing tomorrow morning."

Freeman could no longer take it sitting down. She stood up and started pacing a short pattern near the window.

"This is so unfair and so much a part of Mr. Haller's plan. He brings out the testimony he wants on direct, then pushes Opparizio into the Fifth, and then the state gets no cross, no redress at all. Is that even remotely fair, Your Honor?"

Perry didn't answer. He didn't have to. Everybody in the room knew the situation was unfair to the state. Freeman now had no opportunity to question Opparizio.

"I'm going to strike his entire testimony," Perry declared. "I'll tell the jury not to consider it."

Freeman folded her arms across her chest and shook her head in frustration.

"That's a helluva big bell to un-ring," she said. "This is a disaster for the prosecution, Judge. It's completely unfair."

I said nothing because Freeman was right. The judge could tell the jurors not to consider anything Opparizio had said but it was too late. The message was delivered and was floating around in all their heads. Just as I had intended.

"Sadly, I see no alternative," Perry said. "We'll take lunch now and I'll be thinking further on the issue. I suggest you three do the same. If you come up with something else before one, I will certainly entertain it."

No one said anything. It was hard to believe it had come to this. The end of the case in sight. And things falling just as planned.

"That means you can all leave now," Perry added. "I'll tell the deputy that Mr. Opparizio is relieved as a witness. He probably has the whole media throng in the hallway waiting to devour him. And he probably blames you for that, Mr. Haller. You might want to steer clear of him while he's in the courthouse."

"Yes, Your Honor."

Perry picked up the phone to call the deputy as we headed toward the door. I followed Freeman out and down the hallway to the court-room. I was expecting it when she turned on me with nothing but pure and piercing anger in her eyes.

"Now I know, Haller."

"Now you know what?"

"Why you and Maggie will never get back together again."

That put a pause in my step and Aronson walked right into me from behind. Freeman turned back around and kept going.

"That was a low blow, Mickey," Aronson said.

I watched Freeman go through the door to the courtroom.

"No," I said. "It wasn't."

Fifty-one

My last witness was my trusty investigator. Dennis "Cisco" Wojciechowski took the witness stand after lunch, after the judge told the jurors that all of Louis Opparizio's testimony was stricken from the record. Cisco had to spell his last name twice for the clerk but that was expected. He was indeed wearing the same shirt from the day before, but no jacket and no tie. The fluorescent lighting in the courtroom made the black ink chains that wrapped his biceps clearly visible through the stretched sleeves of the pale blue shirt.

"I'm just going to call you Dennis, if that is okay," I said. "It will be easier on the court reporter."

Polite laughter rolled through the courtroom.

"That's fine with me," the witness said.

"Okay, now, you work for me handling investigations for the defense, is that correct, Dennis?"

"Yes, that's what I do."

"And you worked extensively for the defense on the Mitchell Bondurant murder investigation, correct?"

"Correct. You could say that I piggybacked my investigation on the police investigation, checking to see if they missed anything or maybe got something wrong."

"Did you work from investigative materials that were turned over to the defense by the prosecution?"

"Yes, I did."

"Included in that material was a list of license plate numbers, correct?"

"Yes, the garage at WestLand National had a camera positioned over the drive-in entrance. Detectives Kurlen and Longstreth studied the recording from the camera and wrote down the plate number of every car that entered the garage between seven, when the garage opened, and nine, when it was determined that Mr. Bondurant was already dead. They then ran the plates through the law enforcement computer to see if any of the owners had criminal records or should be further investigated for other reasons."

"And were any further investigations generated from this list?"

"According to their investigative records, no."

"Now, Dennis, you mentioned you piggybacked on their investigation. Did you take this list and check these plate numbers out yourself?"

"I did. All seventy-eight of them. As best I could without access to law enforcement computers."

"And did any merit further attention or did you reach the same conclusion as detectives Kurlen and Longstreth?"

"Yes, one car merited more attention, in my opinion, and so I followed up on it."

I asked permission to give the witness a copy of the seventy-eight license plate numbers. The judge allowed it. Cisco pulled his reading glasses out of his shirt pocket and put them on.

"Which license plate did you want to further check out?"

"W-N-U-T-Z-nine."

"Why were you interested in that one?"

"Because at the time I looked at this list we were already far down the road in our other avenues of investigation. I knew that Louis Opparizio was part owner in a business called Wing Nuts. I thought maybe there was a connection to the vehicle that carried that plate."

"So what did you find out?"

"That the car was registered to Wing Nuts, a courier service that is partially owned by Louis Opparizio."

"And, again, why was that worthy of attention?"

"Well, as I said, I had the benefit of time. Kurlen and Longstreth put this list together on the day of the murder. They did not know all the key factors or individuals involved. I was looking at this several weeks down the road. And at that point I knew that the victim, Mr. Bondurant, had sent an incendiary letter to Mr. Opparizio and—"

Freeman objected to his description of the letter and the judge struck the word *incendiary* from the record. I then told Cisco to continue.

"From our viewpoint, that letter cut Opparizio in as a person of interest and so I was doing a lot of background work on him. I connected him through Wing Nuts to a partner named Dominic Capelli. Capelli is known to law enforcement in New York as an associate of an organized crime family run by a man named Joey Giordano. Capelli has various connections to other unsavory—"

Freeman objected again and the judge sustained it. I put on my best show of frustration, acting as though both the judge and prosecutor were keeping the truth from the jury.

"Okay, let's go back to the list and what it means. What did it show occurred at the garage involving a car owned by Wing Nuts?"

"It showed that the car entered the garage at eight oh-five."

"And what time did it leave?"

"The exit camera showed it leaving at eight fifty."

"So this vehicle entered the garage before the murder and left after the murder. Do I have that right?"

"That's correct."

"And the vehicle was owned by a company that was owned by a man with direct ties to organized crime. Is that also right?"

"Yes, it is."

"Okay, did you determine if there was a legitimate business reason for a vehicle belonging to Wing Nuts to be in that garage?"

"Of course, the business is a courier service. It is used regularly by ALOFT to deliver documents to WestLand National. But what was curious to me is why the car entered at eight oh-five and then left before the bank even opened at nine."

I looked at Cisco for a long moment. My gut said I had gotten all I needed to get. There was still chicken on the bone but sometimes you just have to push the plate away. Sometimes leaving the jury with a question is the best way to go.

"I have nothing further," I said.

My direct examination had been very precise in scope to include only testimony about the license plates. This left Freeman little to work with on cross. However, she did score one point when she elicited from Cisco a reminder to the jury that WestLand National occupied only three floors of a ten-story building. The courier from Wing Nuts could have been going somewhere other than the bank, thus explaining his early arrival in the garage.

I was sure that if there was a record of a courier delivery to an office in the building other than the bank, then she would produce it—or Opparizio's people would magically produce it for her—by the time she could put on rebuttal witnesses.

After a half hour, Freeman threw in the towel and sat down. That was when the judge asked if I had another witness to call.

"No, Your Honor," I said. "The defense rests."

The judge dismissed the jury for the day and instructed them to be in the assembly room by nine the next morning. Once they were gone Perry set the stage for the end of the trial, asking the attorneys if they would have rebuttal witnesses. I said no. Freeman said she wanted to reserve the right to call rebuttal witnesses in the morning.

"Okay, then we will reserve the morning session for rebuttal, if there is any rebuttal," Perry said. "Closing arguments will begin first thing after the lunch break and each side will be limited to one hour. With any luck and no more surprises, our jury will go into deliberations by this time tomorrow."

Perry left the bench then and I was left at the defense table with Aronson and Trammel. Lisa reached over and put her hand on top of mine.

"That was brilliant," she said. "The whole morning was brilliant. I think that the jurors finally get it as well. I was watching them. I think they know the truth."

I looked back at Trammel and then at Aronson, two different expressions on their faces.

"Thank you, Lisa. I guess it won't be long before we find out."

Fifty-two

I n the morning Andrea Freeman surprised me by not surprising me. She stood before the judge and said she had no rebuttal witnesses. She then rested the state's case.

This gave me pause. I had come to court fully prepared to face at least one final tilt with her. Testimony explaining the Wing Nuts car in the bank garage, or maybe Driscoll's supervisor putting the boots to him, even a prosecution foreclosure expert to contradict Aronson's assertions. But nothing. She folded the tent.

She was going with the blood. Whether I had robbed her of her *Boléro* crescendo or not, she was going to make her stand on the one incontrovertible aspect of the entire trial: the blood.

Judge Perry recessed court for the morning so the attorneys could work on their closing arguments and he could retreat to chambers to work on the jury charge — the final set of instructions jurors would take with them into deliberations.

I called Rojas and had him pick me up on Delano. I didn't want to go back to the office. Too many distractions. I told Rojas just to drive and I spread my files and notes out in the backseat of the Lincoln. This was where I did my best thinking, my best prep work.

At one o'clock sharp, court reconvened. Like everything else in the criminal justice system, closing arguments were tipped toward the state. The prosecution got to speak first and last. The defense got the middle.

It looked to me like Freeman was going with the standard prosecutorial format. Build the house with the facts on the first swing and then pull their emotional strings on the second.

Block by block she outlined the evidence against Lisa Trammel, seemingly leaving out nothing presented since the start of the trial. The discourse was dry but cumulative. She covered means and motive, and she brought it all home with the blood. The hammer, the shoes, the uncontested DNA findings.

"I told you at the beginning of this trial that blood would tell the tale," she said. "And here we are. You can discount everything else, but the blood evidence alone warrants a vote of guilty as charged. I am sure you will follow your conscience and do just that."

She sat down and then it was my turn. I stood in the opening in front of the jury box and addressed the twelve directly. But I wasn't alone in the well. As previously approved by the judge, I brought Manny out to stand with me. Dr. Shamiram Arslanian's erstwhile companion stood upright, with the hammer attached to the crown of his head, his head snapped back at the unusual angle that would have been necessary if Lisa Trammel had struck the fatal blow.

"Ladies and gentlemen of the jury," I began, "I've got good news. We should all be out of here and back to our normal lives by the end of the day. I appreciate your patience and your attentiveness during this trial. I appreciate your consideration of the evidence. I am not going to take a lot of time up here because I want to get you home as soon as possible. Today should be easy. This is a quick one. This case comes down to what I call a five-minute verdict. A case where reasonable doubt is so pervasive that a unanimous verdict will undoubtedly be reached on your very first ballot."

From there I highlighted the evidence the defense had brought forth and the contradictions and deficiencies in the state's case. I asked the unanswered questions. Why was the briefcase open? Why did the hammer go so long without being found? Why was Lisa Trammel's garage found unlocked and why would someone who was clearly going to succeed in defending her foreclosure case lash out against Bondurant?

It eventually brought me to the centerpiece of my closing — the mannequin.

"The demonstration by Dr. Arslanian alone puts the lie to the state's case. Without considering another single part of the defense case, Manny here gives you reasonable doubt. We know from the injuries to the knees of the victim that he was standing when struck with the fatal blow. And if he was standing, then this is the only position that he could have been in for Lisa Trammel to have been the killer. Head back, face to the ceiling. Is that possible, you must ask yourself. Is that likely? What would make Mitchell Bondurant look up? What was he looking up at?"

I paused there, hand in one pocket, adopting a casual and confident pose. I checked their eyes. All twelve of them were locked in on the mannequin. I then reached up to the handle of the hammer and slowly pushed it up, until the plastic face came down to a normal level and the handle stood out at a ninety-degree angle, too high for Lisa Trammel to grasp.

"The answer, ladies and gentlemen, is that he wasn't looking up because Lisa Trammel didn't do this. Lisa Trammel was driving home with her coffee while someone else carried out the plan to eliminate the threat that Mitchell Bondurant had become."

Another pause to let it sink in.

"Mitchell Bondurant had poked the sleeping tiger with his letter to Louis Opparizio. Whether intended or not, the letter was a threat to the two things that give the tiger its strength and fierceness. Money and power. It threatened a deal that was bigger than Louis Opparizio and Mitchell Bondurant. It threatened commerce and therefore it had to be dealt with.

"And it was. Lisa Trammel was chosen as the fall guy. She was known to the perpetrators of this crime, her movements had been monitored by them and she came with what appeared to be a credible motive. She was the perfect patsy. No one would believe her when she said, 'I didn't do this.' No one would give it a second thought. A plan was set in motion and carried out brazenly and efficiently. Mitchell Bondurant was left dead on the concrete floor of a garage, his briefcase pilfered on the floor right next to him. And the police showed up and went right along for the ride."

I shook my head in dismay, as though I carried the disgust of all society.

"The police had blinders on. Like those blinders put on horses so they stay on track. The police were on a track that led to Lisa Trammel and they would look at nothing else. Lisa Trammel, Lisa Trammel, Lisa

Trammel...Well, what about ALOFT and the tens of millions of dollars that Mitchell Bondurant was threatening? Nope, not interested. Lisa Trammel, Lisa Trammel, Lisa Trammel. The train was on the track and they rode it home."

I paused and paced in front of the jury. For the first time I looked about the courtroom. It was filled to capacity, with even some people standing in the back. I saw Maggie McPherson standing back there and next to her was my daughter. I froze in midstep but then quickly recovered. It made my heart feel good as I turned to the jury and brought my case to an end.

"But you see what they didn't see or refused to see. You see that they got on the wrong track. You see that they were cleverly manipulated. You see the truth."

I gestured to the mannequin.

"The physical evidence doesn't work. The circumstantial evidence doesn't work. The case doesn't bear scrutiny in the light of day. The only thing this case adds up to is reasonable doubt. Common sense tells you this. Your instincts tell you this. I urge you to set Lisa Trammel free. Let her go. It is the right thing to do."

I said thank you and returned to my seat, patting Manny on the shoulder as I passed. As we had previously planned, Lisa Trammel grabbed and squeezed my arm once I sat down. She mouthed the words *Thank you* for all on the jury to see.

I checked my watch under the defense table and saw I had taken only twenty-five minutes. I started to settle in for the second part of the state's closer when Freeman asked the judge to have me remove the mannequin from the courtroom. The judge told me to do so and I got back up.

I carried the mannequin to the gate, where I was met by Cisco, who had been in the audience.

"I got it, Boss," he whispered. "I'll take him outside."

"Thanks."

"You did good."

"Thanks."

Freeman moved to the well to deliver the second part of her summation. She wasted no time in attacking the contentions of the defense.

"I don't need any props to try to mislead you. I don't need any conspiracies or unnamed or unknown killers. I have the facts and the evidence that prove well beyond any reasonable doubt that Lisa Trammel murdered Mitchell Bondurant."

And it went from there. Freeman used her entire allotment of time hammering the defense case while bolstering the evidence the state had shown. It was a fairly routine Joe Friday closing. Just the facts, or the supposed facts, delivered like a steady drumbeat. Not bad but not all that good either. I saw the attention of some of the jurors wandering through parts of it, which could be taken two ways. One, they weren't buying it, or two, they had already bought it and didn't need to hear it again.

Freeman steadily amped it up until her big finish, a standard summing of the power and might of the state to cast judgment and exact justice.

"The facts of this case are unalterable. The facts do not lie. The evidence clearly shows that the defendant waited behind the pillar in the garage for Mitchell Bondurant. The evidence clearly shows that when he stepped out of his car, the defendant attacked. It was his blood on her hammer and his blood on her shoe. These are facts, ladies and gentlemen. These are undisputed facts. These are the building blocks of evidence. Evidence that proves beyond a reasonable doubt that Lisa Trammel killed Mitchell Bondurant. That she came up behind him and brutally struck him with her hammer. That she even hit him again and again after he was down and dead. We don't know exactly what position he was in or she was in. She is the only one who knows that. But we do know that she did it. The evidence in this case points to one person."

And of course Freeman had to point the finger at my client.

"Her. Lisa Trammel. She did it and now through the tricks of her attorney she asks you to let her go. Don't do it. Give Mitchell Bondurant justice. Find his killer guilty of this crime. Thank you."

Freeman took her seat. I gave her closing a B but I had already awarded myself an A — egotist that I am. Still, usually all it took was a C for the prosecution to triumph. It's always a stacked deck for the state and often the defense attorney's very best work is simply not good enough to overcome the power and the might.

Judge Perry moved directly into the jury charge, reading his final instructions to them. These were not only the rules of deliberations but also instructions specific to the case. He gave great attention to Louis

Opparizio and warned again that his testimony was not to be considered during the deliberations.

The charge ended up being nearly as long as my closing but finally, just after three, the judge sent the twelve jurors back to the assembly room to begin their task. As I watched them file through the door I was at least relaxed, if not confident. I had put the best case forward that I could. I had certainly bent some rules and pushed some boundaries. I had even put myself at risk. At risk based on the law but also something more dangerous. I had risked myself by believing in the possibility of my client's innocence.

I looked over at Lisa as the door to the deliberations room closed. I saw no fear in her eyes and once again I bought in. She was already sure of the verdict. There wasn't a doubt on her face.

"What do you think?" Aronson whispered to me.

"I think we've got a fifty-fifty shot at this and that's better than we usually get, especially on a murder. We'll see."

The judge recessed court after making sure the clerk had contact numbers for all parties and urging us to stay somewhere no more than fifteen minutes away, should a verdict come in. My office was in that range so we decided to head back there. Feeling optimistic and magnanimous, I even told Lisa she could invite Herb Dahl along. I felt it would be my obligation to eventually inform her of her guardian angel's treachery, but that conversation would be saved for another day.

As the defense party walked out into the hallway the media started to gather around us, clamoring for a statement from Lisa or at least me. Behind the crowd I saw Maggie leaning against a wall, my daughter sitting on a bench next to her while texting away on her phone. I told Aronson to handle the reporters and I started to slip away.

"Me?" Aronson said.

"You know what to say. Just don't let Lisa talk. Not till we have a verdict."

I waved off a couple of trailing reporters and got to Maggie and Hayley. I made a quick feint one way and then went the other, kissing my daughter on the cheek before she could duck.

"*Daaaaddd!*"

I straightened up and looked at Maggie. She had a small smile on her face.

"You pulled her out of school for me?"

"I thought she should be here."

It was a major concession.

"Thank you," I said. "So what did you think?"

"I think you could sell ice in Antarctica," she said.

I smiled.

"But that doesn't mean you're going to win," she added.

I frowned.

"Thanks a lot."

"Well, what do you want from me? I'm a prosecutor. I don't like to see the guilty go free."

"Well, that won't be a problem in this case."

"I guess you have to believe what you have to believe."

I was back to smiling. I checked my daughter and saw she was back to texting, oblivious to our conversation as usual.

"Did Freeman talk to you yesterday?"

"You mean about you pulling the Fifth witness move? Yes. You don't play fair, Haller."

"It's not a fair game. Did she tell you what she said to me after?"

"No, what did she say?"

"Never mind. She was wrong."

She knitted her eyebrows. She was intrigued.

"I'll tell you later," I said. "We're all going to walk over to my office to wait. You two want to come?"

"No, I think I need to get Hayley home. She's got homework."

My phone buzzed in my pocket. I pulled it and took a look. The screen said

L.A. Superior Court

I took the call. It was Judge Perry's clerk. I listened and then hung up. I looked around to make sure Lisa Trammel was still nearby.

"What is it?" Maggie asked.

I looked back at her.

"We already have a verdict. A five-minute verdict."

408

PART FIVE

The Hypocrisy
of Innocence

Fifty-three

They came in droves, pouring in from all over Southern California, all brought by the siren song of Facebook. Lisa Trammel had announced the party the morning after the verdict and now on Saturday afternoon they were ten deep at the cash bars. They waved the Stars and Stripes and wore red, white and blue. Fighting foreclosure with the nearly martyred leader of the cause was now more American than ever before. At every door to the house and spaced at intervals in the front and back yards were ten-gallon buckets for donations to defray Trammel's expenses and keep the fight going. FLAG pins for a buck, cheap cotton T-shirts for ten. And posing with Lisa for a photo required a minimum twenty-dollar donation.

But nobody complained. Fired in the kiln of false accusation, Lisa Trammel had emerged unscathed and appeared to be about to make the jump from activist to icon. And she wasn't unhappy about it. The rumor was that Julia Roberts was in talks to play the part in the movie.

My crew and I were stationed in the backyard at a picnic table with an umbrella. We had come early and gotten the spot. Cisco and Lorna were drinking canned beer and Aronson and I were on bottled water. There was a slight tension at the table and I picked up enough innuendo to understand that it had something to do with how late Cisco had stayed at Four Green Fields with Aronson back on Monday night after I'd left with Maggie McFierce.

"Jeez, look at all of these people," Lorna said. "Don't they know that a not-guilty verdict doesn't mean she's innocent?"

"That's bad etiquette, Lorna," I said. "You're never supposed to say that, especially when it's your own client you're talking about."

"I know."

She frowned and shook her head.

"You're not a believer, Lorna?"

"Well, don't tell me you are."

I was glad I was wearing sunglasses. I didn't want to reveal myself on this one. I shrugged like I didn't know or it didn't matter.

But it did. You have to live with yourself. Knowing that there was a solid chance that Lisa Trammel actually deserved the verdict she got made things a whole lot better when I looked in the mirror.

"Well, I'll tell you one thing," Lorna said. "Our phone hasn't stopped ringing since the verdict came in. We're back in business big time."

Cisco nodded approvingly. It was true. It seemed as though every accused criminal in the city wanted to hire me now. This would've been great if I had wanted things to continue the way they were going.

"Did you check out the closing price on LeMure yesterday on NAS-DAQ?" Cisco asked.

I gave him a look.

"You following the Street now?"

"Just wanted to see if anybody was paying attention and it looks like they were. LeMure dropped thirty percent of its value in two days. Didn't help that the *Wall Street Journal* ran a story connecting Opparizio to Joey Giordano and questioning how much of that sixty-one mill he got went into the mob's pocket."

"Probably all of it," Lorna said.

"So Mickey," Aronson said. "How'd you know?"

"Know what?"

"That Opparizio would take the nickel."

I shrugged again.

"I didn't. I just figured that once it became apparent that his connections were going to come out in open court, he would do what he had to do to stop it. He had one choice. The Fifth."

Aronson didn't look as though my answer appeased her. I turned away and looked across the crowded yard. My client's son was at a nearby table with her sister. They both looked bored, as if forced to be there. A large group of children had gathered near the terraced herb garden. A woman in the middle of the circle was handing out candy from a bag. She was wearing a red, white and blue top hat like Uncle Sam's.

"How long do we need to stay, Boss?" Cisco asked.

"You're not on the clock," I said. "I just thought we should put in an appearance."

"I want to stay," Lorna said, probably just to spite him. "Maybe some Hollywood people will show up."

A few minutes later the main attraction of the day came out the back door, followed by a reporter and a cameraman. They picked a location with the crowd in the background and Lisa Trammel stood for a quick interview. I didn't bother to try to listen. I'd heard and seen the same interview enough over the past two days.

After Lisa finished the interview she broke away from the media, shook some hands and posed for some photos. Eventually, she made her way to our table, stopping to ruffle her son's hair on the way.

"There they are. The victors! How's my team doing today?"

I managed to smile.

"We're good, Lisa. And you look fine, too. Where's Herb?"

She looked around as if searching for Dahl in the crowd.

"I don't know. He was supposed to be here."

"Too bad," Cisco said. "We'll miss him."

Lisa didn't seem to register the sarcasm.

"You know I need to talk to you later, Mickey," she said. "I need your advice on which show to do. *Good Morning America* or *Today*? They both want me next week but I have to pick one because neither will take seconds."

I flipped my hand as if the answer didn't matter.

"I don't know. Herb can probably help you with that. He's the media guy."

Lisa looked back at the gathering of children and started to smile.

"Oh, I have just the thing for those children. Excuse me, everybody."

She hurried off and went around the corner of the house.

"She's sure loving it, isn't she?" Cisco said.

"I would be, too," Lorna said.

I looked at Aronson.

"Why so quiet?"

She shrugged.

"I don't know. I'm not so sure I like criminal defense anymore. I think if you take on some of those people who have been calling, I'll stick with the foreclosures. If you don't mind."

I nodded.

"I think I know what you're feeling. You can do the foreclosure work if you want to. There's going to be plenty of that for a while, especially with guys like Opparizio still in business. But that feeling you've got does go away. Believe me, Bullocks, it does."

She didn't respond to the return of her nickname or anything else I had said. I turned to look across the yard. Lisa was back and she had rolled out the helium tank from the garage. She told the children to gather around and started filling balloons. The TV cameraman moved in to get the shot. It would be perfect for the six o'clock news.

"Now, is she doing that for the kids or for the camera?" Cisco asked.

"You really have to ask?" Lorna responded.

Lisa pulled a blue balloon off the tank and expertly tied it off with a string. She handed it to a girl of about six, who grabbed the string and let the balloon shoot six feet above her head. The girl smiled and turned her face up to gaze at her new toy. And in that moment I knew what Mitchell Bondurant was looking up at when Lisa hit him with the hammer.

"She did it," I whispered under my breath.

I felt the burn of a million synapses firing down my neck and across my shoulders.

"What did you say?" Aronson asked me.

I looked at her but didn't answer and then looked back at my client. She filled another balloon with gas, tied the knot and handed it to a boy. The same thing happened again. The boy held the string and turned his cheery face up to look at the red balloon. An instinctive, natural response. To look up at the balloon.

"Oh, my God," Aronson said.

She had put it together, too.

"That's how she did it."

Now Cisco and Lorna had turned.

"The witness said she was carrying a big shopping bag on the sidewalk," Aronson said. "Big enough to hold a hammer, yes, but also big enough to hold balloons."

I took it from there.

"She sneaks into the garage and puts the balloons up over Bondurant's parking space. Maybe there's a note on the end of each string so he's sure to see them."

"Yeah," Cisco said. "Like, here's your balloon payment."

"She hides behind the pillar and waits," I said.

"And when Bondurant looks up at the balloons," Cisco concluded, "*bang*, right on the back of the head."

I nodded.

"And the two pops somebody thought were gunshots but were dismissed as backfire were neither," I said. "She popped the balloons on the way out."

A dreadful silence fell over the table. Until Lorna spoke.

"Wait a minute. You're saying she planned it that way? Like she knew if she hit him on the top of the head it would throw the jury?"

I shook my head.

"No, that was just luck. She just wanted to stop him. She used the balloons to make sure he paused and she could come up behind him. The rest was just dumb luck...something that a defense lawyer knew how to use."

I couldn't look at my colleagues. I stared off at Lisa filling balloons.

"So...we helped her get away with it."

It was a statement from Lorna. Not a question.

"Double jeopardy," Aronson said. "She can never be tried again."

As if on cue Lisa looked over at us while she tied off the end of a white balloon. She handed it to another child.

And she smiled at me.

"Cisco, how much are they charging for the beer?"

"Five bucks a can. It's a rip-off."

"Mickey, don't," Lorna said. "It's not worth it. You've been so good."

I pulled my eyes away from my client and looked at Lorna.

"Good? Are you saying I'm one of the good guys?"

I got up and left them there and headed toward the backyard bar, where I took my place in line. I expected Lorna to follow me but it was Aronson who came up next to me. She spoke in a very low voice.

"Look, what are you doing? You told me not to grow a conscience. Are you telling me you did?"

"I don't know," I whispered. "All I know is that she played me like a fucking fiddle and you know what? She knows I know. She just gave me that smile. I saw it in her eyes. She's proud of it. She pulled the tank into the yard so I would see it and I would know..."

I shook my head.

"She had me wired from day one. Everything was part of her plan. Every last—"

I stopped as I realized something.

"What?" Aronson asked.

I paused as I continued to put it together.

"What, Mickey?"

"Her husband wasn't even her husband."

"What do you mean?"

"The guy calling me, the guy who showed up. Where is he now for the big payday? He's not here because that wasn't him. He was just part of the play."

"Then where is the husband?"

That was the question. But I had no answer. I didn't have any answers anymore.

"I'm leaving."

I stepped out of the line and headed toward the back door.

"Mickey, where are you going?"

I didn't answer. I quickly passed through the house and out the front door. I had arrived early enough to grab a curb slot only two houses down. I was almost to the Lincoln when I heard my name called from behind.

It was Lisa. She was walking toward me in the street.

"Mickey! You're leaving?"

"Yes, I'm leaving."

"Why? The party's just starting."

She came up close to me and stopped.

"I'm leaving because I know, Lisa. I know."

"What do you think you know?"

"That you used me like you use everybody. Even Herb Dahl."

"Oh, come on, you're a defense lawyer. You'll get more business out of this than you've ever had before."

Just like that, she acknowledged everything.

"What if I didn't want the business? What if I just wanted to believe something was true?"

She paused. She didn't get it.

"Get over yourself, Mickey. Wake up."

I nodded. It was good advice.

"Who was he, Lisa?" I asked.

"Who was who?"

"The guy you sent me who said he was your husband."

Now a small proud smile curled her bottom lip.

"Goodbye, Mickey. Thank you for everything."

She turned and started walking back toward her house. And I got in my Lincoln and drove away.

Fifty-four

I was in the backseat of the Lincoln cruising through the Third Street tunnel when my phone started to buzz. The screen said it was Maggie. I told Rojas to kill the music—one of my favorite Clapton cuts—and took the call.

"Did you do it?" she asked first thing.

I looked out the window as we broke clear of the tunnel and into the bright sunlight. It fit with the way I was feeling. It had been three weeks since the verdict and the further I got away from it the better I felt. I was on the road to something else now.

"I did."

"Wow! Congratulations."

"I'm still the longest long shot you'll ever see. The field is full and I've got no money."

"Doesn't matter. You're a name in this town and there's a certain integrity about you that people see and respond to. I know I did. Plus you're an outsider. Outsiders always win. So don't kid yourself, the money will come."

I wasn't sure *integrity* and *me* belonged in the same sentence. But I'd take the rest and, besides, it was the happiest I'd heard Maggie McFierce in a long, long time.

"Well, we'll see," I said. "But as long as I have your vote, I don't care if I get another."

"That's sweet, Haller. What's next?"

"Good question. I have to go open a bank account and assemble a—"

My phone started beeping. I had another call coming in. I checked the screen and saw that it was blocked.

"Mags, hold on a second, let me just check this call."

"Go ahead."

I switched over.

"This is Michael Haller."

"You did this."

I recognized the angry voice. Lisa Trammel.

"Did what?"

"The police are here! They're digging up the garden looking for him. You sent them!"

I assumed the "him" she referred to was her missing husband, who never quite made it to Mexico. Her voice had the familiar shrill tone it took on when she was on the edge of losing it.

"Lisa, I—"

"I need you here! I need a lawyer. They're going to arrest me!"

Meaning that she knew what the police would find in the garden.

"Lisa, I'm not your lawyer anymore. I can recommend a—"

"Nooooo! You can't abandon me! Not now!"

"Lisa, you just accused me of sending the cops. Now you want me to represent you?"

"I need you, Mickey. Please."

She started crying, that long echoing sob I had heard too many times before.

"Get somebody else, Lisa. I'm done. With any luck I might even get to prosecute you."

"What are you talking about?"

"I just filed. I'm running for district attorney."

"I don't understand."

"I'm changing my life. I'm tired of being around people like you."

There was no response at first but I could hear her breathing. When she finally spoke, her voice had a flat, emotionless tone to it.

"I should have told Herb to have them maim you. That's what you deserve."

Now I was silent. I knew what she was talking about. The Mack brothers. Dahl had lied to me and said Opparizio had ordered the beating. But that didn't fit with the rest of the story. This did. It had been Lisa who wanted it done. She was willing to have her own attorney attacked if it would deflect suspicion and help her case. If it would help me believe in other possibilities.

I managed to find my voice and say my final words to her.

"Goodbye, Lisa. And good luck."

I composed myself and switched back over to my ex-wife.

"Sorry...it was a client. A former client."

"Everything all right?"

I leaned against the window. Rojas was just turning on Alvarado and heading to the 101.

"I'm good. So you want to go somewhere tonight and talk about the campaign?"

"You know, while I was on hold I was thinking, why don't you come to my place? We can eat with Hayley and then talk while she does her homework."

It was a rare invite to her home.

"So a guy has to run for DA to get invited over to your place?"

"Don't press your luck, Haller."

"I won't. What time?"

"Six."

"See you then."

I disconnected and stared out the window for a little while.

"Mr. Haller?" Rojas asked. "You're running for DA?"

"Yeah. You have a problem with that, Rojas?"

"No, Boss. But do you still need a driver?"

"Sure, Rojas, your job is safe."

I called the office and Lorna answered.

"Where is everybody?"

"They're here. Jennifer is using your office for a new client interview. A foreclosure. And Dennis is doing something on the computer. Where have you been?"

"Downtown. But I'm heading back. Make sure nobody leaves. I want to have a staff meeting."

"Okay, I'll tell them."

"Good. See you in about thirty."

I closed the phone. We were coming up the ramp onto the 101. All six lanes were clogged with metal, moving at a steady but slow pace. I wouldn't have had it any other way. This was my city and this was the way it was supposed to run. At Rojas's command, the black Lincoln cut through the lanes and around the traffic, carrying me toward a new destiny.

Acknowledgments

The author wishes to thank several people for their help during the writing of this novel. They include Asya Muchnick, Bill Massey, Terrill Lee Lankford, Jane Davis and Heather Rizzo. Special thanks also go to Susanna Brougham, Tracy Roe, Daniel Daly, Roger Mills, Jay Stein, Rick Jackson, Tim Marcia, Mike Roche, Greg Stout, John Houghton, Dennis Wojciechowski, Charles Hounchell and last but not least, Linda Connelly.

This is a novel. Any errors of fact, geography or legal canon and procedure are purely the fault of the author.

About the Author

Michael Connelly is a former police reporter for the *Los Angeles Times*, and is the author of the acclaimed and bestselling Harry Bosch thrillers, including his most recent, *The Reversal*, as well as several stand-alone bestsellers, including *The Poet*. Michael Connelly is a former President of the Mystery Writers of America. His books have been translated into thirty-nine languages and have won numerous awards. He lives with his family in Tampa, Florida.

And for more Michael Connelly...

Please turn this page for a preview of *The Drop*, available in hardback in October 2011.

One

Christmas came once a month in the Open-Unsolved Unit. That was when, like Santa Claus, the lieutenant made her way around the squad room, parceling out yellow envelopes like presents to the squad's six detective teams. They contained cold hits, the lifeblood of the unit. The teams didn't wait for callouts and fresh kills in Open-Unsolved. They waited for cold hits.

The Open-Unsolved Unit investigated unsolved murders going back fifty years in Los Angeles. There were six thousand of them. The unit consisted of twelve detectives, a secretary, a squad room supervisor known as the whip, and the lieutenant. The first five teams of detectives had each been randomly assigned ten of those fifty years. Their task was to pull from archives all the unsolved homicide cases, evaluate them and submit long-stored, long-forgotten evidence for reanalysis using contemporary technology. All DNA submissions were handled by the new regional lab at Cal State. A match between DNA from an old case and that of an individual whose genetic profile was carried in any of the nation's DNA databases was called a cold hit. The lab put cold-hit notices into the mail at the end of every month. They would arrive a day or two later at the Police Administration Building in downtown Los Angeles. Usually by 8 A.M. that day, the lieutenant would open the door of her private office and enter the squad room. She carried the envelopes in her hand. Each hit sheet was mailed individually in a yellow business envelope. Typically, an envelope was handed to the pair of detectives who had

1

submitted the related DNA evidence to the lab. But sometimes there were too many cold hits for one team to handle at once. Sometimes detectives were in court or on vacation or leave. And sometimes the cold hits revealed circumstances that required the utmost finesse and experience. That was where the sixth team came in. Detectives Harry Bosch and David Chu were the sixth team. They were floaters. They handled overflow cases and special investigations.

On Monday morning, October 3, Lieutenant Gail Duvall stepped out of her office and into the squad room carrying only three yellow envelopes. Harry Bosch almost sighed when he saw this paltry return on the squad's DNA submissions. He knew that with so few envelopes he would not be getting a new case to work.

Bosch had been back in the unit for almost a year, following a two-year reassignment to Homicide Special. Now on his second tour of duty in Open-Unsolved, he had quickly fallen back into the rhythm of the work. It wasn't a fly squad. There was no dashing out the door to get to a crime scene. In fact, there were no crime scenes. There were only files and archive boxes. It was primarily an eight-to-four gig but with an asterisk, which meant that his job involved more travel than that of the other detective teams. People who got away with murder, or at least thought they had, tended not to stick around. They moved elsewhere and often the OU detectives had to travel to find them.

A big part of the rhythm was the monthly arrival of the yellow envelopes. Sometimes Bosch found it hard to sleep on the night before Christmas. He never took time off during the first week of the month and never came to work late on a day when the yellow envelopes might come in. Even his teenage daughter noticed his monthly cycle of anticipation and agitation and had likened it to a menstrual cycle. Bosch didn't see the humor in this and was embarrassed when she brought it up.

Now his disappointment at the sight of so few envelopes in the lieutenant's hand felt palpable in his throat. He wanted a new case. He *needed* a new case. He had to see the look on the killer's face when Bosch knocked on the door and showed his badge, the embodiment of justice come calling unexpectedly after so many years. The experience was addictive and Bosch was craving it now.

The lieutenant handed the first envelope to Rick Jackson. He and his partner, Rich Bengtson, were solid investigators who had been with the unit since its inception. Bosch had no complaint there. The next envelope was placed on an empty desk belonging to Teddy Baker. She and her partner, Greg Kehoe, were on their way back from a pickup in Tampa, Florida—an airline pilot who had been connected through fingerprints to the 1991 strangulation of a flight attendant in Marina del Rey.

Bosch was about to suggest to the lieutenant that Baker and Kehoe might have their hands full with the marina case and that the envelope should be given to another team, namely his, when the lieutenant looked at him and used the last remaining envelope to beckon him to her office.

"Can you guys step in for a minute? You, too, Tim."

Tim Marcia was the squad whip, the detective-3 who handled mostly supervisory and fill-in duties. He mentored the young detectives and made sure the old ones like Jackson and Bosch didn't get lazy.

Bosch was out of his seat before the lieutenant had finished her question. He headed toward the lieutenant's office with Chu and Marcia trailing behind.

"Close the door," Duvall said. "Sit down."

Duvall had a corner office with windows that looked across Spring Street at the Los Angeles Times Building. Paranoid that reporters were watching from the newsroom across the way, Duvall kept her shades permanently lowered. It made the office dim and cavelike. Bosch and Chu took the two seats positioned in front of the lieutenant's desk. Marcia followed them in, moved to the side of Duvall's desk and leaned against an old evidence safe.

"I want you two to handle this hit," she said, sitting down and proffering the yellow envelope to Bosch. "There's something wrong here and I want you to keep quiet about it until you find out what it is. Keep Tim in the loop but make sure it stays low-key."

The envelope had already been opened. Chu leaned over to look as Bosch opened the flap and pulled out the hit sheet. It listed the case number of the DNA evidence, plus the name, age, last known address and criminal history of the person whose genetic profile matched it. Bosch first noticed that the case number had the prefix 89, meaning it was a case from 1989. There were no details about the crime, just the year. But Bosch knew that cases from that year belonged to the team of Ross

Shuler and Adriana Dolan. He knew this because 1989 had been a busy year for him, working murders for the Homicide Special Team, and he had recently checked on one of his own unsolved cases, which was how he learned that jurisdiction over that year's cases belonged to Shuler and Dolan. They were known in the unit as "the kids." They were young, passionate and skillful investigators, but between them they had less than eight years' experience working homicides. If there was something unusual about this cold hit, it was not surprising that the lieutenant would want Bosch on it. Bosch had worked more killings than everybody else in the unit combined. That is, if you left out Jackson. He had been around forever.

Bosch next studied the name on the hit sheet: Clayton S. Pell. It meant nothing to him. But Pell's arrest record included numerous arrests and three separate convictions for indecent exposure, false imprisonment and forcible rape. He had spent six years in prison for the rape before being released eighteen months ago. He had a five-year probation tail and his last known address came from the state probation and parole board. He was assigned to a halfway house for sex offenders in Panorama City.

Based on Pell's record, Bosch believed the 1989 case was likely a sex-related murder. He could feel his insides beginning to tighten. He was going to grab Clayton Pell and bring him to justice.

"Do you see it?" Duvall asked.

"See what?" Bosch asked. "Was this a sex killing? It looks like this guy has the classic pred—"

"The birth date," Duvall said.

Bosch looked back down at the hit sheet as Chu leaned closer.

"Yeah, right here," Bosch said. "November nine, nineteen eighty-one. What's that got—"

"He's too young," Chu said.

Bosch glanced at him and then back down at the sheet. He suddenly got it. Clayton Pell was born in 1981. He was only eight years old at the time of the murder.

"Exactly," Duvall said. "So I want you to get the book and box from Shuler and Dolan and very quietly figure out what we have here. I'm hoping to God they didn't get two cases mixed up and send genetic material from a more recent case labeled as if it came from this old one. Like you were about to say, this guy on the hit sheet is no doubt a predator, but I don't think he got away with a killing when he was only eight years old. So something doesn't fit. Find it and come back to me before you do anything. If they screwed up and we can correct it, then we won't need to worry about IAD or anybody else. We'll just keep it right here."

She may have appeared to be trying to protect Shuler and Dolan from Internal Affairs, but she was also shielding herself and Bosch knew it. There would not be much vertical movement in the department for a lieutenant who had presided over an evidence-handling scandal in her own unit.

"What other years are assigned to Shuler and Dolan?" Bosch asked.

"On the recent side, they've got 'ninety-seven and two thousand," Marcia said. "This evidence could have come from a case they were working from one of those two years."

Bosch nodded. He could see the scenario. Due to reckless handling, genetic evidence from one case cross-pollinates with another. The end result would be two tainted cases and a scandal that would smear anybody near it.

"What do we say to Shuler and Dolan?" Chu asked. "What's the reason we're taking the case from them?"

Duvall looked up at Marcia.

"They've got a trial coming up," he offered in answer to her unspoken question. "Jury selection starts Thursday."

Duvall nodded.

"I'll tell them I want them clear for that."

"And what if they say they still want the case?" Chu asked. "What if they say they can handle it?"

"I'll put them straight," Duvall said. "Anything else, Detectives?"

Bosch looked up at her.

"We'll work the case, Lieutenant, and see what's what. But I don't investigate other cops."

"That's fine. I'm not asking you to. Work the case and tell me how the DNA came back to an eight-year-old kid, okay?"

Bosch nodded and started to stand up.

"Just remember," Duvall added, "you talk to me before you do anything with what you learn."

"You got it," Bosch said.

He, Chu and Marcia prepared to leave the room.

"Harry," the lieutenant said, "hang back a second."

Bosch looked at Chu and raised his eyebrows. He didn't know what this was about. The lieutenant came around from behind her desk and closed the door after Chu and Marcia had left. She remained standing, looking businesslike.

"I just wanted you to know that your application for an extension on your drop came through. They gave you four years retroactive."

Bosch looked at her, doing the math. He nodded. He had asked for the maximum—five years nonretroactive—but he'd take what they gave. It wouldn't keep him much past high school but it was better than nothing.

"Well, I'm glad," Duvall said. "It gives you thirty-nine more months with us."

Her tone indicated that she had read the disappointment on his face.

"No," he said quickly. "I'm glad. I was just thinking about where that would put me with my daughter. All the way through high school. So that's good."

"Good then."

That was her way of saying the meeting was over. Bosch thanked her and left the office. As he stepped back into the squad room he looked across the vast expanse of desks and dividers and file cabinets. He knew it was home and that he would get to stay—for now.

Two

The Open-Unsolved Unit shared access to the two fifth-floor conference rooms with all other units in the Robbery-Homicide Division. Usually detectives had to reserve time in one of the rooms, signing up on the clipboard hooked on the door. But this early on a Monday, both were open, and Bosch, Chu, Shuler and Dolan commandeered the smaller of the two without making a reservation.

They brought with them the murder book and the small archival evidence box from the 1989 case.

"Okay," Bosch said, when everyone was seated. "So you are cool with us running with this case? If you're not, we can go back to the lieutenant and say you really want to work it."

"No, it's okay," Shuler said. "We both are involved in the trial so it's better this way. It's our first case in the unit and we want to see it through to that guilty verdict."

Bosch nodded as he casually opened the murder book.

"You want to give us the rundown on this one then?"

Shuler gave Dolan a nod and she began to summarize the 1989 case as Bosch flipped through the pages of the binder.

"We have a nineteen-year-old victim named Lilly Price. She was snatched off the street while walking home from the beach in Venice on a Sunday afternoon. At the time, they narrowed the grab point down to the vicinity of Speedway and Voyage. Price lived on Voyage with three roommates. One was with her on the beach and two were in the apartment.

She disappeared between those two points. She said she was going back to use the bathroom and she never made it."

"She left her towel and a Walkman on the beach," Shuler said. "Sunscreen. So it was clear she was intending to come back. She never did."

"Her body was found the next morning on the rocks down at the cut," Dolan said. "She was naked and had been raped and strangled. Her clothes were never found. The ligature used to strangle her was removed."

Bosch flipped through several plastic-covered pages containing faded Polaroid shots of the crime scene. Looking at the victim, he couldn't help but think of his own daughter, who at fifteen had a full life in front of her. There had been a time when looking at photos like this fueled him, gave him the fire he needed to be relentless. But since Maddie had come to live with him, it was becoming more difficult for him to look at victims.

It didn't stop him from building the fire, however.

"Where did the DNA come from?" he asked. "Semen?"

"No, the killer used a condom or didn't ejaculate," Dolan said. "No semen."

"It came from a little smear of blood," Shuler said. "It was found on her neck, right below the right ear. She had no wounds in that area. It was assumed that it had come from the killer, that he had been cut or maybe was already bleeding. If she was strangled from behind then his hand could have been against her neck there. If there was a cut on his hand..."

"Transfer deposit," Chu said.

"Exactly."

Bosch found the Polaroid that showed the victim's neck and the smear. The color had been washed out by time and he could barely see the blood. A ruler had been placed on the girl's neck to give the measure of the blood smear. It was less than an inch long.

"So this blood was collected and stored," he said, a statement meant to draw further explanation.

"Yes," Shuler said. "Because it was a smear it was swabbed. Back then, they typed it. O-positive. The swab was stored in a tube and we found it still in Property when we pulled the case. The blood had turned to powder."

Shuler tapped the top of the archive box with a pen.

Bosch's phone started to vibrate in his pocket. Normally, he would let the call go to message, but his daughter was home sick from school and alone. He needed to make sure the call wasn't from her. He pulled the phone out of his pocket and glanced at the screen. It wasn't his daughter. It was a former partner, Kizmin Rider, now a lieutenant assigned to the OCP—office of the chief of police. He decided he would return her call after the meeting. They had lunch together about once a month and he assumed she must be free today or was calling because she'd heard about his getting approved for another four years on the drop. He shoved the phone back into his pocket.

"Did you open the tube?" he asked.

"Of course not," Shuler said.

"Okay, so four months ago you sent the tube containing the swab and what was left of the blood out to the regional lab, right?" he asked.

"That's right," Shuler said.

Bosch flipped through the murder book to the autopsy report. He was acting like he was more interested in what he was seeing than in what he was saying.

"And at that time, did you submit anything else to the lab?"

"From the Price case?" Dolan asked. "No, that was the only biological evidence they came up with back at the time."

Bosch nodded, hoping she would keep talking.

"But back then it didn't lead to anything," she said. "They never came up with a suspect. Who'd they come up with on the cold hit?"

"We'll get to that in a second," Bosch said. "What I meant was, did you submit to the lab from any other cases you were working? Or was this all you had going?"

"No, that was it," Shuler said, squinting. "What's going on here, Harry?"

Bosch reached into his inside coat pocket and pulled out the hit sheet. He slid it across the table to Shuler.

"The hit comes back to a sexual predator who would look real good for this except for one thing."

Shuler unfolded the sheet and he and Dolan leaned together to read it, just as Bosch and Chu had earlier.

"What's that?" Dolan said, not picking up on the birth date yet. "This guy looks perfect."

"He's perfect now," Bosch said. "But back then he was only eight years old."

"You're kidding," Dolan said.

"What the fuck?" Shuler added.

Dolan pulled the sheet away from her partner as if to see it clearer and to double-check the birth date. Shuler leaned back and looked at Bosch with those suspicious eyes.

"So you think we fucked up and mixed up some cases," he said.

"Nope," Bosch said. "The lieutenant asked us to check out the possibility but I don't see any fuckup on this end."

"So it happened at the lab," Shuler said. "Do you realize that if they screwed things up at regional, every defense lawyer in the county is going to be able to raise doubts about DNA matches that come out of there?"

"Yeah, I kind of figure that," Bosch said. "Which is why you should keep this under your hat until we know what happened. There are other possibilities."

Dolan held up the hit sheet.

"Yeah, what if there is no fuckup anywhere? What if it's really this kid's blood on that dead girl?"

"An eight-year-old boy snatches a nineteen-year-old girl off the street, rapes and strangles her and dumps the body four blocks away?" Chu asked. "Never happened."

"Well, maybe he was there," Dolan said. "Maybe this was how he got his start as a predator. You see his record. This guy fits—except for his age."

Bosch nodded.

"Maybe," he said. "Like I said, there are other possibilities. No reason to panic yet."

His phone started to vibrate again. He pulled it and saw it was Kiz Rider again. Two calls in five minutes—he decided he'd better take it. This couldn't be about lunch.

"I have to step out for a second."

Bosch answered the call as he stepped out of the conference room into the hallway.

"Kiz?"

"Harry, I've been trying to get to you with a heads-up."

"I'm in a meeting. What heads-up?"

"You are about to get a forthwith from the OCP."

"You want me to come up to ten?"

In the new PAB, the chief's suite of offices was on the tenth floor, complete with a private courtyard balcony that looked out across the civic center.

"No, Sunset Strip. You're going to be sent to a scene to take over a case. And you're not going to like it."

"Look, Lieutenant, I just got a case this morning. I don't need another one."

He thought that using her formal title would communicate his wariness. Forthwiths and assignments out of the OCP always carried high jingo—political overtones. It could be hard to navigate your way through it.

"He's not going to give you a choice here, Harry."

He being the chief of police.

"What's the case?"

"A jumper at the Chateau Marmont."

"Who was it?"

"Harry, I think you should wait for the chief to call you. I just wanted to—"

"Who was it, Kiz? If you know anything about me I think you know I can keep a secret until it's no longer a secret."

She paused before answering.

"From what I understand there is not a lot that is recognizable—he came down seven floors onto concrete. But the initial ID is George Thomas Irving. Age forty-six, of Eight—"

"Irving as in Irvin Irving? As in Councilman Irvin Irving?"

"Scourge of the LAPD in general and one Detective Harry Bosch in particular. Yes, one and the same. It's his son, and Councilman Irving has spoken to the chief and insisted that you take over the investigation. The chief said, 'No problem.'"

Bosch paused, his mouth open.

"Why does Irving want me? He's spent most of his careers in police and politics trying to end mine."

"This I don't know, Harry. I only know that he wants you."

"When did this come in?"

"The call came in at about five forty-five this morning. My understanding is that it's unclear when it actually happened."

Bosch checked his watch. The case was more than three hours old, quite late for coming into a case. He'd be starting at a disadvantage.

"What's to investigate?" he asked. "You said it was a jumper."

"Hollywood originally responded and they were going to wrap it up as a suicide. The councilman arrived and he is not ready to sign off on that. That's why he wants you."

"And does the chief understand that I have a history with Irving that—"

"Yes, he does. He also understands that he needs every vote he can get on the council if we ever want to get overtime flowing to the department again."

Bosch saw his boss, Lieutenant Duvall, enter the hallway from the Open-Unsolved Unit. She made a *There you are!* gesture and started toward him.

"Looks like I'm about to get the official word," Bosch said into the phone. "Thanks for the heads-up, Kiz. Doesn't make any sense to me, but thanks. If you hear anything else, let me know."

"Harry, you be careful with this. Irving's old but he's still got teeth."

"I know that."

Bosch closed his phone just as Duvall got to him, holding out a sheet of paper.

"Sorry, Harry, change of plans. You and Chu need to go to this address and take a live case."

"What are you talking about?"

Bosch looked at the address. It was the Chateau Marmont.

"Orders from the chief's office. You and Chu are to proceed code three and take over a case. That's all I know. And that the chief himself is there, waiting."

"What about the case you just gave us?"

"Move it to the back burner for now. I want you on it, but just get to it when you can."

She pointed to the paper in his hand.

"That's the priority."

"You sure about this, Lieutenant?"

"Of course I'm sure. The chief called me directly and he's going to call you. So grab Chu and get going."